Published by Burrow Press
PO Box 533709
Orlando, FL 32853
burrowpress.com

ISBN: 978-1-941681-61-9
Library of Congress Control Number: 2019933522

Cover Art: Sean Walsh
Interior Illustrations: Nathan Holic
Book Design: Ryan Rivas

BRIGHT LIGHTS
MEDIUM-SIZED CITY

A NOVEL

NATHAN HOLIC

BURROW PRESS | ORLANDO, FL

For my parents, John and Pam Holic. I write so many stories about fractured families and putrid parent-child relationships that they're probably scared to read this. But they're awesome, and it was only through their hard work and sacrifice that I was able to pursue writing. I appreciate them, and I hope they know it.

And for my own children, Jackson, Gavin, and Carson. This book is about a lot of things, certainly, but above all else it is a book about the struggle to be a better person, a struggle I didn't truly understand or appreciate until I was a father. This book is for them, someday, when the world gets more complicated, and it often feels like that struggle is yours alone.

TABLE OF CONTENTS

BOOK I: CHOOSE YOUR OWN ADVENTURE
11

BOOK II: HOUSE TOURS
69

BOOK III: YOUR FATHER'S RULES
157

BOOK IV: YOU ARE NOT YOURSELF
275

BOOK V: FINAL EXAM
489

BOOK I

You are no longer the type of guy who belongs in a place like this on a Friday night, this dimly lit bar in downtown Orlando with its tall hardback drink menus and tiny font and refusal to list anything so tacky as a dollar sign. Yet here you are, pretending again, trying to scratch and claw back to the top with what might as well be cartoon-mouse gloves.

Yes, here you are, sitting at an outdoor patio table at Lakeside Wine Bar, a place you used to walk past imagining yourself as a regular, thinking *that will be the life*. Here you are tonight, though, with your pinot noir coagulating in a floodlight-sized wine glass, and your current life is definitely not "the life" you imagined.

Here you are, a block from the sprawling oaks of Lake Eola, the city's postcard-perfect centerpiece, the spot in the heart of the city most likely to produce a sunset panorama of dog-walkers, joggers, families with strollers, love-struck couples in swan-shaped paddle-boats cruising around the fountain.

But sunset was two hours ago.

And now here you are in the darkness and the faint glow of tabletop citronella candles lit to keep the late-spring mosquitoes away, and you're sitting with Sandra, who detests you, who is married to Jimmy, maybe your last remaining friend in Orlando.

"Isn't that the greatest news?" Sandra asks from across the table. She isn't sweating, and it makes her look inhuman, cyborg-ish, sitting out here on the first viciously humid night of the year with dry plastic skin. Then again, maybe you shouldn't have worn a long-sleeved shirt and jeans and too-thick socks; maybe Sandra was smart to dress so sparing, leaving so much skin exposed, bare legs, just those wedge sandals with the black strap wrapped tight up her calf, and that low-hanging black thing that melts from shirt to skirt.

"Yes," you say. "Great news."

"You were staring at the girls inside. Perv."

"No. I was listening."

"What did I just say, then?"

"You scored tickets to the next playoff game," you try. "Down close, right by the court, where they bring you Rice Krispies Treats and hot towels during the fourth quarter." This is what Jimmy told you earlier, and it's worth a shot repeating.

She leans back from the table. "Lucky guess."

"You give me no credit." You look out to the lake and try to laugh. "No credit" is the least of your worries.

You don't want to be here, not outside where the bugs power through the citronella, and (to be honest) not inside, either, where waitresses pluck bottles from floor-to-ceiling racks decorated with stone and distressed wood to give the feel of a French wine cellar, and where the tables and leather couches are packed seven-deep with intense twenty-somethings who have something to prove, who wear button-downs tucked into shredded jeans, or spandex-tight t-shirts adorned with glitter and angel wings and skulls and fire, and where the women wear whatever looks like it might come off easiest, the whole bar looking like a casting call for an Orlando Real Housewives spin-off, one girl sweeping her hands about in an effort to be the "loud one" and another sitting back quietly, fingers steepled as if she is the "mean, plotting one." Everyone inside—men, women, wait staff—with a role to play. You don't want to be here, because the only role you can play is that of the "failure." But you also understand that if you ever want to get back on your feet and get back into the game of Life, you've gotta start sometime. Jimmy said as much earlier today, when he called and invited you to hang out. "Gotta keep your spirits high, brother. Gotta get you pumpin' your fists again." He said that you aren't fooling anyone, that you're working way too much, acting all depressed, and that you need to stop being a pussy about the whole Shelley thing, grow a pair, start going out and boozing again. "She's just a girl," he said. "Don't let her win." He's been calling a lot lately, God bless him, and you needed to say "yes" eventually or maybe he'd stop calling.

"Thank you," you told him over the phone. "I need this, Jimmy."

"Indubitably, my good man," he said in an unconvincing British accent. "Tonight's another adventure in the big city, just like the old days."

There you were, phone in hand, and you pictured a rebirth of sorts. You pictured yourself downtown with Jimmy, everything the same as it was when you were both fresh out of college, before he was married and before you were engaged; you pictured your new post-breakup life the same as your old post-college life, those days when weekends were not simply a reward for a long workweek but the very reason for working in the first place. Post-college: when it was always Wall Street block parties and Miller Lite and Jack and Coke and shots with girls you only vaguely knew but hoped might sleep with you. God, those were the days.

You pictured tonight as an offbeat romantic comedy: maybe you'd sit beneath the rooftop tiki torches at Latitudes, a bucket of beers on a long patio table that Jimmy had somehow reserved (he has that power), a cluster of girls you'd just met packed around the table taking shots, all of them in their early twenties and still stoked about incredible lives yet to be lived. You pictured a visit from a bachelorette party, a checklist of things the girls would have to do with you. You pictured shots, more shots, laughter. In this movie you would be the "damaged one" who everyone would help get laid. Tonight!

Only problem was, Jimmy had apparently forgotten that he'd also promised his wife a date night at Lakeside. So here you are, third-wheeling the night away. What's worse: seconds after Jimmy tossed his phone on this outdoor table to claim it, he shot inside to the air-conditioning, where he's since been chatting up the manager for the last twenty minutes. Third wheel? Hell. You're just here to keep Sandra company while Jimmy wanders. That's what your glorious night of adventure in the big city has become.

"Do you, uh," you start, "do you come here often with Jimmy?"

Sandra glares at you with what-the-fuck eyes, as if—although you're at the same table—you have no right to talk to her.

"I mean, like, Jimmy probably has to come here a lot, right?" you ask.

Jimmy works for an alcohol distributor. Beer and wine mostly, but he's always talking about liquor stores and vodka sales, too, holding forth on whether Bong Vodka has a chance at longevity. Drives around Central Florida all day, knows every liquor store owner, every bar manager. Samples new products with them at 11 AM. Life an endless line of shots and pint glasses. Even when he's out on a "date night," he can't resist the allure of buddy-buddying the people in charge, scoring free drinks, not just a big swinging dick, but the biggest swingingest dick in the whole joint.

"He never brings me here," Sandra says.

"Oh."

"We were supposed to get cheesecake tonight," she says, locks eyes with you. "That's probably not happening."

You do not want to be here, but you can't leave: this is your chance to escape all that has been haunting you. Your last chance, imperfect as it is, before all is lost.

You must continue. You must. You've got to make the most of this night.

CONTINUE TO NEXT PAGE

Here you are, Lakeside Wine Bar, and you'll try to make the most of it.

The truth, however, is this: there was a time when Sandra was impressed with you, when you'd sit beside her at a packed table and she'd ask how your properties were doing, if you'd made any new sales, and her eyes would light up when you casually tossed out six-digit numbers…but then home values started tanking and your contributions to the conversation became a downer…and then there was the whole Shelley thing…and then Edwin…and then, every time she asked a question, you either snapped and went on a tirade, or you shut down and moped and ruined the vibe, and so now when you talk to her, you spend your night smiling stupidly to look unconcerned and suppressing critical comments about the weather, the traffic on I-4, the dog shit someone left in your front yard, just to convince Sandra and Jimmy that you are not shattered. This consumes the majority of your energy.

You find yourself staring vacantly at the pedicab drivers—kids who pedal their bicycles around the downtown bar scene, pulling four-person carriages behind them. There is one, in particular, whom you fixate upon. He's wearing gray shorts and a red bandana, and always seems to be hauling a cart full of cackling drunk women. Sometimes he'll stop on the sidewalk under the shadow of one of the high-rises, the Waverly or the Paramount, and he'll pop open a pack of Trident, take a swig of his sticker-decorated water bottle, and stand over his bike, feet on the ground, surveying the crowds headed toward the bars on Wall Street or Orange Avenue, or maybe looking back over his shoulder toward the Thornton Park crossroads where Cityfish and Shari and Hue still command martini drinkers until the late hours. He'll stand chewing, chugging water, knowing he can pedal in any direction. You stare and you think, how much money does this pedicab driver make in a single night? How much does he pay in rent? Can he work the weekend and still pay for electric, water, cable, breakfast lunch dinner, internet? Does he own a car? What if he needs to get to International Drive or Lake Mary or Winter Park or Longwood or Sanford and East Orlando…*everyone* needs a car…but this guy pedals a bike around downtown for a living…is he *free* of all that?

"There you go again," Sandra says.

"What?"

"You can at least pretend you want to be here."

"What was I doing?" you ask.

"Yawning."

"I wasn't," you say.

"It's the red wine. Making you tired."

"I drink this all the time. I'm fine." As if to prove your point, you take the glass by its stem and swirl it expertly. You aren't sure what this is supposed to do—release the nose, the bouquet, something like that?—but it's become such a forced habit that you find yourself swirling all drinks in the same way: your morning coffee, your Diet Coke, your beer.

"You're drinking pinot again?" she asks.

"That's right." You look around for Jimmy, but he's still lost in the crowds inside.

"Because that's what Miles drank in *Sideways*, right?"

"Ha!" you say, but she's stolen your joke. Often you've repeated Miles' signature line, "I am *not* drinking merlot!" when out with friends who've seen the movie. Sandra has turned your beloved catchphrase into a punchline at your expense.

"You know red wine stains your teeth purple, right?" She scratches her breast, adjusts the black shirt-thing. Her nails leave a red Florida shape on her skin, and when she sees it she sighs and rolls her eyes. "If you wanted a beer, why didn't you just get a beer?"

"I didn't want beer," you say. "We're at Wine Bar."

Inside, of course, there are more martini glasses than wine glasses. Sandra is saying it but not saying it: you're a fucking poser. "You always do the thing you *think* you're supposed to do," she says, and shakes her head. It's all blonde hair waving in front of you, blonde hair and eyeliner and glitter. Sandra used to be easy to please: you'd repeat a few lines from *Anchorman* and her face would glow like an azalea blossom.

"So how's business going?" she says. The obligatory question. The one you're not sure how to answer. It's like she knows she shouldn't ask it, too, but she's exhausted all other options. So here it is. Here you are, at Lakeside

Wine Bar in the heart of the heart of the city, a crushed man with a chance to show the world—one person at a time—that you're still standing. Show Sandra that you're fun, that you can still have an adventure, that you're the same ambitious go-getter you used to be. Can you do it? *How* will you do it? Here are your options:

Turn to page 18 if you want to discuss today's loan closing. Show Sandra that your business is still going strong, that you're still working hard despite the economic "downturn."

Turn to page 26 if you'd like to talk about the glory days, remind her that you *were* somebody once.

Turn to page 29 if you'd like to tell her about where you came from, regale her with stories about how far you've come in your journey to the top.

Turn to page 31 if you want to discuss your last adventure with Jimmy, thrill her with your super-fun exploits from a few months ago.

Earlier this morning, you closed a refinance deal in the dreamland community of Avalon Park. Sat in the dining room of a townhouse in a dizzyingly long row of identical units. Sat there listening as the owner told you that he thought about walking away from this place because of the mold problem.

"Mold?" you asked. "This place is brand new."

"Foreclosure two units over," he said. "When the people from the bank came and opened it up, there was water running out the door."

"They left the water on?"

"For days. Floors, ceilings were ruined."

You've seen quite a bit by now—all around Central Florida, the population doubling in the last decade, the pine forests and Old Florida swamps and cypress domes leveled to make way for hundreds of housing developments in various shades of beige, the adjustable rate mortgages metastasizing into American Dream fantasies in the minds of winter-weary Northerners and wannabe house-flippers alike—and you make a living off the paperwork. When you started Kwik Closings, an on-the-go notary service (one employee: you), you promised your clients you'd drive *anywhere anytime* to get the right signatures, mail the forms to the title companies, etc., etc. In the past few years, you've been to pockets of town that both time and God have long forgotten, just miles from pockets that sparkle with newness. Still, you'd never seen this sort of thing in a place like *Avalon Park*, some angry douchebag flooding out his foreclosure. Perhaps it was retaliation against the bank, someone pissed off about the "raw deal" he got on his ARM? But in Avalon Park, in this Pleasantville of unprecedented proportions? Didn't seem right.

So there you were, sitting in this client's dining room, shuffling the paperwork and imagining how it happened. What would drive a man to such a—or wait, was it a *woman* scorned? Yes yes, that's it, a woman so pissed off that she'd become a black hole who would collapse the universe around her. Yes, it was a woman. Had to be. In Avalon Park—with its billboards showcasing housewives at the sink, watching children play soccer in the backyard while Daddy walks through the front door, smiling and holding his briefcase—a woman scorned would be fitting. You could imagine her sitting at the edge of her second-floor bathtub and turning the faucet handle one last time, cold water splashing against a stopped drain. The bathroom empty, save for soap scum on the tiles, toothpaste stains in the sink, cracked shower curtain rings on the rod above her. A woman declaring that she would wait five more minutes for her husband—no, her *fiancé*, much more tragic (probably his name was something innocent but suspicious, like Simon)—she would wait five more minutes for her fiancé *Simon* to arrive, and if he did not, she would surrender this townhouse and any dreams she'd imagined for their future together. Yes, yes. Maybe they'd purchased this home together, but now she hadn't seen Simon in two weeks, not since that final fight over…finances? No. Children. Children were more important. That's the kind of fight to end a relationship. Simon (you imagined) was just like you, a man who couldn't keep his home and his relationship alive, so how could he raise children? And you imagined Simon traveled, also like you. All over town. An EMT, that sounded good, and years before, when his then-girlfriend had first met him, he'd just returned from a stint with FEMA in New Orleans, face weathered as if from combat. She'd sensed in him a touch of the adventurous, a dash of reckless ambition. And although she'd chided him for his frequent all-nighters, for the tire marks he left in the front lawn when he grumbled home drunk, she'd always known that this was a possibility, that he might leave and never come back.

"Did you know her?" you asked your client.

"What?" the owner said. He was busy clearing space from his table so you could spread the refinance paperwork out flat and he could sign on the document's necessary lines twenty or thirty times, and then you could both go about your days.

The interior of this particular townhouse wasn't as nice as you expected for Avalon Park: hundred-dollar futon as the living room couch, Wal-Mart dining room table, particle board entertainment center from Best Buy— college apartment furniture. And this guy? It was almost noon and it looked as if he'd just woken up, just slipped on a baseball cap and a pair of jeans he'd found on the floor.

"The woman from the foreclosure," you said. "Did you know her?"

"How'd you know it was a woman?" he asked.

"Oh." You scratched your neck. "Just a guess?"

Lately you've been letting assumptions become realities. You cannot stop thinking of the people in these houses, cannot stop imagining their lives. Even here, you could not stop thinking of this couple, the neighbors, of how maybe—like this man in front of you—they were further from their dream than they even knew.

You imagined her fingers dangling in the bathtub, water level rising. It is an image now etched into your mind, deep as memory.

You imagined the woman taking in her home, empty now, but remembering what it looked like three years ago, after Simon had begged his father for help with a down payment on a townhouse whose monthly mortgage seemed reasonable ("Do you even know what 'adjustable rate' means?" his father probably asked, but Simon was persistent. That's one thing she loved about him, that he was a man and he would *get things done*), after she applied for credit cards at Lowe's and Rooms To Go. "Upgrades," Simon kept saying, "resale value," and she liked that; it sounded smart (and hell, that's the sort of thing *you* said about the house you bought for yourself and Shelley). And so they installed hardwood floors, plantation shutters, custom ceiling fans, stainless steel appliances (all the things you did for your own house, and for some of the other properties you bought to flip). There was a feeling back then, 2006 or 2007, even though she knew (you knew) that they couldn't afford the leather couches and the 52-inch flat-panel HDTV, that this was the start to something great. Avalon Park: a whole new fantasy world constructed at the eastern edge of Orange County, just twenty minutes from downtown Orlando, two thousand acres of freshly built town centers and pastel colonial homes and dog parks and lakes with fountains and new subdivision phases sprouting from the dirt daily. A place to raise children. A place where every day was sunny, and every weekend was a festival. She'd hang a porch swing, buy flowers to plant below windowsills, send children to "A" schools. A dream.

"Yeah, it was a woman," the owner told you. "Hope they arrest her."

"But no mold in *your* place?"

"Thank God, man. Thank God for that. But the next-door neighbors are fucked. We're probably going to see this shit in our next HOA payment."

You laid the first binder-clipped batch of paperwork onto the table, one page immediately stained by a glob of duck sauce or Tabasco. The owner spit on his finger, tried to rub the sauce from the table, then shrugged.

"Almost made me want to walk away," he said, "if I couldn't get this refinance. Everyone else is doing it."

"Here in Avalon?" you asked.

"All the stuff we were promised: it all says 'coming soon,' but who knows if that's happening."

And as this man spoke, the narrative in your mind changed. You imagined maybe this woman had just learned that hers was not even the only home mired in foreclosure. Maybe she'd found herself surrounded by dozens of forgotten-about two-story units with "For Sale" signs pounded into weed-thick front yards. Maybe that's what set her off, finally, after two weeks of waiting for Simon to return. Maybe she drove around the neighborhood, counted the properties whose yards had gone wild, oak branches careening toward windows. They were everywhere, these shattered dreams, she knew it (you know it) but still, she was not concerned about "everywhere." She was concerned about "here," this townhouse that had devalued $100,000 since its purchase, her reckless fiancé. "Underwater," he kept saying, "but I've got a plan." The only problem: Simon's plans didn't include her. (This is where you differ from Simon. *You* included Shelley. It was Shelley who said *she* was finished with your ideas and your investments, who no longer wanted *her name* attached to *yours.* That's the difference. You *cared* about your fiancé.)

Water cresting the bathtub's rim, breaking into one, two, three glassy streams falling over the porcelain. Water collecting at her feet now. She's stripped everything of value from the home: the stove, the fixtures. Everything except Simon's things. If he'd shown up, maybe she'd have stopped the water and helped him pack and they could start over somewhere else, together.

But he left her, and even though both their names are on the mortgage, the bathtub runs; she wants this to happen (*you* want this to happen). Soon, the water will spill into the hallway, onto the hardwood, will seep into the floors, through the ceiling, down the stairs.

Through the wall, she hears the neighbor playing *Guitar Hero* again, so loud that it rattles her mirrors, but she can still hear the noise of the bathtub, water building, building, and this makes her feel good, imagining all of Avalon Park, the entire pastel dream, literally underwater, drowning, the colors bleeding out until it is all nothing.

"We done?" your client asked after signing the final form.

You wondered then (and you wonder now, here at Lakeside) if there is something wrong with you, that this is what you imagine, that no matter where you go, you stare at front doors and into windows and come away with a tragedy.

"You do this shit all day, huh?" he asked.

"That's right," you said, slipping the papers into a FedEx envelope you'd later ship to the sponsoring bank, thus fulfilling your contract and earning a respectable fee.

"Sounds boring."

He'd looked through thirty pages of banking language, but in that time, you'd convinced yourself that Simon was a real person, that his fiancé was your own, that Shelley was waiting for you at the bathtub, and that if you could just rush home, she would still be there. But she's gone now, and still you own your cavernous house in the gated golf course development of Stoney Creek, where you've invested so much you cannot fathom ever giving it up. Somehow your situation feels worse than Simon and his fiancé's, because they all have new lives and you're still trying to convince yourself that there remains a twitch of life in your own dead dreams.

Oh no. This won't work at all.

Try telling Sandra about the next closing.

CONTINUE TO NEXT PAGE

You can't tell Sandra about Avalon Park. That's too depressing. Where else did you go today? Maybe this is what you can tell Sandra:

After you left Avalon, you drove up to the town of Oviedo in Seminole County, to a subdivision called Clear Waters, where there were no lakes, no rivers, only a retention pond, and standing puddles in overturned tires full of mosquito eggs. When you arrived at your destination, the front door was wide open even though the AC was running. You followed a seemingly liquid line of ants as they flowed from overgrown front-yard plumbagos to the welcome mat to the living room, where you lost track of them in the carpet but, even after you sat down with your client, you couldn't stop yourself from checking your legs every few seconds. The house itself looked like a cluttered time capsule for the early 2000s, bookshelves full of Simpsons plush toys, every season on DVD, boxes of Krusty-O's and Buzz Cola from when the Lake Buena Vista 7-Eleven was converted to a Kwik-E-Mart for a month.

"Economy is bullshit," the man of the house said. He wore an Orlando Predators shirt, tube socks over plump legs. Dozens of dusty family photos cluttered the walls, and a large Olan Mills-style portrait stood dead-center on the living room table, its image whited out by a square of light from a bent blind. You wondered what the family looked like, but even with a photo so close, you couldn't quite see them. You wondered if they still lived here, if something had happened to them, if this man lived alone and his Simpsons collection was a substitute for the people he'd lost.

"It's distressing," you said and nodded. "Oh. Don't forget to date, there. Where I highlighted the box."

"When I bought this place, Oviedo was nothing," he said, scribbling his signature on a new page.

"No?"

"You been to downtown Oviedo?"

You've driven through it, and you've seen the chickens that wander the sides of the road, the proud Oviedoans who have "I brake for Oviedo

Chickens!" bumper stickers. You've been to the Oviedo Marketplace, the once-vibrant mall off 417 whose formerly red roof has faded to pink, Gap long gone, Champs Sports long gone, the mall clinging to a Macy's and a Bugle Boy, ghosts of former stores haunting the empty chained and gated interior. Even in a zombie apocalypse, you wouldn't take refuge there.

"That's all there was when I bought this place." He leaned across the table, the square of sunlight turning his face golden, and you wanted to look at the photo in the center of the table now that he'd blocked the light from obscuring the image, but you got the impression that he was saying something important so you kept eye contact. "Even that road. Alafaya. Two lanes, back then. Shit, I remember spending five years with that shit under construction. Every day we told ourselves, yeah it's frustrating but Oviedo ain't cowpoke no more."

"When I moved to Orlando, the road was mostly finished," you offered. That was ten years ago, for college, back in '99.

"We never wanted Oviedo to change," he said. "We still go to the diner. Town House? We still go to high school football. We still go mudding. Someone else, they brought this to us. A six-lane highway? The mall? You coulda left us alone, we woulda been all right." He pointed at you, as if you were not simply a college freshman when this had happened, but the instigator. "Now look at us," he said. "Shit's falling apart. People leaving. *If you build it, they will leave.*" He laughed and nodded to you like he was about to say "Someone should use that in a show!"

You tried to look at the family photo again, but he grabbed your arm.

"All gone, this whole half of my life," he said. "All over."

And it was then that you looked at the paperwork, the names, and put it all together: this was a divorce, and now he was buying the house from his ex-wife, clearing her name entirely from his life and his possessions. And these were *her* things that he was packing, but was he doing it for her, helping her through this difficult moment in their lives, one last moment of partnership and intimacy before the inevitable separation. Unlike you he didn't just leave the house for a night and let his ex figure it out herself.

"Let's finish this up, huh?" he said, as if he hadn't grabbed you. "No time to think about the past. Got work in an hour."

This is the story you want to tell Sandra? This will show her your thriving business, your energy and happiness? No. This story is almost *worse* than Avalon Park. This story will make *her* depressed, too.

Turn back to page 17. **Choose again**.

Remember the time when all four of you—Jimmy, Sandra, your then-girlfriend Shelley—went to the Jason Mraz concert at House of Blues and Jimmy was somehow able to get balcony tables, private bar; Jimmy even got you backstage, and he sniffed a line or two in the bathroom and Sandra was oblivious (well, probably, but she's never seemed *exciting* enough to do coke) and somehow you met Jason Mraz and Jimmy fist-bumped him—*Pound the rock! Explode the rock!*—and you did shots with him and he sang "The Boy's Gone" a capella for the four of you and Shelley nearly died; and you got home at 5 AM and "epic" was the word you used for such a night, Shelley not yet a fiancée at the time, but you'd both been talking about the "future." Remember that?

This was life, post-college. Concerts at Hard Rock, House of Blues, intimate shows at Backbooth and the Social, local bands who'd say "What's up, *Orlando*!" because they wanted you to know it was their mission to defy expectations of what Orlando meant to outsiders: the Mickey-Mouse-eared electrical tower on I-4 that was as much an Orlando "gateway" as the overpass sign near the actual city limits, the Backstreet Boys and NSYNC and O-Town, the Nickelodeon Hotel, the Ripley's Believe It Or Not! Museum and the other I-Drive tourist traps. They were anti-bubblegum, these Orlando bands. To be Orlando was to be *Not Orlando*; that is to say, always living in defiance of what someone outside the city might imagine. So you spent your post-college nights downtown orbiting the axis of Orange Avenue, from the Lodge to Casey's to Chiller's to the Wall Street block parties where it seemed every twenty-something who mattered had convened in the open air, everyone so hammered and loud it was like they were hoping the tourists at Disney could hear it from miles away.

This city, it wasn't New York, but you fucking *owned* it. Hell, in New York, you would be *lost*, you would be a passing face on a crowded sidewalk. But here in downtown Orlando, far from the airport and Universal Studios and Disney World, you slipped from bar to bar with the other locals, shaking hands and kissing cheeks all night long, a greasy slice of Midnight Pizza or a hunk of

Sabrett street meat as night melted to morning, as clusters of sorority girls fell back into their cars and shrank back to UCF, as shiny-shirted post-college frat stars dispersed to different parking garages, different side streets and five-dollar lots, to battered rental houses close enough to downtown to feel part of it; end of the night, but you'd be back tomorrow. They expected you. They knew you. They needed you. The city would not want Tomorrow without you.

It was yours, the city of Orlando.

This was 2006. You were buying houses in brand-new neighborhoods that had—a year before—been swamps and sand and angry patches of snake-infested needle palms. You quit your job at the bank because you thought (correctly) you could make more money off house-flipping and loan-closing, and you met up with your Wachovia cronies for coffee and worked out a contract to be their go-to closer. You stared up at the high windows of 55 West more times than you can remember, looking at the construction cranes hovering over the gutted remains of soon-to-be-reinvigorated Church Street Station and the burgeoning downtown skyline, and you thought, "I'm buying houses today. Tomorrow: condos. Imma own this fucking town!" Someday you'd rent out full floors in 55 West. Hell, someday you'd own a whole damned building.

Orlando was the metropolis of the future, the borders of its sprawl expanding in every direction, unconstrained by ocean or great lake, railroad or river, its wide streets and vast parking lots built for SUVs, every Applebee's and California Pizza Kitchen and Buffalo Wild Wings equipped with enough parking spaces to fit a vehicle for each customer. Metro Orlando. Room to build, room to stretch, square miles upon square miles of *brand new* bars restaurants shopping, but still the city was *demanding* new malls, new subdivisions, new fountains, new arenas, new big-box-anchored town centers, everything to match the sparkle of the pristine theme parks that had allowed the city to rise in the first place. Back then, the newspapers were discussing daily the city's plans for a new performing arts center, a new basketball arena, a new Darden restaurant chain, and every day it seemed some new group was releasing plans for thirty, forty, fifty-story residential high-rises on Orange or Rosalind or Church. Everyone, you thought, wanted to be here. Rust Belt atrophying, Orlando swelling. Metropolis of the future.

Orlando was a *brand-new* American city, after all, an inland speck turned Major Player overnight, and like an 18-year-old gifted with a trust fund, it was now experiencing the rewards of moneyed adulthood without ever having endured the frustration of entry-level work. As far as you could see, Orlando had no scars; there was no awkward 1800s adolescence filled with immigrant clashes and Indian genocide and power-hoarding politicians, no violent riots, no 1950s and '60s midlife crisis that saw residents scatter to the suburbs. Orlando was always just…growing, had never paused.

You'd come from the fire ant piles and weeds of the Valdosta outskirts. You'd fled small-town Georgia for the promise of Metro Orlando. You'd paid your way through college at the rapidly expanding University of Central Florida (30,000 students when you started, 50,000 when you graduated, and probably 60,000 by the time you finish this thought). You'd established your own business in the city, so why *couldn't* you live in one of the new skyscrapers? Why *couldn't* you own and rent out full floors? Why couldn't you have luxury boxes at Magic games? You'd come this far.

You and the city, growing up together: this was destiny, wasn't it?

With hard work, anything was possible.

There was a time when you'd imagined yourself having the VIP tables at every Orange Ave and Church Street bar, every weekend, conversations centered on jet skis and stock purchases and unnecessary but frighteningly expensive techno-gadgets, and you would be the one buying Grey Goose bottles to share with your table at Sky Bar. When the bartender clanged the bell to signal a gigantic tip, it would be *you* who'd signed the receipt.

You were 24, 25, and you were on your way to the very top.

Turn back to page 17 if you think this is naïve, if you want to choose again.

Turn to page 29 if you think this is impressive, and if you want to *further* impress Sandra by telling her about rural Georgia, and how far you've come.

You are from the far outskirts of Valdosta, Georgia, a place whose only claim to fame is a non-Super Wal-Mart, and while there are a thousand Valdosta, Georgias around Orlando, too, a thousand small towns that native sons leave behind for greater ambitions, you'd like to think that your little unincorporated weed-patch was a special kind of rural.

As a kid, you didn't have much, but you worked hard to understand how things functioned. You assembled and disassembled the twin go-karts your father bought for you and your brother Kyle. Your hands caked with red clay and oil, you'd crunch behind the metal wheel—a space so tight your father couldn't even fit, his back cracking as he tried to contort himself—and you'd smash the gas pedal and kick up the sand and stones of the "back trails," as your brother called them. You'd cut corners to plow through fire-ant piles; you'd mow down ferns and weeds to make the trails wider; you'd zip between pine trees, and your father's face and body would disappear behind the thick pine branches and dark needles as you entered the forest, and it was just you and the rumble of the go-kart, and you could hear the engine up-close but you could also hear its echo. Just you and the go-kart, jumping over the first hill, then the mud pit, and you knew your father couldn't see you either, that you'd disappeared, but he could hear your echo. Any time of day, in fact, you convinced yourself that he could hear you. When he was at the shop, when he was out at Darts Lounge, you gassed the go-kart and you thought, *There. Now you know I'm racing, Dad. Now you know I haven't stopped.*

The last time you spoke with your father was Thanksgiving, and he lectured you about debt and family responsibilities and hard work and a man's house is blah blah blah, and you couldn't take it anymore.

I've got some great houses in Orlando, you told him. Get you and Kyle out of here, away from the memories. Mutual benefit.

When someone says mutual benefit, he said, there's only one person benefits. The other only thinks he does.

Things got worse from there. You said something you couldn't take back. In the end, he told you to get the hell out of his house.

You've heard from Kyle that your father is getting worse, that the heart attack and the back problems have taken their toll. No man in the Turner family has lived past 65, is the old saying. Last you talked to Kyle, you told him you'd like to visit, but you can't get away from your job.

Just livin' the life, huh? your brother asked.

He didn't fully understand that you aren't welcome in the home you left behind.

Turn back to page 17 to repress this memory. **Choose again**.

Yeah, tell Sandra about your last "downtown adventure" with her husband. Try to impress her with *that* story.

It was a month or two ago. Tell Sandra about how you ended up at the rooftop bar with the one-word name that would not have seemed erotic in any other context, but here (curvy letters, sign glowing pink like a left-behind lipstick kiss) felt downright sinful. A long fire-hazard line stretched down the stairs, women on the steps in club-ready skirts, douchebag guys trying to sneak underneath the stairs to peek (one of those douchebags was Jimmy, but he got annoyed when he saw other idiots doing the same thing), the world smelling of perfume and cologne and sex and open dumpsters filled with the previous night's half-finished cocktails and discarded fruit garnishes, and even here you felt like you no longer belonged, this rooftop bar, couches on the perimeter with tiki torches and fire pits where mostly naked women (paid by the club) danced and gyrated before the flames orgasmically, and there was a flicker of deep empathy in your heart that night, too, and you imagined finding one of these girls shimmering and wavering like the tiki flames, any would do, and taking her aside, talking to her, placing fingertips on her face and telling her you didn't care how she ended up dancing in front of a fire like a stripper, that *you* thought she was beautiful, not just fuckable, *really beautiful*, and most guys didn't say that, did they?, and she didn't need to be here, doing this. But if you were honest with yourself, it wasn't just some "goodness" in your soul, was it? Because these girls *were* fuckable.

See, your fantasies might begin with noble intentions—you pulling aside the girl with the teal headband, the ankle-high boots, the booty-short panties, the one dancing before a table full of men laughing too loud and saying "retarded" too often, their hair spiked like palm fronds; you, rescuing her, and then the two of you talking and finding common interests and falling in love, the girl looking at you with the eyes of a believer, because here you are saving her, and then the conversation (in your mind) jump-cutting to sex against the wall in the bar's bathroom, but wait wait no, that wouldn't happen, people don't actually *do* that, and so you—in your fantasy—revise so that you're fucking her at your place. Driving all the way back to Stoney Creek, fucking her in a bed once shared with your fiancée, even as this rescued dancer-girl asks why you still have a tall stack of forgotten chick lit books in the far corner of the bedroom, a hair tie on the end table, and (shit! why haven't you taken it down?) a crème-colored canvas hanging beside the dresser mirror, the words "You Are My Happily Ever After" looping across in deep calligraphic red.

Every sexual fantasy deteriorates once logic takes hold.

Anyway.

Jimmy had no such scruples at the bar that night, masterfully scoring a bottle of Three Olives ("This guy loves me," he said of the owner), and sitting down on one of the "Reserved" couches like he'd actually paid money to reserve it. And suddenly a girl in a silver skirt appeared, titties bursting from a silver bra-top, and he was laughing, nudging you in the ribs, saying, "Fucking show us what you got!" and "Nice, nice" as the silver curves flashed upward, the muscles in her legs tensing, the moonlight catching the bounce of her glittered breasts, and he eventually laid his hand on her thigh and she moved closer and you tried to smile but the only thing you could think to say was, "What is this, a strip club?" and it came out derisively, not jokingly, and when it looked like their kissing might turn into fucking right there, you checked your watch and said, "Gotta head out, brother," and Jimmy said, "So soon? Hey babe, say goodnight to Marc," and she said good night and you walked down the stairs, past the crowd, one of the loneliest walks you've ever taken.

Wait. You want to tell this story to Jimmy's *wife*? God, nobody wins with this one. Sandra might be boring, but she doesn't deserve to hear how awful her husband is. And Jimmy is, like, one of your only two or three friends: you want to do this to him?

Turn to page 17 if you want to reconsider, choose another option. Can you? Do you have anything left to talk about?

Turn to page 33 if you see this story as an opportunity.

THIS STORY IS AN OPPORTUNITY.

So maybe, here at Lakeside Wine Bar, you *do* tell Sandra about the girl in the silver skirt. You reveal every detail, in fact, describe how Jimmy's fingers were pressed so hard into the dancer-girl's ass he left behind red handprints.

Inside the bar, as you speak, Jimmy stands beside the manager and holds his beer bottle before the two of them, turning it around like an object on *Antiques Roadshow*. He is pointing out something from the label, talking talking talking while the manager nods. The bottle looks like a Sierra Nevada Pale Ale, but you could be wrong; all your life you've had perfect eyesight, but suddenly here in your late twenties your entire body shocks you with unexpected deficiencies. Like a car in the first month after the warranty expires: sudden engine burps, malfunctioning windshield wipers. You used to be able to keep up with Jimmy, his energy, his drinking tallies, but now you yawn and think about broken relationships.

After processing the story, Sandra's eyes are wide, her breathing shallow.

"Don't worry about him," you say. "Fucking Jimmy. He's not worth worrying about, Sandra."

She hates her husband, you can feel it. Hates that he's always taking her out and then abandoning her. You feel the hate, and you want to make things better for her.

"Let's get out of here," you say. "He won't even notice we're gone."

Inside, the manager hands Jimmy a draft Blue Moon with orange slice, on the house no doubt. Jimmy does not turn toward the window to check whether his wife and friend are still where he left them. He takes you both for granted.

"This is how he treats you," you tell Sandra. "A whole other life. Who knows what he does?"

She looks into her hands, doesn't say anything. But then again, she's always been quiet. This is why Jimmy married her after graduation: he never shuts up, talks incessantly about the Boston Celtics and the Duke Blue Devils and the upcoming hurricane season and the costs of air conditioning and gas prices hitting four dollars and the sad career arc of Vin Diesel and a new ab workout he found in *Men's Health* and he delivers an entire conversation in a single breath without so much as a transition, so all he ever needed was someone quiet to talk at. That's Sandra; she might as well be a mannequin. Now: as long as he's fucking other women on the side, he's happiness personified, drives an Excursion with an "I Love My Wife" bumper sticker so splotched with dirt and pollen that everyone seems to miss it entirely.

"We can go anywhere, Sandra," you say. "Trust me."

She looks up at you with the eyes of a believer.

You wanted to show the world you're still standing. You wanted to rise again, to conquer…you wanted to be a motherfucking hero! So here you are: you are going to *save Sandra*.

Now you're driving, Sandra in your passenger seat, driving away from Jimmy and away from downtown, back to your house north of the city so that you can rescue her and also so that you can fuck her in the bed you once shared with your fiancée (with whom Sandra was good friends, but you'll worry about that complication when the time comes).

"So have you heard any news on your houses?" she asks.

"Which ones?"

"I don't know. Any of them."

You flip the turn signal, pass a slow-moving minivan. Still a few exits to go until the rescue is complete. "Um. Had to lower the sale price again. On all of them, actually."

"Oh," she says. "That sucks."

"Yeah. But whatever. I'll be fine. We'll be fine."

"What are you gonna do?"

You check the rearview. Someone is tailgating you. "Not much I can do. No buyers. We're going to be fine, Sandra."

"We?"

"We," you say. "The two of us." Your finger traces an imaginary connection between the two of you.

"There is no 'two of us.' I'm with Jimmy."

"He cheats on you constantly. This isn't a healthy relationship. We can be together, though, Sandra. I can *save* you from him."

"It smells like 7-Eleven Cuban sandwiches in here."

"I drive all over town. All day long. I work. I work hard."

"I'm with Jimmy. Your fantasy is stupid."

Motherfucker. This fantasy won't work, will it?

And suddenly you're back at Lakeside Wine Bar. Sandra is touching her lips to make sure her gloss is still thick and sticky and too-good-for-you, and she says, "Why did you even come out tonight?"

Turn to page 37 if you want to rejoin the real world. Answer Sandra's question.

Turn to page 36 if you don't want the fantasy to end. Let it go just a bit longer. Like, okay, it's a flawed fantasy, but at least you look sort of noble in it.

You pull into your driveway. You open the door for Sandra, and now she efficiently plays her role in the fantasy your mind has produced. You take her hand, you lead her inside, and you push her onto the couch in the living room and she says "The bedroom?" and you say "No, the couch." It is here that you slip the black shirt-thing from her body and toss it onto the coffee table, rip the thong from her waist, and she slaps your face and says "Fuck me" and she is a naked woman on your couch, and *yeah*, the fantasy is going *just right—*

But you say, "What about Jimmy?"

"This is your *fantasy*, asshole!" she says. "You just threw me onto the couch. You have my panties in your hand, and now you mention *Jimmy*? Do you even *want* to be happy, Marc, even for ten seconds inside your own stupid head?"

Turn to…

Turn to…

Um.

This was a bad idea. Pretend you didn't imagine any of this.

Turn to page 37.

Back at Lakeside Wine Bar, where you never told Sandra about Jimmy's cheating, never left with her or took her back to your place, you stare into the distance and try to seem happy. You've yet to make a single adventurous choice.

"Why did you even come out tonight?" Sandra is asking.

"Why did I…?"

"If you don't want to be here," she says. "Why come out? Why ruin *my* night?"

Inside, Jimmy has his hand on the bare back of one of the waitresses, is leaning in close to tell her something. They are both grinning, both brimming with sexual mischief. That should be *you* in there. That should be you.

Why *did* you come out tonight?

After the closings in Avalon Park and Oviedo this afternoon, you had another condo refinance off Conroy, near the Mall at Millenia, and in the time it took to drive from the suburban outskirts to the congested central artery of I-4, you considered the dreaded weekend ahead. It didn't seem right, how much you've grown to loathe the time that everyone else loves, the time when your schedule clears and you are no longer driving from house to townhouse to FedEx, the two days you could do *anything* but usually end up spending in your empty house or at the gym. A good-looking bachelor in his twenties who hates weekends? None of it seemed right. And there you were, parked in standstill traffic on Conroy, locked behind a series of bright SUVs with out-of-state plates, on the overpass that arches over the I-4 hellscape. This bridge at the southern edge of the city is something of a "gateway" into Orlando: the word "Orlando" is spelled in slender ivory letters along the rails, and spires topped by blue jewels rise at either end of the bridge. This was the first time you'd sat atop this bridge and looked from the inside out, the city spelled backward. ODNALRO. Beyond the guard rail and beyond these letters, the vastness of Metro Orlando spread out before you: Disney and Universal Studios and the clusterfuck of I-Drive and the Convention Center, the 528 "bee-line" to the Atlantic coast, the airport, all of it south of the gateway. Beyond the other guard rail outside your passenger-side window was the much smaller city of

Orlando itself, population somewhere over 200,000, its authority conveyed by a skyline of a half-dozen thirty-story buildings. A mile beyond that, Winter Park. Another couple miles, and you'd be in Altamonte Springs, and Maitland, and Longwood, all century-old towns and cities so close together that—unless you live there—get lumped under the name "Orlando." Why? you wondered. This metropolis: it could have been Metro Kissimmee, or Metro Maitland. Somewhere along the line, Orlando made the choice to assert itself as the center.

The red light changed, and the line of cars inched forward.

And that was it, the moment you decided you needed to start making some real choices about your life. Just a moment on the bridge. But you decided that it would all start tonight. Should Jimmy call you, as he always does on Friday afternoons, you would make the active choice to *not* indulge in loneliness. You would stop ignoring his messages. Jimmy is a bit much to handle, and almost every time you've hung out with him since the dissolution of your engagement, you've regretted it, but Jimmy is one of your few friends who's stayed in contact with you even though you're no longer a viable double-date option. You rarely hear from Steven and Anderson, your few sparing conversations limited mostly to excuses why they can't meet up, Anderson traveling for work and Steven busy with his blog. And the rest of your friends—Edwin, Brandon, Ted—gave up on the city, moved to Atlanta or Dallas or Charleston. But Jimmy believes in you, cares about you, still calls.

So it would begin tonight, your rise back to the top.

Tonight you would go downtown, get some drinks, get back on your feet.

"ODNALRO," you read in your rearview mirror as you merged with the traffic on the interstate. The City Beautiful. The tourist mecca. A place the world sees as magic and sunshine, but a place that smelled to you at this moment of car exhaust and asphalt and swear words shouted from the windows of Hondas zigzagging I-4 at 80 miles per hour through caravans of Ontario vacationers who were just now starting to understand what humidity really felt like. It is style over substance, you decided on the bridge, the sizzle over the steak; that's why the housing boom felt so *at home* here; like a brand-new subdivision, this city was constructed only after its persona had already been workshopped and focus-grouped and advertised to the world. The world was told, and so they believed. Hell, if an entire city could pull off this ruse, maybe *you* could do it too. Maybe if you could force others to see you as the man you thought you were, you could once again *become* that man.

Get it together, you thought. Get it together. Eyes on the prize.

"My drink's empty," Sandra says.

"I'll go inside and—"

"No no no," she says and grabs your wrist. "Don't you *dare* leave me out here alone."

Okay. This is good. You're better than nothing at all. We can work with that.

CONTINUE TO NEXT PAGE

Suddenly there is someone else at your table, standing an arm's length away and paused in mid-step to gawk at you as if you're Justin Timberlake seated here at an unassuming Orlando bar. "Oh my God!" she says.

Across the table, Sandra had finally met your eyes, seemed to be on the verge of conversation, but now she looks up and away.

"Oh my God," the gawker says again, and *no*, she is not looking at you like you're Justin Timberlake. See her eyes, the delight but also the spark of viciousness? The smile, the lilt of the "Oh my God," carried up in tone as if nearly broken by laughter. You are not a JT-caliber celeb. You are Gary Coleman. You are Corey Feldman, Carrot Top. You are a caricature. And the gawker: this is a girl you remember from college: Vicki with an "i" (something you remember her repeating so many times back in business courses together because you—she said—were "Marc with a 'c'! And that means we're both *awesome!* with an exclamation point!"). You remember her short dark hair, face scintillatingly gorgeous except she always looked as if she knew she was better than you.

She places one hand on her hip, still has her mouth half-open like she can't think of anything else to say. "It's been too long!" Vicki says eventually, shaking her head.

"Haven't seen you since the career fair," you say. "Five years ago?"

"I took a job in Atlanta," she says. "I moved back a few months ago."

Vicki is with her girlfriends, four of them, and they all stand behind impatiently like they're waiting for introductions or for seats at the table, or maybe just waiting for Vicki's random encounter to end so their night can proceed. You should know their names—they all look familiar, probably sat beside you in other classes—but in this moment it's just blonde hair and black Coach purses and eyes darting about as they size you up and wonder if you're worth a full conversation. Christina? Lesley? Sarah? You think those are the names, but in the moment they seem interchangeable. One whispers to another, her fingers cupped and gracing the other's ear. They both smile with the cruelty of an under-the-breath insult. Another is texting, wobbling as she does so.

"Sandra?" Vicki asks, now looking past you. "Sandra, I didn't know that was you!"

Sandra rises and holds out her hand to shake Vicki's. They haven't seen each other in forever, they both say, and you're so beautiful and why don't we talk more, and we should totally connect on Facebook, and then they both stretch across the table to hug, long white limbs and the jingle of jewelry and the smell of expensive beauty products, the diamond of Sandra's engagement ring catching the streetlight.

"Oh my God," Vicki says, grabbing Sandra's finger and admiring the twin white-gold bands. "Are you two..." She points back to you, then to Sandra. "Did you two get *married*?"

"She's not my wife," you say too quickly. "Jimmy Bastion."

"Jimmy Bastion?" Vicki's vicious laugh returns. "Girls! You remember Jimmy! Oh my God, Jimmy is still *alive*?"

Sandra laughs, as if she hears this question often.

"He is indeed alive," you say. "He's inside."

"He's right. He didn't die," one of the girls confirms, still looking down at her cell phone. "I saw him...like, he was somewhere once."

"Why don't you sit down? Catch up with us?" Sandra asks. "We don't have enough seats for everyone, but—"

These women are slithering limbs, hands on shoulders, tangled in delicious drunken ways. "They're fine," Vicki says of her friends, pressing her skirt tight against her upper thighs as she slips into a chair. "They need a breather anyway." They look woozy from hard liquor, and now they're all excusing themselves to the restroom to "freshen up," so maybe coke is on the menu? You've never ventured into hard drugs, but old acquaintances—people you'd never suspect—occasionally tell you that they've "graduated from alcohol." It seems so 1980s, so Patrick Bateman, so Michael J. Fox in that New York movie. Cocaine, here in 2009, is still a thing? In Orlando?

"You got married to *someone*, though, right?" Vicki asks you.

"Me?" you ask. "No."

"I swear you were married. Are you sure?"

You hold up your hands. "Nope. Can we, um, change the subject?"

There was a time when you enjoyed random encounters, when you enjoyed sharing the news of your life. But now you proceed cautiously, weighing every option, knowing it took you a decade to build a reputation in Orlando, but a single night could destroy it: all Vicki has to do is tell her friends you've been ruined, her friends tell twenty others, thirty others, thousands, until you are spit from the city like a Kalamata pit.

"No, really," Vicki says. "It said on Facebook that you were engaged."

"That was last year," Sandra clarifies. She perks out her breasts as if delighted to deliver the news. "I don't think he ever changed his relationship status."

"I don't really do the Facebook thing," you say.

"Wow," Vicki says. "What happened?"

"Um. I stopped caring about political rants and cat memes?"

"No! Your *engagement*, silly!"

"Oh. It didn't work out?" You look into your glass.

"Shelley!" Vicki suddenly yells, face alight with discovery, as if some great mystery has been solved, and she nods to you like you should congratulate her. "Shelley was your fiancée's name! Whatever happened to her?"

The thing about broken engagements is there's no good way to tell the world about them. Breaking up with a girl? That's easy. But an engagement is a business investment, and once you start sending out Save the Dates and booking a reception site, it's as if there's a community investment, too. *Wait, you're not engaged anymore? But I have your* magnet *on my fridge!* Or worse: *But I loved Shelley! How could you do this? Now who am I supposed to be friends with, her or you?* And so you put it off, hoped the word would slowly spread and that friends and family would be too embarrassed to ask further questions. You let rumors take shape, and the rumors are so far off that these narratives help blunt the pain of what really happened. You probably only told a dozen people directly, let the news spiderweb from there. You still haven't told your father, and you damn sure never told Vicki or her entourage. Even Jimmy doesn't know the real reason behind the split, not that he is equipped with the right stuff to console you.

"Shelley," Sandra says with her martini glass at her lips, and she sighs sadly.

"I think she's moving to San Diego," you say. "A new job."

"Oooooohh, sorry," Vicki says, but her voice does not sound apologetic. She brushes a strand of hair from her eyes, then whips her head back and brushes her forehead again. "You were always a hot ticket, back when."

You swirl your wine. "I tried."

The pedicab driver is in his familiar spot, popping a tab of Trident. Bandana, long rock-star hair—it will be sweat-slickened by night's end—short-sleeve "Local Celebrity" t-shirt and charcoal jeans, arms and legs etched with definition. He's got the casual cool of Magic point guard Rafer Alston draining a 3-pointer and backing away from his shot, smiling 'cause he knows he's been clutch for the team this season.

"I'm sorry I brought it up," she says. "Let me buy you a drink to make up for it."

Vicki has one hand on your shoulder now. It feels cold even through your shirt. But it also feels smooth, a female touch you've forgotten. Her hand on your shoulder, and you have two choices. You can be gracious, or you can pull a role reversal and be too good for her.

Turn to page 44 to decline her drink.

Turn to page 47 to accept her drink.

"Thanks for the offer, but I've still got a full glass," you tell Vicki. "Good to see you, though." You've signaled that the conversation is over, but she doesn't move.

"Well, tell me about life right now. How's everything?"

"Life," you say. Fuck. You should have just accepted the drink. "What do you want to know?"

"Everything," she says. "All the things we used to talk about when we were business class buddies. Make your first million yet?"

A car drives past the bar, some Lil Wayne song buried beneath booming bass that shakes the metal tabletops. Inside his car, the driver raps along to the track as he scopes the bars, the tables, the pedestrians on the sidewalks flashing past. He is rapping, but he is only repeating the last word of every line. "Knife wound!" you hear, then three seconds later, "Blood!" then three seconds later, "In the mud!"

The drink offer is the same here as it would've been at a casino: shit's gonna go sour eventually, so *take the free drink.*

Way to go, Marc.

Try again. You've got several options for this conversation now:

Turn to page 45 to go home. Abruptly. Just leave.

Turn to page 46 to be daring.

Turn to page 48 to tell her about your job.

Turn to page 51 to tell her about your house.

You always have the option to leave a situation you find undesirable. As a man who owns a car and a house, that is your motherfucking right.

So you do. You leave the two of them at the table, Sandra and Vicki, adjusting your belt and complaining about an upset stomach. "Shouldn't have eaten sushi tonight," you say. Inside, Jimmy doesn't notice that you've stood, that you're walking away from Lakeside, and behind you Vicki and Sandra have crackled into laughter.

Fuck them, all of these people you rely upon for your emotional well-being.

You drive home.

The rest of the night you spend alone as usual, watching Netflix and drinking from a 12-pack of Sam Adams that has been in your fridge forever (the Winter Sampler pack, the kind that, every year, no matter how many you drink, you seem to have bottles of Winter Stout and Chocolate Bock left over until September).

But here at home, you can't stop thinking about Sandra, about Vicki. You know they were laughing at you because you have become pathetic, but still they looked so damned good, and you want to masturbate. This doesn't seem right, and you know it. But you're a man in his late twenties, and sexual impulses still fire across every synapse in your system, and you've spent the night looking at women who've crafted their appearances to seemingly meet your every fantasy, and you're lonely, and so you do masturbate, and afterward you try to convince yourself you were masturbating to the infomercial-length *Girls Gone Wild* commercial that happened to be playing on the television, but you know the truth, right?

Weeks later, you will see Sandra and you will feel guilty and she will just give you the same hateful look and stare deep into your eyes as if she knows she was on your mind when you came.

So maybe this option doesn't work.

Turn to page 46 to *be daring* instead.

"Let's get out of here!" you tell Sandra and Vicki.

"Where?" they ask in unison.

"Across town! Screw this place!"

You stand and motion for them to follow you, and now you are jogging lightly and Sandra and Vicki are holding hands and hurrying and smiling guiltily as they follow. It feels as if you're floating down Central, all three of you in the air, and you're speaking to them and they're speaking to you but there are no words because it's all soundtrack, cymbals crashing, lyrics about house parties and college and keg stands, close-ups of red Solo cups and heads tilted back in laughter and couples kissing beneath the stars and you're in a montage, you realize, a flash of a moment at Wall Street taking selfies beneath the Christmas lights, and then flash to a moment at a rooftop party, and then flash to a moment where you're all three walking down the stairs into Tanqueray's on Orange Ave and the doorman smiles and claps you on the back and the women hug him and there's a gin and tonic waiting for you, and flash to a flash to a flash flash flash and it's as if you've lived an entire lifetime in the duration of a single pop-punk song from your college years and there is no hangover and, yes, if you are daring you will be rewarded with montage. Oh God, you will be rewarded!

You own this city! You're back! All because you made the right decision.

Turn to page 59 to celebrate.

You say to Vicki, "Sure, I'll have another."

Vicki is quick in signaling a waitress from inside, quicker than you have been in years. She raises just two fingers, like a big-city pro hailing a cab, and seconds later Vicki's ordering for you. You haven't seen her in years, but she's telling the waitress you'll take a Jack and Coke because this red wine is making you tired. You are about to argue that pinot noir has a haunting taste, ancient, but Vicki says, "Cut the *Sideways* act."

Sandra chuckles, taps her forehead knowingly. "That's what *I* said!"

"Jack and Coke," the waitress repeats, and when she returns with your drink, Vicki says, "Doesn't that feel better? Not trying to look impressive with your drink?"

You raise the glass to your mouth, ice cubes touching your lips, and it's impossible to disagree.

"I was fine with the red wine," you say.

"Some people say 'thank you,'" Vicki says.

"I'm not ungrateful. I just—"

"Take another drink. A long one." She waits. "There you go. This is the Marc I remember."

"I don't…I never changed."

"So tell me about life right now," Vicki says. "I'll be the judge."

Okay. This won't work. No matter what, she wants to hear about your life, and what are you supposed to tell her? How are you supposed to maintain the façade of success and happiness if she keeps prying? **Turn back to Page 37** and choose again. No, wait. You can't do that. The drink is in your hand and you can't change that. You can only move forward.

Turn to page 48 if you choose to tell her about your job.

Turn to page 51 if you choose to tell her about your house.

Here's what you're going to do: you're going to tell Vicki that you started your own business, that—contrary to how down-in-the-dumps you look—you're still a *big swinging dick*. From your spot at the table, you notice the pedicab driver out on the road. He nods to passing bros in their black Banana Republic pants, motions toward his cab when a couple blondes in black leggings and high heels approach, gives them a thumbs-up as a question: Need a ride? They do. They saunter to his cab and climb aboard. *These are my people*, the pedicab driver is thinking, *this is my city.*

A mosquito lands on your arm and you shake it loose.

No. *Your* city. "I run my own loan-closing business," you tell Vicki.

"Do you?" She's chewing on an ice cube, so the words are wet and conjoined. "What does that mean?"

"It's a mobile signing service. I'm a notary. I work with title companies, drive anywhere they need me to go. I've got it down to a science."

"Are many people buying houses right now?"

"Not really. Mostly refinances."

"That's what I thought. Seems like a lot of houses are going into foreclosure."

The mosquito is back. It hovers. It's on your ear, or is it?

"A lot of short sales, though," you say and slap at your face, but still you sense the mosquito has survived. "And when the short sales and foreclosures die down, the empty foreclosures will sell. Anyway, I get a flat fee per closing, so housing prices don't matter."

"Forecast doesn't look good."

"I'm hopeful." You say this, but your face tells a different story. You've left a handprint on your cheek, and the mosquito might now be skimming your hair; and from somewhere high above, a strand of pollen floats into your glass. For much of early spring, the oak trees are sponge-painted yellow with pollen, which means *all of Central Florida* is sponge-painted yellow, clumps of the pollen collecting in gutters, along curbsides, beneath windshield wipers, the whole world faded to a washed-out mustard color. But that's early spring: by now, the trees are vibrant green, and the pollen should be gone. Yet there it is in your drink, dropped from a looming oak.

"Didn't you work at Wachovia? Or is it Wells Fargo now?" Vicki asks, that familiar mocking tone creeping back into her voice.

"Wachovia, right after college. Then I struck out on my own to—"

"Layoffs, right? My ex-boyfriend worked with you."

"Oh. I forgot." You try to pick the pollen from your drink, swipe at the mosquito as it dances around the rim. "Well, technically, I was given the option—"

"You didn't forget," she says.

You didn't forget.

"So what's your business called?" she asks.

"Kwik Closings."

"Please tell me it isn't spelled with a 'k.'"

Sip that drink. She's about to level you once again. "Um. Why?"

"Never trust a business that misspells its name," she says.

"Okay, so let's talk about you, then," you try. "What do *you* do?"

"I work pharmaceutical sales. No slow-down there!"

You're searching your mind's database for articles you've read about the pharmaceutical industry, searching, but when the hourglass continues to spin without results, you surrender: "Yeah, I guess that's true."

"Living up at the Waverly."

You shake the same damned mosquito from your arm, but there is already a red dot, it has already fed and soon the lump will rise and you will scratch it far more than you should.

"Love it. I walk to work. Walk to the bars. This is the life."

This is it, the end for you.

Vicki is one shovelful of pollen-riddled dirt away from burying you completely. Two choices now:

Go back to page 44. Start over. Decline the drink.

Or: Move forward. Move past this. **Page 50**.

Your life is a stack of Chance cards that forever drag you back three spaces.

Go back to page 44.

That's impressive, right? Your big fucking house!

"Life is good," you say. "Got a house, a pool."

"Very cool," she says. "Where at?"

"North of the city. Maitland. Ridiculous square footage."

"Suburbia! You're like a dad or something. Except, you know, without a family."

Don't say it. Don't tell her to fuck off.

"Long drive," she says, "coming downtown at night."

"Well. Sure. Maitland."

"Don't come downtown often, then?"

"Not anymore. Don't like to drive drunk."

"But I *did* see you not too long ago. That new rooftop bar?"

"Saw *me*?"

"When Jimmy Bastion was almost banging that girl on the dance floor."

You shake your head. "That must be wrong. That wasn't us."

"It was."

"This is Jimmy's *wife*, remember?" You point to Sandra, quiet as ever, who is watching the conversation unfold, still smiling politely, but she doesn't seem to be hearing the words. "This is *Sandra*. You were just talking to her, like, one minute ago."

"I know," Vicki says. "But we're talking about *you*, Marc. We're talking about how easy it was for Jimmy. That's what I want to reinforce for you. It was so easy. Everything is so easy. He's married, and you're single and lonely, and yet you could only sit there while he pawed at that girl's ass."

"This doesn't seem like…you wouldn't say these things."

"He fucked the shit out of her, is what happened. I was surprised, Marc, because I expected *you'd* be the one to get on that. Get over Shelley, fuck some random coked-up bitch in a bar, but it was *this girl's* husband." She points her drink at Sandra, who smiles and nods. "You're pathetic, Marc. I remember, back before you and Shelley got engaged…I remember you at Downtown Beer Fest, when you went home with that Tequiza beer-tub girl. You remember that?"

"You weren't there, either. How do you know about that?"

"Short red top, black shorts so tight it looked like electrical tape on her ass. What a player, you. But now, keeping a friend's wife company while he's inside hitting on waitresses? My friends—back there, the ones giving their attention to other men—were once attracted to you, back when it was you and your best friend Edwin, conquering Orlando, buying homes, gonna make a million easy, blah blah blah. Hell, I remember you emailed me to ask if I needed a place to rent. You remember that? You said you had a few houses?"

"Did I?"

"And I said, Wow. Isn't that risky? Buying so much, counting on ever-rising prices and easy flips? What do they call them, the ARMs, the 2/28 loans? And you said?"

"Let's change the subject. Please."

"I work pharmaceutical sales," she says. "No slow-down there!"

You exhale, brace yourself.

"I'm living at the Waverly."

Fingertips massaging the bridge of your nose. She's still going.

"Love it. I walk to work. Walk to the bars."

"Right," you say and exhale again, any last breath of optimism now gone from you completely. "Smart investment."

"You want to fuck me, don't you?"

"What?"

"You do! You're so lonely, Marc with a 'c.' Don't you see the city moving on without you? Don't you see that it's all over, that you were *someone* once, but now you're just a desperate loser? Don't you *see*?"

Go to page 54 to change the subject, talk about the Magic instead.

Go to page 56 if you agree with Vicki, if you do want to fuck her. Maybe she's offering? Maybe there's a connection here? Maybe this is her way of flirting.

Maybe—but she's probably fucking with you.

Go to page 61 to put Vicki in her place. Tell her what real work looks like.

Here in May of 2009, every Orlandoan is talking about the Magic.

All across town, Orlando Magic banners are unfurled down the sides of high-rises: five-story-tall Dwight Howards, basketball palmed, poised for a dunk, blue flames curling around his screaming face; Hedo Türkoğlu in mid-dribble, directing the offense; Jameer Nelson, Rashard Lewis, Rafer Alston portraits printed beneath the slogan "Blue and White Ignite." It's been a decade since this city last saw a winner, since Shaq left Orlando for Los Angeles, for championships, for bright lights and the big city and bigger exposure than Orlando could offer, leaving the Magic to crumble into irrelevancy, the city's team often tanking early in the season and scrapping its way to .500 winning percentages. The "Heart and Hustle" squads (that was the marketing campaign, "Heart and Hustle," which just meant they played hard, but they lost, always lost). And then Grant Hill—the supposed superstar savior purchased at great cost from the Detroit Pistons—injured more often than he played, and then Tracy McGrady—the next savior—demanding a trade because the Orlando stink was so putrid. A full decade of mediocrity, after you were lured into becoming a fan by the mid-'90s era of Penny Hardaway, Nick Anderson, Horace Grant, and Shaquille O'Neal. Back then, as a child in south Georgia, that was when you first saw Orlando as a city of the future, those black pinstripe uniforms, the star in the logo, the tiny theater lights that lined the stairs inside the O-rena like it was Christmas year-round, Nick Anderson stealing the ball from Michael Jordan and ousting the Bulls in the '95 playoffs. *Orlando,* you thought in your parents' cluttered living room, watching Shaq shatter backboards. It sounded—*yes*—magical, and the Atlanta Hawks had always bored you in a way you couldn't articulate. You and your brother Kyle convinced your father to buy Magic tickets one year as a Christmas present, and you drove down to the O-rena on Christmas day and your mother was still alive and the family was together and was there ever a better day than that?

"Been watching the Magic?" you ask Vicki. A neutral topic, something that cannot be turned against you.

"Who hasn't? Didn't I see you at one of the games?" she asks. After so many disappointing seasons, everyone in town is now sporting Magic shirts again, affixing Magic bumper stickers and magnets to their SUVs. You're about to answer when Vicki says, "By the way, Jimmy fucked this one girl at that new rooftop bar, and you're in debt and lost your fiancé, and your homes are all about to go underwater, and you're pathetic and nobody wants to fuck you. Especially not me. You felt my hand on your shoulder, and you thought: maybe she wants to fuck me? I don't."

"Anyway," you say. "Anyway! The Magic!" And you tell her that this is the year. The Detroit Pistons—the Beasts of the Eastern Conference—they're fading. They've collapsed. Chauncy Billups is gone, 'Sheed a memory. And the Magic just dispatched the 76ers, thrashed them in that final game in Philadelphia, and did you hear the boos from the Philly fans? Sweet, sweet boos. Yeah, okay, nobody expected the 76ers to take it to six games, nor for Dwight to catch a flagrant foul and a suspension for that critical Game Six, but we hit the road and JJ Redick came alive like he was still sinking three-pointers at Duke, and we closed them out and *the 76ers' own fans* booed them in Philadelphia! Ha! Philly fans! Battling adversity, these 2009 Orlando Magic. Yes we can! Yes we can! Obama's in office, the economy will recover, the houses will sell! The Magic are going to overcome the ten-year curse of Shaq. The city is going to overcome. This is our year! Everything that's happened—everything!—can you see the pieces falling into place? *Can you see it?*

"I work pharmaceutical sales," she says. "I live at the Waverly."

Go back to page 16? Or was it page 44? Choose again? No. You've read every possible scenario. You've expended all choices. Wait. Have you been turning pages back and forth? Honestly. Have you been playing along? Did you ever believe you had the power to determine a new outcome, or did you just move page by page and resign yourself to the same old fate, the boring left-to-right, up-to-down, page-by-page machinations you've been programmed to enact since kindergarten? Well. No judgment. But let's keep going: let's tell Vicki how you really feel. **Page 57.** Go!

"Let's get out of here!" you tell her.

"Marc," Vicki says, fingertips steepled, face negotiation-serious.

Strangely, Sandra has disappeared. All around you, the lights have dimmed.

"Across town!" you say. "Screw this place!"

You stand and motion for Vicki to follow you, and you're jogging forward, but then you're looking behind you and Vicki is still at the table and she's not smiling and the montage soundtrack is not starting and your feet are not rising from the pavement and you're not floating and the street is empty and there are no rooftop parties, no toasts, no kisses beneath starlight, no flash no flash no flash. The Lake Eola fountain falls flat. The blue pyramids atop each of the SunTrust Building's four rooftop corners go dark, and then the darkness falls from the 35th floor all the way to the ground, streetlights down Orange Avenue dark, Courthouse dark, neon lights that ride the wave-like roof of the Lynx Central Station snapping off, the streets gone silent and empty and you still standing there alone.

The entire city has faded to black.

Maybe you can rewind?

Maybe you can tell her how you really feel instead?

Turn to page 57.

Rewind.

You never accepted her drink.

You brush her hand from your shoulder.

You tell her you can see right through her.

You tell her you know *her* life is empty right now, too. The *Waverly*? Who is she kidding? Tonight is the night, you say. I'm going to stop pretending I'm someone else, that all is well! Do you care, Vicki with an "i"? Do you really care what's happened to me? *Is there anyone left in this town who cares?*

But here's the thing: she smiles.

"Oh, Marc with a 'c,'" she says. "I hate to see you like this."

And you know this is the end for you. Your father taught you that silence is better than emotion, that no one wants to watch a pathetic display of sadness from a grown man. After all, no one here in Orlando wants to talk about the consequences of this economic meltdown for the city, what the ticket slump at Disney might mean. No one wants to talk about what might happen if Universal Studios' "Wizarding World of Harry Potter" does not set the turnstiles spinning, if Butter Beer is not guzzled by the gallon. No one wants to admit that a long recession will not only kill Disney but Orlando itself, that Orlando's fate could be the same as Detroit's, where the weeds have overtaken house. People *do* talk about NASA, sure, how the Space Coast is withering; people do talk about the overbuilt town centers in East Orlando, the empty stretches of unnecessary commercial complexes, the apartments across Central Florida that overnight reclassified themselves as "condos" and "townhouses" to trick renters into buying for as much as $300,000 but are now going abandoned, the beautiful artist's renderings for high-rise condos that would've changed the skyline but were never actually built, the luxurious Mediterranean shopping centers in Metro West built beside golf courses and gated communities but still waiting for tenants. People *do* talk about the unfinished neighborhoods, sure, maybe admit the mistake of the mostly empty Oviedo Town Center, and use words like "over-valued" and "market correction," nodding in acceptance at the loss of these individual pieces of the city, as if Orlando is now a grandparent with failing body parts. Hips and knees. Bowel troubles. But no one will talk about the heart.

"It's okay," she says. "The city will move on without you. The Magic will improve, even if you stop watching. You are the piece that has given out, and we will discard you and *we* will be all right."

You slap your wine glass from the table, smash the Jack and Coke against the ground, run to the parking garage. You drive home and there is a soundtrack in this scene, too, some heartbroken track from a pop star's failed comeback album, and you don't know what comes next, but like all of your friends who have fled their foreclosures and sinking ideas, you get the sense that you too will flee the City Beautiful, though in the meantime **you will turn to page 59**.

CONTINUE TO NEXT PAGE

Damn it. DAMN IT! How did you end up here?

Is this another fantasy?

Is this reality?

Or maybe this is how you imagined adult decisions at age 7 or 8, back when you read *Choose Your Own Adventure* books. Good and evil so easily defined, when you were clearly the stalwart hero.

Will you choose to use your world-destroyer orb, or will you run back to your space craft?

You wonder what might happen if there *was* a dragon, if it did emerge from some Central Florida sinkhole tomorrow and it did flap its giant wings and soar over I-4 and open its giant mouth to torch a line of cars, yours included. How long would Jimmy or Sandra grieve? Would you only be a passing thought, an "Oh, that sucks" comment on Vicki's Facebook page?

Clearly this is your cue to end the night.

Turn to page 64.

Who is *she* to make *you* feel foolish about your investments? What does she know about hard work? In college, Vicki's sweat sparkled with dollar signs, Kate Spade purse and Coach sunglasses, a brand-new black Lexus even though she only worked maybe ten hours a week at her father's doctor friend's office. *Hard work*, Vicki? Here, now, you'll guilt her with your own story, make her feel like a mud puddle. You'll tell her. You'll tell her the stock you come from.

"You want to make fun of my house, my business?" you say. "Do you understand how I grew up, how far I've come?"

"No clue."

"Georgia. Rural Georgia."

"Congratulations."

"My brother never got his own clothes. Always my hand-me-downs."

"Sounds like you were the lucky one, then."

"Poor. We were dirt-poor."

Vicki can dodge all she wants, but you've seen the middle- and upper-class guilt in the eyes of dozens of friends and colleagues who've listened to just a paragraph of your story. These are experiences she hasn't had, and it kills her (even if she won't admit it) to know that the only adversity she's faced is a sometimes-slow internet connection, a freezer that doesn't deliver ice quick enough.

"Am I supposed to feel sorry for you?" she asks.

"No. I'm setting the scene. All I want is for you to know that I came from nothing. My father practically built our house, too. There was a fire, when I was young. And he rebuilt half the house on his own. Do you know what kind of resolve that takes? We lived in a rental across town for almost a year, and there were holes in the walls big enough for cats to sneak in and out. My parents tried to cover the gaps with furniture so we wouldn't wind up with snakes in our bedrooms."

"We've all got stories," she sighs.

"My father didn't stop. Every night he went to our house. Every night he was over there hammering, laying new floorboards, pounding in the shingles.

Like he was a frontiersman or something, every fucking board. It's a small house, cramped as hell, but he built it back up."

"Sounds like a hard worker."

"The man is a machine. Works from sun-up to sun-down, never stops."

"So you grew up poor, boo-hoo, but he must have money by *now*, hard worker that he is. Does he own his own business?"

"He's an auto mechanic."

"Sounds dirty."

"Filthy. Greasy."

"Does he own the shop?"

"It's…" And as self-satisfied as you were with the details of your childhood, you didn't anticipate this line of questioning, this curiosity about what your father has become and what sort of wealth he's accumulated by now. She wasn't supposed to ask questions. She was only supposed to suffer the violence of your angry rant, allow herself to be reduced to a fraction of herself. "It's complicated," you say. "His best friend owns it. My father works his ass off, and they're practically partners. They had some arrangement or something… John-John was the one who helped—"

"John-John?"

"Yeah. What?"

She's laughing. "One John isn't good enough? Do poor people, like, hoard extra names so they feel like they have more possessions?"

You close your eyes. "John-John is a business owner."

"If you say so."

"My father's got a gentleman's agreement with him, and the idea is that they'll both retire at the same time, and John-John will sell the business and split the money with him. Something like that. I don't know. That's not the point. The point is…*hard work*, are you even paying attention? *Hard work* is the point. It's the most important thing there is, and when you make money from *hard work*, that's ten times more fucking impressive than, like, dating a rich dude."

"Okay. I get it. You came from nothing."

"From *nothing*. I am the American Dream. Paid for college on my own, scholarships and summer jobs and student loans. Unpaid internships to 'do my time,' entry-level position at Wachovia. Work. Hard fucking work. And at my desk at Wachovia, I saw the same names in my emails, the same names on loan after loan, the notaries for the title companies, and I took a chance, left the security of my corporate job, of paychecks every two weeks, of insurance and benefits, and I became a fucking cowboy, a damned eighteen-hundreds *tycoon*, started my own loan-closing business just like all these other people all over town who weren't even half as smart or ambitious as me, and soon I was working half the time and making twice the money, *smarter not harder*, and I'd earned myself the time to invest in house searches with Edwin, to oversee contractors and carpenters on abused properties, to take estimates for landscaping, and I was calling my friends at title companies and signing contracts to become their *exclusive closing service*. From *nothing*, remember! This shit was *all me*. American Dream."

"How could I not be impressed?"

"I just…I just want someone to understand me. It wasn't supposed to be this way. I was supposed to reach the top. That's the reward for working hard, don't you see?"

"Sorry I didn't come from nothing." She shrugs and laughs, perfect black hair shining under street lights, perfect evil eyes. When another piece of pollen helicopters down from the trees, it misses her entirely. This is not how it's supposed to go. She isn't broken, isn't guilted, and the world around you disappears once more. It's just you and Vicki, backdropped by darkness.

"You and Edwin both," you say. "Neither of you can understand."

"Sorry." She shrugs, perfect hair unmoving, checks her phone.

"You probably grew up in a big house with a pool, a foyer, walk-in closets. Edwin, too. You have money, you can just start over whenever something doesn't work out. *Fuck*," you say.

"Go into bankruptcy," she says, "or swallow some pills. Two easy solutions."

Wow. That devolved quickly.

Maybe this is a conversational topic best avoided.

Turn to page 64 to end the night.

If only it were so easy to choose the course of a conversation, as if—like a long string of message-board comments—you could see it all unfurl before you without having to commit to participating.

But in the end, your encounter with Vicki is indeed a combination of so many conversations you did not want to have, questions like "So where are you working now?" that you answer while looking into your wine glass, the deep and resolute red, anything to avoid looking at her victorious smile; you can't escape it, no matter what you choose to say or do; you look at her friends, finishing their drinks, dismissing the young men who purchased them. "I have a loan-closing business," you tell her, and she says, "Oh, that's right!" and, "Too bad about the market. A lot of people really lost their asses, didn't they?" And she says: "I work pharmaceutical sales. No slow-down there!" And she tells you that she lives at the Waverly. "Love it," she says. "I walk to work. I walk to the bars."

It's agonizing, but it's predictable.

"Gotta go," Vicki says. "Drop me a Facebook message or something!" And she's off, headed elsewhere with her entourage, footsteps unbalanced and heels sinking into sidewalk cracks—but when she dips, her girls are there to catch her—and now Jimmy is strutting outside here to the patio, carrying his Blue Moon and looking like he just won a few hands of Black Jack.

"Who killed the party?" he asks. He slides his beer onto the table and immediately pulls a pack of cigarettes out, smacks the bottom of the pack against his rigid palm.

Sandra's straight-line lips crack into a smile. Perhaps she's hoping Jimmy will share some amusing anecdote from his conversations inside, because clearly what she just witnessed out here was a downer.

And the pedicab driver is back, peddling to the group of drunk women who've left your table and are now simultaneously checking cell phones and discussing Sky Bar vs. Ember vs. Lodge, huddled beside a crape myrtle pruned skeletally from winter, the year's new growth just beginning. The pedicab driver adjusts his bandana, tells the girls to climb aboard, climb aboard, choose your adventure tonight, ladies!

Here's a man who occupies his role proudly. Arm muscles taut as he grips the handlebars. An Orlando Magic magnet—the "star ball" logo, just the blue and silver basketball rocketing through an electric stream of five-pointed stars, so bold but so simple—affixed with confidence to the cab's thin bumper. And he's whisking them away to their next destination, wherever that might be. Wherever any of them wants to go. Off they go, the shooting star magnet on the back of the carriage disappearing into the darkness of faraway.

Which is better? you wonder. Which ending? The ones you didn't choose? Or the one you're left with, the one you can't escape?

Up and at 'em, Marc Turner, feet on the floor, out of bed, dressed, forward forward forward, Nutrigrain bar from the pantry and water bottle filled to the brim and travel mug of coffee with just a touch of creamer—just a *touch*, damn it, so much *sugar*—and then out to the car, forward forward forward, weekend over, workday begins, no thinking today, no choices, just listen to this voice, an expert Tour Guide who will tell you exactly where to go and what to do and *ah! ah!*, no thinking, certainly no *over*-thinking, you've done quite enough of that, big guy, and where the hell did it get you except miserable and depressed and dreaming of a life as a damned pedicab driver?, so just listen and follow directions, listen and your Tour Guide will tell you exactly where to go (take a left up here, don't forget the turn signal) and we'll get right back on track, won't we?, no further embarrassments suffered, no further self-loathing (take a right), just listen, no choices, forward forward forward, as we travel the hell that is Semoran Boulevard (ah! ah!, no swearing, even though this is a road where swear words are physically baked into the pavement) until we get to the hell that is the intersection of Semoran and Red Bug Lake Road (okay, you can let out a little swear, a tiny one), and you know where we're going now, don't you?, headed to the first stop on our grand day of tours, inspecting and reviewing all the houses you own and rent out, the real estate that was supposed to get flipped for quick riches but is instead stagnating on the market, all this property you've been avoiding, afraid to visit in the same way that you might be afraid to look under a bandage lest the wound has festered or grown, but if you want to make it back to the top, Marc, good buddy, you need to see where you stand, assess the damage, so follow your Tour Guide, forward forward forward to

STOP #1: CASSELBERRY

And it is here, in a sort-of-suburb called Casselberry, that you arrive for a tour of the first two units that Edwin managed, both of which have been continuously occupied for two years, taken for granted entirely. Of course, Edwin is gone now. "You're on your own, bro," he said three weeks ago, left for Atlanta to live with his rich sister, left you to hold together the depreciating business you started together, sand slipping through your fingers. For all you know, Edwin lied when he told you he was placing ads for the rentals, probably pocketed the cash you deposited in the account for this purpose, spent it instead on gas or Grey Goose or cocaine. Hell, he wasted how much money on his birthday party last November? You never even saw the betrayal coming. Took you until this week to discover that he sold off the staging furniture you'd been using for open houses, the framed art and the wall mirrors and the kitchen tables.

Okay, but we're here now. A tour of your first two properties. Follow, follow! Big smile, too, can you do that?

Both houses are in the same subdivision, separated by three homes in between, and both are rented by the same extended Puerto Rican family. You're greeted at the door by a round man in a Fun Spot polo, and he slaps your back three or four times before letting you in.

"Fun Spot," you say. "The roller-coaster park?"

"My job is a blast! Love it!" he says and takes a swig of Monster Energy. "So your partner's no longer in the business? Too bad. He was a funny guy!"

"Funny, like how?" you ask.

"Oh, like funny! Always made everyone laugh."

Hold your tongue, Landlord. Do not ask, "Do *I* seem fun? Do *I* put you at ease?"

A child shoots past, Nerf gun in hand, knocking the padfolio from your hand; he's followed by another child, this one howling and carrying a double-barrel Nerf shotgun. They crash through the door, and as they move into the yard, you hear their screams joined by a half-dozen others, and then the pop-

pop-pop sounds of dart guns firing, bodies hit. Two houses, and you're not entirely sure which parents and which children live in which house, as the family members drift across the yards and into one another's living rooms at will; hell, maybe they just keep keep accumulating new residents every few months (older brothers, cousins, aunts), and that's why they've built IKEA bunk beds in the garages, and why so many cars and vans are now spilling into the street. Not what you'd envisioned when you first rolled the word "landlord" across your tongue. You'd imagined every tenant just like you, a young responsible guy with a wife or fiancée, steadily building his savings account in order to buy instead of rent. You never really imagined families.

"Shouldn't the kids be in school today?" you ask.

"Teacher work day," he says. "You think I just let them run wild? Ha ha!"

He's joking, slaps your back again, but you know you shouldn't have asked. Edwin wouldn't have. Edwin probably would've grabbed a Nerf gun and joined the mayhem. Where's the quadruple-barrel hand cannon, kiddos? Whoop whoop! Pop pop pop!

You drift into the living room so the father can keep an eye on the kids outside, and from here, you look down the street and see an old man at his window, drapes parted as he watches the tornado of elementary-kid chaos. You imagine this is a regular occurrence, the old white neighbors caught between these two houses, watching from windows and garages, annoyed at the brown children marching across their lawns to get from one house to the next, abandoning their bicycles on the shared sidewalks, playing games of football and basketball that leave marks on every car window down the street, their whole sprawling family giving off the vibe that it's about to annex all land between houses. You picture these old people grumbling and shaking their heads, cursing the day they voted for Obama. But so long as these renters don't knock down walls, you don't care how many are living in each house, what language they speak, or whether they take over the whole damned subdivision: if you get a check every month, you stay afloat a little longer.

Because here's the big takeaway: the round man shows you everything, every square inch of both houses, and there's no damage to either property, and no real threat of the tenants ending their leases. "We like the schools here!" the man says, gulps more Monster. "And the park is walking distance! Why would we ever move?" You nearly cry, it's so reassuring. Not a bad start to the day, is it?

STOP #2: THE WILD BERRY RENTAL HOUSE

Come along, come along, all the way across town to inspect a vacant house you haven't visited in months! The day started great! It's only going to get better, right? Let's see that smile again. Yeah. Big one.

But when you arrive in this neighborhood called Wild Berry the smile gets tougher to hold. You expected you'd encounter *some* damage today, some wear and tear, maybe some overgrown weeds in the front lawn, creepers in the driveway, something cosmetic and easily fixable. But you did not expect to find a large van, paint faded to '70s porno colors, parked in the driveway of the house you own.

There's no one renting the house, haven't been any tenants for six months. Whoever this is, this is not their driveway.

First order of business, then, Landlord: pull into the driveway and park next to the van, like you're challenging it over property ownership.

Then: ask the empty neighborhood, "What *is* this?" and slam your car door. Make sure the world hears you, recognizes your authority. (On second thought, don't shout too loud. There's no one around to answer you. It's mid-day in Florida, that time when the sun reaches such a terrible point in the sky that its rays penetrate and slip around even the largest and fullest of trees, all shade disappearing entirely, shadows reduced to pin-pricks. Adults at work. Cars all gone. And children know better than to play outside when the black pavement is hot as a cast-iron skillet.)

Still. Be assertive. Wipe the sweat off your forehead as you approach the van in your driveway and try to look tough doing it.

Bend to examine the undercarriage: there are cinderblocks wedged under the front tires to prevent the vehicle from rolling into the street.

The first question on your mind is, How *dare* they? How could someone *dare* park their broken-down van in your driveway, so confidently, as if they owned the place? But don't put too much energy into this question. After all, you know the answer. The neighbors likely think this house is abandoned, and they're half-right. This property was part of the first wave of purchases you made with Edwin, back when banks were still giving out loans like lollipops, back when no one needed to worry about down payments—and you rented this house out for *three years* while the value rose and rose, maxing out the life of the low interest rate on the ARM. There was a time when, if you'd sold, you'd have made one-fifty in pure profit. But you waited, Edwin managing it as a rental. When the last batch of renters moved out, you figured it was a good time to sell, but then everything crashed.

So you know *why* someone would park their vehicle here. Why not? It looks like a foreclosure. Soon, it probably will be. Without Edwin and without renters, you can't afford to keep making payments on an empty house. But today? Today you are still the owner—two months late on the mortgage, but *still the owner.*

So the better question to ask, then, is "How can you get it the hell out of here?" This is what your father would think, were he to drive up to the shop one hazy Georgia morning and find someone parked in his lot even though they were shopping in the antique store next door. He'd find them, drag them out, Civil War-era lantern in their hands, and he'd make them move to a properly designated parking space. What's right is right. And if you want to ever rent or sell this property, you cannot abide squatters.

But wait. Stop at the curb, look down. There's an oil spot:

Deep, black, crafted with care. Several drafts, several coats, as if this oil spot was someone's contribution to Orlando culture, some piece of Millennial artwork with all the protest of graffiti and none of the beauty. There's another, not far away, this one sketchy, as if the artist is still laboring in the composing process. Look:

And another stain beneath the van, hidden in shadow.

Walk around the van, let your hand graze the metal. Rust spots here, there. Twin metal wires poking out from beneath the front bumper.

This van has been here for months. At one time, maybe it was running, and perhaps the *preferred* parking spot was its owner's own driveway, but as it began leaking fluids, they moved it to the street, then—when they didn't want their own curb blighted—to the curb in front of your house, and finally—why not?—to your driveway. It's taken awhile to get here, a lot of oil stains and backfires and failed starts. But one thing is certain: its owners are close.

Examine the houses. What sort of person would own this van?

The next-door neighbor, perhaps? It's a two-story house, nearly the same colors as yours, white vinyl fence. Over the fence, you notice the plastic roof of a child's backyard playground, and also a large screened-in porch and pool. You imagine a family, one with money, one that hosts weekend cookouts, ties balloons to their mailbox for their child's birthday party, the sort of family that *might* have allowed party guests to park in your driveway, but only to clear the road and keep the area safer for when they pulled the portable soccer nets from the garage and set them up in the street. Their driveway, of course, is stain-free. This van is not theirs.

Your other next-door neighbor? Mulch bed out front, red and yellow flowers. Marigolds? You know little about landscaping. (It was Edwin who made you invest several thousand in re-sodding the Longwood property, a sweet short-sale deal that looked more damaged than it was, an easy flip. "Imagine if we planted a single palm in the center of the front yard, something as tall and happy as a McDonald's sign," Edwin suggested. "If it's some New York investor buying Florida property from magazine ads, that's what he sees. That's the difference." Fuck, don't admit that Edwin seemed so smart for so long, that these sorts of answers always impressed you.) This next-door neighbor, this is the sort of house whose "curb appeal" Edwin would have commended. The mulch is red as Rutgers, sprinkler heads poised. Concrete pavers in a long, uninterrupted row from curb to backyard fence, clearly delineating the owner's green grass from your patchy yellow sod. *My property*, the pavers say. *And over there,* your *property*. No oil stains over there, either. Walk the curb. Keep walking. Look down.

Oil stains growing, forming a sort of dotted-line trail leading from your driveway to another unit across the street.

Follow the trail, walk across the street.

Yes, it's hot. But follow your tour guide, follow.

And there, notice it now? The home across the street is a mirror image of your own. Weeds high in the yard. Bits of broken porcelain hiding in the bushes and scattered about the yard, as if someone tossed a toilet from the second-floor window and let last year's summer storms carry the pieces wherever they might settle. A number missing in the gold address plaque.

Stand there in your neighbor's driveway, the archipelago of oil stains stretching from your feet all the way down the hot pavement to your own driveway, to the van.

In the window above the front door, there's a trophy. Nothing spectacular, just a white base with an action-figure-sized soccer player atop it, perhaps the sort of award given out on the day when everyone gets a trophy. But it's there, proud, the only thing shining at this house save for the oil slicks.

As part of your tour today, you should walk to the door. You should confront them. *That's my house*, you should say. *You're destroying the value of* my house. *Mow your lawn. Get rid of the* van.

Of course, this should've been Edwin's job, Edwin's confrontation to handle. Standing here, you wonder what he'd do. He had a tendency to act brashly, to threaten legal action against tenants who fought for their security deposits (even when he knew little about the procedures he was discussing). Hell, he left *you* saddled with all these mortgages, not a care in the world that his own name was attached to them. "I gotta get out from under this," he said before he left for Atlanta. "Gotta start fresh." He left it all behind, no thought of the consequences, allowed you to cancel his card and remove his name from the bank account (though not from the leases; you wouldn't give him that escape route). Hell, you know what he would've done. He'd have left the stain, just like he left *you* to hold together these properties, to spend so many long hot days in your car driving cross-town, hundreds of miles a day, interstate pavement, tolls, golf course developments, living rooms, just to keep your modest signing service in the game.

You are not Edwin. You cannot start fresh because you are not bold enough to cut your losses. So ask yourself: Is this really the house? The owners of the van? The evidence appears sound, but if you ring the doorbell, will it be a little girl? A grandmother? And if you raise your voice, "Is *that* your van? Get that out of my driveway!" will they just cower, shut the door, call the police?

No, here is the only conclusion that you can draw, Landlord: this van—rust spattered on the side like mud, tint peeling off the windows—this van *belongs* in your driveway. Because it is *your house* that does not belong in *this neighborhood*, your empty house whose presence is every neighbor's nightmare scenario, not the other way around. Who would live in this house? Certainly you wouldn't. For the first time, will you look at the house? *Look.* Not at the driveway, not at the van, not at the oil stains. The house that you own, that you've been paying for but never visit. Soggy phone books, clumps of leaves, and dozens of old fliers from pizza restaurants and lawn care companies clutter the doorstep. Spiderwebs. Bird shit on the doorknob. The *doorknob*! Wasp nests hanging from the eaves like malignant growths. The house across the street? It's also a nightmare, but at least it's occupied; at least there is life there.

No, in this neighborhood, you can make no demands. So walk back to your car, get inside, blast the air conditioner, wipe your forehead. Spend a few minutes thinking. Is there enough time to find a new tenant before foreclosure descends? You can place ads in a number of local fliers and booklets, everything Edwin was supposed to do. You can contact a property management company, and with the fees they charge resign yourself to losing *hundreds of dollars each month* even when the company finds someone to rent it, the adjustable rate of the mortgage ever-closer to adjusting in the most terrifying way and prying the property from your hands regardless. You can—you can—

Wait, what happened to the positivity?

STOP #3: A TOUR OF YOUR ANGER

Leave the subdivision of Wild Berry. Follow a different road, this one also dotted by oil stains, but the oil stains seem to be leading…inside you, somehow.

Follow them.

Follow the oil stains in here, where you will find the anger that nearly made you scream while standing in the road staring at the van, that nearly made you charge into a stranger's home demanding retribution.

See, there's been something growing inside you, an anger building daily and occupying more and more of the space in your life. There is no square footage large enough to contain it all. You need closets and guest rooms, you need backyard sheds, you need storage units, and your storage units need sheds and storage units of their own. Always it is expanding, always you feel its new blueprints unfurled.

You get angry so *quickly* now, that's the thing. Angry with the roads, the traffic. Angry over the stupidest shit. Driving through downtown last week, you had to wait for a man in a tan suit to stroll across the crosswalk on Orange Avenue even though *you* had the *green light*. He saw you mouth "Oh come on!" as he walked, and so he stopped in front of your car, made you wait longer, held up his arms in a "wanna fight?" motion, knowing you had no choice but to wait, because seriously, were you gonna *ram* him?

And what made you even angrier: later that day, as you crosswalked Robinson in rain slashing sideways, you were almost run over when some jerk-off in a Jeep gunned it through the stop sign. Wet. Fractured umbrella. Almost crushed by a Jeep. Angry. They say that Orlando is one of the deadliest cities in the country for pedestrians, and it made you angry to think of all the ways city administrators and urban planners have failed the people here, the eight-lane highways with only 10-second "walk" signals (or walk signals that don't work), the blind spots, the culture of driving dependency and the shittiness of public transportation in the region, car companies and toll roads fat and rich, the vast conspiracy against walking that almost led to your death.

Anger. On your mind, all day.

There was an open parking spot at Publix yesterday, too—you still remember this, and God, there's something *wrong about you* that you won't let this go—the cars on both sides of your spot had parked over the lines, and you couldn't fit into the spot and you had to drive all the way to the back of the parking lot. You were so angry. You were so angry, and you almost waited for the drivers to return to their cars just so you could pick a fight with the motherfuckers who couldn't just *park within the fucking lines.*

Angry when you stopped at a Mobil and filled a cup with ice only to discover that the Diet Coke button on the soda fountain was out of order. Angry when you stopped at Shell and there were only Pepsi products for sale (*no*, it's not the same).

Follow your anger. More to see, so much more to see.

Angry with sports. *Too often* angry with sports.

Angry with your alma mater's football team, the UCF Knights, which opened its new on-campus stadium in 2007 with grand proclamations that it was ready to challenge the University of Florida and Florida State University and the University of Miami for supremacy in the Orlando market, and then the university—satisfied that they'd made it, that they were one of the "big boys" because they won fucking Conference USA that year—jacked up the season ticket prices and in 2008 went 4-8 in front of bleachers that became progressively emptier as the season wore on, until they were giving tickets away and hoping they could recapture the raucous energy and blistering optimism of the previous year. You called the ticket office and yelled at the joker on the other end: "I pay a premium on my season tickets, just so you can give away 10,000 tickets to the 'local community' when the team stinks?" Your anger increased exponentially with each response the ticket agent gave you, until you threw your phone across the room and vowed not to even use your final ticket of the season. UCF was supposed to be a "sleeping giant" (that's what Coach O'Leary said when he took the job) and, like Orlando itself, the next big thing: 50,000 students circulating through a tropically appointed campus landscape, through resort-style residence halls that looked almost as sexy as honeymoon hotels, through a gym and rec center that put to shame the best that the rest of the city had to offer; 50,000 students and a brand-new stadium, and this university was supposed to not just awaken but *erupt* onto the college football scene, in the process disrupting the entire hierarchy of the state's schools and sports allegiances. But so far there's only been steadily mounting disappointment, anger at their failure to fulfill a destiny you were too eager to believe.

You get angry at loan closings when someone doesn't understand where to sign, even though you've highlighted each space for their signature or initials. You get angry as you plow through 130 pages of legalese that you know—you *know* it, and it *kills* you—is designed to trick the woman who has a screaming child on her lap, whose Marine husband is in Afghanistan and cannot help her sort out the bullshit, who must simply finish the paperwork *now*, today, before she has to drop the kid off with her parents and go to work, this woman becoming so flustered at the language that she stops reading. You're angry at yourself for being a part of this industry, then angry at *yourself* for being *angry at yourself* because *come on*, everyone's gotta work, right?, and this woman—this mother you feel sorry for—she'd take your job in a heartbeat, wouldn't she?

Edwin once told you a story, a really sad story, about this Pennsylvania couple who'd spent every dime of their savings on this phony neighborhood project in St. Augustine, this swampland that wasn't even electric- or water-ready, let alone road- or construction-ready, and they lost *everything*…but Edwin only learned this because the neighborhood was a pyramid scheme, and the Pennsylvania couple was trying to unload *their* steaming pile of shit on *him* and make their money back. "Can you believe these bozos?" he asked you. "Do I look like a rube?" You want to empathize, but no one is innocent; everyone's a villain in different ways, and you get angry both when compassion comes too quickly, or when it seems too difficult.

You get angry when, after searching home prices on Zillow, you experience momentary joy from spotting dips in those neighborhoods where there were boats in every driveway, HDTVs hanging in the Goddamn bathrooms. Good! Greedy fuckers got what they deserved! But it makes you angry that this is the *only thing* that makes you happy, kind of like a fat man who finds momentary joy in a cookie, then gets depressed after eating it.

Anger. *Anger!*

Fat people, too. Oh, they definitely make you angry.

You get angry when you see fat people inside homes against which foreclosure will soon strike, and you think: You can't afford your monthly mortgage, but you can sure afford to *eat*, can't you? Give up the soda and stop buying buckets of ranch dressing and boom: you've got enough money to make your payment. Your motherfucking empty house is going to bring down the value of *every house* around it, you selfish bastard!

You get angry at them, even though you know it's high-fructose corn syrup and French-fried fast food that's behind the obesity, not necessarily some exorbitant budget dedicated to binge eating. You know it's actually more expensive to eat fresh and organic and to pay for a gym membership and to carve out extra time for exercise and healthy cooking than it is to just buy a couple $5 hot-and-ready pizzas from Little Caesars on the way home from work and continue getting fatter, and then—once you come to this conclusion—you are no longer mad at the *fat people* but instead at the *corn industry*, the *U.S.*

government for the corn subsidies, at *Little Caesars* for the up-sale on Crazy Bread for a fat man who doesn't need it, and don't ask him if he needs a canister of butter sauce, either, *come on!*, mad at *yourself* for being judgmental.

You get angry with homeowners for putting up Christmas decorations too early. For putting up Halloween decorations too late. *You fuckers are skewing our perception of the seasons!* But then you think: is it really *their* fault? It's the big-box stores that decide when a holiday season begins or ends, and even which holidays are worth celebrating. Fuck Wal-Mart and Hallmark for dictating how and when we're allowed to celebrate the holidays, the stupid inflatable snowmen we buy to make our yards uniquely decorated (and then we look down the street and see that *everyone* has bought the same fucking inflatable snowman, a whole army of suburban snowmen), and then you're angry that—despite the holiday super-saturation and 10,000 channels on your TV and a billion Christmas-themed TV shows—you once again missed *A Charlie Brown Christmas* and where were the motherfucking commercials for it this year you *need* that cartoon oh God you need that little breath of positivity Linus and his motherfucking Bible story anger anger anger!

Anger leads to anger, leads to anger, until…where did we even start? You even drew a chart of "Things to be Angry About" and "Things to be Happy About" on a dry-erase board at your home office, and there was no competition. Your life entirely, floorplans of anger unending.

Get out now. Get out now. Get out now.

STOP #4: STONEY CREEK

Take a rest. Go home, to your real house, to Stoney Creek, and take a late lunch. Pull into your driveway and—*what?*

There is a pickup truck in the driveway of the home where you *actually* live. *A truck in* your *driveway?* This is a damned gated community. You pay HOA dues that are higher than the rents at some of your houses. You want to ram the tailgate, *ram it!* That's legal, right?

But wait. Let's take this slow, Big Guy. This is not part of the tour. You're not good at making the right choices. Just follow instructions, remember? Take a deep breath and you'll get through this just fine.

Pull into the narrow space still available in your driveway. There's someone in the truck still. Some asshole probably on his cell phone, just loitering wherever he pleases.

Shut off your vehicle. Step out of your car. Clench your fists, because this other driver opens his door simultaneously. And now it's you and him, two men walking to the hoods of their cars, 95-degree heat pressing down and pressing in, humidity so thick your sunglasses fog over when you step out of your car's air conditioning. Rip them from your face, not because the action makes you look tough (it doesn't), but because the fog has made you angrier.

And it's here, the muscles in your neck clenched, eyes squinting, face red like some cartoon character who will momentarily shoot steam from his ears, that—mere feet from this intruder—you realize that you know him.

He is your brother.

"I was wondering when you'd get here," he says, lifts the Georgia Bulldogs cap away from his eyes, wipes a gathering sweat bead pooled in the thick of his brow.

"Kyle," you say.

"Hey bro. Hug?" He holds out his arms.

Breathe in through your nose. Even from here, you can smell the *rural* on him, the gravel and small-town auto shop. Smell the highway on him, too, the distance traveled, the hours, the same junk food that your parents bought on long road trips to visit relatives in Tennessee or Virginia—pork rinds, boiled peanuts, plastic-wrapped chocolate cupcakes, the lowest rung of gas station snack, a sickening but still tantalizing smell. You know this because you drive around town all day closing loans and each time you stop for gas or for a drink, your eye is inevitably drawn to that snack aisle, to the junk food of your childhood. No. Don't go there.

Force yourself to speak. Ask your brother, "What are you doing here?"

"No hug? Too much of a bigshot to show some brotherly love?" He's got the same ridiculous smile that always won you over back in Georgia, like the photo on the cover of a youth group brochure, a mixture of ambition, idealism, positive thinking. You'd see him smile, and you'd think that everything would be all right; why were you ever upset to begin with?

Concede: "Fine." Reach forward for a clumsy embrace, both of you sticky with mid-day back-sweat, your arms stretched awkward and stiff like G.I. Joe action figures trying to fit together. The standard bro-hug. He slaps your back.

"Isn't that better?" he asks. "Don't you feel better?"

"It's Monday." Check your watch. "It's 2:30 in the afternoon on a Monday. Shouldn't you be working?"

"Didn't you hear?"

"Hear what? We haven't talked in months, Kyle."

"Did you see my Facebook posting?"

"Oh. The Facebook," you say.

Spend a moment considering the role that Facebook used to play in your life. It was integral once, an account checked concurrently with myspace and your three different emails and your cell phone voicemail, but now every time you check your account, you feel more overwhelmed and behind, more depressed with all the good news posted by others, everyone going from "single" to "in a relationship," everyone sharing photos from trips to the Rocky Mountains and the Grand Canyon, honeymoons to Paris and Lisbon. Sometime around the election last November, you started burning more energy getting angry that your friends had such amazing lives, more energy wishing ill fortune upon their trips and their ceremonies, then finally more energy *ignoring* posts than *reading* them, and so Facebook stopped being a priority.

Don't tell Kyle any of this. Just say, "I haven't logged on in awhile."

Kyle's still smiling that perpetual aw-shucks smile, like he's on a game show 24/7 and just seconds away from winning a new living room set. He's never been able to grow facial hair, either; he's worked in the shop since he was 16, rubbing elbows with guys who always have scabs healing somewhere, who would've been pirates or mountain men were they born in another century. That sort of work is good for two things: helping you develop an undying appreciation for Pabst, and putting hair on your face and chest. But Kyle still has a baby face, couldn't look gritty if he tried.

"Well," you say. "What are you doing all the way down here?"

"I'd been thinking about it a while. And I just decided: fuck it. Gonna go see my brother."

"Without calling me, you just decided 'fuck it,' and drove four hours to Orlando?"

"Yep."

"And you've been sitting in my driveway hoping that I'd come home sometime?"

"Jeez, bro, don't sound so mad." He smiles again, unbreakable in the storm of your anger, and you realize that, thus far, you haven't looked pleasant or welcoming, not in the slightest. Not unusual: in every family portrait, you appear to be squinting into the sun, your aching lips eager to give up on the forced smile; but Kyle always looks like he was caught in joyful mid-laugh, like Uncle Roger was telling the amusing family anecdote of the time they moved the dresser downstairs and Dad farted and they almost dropped it and—

"Can we go inside or something?" Kyle asks. "I'm melting out here."

Yes, the heat is oppressive, your armpits are wet and your pants are threatening to go swamp-ass, but there's more work to do today. To invite your brother into your house, simple though the gesture might seem, would be to admit that his brash act is acceptable.

"I've got a lot to do today, Kyle."

"Right. You own your own business."

"Yeah."

"But you make the schedule, right? You can take a day off if you want."

"Kyle, that's not the way it works," you say. He doesn't understand. Such reasoning is a slippery slope, one hour of "kicking back" turning to two, today's tasks procrastinated to tomorrow. If you want to survive as a business, now is not the time for lazy afternoons with your brother. Now is the time for buckling down, for bootstrap-pulling, the sort of hard work that has defined your father and your family for as long as you can remember, the sort of hard work that can make you *you* again.

Far away, a car honks, one of those long horn-smashes from a cut-off driver who wants the world to know how angry he is, who won't let it go, who'll continue honking for the next mile as he bears down upon the bumper of the car in front of him. You know him. Often, you *are* him.

Okay. Just say it: "Come inside." (Were you *really* thinking of sending him away? Your own brother? This is why you should just follow your tour guide's instructions. Don't try to make decisions on your own, Big Brother.) Usher him inside and grab a couple tumblers from your pantry, fill them with ice water from your fridge's dispenser.

Inside, Kyle takes a long sip of his water, says, "So. No brews?"

Swirl the ice water in your cup, allow the violent cracking of cubes to calm you down. "It's a Monday."

"God, you're old."

"I don't drink in the middle of a workday, Kyle."

"That's not what you said when I came to visit you at college. Hell, I was looking forward to a little daytime drinking." He holds the water glass up as if toasting an imagined version of your reunion.

"That was five years ago. Six, maybe." Try to remember the specific week he visited. Remember the taste of Pabst Blue Ribbon, the smell of pool-water chlorine and tanning oil, card games, lunches at Burger King, nothing concrete except the vague feeling that you were both drunk the whole time. "That was my senior year Spring Break when you visited. Life was different."

"I'm just sayin'. You kind of disappoint me."

"Sorry." You both sit down on the couches, he on the large sofa chair and you on the middle cushion of the sofa, the material so soft that you sink noiselessly into the excessive comfort. You remember picking out this furniture with Shelley, moving from couch to couch throughout the sweeping showroom and testing every cushion, hoping that—like a cultured wine aficionado, so refined as to know without a label glance which wine came from South America and which from Europe, which wine was aged and which was new—you would find the finest fabric even without looking at price tags. You did, and you felt so proud, but now you're still paying it off.

"How's Orlando?" he asks. "How are things going for you?"

Turn to Page 80 if you want to tell him about your weekend.

Turn to Page 85 if you want to lie to him, to tell him "Just fine."

Turn to –

No! You will not play that game again. Don't turn that fucking page.

No more choices for you. You only screw it up.

Stay *right here* and do what you're told. We're gonna get you back on your feet, but you can't go rogue. Ask: "What do you want to know?"

"Um," he says. "Dunno. Everything?"

Tell him you can give him a tour.

"A tour?"

"A tour of my life. Every damn inch of it."

You could give him the full rundown, a whimsical account of your daily travels, just like Billy from *The Family Circus*, dotted-line footsteps all over town—

You want to tell him. You want to stop living inside your own diseased mind. You want to engage with the world and rediscover what it means to have someone listen to you and care about you and love you.

But listen: that's a little much. Kyle just fucking *got* here, okay? You cannot take him on a tour of all those unseen rooms in your mind. You cannot tell him about tragedy, or about loneliness. Do not listen to the voice that warmly tells you—

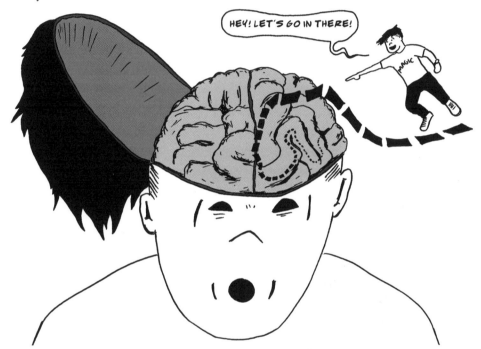

Do not take the tour deeper into your own mind! Do not—

Kyle's now looking you dead in the eyes. "You were saying something?"

"Huh? I was?"

The air conditioner gurgles to a stop and the house is suddenly silent enough that you hear the ticking of clocks and the rustling of old bills under the whip of ceiling fan blades. During the hot months, you sometimes forget how loud the AC can be, how deep and rumbling and taken-for-granted it churns—the pervasive background noise of indoors Florida. Until it stops.

"You were gonna give me a tour? The house?"

"Is that what I said?"

"And you were gonna show me a place where I can put my stuff, I assume."

"Put your stuff? Like, *stay?*"

Don't swear. Don't *swear!*

"So that's my usefulness to this family?" you ask. "I'm a free hotel?"

As soon as the words are out of your mouth, you understand how abrasive they must sound, how mean. After all, you want to reconnect with your brother, right? But do you hear the door creaking open? Do you hear that warm voice again, the other tour guide who is ushering you inside to take a look at what you really think of your family—

IN HERE

IN HERE WHERE IT'S DARK

the FAMILY ROOM

You've had relatives who have passed through Orlando, and you've avoided their calls.

Your Uncle Roger from Hickory. Your cousins from Pigeon Forge, who used to brag that Gatlinburg was a "big tourist hot spot, just like Orlando!" Every time you see them on your caller ID, you think they're looking for a free place to stay. Back when you were in middle school and high school, Uncle Roger and Aunt Sue would swing into town, en route to God knows where but in no hurry to get there, and you'd have to sleep in Kyle's room while your Aunt and Uncle occupied your bedroom, and "staying for one night" would somehow stretch into two weeks, and where were these people going?

They were free-loaders, took advantage of your father's daily grill-outs, his "family comes first" hospitality.

Now that you live in Orlando, you know old friends and family will pass through. The city is a seductive bug zapper, draws everyone in. Uncle Roger, Aunt Sue. Your Aunt Kimmy, who still takes care of your wheelchair-bound grandmother in their Alabama double-wide that always smells like potato salad, a rogue's gallery of Southern caricatures that—were they not family—would be tempting to label "white trash" and discard.

But...you've now lumped Kyle into this category of faceless relatives to be avoided?

HE'S YOUR FUCKING BROTHER! WHAT HAPPENED TO YOU?

"That's a little harsh," Kyle says.

You shake your head. Where did you go?

Smile, crack your neck, roll your shoulders, anything to make it seem as if you've had a long and stressful day and this was just a poor attempt at a joke.

"I came into town to see you," Kyle says. "I just figured…big house, extra bedrooms? Damn, man."

"I'm on edge. I shouldn't have snapped."

"So show me the house, then," Kyle says and takes off his hat, tosses it onto the coffee table. "First I've seen it."

"Is it?" Try not to stare at the hat, the old Georgia Bulldogs hat faded by a decade of sunshine, its bottom half discolored by a white shoreline of salt. The hat that will leave a sweat spot on the table.

"You never invite us down. I had to Google Map the directions."

"If you would have called, I would've—"

"Let's take that tour, brother-man."

"Right. Yes. Yes, let's."

He stands and claps; you notice that he's now left his half-empty cup on the coffee table, too, water dribbling from lip to table where you fear it will leave a ring. "Show me around. Show me how a CEO lives."

"That's not—" Exhale. Rub your hands down your legs. Do not let him believe that you are bigger than you are. You cannot afford to support anyone. "I mean, *owning* a company doesn't mean that I'm…The house, it's nothing much."

"Better than Dad's place. Get up, get up," he says and grabs your forearm, helps you to your feet.

It's been awhile since you've given anyone a tour of this place, but every time you've done it, you've felt too young for the task. *This can't be me*, you think. You are little Billy, but you are no longer playing in the neighborhood. You own this house, are responsible for every square inch:

"A pool," Kyle says from across the room, face and fingertips to the glass of the lanai doors. Outside, the water shimmers in that magical summertime way, sunshine from above and white concrete below and bulbous pool lights beneath the gently rolling surface all producing a nonstop sparkle, as if the water has been siphoned directly from some privately owned white-sands Caribbean island. "Bet you're in there all the time," Kyle says, fingertip tapping the glass.

"Not really," you say.

"You're kidding. When we were kids, Dad couldn't drag your ass out of the pool."

"The community pool?"

"Every time we went there was some big ordeal when he tried to get you out. He'd say it was time to go, so you'd swim farther away from him. Felt like it took all afternoon to leave."

"I don't remember that."

"And a hot tub?" Kyle says. "You got a *hot tub*?"

"It's less cool when you live alone."

"A hot tub, and a pool!"

"I need to get the pool guy out here. I think it needs to be treated."

Kyle shrugs, turns back to you. "Looks good to me." Then he does a 360-spin and takes in the entirety of the great room. "So much frickin' space." He shakes his head. "Show me around, Brother."

"Um," you say. You can't send him away or kick him out, can't pencil him in for a different appointment time, so you motion all around at the open floor plan of your Florida home, natural sunlight sizzling each room from the tall windows, from the skylight, from the long doors leading from great room to lanai, rectangles of sunlight stretching across walls and wood floors. "This is the great room," you say to Kyle. And you point from here to the far end of the room, to the corner nook separated from the living room not by a doorway but by a slope of ceiling and a corner of wall and a hanging ceiling light marking it as *different room*. "That's the, like, breakfast nook." You motion to another chunk of your square footage at the front of the house, chandelier hanging over a table overrun by binders and mail. These rooms are connected, they are one, but the nook's hanging light and the dining room's chandelier dictate that you must place tables there or risk smacking your head on the lights. "And that's the, uh. Dining room, I guess? But, like, I usually eat here on the couch and watch TV."

"Open floor plan," Kyle is saying. "I like, I like."

"It's okay," you say. The best part of the open floor plan, you decide now, is that it's easy to conduct a house tour, to stand in one spot and point and avoid walking the full 3,200 square feet.

"So show me the rest. I'm waiting to be impressed by how my big-time CEO brother lives."

"Big-time CEO. Kyle, stop."

"Country boy conquering the big city," he says and slaps your back.

Ask yourself, Why are you *embarrassed*? Here is an opportunity to feel *good* again! This is the complete opposite of Lakeside Wine Bar. Someone still believes in you!

Show him the master bedroom and the master bathroom, impress him with the cavernous walk-in closet. Afterward, turn on the home theater in the great room, *300* or *Transformers* or something, roll the dial of the surround sound as high as it will go. Own it. Beat your chest and say "This is *mine*. This is the life, buddy."

And for God's sake, ignore that other voice in your head telling you there's a more honest tour you could take him on, that phantom floor plan you've been hiding; ignore the voice telling you to drop the act, to follow the oil-stain footprints. It's not me.

Ignore it. Because if you follow *that* tour guide, you'll reveal rooms Kyle wouldn't expect, more and more of them—

the GREAT ROOM

Open *this* door and you'll remember when you bought this house, how happy you were that it was so open. You'll remember telling Shelley that you wanted a dog, that you wanted to toss a rubber ball from one far end—by the TV—all the way to the front door, the dog tiring himself out while you moved only inches each time, soaking in the latest episode of *Lost*.

As soon as you stepped into this house, you knew that you'd have your first flat-panel HDTV mounted there on the wall. You'd light fires in the winter, and when visitors came to the door, they'd see the warmth of the fire from a hundred feet away, through the frosted entryway window.

The open space is supposed to be bold, each room sweeping into the next, but here's the truth: the open space now makes you feel like you're living in a cave. This past winter, you lit fires and you thought about finally getting that dog, made jokes to yourself about how it was a "one-dog night" or a "three-dog night" as you piled the blankets high in your king bed, but alone in this cave you kept thinking of the dog you'd adopt, and what if it had bladder control problems, or what if it developed cancer and died young, or what if it broke its leash and got hit by a car, and you don't want to invest in more heartbreak right now.

Any relationship, that's all they bring. Friends, fiancés, pets, brothers.

You don't even own a dog, but you damn-near cry thinking about losing one.

Being alone: that's best.

Cabinets

Fire

Cabinets

STUDY

DINING ROOM

"I like the living room couches," Kyle says. "So damn soft." He runs his hand over the cushions like they're the fur of a sleeping tiger.

"There are scratch marks at the far end." Point. "Shelley's cat."

"Shelley had a cat?"

"It wasn't *hers*, technically. She watched it for a friend, sometimes for weeks at a time. Which means, of course, that *I* had to watch it, too. That little bastard made me so angry."

"Look on the bright side, bro. At least your house doesn't *smell* like cat." He pauses, looks around. "How's she doing, by the way?"

You knew it was coming.

You run your fingertips over the wall, over a hole left in the drywall from some framed photo she took with her when she left. "Fuck, Kyle. Why does everyone ask about her?"

"I don't know," Kyle says. He lifts his cup from the coffee table and takes a giant sip of water, another careless dribble running down the plastic, and he puts it back down where this time it will definitely leave a ring on the table.

"What if I asked you about *your* ex-girlfriends?"

"You remember Dad's couches, right? What the fuck are they made of, burlap or something? And shit, that coffee table, brother. Livin' large. Dad doesn't even *have* a coffee table."

"It's a coffee table," you say. "They're pretty common."

Oh, but this one?

Don't go there, don't—

the COFFEE TABLE

No one's ever said that about your coffee table: "living large." Espresso colored, a long circular design with legs like metal teardrops. Glass panel on top, and beneath, a wood slab on which you've stacked magazines and old Pottery Barn mailers.

It's here that you eat, while the dining room table—where several times you tried to impress Shelley with blackened salmon and grilled asparagus—sits unused.

Kyle hasn't walked into the dining room, hasn't noticed the dust on that table, the coffee mug rings on the glass, the cobwebs tight-roping the lights of the chandelier...

Living large? You're living in a crypt.

Open another door, and here's the truth about that coffee table.

Purchased at one of those showroom furniture stores (you'd never bought real furniture before, just cheap particle board sets sold mainly to kids in college towns), with a nightmare delivery process...

The coffee table completes the room, it's a centerpiece, and you were supposed to have it several weeks before the official "House-Warming Party" Shelley had planned at the end of last summer. "We *need* that table," she kept telling you. "This place looks so empty."

she's
HERE

STAY in
HERE

OPEN this DOOR

and you'll remember that the house was brand-new at the time, the air heavy with the smell of paint and cardboard boxes. You made sure the TV was wall-mounted, of course. That was the first thing you took care of, even before assembling the bed, even as you were eating off paper plates.

You weren't going to miss *Sportscenter*. Or *Entourage*. And you were finally catching up with the last season of *The Sopranos*. Plates? Not important.

Anyway, Shelley was making you wait to buy *real* silverware and plates until after the bridal shower, so in your few months living together, it was old dishes, and plasticware swiped from the resort where she worked.

But let's get back to the coffee table, the "centerpiece": it's nothing much, is probably inside hundreds of Central Florida homes...

but—like the pool—it's magnificent to Kyle, more interesting than anything he sees in rural Georgia, where most coffee tables are just repurposed chests or (yes) two-by-fours over cinderblocks. That's how these furniture stores get you: they make you think you've entered a life of luxury, when really you've just entered a life of mass production.

...and we're back at Shelley's housewarming party.

Weeks before, the couches had been delivered on time, but the coffee table and dining room table—matching glass, matching espresso wood, one a miniature version of the other—had been delivered with lightning-bolt cracks down their centers, and so you'd sent them back. The store promised to make it right, and so the furniture was re-delivered, then rereturned because they'd tried to deliver the *exact same* broken product, and finally... after over-the-phone shouting matches, curses, threats, the delivery team gave you a "Friday — Noon" ETA for a new coffee table and dining room table. Friday. The day of your housewarming party. You'd get your table with only a few hours to spare.

OPEN ANOTHER DOOR→

FOLLOW the OIL STAINS

...to the housewarming party: Shelley's friends, and Jimmy and Sandra, and Anderson and Steven and Elaina and Edwin and a dozen others, everyone remarking on how great this place would be for kids, Shelley faux-shuddering.
"Kids... Don't even want to think about that yet!" but you knew that this was just for show.

Out in the GREAT ROOM

...everyone drinking Sam Adams and Terrapin, Smirnoff Strawberry and Sprite from plastic cups, flat-panel TV on the wall playing an episode of *Hard Knocks*, and here was the deliveryman at 9 PM, saying sorry, sorry, just got a little behind, and Shelley getting in his face and saying "Noon! Time is money, asshole. We had *plans*. Do you understand? Nine fucking hours is not a 'little behind.'" And that was the moment you knew you'd made the right decision to move in together. This woman: she was fierce and decisive and took zero shit.

She tore into the deliveryman until he was a cracked breath away from crying, this pro-wrestler-type with lumberjack beard. Everyone at the party clapped for Shelley, and later that night you said "I love this woman!"

...but Shelley said "I shouldn't have done that. I get so angry, and I can't help it. What the fuck is *wrong* with me?"

"This hallway leads to the master bedroom," you tell Kyle, leading him quickly out of the great room and toward the only half of the house currently occupied.

"Art on the wall?" Kyle says, impressed. He's pointing at a long red canvas with spots of white flecked throughout. You've forgotten this painting exists. "Is this, like, surrealism? Damn. My big brother, the art collector."

"Surrealism," you say. "Sure."

Actually, the painting is a Bed Bath & Beyond version of a Jackson Pollack, something else mass-produced and generic, purchased because Shelley wouldn't allow you to hang any of the posters from your old post-frat apartment, the "1 Tequila, 2 Tequila, 3 Tequilas, FLOOR!" and the Tampa Bay Buccaneers wall-sized helmet poster; she found all sorts of abstract shit in the bins at Kirklands and Target, an abstract canvas of the word "HOME" repeating dozens of times in different shapes, colors, and designs. For some reason, you never took them down, can't. Maybe she was right. Maybe she learned something from Elaina's interior decorating blog. Now, when you think of putting up other posters (this year's Bucs schedule, for instance) it seems juvenile. Occasionally you watch *Color Splash* on HGTV and imagine elaborate painting projects to make the room your own, but there's a voice in the back of your head that grumbles questions about your masculinity should you undertake such projects: *a man* doesn't worry about interior decoration.

Kyle cranes his neck and scans the vaulted ceilings, his face aglow with natural light. "Place is a *palace*, brother."

"You should see some of the houses in Heathrow," you say. "Or Isleworth."

"Sounds fancy."

"Out past West Orlando, there's this little town called Windermere. That's where Shaq and Tiger Woods have houses. And this guy, David Siegel, this timeshare tycoon, is building a replica of the Palace at Versailles. It's supposed to be, like, the largest house on the continent or something."

"Orlando," Kyle says. "Fantasyland."

Wait, are you trying to *sell the city* to him? This place that's let you down? Shake your head. Then take him down the hallway: "That's my bedroom in there."

"Where the magic happens, eh?" He elbows you, and you flinch.

Force a laugh. Don't say, "Not lately."

Too late. You've said it.

"Oooh, wheee," Kyle says, walking into the master bathroom. He twirls around again in all the excessive square footage, like a Disney princess in a forest clearing. "This is worth the price of admission! Look at the size of this bathroom. Two sinks?"

His energy is exhausting. "One more than I need." Hell, even when Shelley lived here the second sink was seldom used. You'd tried the "his and hers" thing, one sink for each of you, but the left sink was farther from the door, and so you both naturally were pulled to the same sink out of convenience. "You're too excited about all of this."

Kyle runs his fingers through his sweat-dampened hair. It's a perpetual mess, this hair, always smashed under his Braves or Georgia cap, but somehow he has that unique ability—most common among Abercrombie catalogue models—to make his hair look good disheveled. "Well. You do need to dust in here," he says. "In a bad way."

"Why do you say that?"

"There's dust caked on the electrical outlets, brother," Kyle says.

It isn't dust. It's Shelley's powder.

You don't understand makeup, how it all works: foundation and application, all the aisles and aisles of shit at Ulta and Target. You get the basic idea of mascara and lipstick, those are easy to comprehend, but Shelley had trays of materials, as if she was an artist each morning prepared to paint a portrait atop her face. And the powder—you still remember the smell—floating in the air, turning the white window curtains flesh-colored. She's still here, really, all around you; you're breathing her in every time you step to the sink.

"When did *you* become such a neat freak?"

"Not a neat freak," Kyle says. "Shop knowledge. Don't want to cause a spark."

"Whatever. I worked in that shop, too," you say. "This is just a bathroom. It isn't automotive engineering."

"You only worked in the shop for, like, a year."

"I still worked there."

"No. What *you* did: that's like being a punter in the NFL." He claps your back. "I mean, yeah, you're a football player, but not really. Did you ever pick up a wrench?"

You cross your arms over your chest. He's the Country Brother and you're the City Brother; he is grit and muscle, and you are laptop and dress slacks. He'll allow you to school him on matters real estate, but not on matters electrical or mechanical.

"You pushed a broom, Brother. No shame in it, but let's be honest. You probably don't even change your own oil anymore, do you?"

"Anyway. That's the closet back there."

He laughs and mouths "okay, okay," and then peers inside. It's a walk-in, almost as large as your old bedroom in Georgia. There's a fold-out lawn chair in the center where you sit to tie your shoes. Much of the space is empty, your clothes still relegated to a modest corner so that Shelley could have the rest of the space. But her stuff's gone, save for a rogue hair-tie and a white girl-sock you kind of thought she might come back to retrieve. "Pretty bleak," Kyle says as he scans.

Shut off the light. Motion for him to follow you back out.

Leave the bathroom, but as you do, *do not* glance at the master bedroom. Do *not* allow the master bedroom to come into view, and do *not* listen to the other voice that wants you to—

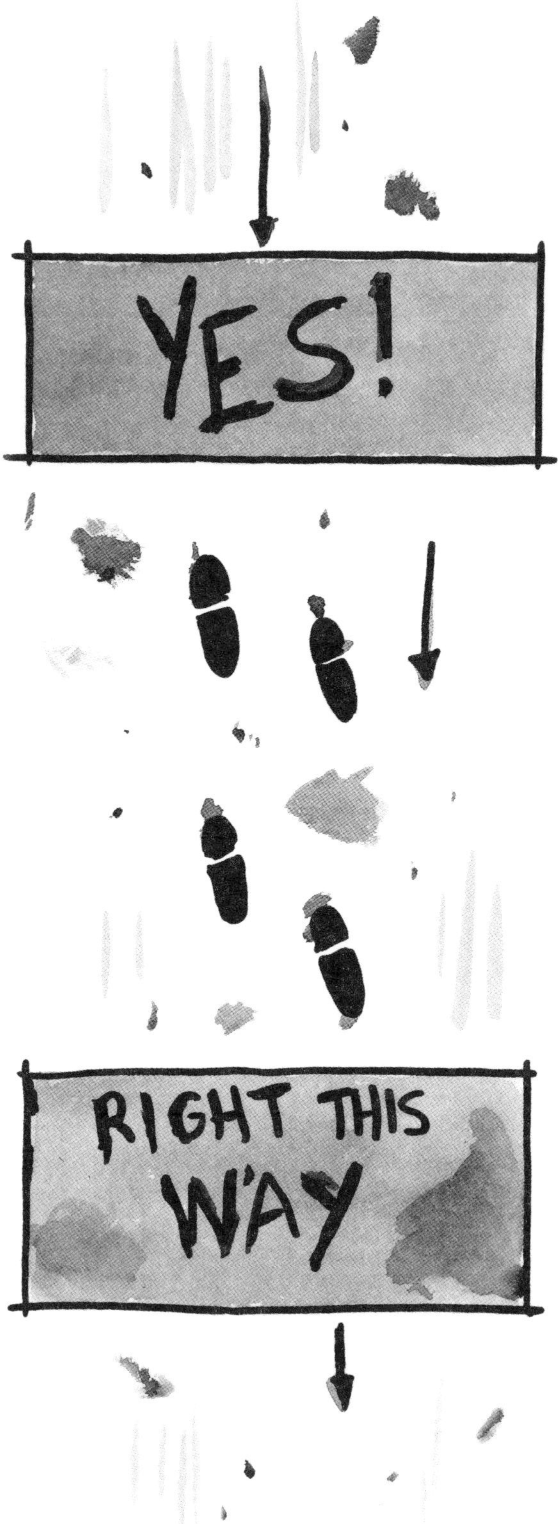
YES!
RIGHT THIS WAY

The bed seemed so large, but you couldn't sleep in the center, could you?

Even now you sleep on the left, never cross the invisible line dividing the bed into Marc's side and Shelley's side, as if you're waiting for someone to come back and reclaim the other half.

You're not entirely hopeless, of course. You're not living in the past *all the time.*

Once, you thought there'd be other women in your bed to replace Shelley, a slew of glittery post-club hookups like you were living an episode of *Entourage,* but on the rare occasions that girls accompany you home from the bars, they a) do not spend the night, or b) sleep in the guest room, or c) take the wrong side of the bed, *yours,* and you spend the night in awkward and uncomfortable positions, wondering why you are where you are. A large family home occupied only by a single man? It's creepy, that's what it is.

Other girls you meet at bars: you tell them where you live and they respond with "Why the hell do you live so far away?" or "Wait, you're married, aren't you? What, your wife's out of town?"

See, here's the thing that maybe no one understands. Up until this house, you'd never had a "master bedroom." A shitty dorm room, a shittier room at the fraternity house, and then an apartment bedroom that existed only as a sleeping space.

You know where Kyle sleeps back home. His **old** bedroom was so tiny that, as soon as you moved to Orlando for college, he pushed his belongings across the hall: he and your father converted his old bedroom into a storage closet.

You can still remember your bedroom there, its narrow spaces, how there was just enough square footage for a full size bed and directly beside it your weight bench, which during the school year accumulated your textbooks and homework.

The mattress was your desk chair, the weight bench your desk. When you worked out, you moved the crap onto your bed; when you slept, you moved it to the bench.

In early high school, when your mother was alive, she'd force you into the living room to use the computer desk. She'd turn off the television, whatever she happened to be watching, *Ellen* or *Rosie O'Donnell*, or whatever.

Focus, she said.

One thing at a time.

After she died, it didn't matter where you did your homework. Bedroom, living room, front seat of your car before you went to the shop to sweep floors.

After your mother died, all that mattered was that you finish the homework, that you get to Orlando, that you get your degree and make something of yourself in the city of your dreams.

Family had been ripped away from you. All bets were off.

There was a darkness inside you, and you no longer gave a fuck about anyone or anything because to do so would be to open yourself up to the most vicious heartbreak imaginable.

Alive one day, not even a goodbye as she slipped into the car, and then an hour later a world without your mother.

And what, now you suddenly care about *everything* and *everyone*?

"You're lucky to have this shit, is all I'm saying," Kyle says.

"Uh-huh."

"You all right?"

"It's just…Sometimes I wish I never bought a house," you say. "I wish I still had my apartment. Somewhere small. Somewhere without so many shadows."

Shit. You shouldn't have said that.

"Grass is always greener," Kyle says. "You want to live in an apartment? Just sell this place and move on. But you'll probably want a house again soon as you do that."

"Ahh," you say. "Sage advice from a man who still lives with his father."

"Well."

"Well, what?"

Kyle's avoiding eye contact now, eyes searching the room for something else to discuss. "Maybe show me the guest rooms."

"Hold your horses. We're getting there." You hold out your hand, fingertips to his chest to keep him in place. He's become jittery, the youth-group smile melting to nervousness. He gets this way when he's keeping a secret. "There's something else, isn't there?"

Kyle chances eye contact again. "I just want to know where I'm staying, is all."

"That word. *Staying*."

"Where I'm staying, yeah. You got a futon, right? Hell, I can sleep on a couch."

"I heard you. It's just that stay-*ing* is different than *stay*." That's how your aunt and uncle would phrase it when they'd pull into your father's driveway. Stay-*ing* implies an indeterminate length of time. You look closer at his face, but he keeps dodging your stare.

"You expect me to get a hotel?" he asks, voice now sounding damaged.

"I don't expect…What are we even talking about here?"

"Well, I was just thinking…You own your own business. And now I'm in Orlando?"

"*Visiting*, I thought?"

He shakes his head. "You've got a sour attitude, you know that? I'm your *brother*. You have a *guest* room. I just need a place for a little while."

"And yeah, see, there it is." This word, *little*, used as a bargaining chip in a negotiation you hadn't known you were entering. "How long is a 'little' while?"

"I mean," he says, "I thought maybe you have a job for me?"

"*Fuck*, Kyle. Hold up. A *job*?" Search the room. Search for problems with the drywall, with the ceiling. Search for something else to look at, something else to absorb your anger. You swallow and say carefully, "What about the shop?"

"What about it?"

"Talking about *jobs*. You didn't walk out, did you?"

He looks down at his feet, at the Reeboks and ankle socks he's wearing, probably purchased from a TJ Maxx knock-off somewhere, an afterthought for a man who doesn't care about fashion in the slightest, weekend shoes because his other pair is safety shoes, slippery with oil and axle grease and that orange-smelling hand cleaner they use in the shop. "What do you want me to say?" Kyle asks. "I couldn't stay in Georgia. Nothing left there, man. I need your help. That's why I came here without calling you. If I called, you'd have said no."

"Perfect logic."

"Come on, brother-man," he says.

"I've got a lot going on, Kyle."

"So let me lighten the load. I'm the perfect man to help!" Before you know it, his arm is around your shoulder and he's hugging you close, almost as if you're some patient who's just confessed to him your depression and loneliness, and he's here to listen and soothe. Then he's leading you down the hallway, back to the couches, arm sliding from your body as he slips back into the sofa-chair and allows you to slump into the cushions. It's been ten minutes, this tour, but it feels like it has taken so much longer.

"What happened with the shop? Did you get fired?"

He stuffs his hands into his pockets to steady them, then pulls them out, picks up an empty photo frame that's been resting face-down on your end-table for six months. "I couldn't do it," he says.

"Couldn't do what?"

"So. You know John-John?"

"What about him?"

Kyle takes a deep breath.

"Still wearing the Camaro t-shirts, pointing out the rips and oil splotches on each one, telling you exactly what cars they came from?"

But Kyle isn't really asking whether you *know* John-John, is he? John-John has worked with your father for longer than you've been alive, has always treated your father like a co-owner, has promised to reward him when he sells the shop. Your father fixes cars and manages the shop for John-John, and that's always been just fine. "What about him?"

"Got into a motorcycle wreck," Kyle says. "Was doing a cross-country Harley trip with a few other grease monkeys from South Georgia shops. They were out in Montana or something. Crested a hill, and there was a stopped semi-truck on the other side..."

"When was this? Is he all right?"

"He was going 60 miles per hour. What do you think?"

"Is he *dead?*"

Kyle makes a swiping motion with his hand to his neck.

"My God. Nobody told me," you say.

"I'm telling you right now."

"When was this?"

"Couple months ago."

"You're just *now* telling me?"

"When's the last time you called? Dad sure as hell ain't calling you."

You hold your head. It feels like the room has shifted, furniture tumbling out. Room even emptier than before.

Perhaps this shouldn't feel world-changing: you haven't seen John-John in forever, haven't talked with him in a decade, but for some reason this news still overwhelms every square centimeter of your soul. It brings to light cobwebbed memories you didn't even realize you'd kept, and it somehow alters your entire view of your future. It's like waking up to hear of a celebrity tragedy, someone whose sitcom you watched so religiously you almost thought them a brother or a sister or a father...It isn't *possible* that any of the people who populate your memories could age or disappear. "Nobody calls *me*, either, Kyle," you say. "You know that, right?"

"Not since you called Dad a prick at Thanksgiving. In the man's own house. That tends to fracture relationships."

"Did I say that?" You lean forward from the couch. "So what happened to the shop?"

Keep your tone neutral. Resist the urge to tell Kyle that you know how this story played out, that your father got screwed out of the shop because he relied on a gentleman's agreement. Your eye is twitching. You're breathing heavy.

Your brother twirls the empty photo frame in his hands and looks into the cavity where you'd once displayed the "cute and playful" engagement photo, the one where you're giving Shelley a piggy-back ride around Lake Eola.

"The shop," you repeat, because Kyle looks like he might ask about the absence of photo.

"It closed."

"For the funeral?" Resist—let *him* tell you.

He shakes his head. "It's done. Forever."

Say it carefully: "What do you mean 'forever'?"

"I mean it closed down. It's done. No more shop."

Now you may allow yourself to shake your head. "I don't get it. It can't just close. Help me understand this, Kyle."

"John-John's brother came in, started selling off the equipment."

Breathe. Resist the urge to scream. Resist the urge to even whisper *I told him, I fucking told him.* "What about Dad? Why didn't he take it over? He's not getting any payout?"

"Dad never got a chance."

"They had an *arrangement*. What about the"—keep the tone neutral, *neutral*—"gentleman's agreement."

"The brother had a lawyer. So."

"Of course he did." Don't say what you're thinking, that most smart people do. "Well, why didn't Dad buy the equipment? Keep it open?"

"You know Dad. Doesn't know anything about business loans, and doesn't have the energy for *anything* right now. At his age, in his health? Place was gutted overnight. Even the land was sold to that antique shop next door so they can sell more bird-feeders and shit."

"Doesn't have the energy?" you repeat.

"You haven't seen him since the heart attack."

"Please. Don't guilt me on that."

"Guilt *yourself*, big guy. I'm just stating a fact."

Push the anger deep into yourself. Breathe. Sit back on the couch. "So that's it, then?"

"What do you mean, that's it?"

"That's all you want to tell me? You don't want to elaborate at all?"

"I didn't want to state the obvious. Dad's not doing well, okay?"

"What about you? You didn't want to take over the shop?"

"I tried to find work somewhere else. Got a job at Tuffy but it was fifteen miles away," Kyle says. "I had to get out of that place, man. I don't want to be stuck in that shithole. I would've left sooner, but…well…some of us have a sense of commitment."

Kyle takes a long drink from his water cup, then places it directly beside the ring stain on the coffee table from earlier. He's a sloppy drinker, water drops sliding from rim to table; by the time he's finished drinking, there will be a five-ring Olympic logo of water stains on the table.

"Okay," you say. "Okay okay."

"What do you mean, okay?"

First, you wanted a shoulder to cry on. Then, you were concerned about hiding from your brother the collapse you've suffered. But you hadn't even realized until now that—if you let him become a part of your life again—you could destroy *his* future, too.

"We'll take this one day at a time," you say, even though you don't want to, even though you'd rather warn him to get out, *get out now*. "I might need help fixing up some of these rental houses. The lawns, especially. I just don't have the money to—" Stop. No need to say more. His mood has transformed in an instant. He's beaming. Why ruin it?

"You won't regret it, Brother."

"Right," you say. But inside your own head, you're screaming FUCK! FUCK! FUCK! Because you're certain that this decision will backfire, will lead into heretofore unglimpsed rooms from which there will be no clean escape. This will lead to heartbreak, you're sure of it.

"I've got to get back to work now. I need to grab something. Have a couple loans to close. Some tenants to visit."

"Can I come?"

"Why don't you just get settled?"

"Sit here by myself? No, I want to talk more, learn about your business."

"Sit this one out, Kyle. Please. Tonight we can crack open beers, watch the Magic game. Get settled. Please."

But Kyle won't be denied. When you leave the house, Kyle is with you. Salt-rimmed Georgia cap, faded blue Braves shirt with underarm discoloration, woven belt through jean shorts, shitty discount shoes.

Breathe. Climb into the driver's seat, smooth your pants, and try not to think about what you've just done.

"Shotgun!" Kyle says, laughing as he hops into the passenger seat.

Drive. Just drive.

DETOUR: THE BACK TRAILS OF GEORGIA

Let's go back to Georgia, shall we? Revisit those winding back trails behind your house, the ones you later learned had been a planned subdivision gone belly-up. Your father would have made good money if he'd just sold your childhood home to the developer in time, but he hemmed and hawed with all things financial, couldn't detach himself from the house and all the work he'd put into it. But for you, back then, the back trails were not some real estate opportunity but rather custom-made for go-karting.

Originally, there had been just one go-kart. Yours. Who knows where your father bought it, where a man finds such things, metal sticks welded into a contraption that—you think now—was probably the least comfortable place a grown man could think to sit, but your Dad did it, squashed himself down to teach you how to drive the thing. And you drove it every day, relished the smell of gas as you refilled the tank, the trembling of the engine as your entire body shook in the hard seat.

When Kyle turned seven, your father bought him one, too. Suddenly there were two go-karters on the graveled pot-holed backroads, the both of you plowing through the weeds of those back trails. Your metal was chipped by kicked-up stones. Bits of wet grass had been pasted to the undercarriage so long they looked like purposeful decoration. Kyle's go-kart was brand-new, blue paint still embedded with that 1980s glitter-sparkle that signified coolness.

And Kyle was faster than you. There was that. He'd somehow always wind up leading you, dictating the left turn down the easy straightaways, or the right turn toward the relatively traffic-free roads surrounding your house. Some days he'd take two quick turns, one right after the next, and you'd follow the exhaust through the tall pines, the tall weeds. It had never crossed your mind before that *you* might be lost by *him*. The grumble of the engine in your ears, the faraway grumble of his. If you lost sight of him, were you supposed to go home without your little brother and hope he knew the way back? You had three years' experience driving these trails, these fields, these swamps. You'd had your own adventures out here. But Kyle was still mapping the land.

One afternoon, the unthinkable occurred. You couldn't see him. You couldn't hear him.

You were at the old construction site several miles away. It was supposed to have been an outdoor shopping plaza, perhaps something to service those subdivisions that never got built, but now it was just sand and clay, only traces of streets and property lines carved into earth overtaken by weeds and young pine trees so tiny they looked like toys. He was your responsibility, Kyle was, and you drove the trails looking for him; when the land grew slimy and impassable, you stood beside your idling go-kart and listened for him, walked the edge of pits filled with rainwater, stepped over left-behind McDonald's bags faded to white, boxes of left-behind nails, a clipboard. There was a sense of apocalypse to this place. You wondered if there were roving bands of *Mad Max* marauders back here, or if this was where the high-school sex and drugs and alcohol happened, and what would the teenagers do if your seven-year-old brother stumbled upon them?

Eventually you discovered the long tire tracks in the clay. They careened this way, that way, going sideways before straightening at the thick trunk of a pine tree. That's where you found Kyle, crying in the driver's seat of his go-kart, its front end crunched inward. He'd been braver than you, had driven over the rough ground that you wouldn't dare. You asked Kyle if he was all right, and what was wrong, and he sniffled and looked up and saw you approaching on foot and immediately turned away.

"Don't tell Dad," was the first thing he said. "Please."

"Are you okay?" you asked again, and after he stopped crying, eyes still downcast, he nodded. A bruise on his arm, maybe on his legs, but you figured he couldn't have been going *that fast* when he hit. "Does it still run?"

He shook his head, more confused than definitive, so you yanked the pull-cord and yes! It came to life, thank God. Briefly, you'd imagined having to get home *on foot*, both of you pushing your vehicles through this rural wasteland, the sun falling, a great journey like *Stand by Me*, two brothers trekking…

But the engine worked.

"Switch go-karts," you said.

"But Dad…"

"I'll tell him we swapped," you said. "I'll tell him I crashed it." Even at that age, Kyle already had an automotive aptitude you couldn't match. More than the fear of parental punishment he might endure, you feared how such a crash might damage your father's outlook on this talent.

And when you got home, your father *was* furious. All manner of what-were-you-thinkings, and don't-you-ever-try-to-be-daredevils. Grounded. Spanked till you could barely sit down. Kyle escaped, though.

That was one of the last times you both rode together. One of the last times you drove your go-kart. You were ten, almost eleven, just a few months from the start of middle school, a new world, new friends. But you knew it was a good thing you'd done, one of those "big brother" moments that would—if your life was a Hollywood movie—be made to showcase the intensity of your goodness. How damn much you cared about your little bro, protecting him, encouraging him. But it's also the only "big brother" moment you can really think of, isn't it? When you were ten years old.

STOP #5: EAST ORLANDO

"So where are we going next, bro?" Kyle asks, the two of you having killed some early-afternoon tacos together before then tackling two closings, back to back. In the close quarters of your car, you've tried to ignore that his mid-day smell has become...pungent. Earlier, you dismissed it as the smell of extended travel, but now (don't say it, Marc, don't allow yourself to articulate this thought) you think maybe he hasn't washed his clothes, like a common damn redneck, or hasn't—

He's your brother. Stop.

"We're visiting a rental property," you say. "My partner used to manage this one, so I don't really know the renters. They called about the garage door so I've got to check it out."

"Fun!" Kyle says. "I didn't know you were doing repairs, too. Getting your hands dirty!"

Convey professionalism. Muster authority. "I try not to," you say. "When you're in charge, you don't need to do the dirty work."

"But that's the best part!"

"Just...just don't touch anything, okay?" Suddenly, in your mind, Kyle is yokeling through your rental property, leaving footprints on the tile floors, knocking over vases, pointing out the "surrealist" Bed Bath & Beyond paintings on the walls, or worse, he's fiddling with the thermostat, checking outlets, talking about "Well, shit, looks like there might be some water damage up on the window there, let's get out the ladder and check!" and "Dang, bro, some of the fence-posts are leaning, let's grab a screwdriver and some boards and fix this up!" and otherwise calling attention to nitty-gritties that the renters probably haven't noticed and that you can't afford to remedy. And shit, God forbid you pull up and the tenants are in the driveway working on their cars. Kyle will go full grease monkey.

But enough of that. He's your brother. Stop.

The drive is long and hot, as are all cross-town Orlando drives in May. As you approach the neighborhood in East Orlando, you are tempted to keep driving past the entrance, to do the same as Edwin, to leave it all behind and start over elsewhere. But listen, Marc. Your brother is in the car, and—stinky and uncivilized though he may be—you are not going to crumble before him. This is the moment when you reclaim authority and confidence, and you will do it in front of Kyle. You will *park your ass at the curb* and *do what needs to be done*. You are a motherfucking Landlord. Entrepreneur. Employer. Big Brother. Act the part, *be the part*.

A few turns through the subdivision and you recognize the house at the end of a cul-de-sac: two-story, stucco, siding the color of an olive that's been left in a martini glass overnight. The lease identifies the renter as "Jake Sims," an innocent enough name. Maybe "Jake" is a responsible father whose children attend soccer camps and whose wife belongs to a scrapbook club? Maybe this will be an easy property to manage?

But you know better.

Pull up. Look around.

Three cars crammed into the driveway (hand-me-down Pontiacs and Nissans from the mid-'90s) and in the street a Silverado with a "Salt Life" decal spread across the back window. You know it immediately: this place will be a disaster. This is East Orlando, spitting distance from the university.

You park behind the Silverado, back bumper creeping across the edge of the neighbor's driveway.

"This neighborhood isn't as nice as yours," Kyle says. He's looking down the long straight street at the monotony of khaki houses, identical exteriors and doorways, identical blank yards, all of it blending together until you can't distinguish one home from the next. The houses are packed so close there's barely enough room to walk the slim yards between homes. It's called "zero lot line," and the tight spaces make you wonder why the developer didn't just build row-houses or townhomes. Why bother with a sliver of side yard trapped in shade all day, with windows whose only view is the exterior of the house five feet away?

"Well. It's newer than my neighborhood, actually," you say.

"It seems emptier on this side of town, even though there are more houses," Kyle says, squinting and pulling his hat's bill down. "Is that possible?"

"No trees," you say, pointing to the row of young oaks planted along the sidewalk, trunks thin as your forearm. "Most of these developments, they just leveled all the land. Bulldozed, built the neighborhood. People were buying houses based on computer renderings of neighborhoods." You point to the newly planted oaks. "All the digital images had trees drawn in the foreground, like the seventy-year-old oaks they'd chopped down would grow back overnight. The computer renderings make every subdivision look as established as Delaney Park. But it'll be twenty years before these trees are anything substantial."

Kyle regards you curiously; he doesn't know the area, so go ahead, feel smarter for a moment. *You* know where Delaney Park is, and *he* doesn't. You are instructive. You are a big brother again, with something to offer.

"Some neighborhoods in downtown Orlando and Winter Park have been around since the 1920s land boom," you say. "Longer, even. You see oaks so old their trunks have split the sidewalks. The trunks just get wider and wider, spilling out into the road, and the city has to keep shaving the trunk every year, digging up roots so that they can save the streets. They post mirrors on the trees so you can see if someone is backing out of a driveway on the other side. But here? Cheaper to start from scratch than to save the old trees."

"Sounds depressing. Why'd *you* buy a house here?"

Why *did* you buy here?

Were *you* one of the buyers duped by the colorful computer renderings?

"Gotta get in quick," Edwin kept saying back then. "Soon as the houses are on the market, someone's scooping them up. Difference of a month could mean ten thousand, twenty. Or it could mean we get frozen out completely!"

Listen, stay out of that room. But you *are* allowed a moment of honesty every now and then. Show him you're human, that you make *some* mistakes.

"Edwin, my partner, his first flip was a neighborhood that didn't exist," you answer. "We did half a dozen like that. No down payment loans, flip within a month or two, walk away with a profit without spending a dime. Other times we'd just borrow against the equity of houses we still had in our portfolio. Some were better than others, but back in '06 you couldn't lose."

"You thought this place would sell quickly?"

"I can't remember the specifics of this place, honestly," you say. "We might've gotten offers on it, but there was this mad rush around here. Somehow it felt like there weren't enough houses to go around, and homeowners—like, people who needed a place to live, people with regular jobs—were scrambling to buy before they got priced out completely. So you had houses like this one"—you motion toward the rotten olive before you—"that were shooting to, like, 400 grand. We didn't know the ceiling. So we held onto some of the houses longer than we needed to. And by the time we wanted to unload, the price was dropping, and the market was flooded with guys like me and Edwin. New condos downtown, townhomes in Avalon Park and Waterford Lakes and Sanford, MetroWest, Harmony, the Osceola Parkway. Now…"

You pull the keys from the ignition. You run your hands up and down the steering wheel. "We've lost 50 grand in five months on this unit."

"Geez, bro. Where's Edwin?"

"Not here, that's for sure. He dipped."

"Wait. So…your business is just *you*?" Kyle squeezes the bridge of his nose. This is exactly what you didn't want, don't you see?

"Well," you say. "Let's take a look at what we've got inside. At *who* we've got inside."

When you ring the doorbell, a frat star in torn jeans and a Georgia Bulldogs hat answers and steps outside, closing the door behind him. He has the aggravatingly carefree look of a twenty-one-year-old who's done nothing with his day, who likely woke up just in time for a late lunch and still wants the world to take him seriously. "What's this about?" he asks, like you're selling magazine subscriptions.

Introduce yourself.

"Oh, you're the *owner*?" he asks.

Beside you, Kyle is once again jolly as a camp counselor, mood likely lifted because of the commonality of headwear and sports allegiances.

"I thought the owner was a different dude," the frat star says.

"You're thinking of Edwin."

"Yeah. Edwin. He sell the house?" He looks to the sky as if remembering something. "He was chill. Super-chill. Where's he at?"

Your mind follows the oil stains, imagining what constitutes "super-chill."

Don't follow the oil stains. Do *not* open that door, Marc.

In here, you see Edwin and the frat star working out together, or maybe taking shots together at some downtown bar, and Edwin telling this kid that he has a rental property he can get him, good price.

Edwin had the same lifestyle as this kid, you know it. Bars at night, sleeping till noon. Every day filled with urgent catchup, near-disasters, like a game of Frogger, always barely surviving to another day. Hell, did you ever meet up with Edwin before lunchtime?

It hurts to consider the things you failed to realize about your old friend who abandoned you.

"Yes, a chill dude," you say stiffly. "He moved to Atlanta. So I'll be your contact now."

He holds out his hand. "Bradley."

Shake it. Follow him inside the house. Look around: Bradley has not yet asked you to take a seat, has not yet offered you a glass of water, but already you're scoping the place for details to confirm your worst fears about the home's condition. Already you're building that bullet-pointed anger list of yours. Here's what you observe immediately:

Four guys on couches here in the living room, none of them old enough to buy beer without heavy scrutiny.

One wears a pair of board shorts and a wife-beater stained by SpaghettiOs, or maybe blood. Neither type of stain is a good sign, and you're not sure which signals greater immaturity.

Only one looks as if he's showered today, and the others look as if they've just come from the gym, still wearing yellow-pitted workout shirts, the smell of tuna and protein shakes hanging in the air.

A pile of dirty towels sits in the far corner, damp gym towels slopped against the walls (stain on the white paint like grease on a paper plate). A long line of empty Bud Light bottles atop the kitchen counter. A forgotten plastic cup flipped over beneath the Wal-Mart dining room table. A flat-panel TV bolted into the wall…but did they mount it themselves? When they leave, will there be a hole the size of your head in the drywall from where they rip it out? Old McDonald's bag wedged under the couch, as if—because there is no area rug to sweep it under—trash must be pushed *somewhere*, right?

Your quarter-million dollar investment is in the hands of *these kids*?

The four guys on the couches stare at you in unison. Eyes unblinking and jaws clenched. Kyle waves hello to each of them, adjusts the bill of his Bulldogs hat, and their icy glares seem to melt a bit. The miracle of sports. Kyle is looking around the room less skeptically, isn't thinking that these four roommates are bent on your personal destruction, is probably instead thinking: *Damn, these guys have a sweet pad!* He never lived in a fraternity house, never spent three years in a party-warehouse that smelled of testosterone and demon piss, and so the thought of four dudes together—four dudes on their own, going to the gym, eating fast food, drinking beer, watching football basketball whatever-the-fuck—is *novel* for him. People *do* this? It's a lifestyle possibility? WHOOOO! Whereas you wince at the old-French-fry-smell wafting from the bag beneath the couch, Kyle is reading a poster on the wall out loud (the title is "The Shit List," and beneath the headline are a series of images depicting different types of shits) and laughing at the descriptions: "Second Wave Shit!" he reads. "Oh man. It's true. It's so true."

Back on task, Landlord.

"So," you say to Bradley, "you said the garage door isn't working?"

"Huh?" Bradley says. He's found a loose thread on his t-shirt, is slowly pulling it out farther and farther and smiling wider the longer it gets.

"That's why we're here. The *garage door*."

"Oh yeah." He yanks hard and lets the thread float to the floor, where it remains, as he steps over it and leads you out of the living room. "It was, like, middle of the night last night. There was a banging noise, like someone threw something against the door? I came out, tried to open it…it just made a tired sound, like a fat guy who couldn't do a push-up."

Kyle laughs. "Say," he says, stopped at the washer and dryer in the narrow laundry room that leads to the garage. "Got some dryer lint on the floor here."

"Huh?" Bradley asks.

"Kyle," you say.

"You guys ever clean out the vent?" Kyle asks your tenant.

"The vent? Bro, I don't even know what that is."

"*Kyle*," you say.

"Everyone knows to clean the lint from the front of the dryer," Kyle says, "but one of the top causes of house fires is actually the lint that builds up in the vent." He's pointing to the wall.

"You know your stuff, huh?" Bradley asks.

Don't interject.

Kyle turns to you. "Any landlord worth his salt is gonna suck out the lint—they make this vacuum tube thing, and we wouldn't even need to come inside, just—"

Lie. Say, "I've got one. I'll take care of it. Let's just focus on the garage today, okay?" Feel good about your lie when Kyle nods, claps you on the back like he believed in you all along, and then follow Bradley to the garage, where he flips on the lights and puts his hands on his hips and sighs too wearily for a kid with zero real-world responsibilities.

Now that you're out here, look around, see what has become of the place. Get angry, if you like, add to your list, but keep your mouth shut. Remember that I am your tour guide, that I am directing where we go and what we do, and that the only thing I am asking—*the only thing*—is to look like you're in control. Stay. In. Control.

Okay. Breathe.

Notice the three keg shells in one corner of the garage, a stolen stop sign leaning against them. Bradley isn't looking in that direction, doesn't even seem to regard these items. They're no different than the big-screen TV or the abandoned McDonald's bag or the sweat stain on the wall, just facts of life. A *real* landlord might confront the issue head-on. Who needs *three* kegs, after all, in a house in a residential neighborhood with "Slow! Children at Play" signs on every corner. Why would anyone host (or attend) a *keg party* in a place like this?

But stop thinking so much. Just breathe. Back on task.

Pretend you are a landlord who understands how houses are put together: search the garage, trace metal wires from wall to door, press buttons, and yes, you've found the problem! One metal line has snapped, the severed point frayed as if a giant rat slithered down from the attic and chewed through it.

"It was fine one second," Bradley says, "then *bang*. The cable snapped."

"You can't lift the door by hand?" Kyle asks. He's wandering the space, running a hand along the wires in a way that suggests he does indeed know how all the parts fit together and why; he tries to lift the garage door, again and again, watching the track, watching the wheels, watching the cable. This is Kyle: Mr. Fucking Fix-It. There is an authority and a confidence to his demeanor that cannot be faked. "Won't budge. Looks like it came off the track."

Bradley looks you in the eye, then motions to Kyle and nods. It's a look that says, *This guy is a savant! A house whisperer!*

"So I've got to call for repairs?" you ask, but damn it! That was the wrong thing to say, Landlord! You should've deflected all responsibility. You should've *blamed* this Bradley kid. You've seen two rooms in this house, after all, and if you were presenting an argument to a jury that this kid was to blame for the broken garage door, certainly you'd have enough evidence to convince twelve reasonable adults that when "something just breaks, suddenly" in a house occupied by people like this, the breakage is not spontaneous or passive. Someone is to blame, and it ain't tough to figure out who. Other items to which we may direct the jury's attention on this garage tour:

A torn white shirt on the garage floor, and what looks like blood stains splashed across it. Excellent! More fucking blood.

A mud-dauber nest in the far corner. Another in the near corner. Colonies of bugs out here in the garage, and no one can be bothered to just swing a broom or open up a can of Raid?

"That's exactly how it happened?" you ask, trying to backtrack into blame. "Just snapped? Out of nowhere?"

"Yeah."

"Nothing else? Nothing you haven't told me?" You feel the anger rising again, that feeling like *you* could snap…and if that feeling occurs in even the most mundane moments of your day then you *know* there is potential for *true rage* if you encounter situations on your *own property*, that the rage could be apocalyptic if you happened to encounter, say, some *college shit-bag* who thinks his rent check entitles him to do whatever the *fuck* he wants—kick the wall or throw beers across the room or let SpaghettiOs splatter the inside of the microwave, or piss on the floor and leave the bathroom tiles sticky-dirty when he moves out, or let the backyard grass grow tall and weedy, or pound nails into the wall just centimeters from electrical wiring, toss empty Coke bottles onto the nether-regions of the roof. These are the things you see in this kid's eyes when he says "Nope, nothing else," two eyes like oil stains that show you everything you've imagined and more, two lying eyes—

—and from here there is no dotted line leading anywhere else, it is just *this kid*, and *these things* he's done to your house, no other option and no other path and no other doors, and perhaps because there's no chance of a child or an old lady coming to the door this time, you know you can unleash your anger in this house, *your house*, you can claim your revenge by evicting them right now, right this very minute: get the fuck off my property, you destructive *shits*! How satisfying that would feel.

"How quick can you get the garage door fixed?" Bradley asks.

"What?" you ask. Fists clenched.

"Do you know how to fix it, or should we call someone? Is it under warranty?"

Fix *their* damage? Is he kidding? This is some security deposit shit, right here.

But don't answer right away. Breathe. Just stare at the garage door opener bolted into the ceiling, which stares back at you like a bat unhappy to be discovered here in the darkness. Breathe. Breathe. Release fists.

But here's the thing: Bradley wasn't asking you. He was talking to Kyle.

"Definitely need to call a professional," Kyle says, still staring at the garage ceiling and at metal tracks and bolts and frayed cables as if in telepathic contact with the machine. "There's something seriously wrong here. I wouldn't trust a home remedy."

"Do you have paperwork?" Bradley asks.

Again he was asking Kyle, but Kyle nudges your shoulder, like he thinks maybe you're sleepwalking or spacing out or something. He doesn't realize he stole your authority. You cough into your hand and ask, "Paperwork?"

"This happened to my parents over Christmas break last year," Bradley says. "It's amazing, the number of files they keep. Maybe it's under warranty."

"I don't know. I have no clue what to do," you say. "You guys just—"

Wait, did you just say you have no clue what to do? For God's sake, you shouldn't have said *that*. That was the *last* thing you should have said, the most damning of comments that a landlord can make if he still wants to hold some thread of authority. *Come on*! I'm trying to show you the way. I'm trying to help you! Are you even listening to me anymore?

"It's not under warranty," you try.

Even if untrue, this is a good comment: you need to *sound* sure of something. Hell, Edwin likely has any warranty paperwork, probably pocketed the security deposit before he left town, too, that motherfucker.

Exhale. "You're sure nothing else happened here. If I call a repairman, he's not going to ask questions about—"

"Bro," the kid says, and he's flipping through his iPhone, searching for something, "it's a *garage door*. Trust me. We don't *want* it broken. I didn't pour beer into it or anything." And his face lights up as he swipes across the screen. "Ah! Here we go. Davis Electric and Repairs. Air conditioners, garage doors, ceiling fans. Want me to call?"

"I should probably find the, um, paperwork first."

"I thought you said it wasn't under warranty?"

"Well, I should price the different repair services, then, and—"

"How about this," he says, his hand on your shoulder. "I'll give them a call, see if they can get out here tomorrow morning. If you find anything in your files, call me and we'll cancel the service appointment. But they're getting five-star reviews, best I see on here."

"Um. I…"

"Sounds reasonable," Kyle says. "I can come out here for the repair, too. Ask some questions, make sure the man knows his stuff."

You're silent, but you need to speak up, Landlord. Right now your brother is making all the decisions, and that's a bad look. How did this happen?

"What website do you use to price your contractors and repairmen?" he asks. "I prefer House Helper. But if your site finds something different…"

"I use House Helper, too," you lie. "So."

"Awesome. Great minds think alike! So I'll set up the appointment for tomorrow?"

"Sounds good," Kyle says, "so long as my brother ain't got me scheduled for anything else?"

"I um…no."

"And we'll pay the bill, and you just deduct that from the rent payment."

Grit your teeth and nod.

Okay. Now. Leave the garage, re-enter the kitchen with Bradley, and try not to think of the numbers: this could cost between $200 and $500, who knows?, but if you *don't* get it fixed then you're taking that first oily step toward *slum lord*, and these kids—despite their inability to place dirty clothes into a hamper, or to place an old McDonald's bag into the garbage can—are too privileged and too savvy to put up with a slum lord, and they'll stop paying the rent, and then it's not just $200-$500 for the garage door, no no, you're out $1,400 every month. What's worse: footing the bill and fulfilling your responsibility as landlord, or losing the monthly lifeline of their rent check? Ten minutes ago, you were fantasizing about tossing your tenants out the front door, and now—the more you consider how crucial they are to saving your life and your bank account and extending the slow sunset of your day as a real-estate investor—you're clinging to their outstretched hands.

Shake your head. Blink until the world comes back into focus.

"Anything else?" you ask. "Anything else I can help you guys with?"

"Something's fucked up with the garbage disposal, too." Bradley points to the sink. "Just today. It's been making a weird noise. Like it's dying."

"Don't look at me," Kyle tells you, now playing with a gas can at the far end of the garage. "I don't know kitchens."

And so, before you know it, you have your hand deep into the throat of the disposal, something you've always made fun of during horror movies whenever some moron got his hand hamburgered by a possessed house. It's stupid to be scared, of course, flashlight shining down there, fingers sifting past chicken fat, tuna, burnt bread crust, because there are no hauntings in Orlando. Not in *these* neighborhoods anyway. There were no Indian massacres when they cleared land for the Housing Boom of 2000-2005, no smallpox outbreaks, no 1920s bootleggers tommy-gunning Capone-style past the coppers of rural East Orlando. Save the ghost stories for the Old Coast: St. Augustine, Savannah, Charleston. Save the ghost stories for Chicago and San Francisco and Boston, for cities where centuries of natural disasters and immigrant conflict and serial-killing and kicked-over lamps and sweeping fires and gang warfare prematurely ended millions of lives, at least some of whom are now anchored to the land and dedicated to wailing about their torment late at night, and spectrally floating through spooky hotel hallways, or appearing as orbs in photographs, or whatever. Save it for them. Because there just isn't enough history in Central Florida to produce quality hauntings in these cookie-cutter Levittowns.

Hand still in the garbage disposal, fingernails scratching the metal teeth. And what's this? Fingertip pricked by something sharp between the blades. Maneuver your thumb forward and pinch, pull. It's a piece of broken glass, and you're holding it up, joyous over your victory, and now that your hand is safely removed from the disposal you flip the switch and the blades spin and blend and liquefy with terrifying efficiency and you've *solved* this problem without spending a dime! Give yourself a round of applause, Mr. Landlord!

"I did it!" you say.

But Bradley is already lounging on the couch with his friends, chatting with Kyle about college football, and no one was watching you brave the spinach-and-raw-chicken depths of the garbage disposal. No one sees the glass in your hand, the lettuce in your fingernails.

"I fixed it. It was just glass, just sort of…blocking the—"

"Oh. Cool," Bradley says.

"I'm just…" you start, but no one is listening so you speak louder: "Where's the bathroom?"

Bradley sort-of nods toward the hall and off you go.

There was a time when this was your life, when you lived in a fraternity house at the University of Central Florida and spent full days in pajama pants or gym shorts or board shorts, or in jeans and t-shirts plucked from floor piles. There was a time when days and nights passed in a present-tense haze of awesomeness, a place without clocks. You never really stopped to think about where you were going and where you'd been, you just *went*. College was a place where possessions and physical properties—the fraternity house itself—didn't seem to matter, where you could get raging drunk and build a beer pong table that swung forth from your wall like a Murphy bed, where you could cut a hole into drywall and create a new haphazard doorway from one room into the next because why not?, you'd be outta there in a year, and then it'd be the next guy's problem. There was a time when you slept 67% of nights in a shitty bunk bed that hovered creakily over your study desk, and 13% of nights passed out on the couch at the far end of the bedroom with the Xbox controller still on your chest and the television blinking the "pause" screen all night long, and maybe 10% of nights at some girl's place or on the couch of some fraternity brother off-campus who'd had a party and you'd crashed there, and the final 10% of nights at undetermined locations, finding your way back to the fraternity house the next morning, drained by intense Florida sunshine (always hottest on these mornings) and twelve-beer dehydration, just picturing the stank-nasty bathroom where you'd throw up so you wouldn't be miserable in class (oh, *now* you remember class!), where you'd promptly fall asleep and later go to the sorority house to copy notes from Trish or Anna or Valerie and—

Oh God. Oh God, those were the motherfucking days.

Wash the tuna juice off your hands, take a piss, then wash your hands again. Wipe your sweaty face on their bathroom towels and stare into the mirror for a moment to be sure you look poised, and then finally step back out into the living room to discover that three girls have arrived. They stand in the living room, one with a bottle of Nuvo. Fuck, what time is it? How long were you in there? Are they drinking *already*?

"We didn't block you in," one of the girls says to you.

Kyle looks more lit-up than usual, as if all the talk of dead owners and closed shops and forsaken fathers and lost fortune was part of someone else's day. Right here and now, Kyle does not look like a man who's sunken into the pit of his brother's despair; he looks instead like a man on the verge of boarding a party bus to his best friend's bachelor party. A house of dudes! And alcohol! And hot twenty-year-old females! Dream come true.

"Are you having a party?" you ask the room.

"Huh? Oh, no," Bradley says. "Just, you know, some people over for the game. Ordering some pizza." He runs his hands over his head, nonchalantly staring at the floor, then pauses, his eyes slowly rolling upward to look at you, a grin creeping onto his face. "Wanna watch with us?"

"I don't know," you say.

"Edwin came over a few times. Told us to always have beer ready for a 'house inspection.'"

"That's awesome," Kyle says. "We were just gonna watch the game at home, so—"

"Kyle," you say.

"You don't have other plans?" Bradley asks.

"Shit, no," Kyle says. "My brother's an old man."

"Kyle," you say. "There's more work that—"

"It's the Magic game," Bradley says. "The workday stops at tip-off."

"It's not tip-off yet."

"Nope. But it's pre-game, and if you leave now, you'll hit rush hour."

"You do *not* miss pre-game," one of the girls says from the couch.

"A compelling argument, Marc," Kyle says. He has his hands out in a what-gives gesture.

"Won't get more work done today anyway," Bradley says. "Come on, Landlord."

As your tour guide—as the one you have entrusted to make decisions, to steer this vessel—I must implore you to *get out of this house*. You are incapable of acting like a responsible and authoritative landlord if you party with these frat-star tenants. You want to turn your life around? You want to change your fortunes? This is *not the way to do it*. Because here's the thing, Marc: tonight's game is not just a game, and the team—the Orlando Magic, your city's only team in a major sports league—is not just a team, not to you. For the last year you've found yourself seeking confirmation of the day's value in the final box score. If the Magic lose, it *confirms* your cynicism, that nothing in the world will work out. Leave this house. There's no telling how you'll act if the Magic lose tonight, if you'll be able to stifle the sourness and the anger swirling inside you and waiting to geyser forth. This will not end well.

"For fuck's sake," you say, "why not?"

"*That's* the spirit!" Bradley says. "Kick your feet up. Help yourself to a beer. Just be prepared: we get a little rowdy."

"What do you think, Landlord?" Bradley asks. "We got a shot tonight?"

"Probably not," you say. "I'm pessimistic about our chances."

"Pessimistic?"

"It's my strategy for coping with sports. If I'm pessimistic about the game, at least I won't be disappointed when we lose."

"No way, Landlord!" he says. "Turn that frown upside-down!"

No one else in Metro Orlando is as angsty as you. How can they be? The Orlando Magic have risen mercurially through the ranks of the NBA's top teams, a washed-out franchise a few years ago but now a *contender*, third straight year in the playoffs, and second straight year advancing to the Semi-Finals. Still, all you can think about is 2004, when the Magic were *garbage*, a league-worst 21-61 record (including a 19-game losing streak at one point), selfish-selfish Tracy McGrady the team leader, and supposed-superstar Grant Hill sitting out *the entire season* while (first) recovering from ankle surgery, and then (post-surgery) recovering from a staph infection that sent him into emergency hospitalization. 2004. What a fucking year to be a Magic fan, but you were there, weren't you? Loyal even then, as the coach was fired, the general manager fired, and rumors swirled of a relocation to Kansas City. Were any of these guys around for that?

Were they around for the 2004 NBA Draft, when the Magic selected Dwight Howard with the first overall pick, and were they around for all the embarrassing losses and excruciating box scores that followed? Or did they just tune in now, here in 2009, as Dwight is finally realizing his potential as the league's dominant *Big Man*, a monster in the paint. The bandwagon fans might not remember that 21-61 season (to them, it might seem as distant as the days before Disney) but *you* remember, and it is a part of the weight you carry with your fandom.

Never mind that your roster is solid, deep, built to win. You've got Jameer Nelson, a bowling-ball of a point guard who drives the lane and makes defenders collapse like pins, then lasers the ball to Dwight, the team's Goliath, who's like a wrecking ball on a bowling lane, not even fair for defenders...Then you've got Rashard, a three-point sniper on the outside. Pick your poison, NBA. *Three superstars.* Not to mention Rafer Alston and Anthony Johnson backing up Jameer at point, and Hedo Türkoğlu, a surefire "Sixth Man" candidate, and rookie Courtney Lee, a future superstar if ever there was one, and Marcin Gortat, the best backup center in the whole damned league, and—

STOP #7: GAME TIME

Sit down on a couch. *Sit.* Run your hands through your hair, that's fine. Do whatever it takes to keep from shouting at the TV. The game has almost started. The second round of the NBA's Eastern Conference playoffs, the Semi-Finals, a best-of-seven series against the defending champion Boston Celtics. *Defending champions.* This is where your pessimism seeps in like hot air through gaps in the weatherstripping. This is why you can't be trusted tonight, Marc.

You spend the first quarter watching everyone else in the room, barely paying attention to the television. You watch the stinky gym-rat stomp upstairs to take a shower. Why would he wait until the game's *tip-off,* until all guests have arrived, to then just leave? God, young people are dumb. But keep your mouth shut, okay?

Watch as the girls pretend to drink their beers and, as Landlord, try not to be concerned over the little things that can be cleaned up in an afternoon, the spilled beer, the knocked-over cups. But still, watch the girls, because they don't have a security deposit at stake. They treat their beers like accessories, sloshing and swinging and sliding them around no different than the purses and cell phones they scatter about on tables and armrests; you imagine chipped tile from a dropped bottle, and grout stained so deep that the house smells like old beer for a decade.

So maybe don't watch them. Look away, Landlord: maybe it's better *not* to see this. Watch the pre-game interview with Boston Celtics Coach Doc Rivers, where he's talking about how it feels to be facing his old team, and the

Magic organization gave him so much, and it's gonna be such a tough game, but beneath this effusive praise is a devilish grumble in Doc's voice suggesting that he's out for blood, that he wants his boys to slit throats and steal souls tonight. It's enough to drain you of hope, of confidence.

"I need this," you tell the room, and everyone laughs like you're joking. "Oh God, I need this so bad."

"Fuckin' A, Landlord!" someone howls. "Give us a win, Dwight! For the big guy here!"

At the end of the first quarter, the Magic go up 24-19 on a three-pointer by the hard-working Frenchman Mickaël Piétrus. Everyone in the living room cheers and claps, but you didn't see the shot because you were looking at a stain on the hallway wall, a splotchy moldy shape that you hope is not growing and—stop it, Marc. Look: five-point lead after the first twelve minutes of the game. Maybe—*maybe*—you should bottle the pessimism and save it for another night. Maybe—repeat: *maybe*—the Magic have a shot.

You watch someone knock over a Bud Lite bottle during the end-of-quarter celebration, your face going sour with principal-style disapproval, but fortunately the bottle is empty so there's no mess, no damage, no broken glass or chipped tile or stained grout. Go ahead, Landlord: congratulate yourself for not screaming or lecturing.

"Can't stop the three-pointers," Bradley says, jabbing his finger at the screen like the TV was talking shit. "It's gonna be raining threes all day long in Boston, baby. All day long!" He high-fives one of the other guys.

"Inside out," someone says.

"Inside out!" Bradley repeats. "Dwight looks like a *beast* tonight, too."

And indeed, here at the break between quarters, the camera zooms in on your superstar center Dwight Howard holding a towel to his face and wiping the torrent of sweat from his scalp. You know he's playing hard because the sweat returns as quickly as he sops it away, beading up like his skin is a pin-pricked garden hose.

"They need to play JJ *all game*," a girl says. You haven't learned their names yet, only know them by the most basic characteristics: the tall girl with the brown(ish) hair and the skin-tight Magic jersey; the one with the "Swim Coach" t-shirt and black ass-hugger shorts; and the blonde one in the jean skirt and the size-zero "Blue and White IGNITE" shirt hand-cut to look sexy (collar cut off, neck line swooping to reveal maximum cleavage). You're aware you've objectified them, these three girls, that you haven't yet said a word to them or even tried to distinguish them in any way but the physical…

Should you be all right with that?

Hasn't this been your problem lately with girls and relationships?

Are you a dirtbag?

Wait a minute. What did she say? They need to play JJ all game?

STOP #8: JJ REDICK

Let's halt the destructive self-examination for a moment to appreciate the stat line of JJ Redick.

He's the "cute" player, the lottery pick from Duke University who looks like he'll wind up on *The Bachelor* if his playing career ends early. He's also one of the main reasons why you remain skeptical of the team: like the entire crestfallen city of Orlando, he is *too* polished, *too* perfect to be a hard worker. This is a city of endless entertainment options, but no gritty American industry. No steel mills. No stockyards. No granaries on the coastline, no fish market to remind you of the thousands of boats pulling in each day with salmon or king crab or shrimp to unload. And thus no sports teams named after them, either, no Packers or Pistons or Steelers or Oilers or Cowboys or Spurs. No teams named after hard-fought battles with the land itself—no Sooners or Mountaineers or Raiders or 49ers or Trail Blazers. No, the city's team is…the Magic. This is just a city filled with dudes in striped button-downs and top-shelf hair product, and damn, is *that* ever JJ Fucking Redick. You want more *bruisers* on the team, more hustlers, more Dwights and Philly-tough Jameer Nelsons and (if you just admit this to yourself) more Boston Celtic-type players, more Rajon Rondos and Kevin Garnetts, guys who will punch you in the gut when you're not looking, and fewer JJ Redicks.

JJ.

There's a rumor that JJ always packs two blow-dryers on long road trips, one in his carry-on and one in his checked luggage (even though it's a charter jet and it seems ridiculous that anyone on such a small plane would have to worry about losing luggage, and also don't you think there'd be blow-dryers in all the hotel rooms anyway?, but hey, it's a rumor). There's another rumor that he signed an endorsement deal with American Crew, and he's now contractually obligated to style his hair for *every* game, and to make passing references in post-game interviews to matte fiber and style putty and citrus mint conditioner. You've also heard him say "gluten-free" and "farm-to-table" in interviews, and so you wonder if the endorsement pipeline is funding those vocabulary choices as well.

The old-school crackers of Central Florida cringe at JJ, even while the women giggle and hold their breath and imagine him sinking a 3-pointer then turning to smile and wink directly at them.

"Mmm, JJ," says the blonde. "Such a tight little ass."

"The things I'd do to him," Swim Coach says.

"JJ looks like a banker, not a baller," you say to the room. "Keep the white guys off the floor. Off the floor."

The room full of white people laughs, so go ahead: feel encouraged. You've finished two beers, and your mood has lightened.

Bradley claps and pumps his fist proudly, like he's successfully managed to force you out of your shell and turn you into a fun-loving Edwin. "Get 'im another beer!"

"Oh, I don't—"

"So, Landlord," he says, "you don't like JJ? Who's your favorite player, then?"

On-screen is a television advertisement for some explosive and CGI-heavy new summer film. A woman—Jessica Alba?, Jessica Biel?, Jessica Albiel?, you get the names of all these model/actress/sexual-icons confused—stands in sexily tattered clothing (soot smeared sexily across her forehead and the sexily sweat-moistened skin of her shoulders and stomach) and points a machine gun into the air and says something bad-ass in a low voice. Sexily. You feel like you've seen this movie before, but over the roar of the commercial, you say: "I'm a Dwight fan."

"*Everyone's* a Dwight fan," Bradley says.

"All bow before Dwight," Kyle says.

On-screen, a monster roars and a stealth fighter launches a missile.

"Dwight can do no wrong," the black-haired girl says. The Swim Coach. At first, you thought she was in nonchalant workout clothes, but now the outfit feels purposeful and maddeningly erotic. Swim Coach: it speaks of another life, one in which she spends all day flaunting this perfect tanned body, one in which she is a *Baywatch* beauty and her boobs bounce in slow-mo. (This happens all the time. You see a purple bra strap and now a girl is suddenly more interesting; a hint of thong, and she is no longer prudish. All these fantasies your mind conjures. It's…holy shit, you need a girlfriend.)

"Not the most creative choice for a favorite player," Bradley says.

"I guess I'm just obvious," you say. "Growing up, I was a Shaq fan."

Kyle looks over at you, laughs, takes a swig of beer. "That's an understatement. You cried when he signed with LA." He's leaning back in his seat, soaking up his first night in a fraternity house. Of all possible scenes you could've imagined for your evening…

On-screen, another explosion, then the low voice of that movie trailer guy saying "When the world needs a hero…"

"I didn't cry," you say. "You're embellishing."

"You had that *Shaq Fu* video game," Kyle says. "You had a Shaq poster on your bedroom door."

"*Shaq Fu?*" the gym-rat asks. He's just arrived back downstairs from his shower, is leaning against the wall, but still is wearing only boxers and a wife-beater, is still towel-drying his hair even as he holds an open Miller Lite.

This age—20, 21?—seems so long ago that you don't understand the logic of anything these kids are doing. Why not just get dressed in the bathroom before coming downstairs? What the fuck? You can see his pubic hair through the slit in his boxers, an image you wish you could erase from your memory.

On-screen, some sort of green creature with tentacles and gaping shark-mouth.

"You guys are probably too young for this," you say. "*Shaq Fu* was a wannabe *Mortal Kombat*. Terrible video game."

"Like, Atari?"

"I'm not that old, asshole. This was Super Nintendo."

The room is looking at you now, former perceptions of "landlord" shape-shifting. Maybe you aren't the stodgy antithesis to the beloved Edwin. Maybe you're the kind of guy who "takes some getting to know" before you "open up." At least, you hope this is the perception you're creating. With a hearty chug, you finish off the last of your second beer.

Kyle says: "Didn't you try to go as Shaq for Halloween, too? And you asked Mom if she'd paint you in black-face, but she wouldn't do it?"

The room erupts in laughter, while simultaneously, on-screen, the white-hot text of the summer blockbuster's release date is branded onto a black background, followed by a smash-cut to one final shot of a smolderingly handsome actor you've never seen before. At the far end of the room, the tall guy is pointing to the screen and mouthing "that looks fucking awesome!"

Try to smile: Kyle isn't un-manning you. He's not trying to ruin your credibility. You're just on edge. Smile. Of all the places your anger manifests itself, do not let it show itself *here*. Do *not* get angry with your brother. He's the one thing, maybe the only unspoiled relationship you can still salvage.

Kyle says: "You destroyed the Shaq poster when he signed with Los Angeles, didn't you?"

"I ripped it down," you say. "Yes."

"Tore it into strips, right? And saved Shaq's head for last?"

"Damn," Bradley says. "That's cold, bro."

"I remember," Kyle starts, and he's staring into the ceiling, picturing something. "You still had his head taped to your wall. For months. Years."

"It wasn't that—"

"You were so angry," Kyle says.

You rub your pants. "I was."

The room is no longer laughing.

The half-naked gym-rat says "Uh, Imma go put on some pants."

On-screen is a man running his hands through his hair while a voiceover asks questions about depression.

"So you're a Dwight fan," Bradley says finally, once the silence has become so oppressive that words are not just necessary but imperative. "But who's your second favorite player, Landlord?"

"This maybe makes me sound obsessive," you say, "but I have the whole roster categorized. Ordered, from top to bottom."

"Oh," Bradley says, in a way that makes you feel like he's reconsidering the benefits of silence.

DETOUR: THE ROSTER

Because you're off, taking them on a tour of your favorite players:

After Dwight, you like Mickaël Piétrus for his off-the-bench energy, then Jameer Nelson ("Short, but dude's got hustle"), then Marcin "Polish Hammer" Gortat ("Anywhere else, he's the starting center"), then rookie Courtney Lee. In your next tier is (sigh) JJ, then "Skip to my Lou" Rafer Alston and Rashard Lewis (though Lewis' $118 million contract sours his likeability for some reason you can't quite pinpoint…oh wait, it's the $118 million), then Hedo Türkoglu and old-as-dirt Anthony Johnson. You've actually written the full three-tiered list into a document on your computer. You rearrange it weekly. Even your bottom tier—Adonal Foyle and Tony Battie and the cluster of players at the far end of the bench whose combined season-total minutes don't equal the number of minutes Dwight plays in a single game—is ordered and categorized. It's comforting, the control it gives you over a team you can't control.

Ugh, don't say that last part out loud.

But *do* tell the room that you hate it when the Magic shoot too many three-pointers. The three-point game is not *sustainable*. No one will ever win a championship on three-ball. You'd rather have a dominant big guy than a bunch of sharp-shooters. That's why you loved Shaq when you were a kid, why you love Dwight Howard so much now. He's a player who *controls* the game, every game, is so powerful that he can *destroy* the other team. When an opposing player runs into Dwight and bounces backward onto his ass, *it makes your Goddamned night*. When Dwight grabs a rebound and pivots, his elbow inadvertently cracking into an opponent's skull, and some poor Bull or 76er collapses to the floor and holds his head like he's been battle-axed, *you scream with uncontainable joy*. Can't fuck with Dwight Howard, D12, D-Twizzy. Biggest baddest motherfucker on the court. When Shaq left the Magic in '96, Orlando basketball was emptiness. You went from championship to futility. But now with Dwight? This is not a team that will be ousted in the first round of the playoffs, not ever again. With Dwight, Orlando is for real. You live under a cloud of pessimism, but Dwight is a window to a brighter world where you will rise again, together, all of you.

STOP #9: SECOND QUARTER

So much of your life has been anger lately, but now—here in this living room, enlivened by your third beer, you're finding bits and pieces of gameplay from which you can almost construct a happy outlook: Mickaël Piétrus twisting inside the paint for a layup and Boston's Glen "Big Baby" Davis falling flat on his ass as he attempts to defend; and later, an offensive foul called on Big Baby, then a Big Baby turnover, then a missed jumper from Stephon Marbury, then a miss from Boston's three-point assassin Ray Allen, then a Celtics shot-clock violation and visible frustration on the Celtics bench, this heralded Boston team collapsing in its own home arena, and Dwight Howard making *both* of his free throws! Holy shit, when *that* happens you know God is on your side. Then another Orlando Magic layup, a jump-shot, and a 54-36 lead at halftime, can you motherfucking *believe* it? *In Boston?*

You see? Doesn't happiness feel good?

STOP #10: HALFTIME

Someone shakes a bottle of Miller Lite and sprays beer over the room like it's celebratory champagne and it splashes the television screen but there's no rush to clean it up because everyone is high on the fumes of a first-half blowout. Even you, Marc. Maybe you've got this. Hell, maybe your tour guide was wrong to tell you to go home.

"Hey-oh!" Kyle says and holds out his Bud Light bottle to clink. Hey, sure! Clink back, Big Brother!

One of the guys is dribbling a basketball on the kitchen floor but, upon trying to execute a crossover, the ball slips, takes a weird bounce off the fridge, and goes sailing across the room, grazes the bottom of the chandelier. Everyone looks at you as the bottom of the chandelier swings lightly, and it's a several-hundred-dollar swing, but the light fixture doesn't actually hit the wall or break or anything. Bradley says "Ooooohhhh!" like it's a middle-school fight, but you laugh it off. You're having fun! Errbody in the club gettin' tips!

Minutes later, a pizza slice whaps against the sliding glass door, pepperoni shooting off onto the blonde girl's leg and she says "Oh my God!" and bends over to unpaste it from her skin. All of the guys look long and hard into the neckline of that low-cut "Blue and White IGNITE" shirt and the other girls know it's happening but they just shake their heads because, well, she *does* have enormous breasts, enviable in their mass *and* their ability to defy gravity, and she's always finding reasons to bend over like this so that everyone can look, and boys will be boys, right?

And now one of the girls is asking if you have any properties you could rent her. The Swim Coach—her name is Valerie—digs through her purse for her phone, inputting your number, biting her lip. Then, the unthinkable, she picks up her drink, gets up from her seat and moves over to your space on the couch, where she sits down *on your lap* in those tight black ass-hugger shorts. "So do you live out here, too?" she asks, and one of her tiny smooth hands is pressed against your inner thigh to keep her balance while she sips her cup of Nuvo.

Kyle's looking your way and nodding with proud-of-you satisfaction. This is a *good moment*, and it's happening in *real life*. Orlando 54, and Boston 36, and girl on your lap!

And now the blonde—her name is Kayla, and her boobs are so damn flawless they look CGI—is leaning forward toward you and asking about properties, too, fingertips tucked into the pockets of her jean skirt as she leans forward more than she needs to, says her lease is up soon and she's looking for a place. And Valerie, there on your lap, looks upset that Kayla has intruded, and you think: *Are they fighting over me? Yes. Yes! I needed this.*

STOP #11: THIRD QUARTER

Look around, Landlord. Look around and take in this joyous moment.

Halftime ends. Valerie stands to fetch another drink and you cross your legs to hide the half-erection, hoping she returns soon to cover it back up. The third quarter begins with a few three-pointers from Gluten-Free JJ and Big-Money Rashard, basketball slipping through net as smooth as water down the drain, the lead stretching to 65-37. A nearly *30-point* lead! The commentators have stopped talking about the game and are instead plugging upcoming TV shows; the camera has pulled away from the basketball court to offer crowd shots, close-ups of despondent Celtics fans whose #1 foam fingers have gone limp. This is dirt on the grave, Stuff the Magic Dragon standing over the plot with shovel in hand. This is Orlando Dominance, something to be relished because this city has seen it all-too-infrequently this decade. The Magic are winning. You…*you* are winning again, buddy.

Across the room: Kayla sucks on the neck of her beer bottle like she's giving a blow job, Bradley beside her telling her to "Go! Go! Go!" You don't know what's happening there, but you can't stop watching. This living room: this living room! Certainly this is a good sign of your future as Landlord, a sign that you can do this, make your money back.

Except.

Except something is wrong here: no one's watching the game anymore. Valerie leans on the kitchen counter scrolling through her phone with a tired look on her face. On the basketball court, Dwight and Company trudge from one hoop to the next while the Boston Celtics sprint and shoot like a team renewed. Suddenly it feels like the Magic are struggling to hold onto a good feeling that has passed, like they've had a dozen beers and the happy drunkenness has turned into sloppy ceiling-spinning disorientation. Kayla slaps Bradley on the arm—not flirty—and says, "Why didn't you *call* her? That's such a dick move," and now it's 74-56 and you're not worried, not really, but *thirty* points has just dwindled to a *twenty*-point lead like (snap your fingers) *that*, and the air feels different now, not like carbonation and sex-in-your-lap and euphoria, but like the cold melted cheese on the bottom of a pizza box, and damn, snap your fingers again and it's 78-62, twenty-point lead shriveled to *sixteen*, and Kyle leans toward you and says, "Dude, who are you snapping at?"

STOP #12: FOURTH QUARTER

When you come out of the bathroom at the start of the fourth quarter, Valerie is at the front door waving goodbye to everyone. She has homework and has to work tomorrow morning. She doesn't even wave goodbye to you, specifically. It's more a general see-you-all-later wave thing. She was on your lap at halftime. She said she'd call you about properties. Now she's a memory, back to swim-coaching in your fantasies.

On the court, the Magic are missing their every shot. It's like the circumference of the basket has contracted. Hedo Türkoğlu bricking free throws and jump-shots. Rafer Alston clanging three-pointers. Anthony Johnson on the floor—the third-string point guard—and he looks so much shorter than any player from the Celtics, *how is that possible?*, did our players *shrink* in the last ten minutes? He bumbles past half-court but has the ball stolen by the younger, quicker Rajon Rondo of the suddenly do-no-wrong Celtics, and then Piétrus—you love Mickaël Piétrus, Mr. Hustle, Mr. Energy—commits two desperate fouls in a single minute, and now it's 84-75 and you look at the score and the clock, and the score and the clock, and the score and the clock, and you think, How can this be? Weren't we just *celebrating* a moment ago? *Fuck!*

Whoa, buddy. Time out. Let's listen to your tour guide again. Let's just… can we just sit and watch the game?

"Dude, are we out of beer?" someone asks from the kitchen.

"There's some Smirnoff Ice down there."

"Yay!" Kayla says. She's still here, but somehow she's no longer attractive. Her face looks pale, mean. There's pizza sauce on her leg that she hasn't completely wiped away. It grosses you out. She wobbles, too, and now her words just sound dumb. Dumb-drunk. "I, like, love that stuff," she says.

Across the room, Kyle's shaking his head and saying "Smirnoff Ice," making a gag face.

"What the *fuck*?" Bradley says from the kitchen. "What else do we have? We still have Jäger?"

Kyle picks up Valerie's warm left-behind beer, grimacing.

Eyes on the game, or maybe not, *shit*, because it's suddenly 89-80 after Brian Scalabrine—fucking red-haired Scalabrine, who looks more like a Will Ferrell caricature of a Boston basketball player than an *actual* basketball player—hits a three. Then, when the Magic inbound, Hedo Türkoğlu squanders the possession by clanking another jumper, Boston's "Big Baby" Davis muscling the rebound and launching the ball up-court to Paul Pierce, who's in the exact right spot to catch the ball and quickly snipe a three-pointer, the Magic's cushion deflating to 89-83. Coach Stan Van Gundy frantically slices the air with his hands in a "timeout" motion.

This is happening.

Oh God. 89-83?

From a thirty-point lead to just six points.

Magic time-out. Magic scared.

This is the most monumental playoff collapse ever.

This game, this day, this house. This house!

This house was a breath away from $300,000, and you were *this close* to selling the property and pocketing the profit, but now the market is roller-coaster-dropping on Orlando all over again. You're watching it *live*. These missed shots, these fouls. These are the oil stains in your driveway, the broken van, the broken windows, the graffiti on your neighborhood's entry sign, the bills piling high, the girl at Lakeside Wine Bar telling you she's "sorry things turned out this way for you." This is I-4 collapsing beneath you, the Suntrust Building toppling, the Orange County Convention Center imploding and Disney World dissolving into the muck of Central Florida swampland. This is *you* buried underground, shot by shot, Orlando returning to palm scrub.

"Shut it off," you tell the room. "It's over. I know how this one ends. Shut it off."

But, upset as everyone is at the collapse, no one seems to think you're serious. Kayla is texting. Bradley is drinking from a water jug.

"It'll be fine, bro," Kyle says.

But you stand from your chair during the time-out, walk to the television screen, use your shirt to wipe off the beer stains lefts behind by the halftime celebration.

"Landlord, no need to be a cleaning service, too!" Bradley shout-laughs.

Okay, that's enough. Smile. Swallow the anger. Smile. Now sit back down. You had your moment.

Time-out ends, and as if to confirm your dire prophecy that the team is falling apart, Boston's Paul Pierce steals the ball from Rashard Lewis, passes it to Big Baby, and a quick Boston Celtics two-pointer sees the lead dwindle further: 89-85, with just over two minutes remaining.

Two minutes left, and the camera cuts to a close-up of Coach Stan Van Gundy, his classic "Master of Panic" face that looks like a porn star who's caught a whiff of a mid-scene fart. The SVG Stinkface, you call it, the sort of disgusted expression that says "It's over, we blew it," and it's the same face you're wearing here in this living room.

Under two minutes left now. Stan is scratching at his turtleneck, looking at the clock and then looking at his players on the floor, up and down and back and forth, like a gambler who's bet everything on the final score. It makes you even more anxious to watch him, and borderline angry too. Depending upon who you ask, Stan Van Gundy looks like either (a) porn star Ron Jeremy, or (b) a used-car salesman. That's the big debate in Orlando. He's got thinning black hair wild over the bald spot that is his entire scalp, a thick dark mustache like a…well, a porn star or a used-car salesman. He also seems to be the only coach in the league who doesn't pace the court in confident shirt-and-tie, opting instead for a loose-fitting turtleneck and blazer, which—while not flattering to his short and stocky physique—at least give him the sort of neck mobility that a buttoned-up collar would prohibit. But really, it doesn't matter whether you think he looks like (a) or (b), because *neither* of these two options looks like a "real" basketball coach; somehow there's this sense that Van Gundy wandered into this job from some other industry entirely (porn or car sales?) and is always a single game—a single quarter, a single *play*—from being ferretted out as an impostor. Everyone believes this. But why are the cameras still fixed on him? Cut away!

35 seconds left. The score is now 91-87. A precarious four-point margin. Keep it together. Don't start muttering pathetically to yourself—

"Please," you say. "Please."

For fuck's sake, man.

The room around you plunges into darkness, an empty cavity of a place with only the television flashing before you. No more Bradley. No more Kayla. No more Kyle. No more cold pizza or empty bottles. You're watching the game underground, in the soil with the earthworms and cockroaches and tunneling ants and the ancient Florida forever before the age of Magic.

Boston calls time-out. You're whispering "Two-possession game, two-possession game, two-possession game," reminding yourself that you *still have the lead*. Boston still has to make *two shots* to pull off their epic comeback.

Orlando inbounds the ball and begins dribbling up-court, 22 seconds left in the game, 19 seconds, and then JJ Redick fouled at 13 seconds. As JJ steps to the line, the Boston crowd explodes in vitriol, waving arms, shouting, spittle flying. A man in the third row in a green shamrock t-shirt points down at the court and screams—so hard and loud his eyes might literally shoot from their sockets—and you can lip-read as the man screams "I'm going to fucking kill you, you pansy-ass bitch, and shit on your American Crew corpse!" It's amazing that HDTV is so crisp, so clear to allow such a visual. A woman in the front row, bone-thin and wearing the sort of heels that could pay your mortgage, also screaming "You shoot like a girl, you low-class cunt!" The arena is a cesspool of hate, quintessential Boston, the TV glowing green as JJ dribbles at the free-throw line and stares down the basket. And JJ Redick, the slick GQ model you were so skeptical about, Mr. gluten-free farm-to-table hair product…you are pulling for him as if he is your own brother. JJ is us, JJ is our only hope, JJ please don't miss, please please please. And he knocks down both his free throws, pads the Orlando Magic lead by two extra points, and it's now 93-87. He wipes the cologne-sweat from his forehead and smiles to the camera.

13 seconds.

"Please," you say. "Please."

Darkness around you. Everything could still go wrong and you know it.

And, as if to fulfill your deepest fears, Boston inbounds and drills a three-pointer with pit-crew efficiency, the Orlando Magic lead shrinking to 93-90. One-possession game. One mistake, Anthony Johnson losing the ball to Rajon Rondo, or Ray Allen twisting a dagger of a three-pointer in the final second of game-play…

"Please," you whisper into the darkness.

Close-up on Stan Van Gundy. "Please," he's saying. "Please."

You are so fucked.

Orlando inbounds. You inhale and hold your breath because you know the ball is going to get stolen and you know Boston will make a three-point shot and tie the game as the clock expires, and you hold your breath and

JJ catches the inbound, soft palms on the ball and it rests there in his organic, pesticide-free hands ready to be ripped out by the aggressive and opportunistic talons of don't give-a-fuck-about-pussy-ass-sustainability Rajon Rondo...

But instead of a struggle for the ball, it's a quick foul. No steal.

JJ hits one free throw, then the next, and the game is over.

95-90. Orlando wins.

After such anxiety, it's over that quickly.

You exhale, and the oil-stain darkness slowly melts down the walls and into the floor, the frat star living room reappearing, Bradley reappearing, Kayla reappearing, the gym rats, the beer cans, the pepperoni on the glass door. The room doesn't feel bright, not really, because even though the Magic technically won, there was no real *victory* here, only an escape.

DETOUR: PARTNERS IN CRIME

And is that the best you can hope for now, an *escape*, when it once seemed as if you had a 30-point lead on the world?

Marc, step into this room here.

Do you remember when Edwin approached you about partnering up?

Picture it. Put yourself back in that moment. Edwin is fresh from that conference or seminar or whatever, down in Cape Coral, is back in Orlando with a binder so large and packed with papers and envelopes and file folders that holding it is nearly impossible; you have to place it on the kitchen table and open it gently, carefully, so shit doesn't spill everywhere, and even then, there are so many thick documents bound by heavy-duty staples that you have to remove them from the rings if you want to even read the text. The binder says "Your Million-Dollar Future as a Real-Estate Investor" on the front, and Edwin is all "This is the blueprint, brother. This is the *blueprint*." And you're uncertain, cautious. Edwin, after all, is the rich kid who back in college bragged that he never wore clothes a second time, always just bought something new (father's credit card, autopay *bitches*) and sold the used stuff to fraternity brothers at half price. He ran a "note-taking" business, too, a front for selling old tests and essays. With that sort of history, aren't you right to be cautious? But Edwin has capital from his father, and before even sharing with you, he invested in a place called Lehigh Acres down by Cape Coral, had already—in, like, a single weekend—flipped his first property for a profit, and (as you look into his eyes now) it seems *impossible* that someone can be so optimistic without having first read this mammoth binder, whose rings you need to lean on with all of your weight in order to effectively close. *Impossible.* Edwin doesn't know shit, doesn't even *care* to know shit, probably won't even read this gigantic home-flipping manual, and yet: clear skies, smooth sailing, world's our oyster, etc. etc. There's something so reassuring about this attitude, something intoxicating.

At first, you tell him that you can't partner up, not now, not with the bank job and the notary business, but he's making sales, cleaning up while you collect the same boring paycheck from Wachovia. Months pass. You thought maybe he'd crash and burn, waste his father's money in the first month and then go back to…whatever spoiled people do when things don't go their way…but this motherfucker is always smiling, always looks like he's headed to the golf course or just came from a pool party. Always "just closed another sale," and there's always one more on the way.

So when, after a few months on his own, he asks again if you want to be partners, you don't hesitate (word is, the bank over-hired, and there are layoffs thinning your ranks), and it takes no time for you to adopt the same smile, the same "We're gonna make so much moola, brotha!" hopefulness. 2005. 2006. 2007. And life is a lazy river, begging you to just float, just float. Edwin: you drink him up. You're sorry to have ever doubted him. "There's a lot of stuff that I don't know," he says to you often (much of it paperwork that confounds him, and that's where *you* come in, why he needed a partner), "but I know how to make money, and that's the most important thing." God, he's right. He's so right.

No, Edwin is not the smartest guy in the room, but he lives a life free of doubt. He has the *binder*, and simply *having* the binder gives him an unshakeable confidence. He jello-molds back into the church-camp mindset of that seminar even when times grow tough; he can ignore the reports of the Cape Coral scandals, the duped families from Pennsylvania trapped in adjustable-rate loans for property they'd been told was soon-to-be-developed into sprawling Mediterranean estates but which actually lay out in the middle of lake-sized swamps without any hope of electricity or water ever arriving to make the property livable and the value redeemable. He can ignore the reports that the seminar-thing was really just a money-making scheme put on by a failed real-estate investor, not an actual *educational* seminar designed to equip aspiring investors with the right tools to succeed. Most of the men and women in the room had paid big money to be there, to *get the binder*, but would never really read it. Edwin understands all of that, hears the words and reads the news stories, but he can filter it out, can still pop out of bed and say "Don't forget about our million-dollar future, brother. It's promised right"— tapping the binder he's barely browsed—"*right here.*"

He never feels the Celtics chipping away at the lead. Just always that damned smile, shrugging every problem away.

"Comps are falling in this neighborhood," you tell him, pointing to one property on your spreadsheet. "We put renters in there, and what happens— long-term—if the prices keep falling?"

They won't. Trust me, buddy.

"Cost of new kitchen cabinets is a little much, right?" you tell him. "For *that* neighborhood?"

Don't shop with your *wallet, my man. Someone will pay for it.*

"Seems like there are a lot of downtown high-rises in the works," you tell him. "You really think they're all gonna get built? Is that a smart investment?"

What am I good at? That's right. *Making money. Have no worries, partner.*

2006. 2007. 2008. The lazy river slows. Purchase prices falling. Falling.

But still the smile, still the optimism. "Opportunities!" he says, grin so wide and so real, and how can you doubt him now? So you buy more.

"What happens if we get stuck with this?" you ask him. "We need to be realistic."

"Marc," he says. "Marky Marc! We got this, man."

"Are you high?"

"Maybe."

"Stop fucking around. Please. And Marky Marc is not a nickname that works for me. The spelling…the spelling prevents it."

"Oh, buddy, don't go to bed angry."

You aren't angry really, not with him. His stupid optimism…Hell, he's the guy who thought the Jon Gruden Bucs would be a dynasty, multiple Super Bowls with Brad Johnson at the helm. He's the guy who thought every Florida-bound hurricane would turn back into the cold waters of the Atlantic. "But what about 2004, the four damned hurricanes we got that fall?" "Well, I was actually out of town for most of that. Took that trip to Colorado?" "But they still came! And Hurricane Charley devastated Orlando!" "Yeah. Awesome. Cleared a lot of bullshit land, made it easier for development."

Unwavering hope. Can't fuck with it. You go to Magic games with Edwin. Watching through his eyes, it's as if every Magic basket is going in, every game a win ("Real improvement tonight!" "You see how many three-pointers we took? Keep that up, we'll be unstoppable!"). Every girl he meets, not just a potential hookup but a potential wife.

But that was then, and this is now, and where did hope and positivity get him, Marc?

Where will it get the Magic, if they're satisfied with this bullshit escape?

Edwin. With his downtown condo, the windows overlooking Lake

Eola, the fully stocked bar. He paid too much for that condo, put down payments on so many other units in development that will never get built. Where did optimism get him? That money is lost forever. Behold Edwin, the cautionary tale!

Maybe if Edwin had gotten angry, as you have? That was his downfall, that he embraced an outlook that allows such a limited view of the world, that he cannot see beyond today's sunshine and clear skies to understand what tomorrow brings.

There's something productive about your anger, do you see it now? Something honest. Anger is *good*. Anger clarifies, cuts through. Anger—real anger, directed at laziness, at carelessness, at idiot decisions as a result of head-in-the-sand optimism—anger means that you're *identifying problems*, which means that you're closer to fixing them. Anger is honesty, and critical thinking, and a refusal to accept the status quo. Anger is good. Anger is right. More people should be angry, and then maybe we could fix this malfunctioning machine we call the United States of America! Thank you, ladies and gentlemen! Thank you, shareholders of Teldar Paper! (Oh God, that speech inside your head feels good. Suddenly you have the power-suit confidence of Gordon Gekko.)

But here's the point of this detour through your memory, Marc. All this time, you've been trying to stifle it, worried about the angry inside you. But what if you *embraced* the anger? Anger is passion. Anger is action. To embrace it is to embrace life itself.

Which tour guide am I, you might be wondering, the devil on your shoulder, or the angel? Does it matter? Just listen to me. Just listen. Embrace the anger, and maybe you'll come out of this all right.

"You *sure* you're all right to drive?" Kyle asks.

"Fine," you say.

"You look a little intoxicated."

"Don't you trust me, Kyle?" You run your hands up and down the steering wheel. You try to will the world back into straight motionless lines.

"I stopped drinking at halftime," Kyle says. "I don't mind driving."

"I saw you drinking a beer that one of the girls left behind."

"That was a joke. I was playing around."

"No. You're my *guest*. You're my little brother. *I* drive *you*."

And what's the worst that will happen? That you'll crash? That everything will end?

Exhale. Imagine the possibility.

"Seriously, I've just been drinking Coke for the last two hours."

"Did you hear me?" You consider the authority that you once exhibited back in Georgia, when you switched go-karts with Kyle. There was no discussion about what to do; there was only your decision, and it was the right one, and you remain proud of that Big Brother moment to this day.

"Marc," he says. "I don't know if—"

"We're going," you say.

Hell, Kyle doesn't even know the way home anyway. He'd look confused as he drove; he'd *look* drunk, and then you'd get pulled over. He probably still has enough alcohol in his system to blow over .05 or .08 or whatever, so here you are again: saving him, doesn't he understand?

Heading home down the 408, it feels like you're swerving each time you blink, but you stick to 60 miles per hour and watch the idiot college students speed past at 70, 80, and attract the attention of any roving police.

Kyle sits uncomfortably beside you.

"So, uh," he keeps saying, "so uh, that was pretty fun, huh?"

Onto I-4, and the drive is silent and the car feels like it's fighting you. But you are a pack mule; you've made this drive so many times you could do it in your sleep. In fact, you could close your eyes right now and try, Big Brother, let the world take you where it may. You could let your hands slip on the steering wheel, let the car veer over *there*, across *that*, and down into *there*, everything becoming darkness and past tense. Yes, wouldn't that be something?

Down the street from your house, there's an old woman who sits motionless in her garage all day, the garage door open no matter the heat or humidity, the wind or the downpour. Always wearing a t-shirt the color of sour milk, and worn-out pants that could either be jeans or sweats. There are cats that crawl through the garage, around the stacks of magazines and newspapers, onto and over an old pool table that takes the space a car should occupy. She sits. She stares soullessly out into the neighborhood.

The old woman does not own the house. You don't think so, at least. The owners are a married couple, thirty-somethings with too much money and therefore (like you) too large a house, and you've concluded that the old woman must be one of their mothers. Occasionally you see them returning home from work: they park in the long circular driveway, walk into the house through the open garage door, step around the old woman and the cats. No hellos, no hugs, no knee-pats or head-nods. No signs of affection of any kind. They seem like average upper-middle-class white people, the sort you see in so many homes here in Stoney Creek: the man wears extra-large dress shirts that blouse out to hide his expanding waistline, and the woman leaves the house in the morning with wet hair, comes home talking on her Bluetooth headset and struggling to hold onto the bundle of home décor catalogues she's retrieved from the mailbox.

You've wondered whether the old woman is even real. She doesn't move, not ever, not even when the cats slither from her shoulders to her lap, claws pressing into her ears and cheeks. Maybe she is a wax figure of one of the Golden Girls—the sassy oldest one, perhaps—stolen from a celebrity wax museum. Or maybe a Bealls Outlet mannequin. Or maybe this is the house of Norman Bates, and she's a stuffed corpse. That would make a fine joke to tell Kyle: I'm living the Orlando version of *Psycho* except, out here, in this bizarre city, you can put the corpse in the garage and no one will even care. Ha ha!

As you pull into your driveway, back with take-out from Buffalo Wild Wings, you make the joke to Kyle, and you expect him to laugh. The sight of the old woman + your delivery = amazing joke.

But he's silent. No smile.

"Maybe it's time you call Dad."

"It was a joke, Kyle," you say, putting the car in park. "I wasn't making fun of Dad."

"You're talking about someone keeping a stuffed corpse of their mother in the garage. These are the things you're saying. It's on your mind."

"He made it clear, his feelings. No need to talk anymore."

You both exit the car, carrying boxes of potato wedges and nachos and mango habañero wings that you will consume while watching the Magic game tonight. All week, you've been showing Kyle different neighborhoods, the tour of Orlando you couldn't possibly have given while driving drunk across 408 and up I-4 on Monday night. You showed him Avalon Park and Waterford Lakes and the area surrounding the university, that recently developed swath of land that he remembered from his Spring Break visit; you showed him Millenia and South Orlando and Dr. Phillips, the acres upon acres upon acres that had once been orange groves and was now Universal Studios; you showed him Conway, also former orange groves bulldozed in the '70s probably, since all the buildings seem to carbon-date back to that frenetic decade for the city; you showed him downtown and Orange Avenue, and spotlighted all of your favorite gas stations, based upon price, based upon your side of the road at a given moment. Oh, you're heading west on Aloma but need to get to a closing in Casselberry? Keep west on Aloma, then go through the light at Semoran to the BP on the *opposite* side of the street, fill up, then right turn back *into* Semoran and head north. Too much of your life is spent at gas stations.

Kyle's been living in your house for almost a week now, and you've created a temporary job for him: yard / handy man. He's been driving to each of your unoccupied properties to help reclaim them from the clutches of neglect and disrepair. The money saved on lawn services alone ($50 every week for ten properties; that shit adds up) allows you to make a mortgage payment here, an HOA payment there, staving off foreclosure and fines and liens and ruin. Next week, you'll brief Kyle on loan-closing documents, spend full days trudging through terms and conditions and FAQs and policies and addendums. Next week, you'll have him ride along to a few more closings to observe the process; then he'll take his notary exam, and in a couple weeks he'll be ready to do the closings himself. Even if he doesn't fully understand the difference between a "pick-a-pay" and a "Frankenstein loan" and a "Fannie Mae," agents and brokers are often present to address a client's questions. What matters is that he knows one page from the next, can gather the signatures and collect what he needs to collect and then get out in one piece. What matters is that he'll be making cash by closing loans on his own, and he can help restock the fridge and contribute "rent." In a couple weeks, if all goes well, you can feel as if you've *saved* your little brother. His life, his finances, his *future*. Let someone call you a shitty brother *then*. Let someone accuse you of abandoning your family.

This is the plan, anyway, if Kyle cooperates. But here in the driveway, now, Kyle is sighing. He's been surly and impatient all day, a temperament wholly out of character for him. "I'm not defending Dad," he says, hands on his hips and thumbs hooked into the belt loops of his faded khaki cargo shorts, the bag of take-out boxes dangling from one hand. "I'm not taking sides. I'm just saying."

You rest a take-out container on the hood of your car. "People love that expression: 'I'm just saying.'"

"It's a good expression."

"It's an excuse to say things you shouldn't."

"Whatever." Kyle holds up his arms. "You can get mad at me for stating the obvious, or you can make amends before you miss the opportunity."

Kyle grabs the 12-pack of Yuengling from the passenger seat, shuts the door, shuffles inside through the garage with the wings and the beer, and you're now alone in the driveway. He shuts the door behind him; he expects you to stay out here and make the call. As your father would say, "What's right is right." Or, "You gotta do what you gotta do." So many stupid country idioms, all of them ironclad arguments against which you can never win.

It's early Friday evening and the last tendrils of sunshine graze the old woman, still sitting as motionless as a stack of sweaters in her garage. Her children are likely inside cooking or drinking wine. Will they come out here to acknowledge her, to tell her dinner is ready? Will they bring her a plate? You want to see. For some reason, it's very important to you that the children forget about her, that they are terrible people.

And in the meantime, you have to make a difficult phone call. But you're already in a foul mood because the Orlando Magic—who, after nearly collapsing at the end of Game One, blew Game Two in Boston by the embarrassing score of 112-94—are probably going to let tonight's game slip away, too. The Magic had a chance to dominate this series, but they're fragile. When someone punches them in the gut, they crumble and cry. Like the city of Orlando itself, they're all flash, all billboard and glossy poster, but hollowed-out and empty of fortitude.

You try to breathe, try to calm down.

You walk to the middle of your front lawn and dial your father's home phone. It rings once, twice. Your father doesn't have an answering machine, so you always feel like you're playing a game of chicken. What will happen first: will he answer, or will you give up? Of course, he doesn't have Caller ID, doesn't have any clue who's calling him—too old-school for that—so the game of chicken is all in your mind.

He answers after four rings. "Yeah," he says.

"Dad, it's me."

A pause at the other end, as if he's deciding whether or not to proceed. You picture him in the dark orange twilight of Georgia, probably drinking a Coca-Cola from that same old yellow cup he seems to always use, the one that actually came as a scoop inside a bag of dog food a couple decades ago but—like so much else at your father's house—was re-appropriated for an entirely different reason. Your father has a dozen of these dog-food cups, some of which he uses for drinking, others for scooping dog food, others (disturbingly) for scooping backyard poop. This has actually become a recurring joke in the family: that your father will slip and use a pooper scooper as a drink cup.

"Just wanted to call and say hello," you say.

"Well," he says. "So now you've said it." You can practically hear him scratching his neck scruff, rubbing his hands down his sandpaper cheeks. You know the shop is closed down, that he isn't working, but still you picture him in his blue work uniform, oil smeared across his forehead. Does he have other clothes?

"I, um," you say into the phone. "You know Kyle's here, right? Staying with me?"

"I do now," he says.

"He didn't tell you?"

"I knew that's where he was headed."

"He hasn't called you since he's been here?"

"Your brother's got his own life to live, is what he said." Again the scruff-scratching noise, then a sound like he's sipping soda from the pooper scooper. Always a Coke on ice after dinner, then whiskey until he falls asleep. "I don't stop him. He's a big boy just like you, and if he wants to make big-boy mistakes, he's free to do as he pleases."

Across the street, the old woman in the garage as still as discarded yard clippings. There's no breeze today, no hope that the heavy air will move or lift or circulate. Even when you arrive home at the time of day when it's foolish to stand in the sunshine for more than a minute, the woman *never moves*, never even raises her hand to her forehead to wipe away sweat or bugs (*does* she sweat?). But somehow, she seems to look at you, always…you can't see her eyes, or the faintest turning of head or craning of neck, but her eyes follow you, bore into you. Right now, she's looking so intently that you're sure she's reading your mind. *Move. Move!* you want to scream at her.

"Kyle told me the shop closed, Dad," you say. "Is that true?"

"Yep."

"And John-John got into an accident?"

"He did," he says. "John-John is no longer with us."

"That's…I'm sorry to hear it. Are you working right now?"

"Are *you*?" he asks. "Or you still just buying things with money you don't have?"

"I *am* working, actually. And I've been trying to create work for Kyle, too."

"How good of you."

"He wanted a job," you tell your father. "So I'm doing my best to find more work, more closings for when he gets up to speed. I'm working with the title companies to expand my business so that *he* can earn some money. I'm trying to do right by him."

"Extra work, huh? Extra contracts?"

"That's right," you say, intoxicated with your own nobility. "I'm a job creator."

"And until then? Until you get those extra contracts?"

"I found him work doing, like, landscaping."

"Drove all the way to Florida to work for a lawn-care company? Shit. Got a lot of weeds around here he could pull."

"Well. He's, you know, doing it for me. For my houses. The ones that need TLC."

"*Your* houses." There's a pause, and the unmistakable sound of your father taking a long sip of soda. "You paying him?"

"Not yet. I mean, he's living here rent-free, eating my food and everything. This is sort of, like, earning his keep."

"Ahh. So it's a step down from a paycheck."

"Come on," you say. "The shop *closed*. He came to *me*. I didn't ask for this, but I'm doing my best."

"And what else you got planned? Make him spend his savings on one of your houses? Give him an 'investment opportunity?'" You can practically hear him making air quotes.

"Okay, this was a bad idea."

"Look at you," he says, "talking to *me* about bad ideas."

You shake your head, close your eyes. "So you're not working, then. Are you in pain? Are you…tired?"

And now, as if on cue: a coughing fit. You knew it would come eventually, but the severity of the coughs catches you off-guard. Each is distinct, like a crashing cymbal, but together it sounds back-breaking, cripplingly painful, one cough after another until it almost seems as if there can be no throat left afterward. "I manage," he says.

Without thinking, you pull the phone away from your ear and shut tight your eyes. You don't want to hear it, any of it. You want those words, "heart attack," to be…words, and nothing more. This is a man whose daily habits of cigarette smoking, red-meat eating, and late evening drinking have taken their toll. Think of something healthy you can do to preserve your body: your father is not doing it.

"I got savings," he says. "Might not've got what I was owed from the shop, but I manage. That's how *I* do it, see. I work with the money I got. No credit cards, none of that. I *saved* money so I'd have it when I needed it."

"And Medicaid," you point out. The need to argue has suddenly dimmed the seconds-ago memory of the cough. "You think nobody's helping you out, but you're getting all this assistance from—"

"Medicaid, insurance, hospitals," he says, short of breath but trying to regain vigor. "All of it is scams, one program scamming the next. Like a hospital stay should cost $4,000. Pssh. I pay taxes, so yeah, I'll take what I can get until my money runs out. Then I'll sit here and die. But I ain't crying about it or blaming anyone."

"Come on, Dad. That's dramatic. You're, what, 60?"

"My father lived till he was 65. Then two heart attacks, and he was all done. I had my one. Next one could come any time now, and I'm ready for it. This ain't a family where men live long, I hate to tell you."

Yes, there it is. The familiar refrain: No Turner man has lived past 65.

"Times are different now," you say. "Medicine is better."

"I don't care. Ain't nothing worse than those final years, no matter when they come. When I've outlived my usefulness, I want to go. No two ways about it."

"You want a lot of things," you say. Across the street, the old woman's arms are folded in her lap; they weren't that way before, you know it, but still you haven't seen her move. Did someone come into the garage and adjust her limbs? "The world doesn't always give you everything you want," you say. "Nor does it owe you anything. That's something *you* used to tell *me* all the time."

"Well, shit," he says. "Aren't you just a font of wisdom?"

"I'm not…" You hold the phone away, stare at it as if it's betrayed you. "You're *impossible*, you know that?"

"I'm practical," he says. "I'm reasonable. I'm consistent." You picture him sitting in his recliner now, stabbing his oil-stained fingernail into the armrest.

"You can be an asshole, too. I call to see how you're doing, and you question whether I'm even working, whether I'm trying to cheat my own brother? Please. What did *you* ever do for Kyle but suck him into that auto shop?"

And now you've called your father an asshole. Shades of your last conversation with him, back at Thanksgiving, the one where you wanted to hurt him so bad you played a card you'd been saving since high school.

"What are *you* doing but sucking him into *your debt*?" he asks. "You love being mad at me, don't you? Blaming me?"

"I don't blame you."

"Ha," he says. "You don't have to agree with me, but I gave Kyle *honest work* at that shop. The things you're doing? *You're* the problem with our country, you know that?"

"I'm the problem? God, you sound like an internet comment board."

"You ain't been here lately, have you?"

"Not since you told me to get out of your house."

"Well. You ain't seen the new neighborhood sprang up on the lake at the end of Plant Road. Golf community, they call it. But I call it empty homes."

"They finally did something with that land?"

"Shoot," he says. "The old builder went bankrupt, way back in the '80s. Land got sold, then someone else went bankrupt. Then someone else. Now someone finally built *houses*, but ain't no one *living there*. Everyone's starry-eyed with big ideas, loves to throw someone else's money at some scheme or another, but no one wants to *work*, do they? That's you. That's what you've become."

"All right, then," you say. "So you sound vigorous. Maybe Kyle exaggerated when he told me about you. He made it seem urgent that I call you."

"My body's tired, no doubt," he says. "But today I did yard work, fixed the bathroom door. The green beans are coming in nicely, and I'm gonna have my first squash soon. What can I say?"

"Good to hear," you say. "Well, then, I—"

"Your house still empty?" he asks.

"I've got ten houses, Dad."

"You know which one I'm talking about."

"Kyle's here." You shake your head. "I've got company."

"That's not what I'm asking. I'm—"

"I'm going to go."

"Still can't just tell me that something didn't work for you, can you?"

"I'm going to go."

"Already?" You hear him take a long gulp of his Coke. "I thought we were getting somewhere. Having one of those father-son talks where we bare our souls!"

"I'm glad you're feeling well today. I hope it lasts."

"Can't you at least tell me not to save the date anymore? At least do me that courtesy? I've got a really hectic social calendar, you know."

"Call me if you need anything," you say.

The old lady across the street is still in her place, a calico cat on one of her shoulders, curled up with one paw dangling across her chest. Is she truly immobile? What sort of strain does that put on a family? Caring for someone like that every day. And how worthless must *she* feel? She's a hundred feet away and you want to hand her the phone and put her into conversation with your father. Here: talk about your ailments, commiserate, drink out of pooper scoopers and sit in sweltering garages and talk about how the world's gone to hell and it's all because your children got too ambitious and greedy and forgot what *real work* is.

Hell, your father *loves* to talk, but even if you got him to talk to the cat lady it would not stop the *imagined* conversations in your head. Because as much as you don't want to admit it, every voice you hear doubting you—devil on one shoulder, angel on the other, asshole tour guides leading you through your life's failures—in all of it, there is your father. You hear him all the time, everywhere. Sometimes it's an honest depiction, true to your father's values and the lens through which he views the world; other times it's a twisted demon manifestation, some tiny facet of your father's character blown up and expanded monstrously. But always that voice—*this* voice—and you can never shut it up.

•

You remember your first real bicycle. Not the bullshit ones with training wheels or the cheap ones from elementary school that broke in a year. Nothing hand-me-down. No. A big-boy bike. And this bike, your father told you when he came home from the shop one afternoon and rolled it back and forth on the driveway, should last you through middle school, even into high school. *Treat. It. Right.* Three words, but in your father's vocabulary, those three words meant dozens of new responsibilities for you, from maintenance to responsible riding.

Your father believes in the mechanics of vehicles, from bikes to muscle cars. He believes in the ability of man to move himself in ever-new, ever-more-powerful ways, as if *machines* were part of man's evolution. He believes in things you can feel under you, machines that grumble like lions, ready to pounce and eat the world. Things that—when you touch the handlebars or the steering wheels—become you. And your father doesn't go cheap with his vehicles. There were go-karts, bicycles, and later, 4-wheelers and dirt bikes, all of it paid for in sweat and blood and callouses. And with a good bicycle—unlike the old go-karts—you were allowed to travel *anywhere*. You could bike out on the quiet country roads and all the way into town, to a friend's house, to the Wal-Mart, and you could chain your bike out front and wander the CD section and never worry about refueling, never worry about which roads were okay to drive on. The go-kart was faster, but the bicycle was limitless and liberating.

Some time around middle school, at some point during your bicycle years, you hung around with a kid named Nick. Other people called him "Nicky," but that dangling "y" at the end always made you feel weird, made his name sound like a candy bar, or like everyone was treating him younger than he was and allowing him to get away with whatever he wanted, so you only said "Nicky" when everyone else was saying it.

You'd bike several miles across town to Nick's neighborhood (he never made the trip to your place), and it was nicer than where you lived, nicer than living out in the country where there weren't even neighborhoods, really, just houses scattered among the trees and fields, and once you got to his place, the two of you would bike through town to a baseball card shop called Locker Room. Nick would flip through the wooden boxes of Topps and Fleer and Upper Deck cards, searching for every Boston Red Sox player they had, telling you how he'd burned his Bill Buckner cards after that World Series error. (As a young Georgia boy, you watched the Braves, not the Red Sox, and you never remembered watching any Boston Red Sox World Series. At some point, you learned that this particular World Series error occurred in 1986, when you were 5, before you or Nick could watch sports with real cognizance. Could he really hate an athlete so intensely at such a young age?)

You're not sure why you hung around Nick. *Nicky.* You didn't like him.

In fact, he made you uncomfortable. He was a rule-breaker.

Inside Locker Room, he'd tell you to "cover him" while he plucked individual cards from the long wooden "singles" box and slid them into the bottom pocket of his cargo shorts. "You don't have to do anything," he'd say. "Just stand there. Block me so no one sees."

It wasn't just the theft that aggravated you. There was a challenge to collecting back in the pre-internet '80s and '90s, especially for rural kids with only a single shop at which to procure cards. To be an honest collector, you relied on the luck of each pack, hoping you'd get what you needed to complete a set, and maybe you splurged occasionally and used your allowance to buy a single Greg Maddux or Ken Griffey Jr. card—that was it, those were your only options. You both called yourself "baseball card collectors." But when you both sat down to compare collections, you were never sure how Nick had scored his best cards, why his collection was always more impressive than yours. How much of his collection had he come by honestly, and how much had been stolen? This nagging question made you hate him.

What made you hate him even more was the way he rode his bicycle. On the rides home from Locker Room, he'd insist on riding against traffic, wheels kissing the shoulder while cars barreled toward you both. "You want to see the cars coming at you," he'd say. "You don't want to get hit from behind, do you?"

But your father had warned about such recklessness. "Soon as you leave these back roads," he'd said, pointing to the pines surrounding your house, "you need to treat your bike like it's a vehicle. Signal when you're turning. Stop at stop signs. Walk the bike across crosswalks. Cars don't always see you, especially when you're coming out of nowhere."

But Nick would just look back over his shoulder as he pedaled, glancing long enough to see if he had a window—you knew the look on his face, you knew what was coming—and he'd *slash* right, *cut* across four lanes of traffic to the other side of the road rather than biking another couple hundred feet to the crosswalk. Cars honking, braking, screeching, Nick laughing and saying something victorious like "Made it!" or "Close one!" when cars swerved and death felt palpable. You never followed, always imagining that one of those cut-off cars might be your mother on a shopping trip, and if she told your father what she saw? Holy shit. Ho-leee shit. You did *what?* That'd be the end of your bicycle.

Nick never seemed to understand that his actions were pointless: *you* still followed the rules, always using the crosswalk, and so he was forced to wait for you at the intersection anyway. Some days, even now, you wonder about Nick. *Nicky*. What became of him? Did he profit from a life lived outside the rules? You don't remember seeing him in high school. Did he move? Did he cheat his way to a better GPA than you? Higher SAT scores? A better college? A quicker graduation, better job, higher salary? Would it ever catch up to him, or would he always cut across traffic and hold his arms up victorious, sneering at you for wasting your time following the rules?

In your father's eyes, of course, your life now—investment properties, loan closings—is probably no different than Nicky's.

Your father taught you to play by the rules, to respect the rules, to live by the rules and die by the rules, and not just when it came to vehicles. This was—*is*—a way of life that you cannot shake. You find yourself constantly wondering if everything that has gone *right* or *wrong* in your life is a result of your having *followed* or *broken* the rules.

Rules.

The rules.

Which rules are *the* rules? Well. You're unable to distinguish sometimes. Everything qualifies: state laws, county ordinances, rules of healthy eating from *Men's Health*, "Man Laws" from beer commercials, HOA regulations, rules for the old community swimming pool in Georgia. They're all lumped together like food on a Thanksgiving dinner plate and you can't scrape any of them away or hide the peas behind the mashed potatoes.

If you have a great workout at the gym, you owe your health and vigor to the chicken you grilled the night before, the broccoli you steamed, the beer you declined. Things went *right* because you diligently followed rules outlined by a credible workout plan you read. Discipline rewarded.

But when things don't work out? Like, let's just say, you postpone an oil change…well, you *deserve* to break down in South Orlando on your way to a loan closing. You owe your failure to rule-breaking. You find oil stains in the driveway of a rental house you've forsaken? That's your own damn fault, isn't it, rule-breaker?

You've become like a zealous Christian who sees God's wrath as a result of Man's adherence (or lack thereof) to Biblical standards. Drought and famine as a result of fornication. Rules are the science of faith.

And you will never escape the church of your father, and his rules.

Your father believes in posted and printed rules, first and foremost: he puts extra stock in speed limits, and he dreams of a world where every car on the road uses its turn signal, and—if you're going to speed a little (a *little*, like five miles-per-hour over the speed limit) you use the *left* lane, and if you drive slower you use the *right*, but you *should not pass* on the right. Only assholes do that. And also remember: you should *never* inconvenience yourself for those reckless speeders doing 90 on the highway; don't change lanes for them; you should, in fact, do whatever you can to make them *slow down*…stay in the left lane, block them, they don't own the road, they're just bullies, and *you stand up to bullies*. (That's one of your father's most important rules, in fact.)

Your father also does not believe in shortcuts. Shortcuts are the opposite of rules, the opposite of discipline, the opposite of a life well-lived. *If you're gonna do something*, he says, *do it right*! It's a cliché to some, but a commandment to your father. He does not believe in "investing" in public companies, no matter how much money can be earned, only believes in savings accounts. It's more honest, he says. You save money that you earn. You manage those savings. No insider-trading, no shorting, no shenanigans.

You've tried to explain the inanity of his argument, how the banks have no similar code they follow, how they invest your money elsewhere, how they *embrace* loopholes and how he's a pawn for trusting these assholes and not taking financial matters into his own hands. *Listen*, he tells you, there is a *set amount* I earn. They stick to their promise and protect my money, and I keep it in savings. I've seen *Wall Street*, and I don't want to get involved with those crooks.

This is how you were raised.

You did not steal cable. You always rewound.

Some religions forbid the consumption of pork or beef or shellfish, but in your father's house, the only sin was food not eaten, food left to spoil. Every expiration date was a rule, a ticking-clock deadline to which you agreed when you made the purchase. You drank expired milk for precisely *three days* after the expiration date, and you always finished the gallon whether you wanted milk or not, because—even if the cost of the remaining milk was negligible and the potential hospital bill for consumption of rotting food astronomical—you *finish what you start*, and you let *nothing* go to waste. He'd pick the moldy crust off bread when making your sandwich, would dump expired salad dressing on grilled chicken just to finish the bottle. He would check the trash can to make sure you hadn't scraped anything worthwhile from your plate, and if you had? Hol-eee shit. Once, he even plucked your discarded chicken bones from the trash to gnaw the tiny strings of meat.

For most of your life, you accepted his rules: you *do* need to stand for something, and if you follow the rules, you *will* be rewarded. Even now, no matter how hard you try to *not* believe it, you still do *not* pass in the right lane. You still drink that fucking expired milk. When you need to problem-solve your life's worries, you still ask yourself what your father would do. So maybe it's easiest to view your life as a rulebook of responsibilities, principles embedded in your mind by your father, algorithms determining correct behavior and reaction.

For instance, what would he do if *he* was a notary, if he encountered an old grandmother in Deltona, as you did, applying for a reverse mortgage only because her children were forcing her to sign each document, standing behind her and making sure of it. "Just sign," the son said over and over. "We need this. We *need* this." She'd owned the house for decades, but it'd gone into disrepair in the years since her husband had passed; her children (and grandchildren) had moved back in, and now the house was like a demented Chuck E. Cheese. There were Led Zeppelin posters on the wall covering old family photos, lava lamps next to Boyds Bears, half-empty bowls of Cap'n Crunch on every armrest of every couch. A pinball machine in the living room, too, and three or four video game systems hooked into the TV, the cables and controllers and game boxes spilled across the floor.

The reverse mortgage would've been perfect for the grandmother, had she any intention of using the money to repair or renovate. But with these people overtaking the home, who knew where the money was going? More video games? A meth habit?

"You sure you want to do this?" you asked the grandmother. She had upward-twisting eyebrows, and she flipped through the documents with a look of genuine sadness. "Is this—the reverse mortgage—is this what you want? You don't *have* to sign this."

"You ain't supposed to influence one way or the other," said her son behind her—a 30-year-old in a shirt that said "Some Beach." You'd spoken just three sentences, each softly and carefully, but now this man was pointing in your face, giving you a menacing stare like you were trying to steal his money.

"I'm just making sure she understands the documents. That's my job."

"She understands. That's why she said she'd do it. All you are is a witness and a glorified secretary. I know my shit."

And so you sighed and flipped to the next page, and then everyone calmed down, and you helped them finish the paperwork, the old woman lifting the pen as if it was heavy as a shovel, and you knew this was a bad thing, an evil thing, children robbing their mother, and you did nothing to prevent it. Driving home, you rationalized by asking yourself, What *could* I have done? I'm a fucking notary. I oversee paperwork, not lives. I get paid by the closing, not by the number of predators beaten away.

But what would your father have done? Would the choice have been simple for him? *What's right is right!* he says quite often. But what happens when right clashes with right? At the shop, would he tell a customer that an oil change could technically wait another 500 miles, or would he simply do as the customer asked and as his employer wanted?

You remember one of your annual Disney World trips from maybe fourth or fifth grade, you and Kyle and your parents. A group of high school kids at Disney, all wearing identical t-shirts as part of some summer school field trip for a physics class or something, all had little notepads on which they were supposed to be calculating speeds and G-forces and so looked especially studious and responsible when you saw them moving in packs throughout the Magic Kingdom. Well. Not *all* of them innocent, because you remember standing in line for Space Mountain, and there were clumps of these kids throughout the line, indistinguishable in those matching shirts, and no one seemed to notice that they were ducking under ropes, two at a time, cutting ahead at each switchback in the snaking 80-minute-wait line because almost everyone else was families, parents trying to herd their children, and these quick fourteen- and fifteen-year-olds would take advantage of turned backs and matching-shirt anonymity, cutting, cutting, cutting, everyone letting it happen.

But not your father. He played dumb, then held out one arm and grabbed some punk teenager—possibly the pack leader, the oldest-looking one, the one who'd failed a grade and was now a man among boys—held out his arm and grabbed this kid's t-shirt just as the kid was ducking under the rope, and your father shot a look back at the line-cutters following this kid, and their sneaky smiles froze and dissolved into fear and humiliation, and you remember the kid saying "Get offa me!" or something that he'd hoped would be tough, and your father clenched his fist tighter and damn-near ripped the kid's shirt. Didn't say a word. Just lifted his other hand and made a "come here" motion, and suddenly there were Disney security guards—security guards!—wedging themselves into the line and grabbing this kid, and finally your father released him and just said, "Going back to the bus, young man, hope you enjoy the rest of your day," and that was it. People throughout the line applauding, whoooo-ing while this little fucker was escorted out of there, and not another line-cutter the rest of that trip. World settling back into place, rule-breakers punished, your father so fucking noble and heroic.

Could *you* have done that? Have you *ever* done such a thing?

Here's the real question: what would your father do with your life *right now*? "Way I see it, you got a couple things you need to do, and you just need to *do* 'em. Hard work. Elbow grease. Suck it up, son. Only one person responsible for your life, and that's you." He'd make it sound simple. Probably he'd use the word "bootstraps."

And tonight, after your conversation with the man, it is now at the forefront of your mind: what would your father do? Should you embrace his commandments once again, recommit like a Christian at Easter, tell yourself you'll go to church again every Sunday? Will life be simpler? Better? Or is it bullshit fried in snake oil? What would happen if you let those rules slide down the garbage disposal once and for all?

It's Friday night, May 8, minutes till tip-off, and you stand in the driveway with your cell phone and a bag of Buffalo Wild Wings take-out while inside your brother watches the Orlando Magic pre-game. The old woman across the street is still staring at you, staring into you like she knows what you're thinking, like she knows how it will all turn out.

Good luck, she's saying. Good luck with all of it.

•

Your father would tell you to "Support your local team," and "Don't bitch," and "Don't boo," and "Stay positive," and even though you want nothing more than to believe that the man's methodology is not simply imperfect but indisputably idiotic, tonight you'll commit to your father's rules, see how far this takes you. You see them, his rules, laid out black and white like wholesome cartoons you used to read in the funny pages.

DO AS YOUR FATHER SAYS.

174

Really, it couldn't be simpler. Game Three. Wings. Beer. Your living room. Your brother. You will be positive. You will cheer: rah rah rah. Just like your father and his simple fucking code. And if it works, this will be the first step in turning your life around. It begins with *attitude*, right? So tonight, as you open the styrofoam box of mango-habañero wings, you tell Kyle: "I've got a good feeling about the game. We're gonna get back on track, Brother."

"Everything go all right outside?" he asks. "You talk with Dad?"

You shrug.

"He's difficult," Kyle says.

"He kept grunting, like he was moving around and couldn't get comfortable."

"Yep," Kyle says. "All night he does that. The grunting from the back pain, then the coughing fits. Tough to sleep, it's so loud."

"Is that why you left?"

"I don't wanna talk about why I left," he says. He's got a potato wedge in his fingers, the ranch sauce glistening in the television's glow. "Let's watch the game."

And here's what happens: throughout the game, you cheer rather than scoff. You say "rah rah rah." Yes, you actually say that (and not ironically). You high-five Kyle, and you eat wings until it's just grease and gristle, and then you eat that too. Because *yum*. The rookie Courtney Lee returns from injury (an inadvertent Dwight Howard elbow had shattered his face) wearing a plastic faceguard, and he plays like a champion. Dwight scores 17, pulls down 14 rebounds, blocks five shots. Dominant. And somehow the Magic win impressively, improve their series advantage to 2-1. They appear to be in control once again.

"You see?" Kyle says. "The power of positive thinking, Brother."

The more wings you devour and the more beer you drink with your brother, the more you think that—like some feel-good Oscar movie—this basketball season is really all about you and Kyle reconnecting: here you are together, just the way you were throughout childhood. The TV is bigger now, and the wings come from chain restaurants, not from a place called "Sports Bar" where there were just two flavors of hot sauce: hot, and no sauce. You remember the

Sunday afternoons in high school, back in the '90s, when the NBA on NBC was an all-day engagement. Games from Madison Square Garden, Jordan scoring 55 in his post-retirement comeback against the Knicks. You remember sitting in the living room with your father and brother watching the Magic-Bulls playoff series, watching Nick Anderson steal the ball from MJ when the still-rusty Jordan wore #45, Nick Anderson cementing the victory and paving the way for the Magic's first (and only) NBA Finals appearance. You remember how Kyle tore off his hat and—like a football player with his helmet after a big win—ran around the room with his hat held high in his hand, ran around the yard in circles until he collapsed. After that game, you and Kyle and your father pushed the basketball hoop into the street and played 21 for what must have been hours, still so giddy over the Magic win. It was rural Georgia, but in those days, everyone seemed to be a Magic fan.

"You remember that old basketball we had?" you ask Kyle, the two of you now drunk from Yuengling, heads swimming from hot sauce fumes. "The one that glowed in the dark?"

"I do," he says. "That ball was the best."

"We'd take it down to the county courts at night, and when someone knocked it out into the bushes, we could always find it. It was like there was an alien in the woods."

"Had a decent grip to it, too," Kyle says.

You stare into the empty container where the potato wedges once were. Now it's just smears of ranch. "Whatever happened to that ball? Is it still at home? In some back corner of the garage?"

Kyle looks at you across the top of his beer bottle, puzzled. "You playing around?"

"No. Why?"

"You really don't remember?"

"Remember what?"

"You threw it into the woods," he says.

"What?"

"You were screaming. You were angry at the ball…or, I don't know."

"That doesn't sound right. Why would I do that?"

"It was after Mom died, remember? We were shouting and you were missing shots, and you launched it. I tried looking for it, too. Later. I thought I saw it glowing in the woods. After you left for college, I just stopped looking."

"I don't remember. I *did* that?"

Hey. *Hey!* The Magic have won Game Three. Don't forget that. Focus on the positives, big guy. Sunday night is Game Four, the second game in a row at Orlando's Amway Arena. Tonight, you put every ounce of your energy into optimism and it paid off, so maybe it'll effect another win in two days?

You try to hold onto the optimism, but it's like trying to grab at the vapor-breath from your father's mouth when he worked on home-improvement projects on cold mornings. Rah rah rah?

You're trying.

The world has changed since the days of the glow-in-the-dark basketball, the family now a shattered thing that can never be the same, but maybe, if only this game, this series, these playoffs, can help you to feel a hint of what you had back then, maybe then it'll all be worth it. Because that's something *tangible*, isn't it? That's not some stupid sports superstition, your troubles somehow paralleling the Magic's struggles, or whatever. That's real: you and Kyle repairing a relationship while watching the game. *That's real.*

ALWAYS REMEMBER, BUDDY.
FAMILY COMES FIRST.

That's the rule.

But while you feel the surge of nobility from your interactions with your brother, it's important to remember that Kyle isn't your only family. Shouldn't you call your father again, try to make it right? "Family Comes First."

And while we're on the subject, why didn't you drive up to Georgia just a few months back when your father had his heart attack? Why didn't you swallow your pride, visit him in the hospital? Hell, you didn't even fulfill the first two words of the rule, "Family Comes," did you?

Okay.

Let's maybe table this rule for now. Let's work on something easier.

TAKE CARE OF YOUR POSSESSIONS.

It's Sunday morning and blessed, by a break in the heat and by a morning without emails or phone calls, you decide to follow another of your father's rules. For too long you've bought bought bought, rarely thinking about the responsibility of ownership, the maintenance, all those notes at the bottoms of instructions manuals, all those tips passed on from professional to consumer, the oil change, the transmission fluid, the wiper blades, the belt, the tires, the battery…Hell, just consider a tiny sample of what you're supposed to do in your house:

- Replace AC filters/ Quarterly
- Test smoke alarm/ Quarterly
- Inspect Fire Extinguisher/ Quarterly
- Bleach Tile Grout/ Quarterly
- Replace Cockroach Bait Stations/ Quarterly
- Clean Gutters/ Each Spring

- Clean Chimney/ Each Spring
- Shop-Vac AC Lines/ Each Spring
- Clean Dryer Vent/ Each Summer
- Vacuum Refrigerator Coils/ Each Spring
- "Hurricane-Cut" Palm Trees/ Each July
- Pressure-Wash Driveway/ Each November

Well, shit. Damned if you've ever inspected your fire extinguisher or cleaned your dryer vent. And your yard? You own equipment, but you've been paying for lawn service. You pay a pool guy, too, to balance the chemicals, brush the walls, and you barely know how to drain rainwater after a storm, let alone change an underwater lightbulb. Maintenance for your air conditioner? For your dishwasher? For your garage door and your oven and your shower and…you just sort of use things until they don't work anymore, and then you discard and replace them. This is the antithesis of your father's rules.

This is going to change. *You* are going to change.

It's a small act, but today—while Kyle is out mowing lawns at your properties, weed-killing along the fencelines, clipping overgrown plumbagos, sweating and callousing and blistering—you will wash your car.

You're not quite sure how many hours the car has sat in driveways or parking lots dusted by pollen and withered oak leaves, how many highway miles it's logged, exhaust fumes and lovebug swarms caking it with a black-ish shell. Your father would be ashamed that you've neglected your machinery. When you first bought the car, you swore you'd take better care of it than the last. And again when you moved into this house, you renewed this vow. Your own driveway, your own hose? You thought you'd be out here washing, restoring the vehicle's finish, every single weekend. This was actually one of the things that made you happiest to be a homeowner.

Sunday is going to be a great day, you decide. A day for discipline.

Across the street, the old lady is still sitting in the garage, hands folded in her lap, as you pull the hose cart from the side of the house, unwind it, a half-dozen lizards and frogs hopping from their hiding places inside the cart and scurrying back to the ecosystem of your yard. You look in the old lady's direction to see if she noticed you flinch when the first lizard jumped out. If she saw, she doesn't register it, so back to work: pour a dollop of soap into a bucket (it's an old Christmas popcorn tin, the kind that came with three different flavors, and you remember sharing the caramel with Shelley, but she slapped your hand away when you went for the cheese flavor—but *shut up* about that, today will be a *good day*.), then back to the side of the house to turn on the faucet. But as you walk to pick up the spray nozzle, your foot slides in the grass, and you go airborne like Charlie Brown missing his football punt, and you slam to the ground, ass on wet grass. "Fuck!" you cry out, far too loud for a neighborhood filled with families. And did the old woman hear you?

Still sprawled on the lawn, you lift your sandal and twist your foot to see the bottom. Oh no. Not mud. You stepped in a pile of *dog shit*, here in your *own yard*, and you don't own a dog. "This is funny to you, isn't it?" you mumble to the old woman, and though it's impossible for her to hear you, you're certain she can read lips, minds. Still, she doesn't lift her head.

You aim the spray nozzle at the bottom of your sandal, set it to "jet," and you spray. The clumps rocket off, and then you aim the nozzle at the pile on the ground nearby. "Fuck you," you say. *Jet*. Blast it. You will break it apart, this shit. You will destroy it, send every tiny shit particle into the sidewalk, into the street, into the whole Goddamned neighborhood, anywhere but *your* grass. Whoever let their dog shit in *your* yard—

Then you stop spraying, reconsider.

You don't have children who play out here. In fact, it is your *neighbors* who have children, children of all different shapes, sizes, ages, and they play basketball in driveways, football in the road. Tag. Ghost in the Graveyard. All of that. You often find tennis balls in your backyard, and you once ran over a G.I. Joe figure on your driveway. Sometimes you see abandoned Kit Kat wrappers, smashed pretzels, Goldfish, Gatorade bottles.

You're not going to step in the dogshit, but maybe *they* might.

So leave the shit for *them* to slide on as they dive for a catch. Let the shit jam the rubber ridges of their sneaker bottoms and smear across their parents' carpets. After all, it was probably one of their parents who let the dog shit in your yard, wasn't it? Can you imagine what would happen if your *father* encountered such a thing in his yard? He'd go door to door to find the culprit. This is something that you Just. Don't. Do. So leave it, leave the shit.

The rules of the car wash, spoken and unspoken, will bring order, calm. *Rules*, remember: One capful of Turtle Wax soap per bucket of water. Let the mitt soak in the soap. Take off your shirt. Enjoy the sunshine. Slather the soap onto the car. In your mind, repeat the word *slather* over and over again. *Slather.* Spray off the soap as you go, one side of the car at a time.

These rules are easy. These rules will not backfire.

You fill your soapy bucket. You drag the wet hose around the full length of your car, yanking when it's caught under your tire, but you stop yourself from yelling, from swearing at the hose as if it's *trying* to frustrate you.

After the chamois, your car looks fresh and promising, and you're reassured about your house and your neighborhood and your ability to live a principled, disciplined, well-maintained life. "I can control my anger," you say. "I've got this."

It could be so much worse: after all, you could be living in a downtown condo with Anderson and Steven, underwater by a hundred thousand. No yard. No hose. No space. Hell, you have a place to wash and store your vehicle, a palace, a swath of green all around, room to breathe and room to punch the air without hitting anyone, a chunk of Orlando all your own. You look at your beautiful, gleaming car and are reminded of the infamous Shit Car. It was sometime last year, you think, a car left parked along the street for two full weeks (was someone staying with a friend downtown, and feeding the meter? You don't remember, and details hardly matter). Central Avenue: the street along Lake Eola Park: a strip of pavement that hugs high-rise condos on one side, and the famous Lake Eola Splatter Zone on the other, an expanse of lakeside cypress trees and tall twisting oaks where the birds gather and seemingly shit in unison like B-52 bombers looking to annihilate the city's most gorgeous walking paths. Engagement photo sessions bombed daily (the spot where *your own* session was ruined, in fact). Sidewalks and boardwalks hosed weekly. And this car, left in a spot beneath the oak trees of the Splatter

Zone, became so completely covered in bird droppings that it made the evening news and was towed away as a "public eyesore."

So breathe. It could be worse. As your father might instruct:

DON'T SWEAT THE SMALL STUFF.

Some dog shitting in your front yard is just that: small stuff. You steered clear of the downtown condo boom. You invested in a gated neighborhood, and it's not so bad, has a few minor flaws, but it's a *good neighborhood* where you—

—where you, from your garage, as you deposit the empty bucket on your shelf, see a man walking his dog up the sidewalk. The man does not notice you. The dog, a beagle, does not notice you. You are hidden in the shadows of the garage. The driveway is wet and the world smells of soap, but they don't know you're watching. The dog walks into your yard, circling, sniffing, and the owner doesn't care. The beagle steps lightly through the grass, finding the right spot, inches from the pile you stepped in… Back arching, knees bending in that familiar dog way and…the dog is shitting in your yard.

The poop hits the grass, and you are out of your garage. Sprinting. You can't help it.

"Hey!" you shout.

This is what your father would instruct you to do, right? A man does not let his dog *shit* on someone else's lawn.

A MAN TAKES CARE OF HIS PROPERTY.

a MAN takes CARE of his PROPERTY!

"Huh?" your neighbor says and takes a step backward. The dog is still bent in shit-pose, oblivious to your outrage, mustering one last nugget, not embarrassed or discouraged in the least by the angry homeowner charging toward him.

"This is my house," you say. "This is my yard."

"Right," the man says. "I know."

"Your dog is still *shitting*!" you say. "Pick him up. Move him or something."

The dog's knees shake, poop pile completed, and it kicks the grass, satisfied.

The owner: you've seen this man before. He lives five, maybe six houses down. Mid-thirties, neatly combed hair. You can smell his aftershave from here, the freshness of his exfoliating cream, his Crest Whitestrips. This is a man who's lived in golf neighborhoods his entire life, who thinks nothing of those who had to earn their way inside.

"Calm down," the guy says. "It's not a big deal."

"I find your shit in my yard all the time," you say. You hold the chamois in your fist, squeeze it. You point to your sandal, but of course, this man has no idea why you're pointing. "I know it's you. Just stop."

The beagle scampers out of the grass.

You are covered in suds and insect parts and hose-water and sweat, and your neighbor is dressed in dry-cleaned polo and khaki shorts. He says nothing. Looks you in the eyes, reaches into his pocket. Pulls out a plastic grocery bag.

"I walk my dog every day," he says. "I *always* clean up after him."

He bends down, beagle straining against his leash as he scoops every poop nugget into the bag, which he then neatly ties and holds in the hand opposite the one gripping the leash.

"Well," you say.

"Have yourself a nice day." He ties the bag to one of his belt loops, mock-salutes you, then walks away with the sort of measured grace you'll never be able to muster.

"Right," you say. "You too."

This is a man, you think, whose dog shit arrives in solid easy-to-scoop chunks and leaves no stain behind on the grass, a man who can walk with the plastic bag of shit and it doesn't stink, who will toss it onto his own yard and marigolds will bloom the next day. This is a man who knows how to sync his iPhone with his computer and his iPod and his numerous HDTVs around his house, a man whose surround sound is built into wireless wall-speakers in his living room, speakers in the bedroom, speakers as fake stones in the back patio around his sparkling swimming pool. This is a man who vacuums his fridge coils each winter, shop-vacs his AC line each spring, trims his palm trees each autumn. You can think of no logical reason why anyone should hate a man who has it so together, but you hate him even more because, listen, here's the worst part: this is the man that your father would probably want you to be.

You know that he'll be walking his dog again the next time you mow your lawn, or you'll see him at the next HOA meeting, should you decide to go. You know you'll run into him at the community clubhouse. This man with his dog.

As you toss the chamois into your garage, you realize your most meaningful relationships in this neighborhood have all been the result of confrontations. Yelling at neighbors about dog shit. Or last New Year, waking up to find burnt-out bottle rockets and bits of exploded M-80s at the base of the drake elm in your front yard, and how you stormed around the neighborhood looking for kids to grab by the collar. And last Christmas, do you remember the line of cars stopped at the gate? Stoney Creek is the envy of the surrounding area, feels like a golf community island dropped into a sea of older and less remarkable neighborhoods, many of them low-income, and they hate that Stoney Creek exists, that down the road there is suddenly this symbol of all they'll never be able to afford. And yet here they were, every night for the week leading to Christmas, dozens of them waiting at the gate for the security guard to record their ID and plate and allow them to drive through and view the decadent lights your doctor/lawyer-neighbors had wrapped around their skyscraper-tall palm trees. How fucking gracious, your neighborhood, letting in the outside rabble, and so you sat in this line as it inched forward, inched forward, just hoping to get far enough to where the road grew to two lanes and you could gas it around the visitors and use the "residents only" gate and speed inside, and one night you couldn't take it and you screamed at the security guard, "I waited for twenty fucking minutes, asshole! Send them away! Send them away!"

This neighborhood. This neighborhood.

And down the block, there's a family. Big: nine people, maybe ten, always unloading a car filled with Wal-Mart grocery bags, Cheetos, chocolate bars, peanut butter crackers. Just like the Fun Spot families in your rental house, except here they're all crammed into a single gargantuan house. Technically, your HOA doesn't even *allow* renting, and yet there's *this* house, at least four adults working jobs to make that monthly payment to a landlord who clearly doesn't respect rules, probably isn't even making mortgage payments anymore, is probably just pocketing their rent checks until the day the bank ultimately forecloses. Once, you tried to start a conversation with one of the adults, tried to warn him that he shouldn't be renting this house. "You're going to get booted," you said.

"Are you trying to *scare* us?" he asked.

"What? No, I—"

"We *pay* our rent," he said. "We will not be intimidated."

"Hey man," you said, "it's the HOA, or it's the bank. This won't last long."

"You're a piece of shit," he said. "You're a real piece of shit."

"Do what you want. I'm just trying to be a good neighbor," you said, trying to sound both tough and reasonable, but you walked to the clubhouse so that this guy wouldn't see where you live, wouldn't follow you home to continue the fight.

Tens of millions of dollars poured into Stoney Creek, into the gate and the basketball courts and the tennis courts and the columns and the brick paver driveways and the plantation shutters and the three-car garages, tens of millions of dollars from doctors and dentists who wanted this place to become another Heathrow or Windermere, lawyers who relocated from the pricier parts of Winter Park, all the money in the world and yet there are dogs shitting on your lawn, twenty-minute lines at the gate, bottle rockets in your grass, and there are investment houses filled with renters who call you a "piece of shit." What is this place? It was supposed to be better than those other shit developments where your own investment properties are—

"Don't even fucking *look* at me!" you yell across the street at the old lady, but the day has grown bright and her open garage feels dark by comparison. Inside, you see shapes, some smooth and some jagged, some still and some shifting, slithering, coming unmoored from the darkness. "Don't," you say, softer now. "Don't even."

And then one of the shapes in the garage stands, comes forward to regard you, crosses its arms, but it's so bright you don't know if this is the old lady, if she's finally standing, shaking her head at you. *She* doesn't even want to be your neighbor, and she's a fucking *corpse*.

Your father. This never would have happened to him, right? Your father knows his neighbors, is friends with his neighbors. Your father *is* a neighbor. No one would allow their dog to shit in your father's yard because they respect him too much, and if it ever happened, your father would know about it before it happened, would have pre-approved the poop.

There's a lesson here somewhere, something you are beginning to understand about yourself, but…but you don't *want* any damned *lessons*. And my God, you've grown even angrier now…it feels like your father is here, whispering into your ear, "I never would have let it come to this," and you scream "*Fuck!*" one more time before stalking back inside.

HARD WORK IS THE
GREATEST OF ALL VIRTUES.

This is your father's greatest rule, the foundation of all else.

Productivity. Industriousness. Hard labor to benefit the family.

This is the first page of your father's rulebook, and the last. All else is just explication.

You still remember—long after the house fire, long after you'd settled back into the house your father and John-John had rescued from the jaws of demolition—your father coming home from the shop at the end of each evening, trudging inside with this beaten look like the cars had won that day, and he'd sit down only long enough for your mother to ask if he needed a—

And then he was up again, saying "Damn it, that hedge needs clipping."

"It can wait," your mother would say.

"No," he always said. "That's the motto of the lazy. One of the branches keeps waving in front of the motion sensor lights, sets 'em off all night long."

"Does it *really*? How would you know? Are you up all night watching?"

Your father would meet her eyes, and soft as he could, he'd say, "Yes," and then he'd be outside trimming.

Other nights it was a piece of rotted wood on the backyard shed he needed to fix, lest the termites come for a snack, and you'd hear the tablesaw buzzing, the new board cut to size, the silence that followed indicating that he was priming, painting, and then at 10 PM the sound of hammer on nail reverberating through the house.

Other nights he spent repairing gashes in the drywall, sanding and repainting chairs that he'd lifted from other people's trash many miles away. *Dumpster diving*, your mother called this habit of his, but for your father it meant fifty or sixty extra bucks each month. The house and the shed (and then the next shed, and the next) overflowed with crap, half-finished projects, and the more that was dumped on his plate the harder your father worked to scarf it all down.

"Will you sit for a second?" your mother asked him each night, and the answer more often than not was "no."

From your place in bed you heard their arguments, muffled. "Someone's gotta take care of this house, don't you see?" "The door didn't need to be fixed *tonight!*" "Then when? When's the right time?" "Your family wants to spend time with you." "My family *relies* on me. They don't need my company. Being a man don't mean being everyone's best friend." And on and on.

Hard work. This virtue, this never-earned prize, this thing he called "taking care of family," this thing ultimately *more important* than family, this rule which you hold and you can't seem to let go, this thing that is your father, this thing that is *you*.

STAY POSITIVE!

On Sunday afternoon, you want to take Kyle out to watch the Magic game, but when you pop into the guest room he's wearing the same shirt he wore yesterday, a faded Georgia Bulldogs tee with a rip in the left shoulder. You want to tell Kyle to put on something that doesn't look like a shop rag, but you're not *there* yet, are you? You're already teetering on "overbearing sibling," telling him to pick up his water cups around the house, to take off his shoes on the living room area rug, to turn off the fan when he's not in his bedroom. He might not have noticed during his first few days in town, but when you told him to close the fridge door while he poured his OJ this morning, he said "Damn, bro. Give it a rest, will ya?" He's still accustomed to living in a house where gray carpet hides the dirt, where no one will complain about clutter or messes because, let's be honest, your father is a hoarder of useless shit. When it's not the booty of a dumpster dive, it's boxes of *National Geographic* and *TV Guide* and *Car and Driver* magazines stacked in corners. For him, a faded t-shirt and high white socks with his greasy shop shoes...what else would a man wear?

So you keep quiet tonight.

"Go out where?" he asks.

You feel like going downtown, out in the real world again. A menu of options appears:

To Ember, where Anderson and Jimmy will be, and where the girls will be bronzed from all-day pool parties? To Wall Street for the block party? To Latitudes, for tiki torches and low-cut shirts? To Zex-Zoo, for both the zex and the zoo?

To the game itself, spending all your money on scalped tickets just to show your brother how to live it up?

Those are all options that would introduce Kyle—in his old Georgia shirt and hat—to your world.

But eventually you say, "How about Buffalo Wild Wings?"

"Wings again, huh?"

"It was good luck the other night."

"I'll wear the same underwear I wore on Friday, then," Kyle says and laughs.

You try to smile but can't.

"It was a joke," Kyle says, but he doesn't change his shirt.

When you arrive, Buffalo Wild Wings is filled with Magic fans, hundreds of them in the dining room, at the bar, and in the outdoor patio. Magic foam fingers, air horns. A table of Hispanic guys all wearing old Arroyo jerseys, maybe serious or maybe ironic. Girls wearing white t-shirts with JJ's face screenprinted across the front. One super-tall dude with a balloon animal like a headband. Someone else has a foam star on her head, kind of like a desperate attempt to replicate the Green Bay Packers "cheesehead" phenomenon. There is a faraway scream of "HEDO!" and a beach ball sails overhead.

"Thanks for getting me out," Kyle says. "I was going a little stir-crazy, staying at home every night."

You nod, but don't tell him about all the other places you could've taken him, if only you could trust him to wear clothes that didn't reek of rural. Let his country-boy mind be blown by the raucousness of a sanitary chain sports bar where you don't know a soul.

When the waitress arrives Kyle smiles a lot and tries his best to make goofy jokes, but—the nasty hat, the nasty t-shirt, a hole under one armpit—it comes across as creepy instead, and you don't speak too much because, should you ever run into this girl again, you don't want her to remember this night.

By the end of the first quarter, it's clear that the Magic cannot sustain the energy from Game Three. They hold a tenuous lead, and the Celtics—Rajon Rondo, in particular—have this look in their eyes, like *this is the best you've got?* Like the Magic are giving it everything they can, and the Celtics are playing with one hand behind their back, just waiting for the right opportunity to explode. Kyle is telling you to smile, telling the waitress to tell you to smile, and she giggles in a way that's encouraging to Kyle but seems incredibly uncomfortable to you.

By halftime, there's a ketchup stain on Kyle's shirt (he doesn't notice) and the Celtics lead by two, are now consistently outplaying the Magic at both ends of the floor. Kyle spills a beer and tries to help the waitress sop it up with napkins, but she says "No, no, please," and he backs off. By the end of the third, Kyle's wiping onion ring grease on his shorts and the Magic are down 79-71. But in the fourth quarter the Magic fight their way back into it, seemingly every player knocking down shots one after the next, Courtney Lee then Mickaël Piétrus then Marcin Gortat then Dwight Howard then Rashard Lewis, and the restaurant has become as loud as the arena five miles from here. Kyle's had six or seven beers, is screaming right along with everyone else, and you've been drinking Diet Coke since halftime, silent on your side of the booth. He's a redneck in a real city, and does he even realize the distance between the two of you, how far he must still travel if he's going to assimilate into a place like this?

Courtney Lee drills a jumper, pulls the Magic to within one, and then the score stays 91-90 for almost *two and a half minutes*, an eternity in fourth-quarter NBA action, when there seems to be a commercial break every other second of game-play. Then, with less than a minute left, Dwight Howard is fouled and miraculously sinks two straight free throws to put the Magic up 92-91.

The crowd in Buffalo Wild Wings. The crowd! The waitress was standing mere feet from your table as he took those free throws, and she turns around, sees Kyle still staring at the TV and clapping, and she launches herself at him and gives him the sort of hug a wife would give to a returning soldier, the two of them a puddle of combined flesh at the back of the booth. Then she peels herself from him, smiles, says "sorry," and is gone.

"Kyle," you say, and you sit up. "Good for you."

He's blushing. "Pays to be positive. The ladies love it."

32.5 seconds left in the game. Magic ahead by a single point.

"How you doing over there?" Kyle asks, dipping a potato wedge into the ranch.

Follow your father's rules, right? Stay positive, and you will be rewarded. (Molested by attractive waitresses, potentially!) Maybe you've been too hard on your brother. You look around: on barstools, there are fat men in softball league jerseys; on high-tops there are thirty-somethings in faded AC/DC shirts with *chain wallets* dangling from belt loops and pockets. This restaurant—hell, this city—is not as polished as you like to think.

"Doin' great," you say. "Let's go Magic. Rah-rah-rah."

"I detect sarcasm."

"Let's win, team," you say. "That's…I can't muster a cheer, Kyle."

"Can you pass the onion rings?"

On TV, Boston's Glen "Big Baby" Davis is lumbering back up-court, trudging with a body that doesn't look built for running, and he's standing almost at the top of the key and the ball winds up in his hands; Big Baby is not a superstar, doesn't take clutch shots at the ends of games; he's a bench player who runs onto the floor in the second quarter and shouts and jumps and pumps his fist to get the team energized while the stars take a breather; in other words, you shouldn't be worried that Big Baby has the ball. And yet here he is, slinking from the three-point line to the free-throw line, just a quick confident dribble around Orlando's defense before he sinks a fifteen-foot jump-shot to put the Celtics ahead by one point with less than thirty seconds remaining. He marches back on defense triumphantly, lower jaw jutting out, eyes cast downward so that his entire face looks long and hard like an Easter Island statue.

Boston: 93-92. Your positivity in a precarious place.

Rashard Lewis powers toward the basket for the Magic, forcing his way between defenders—you need Rashard to make something happen, to earn his astronomical salary—and he raises his arm hoop-ward, and the ball pops out of his hands and there is chaos on the floor, white and green jerseys fighting for position to claim the errant ball, and this is the last fucking thing you wanted, a broken play and a scramble for control and no chance at a good clean shot… *but*, amid the squeaking and scuffling of feet on the floor, there's a whistle—*a foul!*—and now Rashard Lewis is stepping to the free-throw line.

"I see it in your face," Kyle says. "Don't worry so much. This is a good team."

"Sometimes I'd rather cheer for a bad team," you say.

"Why?"

"Everyone expects them to lose. So when they win, it's…I don't know, fun?"

"You'd rather have a losing team just so you don't have to care about the outcome?"

"I think so."

He pops an onion ring into his mouth. "I don't think you'd like that."

"This is too stressful. I don't like the stakes."

On TV, Rashard makes the first of his two free throws. Tie game.

"How do you do it, Kyle?" you ask. He thinks you mean "how do you stay positive during nail-biter basketball games," so he just shrugs, but you're really asking him about *everything*. How is everything so effortless for him?

Rashard raises his eyebrows, dribbles, then nails the second, ball through hoop as naturally as water down a drain. Rashard looks hungry. Unfazed by the expectations of salary, the moment. This isn't a dominant performance from the Magic, not like Friday night, but you've got the lead with ten seconds left, and a 3-1 series advantage is *within reach*. Maybe this is some higher power confirming for you that *positive thinking* is the answer, that defeatism gets you nowhere—

Boston inbounds. "Here we go," Kyle says. "Ten seconds."

Before Kyle can finish speaking, Boston has the ball across mid-court, Paul Pierce dribbling at the top of the arc. Two Magic defenders swarm him because certainly Pierce—the Boston superstar—will take the final shot. But as soon as he's attracted them both, as soon as he exists under a cloak of double-teaming defenders, he lifts the ball with both hands and rockets it to the far corner of the court to—*are you kidding me?*—Big Baby?—Big Baby *again*, wide open. Big Baby stands just inside the three-point line, toes touching the star-trail of the Magic logo on the hardwood, and he jumps—

the ball floats from his hands

floats over the outstretched arms of Rashard Lewis, the hero of five seconds ago

floats, floats

floats until it blends into the backdrop of the crowd and you lose sight of it

floats somewhere amid the black and blue Magic t-shirts behind the goal as the clock hits double zeroes and the glass backboard flashes red to signal the end of the game and you think "we won!"

floats into view again, has not disappeared

oh God

the ball, oh God, the ball, it's still up there

and it swishes through the bottom of the net

—and there is no more game, just a ball bouncing harmlessly on the hardwood.

Silence in the restaurant. The hundreds previously energized by Bud Lite and ranch dressing and fry grease. No one breathing. Everyone gut-punched.

"Wait, what the fuck just happened?" you finally hear from somewhere.

"He didn't fucking make that," someone says. "No way he made that shot."

And then the replays, as if the producer has heard these questions.

"Aw damn," Kyle says. "That's tough."

Over and over, the replays, and the entire arena is a popped basketball. Eventually there's noise, but not cheers. This is anguish. And on TV, Big Baby is mobbed by his teammates, an orgy of Boston Pride for his game-winning shot—and more replays: Big Baby jumping, then stumbling backward after shooting, as if propelled by the magnitude of his shot. Big Baby watching the ball enter the hoop and drop from the bottom of the net. Big Baby's face, pure ecstasy. Big Baby charging from one end of the court—running directly past the Magic bench—charging forward and nearly trampling a referee, who curls forward to avoid getting clobbered. Big Baby charging forward and almost losing his balance as he slips around the referee and then he slaps his hand down on the back of a preteen boy in a courtside seat to keep from falling, and thrusts himself back into his forward charge, knocking the kid to the ground as he barrels toward his teammates in celebration.

The crowd is dead. The game is over. The Magic lost. But still, you must relive it over and over. You watch the replay again: Big Baby...*he hit a kid*. Someone's child, who'd been gifted front-row seats for a second-round playoff series, gift of a lifetime, and is now on the floor with a hand-shaped bruise on his back, struggling back to his feet.

But the producers want celebration and happiness. They must notice the child crumbling to the ground in the replays because the next replays avoid the child-shove, and the new replay footage shows only Boston's coach, Doc Rivers, jumping from his seat as if jolted by electric shock and punching the air and screaming "YES!"

You are standing. Here in Buffalo Wild Wings, face growing red, mind overtaken by rage. "Did you *see* that?" you scream at your brother. "Did you *see that*?" You jab your finger at the television...*did no one else see it*? All around you, Magic fans are gathering their belongings, signing tips onto checks, fitting hats over scattered hair, masking disappointment in whatever ways they can manage. Why is no one as enraged as you? Why is Big Baby not in handcuffs? Why has Dwight Howard not stormed across the court to demand blood vengeance for the assault on the child?

"Tough loss," Kyle says. "No doubt."

"The *kid*!" you scream. "Did you *see* that?"

"Yep, it's gonna be a long series."

"He shoved a *child*! Didn't you *see*?"

"It's one game," Kyle says. "Listen to me, buddy. It's just one game. That's the rule we live by. One game at a time."

"*That's* the rule? *That*...?"

"Take it easy."

"Someone's gotta do something," you say. "The kid…"

"Listen: the kid's fine."

"He's not."

"You want me to drive?" Kyle asks.

You hear him but you don't. You're walking to your car. You're trying the door handle, but you forgot to unlock the doors because in your mind you are still watching the boy fall, over and over. You are still holding onto that image.

•

Late Tuesday morning, you turn off John Young Parkway to finish paperwork for another refinance. Two days ago, this closing wasn't on your schedule, but you've been in contact with another title company that has some big-time contracts all across Florida. They've agreed to "try you out" as part of their "network of notaries." If everything works out, your business output could double, triple. Big lenders—the sort whose daily scandals make national headlines, the sort who, even in a terrible economy, are still doing business— still need notaries. And this—the title company "trying you out"—is not just hope and prayer, this is the real thing, potentially steady work for Kyle. The only thing that matters to you right now is doing right by your brother, getting him a real job, making amends for everything you were supposed to have done years before. You *need* this contract, and if you're going to *get* this contract, you need to make a good impression with today's closings.

John Young Parkway is a busy road in West Orlando, one of those many-laned streets on the outer rims of a downtown where the skyscrapers surrender to shopping malls and two-story commercial complexes, where Bojangles' and Burger King and Chick-fil-A and Taco Bell press down from the corners of every intersection, bleed into Mobils and 7-Elevens and RaceTracs. John Young Parkway: until recently, you didn't even know this road was named after Orlando's most famous son, the astronaut John Young, one of the early space pioneers. Until recently, you didn't know how big a deal that was to Orlando in the '60s and '70s, that the University of Central Florida began as Florida Technological University with the slogan "Reach For the Stars," and that the city thought its future would be a space-based economy, while citrus faded into the history books. One of FTU's first mascot ideas was the Citronaut, in fact, a *Jetsons*-style character with a tangerine body and the head of a spaceman. You get the impression that people in the '60s thought Orlando would soon have flying cars and a launchpad for round-trip moon vacations. But by the late '80s, the city had settled on its now-entrenched tourism-based economy. The orange groves were mostly gone, yes, but the space industry—after the Challenger explosion, which had been not only visible but vivid from any schoolyard in Orlando—was in a recession of imagination. As you careen down John Young Parkway, you spot the occasional cluster of buildings with futuristic designs from the '60s and '70s, now sun-faded and silly-looking and begging to be replaced by Panera Breads and Chipotles and Cheesecake Factories.

The GPS directions have you making a series of quick turns off the bustling parkway until you feel like you're in a different city, twisting through a neighborhood where the houses are sunken behind overgrown bushes and deep shadows, where the trees seem ancient and violent. Thick oaks with more Spanish moss than leaves. There are no palm trees back here, no sunshine, only mildewed driveways and stepping stones through muddy yards, wet wood fences, boards turned green, things living that should have been extinct before dinosaurs roamed the Earth. For someone living in this small corner of town, Orlando is not—was never—about astronauts and space and "reach for the stars!" Street names are the biggest fucking lie that big cities tell.

As you step up the rotting front porch steps, a man comes to the door and lets you in. He's hunched-over, wearing a flannel shirt that seems too hot for the day; the world seems even muggier in this neighborhood, the air thicker and stickier, and inside the house it's no different. Somewhere, a wall-unit air conditioner kicks and clunks, but that does nothing for the smell: burnt toast, wet cardboard, tuna water, old French fries. You can get specific about the smell because you can see each of these items here in the living room.

Sauce-crusted bowls of old ravioli on the couch. Cups everywhere: plastic cups from Chick-fil-A, styrofoam cups from the Circle K, paper cups from McDonald's and Krystal. Gatorade bottles, Mountain Dew bottles, Dr Pepper bottles. Bottles and cups and wrappers and snack boxes with the faces of athletes smiling at you: Dwight Howard, all teeth, ready to bite into his cheeseburger.

The man offers you a seat at what appears to be the dining room table, and something scuttles across the floor as you pull out the chair. Did you kick a bottlecap, or is there a world of living creatures surrounding you, under the tables and inside the cushions and under the rug?

"Is it just the two of us?" you ask.

"Wife's at work," he says.

"Well," you say, "it looks like the loan's in both your names. So."

"So?"

"We need her."

"Let me see that," he says and holds his hand out.

You hand over one of your binder-clipped stacks. A cockroach flashes across the table but then stops at the far end to look at you, to challenge you. *Welcome to* my *house, bitch*, he's saying. *We run this shit.* You shake your head, point to the page that the man—his name is Glenn, be courteous, you need this contract!—needs to see. "Both your signatures," you repeat.

"Let me see the rest of it," Glenn says and points to your bag.

You keep things in careful order. Paper clips and binder clips and manila folders. Duplicate copies and highlighted lines and fluorescent flags. You know that to hand over the full packet of documents to this man—who has left a gravy-covered plate here on the table, which the cockroach is now defiantly inspecting—would be to add two hours to your day, sorting and unsorting, sweating in an Arby's parking lot while doing so, trying to figure out where some missing page went. That's the type of shit that happens when you "let them see the rest of it."

"Listen," you say. "What time does your wife get home from work? I can come back." (You're picturing two or three hours in some nearby

Starbucks, checking your watch, waiting, drinking too much coffee, eating a scone, waiting for the hour when you can drive back to the swamp of this man's neighborhood and get the signatures you need. You didn't set this up, any of it, and in fact you had to postpone *another* signing until late afternoon just so you could get here early, so you could get this contract with the new title company, so you could (pat yourself on the back) create a fucking job for your brother.)

Glenn drops the paper onto the table, done with it, but you see an orange stain developing from the other side: he's dropped the paper into something foul and liquid. You grab it quickly and flap the page to maybe air-dry the goo away? Futile.

"When can we expect her?" you ask again.

"Ten minutes," he says.

"Your wife gets off work in *ten* minutes?"

"Yeah."

You want to jump up and high-five him. "Then there's no problem. We'll just wait."

"All right," he says. "I'm'a go smoke a cigarette."

As soon as he's out of the room and sitting on the dank back porch, and you are alone in the nightmare of his house, you hear it: children playing in the other room.

Your first thought is school: shouldn't they be at school on a Tuesday morning?

Your second thought: it's early May, so is it summertime? Another teacher workday? You have no kids, have no idea about semester schedules. All you know is you hate driving past elementary schools, all the buses, the long line of parent vehicles snaking out of the pick-up zone and backing up traffic for an hour.

Your third thought, not different than when you visited the Fun Spot rental houses awhile back: you know nothing about parenting. Maybe you should shut up.

The longer you sit, the more it feels like you are getting buried alive, so you stand and take a step, accidentally kicking an old OJ container, and then a cockroach is on your foot and you scream involuntarily because it doesn't matter how many hours you log at the gym, cockroaches and spiders still terrify you.

Maybe it's the volume of your unfamiliar scream, or the sound of wrappers crunching underfoot, but seconds later two children are out in the hallway. The boy is six or seven years old, wearing a shirt that should have been retired a few growth spurts ago; it barely reaches his belly button, is smeared with mud and something purple. The girl is maybe a year younger, holds an empty shampoo bottle dented on one side.

"She keeps hitting me with that," the boy says, pointing.

"No tattling!" the girl responds and smacks him upside the head with the bottle.

"Whoa," you say. "Calm down. Nobody needs to hit anybody."

"You see?" the boy says, fingers running over the smacked spot.

"I told you," the girl says and hits him again, this time harder.

"Whoa, whoa," you say. Your arms are out defensively, the same pose you might strike if you were getting robbed at gunpoint in some dark downtown alley. "Please. Stop hitting him. Let's, you know, play nice."

"You can't do nothing about it," the girl says, hits him again.

The boy cries, holds his scalp like he's expecting his head to fall off.

"Your father"—you point to the porch—"he's right there. He's not going to like this."

"He won't do nothing neither," the girl says, then holds the shampoo bottle out in front of her like it's the broken jagged edge of a beer bottle and she might just slit your throat. "Who *are* you?" she asks. "What are you doing here?"

"I'm a notary, a loan-closer," you say.

She jabs the shampoo bottle. "You here to take our money?"

"What? No. I'm just—" and you are momentarily distracted by a sight that should make you scream again, a spider that is creeping across the girl's shoulder. You don't know much about spiders, except that here in Florida, it's the little ones you should be afraid of. And you know enough that this spider—this monster hiking to the summit of her shoulder—is too large to be a silent killer. But still you are deathly afraid of spiders, give them the sort of frightened attention that others reserve for real-man threats like bears and bobcats and rattlesnakes. "Your shoulder," you say. "Don't move. There's a spider on your—"

And without taking her eyes off yours, she brings the shampoo bottle down across her shoulder, so quick the spider never had a chance. Then she points the bottle at you again, a brown smear across its curved surface. *You're next*, her eyes tell you.

"Your father knows I'm here," you say. "He's finishing his cigarette."

The girl's look remains unchanged, defiance and anger and bloodlust, emotions that shouldn't be so easily attained for a girl so young, but in the next instant the front door opens and a woman walks inside, tosses an orange vest onto the floor and proceeds straight to the kitchen without even glancing in the direction of your stand-off with her child. When she finally does come out of the kitchen, Coke bottle in one hand and a Fritos package in the other, she says simply: "Who the hell are you?" She doesn't look scared of you. Not even curious. Just tired, like this happens every day and she's through playing this game.

"I'm—"

"I *been* asking him," the girl says.

"She's hitting me!" the boy cries, pointing to the spider-part-stained bottle.

"I. Told. You!" the girl says and smacks him again.

"Oh, for God's sake," the woman says. "Go to your room!"

"But I don't—" the girl starts.

"But she—" the boy cries.

"Go to your *room*," the woman says and she holds out the Coke bottle in the same menacing way that the girl had been holding out the shampoo bottle. Everyday objects as deadly weapons, and you shouldn't be scared—it's plastic—but somehow you are.

"You gonna hit me?" the girl asks. "With this *man* here?" She says "man" so derisively that you wonder if she thinks her father is something different entirely.

"Look, I'm—" you say.

"Sit down," the woman tells you and points to the kitchen table. "I'll deal with you later."

"Deal with me?"

She doesn't respond, doesn't need to, just stares at you with such power that you do as she commands, that the children run back to their room, and that even the cockroaches seem to scurry for shelter. The woman opens her Coke, takes a swig, then shakes her bag of Fritos in anticipation. She opens the bag, plucks out a single Frito, leans back against the counter, and glares at you as she pops it into her mouth.

Seconds later, the porch door opens and Glenn is back in the kitchen. "Hey baby," he says to his wife.

She eats another Frito, nods at him.

"This is the man closing our loan."

"Is it done yet?" she asks.

"Ain't started," he says. "We're waiting for you."

"Well," she says, "I don't know nothing about that."

"Your name's on the loan!" he says.

"But I don't know nothing *about* it," she says.

You want to interject that they asked for the refinance, so they should know *something* about it, however little, but you fear her reprisal. They argue back and forth about what they know or don't, but soon they're arguing about something else entirely, one of them yelling at the other about a cracked window, the other retorting that they ate rice—motherfucking *plain* rice—for dinner last night because someone—*someone*—burned the chicken, both of them yelling about the kids and about an aunt, an uncle, a grandmother, a failing car, a broken door, a lost job, an aching tooth, arguing long enough that it feels like they've forgotten you, long enough that—despite the shouting—the tension seems to evaporate, like maybe this is the way of life in this home, the norm. The roaches return. They return to the walls, creep back onto the table where you've finally convinced the arguing couple to sit. Occasionally, as you move through the documents and show them the highlighted spaces for their signatures, the woman gives you murderous looks again, like you're trying to swindle her, but you keep repeating, "You don't owe me any money. I'm a notary."

"Nothing's free," she says.

"I'm paid by the title companies," you say. "I'm not an encyclopedia salesman. *You* asked for this refinance, correct? It saves you money on your mortgage. Nobody's *making* you do this."

A crash in the other room, glass shattering. The little boy screams.

"If they busted that fucking window again," the woman says.

"Sign here," you say. "We're almost done."

There is one thought on your mind: get through this unscathed. Power through. Do not spend any extra energy here than you need to. It's going to be a long day.

"They're *your* kids," the man says. "This is the way *you* raised them."

By the time you reach the final page of the documents, the boy emerges from his room. He's crying again, tears of true pain, not just play-smacks from his sibling. "She made me walk on it!" he sobs, and he's limping with bloody feet toward the table.

The man—Glenn—stands up, and you think that the room and the house will change, that sunshine will enter the window at last and the veil of gray will be penetrated and the oak trees will sprout leaves again, that this is the tipping point that will reveal the family's true nature, that beneath their abrasive façade they do care deeply for one another. You sincerely believe this will happen, and there is a part of you that's happy to see the blood on the boy's feet because you know that the healing can now begin. You were poor, too, after all, and there's nothing lazier than stereotyping *all poor people* as stupid and violent and uncivilized.

"You stupid enough to walk on that 'cause she told you to do it?" the man asks.

The child is still crying, but straining to stifle the tears.

"Put on some socks, you hear me?" the man says. "Five minutes. We need five minutes of peace and quiet. Another peep, and I'm'a make you *crawl* over that fucking glass. You think you're hurting now?

Of course, some people *do* match the stereotype.

The boy leaves a blood trail on the carpet as he retreats to his room, and now you can't help it: you're no longer thinking about contracts, or damage to the property; you're thinking about the boy's torn-up feet, and what else he's now stepping on, what is finding its way into the gashes as he marches. The carpet fuzz, the sand, the old Fritos crumbs, the bug parts, the broken glass from a thousand other fights or careless moments. This is a five-year-old boy. This is a moment that begs for intervention.

But it's the final page of the document, too, and then it's done, and for you this is about getting in good with the title company. This is not your house. These are not your children.

Moments later, you are back in the car and texting Jimmy that you just escaped hell and you need a drink. If this was the biggest challenge the title company could offer in order to "test you out," then you *passed*. You even think of your father: could he have performed under such pressure, a bickering family standing around him as he changed their oil? Would he have snapped, told the customers to shut up and get it together?

No. You know what your father would tell you now: "What's right is right."

WHAT'S RIGHT IS RIGHT.

Even as you drive to FedEx with the paperwork, you know you should call the Department of Children and Families. Even now, you know what's right: fight for those who can't fight themselves.

But is this what you want on the first closing of a new contract? To initiate some sort of life-changing legal saga for that family, which could inevitably lead to (at the very least) a complaint to the mortgage company about the snooping sumbitch they sent out? You make that phone call, and suddenly there's an investigation and the parents are in jail and the kids are in foster care and no one is making payments on that refinanced mortgage. This is a new contract, this is for *Kyle*, this is the start of a *real* business for you, with *real* employees, this is a way out of the financial sinkhole: everything needs to go right.

Before even opening a briefcase your father would have been on the phone with DCF, alerting them of the living conditions, the likely child abuse, the litany of details *you* viewed as property damage but that *he* would measure in their human toll.

"What's right is right." Oh hell, it sounds so damn simple, but is it?

God, if only there were a flow-chart.

If only you knew…if only you *knew*.

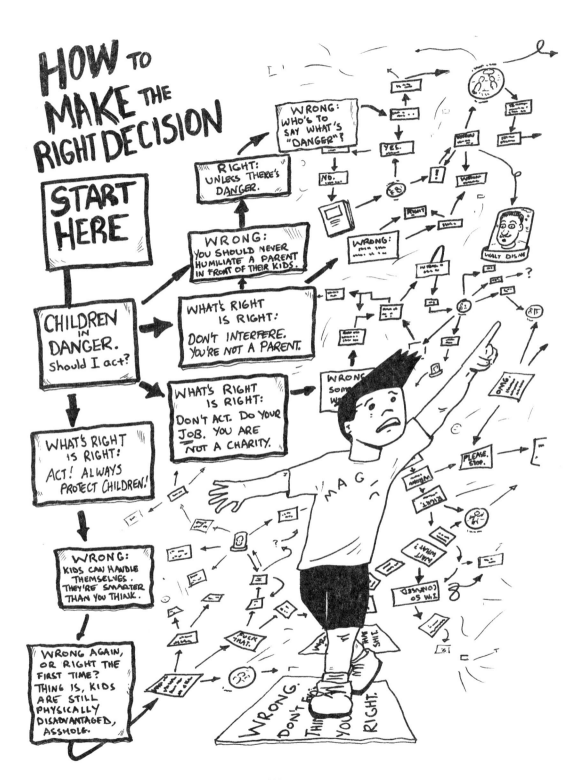

DON'T SWEAT...

DON'T SWEAT THE...

You are a bad human being, an angry despicable man, and you are convinced that, because of *your* poor decision-making, the Magic lost Tuesday night. Because of you and *your* negativity, they are now down in the series, 3-2.

You were angry on Tuesday night after the loan closing. Angry all day Wednesday, too, because you ran out of orange juice in the morning, and you know it was Kyle who finished it, but you told him "what's mine is yours" so it makes you angrier that you cannot get angry about the OJ. All day, you tried not to hold a grudge, tried not to care, but when you stopped at 7-Eleven to grab a Diet Coke, their soda fountain tubes were crossed and you wound up with a cup of motherfucking *regular* Coke, which you didn't discover until you'd already driven away, and because the gas station was at an awkward intersection you'd have wasted fifteen minutes going back for a replacement, and so you screamed so loud in your car your throat was scratchy and raw afterward, and you know this anger was related to the stupid fucking orange juice situation, and if you're truly honest, you were *still* angry about Big Baby beating on that child way back on Sunday. Couldn't let it go. But even before that: surely you could keep flipping back in time to revisit past incidents in a thick ledger of anger, keep flipping and never arrive at a first entry.

Now it's Thursday and you're angry about Game Six, certain that Boston will steal another victory in your hometown. And if they don't, you're already prepared to get angry about *winning* Game Six and then having to travel to Boston for a decisive Game Seven, which the Magic *will not* win. A Game Six victory just delays the inevitable. *Just lose*, you think. Get it over with.

These are the things you're thinking on this sweltering afternoon as you drive the Bee Line to finish two quick loan-closings near Cocoa Beach. You're stuck in the right lane behind a slow-moving pickup truck. "Don't sweat the small stuff," your father would say, like all the world's frustrations are just minor nuisances that don't really matter, and maybe he'd tell you that you choose your reactions, that your anger is your own creation. "Okay, fine," you say. "Today I'll practice patience."

The speed limit is 70 but the truck grumbles along at 60 and you can't change lanes to pass because the left lane runs thick, bumper to bumper.

Don't sweat the small stuff, you say and nod. Don't sweat the small stuff. It'll be okay. You're running late, but it's not the end of the world.

But there's a grill in the bed of the truck, upright and clanging, and a propane tank still attached to the grill. The gas cable between the tank and the grill flutters in the wind. The tank wobbles and slides across the truck bed, the gas cable goes taut. There is no bungee cord, nothing to hold the grill in place. The grill bounces several inches off the truck-bed when the driver fails to avoid a pothole. This is not small stuff. Damn it, Dad! All of these things— *this is not small stuff*!

As you watch the potential explosion in front of you, your phone rings.

"Marc," says the voice on the other end. It's your real estate agent, Samantha. "We've got an interested buyer."

Grill bounces again like a child on a trampoline.

"Holy shit," you say, a reaction both to the grill and to Samantha's statement. "Which property?" For the moment, your anger dissipates, almost like you've flipped the vent in your kitchen and you can actually *watch* the smoke pulled from the room.

"Two properties, actually," she says. "One is Lake Nona."

"Lake Nona," you repeat. Lake Nona is one of your better properties, still unoccupied but situated in a brand-new golf community.

"It's one of the few areas still getting solid offers. Well, that and the communities up your way. Heathrow. Stoney Creek, should you decide to sell."

"Should I decide to sell? I do need a house, Samantha. Can't live in my car."

"Right," she says.

Samantha is a middle-aged single woman living out in Longwood. Straight black hair, always wearing gray skirts and dangling costume jewelry. Thin, like she works out: not just exercise classes at the gym, but free-weight workouts with rusty dumbbells. *Severe* is the word you've used to describe her. When you were selecting real estate agents three years ago, this is the woman Edwin found, based upon his own specific rulebook. "We don't want a male agent," he said. "I don't trust men. They always seem like they're trying to make money, trying to put one over on you." "We are," you told him. "Exactly," Edwin said, "so we want a *woman*. But not a young girl, not someone we'd want to fuck. You don't want your decisions driven by your dick." "A mother, then?" "No," Edwin said. "We want someone without a life. We want some lady who is, like, so consumed by career that she's got no time for kids. Maybe she's got a man, but she's clearly the one in control of the relationship. You know what I'm saying? Yeah. You know." And so Edwin spread out brochures and business cards and you examined all the photos, eliminating dozens immediately. Then you found Samantha, posing in her picture like a kickboxer in mid-punch. And for a while, everything was working well: buying new properties, selling some of them at five-figure profits. But the phone calls from Samantha slowed in 2008, and finally stopped, the home prices falling lower and lower, and you'd reinvested your profits into new properties and you were anything but liquid, and it was like you were reaching for something that was floating away, something drifting over the waves while you kept crashing back to shore, and now—for Samantha—you're just one more douchebag among many who has homes that won't sell.

"Two properties," you say. "What's the other one?"

"We've got an interested buyer for the Wild Berry property, as well," she says.

"The *oil-stain* house?"

"Huh?"

Ahead of you on 528, the grill seems to toss the propane tank across the truck bed, then pull it back in, a swing dance of grill and gas tank.

"No offer yet. But the agent should be calling again soon on the Lake Nona property. It's a professor. Going to teach at the new med school."

"No offer on Wild Berry?"

"Well. That house, as you know, needs some TLC. I think they're looking into the neighborhood more than the house."

"I visited a few days ago. I didn't realize it had gotten so bad."

"Cross your fingers. You want to avoid going into short-sale, but they're going to low-ball you. They'll say the property is a fixer-upper."

"Well, it's mostly cosmetic—"

"It's a disaster. They'll probably come with 160."

"We paid *250* for that—"

"We counter with 220, and hope we can meet at 200, agreeing to a credit for repairs."

"So I'll have to spend for repairs, *and* bring money to close, just so I can *lose* fifty thousand dollars?"

The grill and the propane tank are at a standstill in the truck bed now, staring at each other, finished with their dance and awaiting a score.

"You told me you were serious about avoiding foreclosure."

"I am."

"Listen," Samantha says, "this is a nice deal. This could be a really good week for you. Two properties? In this climate? That's impressive."

"I hope."

"Positive vibes, Marc. Maybe you've got a little house-flipper left in you after all."

Positive vibes. Rah rah rah.

After you hang up with Samantha, you notice with sickening certainty that the tailgate on the truck in front of you has not been secured, it is trembling and—in the next bump—it bangs open, and now the grill is sliding toward the tailgate as you round a curve in the highway, and without even looking to your left or signaling a turn, you slash to the next lane and cut off a Suburban filled with children headed to the beach, the mother honking and the children thrust against their seatbelts, but in the truck beside you the grill finally topples, crashes face-first into the truck bed, then skids across the open tailgate—the grill dragging the propane tank as it slides. One of the grill's knobs catches in the crack for a moment. You wave, hoping you can get the attention of the truck's driver, because clearly he doesn't notice what is happening, and when *you* accelerate to get beside the truck, the driver *also* accelerates, as if he thinks you want to pass him and—just to be a dick—will not allow it. And that's when it happens: at the next curve, the grill tumbles out of the truck-bed and falls directly into the middle of 528, and you hear a horn honking, and then the sound of screeching tires on pavement, the sounds of fenders meeting hoods as the cars in the right lane swerve and brake and crash while trying to avoid the rolling grill and gas tank, and you press harder on the gas pedal because you don't want to see it, any of it. You glance over at the truck driver—you are going 80 now, but he's speeding up and looking in the rearview mirror and mouthing the words "oh shit" and then looking back over his shoulder, biting his lip, gunning it even harder, pedal to the metal, 80 to 85 to 90 miles per hour because he knows what he's done, and he disappears into the stream of cars ahead.

Behind you, far back now, plumes of black smoke.

Small stuff, right. Small stuff. This was small stuff, wasn't it, until it became *big stuff?* This is how it always seems to happen. Does "don't sweat the small stuff" mean "stop caring about the world"? And if the goal is to stop caring about the world, didn't you do the right thing by ignoring the antics of the children in the roach-house?

For the next thirty miles, until 528 delivers you to the beaches, this remains on your mind: a man who couldn't be bothered to secure his grill, who couldn't even shut his tailgate, and who—when disaster struck—wanted no part of the mess he'd caused. Was there an explosion? A fatal wreck? A child killed? What if *you* hadn't switched lanes? Would you be among them? Would it have been better that way, you dead but a child saved? For a while, you are wistful: that would've been the best thing, would've made up for all the poor choices. Mmmm, the sweet taste of imagined martyrdom. But then you're angry for this stupid self-pitying fantasy. Angry again.

When you finally arrive in Cocoa, you're shaking. Your hands won't stop trembling. You want this truck driver *dead*. You want him *dead*. He doesn't deserve to be living, a man who would cause such destruction. It's irrational to feel this way. You know that. But it's the world—it's everything you cannot control, making you angrier, angrier, angrier—

·

Angrier, and it's with you, your anger, always with you, has followed you here to the Panera Bread in Cocoa Beach, where you're waiting to meet a couple different borrowers and gather their paperwork, but really you're searching for that asshole in the BMW who parked so far over the line that he took up two spots and forced you to park several blocks from here in a giant mud puddle. Even after you've closed both loans, you scope out the crowd, hoping to spot him, hoping he'll walk back to his truck at the same time you leave, and then— oh God—this is a man who deserves his face broken…this is a man who—oh, there is no end to the violence in your mind right now, no end, no end to what the anger is whispering in your ear—

·

And at the gym that afternoon, your anger is there, too, nudging you in the side and goading you to yell out that no one ever racks their weights when they're finished, goading you to stare down the skinny high-schoolers who move your towel and your water bottle and steal your bench while you use the bathroom. It's there with you on the treadmill, too, coming through the static of the little TV screen and asking why you pay so much for this damn gym membership when the buttons on these treadmills never work. The speed won't increase quickly enough—run faster!—won't slow despite how hard you mash the buttons. And your anger is there at the complimentary coffee stand in the gym's lobby, laughs as the urn spits hot dregs onto your hand. You don't deserve that. Scream it out, your anger says, scream it out! And do you see these discarded sweetener packets and stirring straws the other sloppy gym-goers have left on the floor? Does no one fucking care about anything anymore? Scream it out!

•

Thursday afternoon melts into Thursday night. You watch Game Six with Kyle, and your anger is there too.

The Magic win and tie the series at 3-3. Kyle stands and cheers as the final seconds tick off. Your anger pats your shoulder, says, You know they won't win Game Seven. Not in Boston.

Thursday becomes Friday becomes Saturday. In and out of days, across weeks to where the wild things are.

You close loans.

Kyle finishes another OJ before you even get to have a glass.

You close loans.

You see a child on a leash.

You buy a packet of lunch meat that turns out to be spoiled.

On Saturday, Kyle passes his notary exam, his face aglow with accomplishment even though you've seen notaries who barely qualify as sentient life forms. "That's a sign, ain't it? We're gonna win Game Seven!"

You should be happy for him, happy you were able to make your brother into a functioning, income-earning employee. But after the exam, he rides along with you on a loan-closing and acts like he knows everything, and your anger says: *Fuck*, it took you so long to learn all this shit, and he thinks he can do the job *just like that*?

On the drive home, over and over, you watch drivers cruise along in the E-Pass lane and then realize at the last possible moment that they should be in the "cash / change only" lane, and so they slam on the brakes and try to reverse, right there in the middle of the highway. "Get! *Fuck*! How! *Drivers*!" you scream, so loud and beastly you spit against the inside of the windshield, your brother beside you holding his breath, and it takes every remaining kilowatt of energy in your body not to turn on him and scream, "You got a *problem* with me?"

Anger sits in the backseat, happy as sin.

•

The next day, Sunday, the underdog Magic beat the Celtics in Game Seven—*in Boston*—the first time a visiting team has defeated the Celtics in a Game Seven on their home floor—*ever*. Maybe you never should have worried, your anger says. The success or failure of the Orlando Magic is not tied to some superstition of yours. And why did you refuse to watch the game with your little brother? Why did you sit silently on the foot of your bed, brooding for four quarters?

You're staring in the bathroom mirror.

Your anger stands behind you, asks, Holy shit, man, why so angry?

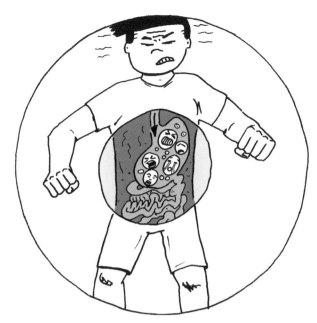

KEEP IT INSIDE.

PUSH IT DEEP.

You knew there would be Diet Coke at the RaceTrac and so there was Diet Coke at the RaceTrac—positive thinking, let's try this again—and now you're back in your car, parked at a pump, when you see a familiar vehicle at the Mobil station across the road. A turquoise Acura, an Orlando Magic sticker on the back window. That's Shelley's car. No doubt about it. That's Shelley, and you could run across traffic right now, run over to her.

Because what are the odds, really? That you would run into her like this, even as—you've heard—she is packing up and leaving town for some new job in San Diego. This is fortuitous indeed, a stroke of the finest luck. Positive thinking?

She's not in her car, of course. She's likely inside the Mobil, buying a bottled water or paying for gas, but what if—just as she arrived back at her car—you were there to greet her? What would you say after all this time, all these months?

The last time you spoke to Shelley—when was it?—she was moving out, packing her final box into that Acura. You remember trying to sound...

masculine. Powerful, tough, together. "Don't show any signs of pain," Jimmy told you. "Don't beg her to come back. Don't ask 'why,' or any of that weak-ass bullshit. It's over." Those were his rules about ending relationships. And really, you'd both known too many friends who'd allowed themselves to be sucked back into relationships that weren't working, or who wouldn't let go and therefore became brittle and pitiable shells of themselves. That was not going to be you. You were important. You were somebody. Shelley didn't want you? Let her go. Let. Her. Go.

"I hope this works out for you," you remember saying, a line you'd rehearsed so that you'd have something memorable with which to leave her. You thought that, in a movie of your life, it would make a strong closing moment before the jump-cut to you going back to work and moving on, sans baggage.

"Hope this works out for…what the hell do you think is happening here?"

"This is a business decision, clearly. You think you can do better, so fine. Go do better."

"Do better? I don't…" Shelley held her fingers to her forehead, then opened her driver's side door. You anticipated a rebuttal, and so you had several options in mind, should she respond in several different ways. "You just don't listen, do you? You don't listen to a word I say."

But that particular response was unexpected, not part of your script.

Don't listen? What tiny quote was she imagining that you hadn't heard? As a boyfriend, as a fiancé, you did everything right. To the fucking letter, you'd fulfilled your contract. The ring! Three months' salary! The house! The neighborhood! But she thought your business was collapsing, so she was bailing before making the all-important commitment.

"I've got to go," she said. "I can't…You do know that I never wanted any of this, right?"

"The house? The ring? I don't remember any protests."

"That's not what I'm talking about, and you know it."

"Oh?" You crossed your arms.

"Or maybe you don't know. Either way." She slid into the car, and from inside she said, "I never wanted to leave, Marc. That's what I meant."

"Oh sure," you said. "Sure. Even as I'm signing the check for the engagement photos, the florist, the security deposit at Ceviche!" But you stifled the urge to say more, thinking again of Jimmy's advice to keep cool. Don't let her see you upset. Then she took off, down the road and out of Stoney Creek. Standing in your empty driveway with the old woman-corpse in the garage across the street, you thought: "Huh. Well that wasn't so bad, was it?"

It was only later, days later, that the pain and the anger—the two of them swirling together—seemed to hit you with the force of an injection. And you felt both equally. The pain: she was gone, the one honest thing in your life, the anchor to a life that meant…etc. And the anger: how could she? To you? After all… etc.

To go over there now, to the Mobil station, to confront her. What would you say if you had one more shot?

"I want you back." No.

"I made a mistake." Did you?

Or, "I do listen. I really do!" But that's a lie, isn't it? Because what did you not hear, what one thing caused her to leave? It was many things you didn't hear, didn't listen to. Maybe you could start with that, but when you look through your rearview to the Mobil station, fucking shit fuck, her car is gone.

"Fuck!" you scream and hurt your throat, and hurting your throat makes you bang the steering wheel and hurt your palms, and hurting your palms makes you want to scream again. This is how your anger feeds on itself, you think, but the feeding does not diminish it, the anger only grows, defying that common theory that energy cannot be created or destroyed. It wills itself larger, never expends a calorie, never even sleeps, just waits. Maybe it's not feeding on itself, then? Maybe it's feeding on you, growing inside you like cancer, and the larger it gets the less you can control it.

Are there people out there who can actually control their anger, you wonder, prevent it from spreading unchecked to their every bodily cell?

If so…if those people exist…you fucking hate them.

A GOOD MAN SPENDS THE HOLIDAYS WITH HIS FAMILY.

"We are all witnesses." That's the slogan that the Cleveland Cavaliers have conjured to sell the LeBron James experience to their fans, as if success and slam-dunk posters and championship rings are all just inevitabilities, and *we are all so lucky* to have the privilege of watching King James hold court. We are all witnesses. LeBron James! King James! But you know that humiliation and disgrace can be remembered as easily as greatness, that the world can witness failure and remember it for just as long, the teams blown out in the Finals or heartbroken after Jordan buzzer-beaters, and that is the poisonous thought now festering in your mind, because that—you're convinced—will be how the Magic go down.

On the night of the first game of the Eastern Conference Finals against Cleveland, Jimmy calls with a set of tickets to a VIP watch party at Ember. "Open bar all night," he says, "and fuck if I'm going to take my wife. Wanna be my date, big guy?"

"How many tickets you have?" you ask.

"Four. Why? You want to bring someone?"

You think of your father's rules, of dedication to family. And you think of Kyle, of how he'd look at a VIP party.

"Maybe," you say. "I'll let you know."

Buffalo Wild Wings is one thing, but you can't take Kyle downtown. He's lived his entire life in rural Georgia, can't even fathom why someone would spend eighty bucks on a pair of jeans. Maybe you can just… leave him a note that you're out for the night?

As you're sorting through your closet to find a blue or black shirt, Kyle steps into your bedroom wearing a polo the sad color of faded mulch, and says, "Can I borrow some cash?"

"Cash?"

"I'm really low."

"What the *fuck*, Kyle?" you say.

"Damn, bro. Chill."

"How much?"

"How much?"

You grab a Crate and Barrel catalogue from the floor—you get these fucking catalogues twice a week, it seems, all these images of happy couples in their chic urban lofts—and you roll the catalogue up and smash it against the closet door like you're swatting a ten-pound bug, a swat for every word: "How much *cash* do you need?"

He stands motionless before you. "Are you going to *hit* me?"

This is how quickly the anger surfaces.

You toss the catalogue back onto the counter and run a trembling hand over your forehead and into your hair. "Okay," you say after a too-long exhale. "You need cash. What do you need to buy?"

"It's not a big deal. Forget I mentioned it."

"*Don't*—" you run your hands over the wicker baskets on the catalog cover, baskets that you'd rip apart if they were here right now, unraveling the twiggy ropes and mutilating them until no one even fucking knew that they were wicker baskets *ever*. "Don't do that," you say. "You said you needed money."

"It's just…I don't have a whole lot to my name."

"Well, I'm paying your rent. Electric. Your food. So I guess"—*breathe*—"I just don't think I understand"—*breathe*—"what you need."

"Did you see my suitcase?"

"You have a suitcase?"

"Exactly." He motions toward the guest room. "I have two gym bags, and a PlayStation. That's, like, everything."

"Don't be dramatic. That's all you brought, but—"

"That's all I've got that's worth anything," he says. "That and my truck."

"Come on."

"Shit, I had five or six work uniforms, all covered in oil and blood and fuck-knows-what-else, but I didn't bring any of that." He holds up his hands. "When I started packing to come down here, I went through my dresser, and I realized something…I mean, there was still underwear from when I was in high school. There were t-shirts that haven't fit me in a decade. I was about to grab my suit out of the closet." He shakes his head. "Marc, it was the same suit I wore to Mom's funeral."

"That can't be true," you say.

"When do *I* ever wear suits?" he asks. "I wear the same shirt every day of the week. And this polo? I wear this shit *every* damned Saturday night. I've gone through everything I own, and I've only been here since the start of the month."

The story feels true. For the last two weeks, Kyle has been borrowing the occasional too-big pair of khaki pants from you, the occasional polo, but you've got a thicker neck and shoulders from those Men's Health workouts, a thicker waist, thicker biceps, and Kyle has the typical backwoods skinny-guy physique, and when he wears your khakis and your polos he looks like he's (no other way to say it) borrowing clothes, like he's a poor redneck who can't afford his own.

How to take care of your younger brother? How to make up for the way you treated him during childhood, the way you abandoned him after high school? Because yes, you remember trying to convince Kyle to go to college.

You remember his two or three futile semesters at Valdosta State, still working at the shop, still living at home with your father and commuting to campus, still spending Friday nights in his work clothes at the Hole in the Wall, Saturday nights at 8-Ball, maybe backyard bonfires here and there, long Sundays watching NASCAR races with his high school friends while his college textbooks remained unopened. You remember—from a distance—hoping he'd gather himself, hoping he'd find a way out, but he worked with your father and John-John, with guys who looked and acted like Larry the Cable Guy, and he probably listened to every stupid word they said about the money he was "wasting" at school. And then it was Christmas one year and you were back in Georgia and you asked Kyle about college and he said those horrible fucking words, "It's not for me," and you knew that his mind was made up and it would never be unmade and you'd let it all happen. Big brother, you could have called more often, visited more often, encouraged him more often.

Where was your father in all of this? Oh, he was around, probably saying something like, "Every man makes his own path in life," to justify how he didn't push Kyle harder. That's what your father's rules did for Kyle: they dropped him off on your doorstep with no money and no college education. You see? *You see?*

"So you need cash for new clothes?"

"I do," he says.

"This is an investment for me, then?" you ask. You slap the catalogue cover, self-satisfied. You've got to find a way to feel good about this, lending your brother money, or the anger will burst from your chest.

"What?"

"I'm your employer. I'm investing in you. Can't send someone out into the world in old K-ROC shirts and Puddle of Mudd concert tee's. The new clothes will be an *investment.*"

"Oh. Right," he says.

You rap your knuckles against the countertop. "This weekend—" you shake your finger, as if this is a brilliant idea—"this weekend, we go to the mall. I pick out your clothes."

"Dude, I can pick out clothes."

"No," you say. "You can't, or you would have by now."

"Come on. This isn't *Clueless*. I don't need a makeover. Guys don't do this."

"We're brothers," you say. "But more importantly, I'm an investor. I'm investing in your future, Kyle. No more of these cheap rubber flip-flops, or old Big Johnson t-shirts."

"I only have *one* of those."

You laugh. "One is too many." It's a strange feeling, to laugh, the rage trembling just on the other side of the joy.

"So what's the plan for tonight?" he asks. "Where we watching the game?"

"Oh," you say.

"What?"

"Nothing, I just…" You feel your pocket, the phone inside still burning from that invitation from Jimmy. "I've got a date tonight," you tell him. "I'm…I'm sorry."

"Oh shit," he says and claps you on the back. "Why didn't you say something? I understand, bro. I'll find a barstool somewhere, no worries." He laughs and shakes his head. "Holy shit, my man. Getting back on your feet, ain't'cha?"

When he leaves, you turn and are startled by your reflection in the closet mirror. "What the fuck are *you* looking at?" you say, loud enough that you startle yourself again, that you suck in your breath and listen for any sign that Kyle might have heard.

•

You spend holidays with your family, that's your father's rule. No matter how long the drive, no matter how exhausted you'll be when you head back to work the next day. During college, you didn't miss a Thanksgiving, a Christmas, even (back then) a Memorial Day or an Independence Day. "Family comes first," he'd often say as he started the grill and scraped away the burnt gristle. "A man commits himself to his family, takes care of his family." Then: ten bratwursts on the grill, potato salad opened, '70s rock on the aging back-porch speakers.

A man takes care of his family.

And yet you didn't visit your father after his heart attack in January, did you? And you didn't see him in December, either. You skipped this past Christmas because of Thanksgiving. That was the last time you were back in Georgia: Thanksgiving of last year. Shelley had moved out months before, and still you couldn't tell your father the engagement was over. Late at night on Thanksgiving eve, drinking beers and eating wings with Kyle at 8-Ball, you finally leaned over and said, "So, uh, sorry to tell you, but you'll have to wait awhile for my open bar."

"What are you talking about?"

"The wedding," you said.

"What about it?"

"It's, uh," you said, "it's not happening."

"Not happening? Like, it's been pushed back?"

"Nope. No reception. No open bar, brother. The engagement is over."

"What are you—" he started. "Stop it with the open bar stuff. Did something happen to Shelley?"

You opened a wetnap carefully, as if you weren't bothered by the news, as if it was no different than telling him you'd cleaned out your closet and taken an old stack of sweaters to Goodwill. "She got tired of me. She didn't like my job, couldn't marry someone who was so business-oriented."

"My God," Kyle said. "I'm so sorry."

"Life goes on."

"That's what she said? About your job? That doesn't sound like her."

"She turned out to be different than I expected." You tossed the used-up towelette onto a plate of picked-clean bones. "But whatever, you know."

"Are you all right?" Kyle asked.

"How do I look?"

"You look…" He paused, considered you anew. "Happy? I never would have guessed."

"Everything's fine, Kyle. Business is good. Everything's fine."

"The economy," Kyle said. "We just spent six months watching campaign ads about how bad everything is. This isn't…you're not…?"

"I'm smart," you told him, tapping your head.

But there were a thousand things you *didn't* tell him that night, things you wouldn't yet admit to yourself. You'd just gone out for Edwin's birthday party the night before. Ceviche on Church Street (the tapas place where you'd originally planned to have your wedding reception). Long table, maybe thirty people total. Edwin, Mr. Popular. Sangria, chorizo meatballs, paella, hummus. "They say this place is haunted," Edwin said when his birthday cake came. "But tonight, we're gonna drink those ghosts under the motherfucking table!" All night you wanted to ask him about the houses, about whether he'd heard from Samantha, about how long he thought you'd need to keep renting these properties before you could find buyers…but you'd somehow wound up on the far end of the table with a group of twenty-two-year-olds who wouldn't shut up about how fucking awesome it was that they'd found a place to live downtown ("Bro, bro, bro," one kept saying, "it's a condo, a fucking *condo!*"). You could never get Edwin's attention, not before dinner, not during, not after, and looking back now you could sense how the business of home-flipping and investment had overwhelmed him, so deep was the debt and so impossible any way out, and still Edwin took the check when it came and paid the whole damn thing and said, "Economy? Fuck the economy!" You weren't sure how he could afford such a lavish expense, but it's clear now that this dinner was funded entirely by mortgage money from the business account, that—while it would take a few more months for him to break the news to you, to *officially* dump the properties on you and call it quits—he'd already decided *that night* to walk away from it all.

"Fuck the economy," you said to Kyle, back at 8-Ball on Thanksgiving eve, and you paid the check to set aside any doubts.

You didn't know how to tell your father about Shelley, about the big empty house you slept in every night, because your father has no rules about conversation among men. A thousand rules about the turkey, though, and about the mandatory side dishes that no one ever seems to eat, the cucumber salad Aunt Kimmy brings, the slab of cranberry, the steamed-to-soggy asparagus, the moonshine Uncle Roger brought and made you all shoot after you'd stuffed yourselves with pumpkin pie. Your father's dog lay across your feet during Thanksgiving dinner, brushed back and forth against your legs every time you walked around. "He likes you," Kyle said, and because back then you were so consumed with artifice and persona and chiseling a smile that could still fool other people, you said, "He's got good taste in friends!"

Fooling *other people*. Not your father. He wasn't buying what you were selling.

After dinner, while you smoked cigars on the back porch with Kyle and Roger, he came out and lit up, stood at the screen and didn't make eye contact with you.

"Forgot my smoking jacket!" Uncle Roger said. He wasn't joking, either. He'd found a smoking jacket at a thrift store several years back and brought it to every family holiday.

"You're all here," your father said. "That's what's important." He looked at you. "Glad to have you this year, Marc."

The previous year, you'd spent Thanksgiving with *Shelley's* family at their home in Sarasota. They were a disconnected family, the kind that spoke once every six months, the kind for whom holidays were never mandatory, never overflowing with brothers and sisters and cousins and uncles. Holidays were just days. Shelley frequently told you about how her own family, when she started one, would be different, would be a regular '80s sitcom. She hated feeling like her relatives were all strangers, but *you* didn't mind so much. After all, how could you feel guilty or sad or angry about family when you'd decided that family wasn't a big deal?

"I come when I can," you told your father. "I've got a life down in Orlando. I work my ass off."

"Roger and Sue live in North Carolina," your father said. "Kimmy lives in Alabama. Last year, she even brought your grandmother."

"If you're trying to make me feel guilty, you know why I couldn't make it last year."

"The fiancée."

"The fiancée."

"And where is she today?"

"Not here," you said.

"Nothing else to report?"

You shook your head. "Nothing that's any of your business."

Your father nodded, shrugged. "I get it, a holiday with her family. No problems there. But this is what I don't understand," he said and sucked on the cigar, removed it and let the smoke seep from his mouth and through the screen into the crisp night. "You can go to Shelley's family, but you never bring her up here?"

Kyle said, "Dad, I think he's got something to tell—"

"Kyle," you said and gave him a shut-up look. "How about this, Dad?" you said, redirecting your attention that way. "Clean the place up, and maybe I'll bring a visitor."

"Oh, it's the condition of my house, is it?"

"It's overflowing with junk," you said. "Yard looks fantastic, as always, but where the hell would we even sleep if she came up here with me? In tents? Out in those sheds? Or if we stayed inside, maybe she'd sleep on the couch while I sleep on the floor?"

"This is my house. You insult my house, you insult my whole *life*."

"Please. I've got some great houses in Orlando," you said. "I could get you and Kyle out of this town, away from the memories. Mutual benefit."

"When someone says mutual benefit," he said, "there's only one person benefits. The other only thinks he does."

"You could always stay at the hotel, with us," Roger said and winked.

"That place is a whisper from being condemned."

"Can't rough it a little?" your father asked. "Shit. All the road trips we took with the two of you way back when—"

"I can handle travel," you said. "That's not the point."

"Yeah. How much you travel last year, big guy?"

Big guy. You were the one living in a big city, the one making money, and he was up here in this fucking shack in the woods *condescending* to you.

"Atlanta, twice," you said. "Savannah, obviously, when we met up with Kyle. Chicago for the football game. New Orleans. Miami, twice. I don't know. A couple other trips."

"Well-traveled," your father said.

"I know how to pack. I know how to move from one place to the next quickly, how to coordinate with Shelley, how to work with her. It's not a matter of *roughing* it—"

"And not once. Not once you come here."

You stopped. He knew you'd turn braggart. He was leading you here all along.

"Lotta money, all that traveling," and he blew smoke again and shook his head.

"I'm here now. So let's take it easy."

•

No question that "dedication to family" was life's very foundation for both your mother and father, but they had different ideas of what that meant. For your father, it was *hard work*. For your mother, it was time spent together, engaging. "Will you sit down?" your mother always asked him. "Will you just put down that screwdriver and sit with your *family*?"

For years you fell on your mother's side of this argument, that one should appreciate one's family by spending time with them. For years, even when you'd never vocalize it, you agreed with her, just wanted the man to plop down in the living room and play some fucking dominoes. Or hell, just be home in time for dinner. It wasn't until your mother died that you began to question this.

During high school there were arguments between your parents over finances, arguments about your father's constant absences, his too-long days at the shop, days which bled to nights out drinking with the shop boys, grumbled late-night arguments about how he took *care* of his family so let him have one night, *one night* damn it, followed by a week's worth of exhausting house, garage, shed, and yard tasks that consumed his guilted life from the moment he arrived home from work until the moment he went to bed, if he ever did. One night, there was an argument between them, and then your mother was leaving the house, and then there was the car crash, and a family without a mother, and even though no one spoke of the night leading up to that crash, how could you ever again hold up this fractured ugly thing and claim it was a gift to be treasured? *Family?*

After her death, your father became a ghost.

Your senior year of high school, you saw him an average of ten minutes a day, if even. Your monthly conversations with the man could've been recorded, collected, and viewed in less time than it might take to watch an episode of *Friends*. He never left the shop. He slept there some nights. No, you don't think he was drunk; and yes, things could've been worse; he could've been destructive, abusive, could've ruined lives in the wake of your mother's accident; no, he was just…he was the cold vacuum of space, and you spent your final year in Georgia taking care of your brother, waking him up in the morning, helping him study in the evening, showing him how to conquer the tedium of the SATs and college applications, and then he took his summer job at the shop just as you were leaving town.

Your father worked and worked and worked. "One thing a man can control in life," he said, "is how hard he's willing to work." For so long you'd assumed that this sentence ended with the words "for his family," as if the *point* of all work was not just providing for a family, but *honoring* the family, that the two rules—work and family—were intertwined, symbiotic, but this work hadn't been for you or Kyle or your mother, not really. This—the long hours, the house projects, the gruff self-exhaustion—you now realized that this was something he did for *himself*.

As you readied yourself for college, you figured it out. For your father, family was just an obligation. And if that's all a family was, then *fuck it*. Why be so precious over this thing that did *nothing* for any of you?

You were angry at the very idea of family, of hard work in the name of family, furious at the both of them during that Thanksgiving night, as you nursed a bourbon on the back porch and watched your father sweat, tossing the turkey carcass into a pot of boiling water with sliced carrots and celery to make soup for the next week and ensure that no single morsel of meat would be wasted.

After the cigars, it was shots of Roger's moonshine, moon rising higher in the sky, the holiday gathering officially over, goodbyes to the family who'd traveled far and wide, Roger and Sue back to the hotel, Kimmy back to Alabama, cousin Frank and his wife Kate back to Valdosta proper, insert from the dining room table removed and slid back into its hiding spot behind the china cabinet, now just the three of you—you, your father, Kyle—collapsing onto the couch and the recliner. Your father was so intent that everything be finished tonight, every dish, every napkin, every tray, all of it restocked, extra chairs returned to the backyard shed, bathroom toilet paper replaced, trash taken out, nothing waiting until tomorrow, and it was close to midnight and you'd missed the prime time football game.

"There's more to life than work, you know," you said to him, and this was the beginning of the end.

"What's that supposed to mean?"

"I try to enjoy life."

"I enjoy life, too."

"No," you said. "You work. You're working yourself to an early damned grave is what you're doing, and then you're lecturing me about where I go, what I do with my money—"

"I didn't lecture you."

"Spent all night cleaning up, couldn't even enjoy ourselves and watch the game."

"You work hard, then you can—"

"Yes, yes. Always tomorrow. The fun always happens *tomorrow*, doesn't it?"

"You prefer debt, then?"

"It's not that I *prefer* debt. I just don't think my life has to wait until later."

"Told you a million times, it's smart to save," he said. "You see where this gets you, this lifestyle of yours."

"This lifestyle? And what's *your* lifestyle?"

"My lifestyle is I earn what I have."

"Your lifestyle is, this is the second time we've spoken today. For a man who talks so much about family, you spent more time today with the fucking turkey than you did with any of us."

"The language—"

"You're *consumed* with work," you said. "You don't know when to quit. You work because you don't know how to have real human relationships."

"Slow down, son."

"You're afraid. You say you want to see me on holidays, but it's just a formality, isn't it? You're just fucking scared of real people."

"You need to watch what—"

Throughout all of this, Kyle sat, too afraid to interject and too stunned to take another bite of the late-night slice of pumpkin pie he'd cut for himself just moments before this argument had ignited.

"Who are you to give advice?" you asked your father. "You're the reason she died."

It was the trump card you'd always kept in your back pocket but had never played. It was too terrible a thing to say, something that couldn't be unsaid, but here was your father, and here was Kyle, and here was your anger, and there was no better time to play it.

"It's your fault what happened to Mom," you said. "That night, she was *leaving* you, wasn't she? And then after she was gone, you weren't there for *us* either."

•

Still guilty over deceiving your brother for the rich pleasures of the VIP watch party, you tell Kyle you're taking the afternoon off on Friday and driving him to the Mall at Millenia. Over the ODNARLO bridge, past the crème and seafoam jewel-topped Tower of Light pagodas, through the mall's double doors and into a place that feels like you're in the very center of a diamond.

It's a slick consumerist palace, Millenia, every square inch smelling like a magazine advertisement for cologne. It's all high-end here. A Tiffany &

Co. with glass windows and a front door that looks like a bank's secret vault. Burberry and Coach and Louis Vuitton and Gucci. It's a place with spurting fountains and valet parking, where people dress up to go shopping. Encircling the mall are dozens of other shopping centers all decorated with the same audacious ultra-modern "pagoda light tower" motif: high-end furniture stores, salad restaurants, smoothie shops, a Mercedes-Benz dealership tucked next to a Best Buy. Less than fifteen minutes away is the Florida Mall, the old prize of Orlando indoor retail (complete with on-site hotel!), but the Mall at Millenia makes the Florida Mall look foolish, cheap. Another fifteen-minute drive south takes you to the outlets, to the J. Crew and Coach and Banana Republic discount stores, but the outlets are an ant colony of tourists, mostly Brazilian, swarming in and out, in and out, buying stacks of Calvin Klein button-downs and boxes of Nikes and then buying extra heavy-duty suitcases *right there* and stuffing and packing away all this booty just fifteen feet from the Oakley Vault, where they'll stop in to grab some new sunglasses for their beach trip tomorrow. The traffic to get into the parking lots at the Outlets is enough to make you swear off ever going back. Mall at Millenia is the only option. It makes you feel wealthy. It trumpets pride in appearance, makes you forget about failure.

You tell your brother not to gawk at the women wearing tight black pants and low-cut black shirts who smile and urge you to smell the cologne that— here, one little puff—will make you irresistible, give you superpowers tonight.

"Ignore that, too," you tell him as you pass the shirtless male models standing in the entryway of Abercrombie.

"The fuck?" he says. This is a different world for him.

You punch him in the arm when he stares too long at a Brazilian woman leaning against a wall. She's wearing the brightest fluorescent green pants you've ever seen, maybe the tightest too, has the most tanned and toned mid-section you've ever seen, and she's got all the right bags dangling from her fingers, but her boyfriend is likely within twenty feet, maybe at Tommy Bahama or something, and the last thing you want is to peel your brother's punched-flat carcass from the floor. "Move along," you say. "Move along."

"I just want to—"

"Listen to me. We go where *I* say today. I'm, like, your tour guide."

At Banana Republic, you pull three belts off the rack, four pairs of pants in various shades from caramel to stone, even more shirts, and pile them into Kyle's arms. When a wandering sales associate approaches, you tell the man to open a changing room post-haste. Kyle barely says a word, just waits for your direction. "Let me see those pants," you say and he emerges from the changing room, walking like a twelve-year-old boy forced into church clothes. "Okay, we'll also try heather-gray," you say to the associate, and Kyle says, "Aw fuck," and walks back to try on more.

At Macy's you get him measured for a new suit.

At Starbucks you get him a travel coffee mug.

At the Sunglass Hut you spend two hundred bucks on a pair of Ray-Ban aviators. "No more Oakleys," you say. "Hey. Listen, wandering eyes. No more sunglasses with a strap or lanyard or whatever."

"But I like—"

"We're not in Georgia," you say. "When you go out to the lake, or you go mudding, you wear the Oakleys. When you go out to downtown Orlando, you wear what I tell you."

"Ooo-wheee! Victoria's Secret!" he says and slows to peer in.

"Come on. Have you really never seen one of these?"

He shrugs and chuckles, and you realize: my God, he *hasn't*.

And then it's Express, and Kyle shakes his head and holds up boxer shorts with fake kisses across the crotch. "Seriously?" he says. "What self-respecting man would wear these?"

"Can I help you?" an associate says from behind him, a who-the-hell-is-*this*-clown? look on his face.

You close your eyes, rub them. This is like a scene from *Encino Man* or something, the Neanderthal brought into the twenty-first century. "We've been looking for some heather-gray pants for him," you say.

"Why is my waist size different at all these places?" he asks.

And, "This shirt just doesn't *feel* right."

And, "This is, like, totally not my style."

"You don't *have* a style," you say eventually. "*That* is why we're here. Can you just *stay quiet* and let me handle it?"

By the time you leave the mall it's Friday evening, but Kyle looks downtown-appropriate. "You have graduated, come of age," you tell him. "Still need to work on your hair, but you can definitely fit in."

"Downtown." He jabs you in the ribs. "And here I thought you were getting old on me, bro. Been wanting to go downtown ever since I got here."

The Magic are playing tonight, Game Two versus LeBron James and the Cleveland Cavaliers, so you tell him you'll be going to the block party that is Wall Street. Jimmy wasn't able to score tickets, so he's watching the game with you, the way ordinary folk do. "They put the game on a projection screen outside," you tell your brother. "A lot of rowdy fans."

"Love me some rowdiness," Kyle says.

"That shirt looks good on you. I'm not joking about that."

"Feels funny. Too soft." He pulls at the bottom, grimaces.

"Own it," you say. "Own your look. Nobody looks good when they're uncomfortable."

You feel terrible judging your brother, but those feelings are diminished by the glow you feel from having helped him. A whole new wardrobe? You've changed his life!

And surprisingly, you're now excited to immerse your brother into the city life. Oh no, this isn't Chicago, nor is it Los Angeles or New York or Miami, all places that you visited with Shelley or Edwin or Jimmy, either for a weekend mini-vacation or for a Bucs road game. But it does have a personality all its own. "Orlando on game night," you tell your brother. "This city…people give us a hard time about not having a real culture. I'll show you the real Orlando."

"Sweet," Kyle says. "I want to get hammered tonight."

You sigh. "Play it cool. Don't go overboard."

"We hanging out with your friends?"

"Jimmy, Steven, Anderson, maybe a couple others. You haven't met them."

"I remember a few from the frat house," he says.

"All the way back then?"

"Your girlfriend gonna be there?"

"Girlfriend?"

"The date you had on Wednesday?"

You almost say "what date?" but catch yourself. "No, no. I don't, um, think that's going to work out."

"Bummer. Was she hot?"

Change the subject. "Are you wearing that hat tonight?"

He removes it to reveal terrible hair, a broom mashed into the floor.

"Oh God, put it back on," you say.

A night at the bars that line Wall Street and Orange Avenue: you've spent a decade learning how to fit in, making fun of the tourists who wander from their edge-of-the-city resorts and into downtown Orlando. Your favorite days are the ones surrounding New Year's, when visiting Michigan State and Wisconsin fans flood the bars after the Citrus Bowl, only to discover themselves dramatically under-dressed, winter-pale among still-tanned-in-January Floridians, or (worse) sunburnt from a single 75-degree afternoon at the stadium.

"So where are we going?" Kyle asks.

"Orange Avenue," you say, because saying "Wall Street" would confuse Kyle.

In the daytime, Orange Avenue—and all of downtown—is bankers and lawyers and city administrators. At one end of the strip is the towering Orange County Courthouse, in the middle are the high-rise Bank of America and SunTrust Buildings, and at the southern end is City Hall. When the clock strikes five, the streets flash into happy hour crowds, and then—when rush hour fades and there's no lingering workday headache—Orange Avenue is overtaken by button-down zip-up flesh-pack late-nighters.

There are a scattering of restaurants, most of them on Church Street, the downtown's old tourist sector that has since struggled to assert itself as anything more than a curiosity. For most of the early 2000s, it felt like a shut-down theme park, places like Terror on Church Street and Howl at the Moon closing one after the next, but the bars and clubs—Chillers and Latitudes and

Antigua—mostly survived, and the restaurants—Ceviche, Hamburger Mary's, Kres—kept enough of a "destination dining" vibe to keep ticking. But really, when you think "Downtown Orlando," you don't think "restaurants," you think perfume, cologne, hair wax, sparkling jewelry dangling between fake boobs; you think of your early twenties, of those pedicabs, of packs of *whoo!*-girls hauling their drunk friend out of One Eyed Jack's; you think of Semisonic's "Closing Time," and security guards screaming at the 2AM crowd to "get the fuck *out!*" And you think of late-night pizza curling away from your mouth as you try to bite it, pepperoni falling onto your shirt; you think of Miller Lites pulled from beer tubs, Jack and Cokes made by bartenders who can barely hear you and who sift through three dozen credit cards when you tell them to put it on your tab; you think of a hundred different girls looking past you as they talk, and you looking past *them* to the next girl as they talk, everyone's gaze wandering to the next slip of flesh, flex of bicep; you think of Shelley working the beer tub outside Slingapour's when she was still in college, and— back then, before you were dating—you'd always buy your drinks from her no matter how long the line, just so you could smile and make a stupid joke. Most of all, you think of your brother, who is unprepared for the grotesquery of it all, the toxic cloud of performance that is Orange Avenue and Wall Street. You worry that *he* will be a mark tonight; you worry that you'll lose track of him, or that he'll be overwhelmed, drunk by 8 PM, dancing on the bar or puking on the sidewalk or some other such nonsense. And then, well, *We are all witnesses*, as they say, and Orlando is not so big a city that embarrassment at the bars cannot follow you like the stink of the Skunk Ape.

ROOT ROOT ROOT FOR THE HOME TEAM!

AND REMEMBER: IT'S JUST A GAME,
AND GAMES SHOULD BE FUN!

You live north of Orlando, in a city called Maitland that a striking number of residents lump in with Orlando (while an equally vocal number make great efforts to assert is *not* Orlando), and getting downtown to the raucous bars of Orange Avenue requires that you shoot *south* on I-4 *West*. Technically, I-4 runs from Tampa on the Gulf Coast to Daytona Beach on the Atlantic coast, which makes it an even-numbered, east-west interstate. But Daytona sits at least sixty miles north of Tampa, and so the interstate slants diagonally across the state and often goes pure north-south, especially as it barrels through downtown Orlando, bisecting the 408 East-West Expressway so perfectly that the very heart of the city is a tangle of roads with names that do not mean what they should.

Driving south into Orlando on I-4 reveals the skyline first as a packed-together community of high-rise glass and steel and concrete, the teal pyramids atop the SunTrust Building seeming to appear directly next door to the rounded roof of the courthouse and the needle-spires and blue-steel setbacks of the Bank of America building. This is because the buildings all sit along Orange Avenue, and when you're driving directly south you're basically staring *straight down* Orange. But as you round a curve and the highway goes east-west for a stretch called the Fairbanks Curve, the skyscrapers drift apart block by block and downtown separates from itself. Yet another Orlando illusion.

"Remember when we were kids, coming down to Disney," Kyle says, "and you always wanted Dad to go through downtown so you could see the buildings."

"I liked skyscrapers. I was fascinated."

"'What the hell's in downtown?' he always said. God, you got so pissed. You wanted to see the basketball arena, too. 'Just concrete,' he said. 'Ain't like you're seeing the court.'"

"This is funny to you, my childhood dreams snuffed out."

"Still picture your whiny-ass face."

"He never once drove us into downtown," you say. "Always the damn Turnpike, skirting the city. 'Ain't dealing with that traffic.'" (Your impression of your father is vastly superior to your brother's, but who's competing?)

"Can you blame him?"

"Everyone drives the Turnpike when they come down to Disney. On a daily basis, do you know how many cars avoid this city?"

"Holy shit!" Kyle shrieks, as two cars—right lane and left lane—simultaneously cut you off and nearly smash into one another. "That shit right there, that's why!"

"Turnpike is just as busy, just as assholey," you say. "That's all I'm saying."

"I rescind my offer to drive you home tonight. Not on this damn road. We should take the subway or the el or something."

"There's none of that in this town. You know that."

If all goes well tonight, though, maybe you and Kyle *will* be out every weekend together, each of you trading off on nights as designated driver, or taking turns covering the bar tab, or double-dating, or…well, you've updated his wardrobe, but he's still a redneck of the highest order, so let's not get ahead of ourselves.

The thing is, there are rules for how to behave in the downtown bar scene. This is a place where *your father's* rules do not apply. He wouldn't even drive through the city, so you know he'd never *live* in the city, and even if he did, he damn sure wouldn't go to downtown bars. Such an experience would send him into another cardiac arrest. No no, *your* rules win out tonight; they hang in the back of your mind like a breakroom poster:

- Always pretend to be positive while bar-hopping. Laugh too loud, so that the people around you know you're having a better time than they are. Always strive to look like you're in a Budweiser commercial.

- Move in a pack, call your friends "your boys," and search for women who refer to their friends as "the girls" and who likewise travel in packs, ideally with membership exactly equal to yours.

- If left behind (i.e. your boys move on to the next bar), pretend it was purposeful, even while you frantically call and text to figure out where your boys have gone.

- Pace yourself: do not take jell-o shots from the girl in the pink cowboy hat unless you've met a girl who *really really* wants this, and thus taking the shot gives you…well, a shot. Drink beer, or Jack and Coke. Make it until the end of the night without deteriorating into a mess.

- Because there are only a handful of bathrooms throughout Wall Street, hold your bladder so that you only have to piss two times throughout the night, *tops*; standing in line for bathrooms is not a pleasant way to spend your night, nor is the inevitable moment when you find yourself pissing into a toilet or sink with three other dudes because you've all waited so fucking long to pee and you've decided to expedite the process.

- Always accommodate bachelorette parties, those packs of girls wearing pink boas, their bride-to-be leader wearing some sort of sandwich-board-style checklist (Kiss a Boy Named Sue, Take a Shot

That Scares You, etc.). If they need your underwear, or need a picture of you shirtless, or need you to arm-wrestle the largest girl in the pack, consider this rule a law: *do it.*

- Do not *stare* at the hot girls, even though they'll be dressed like strippers and will want nothing more than to be stared at (provided the stare traces back to an attractive man, of course). Constantly look around, noting where the hottest girls are so you can sneak quick glances to the locations that matter. It's a tricky business. Looking at your cell phone, but holding it out as if searching for service, so that the phone is eye level with a hot girl's ass: good strategy.

These are, of course, not things you can articulate without sounding like a jackass or a pervert, so when you first arrive on Orange Avenue and Kyle says, "Damn, that girl is fucking *smoking!*" as if he's watching TV and the actress cannot hear him, you say, "Easy, tiger. She's ten feet away."

"You see that dress? *Holy shit.*"

"I see it."

"There's girls everywhere."

"Yes. Yes, there are."

It's going to be a long night.

Kyle follows your lead past the colorful clock-adorned archway and into the brick-paved outdoor courtyard of Wall Street. Soon you're both holding Miller Lites, standing in the center of a thick crowd thirty feet from the projection screen where the Magic pre-game show is starting.

At one point, maybe Wall Street was a real street, something no-doubt financial, cars bouncing over the pavers, real businesses in the bottom floors of the 1920s and '30s red-brick high-rises, but who really knows or cares about the history of Orlando? Even for residents, the city is a theme park, with Wall Street as the manufactured "downtown city street" attraction, so meticulously detailed that maybe you'll actually feel like you're in a real downtown. Twenty minutes south of here, at Disney World's Epcot Center, you can wander from Fake Mexico to Fake Britain, switching margaritas for Guinness pints. No different here. Everywhere is crafted for your amusement. On Wall Street the bottom floors of the old brick buildings are occupied by bars: One-Eyed Jacks, Loaded Hog, Wall Street Cantina on Orange Avenue on the west; Slingapour's, the Globe, and Monkey Bar on Court Avenue on the east. Much like the name "Wall Street," the name "Court Avenue" no longer carries any meaning: at one time, it was the original address of the Orange County Courthouse, but that structure was decades ago converted into the History Center. It's visible beyond the barricades of the Wall Street block party, though of minimal interest as it serves no alcohol.

It's a humid night, so muggy it seems you have only two options to make the outdoors bearable: jump into water, or consume as much liquid as possible. Kyle, within five minutes of arrival, has nearly finished his first beer.

"Slow down, Kyle. Got a whole game to watch, and beers ain't cheap."

"I told you," he says. "I want to get hammered. I'm a notary now! We're in *business* together, bro!"

It's going to be a long night.

"Those bars air-conditioned?"

"We've been out here for ten minutes. I thought you were tougher than that, Kyle."

"It's these clothes. These jeans are so thick. You wear this shit outside?"

"You don't go into battle without armor," you say.

"Armor? Shit, man, who we fighting? Who cares what we look like?"

Who? The girls, first and foremost, the ones out of your league but also the ones with whom you have a chance, and their friends, because one must often impress a full cheer-squad of friends to…ah, fuck it, too much to explain. Let the answer reveal itself in time. "Follow me," you say and lead him inside.

On the TV bolted above the bar inside One Eyed Jack's there's a looping replay of Rashard Lewis' shot to win Game One, then the disastrous look on the faces of Cleveland fans: they wear shirts that say "We are all Witnesses," but they didn't expect that they might witness a defeat on their home floor to the Orlando Magic. The TV replays the final-second reaction of Mo Williams, Cavaliers point guard, his expression a case study of disappointment and soul-wrenching betrayal, like someone stole the victory that was rightfully his. The Cavs are the favorites to win the 2009 NBA Championship, of course. This is supposed to be *their* year, LeBron's year. Next on the TV is LeBron James talking at his press conference about how Cleveland can still win the next four in a row and end the Orlando Magic's season. You watch the interview, and you believe him. It's *King James*, after all, the biggest sports superstar since Michael Jordan, a man seemingly molded of strength and confidence.

"Do they serve food in here?" Kyle asks.

"No, Kyle," you say. "At night, the bars are *bars*. Just drinks."

"But they have menus. I see them on the tables."

"Nobody orders food at Wall Street. It's, like, a *rule*. We'll get street meat or pizza or something afterward."

"How can you watch a basketball game without eating wings?"

"Kyle, you've got to trust me. Look around you. Every ten seconds, someone's bumping into you. Do you really want to hold onto a basket of greasy wings?"

From here inside One Eyed Jack's, you can see the fans crowding the Wall Street entrance. It's a long line now that the sun has set, packs of graduated frat stars who rent giant houses together in the nearby neighborhoods; packs of graduated sorority girls made over in sparkling sexy Magic gear, extra-long jerseys cut up and repurposed as shirt/skirts; packs of young professionals fresh from work, coats discarded, blue ties as headbands. "We don't have a waitress," you say. "We don't have a table. I don't even think they have silverware or napkins. Are those conditions really conducive to eating wings?"

"All right, all right," Kyle says. "I'm out of beer, though."

"Holy shit, did you spring a leak?" you say. This is going to be a long, long night.

A couple Cleveland fans stand at the bar, loud and crude, pointing at one another and taking every opportunity to flex while talking, conspiratorially checking out the short-skirted servers as they walk past, somehow looking both jovial and wound up, eyes wide as if ready to crack into 'roid rage, hands so tight around beer bottles you expect the glass to shatter and the guys to simply keep drinking from jagged necks, maybe bite and swallow the broken shards. They don't look like Clevelanders. They look like Jersey Shore, or maybe South Beach rejects. One sits on a stool, a LeBron jersey stretched tight over his well-muscled frame. Shaved head, goatee. The other stands beside him with arms crossed like a bouncer. They're watching one of the TVs overhead, a SportsCenter clip of previous Magic-Cavs matchups. Dwight Howard frustrated at the free-throw line, having just missed a key shot. One of the Cavs fans laughs, points at the screen and says, "Fucking fraud!" A few feet away, a scrawny guy in a Magic jersey says, "Dude, shut up." The Cavs fan lunges as if to throw a punch, and the Magic fan ducks and covers. "Pussy," the Cavs fan says as the Magic fan retreats, humiliated.

You'd like to keep watching this shit-show, but a moment later, you spot your good friend Jimmy Bastion wandering into One-Eyed Jack's. You wave him over, but he's got some sort of radar that allows him to always find a friend, so he was already on his way.

"What's going on, big guy?" Jimmy says, slaps your back. Leaves his hand there, like he wants you to know how awesome he thinks you are (he does this to everyone, very much like a politician or a rush chairman, but somehow you still smile each time and revel in the self-esteem boost that comes from perceived awesomeness).

"Where's Sandra tonight?" you ask Jimmy.

He shrugs. "Spending my money. I don't know."

"It's a Friday night, and you have no clue where she's at?"

"I'll see her at home," Jimmy says. "Or not, if I'm lucky."

"How can anyone get married with so many girls around?" your brother asks. A brunette in white shorts brushes past, the frayed cut so far north that two-thirds of her bare ass is exposed: you look away instinctively, knowing that you're allowed only a split-second glance, but Kyle stares dangerously, like a child who's just spied the sun for the first time.

You slap the back of his head. "Not so obvious. Calm down."

But no one noticed the gawking. The tide of the block party is still rising around you both.

"This is my brother Kyle," you say to Jimmy. And here it is, the first of many nervous moments of the night, introducing your family to your friends.

"Kyle, huh," Jimmy says.

"Kyle," Kyle says.

"Didn't know you had a brother."

"I do," you say. "He lives in Georgia, so…"

"We actually met a couple years ago, when I was in town." Kyle stands with his hands on his hips, and you can't tell whether he's standoffish at your friend, or if he's upset at you. The new clothes, the constant talk about the "rules of downtown," have you gone too far? When you reprimanded him about gawking at girls, was this a hint of the Old You coming out, the bad brother? For the first time, you realize this night could be disastrous not just for your relationship with your friends, but also for the relationship with your brother that is in such need of repair.

"Georgia, huh?" Jimmy asks your brother.

"Near Valdosta."

"Is that, like, *Deliverance* country?"

"Um," Kyle says.

"Sorry if that was indelicate," Jimmy says. "Allow me to rephrase. What I mean is, is that the geographic territory wherein cousin-fucking is socially acceptable?"

You cough, a mist of Miller Lite projecting from your mouth. "We grew up there," you interject. "It's like any of these Central Florida towns. Damn, Jimmy." And now your trepidation has taken a 180, and you want to warn *Kyle* about *Jimmy*, offer pointers about how to handle your abrasive friend.

"I don't buy into political correctness," Jimmy says.

"I see that," Kyle says.

"It's the charm in me. I say what's on my mind. No filter."

"Well, sometimes a filter is a good—"

"Cousin-fucking off-limits. Got it. But you eat raccoons and squirrels?"

"Not…lately."

"And you've got like ten guns?"

"My Dad has—"

"And you *definitely* hate black people up there, right?"

"No, I—"

"Sorry, sorry, I was being too PC again. I mean, you hate—"

"No!" Kyle says.

"Lotta meth, though, right? Fucking Georgia people love meth."

"Why does everyone think—"

"Oh, and the gays, you *really* hate the gays." Jimmy pauses. "That wasn't a question."

"Listen, I think you're a little off-base about life in the true South—"

"You go *muddin*?" Jimmy says "muddin'" as if it's in quotation marks, as if the word would never pass unsarcastically from his own lips. "Big fucking trucks, big fucking tires."

"On occasion, yeah, I—"

"I'll be honest. That shit gives me a boner. You drink Budweiser, the classic red label?"

Kyle exhales, shrugs. "This is America." He's given up trying to fight.

"All right then, brother," Jimmy says, "you're all right with me. Come here, you!" He puts your brother in a headlock, gives him a noogie, and this scene—the two of them laughing and wrestling and pushing—feels almost familial. How was it possible for this to happen so quickly, Jimmy to go from villain to jolly good fellow, and to insert himself into a scene that looks more like sibling horseplay than any moment you've thus far had with Kyle?

"Break it up, you two." You pull on limbs and torsos and free your brother from Jimmy's embrace.

"You been in Orlando two weeks," Jimmy says, "and this is the first you've brought him downtown?"

You take a sip of your beer and make a "so what?" face.

"Why didn't he come to Ember with us?"

"Ember?" Kyle asks. "When was that?"

"He was busy," you say quickly. "He's been…doing a lot of work for me."

"You're a bad brother," Jimmy says and makes a tsk-tsk motion with his finger, then reaches around your shoulder and traps *you* in a headlock. "A bad, bad brother," he whispers. "I mean, how could you deprive little-man of—" and Jimmy tugs you this way and that, searches the crowd, and you think he's going to talk further about the VIP watch party, the free top-shelf vodka, but he spots a girl wearing a black shirt that, were she to bend over to pick up a straw, would expose things men would pay to see—"*that*," Jimmy finishes and points. (He, of course, does not pay attention to Downtown Rules regarding oversexed rubbernecking. Jimmy pays attention to Jimmy Rules, and you're often surprised that this has allowed him to remain among the living.)

"I, uh…" you start. Do you tell him the truth, that you've been hiding your brother, that dedication to family is a rule only followed when it doesn't embarrass you? But then, mercifully, you see Anderson and Steven traipsing into Wall Street, a quick stroll from their Lake Eola condo, both of them looking freshly showered and stepping with the sort of pre-game joy and positivity that you simply can't muster. You tap Jimmy's forearm. "Let's go back outside, we've got company," you say, and Jimmy lets you free but gives you a good-natured push toward the door.

Seconds later you're all three once again swimming in the humidity, sloshing through the crowd to greet the new arrivals. Anderson slaps hands with you and Jimmy, always quick to exert his Hulk-strong handshake. You elbow Kyle and say "Shake hands with him," and though you want to say more, want to tell him to look as joyful as an extra in a beer commercial (it's a *rule*, Kyle), you swallow the comments and let the introductions happen as they do.

Steven performs an ironic bow. He's wearing a vintage Penny Hardaway shirt from the mid-'90s: a graffiti-style "ORLANDO" at the top and a cloud of blue at the center, from which a cartoon Anfernee Hardaway leaps—poised to dunk—over a big-headed Little Penny. Only Steven could find a shirt like this, and only Steven would think to pair it with seersucker shorts and tall black-and-blue striped socks. "Are you gentlemen excited?"

"Are you trying to grow a fucking beard?" Jimmy asks, backing away from Steven.

"I was thinking…just started it a couple weeks ago, and—"

"That little bit of testicle fuzz is *a couple weeks* old?" Jimmy shakes his head. "You're way too desperate to be a hipster, my man."

"I'm not a—" Steven starts, but knows the futility of arguing with Jimmy, and stops. "I've got to shave it for the wedding anyway. It's just an experiment."

"Take it back to the lab, brother," Jimmy says. "Put that shit out of its misery."

You lean to your brother and say in a low voice: "Steven is our creative friend. Graphic designer. His fiancée restores furniture, interior design, something like that. He's a bit of an Orlando freak, too. Whatever you do, don't ask him if he knows any good places to go. It gets irritating."

"Good places to go for what?" Kyle asks.

"Anything. He's like an archive of internet list articles. Here are the ten best coffee shops. Here are the ten best places to read a book outdoors. Here's the best three places to buy, I don't know, unicycles. He was normal back in college, but somewhere along the line, he went hipster."

"Feeling good about tonight, gentlemen, feeling really good," Anderson says and intertwines his fingers behind his head, massive biceps popping as he does so. It's his usual stance, a not-too-subtle performance to showcase his physique.

"Damn," Kyle says. "Dude looks like the Rock."

"Don't encourage him," you say. "Anderson's ego doesn't need a boost."

Anderson relishes his role as the *thick friend*, the guy with granite boulders beneath his skin, with GNC buckets throughout his condo, stacks of bodybuilding magazines in his bathroom. In college he carried a gallon water jug wherever he went, always smelled like tuna or peanut butter, and without fail carved out eight solid hours of uninterrupted sleep each night, and while there were steroids rumors, and strange stories about Anderson experimenting with GHB ("Just a bottlecap will get you effed up, and zero calories consumed!" he once joked), you found it difficult to believe that a man so disciplined could ever take health-risk shortcuts. Now, he's 28 years old, still gigantic, and—unlike so many of you—still making money. Or claims to be.

"What do you do?" Anderson asks your brother.

"What do I *do?*" Kyle says.

Anderson looks at you like *is this guy for real?* "Like, *work*. Where do you work?"

"Oh," Kyle says. "I work with my brother."

"This loser? Want *real* work, let me know," Anderson says. "Lot of inventory to move." Anderson works in timeshares, a market that has admittedly slowed, but—even while he mocks those who buy the timeshares—he's so far refused to acknowledge that *he* could be in the same trouble as all the real estate agents and mortgage brokers and house-flippers caught in the bubble-burst. Perhaps because his superiors are afraid of him, he's been promoted so far up the company ladder that his paycheck is no longer dependent upon sales commission and upon persuading someone without money to take out a loan and buy a shared vacation home.

Anderson turns his attention to Jimmy. "Where's that wife of yours?"

"Taking it up the butt from Rondo, for all I know," Jimmy says. When Anderson's around, Jimmy grows even more vulgar. It's become sport: how far can he go before Anderson tells him to watch his language? Anderson, large and destructive as he looks, is the opposite, says "*eff* this" and "*eff* that," rarely swears. You're not sure if he finds the language offensive, or if it's just a show of discipline: look at how controlled I am with my language, how controlled I am with every aspect of my body.

"Damn," Kyle says again. To you: "That's a little much."

"That's just Jimmy's way," you whisper. "He's a piece of shit, but he's *our* piece of shit. You just have to roll with it."

"Why do you have to *have* a piece of shit?" Kyle asks, a question to which you find it extremely difficult to find an answer.

Meanwhile, Steven is saying "You know, Sandra *is* your wife, Jimmy. The way you talk about her sometimes…"

Jimmy shakes his head. "Oh Steven, are you getting nervous?"

"Nervous?"

"That you're not going to have a lifetime of marital bliss? When Elaina makes you shave that pussy beard of yours, I guarantee it won't be the last concession you make."

You explain to Kyle that Steven's getting married soon, and after the wedding will be moving out of the shared bachelor-pad condo to live with his wife. "We used to go out with them a lot, me and Shelley," you say. When Steven announced his engagement, in fact, you remember Shelley saying, "Oh yay! Another couple!" as if the world was one giant continent slowly separating into married and unmarried islands.

"How's the wedding planning going?" you ask Steven.

"Same bullshit, different day. I mean, you know what I'm talking about."

"Not anymore, I don't," you say.

"Shit, that's not what I meant." He winces, shrinks into himself. "Wedding planning is fine. Just finalized the menu at the History Center. We're going to have an espresso bar at the end of the night."

"My man here," Anderson says, slapping Steven on the back, "such a cultural advocate. Wedding at the effin' History Center!"

"Trying to make us all learn, even on your wedding night?" Jimmy shakes his head. "Weddings are for two things, pal. Drinking, and fu—"

"Any news on Jameer?" you ask quickly, desperate to staunch the flow of expletives from Jimmy and preserve for your brother some hope that you are a decent person who surrounds himself with other decent people, and so you point to the TV where the pre-game show loops a clip of Jameer Nelson threading the ball through a defender's legs to Rashard Lewis, who scoops the ball without looking and delivers it to the basket, a move so unthinkingly quick and organic it could only have been born of countless hours of shared practice.

On the sides of buildings across downtown are Magic banners, a ten-foot-tall Hedo Türkoğlu unfurled on the brick building to your left. The beer tub girls are wearing baby-sized Magic jerseys, the fabric tight over their breasts, their full flat stomachs exposed. They reach into the beer tubs and it's as if they know how to let the beer bottles drip melted ice *just right*, water splashing skin, belly buttons—

God, *look away*! Look away, pervert! That was *twelve seconds* of staring.

"No news," says Anderson, scrolling through his iPhone, reading player reports. "Van Gundy still playing Rafer Alston at point. Jameer still out. Let's hope Rafer doesn't do something stupid and get suspended again."

"Rafer, so fucking inconsistent," Jimmy says. "Fuck fuck fuck, fuck fuck."

Kyle leans into you: "That sentence was all fucks."

You throw up your hands. It's impossible. There's no conversational topic that will transform Jimmy into someone more decent. But still, Jimmy now has his arm wrapped around your shoulder, is holding up his beer bottle to give you cheers, is pinching your cheek until you smile. How is it possible to be mad at a man so jolly, a man whose vulgarity—once it passes—seems not to have happened?

"You follow the Magic?" Anderson asks your brother. "Wait. You're from Georgia. Hawks fan?"

You open your mouth, ready to answer the question, but Kyle beats you to it.

"No one is a Hawks fan," Kyle says. "Come on."

"Joe Johnson, right?" Anderson says. "And Josh Smith? What do they call the Hawks? The Human Highlight Factory or something?"

"Nobody says that," Kyle says. "Kobe Bryant jerseys outsell Hawks jerseys in Atlanta."

"Kobe's a popular dude."

"In the *arena*. In Atlanta's own stadium."

"Hmm," Anderson says. "Not the best business model."

"Anyway, we're not exactly close to Atlanta."

"We were raised as University of Georgia fans," you say. "Dad cared more about the college teams than the pros. We always watched Magic games, but if we would've cheered for Auburn or LSU, his head would've exploded."

"Georgia Bulldogs," Anderson says, looking your brother up and down, upper lip curled in a way that you can't tell whether it's good humor or disgust. "You know what they say: if you ain't a Gator, you're Gator Bait."

"It's been a rough couple of years, for sure," Kyle says, takes a swig of his Miller Lite.

"We sure we want to be talking Florida-Georgia?" you ask. "We just met, guys. This is a sensitive—"

"Ready for another spanking from my man Tebow this season?" Anderson asks.

At the mention of Tebow, there's a decided darkening of Kyle's energetic youth-group face. There's only so much that one man can take, and Kyle might be approaching his breaking point. (To be fair, of course, Tim Tebow is the breaking point for the vast majority of sports fans, a system error crippling thousands of once-civil conversations.)

"Georgia Bulldogs. Jaw-ja Bool-dogs," Anderson says in his best mock-Southern voice. He takes the bill of his cap in one hand and squeezes it for a more violent curve. "You go to school there? U-G-A."

"Just a fan," Kyle says. "Bulldog born, Bulldog bred."

"And when you die, you'll be Bulldog dead." Anderson nods. "But you didn't go to school there."

The college question. You didn't want this. Not here, not downtown, not with a drink in your hand. You wanted good times tonight, not a reminder of your greatest failure as a big brother.

"So where'd you go to college?" Anderson asks.

"I didn't."

"*What?*" Anderson says, as if your brother has revealed himself to be a lizard person. "Need a degree to get ahead, my friend."

"I started. Just didn't finish. Wasn't for me."

"Marc didn't go to UGA, either," Anderson says to Kyle, then motions to you with his chin. "In fact, I've never seen him wear Georgia colors in my life. Didn't even know he came from a family of Bulldogs."

"I gave it up when I started school in Florida," you say. "Embraced my new state."

"The things I don't know about you," Anderson says. "The things you never tell anyone." Anderson turns back to your brother. "That's the problem with Georgia fans, see. Everybody in that state is a pretender, high school dropouts buying Bulldogs shirts at Wal-Mart and then talking trash to Florida grads."

"Florida grads. Where'd *you* go to school?" Kyle asks, with more indignation in his voice than you would have advised.

Anderson spits. For someone who chews neither tobacco nor sunflower seeds, Anderson is (strangely) always spitting. "UCF." Takes a sip of Mich Ultra, shrugs. "Family lives in Orlando. Had to stay local."

"So you're no different?"

Anderson doesn't answer. And you worry there will be a confrontation, that Kyle has taken offense to the college conversation, that he was made to feel small and stupid and inconsequential and that there will be an argument of the sort that drags on everyone's moods for the whole night, but they're laughing together now, the two of them, each extolling the virtues or decrying the failures of his own head coach, quarterback, running back, defense, Urban Meyer and Mark Richt and Matt Stafford and Tim Tebow and Percy Harvin, and it happened *that quick*, and how is it that *others* can embrace your brother without reservation while you question him so relentlessly that you're only satisfied if his actions mirror your own?

And, just as unsettling, how is it that others can bond over sports but *you* only grow angry? Case in point—even as new friendships are being forged mere inches from where you stand, your gaze wanders to the inside bar, to the musclebound Cavs fans who stand behind their empty barstools, arms pressed onto the seats as if claiming them. There are only a handful of seats, and yet these two bozos are hoarding stools…only to *not* use them? One of them shouts at the television, shouts and punches the air so violently you expect to hear a crashing noise, air shattered like glass; you see his spittle fly, too, hard drops of it launched into the bar, and this makes you angrier. *His* spittle on *your* hometown bar. *His* words polluting *your* Florida air as he shouts "You fuckin' suck!" at Dwight Howard on the screen.

When the pregame show transitions to a clip of Anderson Varejo, power forward for the Cleveland Cavaliers, the two meatheads clap. The one with what appears to be the Monster Energy logo tattooed on his upper arm repeatedly slams his glass onto the bar with such force that it actually causes a tsunami in a girl's Cosmo three stools away, pink liquid rolling over the lip of her glass.

Farther back inside the bar, in the darkness that you cannot see from out here on the patio, there are even more Cavaliers fans cheering, too, more LeBron jerseys, a Mo Williams jersey, a Delonte West jersey; a few Magic fans look their way, perhaps annoyed, but no one answers the challenge and screams "Boo!" or "Go Magic!" What the hell is wrong with your hometown? You want a coordinated Magic cheer, loud support. You want Anderson to crunch his ballcap's bill and boom "*Shoooosh*" in his deepest dead-lift voice.

Your father. He wouldn't stand for this sort of invasion, would he? He'd walk up to the Cavs fans, tell them to *watch their language*, that this isn't their home, they are visitors, *guests* in Orlando. *You do not behave this way in my house!* Or maybe he'd rally others to a "Let's go, Magic!" chant. Or maybe he'd avoid violence and take the "Don't sweat the small stuff" route. For God's sake, it's tough to figure out what he'd do, which rule matters most, which ones contradict others…

These Cleveland fans, why are they *here*? Until LeBron came along, you don't recall *ever* seeing a Cavaliers jersey in a bar in Orlando. And worse, these guys look like South Beach transplants, not Midwesterners: dark tanned skin that could be Italian or Hispanic, bodies sculpted from three-hour gym days, linen pants. Sunglasses at night. (And oh, how you hate grown men who wear sunglasses at night.) When did *Cleveland* become an All-American team? Why are *they* able to get away with this sort of thing here? This is why your city has a reputation for being soft.

"How much you wanna bet those guys aren't from Cleveland?" you ask.

Anderson drinks from his Mich Ultra, inspects. "They have nice tans, so probably not."

"What does someone from *Cleveland* look like?" Jimmy asks. "Pale? Broke? Covered in rust and regret?"

"It's Cleveland," you say. "Not Soviet Russia."

"In any case, they were smart to move here," Steven says.

"Oh no," Anderson says. "Here it comes."

"Though I do wonder," Steven continues, "how they can come here— downtown Orlando—and look around, and seriously still feel good about wherever they're from? I mean, it's no accident that we're the most-visited city in the country. You guys know that, right? *Most visited*. When people have a choice of where they want to go—" Steven, ever the hometown champion, goes on for a while, reciting travel statistics, a new Top 10 Unexpected Things to Do in Orlando list that just appeared in *USA Today*—

"Okay," you interrupt, "how much you wanna bet they've never even *been* to Cleveland?"

"What's it matter?" Anderson asks.

"They're wearing Cavs jerseys. Isn't it a little pathetic to paste Cleveland shit all over your body, but you never cheered for the team before the world's biggest superstar got there?"

"People cheer for winners," Kyle says. "It's why nobody cares about the Hawks."

"Those guys look very South Florida," you say. "They should be Miami Heat fans."

"Probably were, when they won the championship," Steven says. "Then Shaq left. They moved from one bandwagon to the next."

"That's what I'm saying," you say. "Support the *hometown* team. Don't jump ship at the first sign of struggle."

"You sound like Dad," Kyle says.

"I hear you," Steven says. "I'm with you."

"So what happens when LeBron leaves Cleveland next year?" you ask. "After his contract's up?"

"LeBron won't leave," Kyle says.

"Why not?"

"Loyalty," Kyle says.

"Ha. Loyalty," Anderson says. "NBA's a business."

"That's his home," Kyle says. "You don't turn your back on your home."

"So it's okay for *you* to leave *your* Georgia hometown?" Anderson asks.

"Where I'm from, that's not a place that can be saved," your brother says. "That's a Wal-Mart town, where your greatest ambition is being *manager* at some chain store."

"He's gotta be loyal, but you don't?" Anderson asks.

"I don't live in a world of absolutes."

Wait…how did Kyle escape the tyranny of the rules that still control *you?*

Jimmy returns with beers for the crew. Steven grabs one, then leaves to stand in line for the next round. It's a merry-go-round, and everyone will take time in the beer line.

I don't live in a world of absolutes, your brother said. And shit, Jimmy obviously doesn't play by the rules, either, especially not in his marriage. And Steven? Look at those fucking weirdo socks. Is this a losing battle, your attempt to adhere to a code? The city itself…it doesn't play by the rules of ordinary sports fandom and conduct. In the security line outside, there are too many Cavaliers fans, even a girl who wears a LeBron James jersey *and* a Magic hat.

You feel like you're close to understanding something significant, but then the projection screen goes dark, the TVs inside go dark, and Wall Street remains lit only by neon bar signs, strings of Christmas lights, and the glow of open cell phones. It's the opening ceremony in Cleveland, the players introduced one by one under spotlight, cheers pouring from the loud speakers here at Wall Street so that it almost feels like you're inside that Cleveland arena. On-screen the Magic players are introduced to booooos, made more intense by the scattered Cavs fans here who've put their full lung power into their own boos, the two South-Beachers inside the most animated of them all. And then the arena's lights flash on and the hardcourt is all reflected glare, so smooth and bright and crisp that it almost looks CGI; the camera switches to a close-up of LeBron as he coats his hands in baby powder, claps them together like a magician who's just made something vanish—*poof.* Quicken Loans Arena goes wild even though they've seen it a hundred times, because they're all thinking that the thing he's made disappear is the stench of the Cavaliers' Game One loss. *We are all witnesses.*

When the game tips off, the Magic fans around you finally unleash their applause, a wave of cheers and whistles and throaty "YEAAAHHHHH"s that flood Orange Avenue. From one corner of the block party comes an air horn, and as you turn to look, you see a stream of silly string shooting high from the center of the crowd like an erupting volcano; it keeps going, keeps going, and there are shrieking women, giggling frat boys all bumping through the crowd to get away from it. Seconds later, you watch a girl run past laughing, her body covered in blue and white silly string.

And then everyone's back. Jimmy, Steven, Anderson, Kyle, your Orlando family, and you're filled with the warmth of community and love and purpose. You're all here together, in this together, and you know what? This is what it's all about. Rah rah rah! Support the home team! No negativity! Because sports teams *are* community, *better than family*, especially for the man who's lost his mother, who's left his father, who's struck out on his own and lost his fiancée in the process. This—the togetherness—this matters.

"Look at this motherfucker!" Jimmy says, and he's clapping hands with a guy wearing a necklace of flashing blue and white lights who gives you a head-nod as if he knows you. To your left, Anderson is saying "Thomas!" and embracing a fellow gym rat. Steven has been pulled into conversation with a group of girls in librarian glasses who stare at him as he talks like he's the hot professor in a campus comedy. Someone claps you on the shoulder and says "My man, Marky Marc!" but when you turn they've already passed. A moment later, three girls slink past in shiny blue Magic shirts, and the one in the middle screams "MARC!" and breaks free of her pack to give you a hug so all-consuming that this—soft smooth fabric, smell of girl, brown hair in your nose and your eyes, flesh beneath your fingertips—is for five full seconds your entire world. When she releases you and says "Gotta follow my girls, but we'll catch up later!" you are feeling so high, a place that is the absolute antithesis of the godforsaken pit in which Vicki left you at Lakeside.

"Seems like ya'll know everyone down here," Kyle says.

"Yeah," you say, and everywhere you look, you see faces in the crowd that you recognize and it feels good. It's *your* city, *your* time, you—you—*you will rise again*!

But then, just a few possessions into the game, your crew breaks apart again. Kyle remains beside you, yes, but Steven vanishes, and Jimmy is back to the inside bar to grab more drinks. You see him in there, working his way past a dozen others waiting for the bartender to notice them, before finally settling in next to those two damn Cleveland fans. You want to text Jimmy, tell him to talk trash, make fun of their jerseys, maybe something like "You're in *Orlando* now! *Respect*, bitches!" Jimmy can get away with it; he knows the bartenders, the owners, everyone who matters. If Jimmy—*Jimmy*—makes fun of the Cavs fans, everyone would join in. The bartenders, the regulars, hell, the managers even: they'd tell these jerk-offs to get their asses back to the tanning salon, to get their arms off the stools, either sit or stand, one or the other. Maybe the Cavs fans would mouth off. Maybe Jimmy and the managers would snap their fingers to have a gang of security guards put these assholes in headlocks. Oh man. You're breathing heavy with anticipation.

But Jimmy just shakes the manager's hand, gathers more beers than he should reasonably carry, a plastic cup of Jack and Coke clenched by his teeth, and then he leaves the bar—glancing over his shoulder at the Cavs fans, face contorting in puzzlement—has he just *now* noticed them?, is he going to say something?—and then Jimmy nudges one of the guys with his elbow—oh man, it's *happening*!, Jimmy's gonna put him in his place!—and says something with teeth still clenched and cup still hanging from mouth, motions with his chin at the beers in his grip, and then the Cavs fan says "Yeah, sure," and takes the Miller Lite dangerously dangling from Jimmy's clasped pinky. "Thanks," the guy says.

Wait, what?

"Beer for the enemies?" you when ask Jimmy returns.

He cranes toward the high-top, gently drops the Jack and Coke from his teeth to the table. "Ah, that one was gonna fall," Jimmy says. "It's all free, anyway." He hands two beers each to you and Kyle, sets down four more on the table for him and Anderson. It doesn't seem possible that a man could carry nine total drinks by himself, but you've seen him carry four pitchers without spilling a drop.

"Well, then." You exhale. "Cheers."

As you raise your bottle to clink with Jimmy, you see on the far end of

Wall Street a short guy with spiky hair laughing too hard at his skinny friend's story, and though it's dark and difficult to see, you suspect that this could be Edwin. Stocky, hair-spikes so thick and solid they could pop a balloon. Even his mannerisms evoke Edwin: the way, after a laugh that has him doubled over, he immediately pulls back his shoulders and tries to stand taller, constantly worried about others' perception of his height; the way he wipes his nose with the full length of his forearm, as if he doesn't want the world to think he's wiping away snot, but instead maybe wiping sweat from his forehead. No. Edwin's in Atlanta. He isn't allowed to be part of your community here.

"So, um," you say to Jimmy, struggling to strip all emotion from your voice, "have you talked to Edwin lately?"

"Week ago," Jimmy says. "At the Magic game."

"He was in *town*?"

"He comes back here like every other weekend."

"Are you…" You shake your head. "And you see him out? Like, often?"

"Occasionally. He bought me a beer at the game."

Isn't there some loyalty clause, that if Jimmy is friends with *you* then he should *not* be friends with your sworn enemy? "That's…" you say, a sentence unfinished because you can think of no other words that aren't ruinous. It's taking far too much of your energy to resist gritting your teeth.

And worse, on the projection screen, the first half of the game is proceeding sluggishly, the Orlando Magic out of rhythm, Dwight Howard moving like a man in concrete boots. Maybe it's the defensive pressure, the way he's swarmed and fouled so often. Maybe he's sore from the first game. Maybe the win went to his head and he expected this to be easy, but the game is a slugfest, like a football contest played in rain and mud. There's a brief moment of joy when, late in the first quarter, the frustration of the lethargy bleeds into the Cavaliers roster and point guard Mo Williams launches the ball at Dwight's back, a petulant middle-school move. There's no resulting foul, though, and the crowd at Wall Street begins chanting "Fuck you, refs! Fuck you, refs!" which Kyle gleefully joins, and you're relieved that he looks so comfortable out here, like a child finally able to wander a theme park without parental supervision.

By the end of the first half, the score is 56-44, Cavaliers with a 12-point lead.

"Hey," Kyle says, holding up his hand to whisper in your ear.

"What?"

"Thanks for the beers."

"Those were from Jimmy."

"I know."

"So thank him."

"I've got a problem," Kyle says.

"For God's sake, what? The game's on."

"Everyone else has bought a round."

"So?"

"The next round's on me. I don't have any money."

"Okay? Then I'll get the next round. Nobody cares."

"But I don't want to look like an asshole," he says. "I don't want to look like—you know—like I need my big brother's help."

Oh, for fuck's sake. Here's something you didn't anticipate: not just that you'd need to play the role of Big Brother, but that you'd need to discreetely *not* play the role of Big Brother. That you'd need to follow *Kyle's* rules of honor, too.

"Use my credit card," you say and slip it in his palm. "When the time comes, just go to the inside bar. Where Jimmy went."

By the start of the third quarter, the two South Beach Cavaliers fans have taken to chanting "BRICK!" when Dwight is at the free-throw line. They laugh when Rashard Lewis misses a 3-pointer, and raise their arms up to the crowd as if this is a gladiatorial match and they will take all challengers: "Can't make *shit*, can you, *bitches*!" Still, no one tells them to quiet down. Anderson seems oblivious, so absorbed in the game, watching on the projection screen in the outdoor courtyard and not even sneaking a peek at the TVs mounted above the inside bar, where the two Cavs fans are causing their scene. Steven is still missing, probably on the phone with his fiancée. Jimmy still stands beside you, of course, but he's equally absorbed in his own orbit, talking to a cluster of girls in Miller Lite outfits who are passing out blinking bottlecap pins and flirting with any man whose beer bottle is close to empty.

At the break between third and fourth quarters, it's Kyle's turn to buy drinks. "Just grab me a water," you say. "I've gotta drive us home tonight." (Ahh, responsibility. Marc, you are a good man.)

Jimmy shakes his head, though: "Ain't getting off that easy, little bro! I'll take his!"

And then Kyle's off to the inside bar, tentative in his approach, too kind as he tries to squeeze past the clusters of other bar-goers waiting to buy drinks. He knows you're watching him, critiquing his style, so he pushes forward, albeit with constant apologies to anyone he bumps or brushes. The politeness is overwhelming, this elementary school innocence that you surrendered so long ago, it breaks your heart, really, to see how wide the gulf between you two. There's Kyle, tapping someone on the shoulder and saying "excuse me" so he can get past, and here's you, feet planted and elbows out so no one can knock you over. You wonder if—as part of his makeover—you should toughen him up. Or would this ruin him, steal away the youth-group smile forever?

You turn away and try to engage with Jimmy and the Miller Lite girls. One of them says "Heeeeey, looks like you're almost out!" And another says, "Can I put this button on you? Where do you want it, shirt or—" naughty look—"pants?"

How could any man choose shirt over pants? But you do. For some reason, you feel it's important that you not surrender to impulse, that tonight you remain careful and measured. "Just the shirt, thanks," you say, "I'll wear it proudly."

Quickly, you learn that you've wandered into a conversation about downtown condos, the hottest place to live, and Jimmy says, "My man here has some rental properties!"

"Oh really? Where?"

When you tell the girls, they scrunch up their faces, disappointed because these are not "hot places," and you feel like a fraud, a D-league basketball player trying to impress a girl by telling her he "plays pro ball…in South Dakota." Rental properties in the *suburbs*? Even the girl who gifted you with the flashing button looks as if she wants it back.

When you turn back to check on Kyle's progress, you see from a distance that his hands are filled with beers, and in his mouth (teeth clenched like Jimmy) is the water cup you requested, dangling and spilling out crushed ice cubes. He looks like a pro, too, a downtown veteran. And then: the unthinkable. He's walking slowly and carefully past the asshole Cavs fans, and one of them pushes back from the stool he's been hovering over, and Kyle is right behind him, and the Cavs fan knocks into Kyle. The water cup falls straight down and splashes across Kyle's crotch, two beers following in descent from hands to floor.

"Fucker!" the Cavs fan says.

"Shit," you say.

"Oh God, sorry!" you see Kyle saying, despairingly.

The Cavs fan looks ready to throw a punch, and his friend is now right behind him saying, "This fucker looking for a fight?" but the first one brushes his pants, his shirt, inspects himself for damage, sees no wetness, and says, "Naw man," and to Kyle: "Get the fuck out of here, piss-stain."

Kyle does. He indeed looks like he's pissed himself. He scurries back outside, two drinks lighter, and arrives before you looking like a kid who's failed during potty training and now must ask Mom for a new pair of pants.

"It's okay, bro," you say.

"That's rough, man," Jimmy says, motioning to the wet crotch. "You should probably spill some on your shirt, too, so no one'll think you peed yourself. Make it epic."

Back inside, one of the Cavs fans kicks the empty plastic cup that held your water. Rolls his eyes and shakes his head.

You must be careful. Measured. You must not surrender to impulse.

But this is your *brother* they've disrespected; this is the man for whom *you* are responsible. This is something you can't forget, no matter what happens the rest of the night. Dedication, loyalty to family? To your entire *community*?

By the end of the fourth quarter, you're praying for a Magic comeback just so these Cavs fans will shut up. The all-night tirade, the beer spilled on Kyle: it's all worth it if Dwight slams one final bucket, or Rashard drains a three, and the Cleveland fans at the Q go silent for the second game in a row, and the South Beach Cavs fans here in Orlando swallow their insults; there's no greater argument than "Scoreboard!" and because no one on Wall Street will act to defend the city's honor, you need the Magic to do it.

And then: destiny.

With 48.7 seconds left, Hedo Türkoğlu hits a 3 to tie the game at 93-93, and all around you, the City Beautiful is on fire with hope and optimism. The silly string. The screaming. The air horns. The blinking bottlecap buttons thrown high into the air. The ecstasy of near-victory. The game tied after having been down by *23 points* at one time! 23-point deficit, the announcers keep saying. 23, 23, the number on the back of Michael Jordan's jersey when he made the most infamous shot in the history of Cleveland basketball, a last-second jumper that helped the Bulls upset the Cavs in the '89 playoffs, a game-winning shot that marked the start of the Jordan-Bulls dynasty and the most devastating of Cleveland Cavaliers collapses. 23, 23, the number on the back of LeBron James's jersey, a not-too-subtle nod to the former King Jordan. 23, the number of points overcome by the scrappy Magic, the curse of Cleveland!

The Cavs have possession. Mo Williams takes his shot—*blocked* by Dwight Howard!

LeBron scrambles for the rebound, and—*WHISTLE!* Traveling on LeBron James! MAGIC BALL! 30 SECONDS LEFT!

Five feet away, one of the Miller Lite girls throws herself into your brother's arms and hugs him so hard you think they'll both pop. (How the fuck does this always happen to him? Is it his goofy nonchalance? You'll take credit this time. It's the clothes.)

Pandemonium on Wall Street. The place so thick with celebration that when you look inside for the meatheads, you can't even see them through the chaos.

"How you like that?" you scream at the inside bar, and hope they hear.

"Yeah!" Kyle says, the Miller Lite girl still in his arms. You can tell he's now having trouble breathing. "How you like that?" he screams at the projection screen, at the deflated Cavs fans in Quicken Arena, but in your mind he's screaming at the meatheads with you, also.

And then it's Hedo Türkoğlu—Hedo again!—driving the lane, pulling up, and from twelve feet *nailing* the go-ahead shot—95 to 93, Magic!—and the game is over, the game is over, the Magic have—

No. One second left. Cleveland timeout.

Victory celebration premature.

Whatever. One second left.

"This is Orlando's moment," you tell Kyle.

The Miller Lite girl has dismounted, but he's still got his arm around her, and she giggles. "What the hell is a *Cavalier*?" she says.

Inside, you spot the two Cleveland meatheads directly below the big-screen TV, and you again wonder how they were able to score such a fantastic spot. They have their arms around one another, a tight embrace the likes of which you might expect from an easily scared girlfriend at a horror movie.

Kyle puts his hand on your shoulder. "Last play. It worked out in Game One."

"Rah rah rah," you try.

Time-out over.

Mo Williams inbounds. One second remaining, but time stands still.

The outdoor crowd has hushed collectively, or maybe your focus is so intense that you can't hear anything anymore.

Ball lasers across the court from Williams to LeBron in mid-stride, clock already under a single second at the very moment LeBron's hands touch basketball, already draining down to milliseconds, and LeBron doesn't even dribble, just moves the ball smoothly from two-handed *catch* to two-handed *jump-shot*, body's momentum carrying him upward, and though there are only milliseconds left, fractions of fractions of milliseconds, it doesn't matter, time expands to twice its normal length, the moment just as long as LeBron needs it to be. He rises, shoots the ball from behind the three-point line and— perfect as a fantasy—the ball sinks as time expires.

Game over. Cleveland wins.

Positivity, Dad? Posi-*fucking*-tivity?

After the glimmers of hope—that Game Seven victory in Boston, that Game One victory in Cleveland, that phone call from Samantha about the interest in your properties, the notary exam that Kyle passed, his makeover—you are returned to dark reality. You still need to empty your bank account to sell that house, don't you? Nothing's changed. Really, things have only gotten worse. And this: LeBron James, a three-pointer from 23 feet. Are you kidding me? *23 feet?* This was preordained. This was Biblical. Witnesses, indeed.

You've done everything you can to follow the fucking rules, your father's rules, your city's rules, all the rules of all the world, and yet *this* is what happens?

Suddenly the world is at full speed again, the noise rising in the block party like a wave about to break, the crowd a cacophony of screams and shouts, a crash of released emotion, and so your anguished scream blends into all the other anguished screams. The crowd: it's in agony over the loss, but *you* are focusing your vitriol on the asshole Cavs fans. You stare at them. They are boisterous as ever.

"Fuck you!" you scream at them. "Fuck you, you goddamned fucking posers! You're *dogshit!*"

That's right. *They* are the dogshit. *They* are the dog's owner. They are the driver whose grill spilled into the highway while you dutifully followed the rules of the road. They are Nicky, biking on the wrong side of the road. They are the truck parked over the lines. They are Edwin. They are 100-degree heat too early in the year, and tenants who haven't paid rent, and speculators who fucked over your business, rule breakers who never suffer any damned consequences and *they* are the *motherfucking problem.*

Breathe.

Your father's rules exist precisely for this sort of situation, right? Rules that pulse and beat within you, that prevent you from thinking too hard and growing too angry, that call you to action as if by alarm:

Do not let anyone bully you.

Defend the honor of your family.

Well, shit.

These two motherfuckers were fucking with your *family*, with Kyle, with the whole city of Orlando. According to your father's rules, that cannot stand.

You will do what's right.

What's right?

What's *right* is right, *that's* what's right. Dad's own rules, once again!

You pull the blinking Miller Lite bottlecap from your shirt. The meatheads are in the middle of self-congratulation, have just knocked someone else's beer across the bartop and they shrug and laugh it off because—hahahaha!—they've won the game and can get away with whatever they want. The bottlecap. You toss it across the room and magically, carried by destiny, it strikes the bald one in the back of his head. Strikes him hard enough to leave a jagged red mark you can see from here.

Holy shit, that was a great throw.

But now you reconsider. You didn't do *that*, did you? Oh fuck, that was the *wrong* thing to do. Maybe your interpretation of the rules suffered poor guidance. What if your "city" is *not* the same thing as "family"? Are you still allowed to defend its honor in whichever fashion you choose? *A bottlecap across the bar*? An epithet at a distance? There are rules for altercations, rules for retribution and revenge.

Do not kick a man when he's down.

Do not kick a man in the nuts.

Do not throw a punch, then run away.

Do not hit a man in the back of the head.

You thought you were following the rules, but did you *break* a rule somewhere along the line?

Too late to think about that. The bald meathead looks around, searches, spots you—the only person staring back at him. When he locks eyes with you, you nod slowly and assertively. *Yes*, you are telling him. It was *me*. I threw the bottlecap. *Do something*. Bitch.

And all of your anger has been building toward this moment, hasn't it, this moment when you shout "Fuck Cleveland!" as loud and deep as you can, hoping that it's not just a declaration but also a rallying cry for every

Orlandoan in the bar. In your mind, they join you: they slip into their metal-mesh armor and charge against tyranny, a whole bar of Orlandoans chanting "*Fuck Cleveland!*" with you. In your mind, their honor—not just yours—was called into question by these two assholes. In your mind, Anderson is itching for a fight, ready to rampage Hulk-style, and Jimmy already has the manager's ear, has enlisted the help of the security guards, and Steven is there, too, and so is Kyle, everyone ready for vengeance.

The Cavs fan grabs his friend's shoulder, points to you—and it's as if you are spotlighted suddenly, just as in the game's opening intros—the bald one speaking into his friend's ear, both of them rolling their shoulders and standing taller, straighter, and how is it that they seemed shorter a moment ago, but now seem Dwight-Howard tall? They've both grown by six inches, and now that they're approaching, they look thick and destructive as defensive linemen. Earlier you scoffed that their physiques were soft, gym muscles, not real-world muscles, but now you wonder if such a distinction matters.

The Wall Street crowds are dispersing, streams of Magic jerseys dissolving past you to the exit gates, your allies disappearing without ever having noticed the battle you expected them to join, and now that your anger is fast dissolving also (God, why did you care about this so much just a minute ago?), you could easily turn and join them. With all the people swirling about in so many directions, the Cleveland fans are trudging against a heavy current, battling for every inch of progress in your direction. Surely if you turned and joined the exodus you could get away…you could be five blocks away by the time they even got out of Wall Street.

But you don't leave.

Some part of you is saying that there's principle at stake here, that this could be the one good thing you do, that it could make up for your negligence at the roach-house this past week, or your irresponsible home-buying, or your absence as a big brother for so many years.

Right now, with six or seven beers fueling your courage, you resolve that you will never again run when things get tough. You will never again rationalize cowardice. There will not be another child abandoned. This—right now—is the moment when your life is going to change. *You will not run away.* Is that one of your father's rules?

You look left and say to Kyle, "I think I pissed these guys off," and you chuckle to show how little seriousness you attach to the approaching threat. Ha ha! Courage!

But Kyle is not there. You look right, then left again, then in a circle, and there are still a hundred Magic fans walking and clumping, but Kyle's nowhere to be found. Jimmy's gone, too. And Anderson. You're all alone, spinning in every direction like a man in a burning building searching for an exit route.

The Cavs monsters nudge past a girl in an XXL Magic t-shirt fashioned into a dress, and they push a scrawny kid in glasses, who spills his beer on his feet and says "Fuck, man!" This is enough to pump your blood again, this reminder of disrespect, this reminder of what they did to Kyle, and even though you're all alone, you remember that you are on the side of righteousness. Surely the city will endow you with some sort of power. You are *Orlando.*

"You the motherfucker threw that bottlecap?" the bald one asks, inches away now. He leans into you, so close you smell the cigarette smoke on his breath. He scratches his nose and narrows his gaze. You could kiss him, he's so close.

"That was me," you say. "Good aim, right?"

"Tough guy, throwing shit across the bar," he says and now he jabs his finger in your face. "A real tough guy."

"Bet he does this all the time," his friend says. "This is the type of prick that needs to get his ass kicked."

"Thinks he's tough, but always hides at just the right time."

"Sure," you say. "The both of you are going to teach me a lesson, huh? Right here?" And you hold up your arms as if you have the full support of everyone in the bar, everyone who's ever lived in the city. Perhaps you could cry out to the security guards and be immediately rescued, but you don't think that's even necessary. Not here, not among your people.

"As good a place as any," the bald one says and shoves you hard.

You weren't expecting it. You thought there'd be more talking. You stumble backward and fall into a girl whose bony shoulder clips your jaw, and her boyfriend grabs you and lifts you up and you think "ALLY!" but he says, "Get the fuck off my girl, douchebag!" and he shoves you back to the Cleveland fans.

A crowd is watching now. It's not quite a middle-school fight—there's no perfectly formed circle around the combatants—but the opening move was enough to attract attention, to turn the heads of those who were still at the bar and waiting for their tabs. The crowd *does* want this, you now realize, some sort of bloody death match to release their post-loss anger, but they damn sure don't want to *participate*. They're all dressed up, and there's a whole night of bar-hopping ahead for them.

"Fucker was throwing beer bottles!" the taller Cavs fan says to the crowd.

"I wasn't—" you start.

"Drunk as fuck, starting fights," the other Cavs fan says.

"Fuck him up," says the boyfriend of the girl you knocked into.

You're trying to stand tall, but the bald guy shoves you again and you fall into someone else you never see, who shoves you back again, and it's like you're in the center of a mosh pit. No one will defend you. No one will help you to your feet, help you to balance. They cannot take out their anger on the Magic. They will use *you* instead.

"Throwing beer bottles," you hear someone else say derisively, and you feel hands on your shoulders. A girl places her hand on the bicep of the tall Cavs fan and says "We're not *all* assholes." And when the *fuck* did everyone get so *gracious* after a loss?

When you stand up again, face to face with the bald guy, you see spilled beer all over your shirt, all over your jeans, much worse than Kyle's tiny crotch stain, and you say, "I never threw any—"

But he's just spit in your face, and the crowd around you roars. "Ha ha!" his friend screams. And you know *that's* a rule, right? You. Do. Not. Spit. In. A. Man's. Face. Not just your father's rule. That's *every* man's rule. It's crass, cowardly, and you can't believe it's received positive acclaim from your hometown crowd.

Rules. The Rules. Your father's rules, the world's rules, your own rules. Nobody else cares, do they? If Orlando followed the rules, it'd still be citrus groves. Rules are just another illusion, aren't they, a ruse to keep the animals under control, a lie a man tells himself so that he can believe he has it all together and he's living right, "doing the right thing." No one follows the speed limit. No one uses a turn signal. You're a sucker. Live your life according to the rules? This was the worst fucking decision you ever made. Well, shit, you're *not* going to be controlled any longer. You're done with rules. Done done done. You will *be* the douchebag who profits, rather than the notary who goes house to house imagining tragedies. You will be the douchebag who claims a stool but doesn't sit in it, the douchebag who doesn't secure his grill to his truck, who steals a parking space, who runs the red light. If no one else cares about rules, why should you? It worked for you once before, and if you're going to return to the top it'll work for you again. And you're going to say this. You're furious that you've been tricked for so long, and you're so eager to articulate this that you're on the verge of tears, and so you raise your hand to point in the face of the Cavs fan and suddenly your entire finger is caught in something—his grip—he has hold of your right finger. And he doesn't say another word, just swings and—

·

There is darkness, and then there is light.

Your immediate thought is that it's morning, that the sunshine is coming through your blinds and it's time to get up and get to work. But fuck, why do you feel so damned groggy? Your head. Your jaw. You didn't drink *that* much last night, did you? You drove, after all. Why does it feel like you're still in last night's clothes, your shoes?

But the light clicks off, and though your vision is hazy and burning with afterglow, you see red and blue lights flashing in your periphery. And you know this isn't your bedroom because you hear voices. Only a few at first. Then more, and more, until—by the time your vision clears—you see a whole crowd. Hands on your body. And you feel something slide beneath you, and you know it's a gurney, but how did you get on a gurney? All thoughts of a bedroom ceiling give way to stars, to blue and white Christmas lights strung back and forth between two old brick buildings, a Magic banner dangling by one rope from a colorful archway. The smell of alcohol and vomit is in the air, there is laughter, and you hear a girl say, "*Not* driving!" and she cackles, and as the gurney moves and bumps over the street, you turn and see a big-screen television on the building across the street playing local news to an audience of no one. From a distance, carried on the breeze, are the nightly arguments between the "You're Going to Hell!" people and the drunk late-nighters who don't want to be told they're going to Hell, and everything is still so fuzzy that you can't figure out which side you should be on, but when an EMT snaps his fingers in your face and asks you, "Do you know where you are?" you are ashamed to answer with clarity, "Orlando. Downtown Orlando."

BOOK IV

YOU ARE NOT YOURSELF

You are not yourself.

You are not yourself.

You are not yourself.

You see a neurologist and he tells you to treat your head as if it is a porcelain bowl that could shatter if not protected. He pantomimes the dropping of a bowl to illustrate, and tells you to avoid physical contact of all kinds. No more fights, he says.

I wasn't in a fight, you remind him. I was assaulted.

Well, he says. No more of that, either.

You are not yourself at the dentist's office, where a technician repairs your chipped tooth by coating it with some sort of liquid enamel, then polishes it down to look natural and smooth, and you know what the dental associates and hygienists are all imagining: they see the black eye, and they see your cracked lips, still torn and only just now scabbing, though every time you open your mouth the scabs break. The pain inside your mouth is perhaps the most intense of anywhere on your body, your teeth having cut into your gums when the two assailants smashed your head repeatedly with either fists or feet, or maybe fists *and* feet.

Assailants. That's the word you've been using when you describe the night; it sounds so much more serious than saying, "The guys who beat me up." Or just, "The two Cavaliers fans." *Assailants*. The word makes you feel wronged, victimized.

When you drive across town for a loan-closing, MetroWest to Avalon Park, you cannot get comfortable no matter how you sit. Your ribs aren't broken, but they're damn sure bruised, and you're glad that you have no prior experience allowing you to articulate the difference. It hurts to breathe; you can't speak long without taking a breath, and you grit your teeth because you fear the long lung-filling inhalation you must make.

When you explain to a 65-year-old woman the documents she is signing, she pats you on the back as if you share a common ailment, asthma or emphysema or something. "Let me get you some water," she says, and you want to tell her that water won't help (*have you seen my* face?) but you take it anyway and try not to wince as you swallow and finish explaining the documents.

You are not yourself.

During mid-day loan-closings, you forget how to respond to questions. You stare blankly. You zone out. A cat was in your lap at one point. You were staring into a woman's breasts at another, and they were not the type of breasts that should attract your gaze.

Your brother snapped his fingers in your face the other day and you didn't notice.

Hey, he said. *Hey.* And how many times had he said "hey" before you turned?

The other day this happened. When was that? The other day?

I don't feel right, you tell the neurologist.

There doesn't appear to be brain damage, he says. But you had a concussion. It's natural to feel groggy.

A *concussion*, you say.

Like the word assailants, *concussion* is serious enough that you repeat it at every opportunity. You're not just some asshole who got into a fight in downtown Orlando. No, you're a victim of two *assailants*, and you're recovering from a *concussion*.

On…one morning, late in the week…what week?…whatever, just roll with it, stop asking questions…you are driving east on I-4—no, north, it's technically *north* as the crow flies, but damn it, it's I-4 *East* —out to DeLand where you've agreed to close two loans. That new contract has been sending you to closings as far as Daytona, St. Augustine, several long-distance jobs lumped together so you don't have to make the same drive twice. "Don't want the gas costs to bankrupt you," an anonymous voice on the phone assured you, and you spend hours wondering whether it sounded cheerful or phony.

Traveling I-4 East away from downtown Orlando, the city eventually disappears, is replaced with greenery on both sides of the highway. Oaks, maples, long swamps ringed by cypress trees. Scrub land. Deep forests of pine. You are driving through the green fog of the Florida Wild, the other cars a multi-colored smear shooting toward you, shooting past you.

At mile marker 101, Interstate 4 is joined by the 417 Greenway toll road, and this merger is the northernmost edge of the Orlando metropolis, the last gasp of major civilization for another thirty miles or so, before I-4 itself expires at the Atlantic coast. For these thirty miles, I-4 cuts through Old Florida. Small towns. Exits leading to two-lane roads, to fruit vendors and decades-old Shell stations, thirteen-foot alligators on display in faux cages out front, the smell of boiled peanuts heavy in the air. Thirty miles of swamps, of wilderness so primal and powerful that you could bulldoze it today, and it would return to Florida by the next summer. Out there: gators, snakes, spiders, mosquitoes, the same mud that swallowed Spanish explorers, the same trees atop which the guerrilla Seminoles fired upon Union soldiers, the same branches from which dozens of runaway slaves were hanged. Out there: fire ants. Scorpions. Out there: the Skunk Ape is wandering, and the Mangrove Man is lurking. Out there: the distant "Oviedo Lights" appear to descend and float away to the horror and delight of necking teenagers on old back roads. Out there, just an hour from the Happiest Place on Earth, is monstrous muck and violent vegetation; there is nowhere on the continent as sinister and darkly magical as the Florida Wild, nowhere so alive and yet so lusty for death. Within this stretch of I-4 is the city of Cassadaga, the Psychic Capital of the World, a hub of spiritual energy, a reminder to travelers that the air is thick with something more than humidity. Within this stretch of highway, too, is something called the "I-4 Dead Zone," which is usually discussed on local newscasts around Halloween every year.

In fact, just after you pass the I-4/417 interchange and approach the long bridge over the mighty St. Johns River where it kisses the sprawling Lake Monroe, you know you are entering the Dead Zone. It is here where cell phone reception (allegedly) goes sour, where the radio flickers in and out, where a thousand motorists a day smack their dashboards and wonder why their XM has been swallowed in static. Here, brakes seem to stick, and brand-new tires seem to pop, and windshield wipers seem to fail against the rain; cruise control accelerates or coasts unexpectedly; on this stretch of highway leading up to and over the St. Johns River, anything is possible. Some motorists are skeptical of the Dead Zone, but the Dead of Florida don't give a fuck about anyone's skepticism.

Usually *you* are skeptical too, and you don't think about these sorts of things. You don't get spooked about ghosts, superstitions, don't even think Florida is an old enough state to have quality hauntings. Once, Shelley actually took you out to Seminole County to see those so-called Oviedo Lights. She took dozens of pictures and pointed out the mysterious orbs appearing in each frame. Ghostly energy, she said, spoo-*ooooo*-ky! But you were thinking about a house you'd just bought and sold in a subdivision two miles from where you sat on blankets drinking wine and watching for ghosts. Shelley did these things sometimes, made you take picnics, made you get away from the obviousness of the city. She had a book called *Weird Florida*, and her goal was to see every oddity in the book. You'd helped her check a dozen or so items from her list. The Oviedo Lights, Spook Hill in Lake Wales, The Senator cypress tree in Sanford. But at some point, you started dodging her requests for day trips, deploring the idea of traveling fifty miles to some sticky roadside attraction without air-conditioning, all for the sake of immersing yourself in "Florida culture" or whatever.

You are not yourself.

Here deep within the Dead Zone, you do not feel in control of your car anymore. On a whim, you lift your foot from the gas pedal and your hands from the steering wheel, and still your car stays the course. You watch as the turn signal blinks of its own accord, and your car smoothly passes a semi without your assistance.

This isn't happening, you say, but who's to say what's real and what isn't? The pain in your face is disappearing, too, the world going brighter, the horizon of trees dissolving, the fog of the world burning away.

The legend of the Dead Zone goes like this: before there ever was an Interstate 4, before there was even a Dixie Highway, there was only a tiny sand road leading from the Atlantic coast to the massive St. John's River, whereupon a ferry could deliver you safely to another sand road on the other side of the river, on which you could then travel all the way to Winter Park and Orlando and Kissimmee.

The wilderness surrounding the southern shore of the St. Johns River was owned in the late 1800s by a diplomat named Henry Sanford, who, in one of the thousands of schemes to get rich quick off Florida land, developed a colony called St. Joseph's to lure Germans into the heart of Central Florida to buy the land. Sanford's name is remembered through the name of the small city on the banks of the St. Johns, but the colony was not one of his better ideas. Only a handful of families took his bait, and when smallpox swept through the colony (wiping out one German family and scaring away the rest), the real estate venture was doomed. But not just the real estate venture: the legend of the Dead Zone tells us that the land itself was soured by the dead Germans buried beneath the dirt, their graves having been disrupted first for farmland (ultimately unprofitable, thanks to the ghosts), then for the construction of I-4 in 1960. During the construction of the interstate, Hurricane Donna gathered her strength and—in league with the haunted land—powered directly across the I-4 Corridor from Tampa to Daytona, *directly over the Dead Zone*, halting construction and delaying the interstate's opening for months. And now, daily, the land exacts its vengeance on motorists who travel I-4 over the former colony of St. Joseph's.

That's the legend.

And you know this story because *the land* is telling you, whispering and flashing images in your mind even as you close your eyes. "This is our road," it breathes. "This is our land."

"*Really?*" you say in your best sarcastic voice. "Ghosts? Come on."

You are not yourself, but you're not fucking stupid. You are a critical thinker, and you are not easily bullshitted. *Really?* you say again to the ghosts in your brain. *Really?*

Still, the car is *driving itself*, isn't it?

Through the windshield, the land and the road seem to de-age like a flipbook in reverse, trees changing size and shape, forty years flashing by, *fifty*, car frames shrinking then expanding, and suddenly you are watching a frozen-shrimp truck speeding along on the fresh asphalt of the just-opened interstate. You see it through the windshield, the truck approaching the brand-new bridge over the St. Johns, and then you see it cinematically, a close-up, the driver checking his watch and marveling at the time he's making. He looks back up, and to his surprise there are headlights approaching *in his lane*. He slams on the brakes, the entire trailer of frozen shrimp skidding of its own accord, folding in toward him, and then there's broken glass and blood and ice cubes and cracked coolers of shrimp across I-4 and this brand-new highway is open for business, yessir, but the Dead Zone has made it clear how business will be conducted.

You are watching a man in a Corvette, years later, speeding down I-4 late at night, approaching the St. Johns River, and suddenly *he* sees headlights in *his* lane, too, and he screams and jerks the wheel, smashes into a pine tree on the roadside.

Headlights, always the headlights. That's how it starts.

Unless the lights are not headlights.

Unless the lights are floating high above street level, watching as patiently as the gators on the river's banks.

You are watching a biker grumbling toward Daytona for Biketoberfest, middle of the day, and as he drives his helmet feels suddenly hotter. He wants to pull over but can't; the bike is no longer under his control. The lights are everywhere around him.

The lights are everywhere and then he is in the lights, he is one with the lights, with every other driver who has crashed here in the I-4 Dead Zone, with the German family whose gravestones were moved but whose bodies remain below the concrete.

The Dead Zone.

The lights were here before the road, of course.

The lights were here before the colony, before the wars, before the pioneers, before even the natives. The lights are part of the land; they've always watched over the land.

The lights *are* Ancient Florida. They are every dead Seminole killed here before there was even a thought about a "St. Joseph's Colony," they are every soldier killed, every native Timucuan buried deep, millions of years collected here like insects frozen in petrified sap. *Dead Zone?* Nothing "dead" here. No, this pavement merely allows the world to travel through the Ancient and pretend they have power over it.

You are not yourself.

You are not even inside your own car, your own body.

You can see your car still traveling I-4, but it's far below you. You look south toward Orlando, to the haze that is the city, the hint of a skyline, and you hear voices all around you.

"You are Orlando?" one of them asks. "*You* are the city? Is that what you think?"

"It's what he *wanted*," says another voice.

"*This* is Orlando," the voice says. "This is where we all end up eventually."

"I don't understand," you say. "I don't understand what's happening."

"Do you think you're the first?" the voice says.

"The first?"

"The first to try his hand at conquering."

Below, the cars whoosh by. You've lost track of your own vehicle, suspended as you are in the sky. You don't know where it's gone, if you're asleep at the wheel, if you've slid off the road, if some otherworldly force nudged the wheel ever so slightly to the left and sent you into mud and death and Forever Florida. Maybe you are dead. Maybe this is what Dead feels like. All you know is that you are not yourself, and you understand that the world is not what it was. Or what you *thought* it was.

One voice says, "You think you're special, don't you?"

"No. I'm not myself lately," you say. "It's my head. The concussion. I was *assaulted*."

"You will join us," the voice says. "In the mud and in the light. You will join us. You will see how small is the intruder, how meaningless."

You are not yourself.

You are not yourself.

You are not

YOU ARE STARING AT YOURSELF. And not in a mirror. You are walking down a brick pathway in deep-summer humidity and you are *someone else*, literally inhabiting someone else's body, someone else's mind, and you're watching yourself—*Marc*—talk, and he's saying, "…a chance of thunderstorms. I mean, is that *really* a risk you want to take?"

"Of course," you're saying, but you have no control over whether or not the words are said. This is like watching a movie, not like playing a video game. You see, and you feel, and you listen, but you cannot change the course of what's happening.

It's hot. It's summer. You are walking the pathways and boardwalks of Lake Eola Park, dangling your hand out to Marc so he can take hold, but he doesn't. You are not yourself, but you know the date and time, that this is summer of '08, and that Marc (you, but not *you* anymore…) just proposed two weeks ago, and now it's time to talk wedding. No more self-congratulation. No more phone calls to friends, no more YAY!s and afternoon margarita toasts with the girls. Down to business. And, as a professional event planner, you're so fucking ready to show the world who you are, what you can handle. You're sick to death of people (the older women at Alumni Club, especially) taking you less than seriously because you're four inches shorter than everyone in the room, face so bright and smooth that—just last week—when you answered the door for the maintenance man at your apartment, he asked if your parents were home. This: the wedding, the planning: this is how you signal your arrival.

In fact, wedding details commence this very afternoon: you're meeting the photographer in thirty minutes on the far side of the lake, over by the bandshell, for your engagement photos.

"It's Florida," you tell Marc. "It could rain no matter what month we get married."

"Right, but—"

"A few years back, we had a tropical storm in, like, November. You remember that?" You were in high school at the time, a waitress at Daiquiri Deck on Siesta Key, and you worked through the storm, winds so hard they pulled umbrellas out from tables and shot them into the parking lot. "We could get rain any time of year. But an *early*-summer wedding? Late May, early June? Think about it. That's the dry season. Less chance of a hurricane. Everyone's kids are out of school. And we can honeymoon *anywhere* without worrying about weather." You say these things as if you just now thought of them, but really you created a chart and mapped out the pros and cons of every single month. June won.

"It's so hot," Marc says. "Why not December?"

"The *hol*-idays, for crying out loud," you say. "Nobody likes a December wedding, not with all the other crap they're dealing with. When it comes to the planning, trust me, baby."

Marc still hasn't taken your hand. You wonder if he realizes how awkward this is, a couple on their way to engagement photos and yet he won't hold his fiancée's hand. He turns away, slumps onto a park bench. "When's the photographer getting here?"

"Wow. Excited much?"

"I just…I've got…" He squints, feels in his pocket for his cell phone but doesn't take it out. "I'm excited, yes. I can't wait for pictures. It's just so fucking hot out here."

Orlando heat was nothing compared to the Osprey heat where you grew up, back where the trees seemed shorter, the parking lots longer and blacker and your dashboard always sizzling, back where every house on the block had shells for yards and even when you were nowhere near the beach, you got hot sand in your eyes.

"Quit being a wimp. We're in the shade."

"The shade." He blows air up his face. "Ninety-degree shade."

"I'm the one whose hair is affected by humidity, and you don't hear *me* complaining."

Marc wipes the sweat from his forehead dramatically, shows you his wet palm.

"And anyway," you say, "you've lived in the South all your life. Just 'cause you spend all your time in AC now, don't pretend you can't handle an hour outdoors."

He looks away to where a homeless man is napping at the base of an oak tree, an image that efficiently captures the dual nature of Lake Eola Park. "Why are we getting the pictures taken here again?" he asks.

Lake Eola Park. The background of a thousand other engagement photos, symbols of all the city aspires to be and all the city has been, an iconic fountain in the lake's center, a statue of some old-timey soldier at the east end, flower gardens and memorial plaques for veterans and famous citizens, boardwalks and cypress trees and swans, a seafoam-colored bandshell sponsored by Walt Disney World, all of it, just like Grant Park in Chicago or Central Park in New York, built tight against the downtown skyscrapers. But the homeless men who loiter at the statue and wash themselves in the public restrooms at either end of the park are an important part of this place, too. Orlando proper is not a theme park. It doesn't hose down the streets and start fresh each morning like Bourbon Street. "Let's hope *that* doesn't wind up in the picture," Marc says, and chin-nods at the homeless man. You knew he'd point this out.

At the northeast end of Lake Eola Park is a red pagoda, extending from the grass and sidewalks and out over the water. Not far from there is a playground under the shade of hundred-year-old oaks. At all hours of the day, it seems there are mothers on park benches, children stomping across the bark nuggets, sprinting from swing sets to slides. Strollers and diaper bags. A single corner of the park where no one ages.

"Hold on," Marc says. "Gotta take this call real quick."

Marc sees the homeless man, sure, but you wonder if he sees the playground. Has he *ever* looked in that direction, or will he always—at the sound of children—make that face, that same one Jimmy makes, the one that says "I want to be 25 forever," the one that treats the idea of "family" as something to be escaped rather than embraced. You wonder if Marc has ever imagined himself on those park benches, stroller at his side, child at the top of the slide yelling for him to watch. To be a *man* without a family is *cool* in an anti-hero sort of way. But to be a woman without a family? There's no way to quantify the amount of question-dodging, the number of times you've had to tell your mother that *yes*, it's serious, and *yes*, it'll happen, just be patient, okay? To be a woman in your late twenties is to live under the tyranny of the wedding clock, as if you don't have your shit together if there isn't a careful month-by-month timeline to familyhood available for all to see.

"No, seriously," he's saying into his phone. "Gonna need a drink in about thirty minutes. Huh? No, she'll be there. It's…engagement photos. This is *her* thing."

You once asked Marc if he wanted to take a swan-boat ride on the lake, part of a checklist of "Orlando experiences," a sub-list of your *Weird Florida* list that Marc gives you such a hard time about. Marc looked at you like you'd asked him to wear your panties. *Do I want to surrender* all *of my masculinity*? he said. You were going to Lakeside Wine Bar that night. A date night: wine, a cheese plate, maybe gelato afterward. Date night meant *just the two of you*, not crowds and beer tubs and skull-cracking bass, but the way *he* saw it, date night just meant the opening act before meeting up with his friends and dissolving into Wall Street.

It occurs to you now, here in the park, that you've never asked Marc whether he even wants kids. For so long, you just wanted him to propose, just fantasized about how the women of the Alumni Club would regard you with a ring on your finger: never again Little Shelley the Party Girl, but instead Shelley the Serious Professional.

For six months, you've been going to Alumni Club meetings, and for six months you've been trying to ignore their eye-rolls and their fake smiles (too many of them know that you wore low-cut shirts and served beer out of a tub downtown, but while you've tried to change the narrative by mentioning your time as a nanny (freshman year of college), this somehow made you seem even younger—a girl who plays with babies all day?). Months of these weekend brunches, high teas, evening mixers with women mostly in their forties, whose husbands made in their spring bonuses what you make all year; most of them speak about children in the past tense, but some do complain about the difficulty of dropping off kids at daycare while wearing heels, the difficulty of having three kids in three different schools, so you know there are women at Alumni Club in that nebulous region of "your generation." Still, you feel like the youngest no matter which table you sit at. "Where do you and your husband live?" you're asked at each gathering. Explaining that you have a long-term boyfriend, and that you're going to move in together once your lease expires, has only gotten slightly less excruciating when replacing the word "boyfriend" with "fiancé." When the other young women introduce themselves as married, the conversation is allowed to move to the woman herself, to *her* career, to *her* goals, but with you, until the day of your wedding, everything seems to stall awkwardly at "Oh. I see," with the unspoken parenthetical aside of "(Come back once you've grown up.)"

So yes, the idea of marriage and house and car and the women *taking me seriously*, you want it so badly you've barely considered the particulars of life with the man to whom you said yes. Children, for instance: would you know Marc's answer if you asked him here, now, whether he wants children? It occurs to you that you're *scared* to ask him this question, to interrupt his high-stakes phone calls, because you don't know how he'll react. If he tells you he doesn't want kids, what's next?

You spot a young mother at the playground, holding her baby girl, lifting her up so the girl's face is illuminated by sunshine, Orlando skyline as a backdrop. It's like a damned *commercial* for having kids. If you stay in the city, this is where you'll have your first family photos taken, too, where you'll have your maternity photos taken, and yet—

"Personally, I don't even know why we need engagement photos," he says into the phone. "I know, right? Everyone knows what we look like. Money better spent elsewhere."

"Is that Jimmy?" you ask him.

"Huh. Hold on," he says. "No, Edwin. He's about to sign a lease with some renters."

"Oh."

Marc looks at you, then at the phone. "Gotta go. I think she's pissed at me. No business this afternoon, she said."

He shuts the phone and walks to you, takes your hand gently. For a moment it's encouraging; this is what the day *should* feel like. "What's on your mind?"

And you can't believe he asked. You were staring at your own feet, but maybe he saw you looking out to the playground. Maybe he wants to talk. Maybe he'll make sure that the smiles in your engagement photo will be genuine.

"Orlando Reeves," he says.

"What?"

Down at your feet. He's staring down at your feet, and you realize you're both standing in front of one of the many historical markers scattered throughout the park and mostly ignored by the children and parents and joggers. Marc bends down and reads: "'In whose honor our city Orlando was named. Killed in this vicinity by Indians, September 1835.' Huh. Learn something new every day."

"Something I should've added to our Orlando checklist, things to see, things to find."

"I love your lists, Shelley. You know that, right?"

"I know," you say and exhale, and for the first time today you feel light enough to be carried. Maybe you were wrong to worry. Maybe everything is going to be just fine.

"These photos are gonna look great," he says. "They are. You're so damned organized, and I'm impressed by you every day. God, I'm so happy I get to marry you."

"Thank you for saying that, Marc. Thank you. I needed—"

"Oh! Hold on," he says. "Phone's buzzing!"

AND NOW YOU ARE standing beside a car, and it's 1924, and the road is a snaking trail of gravel and mud puddles and downed oak branches and palmetto fronds, a far cry from the route you traveled for most of your journey from Albany. That road was a modern marvel called the Dixie Highway, and it leads all the way from Michigan to Miami, connecting the muscular continent of North America to this muggy peninsula dangling from the southern coast. Coming from Albany, linking up with the Dixie Highway in Toledo was a tad out of your way, but it brought you down uninterrupted to Daytona. Then, to get to your property in Florida's interior, you had to leave the highway behind and push to the center of the state on roads less friendly to motor vehicles. Now, you're headed to a town called Winter Park where you're confident there is land that can make you rich. That name: *Winter Park.*

The advertisements for this state proclaimed, "Tourists can enjoy more than 1,000 miles of paved roads!" but it's bullshit. Three tires you've shredded since bouncing into Florida. You had one spare, and you had a patch kit, and then you had to stop and buy two damn more, and finally that was good enough to get you to the St. Johns River (which you ferried across with your vehicle) and then here to this autocamp in Maitland, where the air smells of oranges and limes and…smoke. Yes, it smells perpetually of smoke here in the state's interior. For every one thing that's expected in Florida, there's something else you could never have predicted. You expected alligators, for instance, but you didn't expect alligator *wrestlers* as a roadside diversion, or *fried gator tail* at the autocamp in Jacksonville, one man wearing a necklace of gator teeth, an old gator-bite scar tattooing his calf.

Some of the autocamps have been deplorable in condition, too, though you don't mention this fact in your letters home. "This is paradise," you wrote on a postcard yesterday while parked outside Daytona. And for a few moments just after you parked, it was. The salty air, the breeze, the palm trees. The roads kept going from pavement to sand to pavement to sand, but you'd driven onto the beach through a gap in the dunes, and you stood beside your car and stared east into the vastness of an Atlantic Ocean so much more inviting than the one you'd left behind in New York, and then you turned around and stared west into the sand dunes and the wilderness beyond, all of it dangerously enchanting, the land feeling more powerful, more alive than anything in New York or Ontario.

Last night, the Daytona "autocamp" was, truthfully, just a tent in a rancher's backyard. A chicken wire fence surrounding a dusty, weedy lot. The tent provided the only shade as far as you could see; everything was flat land and squat vegetation, dirt roads leading in and out of the ranch, cattle grazing in all directions and crowding under the few trees poking from the grassy fields. You've been wearing jacket and tie for this entire trip, but the rancher—a man named Travis with skin like a bullwhip—came to greet you at his gates with chicken blood speckled across his forearms. He looked you up and down.

"Am I the only one here?" you asked him.

"They's more comin, always is," he said. "We's a stop on the way, not a destination."

And sure enough, by sundown the lot was full of mud-spattered Tin Lizzies, fifteen other travelers headed in as many directions. To Palm Beach! To Miami! To St. Petersburg! A man and wife excited to see The Senator cypress tree, a living wonder older than Moses. A 16-year-old kid who'd stolen his father's car and intended on making a life down in Miami. An unsavory Italian man who smelled of whiskey and guarded his car like there was something inside worth hiding. A couple veterans who'd been making this trip every year since returning from Europe.

"Anyone headed to Orlando?" you asked. "Winter Garden? Winter Park?"

"Where's that?" the Miami-bound boy asked.

"Center of the state," you said.

"Cracker country," the Italian said.

"It's just past Sanford," you said, nodding toward the married couple.

"What's in Orlando?" the husband asked.

"Oranges, celery," you said, "and opportunity."

"You a developer?" the Italian asked.

"I don't reveal my secrets," you said coyly, "but maybe."

So far, you've been playing the part of tourist: you want to experience Florida the way these other travelers might. What brought them here? How do they spend their time? So you stood on a 100-foot-tall live oak with ladders and look-out decks built up its trunk. You cooked fresh-caught fish in a cast-iron skillet at riverside. You bought fresh-picked oranges from a road stand called Stuckey's. You drove through flooded roads, unsure whether you'd make it out alive, but exhilarated at the adventure of it all. Too young for the Wild West, Florida is your only chance at frontier. You stopped at a train depot in Jacksonville just to see the hustle and bustle, to hear the excitement, and the words on everyone's lips were *land boom*! Snatch up what you can, 'cause brother it's going *fast*!

"Stick to the coasts," the Italian said. "Nothing of value in Orlando."

You shook your head. "If you buy what's hot, you're already too late."

"You have something better in mind?" The Italian rarely looked up, just kept sharpening a knife there in his lap.

"If you're going to make a fortune," you said, "you don't follow everyone else. You go where they haven't gone yet, but where you know—sooner rather than later—they're gonna be." You saw it already. The Atlantic coast is bought up, and it'll be a different place in a year, Miami and Miami Beach and Palm Beach a string of gems for the rich: hotels, mansions, golf courses. St. Augustine, too, and Daytona. And the excitement over the Gulf Coast, over Naples, over Tampa Bay, where someone is conjuring islands from dredged sand, an *island of millionaires* where before there was only ocean. If you want to develop the coasts, the prices are too high to make money. But if you're willing to drive into the untouched heart of the state where the land is still dirt-cheap, and where the highways are certain to come next? Lakefront living far from the terrors of the seas, but close enough for easy trips to the beach.

"So you're buying into Orlando?" the husband asked. He was now leaning close. "Tell me more."

"Honey!" his wife said. "This is supposed to be a vaca—"

He held up a hand to her face. "Quiet."

"Already got the property," you said. "A small town's worth of it." In fact, you'd met a man with a full binder of property deeds for sale. Florida land is in such high demand that they come to the train station—Binder Boys, they call these men—and sell property to passengers exiting the train. You waited until you found a man with property in Central Florida, acres and acres of it in Winter Park and Orlando and Winter Springs, names catering to the imaginations of Northerners, names that speak of a new life where your bones don't ache from the cold. Names that, for you, speak of a fortune to be made, and that—when you first heard them months ago—convinced you to put the hotel in Madeline and Jim's hands and take a scouting trip. But there at the train station in Jacksonville, you bought sight unseen, a land mass bleeding across the city limits of Orlando and Winter Park.

"Orlando," the husband said. "Orlando. I like the sound of it."

"Not as pretty as you think it is," the Italian said. "Saw a man fed to—" He stopped, reconsidered. "I've seen things on my drives across the state. I'm telling you. If you's a tourist, stick to the places in the brochures."

But that night you wrote to Madeline, "The state of Florida is paradise," and it was a cheesy sentiment lifted from all the advertisements circulating the Northeast, and you knew it wasn't true, because if you wanted to write something honest you would've written, "This state is a swamp populated entirely by thugs, whip-cracking cattle ranchers, horrifying Indian/Negro couplings straight from a penny dreadful, and toothless yokels too bizarre in appearance even for the darkest reaches of Appalachia—all of it terrorized daily by prehistoric creatures that could withstand and repel a Biblical plague." This place is paradise for five seconds, hell on Earth for the next ten. You've no delusions. You did not come here as naive as some foolish Yukon gold-rusher, eyes sparkling like precious metal, dreams soon to be washed away by the reality of the land, how brutal the journey and how little gold actually glowed beneath the frozen mud. You've known all along: the land is here, and the land spreads out before you in every direction waiting to be taken; and angry as it is, the world can be scrubbed, made palatable, safe-seeming. And if your eventual development doesn't look like solid gold, well, you can still lie about the beauty of Florida paradise. Everyone will believe your lies, everyone *wants* to believe.

So yes, your postcards have been dishonest. In fact, as far as Madeline knows, you're just another Tin Can Tourist clanking from snowy winter to Sunshine State. She believes this is just some minor investment opportunity, a winter home, but you haven't told her you plan to make Central Florida *yours*. You haven't told her how much money you've already funneled from your account in order to make your vision happen.

Today, as you approach the Maitland autocamp, the live oaks creating a sort of tunnel through which you drive, ten thousand thick branches offering shade and promise, you're thinking: Why *not* me? Why *not* Central Florida? Measure off the plots, start placing ads in the Northern papers. Eden is calling! *Winter Park.* Live in sunshine while the rest of the world slips on ice and chops firewood. Even the name *Orlando* sounds warm, suntanned as a Spaniard. You picture the advertisements you'll create: the lakes, the boats…That's how to make money: advertise first, *then* make the world of the advertisement real.

You swat a mosquito at your neck. Maybe don't mention the bugs.

You're sweating (don't mention that either), but still you do not remove your jacket or loosen your tie. Tonight you'll learn the names of the men who matter in these towns. For the next couple weeks, you will lurk on the periphery of their community meet-ups, and you will sweat and persevere through the discomfort. But on your drive back North, after construction has begun and you are assured that you've got this place figured out, you will ride with your jacket off, your tie wrapped around the rear-view mirror, the papers for a full world of possibilities tucked safely in your briefcase on the passenger-side floor.

You are sweating at the gateway to the Maitland autocamp, sun bright through the tunnel of trees, the brightness bleeding in, brighter, brighter, brighter

AND SUDDENLY YOU ARE standing before a three-story image of yourself, a massive banner stretching down the exterior of the RDV Sportsplex, just unveiled today while you were in practice, and you're taking it in, the curves of your every damn muscle, the godlike shoulders, and you're saying to the banner, "Why hello, Dwight. You're a sexy man, you know that? A *sexy* man!"

You nod, as if the banner is speaking back.

"What's that? *I'm* sexy, too? Oh, thank you, Mr. Howard! Too kind."

Dwight. Howard. You are Dwight Howard. In practice today, you shattered a backboard, swatted one of Jameer's shots into the wall. You flexed afterward, and your muscles swelled, kept swelling until it seemed they'd overtake you entirely. Can a muscle swell so much that it *explodes*?

Dwight Howard. You are *Dwight Howard*—have you mentioned that?—and when you order chicken fingers for every meal (even during your first fancy dinner with the General Manager down here in Orlando, against the advice of your father who told you to order steak) everyone laughs.

He's so funny! they say.

Such a nice young man.

So clean-cut, so well-spoken.

Movie-star good looks.

And he's always smiling. Always happy. That's why he'll be a superstar.

A big kid. Joyful, like a child!

Perfect spokesperson for, like, McDonald's.

The next generation of athlete-superstar-celebrity crossover!

Oh, Dwight Howard, he's a guy to be around! One second, he's swatting basketballs and looking like the second coming of Shaquille O'Neal, and the next he's channeling Samuel L. from *Pulp Fiction*, quoting Ezekiel 25:17, "And you will know I am the Lord when I lay My vengeance upon you!" or he's ripping a ball from its mid-air trajectory and then holding it up like Mufasa in *Lion King*, scream-humming the theme from the movie, everyone laughing.

"We are building this franchise around you, son." That's what they told you on draft night, and though it's been slow-going here in your first two years in the NBA, everyone agrees. You have so much talent. Sky's the limit. If there's a sports cliché about potential, you've heard it. *Tell me something I don't know*, you think but don't say because you're also thinking, *Nah, keep telling me what I love to hear*! When you palm a basketball and hold it skyward, people gasp. They literally gasp at your wingspan. You are an evolutionary marvel, and it doesn't seem possible even to you, this body, the possibility.

But, of course, there is the problem of humility.

After draft night, you spoke with the national media about setting an example, being a role model, spreading Christianity through the league. The city of Orlando—and especially its old-school Baptist element, its contingent of churchgoing women west of Division—seemed to have a collective spiritual orgasm. It was 2004, and the NBA was mired in a publicity nightmare with its thuggish-ruggish superstars: Allen Iverson, Ron Artest, Latrell Sprewell strangling his coach, Rasheed Wallace and his "Fuck what you heard!" t-shirt, the entire Portland Jailblazers team, and Kobe Bryant simultaneously raping women and cheating on his wife and yet held up as an exemplar because—like Lloyd Banks said—he moves from basketball court to the courtroom—and Orlando, gifted with a star player who was also a role model, rejoiced!

Daily, though, you think about what a mistake it was to open your mouth with such a decree: *spread Christianity throughout the league*. That was your father speaking; that was *you* playing by *his rules*, trying to do what he would do. But you were 18 when you were drafted, when you were made a millionaire overnight, and come on, you *had* to say something grandiose. You just didn't realize how hard it would be to live up to that promise.

Because you had to celebrate, too. Just a pinch of sin for the newly minted millionaire.

You had to see Orlando when the sun went down. Orange Avenue, downtown, the bars, the clubs. You promised yourself you'd never become a stereotypical "baller," but you wanted a taste of the baller lifestyle. Just a taste. A club owner lifting the velvet rope and bringing your table a bottle of champagne *on the house*, a night that would feel like a rap video in the making.

This is something your father wouldn't have allowed, something the church women would've looked down upon. All of them would be disappointed with the way you were thinking, with *what* you were thinking, the lusty pornographic fantasies multiplying inside your mind when you took your first look at photos of Orange Avenue on a Saturday night and imagined yourself motor-boating through a sea of boobies—oh man. You wanted to be *you*, not some brand pre-determined by all these other people, by some statement about Christianity that *was* a part of you, but just a part, and now you couldn't take it back.

So you stormed out to the clubs fueled by testosterone and sinful thoughts, and you rolled thick with men you didn't know, men hired to watch and handle you. Even then, before ever playing a single NBA game, the world recognized you wherever you went. It took just ten minutes on the street before this happened: a tiny girl with fake boobs and shiny crimson hair, white skirt so short that her ass bounced out as she ran to you, jumped into your arms and wrapped her fingers around your neck and told you she loved you, and *oh my God*, you're so big, *so big*, sooo biiigggg, each big directed at a different muscle that she traced with her fingertips, and she didn't seem to mind that you were staring down into her boobs as they pressed against your chest, looking big as bowling balls—there in your arms, the girl light as a basketball, her skin touching yours, and you were damn-near drooling and you forced yourself to say, "No baby, I'm…uh…I'm a good Christian boy," and she plopped down out of your arms, her breasts gliding across your forearms, nipples for one instant brushing your fingers, her fingertips nonchalantly grazing your half-erection, and she said, "Oh. I thought we could have some fun."

Good Christian boy.

Because here was the other thing about Orange Avenue. It wasn't just bars and clubs and glitter and shots and fake boobies. It was also church people. A spread-out cluster of church people at the corner of Orange and Central, all holding posterboards with messages like "Jesus Saves" and "Hell is Forever" and "You are Pornography." A few of them old, 50 or 60 years old with gray beards and goatees and veins that popped out of their forearms, grizzled and weathered like they did this every single Saturday and yet still woke up early for church on Sundays, maybe even set up all the A/V equipment and organized the chairs for the Sunday school classes. There were kids, too, 18 and 19, same age as you, looking more tentative than the old men in charge, yet they were still here, none of them saying a word to the crowds passing around and through them, the streams of drunk people arguing with them ("You think I'm going to hell, you fucking prick?"), cops on horseback a block away the only thing keeping the sinners from shoving the church people, and yet the church people remained quiet as they held their posters, didn't say a word to you or anyone else…But you know they recognized you.

That night, you learned how big you were. How biiiigggg. Not just big lats and big pecs, not just big legs and big hands (and you know what they say about big hands, right?), but big big *BIG*. Biggest celebrity in town. Face of a franchise, face of an entire city. And you knew that you couldn't enjoy it, not really. There were the church people who recognized you, yes, but you were quickly attracting a crowd on Orange Avenue, and my God, where could you go in Orlando where you *wouldn't* be mobbed, where these little girls *wouldn't* jump into your arms and pout their lips and shake sex in your face, where the frat boys wouldn't crowd around and try to fist-bump and tell you they believed in Magic, black guys giving you head-nods like *they* were the cool ones who actually knew you and the white guys were wannabes. You were 18, and wanted to have fun, and that first night when you seemingly flew like Superman down Orange Avenue, you came to the realization that you couldn't enjoy *any of this* because it all ran counter to your already-established brand. You were 18, and everything had been decided for you.

Or maybe not. Maybe no one would notice one little…Maybe?

The girl with the crimson hair lingered in her disappointment, but she didn't walk away, and you leaned down and whispered in her ear. "Tonight, baby, I'll be a sinner. Tonight and tonight only."

She looked into your eyes, joy flooding her face. This was the power you had, the power you have. She tried to answer and couldn't, mouth open but shocked to silence, face looking like you were already deep inside her. She'd jumped onto you as a joke, but had never expected…oh God…had never expected that…maybe you'd really…oh God, this was happening!

"I got a room at the Marriott tonight," you whispered. "The one by the arena. Bring a couple friends. If I'm gonna sin, I'm gonna sin big."

You shed your entourage, your handlers, tell them you were sleepy, and you high-tailed it back to the hotel. So you couldn't go to the clubs? So you couldn't be seen on the streets without the church people recognizing you? No big deal. You could still get your dick sucked pretty easy. Not a bad life, Dwight. Brighten up.

So you waited there in the hotel room.

11 PM.

Midnight. Watching *Happy Gilmore* and dreaming of wild end-of-the-world sex with a room full of porn stars.

1 AM, 2 AM.

There was no other Marriott by the Amway Arena, was there? At this point, you barely knew the town, hadn't yet purchased your castle in Casselberry. Maybe you'd made a mistake. Your mother was staying at your rental condo until you could find the right house, so you couldn't bring an orgy back *there*. It had to be *here*. Make it easy for everyone. Maybe you'd even shatter a mirror or destroy a TV, your first night as a rock star. That could be fun. But 2 AM? What if you'd given them the wrong hotel…oh God, a troupe of delicious sex kittens slinking into the wrong hotel, all flesh and hot sex, ready to go, and then…someone else got to scoop it up?

You walked down to the front desk, talked to the clerk.

"Mr. Howard," he said, starstruck. "What can I do for you, sir?"

He was transfixed. You could have asked him to go wander into I-4 traffic, and he'd have done it happily.

"I'm, uh, expecting someone." You told him your room number, asked if there were any messages.

"Actually, yes," he said. "Someone left a message not long ago. I was on break."

"A message?" Oh, hell yeah.

The clerk handed you a small envelope with a handwritten note inside. "So sorry," the message said. "I couldn't do it. You're too important, Dwight. We need you to be *Dwight Howard*. I couldn't ruin that. You're our everything. This city. All of us. Be good. All my love."

Um.

Couldn't *ruin* that? Be *good?*

"All my love" was not the same thing as a good hard fuck. Not the same thing at all.

Ain't an 18-year-old man in the world who wants an "All my love" note instead of boobies in his face.

You shook your massive head, knocked your hand into the edge of the counter and set off an explosion of pain up your entire forearm. Your body felt silly suddenly, too big for the world. So much strength and you couldn't even stand up straight.

You crumbled the note.

"Thank you," you told the clerk.

"Can I do anything else for you?"

"Just…" You closed your eyes. "Don't tell anyone I was down here."

"Of course. But…well…could I get a signature? I won't tell anyone where I got it."

You tried to smile, and you tried to oblige with happiness in your eyes, but the act of signing the scrap of paper he gave you—why did this feel like the worst kind of chore, like the world had already turned against you?

AND NOW YOU'RE HERE with Marc at one more house that looks so agonizingly similar to all the others across Orlando that you almost vomit as you coast through the neighborhood. Everywhere you go, it feels like Orlando's multiplying, and even when there's some relief (a thick sea of pine trees that you think is a forest, say) there's always a subdivision on the other side. This— where you're at, right now—is the fifth house in the last two days that Marc's visited with you in his quest to make you into a loan-closer, a mini-Marc. This is what you wanted, and you've tried your hardest; together you've closed loans not just in living rooms like this one, but also at a Wendy's, a Starbucks, and a Chili's. One client tried to get you to meet him at Golden Corral to finish the paperwork, but Marc told him, "You know I don't *pay* for your lunch, right?"

"You don't?" the man said.

"Not part of your refinance, I'm afraid."

You've driven with your brother to Lake Mary and Heathrow, communities north of Orlando teeming with doctors and dentists and swimming pools and Lexuses and enough columns and granite countertops to refill some Pennsylvania strip mine. You've seen at least one seven-bedroom home (walk-in closets in each bedroom), and it had *three* Hummers in the front yard. "Rich get richer," you said and whistled, thinking maybe this was just one step up from where your brother was at, and shit, maybe in a couple years you'd both be living in a place like this.

But Marc popped that balloon. "It's the *wealthy* who get wealthier," he said, "and you don't see *them* buying three Hummers."

"Debbie Downer," you said. "Marc, this could be *you*. You should get a Hummer."

"Kyle, this is stupid. There's a bottom here that's a few months from falling out completely, and these idiots still don't see it coming."

"You seen the size of their pool?" you asked as you wandered to the edge of the yard. These guys were living a sweet life. If Marc owns ten properties like he says, then why isn't he swimming in toys? He's gotta have more money than he's letting on.

"These guys are in their twenties," Marc said, "just like Edwin and me when we were starting out. They're textbook douche-preneurs. Probably never passed a single business course, but when we go in, they're going to pretend to know *everything* about *every* form we have them sign. They don't know *shit*, but they want the world to think they do. They'll talk louder than necessary, like loud voices equal success. Just wait."

Sure enough, the loan-closing was as he'd described: three gym rats who lived together and talked about their website and their big ideas and the properties they were scooping up. "Fucking morons bought too high," one of them said. "Now's the time to buy. Cheap."

"Right, only morons were buying during the boom," Marc said to them. "The smart people just wait a full decade for everything to crash?"

"We got a few properties, know what I'm sayin'?" one gym rat said. "Own half a development in Lake Nona. That area's gonna blow up for sure, soon as the medical school is finished. Paid in cash. Straight cash, homey."

"We got properties, too," you said. "One in Lake Nona that I was just mowing yesterday. Tell 'em, Marc."

"Sign there," Marc told them, and glared at you so hard you quieted down. "Sign here, too, and don't forget the date."

"Cash deals," you said. "How'd you guys get the money to get started?" It sounded so easy, all of this buying and selling. Marc refused to talk about his own mortgages, how he'd scraped together down payments, how he could afford so much, but if it was so easy for him to buy ten houses— and you know exactly where *he* came from—why wasn't *everyone* doing it? Why hadn't your father? Why hadn't *you*? You were here in Orlando now, but Marc was always whining about money problems, lecturing you not to leave the fridge door open or take too-long showers or whatever. And these idiots? How had they…?

At your question, though, the three douche-preneurs grew sheepish.

"Know the system, work hard," one said.

"Watch the listings. Always be watching."

"That's it?" Kyle asked.

"Gotta be smart," one said, tapping his temple. "That's what it's all about. That's the main, like, determining factor of success. Who's the smartest."

"Right," Marc said and rolled his eyes. "Timing has nothing to do with it."

"If you're smart enough, you make your own timing."

"Right," Marc said. "You're how old?"

"Do I have to put my age on the form?" the gym rat asked.

"No. Just wondering."

"Twenty-three."

"Just graduated?"

"A *year* ago," he said proudly.

"Tough to get loans now," Marc said. "A lot of scrutiny. If it was still as easy as '05, '06, everyone would be buying up foreclosures at rock-bottom prices." He narrowed his eyes, almost like he knew where the conversation was going next. "Now, you need cash to make the purchases happen. Wish I had that kind of cash handy. What's your secret?"

"No secret," one said. "Just brains, my man."

"Recent college grad, just now coming into the market with sacks of cash?" Marc flipped through the paperwork one last time, checking for signatures. "You're self-made, huh?"

"Gotta have, like, *some* family support. I mean…" one said.

"Yeah, like for the initial cash sales and stuff," another said.

"—just to get started, you know, and everything after that is *brains*—"

"—will pay my dad back when I—"

"—totally not a big deal, totally has nothing to do with, like, business acumen—"

"Time to go, Kyle," Marc said and nodded at the douche-preneurs.

There'd be no convincing these guys of their good fortune, but Marc had engineered this conversation for *you*: he wanted to prove a point. Everything was easier if you had a pocketful of cash to get started, if you'd inherited it, or were gifted it, or took a "loan" from your parents, all at the exact moment when prices were at their lowest and inventory was at its highest. With a flush bank account, it was easy to buy some depressed properties and invest in repairs and then flip and think yourself a genius. If you were overextended, on the other hand, money already tied up in ten underwater properties and no safety net from wealthy parents, these opportunities were not available. When he'd earlier confessed to you how much trouble he was in, you hadn't taken him seriously; now, he was leaving no doubt.

"Back to the house," Marc said in the car. "We've got highlighting to do."

Marc owns a shoebox full of highlighters, and every night for the past week has handed you the shoebox, a stack of forms, and said, "Get to it."

When Marc attempts to teach you something new about notary work, the lessons come swift, and the practice is boring as hell. It hurts your head, the things you've gotta do. "Get to *what?*" you asked the first time, a week ago.

"I'm printing out the documents for tomorrow," he said. "And we need to highlight every spot for their signatures or initials."

"Can't we just point it out? Say, 'sign there'?"

"Sure," he said. "That's how I started. Flipping page by page through the packet, pointing, losing my place. Watching them go cross-eyed. Losing *their* place. Took me twice as long for each closing."

So tonight, when you get home from the three-Hummer-house, you watch the Magic game together, Game Five vs. Boston, and Marc declares that you'll spend the entire three hours prepping documents. "Follow my lead," he tells you, and he goes page by page in the tall stack, highlighting highlighting highlighting, till one marker runs dry, and then the next, and he's moving so fast he's sweating, and you look down and realize—by the time the game's first half is over—you've only gone through ten pages.

Marc stares at your stack and says, "What gives?"

You point to the TV and tell him not to worry, just take it easy, the Magic are winning.

"Why would you *say* that?" Marc shakes his head. "Don't ever jinx a lead." Then he gets back to work, says to the TV: "Please, Magic, my brother knows not what he does. Do *not* blow this lead."

Minutes later, Stephon Marbury leads a furious second-half comeback for Boston, brings the Celtics from 14 points down to *win the game* and put the Magic on the brink of elimination in the Eastern Conference Semi-Finals.

"Master of Panic!" Marc screams at Coach Stan Van Gundy. He throws a highlighter at the screen. "*Fuck* you, Van *Gundy!*"

The next day, you're closing loans again.

Other rules Marc teaches you along the way: always carry a full box of blue pens, and be prepared for one to go missing at each closing. "People love stealing pens," he says. And remember: *blue* pens, not *black*. Why? Who knows? Also: before leaving home to close a loan, plot out the closest FedEx from that location. Learn how to use a fax machine, too. Carry a Ziploc baggie of extra binder clips and a snap-shut case of hanging file folders for any papers you accumulate. A disorganized car's a disaster waiting to happen.

Marc is hyper-focused during the day, as if an extra ten minutes at one closing will kill his productivity for the whole day ("We can*not* fall behind schedule, or we'll be working all night," he says). More and more, you see him unwind at night by watching Magic games, but his temperament is… violent…flashes of desperation. No amount of "it's just a game" consolations will ease him down from the ledge, and you're worried about what he'll do if the Magic get knocked out of the playoffs.

On Thursday, when Game Six arrives, you expect the worst. You expect the Magic to crumble. The Celtics to push them around and win the series with ease. You expect to see Marc throw a pint glass at his own TV or something.

To advance to the Conference Finals, the Magic need to win Game Six, and then (if they win, and that's a big *if*) they have to travel back to Boston and win Game Seven. Marc reminds you again and again that no road team has ever won a Game Seven in Boston, and there in your brother's living room with highlighters and binder clips strewn about the area rug, you sense the Magic's playoff run is over. The way Marc looks, it seems like the city itself is on the brink of elimination. His business, too. Everything. And this is the first moment that you *know* something is seriously wrong with him, that he's been burying something deep within himself.

For much of Game Six, it seems his prophecy will be made reality: the Magic can't hit a shot. It seems as if the Celtics will bully and bruise past the smoke-and-mirrors Magic. But in the fourth quarter, the boys in blue flip the script.

Rafer Alston—"Skip to My Lou," they call him, the playground legend—nails a three, and then it's Hedo Türkoğlu sinking a shot from long range, the Magic scoring eleven of the game's final thirteen points to win 83-75. You look at the stats—Boston with 19 turnovers, and whistled for 26 fouls to the Magic's 15—and the Magic, you realize, just won a gritty game, a *bruiser*, and this playoff series is going to a damned Game *Seven*. You watch Marc run his hands through his hair, shut his eyes, and you expect a positive change in his mood (maybe even "Do you *believe* it? We've got a chance!"), but he just says, "Doesn't matter. We're still gonna blow it."

A new day, Friday, and more loan-closings. More practice, and more of Marc's rules.

You visit Delaney Park for a cash closing with a man who's just come from the golf course and who doesn't appear to have anywhere important to go afterward. "Never get tired of this feeling," he says, holding up the key to the house he's just purchased.

Out here, just southeast of downtown, the streets go to brick and the houses go historic, cinderblock bungalows with front porches, sixty years old, seventy, small houses with deep backyards, and guest houses under the shade of Spanish-mossed oaks. Beside the historic homes are faux-historic mansions, part of some slow but long-running effort by the wealthy to return to the shade-cooled brick roads after having scattered to golf neighborhoods years ago, to reclaim Delaney Park two lots at a time and build unnaturally colossal homes that are supposed to look like they've been there forever. It goes old house, old house, new mansion, old house, new mansion. When you come upon a lake (you were surprised to discover there are hundreds throughout Orlando), it just goes mansion, mansion, mansion—porches on the first floor and porches on the second, boats and docks and boathouses with locked gates at the sidewalk. It gets especially egregious when Marc drives you out to Edgewater and Lake Ivanhoe. These are the sorts of houses whose Christmas lights you can't wait to see, whose Fourth of July parties are probably unlike anything you've ever experienced.

"Someday, right, Marc?" you say and nudge him.

"Fuck them," he says. "Fuck their houses."

And then it's Sunday, Game Seven of the Orlando-Boston series, and you're out at the Ale House where the nacho plate seems to occupy the entire table, and it's you and you alone because Marc refuses to watch the game. You weren't allowed to turn on the television at his house and you decided that you had to get out of there and escape the airborne toxic event of his attitude, and so you sit at the bar with your mountain-sized nachos and watch the Magic win the game (and the series) with ease. There's no drama; quite simply, the Magic win. And everyone's clinking glasses at the bar and at every high-top, waving foam fingers and blowing blue-and-white victory kazoos. The Orlando Magic are moving on to the Eastern Conference Finals!

But when you get home, Marc seethes: "Shit. Now we've gotta play LeBron."

It's too much, your brother. Too much for you to process how this life— one in which you've got a giant bedroom, working AC, a pool, a bathroom with meticulous tile-work—this life, the one for which you left muggy backwoods Georgia—this life, the one that was supposed to be better, happier, because you wouldn't be a bedroom away from your old man—how can this life feel just as soul-sucking as the one you thought you'd escaped?

AND HERE YOU ARE, pushing the record button and saying, "Uh. Where to start, where to start? Well. My favorite foods are Scotch and soda. Scotch without soda. Scotch any old way." Your wife bought you a tape recorder, insisted you keep a record of your time in office. The world will want to know the history of the city's most important decade, she said, and she drafted pages and pages of questions to help you with the process, so your book would feel more like an interview than a memoir.

You can't think of anything else to add, so you walk to the end table where you keep your decanter and a couple stacked rocks glasses. You pull the top off the decanter and pour yourself a Scotch. "Writing is tough damn work," you say and take a quick burning sip of the Scotch to confirm its greatness and importance, then shut off the recorder.

Orange Avenue outside your windows, the mayor's office your prize. Wood-paneled walls, as God intended. You're wearing a cowboy hat and powder-blue leisure suit pants, the jacket draped over the rocking chair. You're standing tall in an office full of American flags and framed photos of yourself shaking hands with LBJ, holding hunting rifles with Richard Daley.

What a time to be in charge! A new golden age for the city, there on the horizon: Disney World under construction, I-4 finished, the promise of a new Orlando within reach. Ten years from now, ain't no one gonna call you "podunk" or "backwater" or "off the beaten path." And when they talk about who brought 'em into the future, they'll be talking about Carl T. Langford.

Of course, just a couple months in, you were handed a catastrophe in the making: the city had just bought this million-dollar incinerator, supposed to burn up whatever garbage you could throw in there, like some science-fiction movie, reduce a couch to a pebble of ash. But hell, technology and progress, and this incinerator…it's like the incinerator didn't like his job, like he was some Got-damn hippie on a protest against burning trash. *Save the coffee filters*! *Save the half-eaten oranges*! Sum bitch just up and quit.

The city's landfills were all packed solid, see. And so you had garbage comin' in, five and a half pounds per person, every damn day, and the hard-asses in Orange County, they wouldn't take any of your 170 tons of daily garbage, and you're landlocked, see? You can't just take the garbage out to sea, or whatever the coastal cities do. New York, with their garbage island. You couldn't sneak into Daytona and dump it on their beach. And you couldn't make people take their trash *back*, bury it in their backyards. You were stuck with it: mayor of a small town turning to Big City overnight, garbage leaking from every pore.

"The sidewalks," you said in council meeting. The idea came that quick. (Well, you'd first suggested Lake Eola Park; nobody'd notice 'cause you'd bury the trash in the dead of night, and it'd create some beautiful rolling hills in what was currently a flat park. But that idea went over like a turd in a punchbowl.) "At night," you said, "lift the sidewalk panels up. One by one. Dig a hole, then dump the garbage down in there. Put back the pavement like we're just repairing some underground pipes or something, right? New grass, new landscaping. Some pretty flowers. Hell, long as the new trees don't blossom old milk cartons, we *golden*, ain't we?"

"Sir," your assistant Greg said, "is this really…"

"Anyone got a better idea, they're welcome to share," you said, but who was going to challenge the World War II hero in the cowboy hat, the man who wore a Superman cape to his first council meeting, the man who rode a damn elephant through the streets of downtown for the Presidents' Day parade? You lean over the table, seeming to occupy more space than all the rest of 'em combined: "Clandestine, gentlemen. We need to act quick, and we need to keep our mouths shut."

Leaders lead, and followers follow. First month in office, and the council fell in line.

About town, not a damn soul knew.

Hell, by summer you were toast of the town, invited to speak at every damn civic club worthy enough to have its logo stamped on Orange Blossom Trail's "Welcome to Orlando" sign. Kiwanis, Shriners, Italian-American Society, all of 'em Good Old Boys at once excited and terrified by the future of the city, but you were there to slap backs and reassure 'em that ain't nothing they loved was gonna change. So they invited you, just months into your political career, to feel good about themselves, to maybe boost their meeting attendance and make sure they had quorum for their annual officer elections. And month after month you stood up there, the man who'd buried garbage under their noses for ninety days, acting out the persona of mayor you knew they wanted, making a few jokes about politicians, maybe dropping a General Patton quote, or hell, something from Walt Disney himself (people love that bullshit), some inspirational gobbledygook you've repeated so much it drips from your mouth like dog slobber. Hell, you say "dadgum" so much in your speeches (people *request* it) that now you're saying it at home, too, and that ain't right. Fuck that silly-ass word. Behind closed doors, you love the purity and honesty of the word "fuck," but that shit ain't family-friendly, ain't Kiwanis-approved. This meeting, that meeting, and someone with a sash to inevitably say, "The man who put Orlando on the map!" as he introduces you, and you know that everyone in these audiences is thinking *Yes! The man who brought us Disney World!*, even though you had nothing to do with that, but you can't correct anyone without seeming ungrateful. And this man with a sash, he stuffs his face into the microphone almost like he's gonna eat it up: "Gentlemen! Please welcome Hizzoner the Mayor, Carl T. Langford!"

"Ho-ho!" you say in return, every damn time, strutting up to the stage or the podium or whatever with a hand out like, *No, no, no, I don't deserve this. Please, you're too kind.* All that. Jolly Old Mayor in his cowboy hat, a man who'd be a caricature if the whole damned town wasn't populated with Southern movers 'n' shakers—Got-damn editorial cartoons come to life.

You don't know what's going to happen here in ten years, fifteen, twenty. How many more civic clubs will give you plaques and thunder "*Hizzoner* the Mayor!" to electric applause, how long this whole charade will last, you the face of Metro Orlando on *60 Minutes*, the Age of Disney World your gift to the world. You don't know what will come. All you know's that there's garbage under those streets out there. That one. That one. Every sidewalk in the city. Beneath every park, every swingset. A few tons here, a hundred tons there. By the airport, by the Air Force base. Tens of thousands of tons, the bulk of it in an empty stretch of land on Central near Dickson Azalea Park, right by the Reeves Terrace projects, buried behind the tall oak trees and thick palmetto scrub so no one could see what was happening. Three months you buried the garbage, dead of night, until the incinerator was fixed and a new landfill site was designated. It's out there, and you know sooner or later it'll come bubbling out the storm drains. Sooner or later the world will see what the city has been built upon.

AND THEN YOU'RE SITTING at a high-top lunch counter ripped from the background of a *Forrest Gump* flashback, a wax paper-wrapped hot roast beef sandwich before you on the cafeteria tray you used for transport, a side of tots and a collection of barbecue and horseradish dipping cups surrounding it. "This is what makes the city *the city*," you're telling Elaina, dipping a tot into Hot Barbecue. "This is where the locals eat. Best sandwich in town."

"Steven," Elaina says, eying her own sandwich with distrust, "it looks rundown. There are clown dolls on trapezes above the trash cans, for God's sake."

"Don't trust me?" you ask.

But the physical space *has* seen better days. It's 2007, the moment in Orlando's history when the big box takeover and the Dardenization of cuisine has reached a nauseating peak, and yet Beefy King persists, this relic of the late '60s, fueled by some combination of charm and nostalgia and…what? An honest love for its sandwiches but a disregard for its appearance, as if it doesn't *want* new customers? It isn't unclean so much as it is anti-slick, the decades-old sign outside—"Beefy King" spelled out in space-age *Jetsons* font, a cartoon bull in gold crown breathing steam out its flared nostrils—still cracked from Hurricane Charley debris. Inside, the floor tiles are yellowed with age, and to access the bathroom, customers have to walk outside and nudge their way through the cars in the drive-through line, the exact opposite of convenience. And the clowns. Straight out of a low-budget horror movie. But still there's a line out the door for those amazing roast beef sandwiches, every damned day.

"Think of it this way," you say and motion around you. "This is all just the wear and tear of a life well-lived. These new restaurants that you love so much—the Cheesecakes Factories and the Bahama Breezes—they're too new, too corporate to have any interesting scars."

"Okay, okay," she says. "First bite."

You take a deep breath, fingers clutching the ancient countertop, and her approach—eyes closed, mouth wide, a hearty chomp—would be commercial-worthy, if only Beefy King cared to film a commercial.

"It's good," she says after a few moments of this, her eyes reopening. "You're right."

"Life-changing?"

"With the horseradish," she says. "Life-changing."

"Homemade, too, that horseradish sauce!" And in this moment, you realize you're coming on a bit strong, your finger pointed directly at the food in your girlfriend's face, the manic Joker grin you're making, the overwhelming urge to shout affirmations about this place and to make her love it as much as you love it…one might find all of this a tad off-putting, creepy, especially because these are still the early days of your relationship with Elaina, and you're not yet sure which of your quirks are endearing and which are annoying. You are eager to use the words "I love you," to use them every day, but you remain guarded about how you act and what you reveal about yourself, lest Elaina realize she is leagues above you in looks, intelligence, personality, good will, ambition…and self-esteem, obviously.

"Can I take a picture of you?" you try.

"Eating?" she says.

"I mean. If you don't want—"

"Oh, for your blog! Yes, yes! Sorry! Just wait." She dabs at her face with a napkin, examines her reflection in the window, then returns to her sandwich and her tots. "Make sure it's cute. And I get final say."

Sometime after college, you registered a blog called The Other City Beautiful, and while you initially conceived it as a showcase for your concert photography, all those pictures you took at the dark and dirty punk shows of your Orlando youth, it didn't take you long to imagine something grander: a blog that would do battle against the stereotypes foisted upon Orlando by the outside world (and too often accepted by its own citizens), a blog that—through elaborately written, immersive set-piece narratives— would place the reader directly into *authentic* Orlando. You—Steven Hart, freelance graphic designer by day, Orlando culture warrior by night— would single-handedly create a grassroots campaign to *rebrand the city*. When you're done, the world will not see Orlando as Theme Park City, nor as the plastic bubble-gum O-Town of the boy band era, but a city with a vibrant personality all its own.

Now you're snapping photos: of the sauces, of the kitchen staff, of Elaina giving her sandwich the "I'm gonna eat you" stare, of Elaina biting and chewing and generally looking fantastic. Out of fear that she'd find your unwavering enthusiasm for your blog too geeky, borderline obsessive, this is the first you've dared to ask her along on one of your blogging adventures, and it's certainly the first time you've asked to do something so bold as take photos of her, though it's a good sign that she's fine with them going online, an undeniable announcement to the world that the two of you are serious. That's big.

Then again, maybe not? Elaina has her own blog, after all. Ever since college, she's been restoring furniture, creating inexpensive interior design accessories from cast-off crap. Weekend projects: custom furniture, wall art, each project netting a couple hundred bucks, each project photo-slideshowed on a blog that has already (through no conscious planning) made Elaina into a brand. "Ten Things You Can Do With Old Wrapping Paper," "Five Ways to Recycle Old Toys as Wall Decorations," that sort of thing, her friends frequently deployed as models for the tutorials, or for party scenes, sitting on pallet chairs holding custom-painted martini glasses.

"This right here, this is the city of Orlando," you tell Elaina, sitting back down. "See, the problem is, too many people think it's *there* on the outskirts. The subdivisions. The golf courses." (You stop yourself from saying, "Where *you* live, Elaina." God, how disastrous that would be to indict her when you instead want to inspire her.) "That's not Orlando. That's, like, some fake appendage that the transients *think* is Orlando."

"So I'm a transient?" Elaina asks. "I've lived here six, seven years now."

"Uh," you say. Shit. You are not yet willing to risk the relationship's settling foundation over a semantic argument. "But you've now experienced the *real* Orlando"—you point to her sandwich—"so not anymore, you're not."

Nice recovery.

"So why do you care so much about this?" she asks. "What does any of it matter?"

"You might as well ask, why does it matter where you live? You came to Orlando for a reason, right?"

"I came for school."

"But you had options."

"I came for school, and I stayed for a job."

"That can't be all there is."

"Love what you do, and love the ones you're with," she says and pops a tater tot. "For me, that's all there is."

The "L" word. It was there, the sentence not yet constructed in the way you hope it will someday be, but it rolled off her tongue nonetheless and you heard it. You'd love to stay there, to linger in the warmth of that word, but at the same time you sense that this conversation—here, now—is your chance to finally move forward and explain to Elaina how much all of this matters to you, to reveal your interests fully and hope—*pray*—she doesn't just dismiss you as some weirdo nerd. She knows you have an Orlando blog, and she knows that this is your favorite restaurant, but does she know the depth of your love for this city? Does she know that you spend much of your workday deep in thought, lamenting—as you paint pixels onto digital images one by one—how the outside world views Orlando?

You post all kinds of stuff on your blog—concert photos, restaurant reviews, profiles of "Outstanding Orlandoans!", a dozen categories—but the most important feature by far is your long-running series of location spotlights, the top fifty places in Orlando that define the *real* Orlando. Fifty entries. An Orlando Manifesto. Your *Orlandofesto*, if you will, in which you painstakingly lay out the city's past, present, and future, all it has been, all that it can be. The list started with #50, and now that you're down to #18 (Beefy King), you're mad that you didn't start with #100, because, in the cocktail napkin drafts of the final spots, there's no room for Nora's or Greenwood Cemetery or the floral sundial at Leu Gardens. So much to love in this city. So much. The naked-lady wallpaper at Wally's, the checkered tablecloths at Linda's La Cantina, the mission-style Amtrak station from 1926, the miniature Statue of Liberty leading into Ivanhoe Village. If only you can convince Elaina that this is not some bizarre obsession, but a cause that *matters*…if only you can get her on your side…

"Doesn't it bother you just a little?" you ask Elaina. "How everyone thinks we're some theme park city?"

"Why would it bother me?"

"This is our home. This is how people see us. I mean, it's 2007, thirty-six years after Disney World opened, and most of our own population doesn't even realize that Disney isn't 'Orlando,' but this, like, shady dystopian-novel entity called the 'Reedy Creek Improvement District,' and it regulates itself and only answers to local government as a courtesy, and—"

"Please. Who doesn't love Disney World?"

You chew your sandwich, shake your head. So many things you want to say on *that* topic.

"Listen, Steven. All I'm saying is that I prefer to not be defined by things"—she waves her hands around to indicate the city, its population, its businesses, its reputation, even its sandwiches—"that I can't control. I am me. You are you. Regardless of zip code."

You imagine just giving up, laughing it all off, tabling this conversation and hoping a new moment someday presents itself, but at the same time, you *can't* imagine being anywhere else. In the first twelve years of your life, you lived in five different cities, your father an assistant football coach with a new team seemingly every year, not even a *head coach*, nor a *coordinator*, just some assistant with different bitchwork, first at the University of Kansas, then a big step up to the Kansas City Chiefs, then down to Mississippi and over to Virginia Commonwealth and a strange journey to the semi-big-leagues of the burgeoning Arena Football League with the Tampa Bay Storm, before finally taking a front office role with the Orlando Predators, where he's been ever since. Almost every year throughout your childhood, a new town and a new school. Worse than a military brat: a coaching brat. No friends who stuck, no place that felt like home, always nasty looks from the other kids at school, like *who is this impostor* (all the while hating the game of football)? But here in Orlando: this was the first place where everyone felt as displaced as you did. This was allowed to be *your place*.

"But what if I *could* control it?" you ask.

"I'm not sure I follow."

"How much do you Nona?" you ask.

She pops a tot, cocks her head to the side. "Now I'm definitely confused."

"That was a billboard I saw awhile back," you say. "'How Much Do You Nona?' A sign for the new developments out at Lake Nona."

"Lake Nona? Is that where the med school is going?"

You nod. You remember the day you saw that billboard, how intensely you hated that stupid catchphrase. Still, the pun infiltrated your brain, and—after a little Googling—you discovered that the phrase was referring to the new "Medical City" rebrand for the Orlando region called "Lake Nona," a gigantic spread of undeveloped land southeast of the airport that'd soon house UCF's newly approved medical school and new hospitals and research centers and medical start-ups and dozens of new gated subdivisions and golf courses for all those high-income jobs. According to the city's colorful online brochures and press releases, all the research money and all the medical jobs will transform and diversify Orlando's economy and identity, and nobody will ever see the city as Mickey Mouse Town anymore. Lake Nona is Orlando's *future*! Currently, of course, Nona is mostly cow pastures and billboards on scrubland far from the city center, the rebrand a far-off fantasy for the developers who are busy building thousands of five-bedroom homes and betting on their future Orlando.

You tell Elaina about this, about how—the more you sifted through old Tourism Bureau brochures and pamphlets from decades gone by—the more frustrated you grew. For so long, the city's marketing materials seemed to boast only of future development, like they were ashamed of what the city was. Always looking to some outside "visionary" to *remake it*. Always a strained comparison to Miami. Orlando was a citrus city, until that was outdated and uncool, and then Orlando was a Tupperware city, and then a military and space city, and then a theme park city, and then a hotel and convention city, and then, in the late '90s, there was the "Innovation at Work" campaign, when Orlando wanted the world to know that the theme park Imagineers were taking their modeling and simulation talents into into defense contracting. Posters, brochures, banners: "Innovation at Work," the words written in this bubbly neon font straight out of a roller rink. You searched and you searched, but you couldn't find a marketing campaign that captured the city's real history and personality: the way that Colonial Drive feels, driving away from the new downtown high-rises and through Little Vietnam, the decades seeming to go in reverse, block by block, driving past businesses that have been around since the advent of the word "astronaut," neighborhoods and shopping centers that still look like 1965 and still beat with the same goofy positivity of "It's A Small World."

Culture is not a thing to be decided upon at an institutional level, you tell Elaina. Culture is not a thing to be dictated and defined and constrained by political decree. No proclamation can bring to life the artist or writer or culinary wizard whose work will reflect perfectly the way people feel about the city, the way people *live* in the city. Culture is an organic entity, and a leader can't *force* it into being; a true leader can only ensure it is showcased, curated, amplified, celebrated. You tell Elaina that the Lake Nona billboard helped you realize *you* could be that curator, the one to show the world the "other City Beautiful," *your* city beautiful. This is a *culture war*, and you want to dedicate your time, your energy, your whole life, to winning hearts and minds. Someday, perhaps, Orlando Culture will even look back and thank you.

You stop. You've been pointing a tater tot at her for several minutes. "Shit. That was a rant. I went on a rant. Oh God." Tot dropped. Hands in your hair. Eyes fixed on the remnants of your sandwich, afraid to look over. "You're still here, right? Please tell me you're still here."

"I'm still here."

"I mean, like, here…or *here* here?"

Shit, that made no sense. Damn it, Steven!

"I'm glad you're passionate," Elaina says finally. "It's what I love about you, Steven."

What I love about you.

And against your better judgment, you lean over the counter and grasp the back of her head and give her the sort of full-face kiss that you've only ever seen in movies. *What I love about you*: how could she know that this was the best possible thing she could've said? "You have no idea what that means," you tell her after you've backed away. "No idea."

With a closed mouth, she laughs, then wipes her lips with the back of her hand. "You know there's still sandwich in my mouth, right?"

"I'm sorry," you say. "I just…"

"Don't be sorry, Steven," she says. "You know, I feel like I get you now, in a way that maybe I hadn't before? I feel like we shared something just now. Besides, um, roast beef?"

You exhale, allow yourself to laugh.

You understand immediately (but would never dare to speak the words aloud) that the two of you are a perfect match, two artists who've found weekday jobs in your industries of interest, but who've scratched out artistic endeavors on the weekends. A perfect coupling, like a listicle meeting a tutorial. You will not write this scene into your blog post about Beefy King, the #18 spot on the list of Fifty Places in Orlando That Define the *Real* Orlando; you will not trumpet your own personal love story, the things you realized while eating hot roast beef sandwiches, even as you post the sexiest damn sandwich-eating photos the world has ever seen. But for years to come, you know this place will matter as much for its meals as for this moment you shared here with your future wife, the moment when you vocalized everything you ever wanted in the world and found in Elaina an advocate.

But the moment is fading, the perfect moment, it is gone, and

AND YOU'RE BACK at Lake Eola in the summer of 2008, waiting while the photographer sets up his equipment for your engagement shoot. "The swans," you say to Marc. "So lovely."

"You say that every time we come down here," Marc says. He's texting someone.

"So? Is it wrong to appreciate something beautiful?"

"Look past the swans," he says, pointing. "You can see the bird shit from here. That little island in the lake." You see it. You've seen it many times: the stones that from here look white and sun-bleached, but up close it's Bird Shit Island. The birds hang out high in the trees and drop bombs all day long. "Make sure *that* doesn't wind up in our photos."

It never ends.

You toss a twig into the water and the swans regard you curiously. "You can see the negative in *anything*, can't you?" Throughout Lake Eola Park, signs implore you not to disturb nature: do not feed the swans, do not pet the swans, do not grab the swans, do not jump in the water with the swans, all of the signs written with a sigh, the sort of tone that indicates each rule was a reaction to some asshole doing each specific thing. "We wish we didn't have to tell you this," the signs seem to say, "but please don't try to *ride* the swans. Seriously. *You, yeah you*: get off the fucking swans." The swans are just as vital to Lake Eola as Lake Eola itself; there are even small concrete ramps around the lake so the swans have an easier time waddling in and out.

"These swans cost, like, 10,000 bucks apiece," Marc says. "Do you remember when someone stole a couple? Tried to smuggle them to Jacksonville and sell them?"

"I remember," you say. No sign for *swan theft*. (Well. Not yet.)

"Smart idea. If you've got a buyer. That guy only *thought* he had a buyer."

"No buyer," you say, "what an idiot." You try to sound sarcastic, but you wonder if Marc is actively listening, and therefore capable of detecting subtext, of applying this subtext to his knowledge and understanding of his own financial dealings. His life is an orgy of multitasking, of partial commitment to a thousand tasks at once.

"Really," Marc says, then laughs at something on his phone.

"I mean, seriously," you say, dropping the sarcasm to see if he'll hear you, "who would take an *insane* risk—something that could *ruin* their life—something like stealing a swan, or—hmm—putting all their money into house-flipping—without having a buyer in mind?"

Marc doesn't acknowledge. At this very moment, he's likely discussing additional "insane risks" with Edwin, new opportunities even as the real-estate world teeters on the brink of collapse, but the two of them are encouraged by the sales they've recorded, as if the sky's the limit because they've had just a taste of success. They're looking to buy properties whose owners have lowered their prices by forty thousand dollars, but they've refused to lower their own inflated asking prices: do they even see the stupidity of this?

Next weekend, your apartment lease expires and you will officially move in with him. In that too-big golf community house of his, the one with empty rooms and old Target furniture from his college years. It's as if Marc has ideas about all of Life's Big Moments, and all of Life's Sacred Institutions, and they're all misinformed. In order for marriage to be successful, for instance, he thinks he's got to have some big house in an upper-middle-class neighborhood. Even if you don't need the space, *get a big house!*

Or take the engagement: he had to tap the wine glass at a fancy restaurant, had to say, "Everyone, can I have your attention?" He kept tapping even though no one was looking. Had to get down on his knee. He'd paid the waitress to start clapping and try to rally others into applause, but the place was too loud and too dim and no one really knew what was happening until it was all over. There's a trace of good intention in his ideas, but it's too often drowned out by some imperative to "do this because *that's what people do*," regardless of whether it makes sense. He should've proposed outside, where it was quiet, where it was about *you* and *him*, not the people watching. But he couldn't part with his own fantasies. It's like he lives by some inflexible set of rules tragically unsuited for real life.

The photographer is peering into one camera, moving it close and then pulling it far, like he can't decide if he's farsighted or nearsighted. He's a gap-toothed bald man in a bowtie, not at all what you'd expected from watching so many wedding movies and TV shows. He seems to bumble far too much, pulling cameras from a case only to immediately shove them back in like he's unsure why he brought them, and you worry if you made a mistake in hiring him.

This is just the first of many worries, of course. Three weeks from now, you're hosting a party at the new house that will double as "engagement celebration" and "housewarming," and you've invited all your friends from work and from Alumni Club. You've no idea what expectations formed in Marc's mind when you said "housewarming party," if he's still stuck in his early twenties, thinking drunken bounce house! and ice slides! and bottles of Jack! and all the sticky frat star accoutrements that were fun when you first met him but are now nauseating to consider. Or maybe he's just taken all these images and slathered them with the Krispy Kreme glaze of a life more moneyed; maybe he's picturing a caterer, and thousands upon thousands of egg rolls and fried avocado wedges and Key lime shrimp (but still the bounce house).

Either way, you're worried. The party must reveal to all these women *the perfect version of you*, not Short Shelley who could still be a high school cheerleader, but Shelley the event planner, Shelley who's designed flawless Save-the-Dates, Shelley who's grown up, who's moved past beer tubs and tight shorts worn for tips, who no one will ever again see dancing on a bartop, who'll never again close down One Eyed Jack's on a Tuesday night to impress the older man she's been dating, who'll never again walk into a classroom during her senior year twenty minutes late and dressed in a hoodie and track pants and—just a short while later, during an especially quiet part of the lecture—hurry for the exit so she can throw up in a trash can in the hallway (not to mention withdraw from that course out of embarrassment, which delayed her graduation one semester, though she told everyone she stayed in college an extra semester so she could "find another internship"), who'll never again miss a morning at her internship during her *second* final semester because of *another* Tuesday night out with sorority friends. No. You must show these women the Shelley who has it together, the adult Shelley.

"Okay, let's start off with solo shots," the photographer says, and it might just be your imagination, but you swear you can hear the gap-tooth in his voice.

"Sounds good," you say.

He photographs the ring from several angles, the Lake Eola fountain in the background of one, the swans in the background of another, the long stretch of condos in the background of another. These feel silly to pose for, but you know that it's all about lighting, and focus, blurry background so that the bird shit doesn't look like bird shit. You hired the man. Trust the professional.

He shoots Marc standing on the boardwalk and looking at the fountain. He shoots Marc in ways that make it seem like you're not even in the center of a city, Marc at lake's edge, Marc sitting on the grass and laughing like a man without a care, while behind him the cypress knees rise like petrified drip castles from the water. What the pictures will never show: you had to take Marc's phone so he wouldn't check it between shots.

The photographer shoots you with your fingertips on a palm tree, looking around as if coming out in a game of hide-and-seek. He shoots you on the grass, as if at a picnic (and it takes every bit of your self-control to ignore the bugs).

"Okay, let's get some fun shots to loosen up before the formal stuff," he says.

"Fun shots?" Marc asks. He's looking toward his phone, which rests atop your purse twenty feet away. "Those weren't fun?"

"Candid stuff," the photographer says. "Just a couple having fun?"

"Um. What am I supposed to do?" Marc asks.

"Just act natural," you say, and play-hit him. "Natural."

"I don't…" Marc holds up his hands. "What's *natural?*"

The photographer looks as if no one has ever before asked how to be candid. "Like you're a couple," he says. "Like you love her."

"Like you love me, Marc."

Marc closes his eyes, breathes slowly. Fingers squeezing the bridge of his nose. "Seriously. Just tell me what I'm supposed to do."

"Kiss me, for God's sake," you say. "Hug me. Look *engaged.*"

You feel the blood rising, a more-and-more familiar feeling, a fuse being lit. You're grabbing at his hand and he's pulling away from you with this even-angrier look in his eye.

"What does 'look engaged' even mean?"

"It's…fucking *love* me, okay?"

"—so abstract—"

"—should be fucking *second nature*—"

"Why can't anyone just—"

"—look like you're in love, can't you just—" you're saying and the sweat is beading and it will ruin your fucking makeup—

Breathe, Shelley.

It's only the start of the shoot, but there's a bad feeling in the air, a volcanic flow beneath your skin that until now you've been able to suppress, and you don't know how you should proceed, what to say in order to prevent yourself from sweating more, and prevent that inner heat from rising further and prevent—here, and twenty years from now—an association of *anger* every time you think about or see your photos, every time you think about your engagement, and by extension your marriage, and by extension (eventually) your family, your whole fucking *life*.

This isn't you, this anger, but you can't shake it, you can't

AND YOU FEEL DAMN GOOD that you bought just in time, scooped up vast swaths of swamp and forest while the price was still manageable, but the land purchased is so confoundingly thick with palmetto scrub it's nearly impassable. Still. Little by little, you clear it, bloody your hands lifting the saw-toothed stems of palm fronds, pick ten thousand sandspurs from your sweaty socks. You eat gator tail with the grizzled Florida Crackers you hire to do the heavy lifting but who rarely speak to you and never smile; they measure off this from that, tell the Negroes where to dig, which trees to "X," and you know they don't trust you or appreciate what you're doing. Probably they call you "carpetbagger" behind your back, and this wouldn't bother you if you'd chosen to buy land in Georgia or Alabama, but this is central Florida. This is supposed to be the frontier, a new Manifest Destiny for America, a blank slate upon which you'd build paradise, but too often it feels like some imbecile brother to the rest of the South. The people here, the Crackers and the Negroes and the mostly-shiftless Seminole descendants, all act like you're encroaching on their turf, like they didn't *want* this, like they're plotting together to ruin it all as soon as your back's turned.

No matter.

Day by day, the land's cleared. A dozen men walk into the thickness of the palmetto scrub with machetes whose blades are stained green from all the chopping, and at the end of the day they emerge covered in mosquito and spider bites, flesh torn and split in a hundred places, but the scrubland's beaten back inch by inch, foot by foot, acre by acre. In other spots less dense with vegetation, what started as thick swamp and cypress forest is now flat and sandy, an impressive transformation that would've taken twice the time back in rocky New York. Here, flattening cleared land is just like ironing wrinkled pants.

You've hired the architects, too, and you're thinking big: you're thinking of a centerpiece Mediterranean hotel like the ones in the brochures for Miami Beach. You're thinking of draining this swamp-lake here in the center of the land, casting out the critters, digging deeper to make it into something rounder and more symmetrical, and you'll even bring in Atlantic Coast sand and make a beach right here, by God. That's what everyone wants, after all. They just don't want the waves, the sharks, the storms. You watched those tourists in Jacksonville, in Daytona, men from Omaha and Chicago and Buffalo, how they tiptoed into the Atlantic and then ran away when the waves crashed, laughing like they conquered the ocean when really they were scared of it. But here? An ocean without waves, that's what you'll call it. No jellyfish, no crabs. Biggest pool in the world. And right there in the center of your inland ocean, you'll plop a pile of Atlantic sand and make an island, plant a few palm trees, build a restaurant accessible only by private ferry. This will be the most famous development—no, *attraction*—in the U.S.

But what to call this centerpiece, that's the question. The Grand Floridian? Swamplandia? Tomorrowland? The Island of Adventure? Wet and Wild? So many options your head swims.

For now, the first neighborhood will be called Paradise Park, and you've already constructed the gates, the most essential element. That's what you learned when you joined Walter Fuller and Doc Davis for golf and steaks over in St. Pete Beach. The houses don't matter. People'll buy the *promise* of a house so long as the gate—the image on the front of the brochure—inspires dreams. Plant some orange trees and magnolias on the central boulevard, lay sod and colorful beds of marigolds. The land is yours and now *you've* got Binder Boys working the trains, flashing watercolor renderings of the gate, the towering palms, the sweeping greens. Sell the plots on the opening boulevard, and you'll have the money to build that inland ocean, that hotel, that clubhouse, the polo grounds, the golf course, all the things you're promising, and then sell the next phase and you'll have money for another development in Orlando, and then you'll branch out to Kissimmee and maybe Ocala…so much land, an *empire* really. Someday you'll be the Emperor of Central Florida, you can feel it.

"When will I see you?" Madeline wants to know.

"This will be your last winter without me," you write. "The Fall of 1926 will be your first here in paradise, in our new palace. Just you wait."

Two years ago you were struggling through Albany winters with your hotel, but now you've taken every penny to your name, your full inheritance from your father, and you've invested it in Central Florida. There's barely enough money left to run the hotel up North, but no matter. You've put *that* on the market, too, though Madeline doesn't yet know. Every penny is coming to Florida, and it doesn't matter if the Crackers never thank you, or never trust you, because you're going to *own* the interior of the state, and down here, you're going to be the man you were always meant to

AND THIS YEAR, you're sitting at the table for Vanity Builders, a company that constructs upscale golf-course communities and timeshare developments throughout the South, though you get the feeling that the men at this table have probably never lifted a hammer themselves.

It's your fourth year with the team, your fourth go-round at the Orlando Magic Youth Foundation's Black Tie and Tennies Gala, and you're no longer the bright-eyed rookie aw-shucks-ing your way through the league. You are a man on the rise. A *man*.

At the table over there is attorney John Morgan, his famous "Morgan and Morgan: For the People!" commercials making him a celebrity as recognizable as anyone else in the region. And a few tables over: attorney Dan Newlin, who probably wishes his own commercials could generate for him the same degree of law-fame. And over there, Joey Fatone and Lance Bass and Chris Kirkpatrick. And timeshare mogul David Siegel and his gigantic-boobed wife, the one they call the Queen of Versailles. And Tiger Woods. And a full table of Darden Restaurants executives. And that crazy Asian dude who always wears a t-shirt and jean shorts in those Appliance Direct commercials (your imitation of him is spot-on!). There's Mayor Buddy Dyer and Orange County Commissioner Rich Crotty, and an older woman whom you recognize as an anchor from Central Florida News 13. If this was a superhero movie, the Joker would burst in at any moment to steal the jewelry from the screaming socialites. The Orlando Elite.

And you.

In this room, you're the biggest of all of 'em. In this room, the Joker would bow to *you*.

Your fourth year in the league, and these people—no matter how important, or rich, or whatever—they fucking worship you.

Everyone at this event is dressed in tuxedos and evening gowns, and yet before you is a plate of chicken fingers. A plate? A *bowl*, really. Larger than the salad bowl shared by the entire table. Everyone else has these little side plates for purple-lettuce salads drizzled with nameless dressing from a silver boat, but—as per your request—you are never served tilapia with lemon-dill sauce, never asparagus and hollandaise, never chicken satay and cranberry chutney, none of that bullshit. Instead you are served a plate of *chicken fingers* and *French fries*: you have the power to eat what you want when you want, and you ain't gotta bother looking fancy for no one, even if the room is filled with the Orlando Elite. Tables spread out across the floor of the Amway Arena, a center-court stage book-ended by sparkling black curtains from which you emerged pre-dinner to earthquake applause, wait staff hustling through the tables with freshly popped Heinekens, bar in back pumping out cosmos and gin and tonics. *Earthquake applause.*

Power, ya'll.

Of course, your handlers don't let you drink. That's something you can't control, a demand they won't hear. Hell, they barely let you go out anymore, so careful are they about managing your brand. So there are some checks on your power, but…

"So Dwight, what'cha think about those chicken fingers?" asks the man beside you. He's leaning over with too much familiarity, like the check his company wrote for this event bought him not just a plate of food and a seat, but real friendship with a basketball player as well. Only the biggest donors get a player. You nod to JJ Reddick sitting with some law firm or another, to

Rashard Lewis with Disney. Before you took your place at this table, there was a silent auction out in the concourses for which you had to sign a few jerseys, a few commemorative basketballs; someone even bid twenty grand to golf with you (and hell if you know how to golf, aside from *Golden Tee*). Who knows how much Vanity Builders paid for this table?

"Oh, you know," you say to the table, smiling wide. (They expect the smile. They want it. Polls have shown that it's your greatest attribute, and your agent is currently working on a mega-endorsement deal with McDonald's because they say your smile is the embodiment of the McDonald's brand.) You dip a fry into a pool of ketchup and chomp down. "Ain't nothing like McDonald's mustard sauce, but I'll get by." You're unsure why you just felt the need to name-drop the brand—are you practicing already?—but the man beside you convulses in laughter and slaps your back. A split-second later, though, he pulls his hand away and holds his wrist in pain, like he just smacked a concrete wall. These people: they expect the smile, love it because it makes you appear human, but you *aren't* an ordinary human made of regular old flesh and bone, you are *Superman*. Don't slap Superman's back and expect to come out unscathed.

"Dwight, those look *delicious*," says the woman to your left, her fingertips on your forearm. Slender fingers, nails painted in alternating Magic silver and blue. No matter the price of the gowns or tuxedos, the kitschy fan ornamentation is a subtle reminder that this is supposed to be about *sports*, not just about celebrating wealth. There are rich ladies in corny Magic sunglasses, rich teenagers in headbands with their tuxes, and everyone's wearing tennis shoes: Black Tie and Tennies is the name of the event *and* the dress code. And the more outlandish the tennis shoes, the better. One woman has G.I. Joes painted as Magic players glued to her navy-colored Nikes, and one lawyer-type has model basketball courts constructed atop his Reeboks. It's silly, the amount of money spent on the outfits and the decorations and the food and the liquor. The event itself is silly, over the top, but despite the ridiculousness all around, these people want to comment on your chicken fingers? The past couple years at this gala, the chicken fingers have been a symbol of your happy-go-lucky personality, and a hint at the millions of dollars you'll soon earn just by flashing your smile and making people laugh (You like to make people laugh, you really do. What's better than being the most-liked guy in the room?). But this year, you're starting to worry that the chicken fingers are also evoking…a different kind of laughter. You saw the lawyer give a snort-laugh. At first you thought nothing of it, but now you can't stop yourself from wondering: was he laughing *at* you?

This is not a pleasant thought. This puts a dent in your happiness.

"We all watched the Slam Dunk Contest," the woman says. "Everyone in our office."

"Oh yeah?" you ask.

"We never watched the Slam Dunk Contest before."

"No way," you say. "Ha ha. If I'm not in it, what's the point, right?"

"They're saying you saved it, that the NBA was probably going to cancel it next year, but you *saved* it." Her hand is creeping farther up your arm, is now at your elbow, the touching deeper and more intimate than probably is appropriate. She's twenty years older than you, has to be, her husband just two chairs down, but damned if she doesn't look like she wants to fuck right here and right now. Rip your jacket off, rip open your shirt so the buttons pop off and scatter across the floor. It's a possibility you never considered, an older woman, but her body's tight as a Magic dancer, her whole look more confident than the squeaky little girls that your handlers beat away when you're out and about, and you're actually wondering how it would go down. Shit. Maybe she's an absolute freak? What would she do to you? Finger higher up your arm.

"The Superman cape!" exclaims a man on the far side of the table. "Perfect! Perfect!"

"Ha ha," you say to hide your heavy breathing. "Needed something different, you know? Had to keep it interesting."

Tight body. Fake boobs. Experience.

The woman's fingers slink away as she takes a drink, and you're disappointed when they don't come back.

You shake your head and think about chicken fingers and skittles and Superman, anything but sex. You've gotta be the Ultimate Christian, remember? Market research shows that this one characteristic you barely care about anymore, the Christianity, saves you from all the derogatory race-tinged characterizations, labels like "thug" and "immature punk." Jesus saved Ray Lewis' career, and he was, like, a *murderer* or something. But the obvious drawback is that you are increasingly unable to get laid, your handlers an impenetrable wall against the admirers, and you feel now in your twenties—as a damned *millionaire*—as sex-deprived and anxious as a kid in one of those *American Pie* movies. "The girls are short-term. Think long-term and hold tight to the Christianity," the Guru told you. He was hired by your agent, and though you've never seen the man's face, you've heard his voice enough; he's in your ear on a daily basis, constant critiques and suggestions. "Mention the Christianity once every few weeks," he said. "No one wants you on a pulpit. But you need to remind everyone that you could *never* be Rasheed Wallace."

"And Shaq can just shut his dumb mouth!" says a woman several seats away, maneuvering into the conversation. She's consumed four or five glasses of Sauvignon Blanc since you've been sitting here, her face red and sloppy, the perfect come-down from the elegant sexiness of the lady beside you.

"Shaq?" you ask. "What'd he say about me?"

"About the Superman thing," the woman says. "He said you were unoriginal."

"Oh, that," you say.

"He *left* Orlando," the man says. "He made his bed. People 'round here ain't want nothing to do with that man."

"Far as we're concerned, there's only *one* Superman," the drunk woman says. "It's you. And fat-ass Sha-*quille* O'*Neal* can just…" She pauses, searching for the proper way to describe her anger toward Shaq, but finally she just shakes her trembling fists and settles for: "Ooooh, it makes me so angry."

"It's all right," you say. "He's just playing around." You toy with a chicken finger, take a bite, but man, they really *would* be better with McDonald's hot mustard sauce.

"That's right," the man says. "When you see Shaq on the court, we'll see who the real Superman is."

"Yeah! The *real* Superman!" The drunk woman pushes out her breasts.

"You're the *new* Shaq," one man says. He's got a piece of tilapia skewered on his fork, and it's breaking apart under the weight of the dill sauce. Both of these things—tilapia and dill sauce—make you sick to your stomach, but you smile and dip your chicken in the bowl of ranch.

"New and improved!"

"Shaq 2.0!"

You smile harder, try to keep up with the compliments, but they're coming too quickly.

"You have such a good voice. I can see you doing voices for Pixar movies."

"I see you as a parakeet. A wise-cracking parakeet."

"A parakeet? Come on!"

"An iguana."

"No, a polar bear. Definitely a polar bear."

"Dwight, do your Shaq impersonation!"

Ha ha.

Every conversation comes back to Shaq, doesn't it? And you don't want to be Shaq. Not *Shaq 2.0*, not the "better-looking version of Shaq." None of it. No matter what kind of power you have, no matter how many people love you, it'll always be a sliver of Shaq's own power. This is something your branding and marketing people have yet to tackle. Really, while you were donning the cape at the Slam Dunk Contest, you were barely aware that Shaq had ever called himself Superman. You just thought Superman sounded tough, and supercool, and you wanted to be tough and supercool. The comparisons grate on you. Maybe you could have your people do research on Shaq just so you can avoid his career decisions, just so you can avoid the moments when someone says, "I remember when Shaq did that, *too*."

"You must really hate Shaq," one of the men says.

"I mean," you say. "He's just a guy…"

"But your voice really is better. When Shaq talks, it's like mumble-mumble-mumble."

"Come on, Dwight! The Shaq impersonation! It's so good! You're so funny!"

And really, do you even like chicken fingers anymore? These taste terrible tonight, yet you feel compelled to keep eating them, as if the crowd expects it. Shit, you suddenly *want* that tilapia. When can you stop being the persona you created for yourself? Are you actually the Big Kid, or the Ultimate Christian, or the Savior of Orlando? Are you any of these things? The way the Guru talks, each is a refined "element" of your brand, "like toppings on a pizza," he said, but some days you don't *want* these same fucking toppings. If it was up to you, you'd just be a 22-year-old basketball player out on the town, enjoying your youth. VIP velvet rope, dancing with hotties, chugging whipped-cream vodka. What's so wrong with that?

"Stop talking about Dwight's *voice!*" someone says. "It's his *face*. Shaq doesn't have an A-list face like our boy here. Shaq had to play monsters…what was that movie? *Kazaam? Steel?* Monsters. Dwight could be a leading man."

Leading Man: there's a persona you could enjoy. You shake your head, try to stop thinking so hard about the personae you inhabit. Smile again. Enjoy yourself, Dwight.

"Such a *smile*, too! So non-threatening!"

"Will Smith, move aside!"

"Denzel, find a new line of work!"

"He's a younger, happier…um…what's the name of the guy that played Stringer Bell?"

Then, a moment of silence. This table full of white people has exhausted their knowledge of black movie stars.

"Dwight," someone says, "you should get together with *Tyler Perry!*"

Oh, super, they've got more.

"It could be a whole universe of possibilities, oh my God! Romantic comedies. Dramas. *Madea Sits Courtside.*"

"Ha ha," you say, but the smile is heavier to hold.

Someone spills wine, but that doesn't stop the carnival from screaming along.

"Or Tyler Perry's *Diary of the 7-foot-tall Kid*. You hear that, Dwight?"

"Get his agent on the phone!"

"Tyler Perry's *On a Mission From God*!"

Ha ha.

Smile, laugh. What you wouldn't give to take back all that Christian talk from those old damn interviews. Dennis Rodman never had to worry about this. Ron Artest. Even Michael Jordan: he chose McDonald's and Hanes and motherfucking Looney Tunes as his endorsements, and they didn't care that he gambled and fucked different women every night. What you wouldn't give to have ordered steak on your first meeting with the GM.

"Tyler Perry's *Women Love the Slam Dunk*!" one man says.

"Tyler Perry's *Think Like a Basketball Wife*!" says his super-hot wife beside you, and she's leaning forward so you can see her cleavage, but you know— truthfully—she wouldn't fuck you, because, like so many other women, she doesn't want to ruin you. Dwight Howard The Big Kid. Ultimate Christian. Savior of Orlando.

"You've gotta think *romantic comedy*, Dwight."

"Ooh, what about those Big Momma movies. Except, instead of fat people, it could be tall people."

"*Tall Momma's House*!" one guy says, holding his fist out for a bump but he's too far across the table.

"Oh brilliant!"

Ha ha.

You can't help but wonder, what happens when the McDonald's deal goes through? Or Best Buy? Or Wal-Mart? What will *they* impose on you, these corporations stricter than your father ever was? Who will *they* want you to be?

Smile, smile, through ten more movie pitches, smile through twenty more minutes of sequels and spin-offs, TV shows and cartoons and video games, board games and theme parks. "Have you ever thought about a partnership with Holy Land Experience?" someone asks. Shit, is that the Bible-themed attraction off I-4, the one where Jesus walks around reciting New Testament parables through a hands-free microphone, and kids take pictures with costumed Moseses?

Ha ha. Smile. Smile for the drunk white people.

"Tyler Perry," you say and smile. "Martin Lawrence. Ha ha. Oh, that's funny. You're really funny. Ha ha. I'll remember this. Ha ha. I'll remember all of you. Ha ha ha ha ha ha ha ha ha ha ha

AND YOUR PHONE is telling you that it's May 20, a Wednesday, which makes it three weeks in your brother's house and you're still not comfortable.

All morning you visit neighborhoods in South Orlando by the airport, heavy transatlantic flights rattling the earth below. South Orlando neighborhoods behind SeaWorld, once-quiet '70s suburban enclaves that pre-date the dolphins and shark tanks and theme park traffic. South Orlando, where you're muscling for space on the 528 as pickup trucks clunk along with their boats or jet skis, whatever these people are taking out to Cocoa Beach for the day (boating on a random Wednesday?). It's hot and still and stagnant in Central Florida, here inland where the heat and humidity seem to collect and wait breezelessly, but on the coast it's several degrees cooler, breezy, so you savor the chance to drive the Beeline out to the Space Coast, escape from the city.

More loan-closings in the afternoon. More time in the car, more time in strange living rooms. More time to wonder if you made a mistake by moving here to live with your brother. You thought *independence*. You thought *make something of myself*. You thought *think for myself, do something worthwhile*. And yet...

Back in middle school and early high school, there was a time when your brother was the only thing in the world capable of making you happy. The days and weeks and months after your mother died, when he'd pop into your bedroom in the morning to wake you up, recite *Simpsons* quotes until you finally smiled—first thing in the morning and *who has that kind of energy?*—then came home from his after-school job at the shop and made you dinner (usually just grilled cheese or a frozen pot pie or pan-fried Bubba burgers and tater tots). At night he sat with you to memorize vocabulary flash cards and read passages of "A Modest Proposal" while your father worked at the shop late, later and later as time went on. Never home. Some days, you recall your brother bursting into anger, suppressed grief unleashed suddenly and terribly, and it was on those days that you smiled the hardest, recited your own *Simpsons* quotes, played court jester until *he* calmed down, because if you showed even a hint of your own sadness in those moments, then the situation would spiral out of control. By his senior year, you rooted for Marc to get the hell out of Georgia and away from that house. You rooted for him to become something, and in the back of your mind thought *maybe I can join you someday.*

But then, what happened to you? It's almost as if you grew comfortable with life as a fixture in your father's house, no different than some forgotten lamp, just this thing that kept existing. The shop during the day. Video games deep into the night. Repeat.

Now. Thursday. New day, and more closings.

You ride with your brother up and down I-4, over Lake Ivanhoe and past Ivanhoe Village (Antique District, according to Marc). He tells you about College Park, just north of there, home to Dubsdread, where he paid a lot of money to learn golf and failed miserably in the summer heat. "One of those stupid couples things I tried with Shelley," he says. "I think she just wanted the pink gloves, the golfer outfit." You pass Winter Park, what Marc calls the "cultural hub" of the region. Rollins College. A Tiffany Museum, stained glass and diamonds and what-not. Another "stupid place" he went with Shelley. Farther north on the interstate, Marc points to a sign for Eatonville and says, "Zora Neale Hurston is from there."

"Who?" you ask.

"Zora Neale Hurston. She's, like, the only author to come from Orlando."

"The *only* author?"

"The only one that matters, I guess. She was an Oprah book."

Marc tells you he never actually read Hurston's *Their Eyes Were Watching*

God in his sophomore lit class, though he was supposed to. He knows the book is important somehow, that there's a Zora festival each year in Eatonville (again, he knows no details except what his friend Steven has blathered about), and he knows (from that lit class, and from his crazy liberal lit professor who canceled class the entire week after George W. Bush was sort-of elected president) that Eatonville was a clear loser during the construction of I-4. From what Marc tells you, I-4 was built mid-century to link Tampa on the West Coast and Daytona on the East and was apparently destined to barrel through Orlando. The political movers and shakers *demanded* it, lest the city cede its power to Sanford or Tavares. Highways were the new waterways, the new railroads. A city inaccessible by interstate highway was, well, just a *town*. "So I-4 came," your brother tells you, "with the original plan set to lay pavement through the heart of Winter Park."

You enjoy these moments. It's as if Marc is sitting with you at the kitchen table during freshman year of high school, helping you to calculate the angles of a triangle, helping you understand the motivations of each participant in the first world war.

"Winter Park," you say. "Home of the Tiffany Museum you hated?"

"Right. Cobblestone roads and old-Florida mansions. White people paradise. Well. That's what my crazy liberal professor called it. Now that I think about it, though, he also said that's where he lived… Anyway, the path of I-4 got shifted to the west to avoid Winter Park, and—whoops, sorry, Eatonville. First incorporated black town in the country, and the heart of Eatonville gets halved by the highway."

"That's all true?" you ask.

"Truth is relative, was my professor's point," Marc says. "He showed us five different texts, showed us how each one took a different argument toward the construction of I-4, how they all tried to assert a viewpoint. The interesting one," Marc says, "was actually the first official history of Eatonville. Written by a black man in the 1980s. And this author tries so hard to make the highway sound *good*, like having an interstate plow through your small downtown is *special*. But it's—I still remember it—the whole passage in that book is heartbreaking, really, 'cause he knows the highway devastated the town."

"Huh," you say.

This is probably the reason you never went to college: what's practical about statements like "truth is relative"? Imagine if you took that theory to engine maintenance manuals, like maybe they were only telling you to get certain things checked and flushed so they could keep certain sectors of the auto-repair industry going strong, the shops making extra money off crap that wasn't really necessary, and…well, shit, maybe not so far-fetched. "So you agree with your professor?" you ask. "The highway's bad for Eatonville."

"I thought it was, back when I was in college," Marc says. "I thought all professors were—I don't know—obligated to tell the truth. It never occurred to me that your professors have their own agendas. My first business professor actually told us to forget all the bullshit from our liberal arts professors, that it was all lies designed to make us hate capitalism. I don't know. College is whacky. After that, I just decided to parrot what the professors said in order to get the grade. Just roll with it. The same as these mortgage documents. I don't need to make judgments about whether someone should or shouldn't do a reverse mortgage. Not my job to make that call."

Farther north on I-4: Maitland, Altamonte, Lake Mary, Longwood, all towns that are Orlando and not-Orlando. To call them suburbs is inaccurate: they've been here as long as Orlando, and given the right confluence of circumstance, a twist of I-4 or a bend in a river or the freezing of a particular citrus field or an entertainment mogul's decision to buy land right here instead of right there, any of these towns might have become what Orlando is now.

Apopka is your favorite stop so far: outskirts of the metropolis, kinda country, but a town rich with recreation, a state park and a gigantic lake, some history, but also the not-overwhelming influence of the commercialized present: McDonald's, Burger King, CVS.

"Apopka," Marc says to you. "Otherwise known as Meth-lando."

"Meth-lando? What's that mean?"

"You know. Like, meth?"

Meth-lando. Did you miss something? The long stretches of undeveloped land and thick pine forests, the boats sitting in gravel driveways, bonfire pits in backyards, men wearing camo as they lug bags of mulch to pickup trucks. This feels like *home*. Orlando's been interesting, but it's so packed with houses and strip malls, no space to breathe, and for the first time you question what your brother really knows. He's been reeling off his own rules, his own views on the city, and you've been accepting it like a lecture from a professor. *Meth-lando*. Does he know this place, or is he just talking shit? "Why do you say that?" you ask. "Meth-lando?"

"It's like...the sticks. Like, impoverished."

"So what?"

"The sticks. Like, a lot of toothless idiots? Like, drugs are really big out here? Meth-lando? Like, Orlando, but with meth?"

At a red light you watch an old man hold the door at a McDonald's for a woman and her child. "Looks all right to me."

"If you don't get it," he says, "I can't explain it to you."

"What, it's a *local* thing?"

"Yes."

"So how often you come out here?" you ask.

"Often enough."

"Sure," you say. "Sure."

Two in-home closings in Apopka, a third at Wendy's. Marc tells you story after story to—in his words—"prepare you for the unique tragedies and heartbreaking success stories that come with closing loans in 2009." He tells you about the girl who quit college to help her grandmother pay the bills, the refinance that saved their lives, and the way he says it, it's like he wants credit for it, like it's proof that this job matters. But in the next breath, he tells you about the husband who left his wife in Avalon Park, the couple in Conway who tried to cheat the system by closing on two different loans on the same house in the same day, how he knew something was fishy and so he drove down the block and staked out the house, watched a different car pull up an hour later, some sort of scam, and if he'd turned in the final paperwork, the fines would've devastated him. He's telling you what to watch out for, keeps reiterating that "this is an entirely different world than auto repairs, brother." This is not some easy step-by-step instruction manual, he says.

Maybe not, but is this job—loan-closing—is this *making something of yourself?*

You visit houses, see how people live, see what they waste their money on. You see DVD box sets of *MacGyver* and *Unsolved Mysteries*, but front doors that won't close because the wood is humidity-warped. You see granite countertops collecting dust on living room floors, money spent on materials, but clueless owners with no cash left for installation.

"You ever offer to do that work for them?" you ask.

"I close loans. I don't fix doors."

"But it seems like…I mean, that's a whole *business* right there."

"That'd require me to stay in their houses longer," he says. "Most of these places I'm happy to leave."

"But you could *help* them. Leave them better than when you got there."

"You saw me with the garage door and the garbage disposal. Does that look like something I'm good at? I'm a terrible landlord. There's a reason I can't flip my houses."

"You only learn by doing. You fiddle around, find out how something works, you fix it."

"You waste your time doing that," he says. "Trust me. Learn one thing, then do it well. Best business advice I could ever give."

"Business advice," you say, but you don't tell him what you're thinking: every day, his advice means less and less.

"We're closing loans, Kyle," Marc says. "I told Dad that I never wanted to work myself to death, and I'm telling *you*, too. These are not your houses, your problems. Shit like that, it'll wear you down."

"But you *are* worn down. You're angry at every little thing."

"I'm just *intense*," he says. "This requires *focus*. This is a *challenge*."

"I'm up for a challenge," you say again and again, and this is true. You left Georgia because you were a fixer with nothing left to fix. Shop was gone, and you couldn't fix your broken father. You left, and justified it by telling yourself that the old man needed distance, some time alone to come to terms with all he'd lost; the truth was that it was *you* who needed a change in scenery, a chance to go somewhere and feel good about your life, to not feel stuck with a problem that couldn't be solved. Then you come here and it's your brother who's broken. Everywhere it's the same broken-down ruin…it's rural Georgia and the city of Orlando, it's a father and son collapsing in on themselves. This isn't the challenge you signed up for.

Thursday's done and Marc says you both can take Friday off. It's Game Two of the series against the Cavs, and he's taking you downtown to watch the game, but first you've gotta spend the day at the mall because your clothes aren't good enough for downtown. Day off, my ass. And then he's telling you that you're trying on this shirt and then that one, and put that fucking belt back, Kyle, seriously, a *woven belt*? Your redneck is showing, buddy. And these jeans, not those. And yes, this shirt costs as much as a full day's work, but *look the part, act the part*, okay? Your brother tells you what cologne to splash on, how to act once you leave the car, and hours later downtown Orlando is such a circus of game-night madness that it's impossible not to smile, but still: Marc's rules, Marc's friends, Marc's life. Every chance you get, you try to wander away, break from your brother so that he won't judge the way you're standing or the jokes you're making or whatever. But then there's beer all over your pants and once again you look like a damn buffoon to him, don't you?

Eastern Conference Finals, Game Two, and you need the Magic to win, because you want this thing between you and your brother to work out. Win or lose, it's a sign. Shit. Spend enough time with Marc, and now you're thinking just like him.

You shake your head. You need air. You need to get away. You're walking off to a spot less packed, but then the game's back on and you look up and it's LeBron with a buzzer-beater to win, and the crowd is chaos, and if this *is* a sign then it's crystal fucking clear, ain't it? But then the noise of the crowd changes. There's shouting, a stampede, a fight, and when the bodies clear, there is Marc on the ground, bloody and unconscious, broken even further.

How did this happen? In his city? With you by his side…

Or had you already left

HERE YOU ARE, Mr. Mayor, end of your first year and you got everyone so damn excited about the future of the city, but already the world is on fire, and you don't know what the hell you can do to stop the flames. You ain't speaking in metaphors, neither. There's literal fire sweeping the country.

That's what it looks like, anyway, if you're a mayor in 1968 and you watch the evening news. Last year it was Houston, Detroit, Minneapolis, Buffalo, Newark. Now it's DC, Baltimore, Chicago… Chicago: you watch the smoke, the lick of flame, the trash cans through shop windows. Power lines toppling, street lights fizzing and crashing into pavement. The ghettos consuming themselves, the Blacks seething and boiling with *can't-take-it-no-more* fury, exploding in violence after the death of Reverend King. This here's the curse of American prosperity, Chicago worst of 'em all, a million immigrants and minorities fed into the meatgrinder to build that damn city. Maybe Chicago wasn't the cornerstone of the slave market, cursed to some voodoo doom like New Orleans, but that city damn sure consumed the Slavs, the Poles, the Irish, the Italians, the Russians, the Lithuanians, the Czechs, and yeah the Blacks too, all of 'em compost for the Midwestern Metropolis. You read *The Jungle* back in high school, didn't you, Mr. Mayor? You know. Chicago: days after the riots, there's smoke still drifting through the crumbled apartment buildings, the twisted skeletal rebar, poor folk on street corners clamoring for food and waiting for volunteers to truck it in.

1968 and you are the mayor.

And *what*, you thought *Orlando* would be spared from all this? 'Cause you wear yourself a cowboy hat, and 'cause the Kiwanis Club kisses your ass? 'Cause you call yourself a small city even though the world knows what's happening here and in Las Vegas, cities without industry that through chance and circumstance have now been gifted with the opportunity to rise up as the Chicagos of the next century? You think Orlando didn't make a deal with the devil? You burying garbage under the sidewalks, and Walt Disney leveling the Florida wilderness and building carousels on the wetlands. Only five years ago that Disney began making land deals, all the politicians and media-types working hard as you all could to keep it secret so land prices wouldn't skyrocket and Walt wouldn't take his park to St. Louis or Maryland—or worse, Ocala or Jacksonville. You kept quiet, didn't you? Pulled the right strings, made it so Orlando would never be the same. Your city'd rise, most assuredly, but did you think that the Spirit of Old Florida wouldn't make you pay your pound of flesh? It's late '68, summer passed, the riots up North over, the cold settling in, the crazy drifting south, the riots about to overtake *your* streets.

Your assistant Greg bursts into the office, waving his arms to get your attention. "They're marching, sir," he's saying and it's late-night, dark here in your office. Ain't no one here but you and a few staff members roused from their homes, called to service after sundown at City Hall under threat of the same conflagration overtook them northern cities don't know how to handle their Blacks. Newark, Chicago, Baltimore, the cities that fought the War to free the slaves but then forced down the Blacks soon as they took up residence. Outside your office, you got staffers racing through a binder containing lists of the prominent black men in Orlando, the ministers, the business owners, the high school coaches, combing through the lists of known trouble-makers, making contingency plans should *your world* find itself on fire this very night. Got-damn.

"You know that for sure?" you ask Greg. "They're rioting? For sure?"

"Janice called, confirmed it."

Janice. Secretary. Lives with her daughter out in Parramore. Black neighborhood.

"What'd she say?"

"She said there's fifteen of them gathered in the street outside. Fixing to march."

"Fifteen ain't so bad," you say. You're standing tall now, cowboy hat damn near touching the ceiling. Roused from your home and your pajamas, but you got your cowboy hat on, even brought the baseball bat you sometimes carry in emulation of ol' Teddy's "big stick" policy. "Only fifteen," you say. "Shit, Greggy Boy, let's wrap this up and call it a night." Fifteen, by God, that's the type of mob quelled by *two* patrol cars! What the hell were you worried about? See, Orlando ain't such a big city, after all. Not yet. Maybe 30 or 40 years from now, when Disney World is finished and bustling and the city's—who knows?—the next Birmingham or whatever, *then* they can riot. But not 1968. Not during *your* time as mayor. You clap and then open your hands wide as if your palms are an exploded bomb.

"Fifteen in the *street*, Janice said."

"Yeah. So?" you ask.

"The rest are knocking on doors."

"The rest?"

"Spreading out everywhere on the other side of Division. You know there aren't *fifteen* total Negroes in this city, right? It's a storm gathering, sir. The fifteen are…they're waiting for the others. And if a patrol car shows up to confront them? All hell's gonna break loose."

You grab the bill of your cowboy hat, tighten it against your bald head. Maybe you're checking that the hat is still there. You often joke with people: What's the difference between Superman and Carl Langford? *Mayor Langford* looks good in a *hat*! Haw-*haw*! Applause every time! But hell, sometimes you wonder, if you didn't have this hat, what would you be? *Who* would you be?

"Where's my big stick?" you ask.

"The floor," Greg says. "It's probably not a good idea to carry a—"

"So what're they gonna do, these Negroes?" you ask.

"How do *I* know?"

"You were the one talked to Janice!"

"She was watching through her kitchen window," Greg says. He's got both his hands out, like he's pleading with you to stop being an idiot. He always looks this way, like *how did I get stuck working in this backwards town, working for this backwards-ass mayor*? Makes you furious. Like you got elected as a gimmick, and Greg thinks he's the real brain. "She was scared out of her mind," he says. "You think she wants to go out there and ask a *mob* what they're doing? She doesn't want this, just as much as we don't."

You imagine what the city of Orlando would look like in flames, some decades-later vengeance for every damn massacre the Black Man has suffered in this region. You picture that awful mess back in the '20s, not more than five miles from here. Black section of Ocoee burned to the ground after one of their people brought a shotgun to the voting booths, claiming he was defending his right to vote or what-not. End result was hundreds of blacks slaughtered in the streets and sent screaming into the citrus fields, their homes reduced to ash. You imagine Ocoee in reverse; you imagine the white man's citrus groves aflame, the oranges and yellows and greens sizzling and popping and blackening, air misted with the smell of hot rotten lime. You imagine the black mob crossing Division and then I-4—the two barriers that separate *their* town from *yours*—crossing into downtown with…torches? Do rioters carry torches and pitchforks, like they're hunting Frankenstein? What the hell do they carry? All summer the news has been showing flipped cars, broken windows, that sort of thing, so that's where your imagination goes: up and down Orange Avenue, broken windows on the department stores, light posts careening into the glass on the bottom floor of the American Building, mattresses tossed from the windows of the Angebilt and the San Juan Hotel, Woolworths and McCrory's Five and Dime hollowed out from looting, the fire and the chaos dragging Church Street to hell. Thank God Disney World ain't marching distance from downtown, or there'd be angry Negroes in Mickey Mouse ears hijacking bulldozers and bringing down the foundation of Space Mountain.

Carl Langford, with the cowboy hat and baseball bat. Carl T. Langford, *Hizzoner*, Superman of the City Council. It's 1968, and you could be the greatest mayor the city has ever had, taking Orlando where it never dreamed it could go, all your garbage buried and forgotten. Or, in one night, you could be the man who lost it all.

IT'S A HOT SATURDAY afternoon and you're wandering the aisles of the 7-Eleven on Summerlin with Anderson, your mind awhirl with concern over the future of your blog. Elaina told you to have fun with it, that it shouldn't just be this thing that you worry and obsess over, but you can't stop thinking of "likes," the ones you do earn but also the ones you feel you deserve but never arrive, and comments, both from people who praise you and from people who just don't get it, and replies, and replies to replies, and arguments, and counter-arguments, and—

"Bud Lite?" Anderson asks.

"Huh? Oh, sure."

You and Anderson are on a beer run, both of you in board shorts and sandals, having just come from the rooftop pool of your condo building. Well, not *your* building. *Anderson* owns a 3/2 unit, is underwater by maybe a hundred grand, regrets having bought it but never expresses this regret to anyone but his parents during somber long-distance phone calls that you pretend not to hear through the condo's thin walls. For the past two years, despite your own long-standing dream of living in an authentic-Orlando bungalow in Colonialtown, you've lived with Anderson in this condo as a favor, helping to offset your friend's massive mortgage payment. You live there, and now you're both wet and cold in the convenience store AC, here to replenish your afternoon with a new 12-pack.

"I don't know if I can keep doing this," you tell Anderson.

"This?" Anderson's holding the Bud Lite box, twirling it around to look for whatever he's missing. Nutritional information? Alcohol content? "Oh, your blog. Yeah, people don't have to time to read the novels you're writing, my man."

"They're not novels! They're articles. Just a few thousand words."

"How many thousand?"

"Well maybe six thousand on average. But they're immersive, designed to put the reader into authentic Orla—"

"Yeah, nobody's got time for that. Keep it quick. Snappy. Isn't that what your girlfriend does? Slideshows. Lists. And she's got like a million subscribers."

"Forty thousand."

"Forty eff-ing thousand. Can't argue with the numbers."

You've written hundreds of blog posts by now, from "Top Orlando Restaurants You've Never Heard Of" to "Five Best Spots For Coffee in Orlando." You've written glowing profiles of civic and grassroots heroes (the married couple who famously fought to make front-yard gardening legal in

College Park, the woman who got laid off from her job in real estate marketing and started a children's literacy nonprofit, the little girl who sings the national anthem at Magic games). Hundreds of shares. People *do* know you. You are having *some* success.

"Elaina's writing pictorials. How-tos. It's a totally different—" You shake your head. The conversation's getting away from you. "Anyway, that's not the problem. I write short stuff, too. It's been reblogged all over the place, *Huff Post* and *Buzzfeed* and *Context Florida*. And I've got three thousand subscribers. That's pretty good. It's just—I've been blogging for a while now, and I'm getting nowhere, accomplishing *nothing*."

Anderson shakes his head. "Accomplishing nothing? You want a ribbon or something?"

"No," you say. "Ha ha." But a ribbon would be nice. Ever since you started writing your *Orlandofesto*, you've played in your mind a fantasy montage of your future: it opens with a long shot of you at the bars on Mills, downing OBPs with your crew; the camera pans out to capture a pack of twenty-somethings strutting past in the vintage "Ivanhoe is My Hood" and "Tangerine Bowl '79" t-shirts *you* designed and sold from your website (you've imagined a hundred different slogans, sketched dozens of designs, but you haven't yet printed a single one); jump-cut to a close-up of the "Make Orlando Weird" bumper sticker *you* thought up, and that—as the camera pans left to show a long line of cars parked along the street—is affixed to every car (you plan to sell *this* from your site, too, but alas, it currently exists only in your mind); cut to the downtown Tijuana Flats, a huge table of diverse and upbeat couples sharing chips and queso, and over their shoulders, there on the wall of celebrity photos, is a picture of Steven Hart with his arms around three or four of the beaming bouncy Flats Girls, *your* picture just inches from the photos of Shaq and Dwight Howard; cut to steadicam footage of you walking the concourses at a Magic game, high-fiving with the common folk, then sitting in a luxury box as the distinguished guest of Mayor Buddy Dyer, then footage of you at the Orlando Chili Cook-Off sampling pots as an honorary judge, then as grand marshal of the UCF Homecoming Parade, *you, Steven Hart*, the man who transformed Orlando's identity!

You shake your head. Such fantasies seem downright silly in the light of day, away from your keyboard. So damn naive, too, when you consider what's happened lately.

Anderson lifts the 12-pack onto the counter and says, "I got this one," because he must always preserve the illusion that he's rolling in cash. "You gotta stop believing in stuff, man. You want to make money off that blog? Want clicks? Or do you want something that *you* love but no one else cares about?"

"I don't need to make money, necessarily."

"Oh, right. It's about starting a movement."

"Right."

"A movement to save the save the city's culture."

"Yes!"

"But money would be nice, right?"

"I mean. Like I said, I want to eventually sell t-shirts, and bumper stickers... I'd love to do this full time, and—"

"So what's the eff-ing problem, man? Why are you whining to me? You've got a plan, but things are just going too slow? Join the club, homeboy."

Once a man tells you that you're whining, it's futile to continue. How to tell Anderson what you're feeling without facing scorn or humiliation, without hearing that inevitable and reductive toxic-male advice of "suck it up"? How to tell him that, for so long, you've wanted The Other City Beautiful to be unflinchingly serious, the love letter to Orlando that won't quit, every damn word of every damn 6,000-word blog post a defense of the city and its culture. This is a *culture* war, and wars are deadly serious. How to reveal to him the joy you felt when those first few months of comments from your readers were all "so glad you're writing this," and "right there with you!" and "keep fighting the good fight"?

How to reveal to him the moment it turned?

The trolls.

They came just as you hit 500 subscribers and the future felt bright and your dreams attainable. "Dumb fucking blog," one hater wrote, "there is no 'Other City Beautiful,' just ONE BIG CITY UGLY!" That was disheartening enough, but then there was "How u gonna write 50 damn blog posts about Orlando and not one thing about Disney? Fagit." Had this one not even read the title of your blog, the "About This Site" page, the whole fucking mission? Trolls. Dozens of them, waging their own little online culture war with no objective but anarchy. Trolls. No, *gremlins*, slashing into the machinery of your dreams. And Lord help you, you knew their game, know it now, know that their sole joy is antagonism, is wasting the time of people who care about things, but you've thus far been unable to resist responding to each and every one of them. Long back-and-forth threads dissecting and rebutting their stupid arguments, consuming entire afternoons, consuming entire nights. Entire nights following the trolls to the comment boards for *other* Orlando institutions you love, scanning for negative comments and for familiar usernames and avatars and catchphrases, scanning for arguments in which to engage. "Shitty tables and a gross area," someone wrote on the National Sandwich Review comment board for Beefy King. "Oh, fuck no," you said, and your response to this commenter was so scathing that you almost felt bad about it. "Stay away from downtown Orlando, too many homeless people," you read under one article about Church Street Station, and oh, the flood of expletive-enhanced vitriol that you heaped upon this poor soul. "UCF is a crap school. East Carolina is gonna kill them in football this yeer." God help the trolls who fail to catch their typos. Night after night, you stay indoors and rip them apart, slashing back, slashing and slashing until you've defended your city on more than a thousand comment boards, and isn't that a far nobler thing than to join Anderson when he asks if you want to come out to Wall Street on a Friday night? Isn't it better than to go see a movie with Elaina on a Saturday? Destroying some douchebag who *really* believes that downtown Tampa is better than downtown Orlando?

Every hour of every day, you defend this city.

And now you're depleted.

Your magnum opus, the "Fifty Places in Orlando That Define the *Real Orlando*," has stalled at #10, too many entries still in severe conflict in your mind, too many imagined arguments every time you sit down to begin drafting your #9 spot. What will the trolls say? How will you be forced to defend? What if…And what about…How do you wage a culture war when there are so many combatants you didn't anticipate? This list has been years in the making. This Orlandofesto—it's everything to you. But…

"It's getting wearying," you tell Anderson, there at the counter of the 7-Eleven. Just a few feet away, the cashier rolls his eyes, this look on his face like *How 'bout we trade jobs, kid, and you see what* wearying *really means.* "Didn't get any comments on the last post," you say. "Not even a like. It's been up five days."

"The novel about Freshfields Farms? Yeah, that was tedious, brother. Maybe—here's a bright idea—try to have some G.D. fun with it again."

"I *am* having fun!"

Anderson exhales. "If you say so, man. A second ago you said it was wearying." And he holds the door open for you, and you're back outside. "You're at number nine, right? Maybe just make 7-Eleven your next spot. Just to eff with everyone."

"That's ridiculous," you say. "I'd lose all credibility."

"Credibility? It's an eff-ing blog, brother. Stop worrying and live a little."

It makes sense, though. That's the shit of it. It makes sense.

7-Eleven is about as *Authentic Orlando* as it gets. After all, it's here, just a block from Lake Eola, on the brick roads of hyper-gentrified Thornton Park, a stand-alone building holding strong beside downtown high-rises and wine bars, gelato bars and boutiques, a short walk from million-dollar restored homes, from wraparound porches and lakefront balconies. For better or worse, it's *everywhere*. To include 7-Eleven in your *Orlandofesto* is to anticipate the online trolls, who will argue that "Orlando is a dirty city," who submit photos to the "People of Orlando" Tumblr, photos taken where else but at 7-Eleven, of Central Florida's most gloriously hideous and hopeless-looking citizens, buttcracks hanging out, grown men in Tigger outfits, shit-stained pants. To include the 7-Eleven is to show the world that you are aware of your own quirks, aware of (though still in love with) your dumpier side.

Above all else…it's *fun*, an effusive tongue-in-cheek posting about the 7-Eleven, with its Super Big Gulps and Slurpees, its red vests and donut display case, its plastic-wrapped cupcakes, its pizza slices and chicken wings and chicken-wing-pizza-slices dried out and forever baking beneath heat lamps! Days upon weeks upon months, building this blog, your spirit weighed down with the seriousness. But now? 7-Eleven is #9. Laugh it up, trolls.

Back at the pool, while Anderson is showing off his abs and sharing Bud Lites with a couple of girls in purple bikinis, you sit alone on your chaise lounge and let your creative mind take you where it will: deep in reflection, you realize that your whole approach has been wrong. This was never supposed to be about *one man* defending the city. This was supposed to be about *community*, about *everyone* fighting for their city's culture.

Anderson flicks a beer cap at you and asks if you'd like to join him and his new friends for Chipotle. You mumble something that makes the girls giggle and that you hope communicates "No thanks." You're drunk, sunburned and drunk. But beneath the dampening influence of the alcohol is the flame of inspiration, long dormant, and you want to set fire to page and see what happens. So you head back to your bedroom and park yourself at your work desk and flip open your laptop, your head spinning with ambition. (Writing blog posts? Typing replies when you can barely stand? Maybe not bright, Steven.) But you're thinking *be fun again*, and for some reason this *is* fun (despite the multitude of typos as you mash the keyboard with dumb-sloppy fingers), and you're thinking *community*, and you've got an idea and you don't want to wait until morning and chance that you might forget it. So you spend Saturday night finding every Orlando blog that you can. Fan sites for the Orlando Magic. Fan sites for the UCF Knights, for the Orlando Solar Bears. Orlando Ghost-Hunters. Tasty Chomps, the site for Orlando Foodies. Orlando Literati. Orlando History Buffs. Central Florida Mediums. Active Seniors. Scrabble Enthusiasts. Craft Brewers of Avalon

Park. Orlando Mommies. Orlando Cosplayers. Orlando Unicorn Hunters. Orlando Horror Society. Each leads to another, all of these glorious and weird subcultures, and you will unite them all on The Other City Beautiful. You will be the community hub. *You*. You will build an army, and you will

AFTERNOON TURNS TO EVENING in Lake Eola Park. The photographer assures you he's got the most Perfect. Shot. Ever. When the sun sinks past the skyline, clouds pasteled across the sky, it'll look like a cruise ship photo, too good to be real, he says. "This is the one you'll want to use on your Save-the-Dates," he says. "The one you'll want on your wall."

You picture the Save-the-Dates magneted to the refrigerators of your old sorority friends, the ones who stopped talking to you after you were written up to Standards Board senior year, the ones who told you that "maybe you need to work on your *adulting*." The same ones who came back around once they learned that you not only have a fiancé, but a real *career*, surprised how quickly you went from "Girl Least Likely to Succeed" to "Girl On Her Way."

Six months after graduation, after you'd turned in your sorority pin, you weren't sure you'd ever see them again. But then you landed your first real job at the Golden Citrus Golf & Resort, sat down with David, the Senior Account Exec, and the first item on the agenda was the "contacts" you'd brainstormed during a workshop about "living and thriving with a networking mentality." (Really, the goal of that afternoon had been to fresh-squeeze as many leads as possible for the sales team, and to reinforce for the entire staff that conferences were the lifeblood of Golden Citrus.)

"I see you wrote down your sorority," David said. "Very good. I'm part of my fraternity's alumni association. Over 1,000 members in this region. Do you know how many alumni of—pardon, what's your sorority?" Shelley told him. "Yes, do you know how many women there are in this city alone? Not to mention the regional association, and the national conventions? Gold mine of opportunity. Why *wouldn't* they want to have their conventions in Orlando? Why *wouldn't* they choose Golden Citrus?"

"I sort of"—you almost said "got kicked out," reconsidered—"quit during my senior year."

"Everyone quits!" David said. "It's *college*! Okay, here's what I need, Shelley. I need you to get re-involved. Become a regular attendee of your association's meetings, speak up, lend your expertise to their events, let every last woman know who you are, where you work, what we can do for them. Network until it feels like you don't have any breath left to make another introduction. That's how we fill the calendar."

And you did. You found Alumni Club, poured yourself into it like a martini into a glass. You reconnected with your sisters from the UCF house, recruited them to the brunches, the mixers. This—the Golden Citrus Golf & Resort—was your first real job, and you wanted to out-work *everyone*, even the event planners far above you on the hierarchy. The next time David asked, you'd tell him how many networking hours you'd logged with these women, how many business cards you'd passed out.

But every minute at Alumni Club has been a struggle, thrusting yourself into conversations with 45-year-old mothers of two who swipe through their phones to show you their master bathroom renovations. "35,000 dollars," Amanda Linda said, "but feeling the heated floors on your toes…so worth it." Photos of walk-in closets so big you can't imagine owning enough apparel to fill them. And yet these women at the Alumni Club, they all managed without fail to over-stuff those closets. You will, too, they assure you. The goal, you've learned, is to *have it all*. Those are the words repeated again and again: "I don't want to give anything up. I want a husband, and I want children, and I want a career, and I want a nice house, and I want nice things. I want to *have it all*, and I don't see anything wrong with that." No no. Not unless you're the only woman in the room who doesn't even have the first thing. To be a woman without a husband or children? To be a mother without a career? That's cheating. The Alumni Club snubs these women. The key word in "have it all," remember, is "all."

"We had to repair the solar heater for our pool," Cassandra told you. "Lord knows we don't ever use it, but there the panels sit. You know the funny thing about pools?" You shook your head. "You swim all the time when you first get one, but now I can't remember the last time I used ours."

So much damn time at Alumni Club, and you still aren't sure where the *real women* are, the ones who are down to earth and who have homes with a reasonable number of bathrooms. Amanda Linda, the attorney, initially gave the impression that she thought the whole Alumni Club atmosphere was excessive, but you've noticed that she always follows up her criticism with some hint that she secretly enjoys it all: without a shred of self-awareness, she will groan over Cassandra's "absolutely frivolous" patio expansion, then brag about her latest adventure to Bologna. There at Alumni Club, among the women who *have it all*.

But you're engaged now, your first house a week away from reality. A husband soon to follow.

Speaking of, where *is* Marc?

You scan the lake, the swans, the trees, and spot him in a square of shade beside the bandshell, on the phone again. You wave him over, will the sweat away as it forms under your arms. "It's time to take some shots together," you say.

"Ready, kids?" the photographer asks.

In order to get to the *perfect spot* for the *perfect shot*, he leads you down the sidewalk and through the park's "Splatter Zone," where the pavement goes from gray to white, and where the birds hide like snipers in the twisting oak branches above. A plop on the grass here, a splatter on the street there, no pattern. But you hear it. It's like a war zone, and the photographer speeds through the Splatter Zone like some salty war vet who knows where the landmines are buried.

You approach tentatively, Marc beside you looking into the trees and trying to calculate the route least likely to result in shit on face.

A mother walks past with her two children, all three of them rigid in their gait and grasping hands with bone-breaking intensity. The little girl trembles, says, "Mommy, we're not going to get *hit*, are we?"

Seriously, though: it's just, like, twenty feet you have to walk.

Marc looks around anxiously, perhaps more nervous than anyone else, like his life is on the line, so you say, "It's just bird shit. Let's go." And you grab his hand and pull him forward and you don't expect anything to happen, but then it does—

—one second Marc is looking into the trees and sprint-walking past you (pulling away from your hand, leaving you behind), and the next he's turning around to say something and his face is gone entirely, seemingly whited-out from the world.

Things happen more quickly after that.

He's touching his face. He's screaming "Fuck! Fuck! *Fuck!*"

He's wiping at his face with his shirt, shit smeared everywhere. Into his eyes.

The woman with the children is horrified. She's trying to herd her children past, but he's flailing and screaming "Fuck! Fuck! Fuck!" and almost knocking them off the sidewalk, and she's simultaneously trying to hold her kids' hands and also cover their ears and—

Marc's eyes are clean now, and he sees the family staring back at him like he's a maniac, and so—without even processing the moment, without even the briefest pause to consider who he's talking to—he screams: "What the *fuck* are you looking at?"

And it's at that moment that one of the kids is himself nailed by bird shit. The little boy.

The photographer, of course, is far ahead, safe, equipment untouched, hair and face and clothing still clean and fresh, and he seems to only now realize that you're both stuck in the dead-center of the Splatter Zone and pinned down by the doom from above. He yells for you to just run, *come on*, you're almost there, we got photos to shoot!

But now the mother is yelling at Marc—"use that language in front of my *children*!"—and Marc is yelling at her—"the fucking *people* in this city, for fuck's sake, get over it, it's a public fucking place!"—and it's getting worse between them, more heated, the little boy and the little girl wailing and the bombs still dropping and there's bird shit everywhere and—

And it all becomes background noise.

Things slow down.

You've got wet-naps in your purse.

You approach the little boy. You lean down, wipe his face. Shit is streaked in his hair, and you can't get it out entirely, but he's not crying anymore, just sort of whimpering with his bottom lip. Scared because your fiancé is yelling at his mother and maybe is going to attack her or something. You go through wet-nap after wet-nap, until all becomes quiet and the boy is glistening and moist but no longer shit-stained.

You didn't want this to happen, this sort of moment where everything focuses and forces something inside you to shift. It's here in the park, at the end of your engagement photo shoot—that's right, the end, there will be no final "perfect shot," not with your fiancé so disheveled, physically and emotionally, red-faced, sweating, a beyond-salvage wreck—that you first picture what *marriage* and *family* might actually be like in ten years with Marc. It's here that you wonder how he'd react if you told him you were pregnant. Who would he be at your child's first birthday party, and who would he be when the baby flung mashed potatoes onto the TV screen? How would he handle a joint bank account, a college fund? Will his life descend into investment schemes, your family's money siphoned from your savings to feed his fantasies? If he's this angry now, how bad will it get? Is he destined to become a Lifetime movie villain?

Days before you're set to move in with your fiancé, weeks before the housewarming party, these are thoughts you don't want, because *there's no turning back now*, because you're an *adult* and you're in a *relationship* and everyone at work knows it, and every woman at Alumni Club knows it, and if you think they looked down at you when you were single and minglin', think about what they'd do and say if you became that little girl whose engagement cracked apart, that little girl who was only pretending at real-world relationships. Imagine Samantha with her cold laugh saying something like, "Not ready to be a grown-up, honey?" No, it's too much. You shake your head until the thoughts go away, go away, go away, until you are just a woman and a man at the end of their photoshoot and nothing is wrong, nothing is wrong, nothing is wrong

YOU FEEL THEM WALKING ON YOU, the residents, the outsiders, digging into you, pouring concrete into your open wounds, setting foundations, lifting frames. You feel them taking pictures on the banks of Lake Lucerne and Lake Eola and Lake Rowena. You feel this thing they call the San Juan Hotel rising in what they call "downtown," 250 bedrooms, so much weight on your back; you feel their courthouse rising, its columns and its stone, its gravity. You feel the grass trampled to dirt. You feel trees uprooted, machines churning your soil, Crackers burning chopped branches. You feel signs pounded into the ground, directing cars toward swaths of just-leveled land, signs one after another asking questions and making promises: "Will we have water? Yes! Will we have front porches? Yes! Will we have a golf course? Yes!"

It's the Spring of 1926 and they are calling it the Great Florida Land Boom, and you feel yourself divided into parcels, traded. Imagine that. Chopped apart like a cow hanging from a hook. You feel the flash of the camera once the gates to a new subdivision have been constructed, photos pasted into newspapers distributed in New York and Canada. You don't know *how* you feel the gaze of those money-hungry eyes up North, but you *do* feel it. Their eyes, the money changing hands.

You feel them come from far away. Sometimes they build houses. Sometimes they stay. You hear a man named Walter Rose—*Walter Rose*, he booms and shakes a hand, then turns, and *Walter Rose*, he booms and shakes another hand—spreading his arms wide and selling his dream of College Park on the northwestern edge of the city, "streets named after the great universities of the North!" he says, "Princeton! Cornell! Harvard! By God, we can civilize this place yet or my name isn't Walter Rose!"

Sometimes they build, and stay. More often, though, they buy land, build a gate, take a picture, and then leave. They pass the picture from one man to the next, deeds handled in sleeves and binders, a slickster from Palm Beach holding title to a small piece of you, then selling it to a hopeful idiot from Cleveland.

You feel it all, and despite the violence of your own long history, it feels dirty. You embrace what you are and have always been, the millennia without human presence, the swamps and the mosquitoes and the citrus, then the natives who went by dozens of names but never disrupted the natural order of things, then the cattle and the Crackers who rode over flat land on horseback, then the Seminoles and the soldiers, and now the roads and trains and salesmen taking photos of gates staked into your skin. This is you, and you are it.

They call you "Orlando."

You hear them making deals as they stand on your back, so many conversations about your future, what they can make you.

What do you want *from me?* you want to ask. *You people. What do you* want?

You are not against progress, people living on you, people building homes and living in communities, but this doesn't feel right. You worry what it will feel like to be a *city* with great massive crowds of people living and working and loving and hating. You know that some cities fail, too. Resources mined from the Earth, then empty general stores left behind to rot on useless land. The flash of camera, money changing hands, trees felled and lakes drained. Trains in and out of Church Street Station, in and out, in and out. A man selling off his "College Park." A doctor building his hotel for blacks on the other side of Division. A woman racing in from the North—Grace is her name—announcing that she's building "the biggest dang swimming pool anyone can imagine!" A man laughing as he creates an advertisement for his own hotel that reads "Orlando, Florida: Gloriously Free of Mosquitoes!" And another man, a phony doctor, claiming all the acres he can for his orange groves, endlessly experimenting with the fruit to change its taste, to prevent spoilage, hoping he can export Florida juice to the world. A sightseeing bus chugging along Orange Avenue, tourists on their way to see the exotic caged animals at the far end of Lake Eola. A man posing as one of these tourists, sitting among them, scheming to involve others in his imagined Florida fantasy land on the acres he bought but could not afford.

You are just soil to them.

You are just soil, and these people want to break and tame and transform you.

This will end badly for you, you say, but all anyone hears is the wind through the trees.

AND THEN YOU ARE HIGH ABOVE THE EARTH, soaring through the clouds in your red cape, the eyes of Orlando—the eyes of the *world*—upon you as you fly. Up in the sky! It's a bird! It's a plane! It's…well, actually, it *is* a plane and you're looking down at Orlando as it shrinks away. But, down on the ground, everyone knows you're *on* the plane. Everyone saw you climb aboard, tuck your gigantic head and shoulders inside, everyone watched you take off, the Great Dwight Hope shooting into the sky, headed for Los Angeles and the first game of the NBA Finals.

Thursday, June 4, 2009.

Kobe vs. Dwight.

LA vs. Orlando.

Lakers vs. Magic.

Sweet revenge on the city that stole Shaq so many years ago.

When you land in California, you'll begin the process of winning your first NBA Championship, bringing the trophy back to Orlando and officially taking the crown from LeBron as Most Popular Player in the League.

You've made it, that's the point here.

This year, the NBA and Nike and everyone else wanted LeBron vs. Kobe in the Finals. Those puppet commercials, Puppet Kobe squawking at Puppet LeBron as if they were the only two superstars in the league. Well, now *you've* arrived. Next year, there'll be Dwight puppet commercials, and Puppet Dwight will tower over all others.

Rafer Alston is sitting across the aisle from you, hands folded in his lap, seat reclined, eyelids fluttering as he falls sleep. Rafer still carries the cocksure confidence of a one-time streetball legend, facial expressions almost always approximating smirks rather than genuine smiles. Wiry, too, a kid whose lean physique and gritty saunter never let you forget that he— like Allen Iverson—grew up ballin' in outdoor chain-link-fenced basketball courts with deep gashes in the surface, with triple-reinforced rims that required a 100% swish for a ball to fall through the chain-net, the sound not quite *swish*, but a reverberating *swa-shunk*. Rafer, he dribbles the ball so fast he's like a hummingbird, and he's quick no matter what he's doing or where he's moving, dodgy, always squirting between people. *Squirting*, that's the best word you can think of to describe the way he moves, how small he is, how easily lost.

Rafer. What kind of name is that, anyway?

"Yo, Lou," you say to him. You sprawl over your seats, into the aisle. Rafer's been in the league for almost a decade. He's old, maybe only has one or two good years left, and he's played for so many teams the commentators call him a "journeyman." But really, doesn't that just mean he never found a place, that his time has passed? Contrast that with Dwight Howard™: next year, you'll demand your own motherfucking plane. You'll *always* be wanted.

"I told you," Rafer says, closes his eyes like maybe you'll stop talking if he makes it obvious he wants to sleep. "No one calls me that anymore."

"Lou," you say and shake your head. "Come on now. 'Skip to My Lou.' That's one helluva nickname."

"That was twelve years ago." Eyes open now, annoyed. "You were in grade school."

You laugh in that good-natured, big-smiled way that you've got, the same jovial face you made when you shook hands with Paul Pierce after you conquered Boston in Game Seven, the same face you made when you slapped Zydrunas Ilgauskas' back after you mopped the floor with the Cleveland Cavaliers in six games. The same happy face you wear every day when Coach Stan tells you to position yourself here, to hustle there, *move quicker*, and "come on, Dwight, you're supposed to set the tone for everyone," the same face you wear during televised games when—after a poor shot or blown-up play—Coach makes his stink-face and the whole world looks from him to you, from dissatisfied Stan Van Gundy stink-face to Dwight Howard™ happy-face, and everyone concludes that you are *the happiest man alive*, not one Goddamned mean bone in your body. Positivity. Best Person Ever (you should trademark that). The Guru made you watch hours and hours of film, showed you the disarming effect of your smile, made you practice. "Here we go again," you say to Rafer. "Dwight's the baby, and Lou's the Elder Statesman."

Rafer sits and stares, one earbud of his iPod popped out so he can listen to your ribbing. It's an unspoken expectation of your every teammate that Dwight Howard™ jokes must always be listened to, that smiles must always be returned, fist-pounds reciprocated, joviality matched with joviality. No one is allowed to argue with Dwight Howard™. You are their leader and they do what you want or they're traded the fuck out of town. When you hand someone a Skittle, *they eat it.* When you hand someone a video game controller, they play. Some commentators assert that your "big kid" personality reveals immaturity, but the Guru counters that this characterization is important for your endorsement branding. The "team leader" characterization is (admittedly) not yet a viable component to your brand, he says, but that'll change when you win your first championship. "Dwight," Rafer says, "I don't want to get into a—"

"Call me *Superman*, Lou," you say. "Call me Superman so we can always, you know, share the delight of one another's nicknames."

"I need some rest, Dwight. Didn't sleep well last night."

"'I need some rest, *Superman*,'" you say. You pop a Skittle, chew, cabin bright as a rainbow around you. "Say it like that."

"I just—"

"Say it."

"Dwight…"

"*Superman*," you say. "Ain't tough. Say it."

All around the plane now, your teammates are looking at you. Jameer up front playing cards with Courtney Lee, Anthony Johnson peering out from behind the biography of John Adams he's been reading throughout the playoffs, JJ Redick preparing cheese and crackers in a Tupperware dish and pausing with a slice of smoked gouda centimeters from his lips. Coach Stan's in the back of the plane talking game-plan with Patrick Ewing, a clipboard between them, but they're now both frozen, mouths stuck mid-sentence, mid-word, Coach Stan looking out over the top of his reading glasses. Coach Ewing looks old and disappointed as usual, a man who wants to live vicariously through Dwight Howard™ but who can't accept that you're not him (that's the thing: Dwight Howard™ is better than *he* ever was, and so

Coach Ewing's gotta pretend he's teaching you "valuable skills" so *he* can feel better about *his* failed basketball career). Jealousy and envy everywhere. Ice has overtaken the cabin, has overtaken the entire plane, threatens to weigh down the wings and send it plummeting before you ever get a chance to slap a basketball out of Kobe Bryant's hands. Coach Stan. Icy Coach Stan, with that *judging* look again. *He's* the one who's frozen the plane. Can't take a joke, can't have a good time. So you smile, as if in defiance of Coach Stan's seriousness.

"Haw *haw*," you say and clap Rafer's knee with your giant hand. "Just playin', buddy!"

"Whatever," Rafer says and closes his eyes. "Let me sleep."

The ice thaws and the team goes back to their in-progress activities.

"Haw haw!" you say again. "Someone get me more motherfucking Skittles!"

Los Angeles-bound. Up to *you* to try to lighten the mood, 'cause the coaches damn sure ain't gonna keep the team loose. Up to *you*. Best Person Ever.

Before Game Six against Cleveland, you smiled at LeBron James and said softly to him, "Witness *this*, bitch," and then you won big, and after the game, after his Cleveland Cavaliers had lost to your Orlando Magic, you could see the pain in his eyes when he stalked off the court without shaking hands, then skipped his media session. "Haw *haw*!" you said and elbowed the rookie Courtney Lee; you aimed for Courtney's ribs, but you wound up hitting his shoulders, and Courtney reflexively grabbed and protected his facemask, the lingering injury from the Philadelphia game a few weeks back, when you accidentally elbowed him and fractured his sinus. "Guess who ain't gonna re-sign with Cleveland in two years," you said. "Think we done *killed* this team, brother. Ripped out their motherfucking *souls*." Courtney flinched again, even though you barely moved.

So they call you a "big kid" because you eat Skittles and chicken fingers? Whatever. You live the life *they* all wished they could live. "Witness *this*, bitch," you told LeBron and then you won the game. Boom! Leadership.

Of course, Coach Stan said he'd heard what you said to LeBron. "You're my guy, Dwight," he said, "but those kinds of comments, they're not gonna help you."

One more voice, tellin' you who to be.

"Lemme guess," you responded and then switched to your geeky white-guy voice: "The comments reflect a certain, um, immaturity in my approach to the game?"

"Well," Coach Stan said. "That's right, yeah."

"You've said it a dozen times, Big Stan. I hear you. But you gotta understand: Superman gon' be who Superman gon' be."

And lately you've been thinking, Superman's gotta fly. You're flying right now, toward the bright lights of Los Angeles: a real City of Dreams to which Podunk Orlando cannot even compare. Orlando is all mirage, the illusion of paradise, a hundred theme parks replicating the world's more interesting places. Los Angeles actually *delivers*. Sure, it has theme parks because why not?, but *the city itself* is paradise. Beverly Hills. Redondo Beach. Hollywood. Malibu. Pasadena. Ain't none of that in Orlando. You only got replicas.

What's left for you in O-Town, anyway? Streets too tiny for your feet. Restaurants with ceilings too low, VIP sections at bars where you're rubbing elbows not with celebrities but some guy who owns a car dealership in Maitland? A time-share mogul? That shit ain't impressive. There are bright lights in Orlando, bright lights on I-Drive and at Disney and at Universal Studios, spotlights circling the sky and fireworks nightly, but the bright lights are not Orlando, the bright lights were built by millionaires from other cities—Walt Disney never lived in Orlando, and Rich Devos owns the Magic but doesn't live in Orlando—and those lights would shine regardless of whether the city of Orlando itself shriveled up and foreclosed. People would still visit the theme parks even if there was no town to the north. This city's motherfucking Krypton, a dead planet, and they know you're the only hope they got. So sure, you'll give the city its championship, scream "I'm going to Disney World" into the cameras, pop the damn champagne and ride the damn float down Orange Ave. But mark it down: 2009 will be the year that you officially became bigger than the city. No question.

You're going to beat the Lakers, and then maybe you'll take over LA, too.

Still, you have this weird feeling that…even though you've sacrificed your teen years, your early twenties, to be a sports superstar…even though you've done everything possible to give everyone what they want, the most perfect persona that money can buy, more sustainably likeable than even Michael Jordan…you have this terrible feeling that people will *never* stop making you into something you're not, that—like the city you've outgrown—your own identity was leveled so some developer could make something he felt was more beautiful. And what happens if you can never get it back, your essential *you*-ness? No. Nonono, good buddy. Best Person Ever. Don't think like that. You're a conqueror. You're *you*! You're…you're

YOU'RE IN SECOND GRADE, and a new boy has moved in down the street from you. Jeremy. He says "shit" in front of his parents, has a pellet gun and shoots lizards, carries a switchblade. "Edwin, you gotta stop trying to be a good boy," he says, and it's the first time you've ever questioned whether "good" is indeed good. Jeremy's family is vintage Georgia, their wealth stretching back generations, and there is an effortlessness to their spending that your own father—a Yankee transplanted here to Atlanta, a man who never misses the opportunity to remind you that he "earned all this"—will never allow himself. They spend their weekends boating, renting cabins and hunting, driving across state to golf. Jeremy has everything he wants, does whatever he wants. He's three years older than you, too, and your father warns that something's wrong with the kid. "Why else would he hang out with *you*?" Dad asks, and though he means, "Why else would an *older kid* hang out with *someone three grades younger*?" you can't shake the phrasing, the implication. Still, you visit Jeremy's house often. He's got a Nintendo. He's got *A Nightmare on Elm Street* on VHS, and his parents let him watch it in the living room. He's got Playboys, Guns N' Roses cassette tapes, all the stuff you've been denied, despite your father's money. Best of all, Jeremy's got a tall Garbage Pail Kids poster on his wall: Mean Gene is the character, a mohawked badass with a machine gun and dynamite. When he catches you staring, he says, "You want it?"

You never expected this possibility. "I can *have* it?"

"We'll do a trade," he says, and tells you that the bigger kids—"kids *my* age," he says and grins—swap cards, one for one, but that the poster is way bigger than a baseball card. "How many cards fit on top of the poster?" he asks. "That's how many I should get. Shake?"

You shake hands, and he tells you the deal is sealed, no backing out now. It sounds fair to you, and there's an exhilaration to finding yourself skipping ahead three grades to big-kid behavior. But when Jeremy brings the poster to your house and rummages through your closet to collect the cards he's owed, you get a bad feeling. Your father bought you a wax box of the new Upper Deck cards a month ago, along with a binder and page sleeves, the gift a Trojan horse into some lesson on patience and valuation. You dutifully opened the packs and used the checklist to file them in the sleeves by number, but you were intimidated by the thick Beckett guide that your father provided, and couldn't follow his lecture on how to track card value and record numbers, and in the end you gave up, and now it's all in your closet, next to the xylophone and the model dinosaur kit. But Jeremy finds the binder, goes straight for the Star Rookies. Ken Griffey Jr. Gary Sheffield. John Smoltz. Takes them all, full binder pages, placing them atop the poster to show you how many fit upon its surface.

"I don't think my Dad would…" you start. There are two Griffeys. That's a name your father kept saying as you opened the packs. Rookies are important. And All-Star guys. And "error cards," of which he identified one particularly valuable example.

"We shook hands," Jeremy says. "It was a deal."

You don't know how many cards he swindles, but you know in your soul that you lost this trade. When your father learns of the transaction, he's apoplectic. "For this Goddamned poster?" he yells at you. "*This* ugly thing? You're not putting this up in my house, on my walls! That's the last time," he says. "That's the last time I throw my money away."

He's been mad before, but something is different this time. You've let him down in some way more personal than you could imagine. Strangely, things change between you and your father. You can no longer do anything to his satisfaction. Always there is something wrong with your behavior. He cuts off the "Happy Birthday" song at your next party because you aren't smiling enough. "Gratitude!" he roars at you. "For everything you've been given. Smile for these people!" These people: your friends, other 8-year-olds who, like you, just want to slam cake in their faces and go back to playing Skee-Ball, and now they're terrified.

Time passes, and this scene replays itself again and again, your father arriving late to some event just to reprimand you, to correct some behavior of yours. It happens at Cub Scouts, at karate, at tennis camp, and you are often too humiliated to return, your ability to make new friends severely hampered. Hell, it's as if the other kids receive permission from the old man to treat you poorly, all of them breathing in his negative energy and feeling emboldened by it, and so—in addition to the daily punishments visited upon you by your father—you soon become the target of *their* dodgeballs and spitwads, too.

At home, the few times your father sits with you to complete schoolwork, he makes you feel like an idiot for not knowing what he knows. All the time, patience, and attention he once bestowed up on you he now grants to your younger sister. She is the future him. She takes no shit. She corrects *him* when he screws up a fraction. She knows how to fake a smile and make someone feel loved, even when they are held in extreme contempt.

Your father orders you to toughen up, but then doesn't let you play sports because (he claims) he's concerned about your size, about broken bones and emergency rooms. Really, though, you suspect that he's protecting himself, that your lack of athletic ability brings him deep embarrassment. And so the other boys get bigger, stronger, faster, and all through middle school you remain this diminutive growth-stunted outcast without any close friends. Edwin: the rich little weirdo who can't catch a baseball, can't throw a football, can't even swing a tennis racket. P.E. is a particularly rough period of your day, mostly spent avoiding physical contests and praying you don't wind up as "skins" when half the class is forced to remove t-shirts to distinguish between teams.

Years pass. Your father works long hours, and you are relieved when you go to bed at night without seeing him. And then, during your junior year of high school, your father calls you a *disappointment* for the first time—it's been communicated to you in a thousand other ways, of course, but the word itself has never left his lips except in the oft-repeated phrase "I'm disappointed," or "This is disappointing." You scored a C in Economics, which, given your father's varied business ventures and investments, he views as an affront to all that he is and all that he believes in. "Mr. Ehren is a close friend," he says. "I guest lectured for him when he taught community college. Do you know how this makes me look, my own son?"

Your father. Daily, you wonder what sort of life you'd be living if you'd been given a different one. If he'd encouraged you. If he'd taught you. This is an old story, re-told a million times, with a million tragic sons the outcome, so why couldn't your father have just read the damn story himself, seen the ending so you wouldn't have to suffer?

At some point, fear of your father gives way to rage. You want the friends you feel you've been denied, even if it costs your father a thousand fucking dollars. You will make those friends, you will make the world love you.

During your Senior year of high school, your parents buy a plot of land in an exclusive Atlanta neighborhood and begin constructing their dream mansion, rooms upon rooms upon rooms, a place—now that you're set to leave for college—you will never live. When they leave town for another weekend trip to Hilton Head, you decide you're going to throw a party for the whole damn Class of '99. So what if you're the kid no one really likes, Edwin the weirdo, the short dude whose polos always seem too long, whose hair always seems greaser-shiny even when he doesn't gel it, who always forgets how to read poetry aloud (stopping at the end of every line as if they're all meant to rhyme) and embarrasses himself in the Honors English class he doesn't deserve to be taking but into which his mother fought for his inclusion? Who cares, who cares, who cares? You've never hosted a party, have in fact never *attended* a true high school party—the type from teen comedies, where kids spill out the doors and girls give BJs in upstairs bedrooms—because no one would ever think to invite you, but fuck it: you invite *everyone*.

The new house is all wires and sawdust and just-laid kitchen tile, and on the one hand it's perfect for a high school party because there's nothing to break, but on the other it's like a body without skin, everything bare and susceptible to terrible injury: you picture a drunk girl spilling her beer into the guts of what will be your father's new home theater; you picture the football team arriving and stomping on the piles of sheetrock, the baseball guys pissing in toilets that don't yet flush, the pot-smokers lighting mounds of sawdust because *whooooaaaaa*, someone taking a shit and leaving it between the walls, all these kids you barely know and who don't respect you feeling free to raise hell inside this unfinished mansion. But after another dismissive comment from your father—you told him you'd been accepted to the University of Central Florida, and he rolled his eyes and said, "Didn't do the work to get into Athens, did you?" like your acceptance is folly rather than achievement— you actually crave the carnage that such a crowd would create.

In fact, as soon as your parents leave for the beach, you pack up your father's tightly maintained liquor cabinet into plastic milk crates, pluck dozens of wine bottles from the basement, unhook the keg from the porch's kegerator and dolly it to your pickup. Thousands of dollars in alcohol, enough to impress even the most uncharmable of rich girls at school. Hennessy. Wine from the '70s, dust thick on the curved glass. All of it you transport to the half-finished mansion. You spread stacks of solo cups and wine glasses across the kitchen table. "Drink it!" you say to the world. "Destroy this fucking place!"

But in the end, your sister doesn't help you enlist any party-goers. That night, she just goes to a movie with her boyfriend, and only three or four kids show up to the half-mansion to drink your father's booze. You smash a panel of sheetrock, just to feel like you've done something productive, but you still feel annoyed when one of your guests tracks muddy footprints across the kitchen tile. It feels like you're trying too hard. And indeed, it's a pain in the ass to re-pack all the liquor, the keg, the glasses, drive it back home without any breakage, rearrange it in the bar and on shelves and in the basement, all exactly the same. All for a failed party.

You consider dumping out the liquor, and just lying to your parents. You *did* have a party. It was insane! But you know your sister—the good child, the smart one—won't lie for you. "There was no party," you can hear her scoffing. "He just *wasted* your alcohol." And how insignificant this would make you seem. Worse than trading your best baseball cards for a dumb poster.

When your parents return home, the only thing your father says to you is, "Someday, when you get a house of your own, maybe you'll learn how to do dishes." He holds up your empty pizza plate and shakes his head. You know immediately that he'll never see the sheetrock you smashed, the footprints on the tile, the empty solo cups you left on the concrete floor of the half-mansion's living room, that all of this will only be a nuisance to the construction workers, who'll wonder what kind of asshole drives all the way out to this place—a half-built neighborhood for the too-rich—to drink a bottle of Grey Goose?

Days pass. Weeks. Months. High school ends.

You leave for Orlando, and you are elated to leave behind your Georgia past, the father who is always disappointed by your inadequacies as a potential heir, your sister who can do no wrong, your mother who is always fucking absent when you need her. You chose UCF because it is not UGA, and Orlando is not Atlanta. Maybe your problem has been one of scale. You were never meant to succeed in a city as large as Atlanta, its established private schools, its old money, just as your own father had to downsize from New York City to make his money. Maybe Orlando will be easy. Smaller town. Maybe they…maybe they'll have never seen someone like you, with your experience, your big-city smarts? Maybe you can take the place by

AND EVEN THOUGH MARC is still supposedly "training" you, today he had a meeting with a graphic designer friend about his "digital presence," so he left you to your first *solo* loan closing.

If you can do this, he'll give you more loans to close on your own, and you can pocket the full fee. He can look for more banks, too, more title companies, more income opportunities. "There's a lot riding on this," he told you from the couch yesterday, staring up at the ceiling. "If you can do this, my business is not just me. My business is a business."

But Marc is not himself. Ever since he got his ass kicked downtown he's been going through these stretches where he stumbles around like a zombie, missing appointments, mumbling "I am not myself" and "Assailant" and "Concussion" and (most bizarre) "Dead Zone."

Last night, you both watched Game Four of the Magic-Cavs series, and you wanted him to get angry as he watched, to throw highlighters, to scream every time the Magic missed an open shot. Anything to show he was still alive, but he just stared at the screen, unblinking.

The Magic won in overtime, 116-114. Exciting game. Magic up 3-1 in the series, one win from the NBA Finals. History in the making. Pandemonium on the streets of Orlando. Marc just turned off the TV and went to bed. It was frightening how little he cared.

So today you're in MetroWest, a slice of Orlando you've never before visited. Your hometown in Georgia was not sectioned into these sorts of chunks, directional or otherwise; there was no East Orlando, no South Orlando, no MetroWest, no Dr. Phillips, no University, no Waterford Lakes or whatever. There was only "in town" and "out in the country." And out in the country, you knew where you were by access roads, by industrial monuments. "I'm out by the fertilizer plant," or "I'm at the Johnson Ranch," or "that old Citgo on County Line." Here, there are so many little designations you often wonder which are towns and which are just neighborhoods or nicknames. Union Park, Delaney Park, College Park. The city limits snake and tentacle to avoid or absorb land. What's city, what's county, what's autonomous?

MetroWest, you discover, is a land of golf courses, long boulevards lined with new trees and middle-of-the-workday joggers, the forever smell of just-cut grass floating over it all. Thick brick walls with black and gold plaques, golf community subdivisions with gates and guards. Red Spanish-tiled roofs on the houses, yes, but also on the grocery stores, on the gas stations. From here, looking toward downtown Orlando to the east, the skyline exists in that hazy blue-gray heat-shimmer of a hot afternoon, the blacktop below sizzling, the buildings a mile away like faded photocopies of themselves glimpsed through poolwater-eyes.

MetroWest on a Wednesday, and you kill it, answering questions with the confidence of JJ at the free-throw line, moving quickly through documents, pointing to the highlighted slots with your pen, saying "Just a couple more" like a nurse taking blood samples, binder-clipping papers and slipping them into a FedEx envelope, shaking hands; you're finished in no time, and though there were moments when you suspected that Marc (if here) would've been holding his breath and waiting for you to fail, nothing terrible happened.

"They're not all so easy," Marc tells you when you brag to him over the phone.

"I know," you say.

"You never know what's easy and what's tough until you get there," he says. He's told you the horror stories, but these all happened in a pre-Kyle Orlando. The thing is: you nailed it. Easy money. You should feel fantastic.

But in that living room with that family, you had to bite your tongue to keep from asking whether the father wanted someone to fix his wobbling ceiling fan, maybe patch up the holes in the drywall and repaint the place. The thought of these things—the smell of sawdust, the feel of a screwdriver in your hand—was enough to make you dizzy with fantasy as you held the stupid little pen and the soulless self-inking stamp.

You're okay at this, notary work. But by the end of the day, three more closings on Good Homes Road beneath the world's most gigantic white cross, then two subdivisions in East Orlando filled with empty year-old houses, and you were ready to puke. The uniformity: a house in Sanford identical to a house in Andover Lakes identical to a house off Chickasaw. Identical townhomes in Lake Nona, Oviedo, Kissimmee, same nauseating new-carpet smell. Same quick-construction craftsmanship: sagging cabinets, bedroom doors that won't close over already-buckling wood laminate floors; windows without blinds. The things that kill you the most are the errant brush strokes of bright paint slopped onto the ceiling, the bad bubbly caulk jobs, the fire-ant piles growing up the sides of houses, the thousands of things that could be fixed in an hour if someone just gave a shit. A new home should be a dream come true. But these homes are McDonald's burgers sitting under heat lamps. When you see one that is "fixed up," it's only because someone was willing to pay extra for a different showerhead.

Only a couple weeks doing this job, but you're...yes, you're certain: you fucking hate it. Hate going into these houses. Hate the highways. You'd rather drive your ass back to Georgia than keep doing this. Two more signings on Wednesday. Three on Thursday, and the Magic lose to Cleveland in Game Five and you can see how this happened to Marc: you were crossing your fingers for that game, thinking that if they won, life would get better. But you know it won't. And pretty soon now, you're going to have to tell your brother: *I quit.*

So you search the paper for other jobs, thinking it'll be easier to quit if you already have another offer in hand, and that's when you see it: Friday night! school bus races! hot rods! and it's like a godsend. Demolition derby!

It's Rural Georgia come to Metro Orlando.

It's a sign. It's your last chance to love this place, to love your brother again.

It's everything you needed, it's

CITY HALL, GLASS OF SCOTCH in your trembling hand, Greg telling you a riot is coming. You sip the scotch and then immediately grab the decanter with your free hand for easy and continuous refills, because you want your body—your throat, your stomach—to feel the fire, to be prepared for the flames coming downtown. They're going to destroy everything, and why? *Why?*

You close your eyes, try to think of the plight of the average black man in Orlando.

Sip scotch, deep breath. Try to understand how it feels to be someone else.

You squint, hold the bridge of your nose. Aw, hell. Plight? This ain't the *North*, okay?

Up there, the Blacks moved in and they overtook the old white sections of town, and it was *all at once* and it wasn't pretty. Up there it's…it's… it's Cabrini-Green in Chicago, Tasker in Philadelphia, Pruitt-Igoe in St. Louis, you seen the news. Those people can't pay their $40 rent let alone throw away their garbage properly—old bottles and tin foil and diapers flooding every hallway of those towering projects. White flight, that's what they called it, but who wants to live surrounded by garbage? Can you blame the white families for wanting to escape living next door to *that*? Some old Midwestern couple who all they care about is Cardinals baseball and bratwurst, can you blame them for wanting to get away from those cesspools of depravity built into their backyards?

White Flight is *perfectly understandable*. Carl T. Langford ain't a racist, but that shit up there is animalistic. You don't see no White Flight here in Orlando. You don't see no scared white folk cramming into station wagons and peelin' out to some silly suburb. Nossir. Here, you got folks—black 'n white—that believe in the city. You're sure of it. There's a reason why Eatonville was the first incorporated black town in the country: Orlando is the happiest Got-damned place on Earth for the Black Man. You remember the billboards the city put up earlier in the decade, right when all this civil rights talk was heating up: "What's black and white and friendly all over? Orlando!"

Sip the scotch. Greg on the phone, talkin' to God-knows-who.

Finish the scotch.

Black plight. Pssh.

Someday this will go in your book. You'll record your thoughts for all time. You understand race relations. You *get* it. Someday, the book. But tonight there's a riot on the way, and now the alcohol has calmed you. Thanks to the Scotch, you are Superman again, and you're gonna squash this shit.

"Mr. Mayor, they're on the move," Greg says.

"I hear you." You pour yourself another from the decanter. "Sit with me, Greg," you say and pour out another glass, point to one of your leather chairs. "Have this. Could be a long night."

"Mr. Mayor."

"Sit, I said."

Greg sits but doesn't drink. What kind of man refuses a glass of scotch in a situation like this? What kind of egghead glues himself to the phone and the textbook?

"Drink," you say. "Ain't tough."

He floats his hand toward the glass and sort-of lifts it, sort-of puts it to his lips, but he's like a child with a spoonful of peas, distaste in his eyes. He makes as if to place the glass down instead of drinking. "Mr. Mayor, I think we need to—"

You slam your fist onto the table. "Put it to your *Got*-damn *lips*."

"Okay," he says. "Okay." Like you'll ground him for a week if he disobeys you. And he does lift the glass, shakily. His uneasiness makes you feel good. Greg is a law-school type from up North who never swung no axe, never went hunting. He don't know Orlando, don't know Florida. Hell, maybe he never even met a black man who didn't work for him. *Greg*. Greg's deficiencies as a man make you calm.

"Don't sip it like some damned pansy," you say. "I pour you a glass, you take it down."

"Sir, I don't think that now is—"

"Shut. Your. Mouth. This ain't *Harvard*."

"I didn't go to Harvard."

You pour again.

"*Drink*," you say.

He does, his face contorting into agony as he swallows. Cheeks already flushing red.

"Imma pour one more, and we're gonna talk strategy. Like men," you say. So you pour, and you knock it back, and you watch him struggle to keep his down. "All right, let's talk," you say. "They're marching?"

"They're *moving*, sir, literally *marching* and not just gathering." Greg holds his hand over his mouth like he might vomit, takes a long breath. "People are scared."

You run your hand down the decanter, a gift from Chicago Mayor Richard Daley. Met him at a retreat in Oklahoma, and the *man* could *hunt*: you were on a team together, and you thought he'd be the liability, the big-city mayor; but he shot a deer almost *before* the hunt had started, and after he did it he said, "Nothing like hunting a man. Now that's a challenge." Oh man. Daley. And yet his city burned. You'll show them what makes a mayor. "Okay," you say. "What direction they marching? What destination? Or they just gonna destroy their own neighborhood?"

"The destination is *City Hall*. Orange Avenue. They've got wheelbarrows full of bricks, shopping carts full of liquor bottles. They've been stockpiling."

"Better than torches and pitchforks!" you say and knock back your glass.

"What?"

"Frankenstein joke," you say. "Read your lit-rature, Greg."

"Shotguns, too," Greg says.

"Shotguns." You nod, trying to show some respect for their weaponry, but Greg has become a siphon of fear, has sucked it all out of your soul, and damn you feel good watching him tremble. "Okay, Greg. They got themselves a militia, do they? They gon' burn us to the ground?"

"Sir, this isn't a joke."

"I ain't laughing," you say. World on fire. World on fire. Under *your* watch? You ain't laughing, no, but you ain't quaking with fear, neither. Where's your fucking baseball bat? You ain't afraid. "This is Orlando, Greg. My city. I *run* this shit, you hear me?"

"What are we going to do?"

You pour another drink for Greg, slide him the glass.

"You're gonna take this drink," you say. "And me: Imma go outside. With my hat. With my bat, yes. And I'm gonna wait for the waves to hit my toes, and it ain't never gonna happen. Know why?"

Greg rises and points. "Sir, they're—"

"This is the City of Dreams, my friend," you say.

"Sir, that's a Goddamned *marketing* slogan. It doesn't—"

You rise from your seat and—quick as a linebacker—you rush Greg and pin him to the wall with your elbow. His head makes a thumping noise against the wood paneling, face scrunches up in suffocating pain. "You take the Lord's name in vain again, you Yankee prick," you breathe into his face, "and tonight *you'll* be the one facing hellfire." You're not Superman, no, you're something better; it's as if the scotch has summoned the spirit of ancient Florida, and Greg can smell the history on your breath. He's squirming in your grip, arms flailing.

"I'm going outside," you say, but you don't release him. "You tell dispatch I don't want a *single* police officer cruising west of Division tonight. Not a one. Pull 'em all. Let 'em burn their own neighborhoods should they desire, but don't let anyone say it was some white cop caused problems."

"Sir," he coughs, "can't…breathe."

"You tell them what I said." Deeper into his neck your elbow goes, the walls straining against his skull. You got yourself a plan, yessir, and you will accept only surrender. "Then you get me Father Pinder. Get him here *right away*, even if you gotta drive over there yourself. Through the mobs and to the front door of the church."

"Sir," he croaks.

"And you look through that binder. Call each of the football coaches for the black schools, and you tell 'em to meet me out front here."

"Sirrrr…"

"Maybe we gon' have fire tonight," you say, "but I tell you what, son. I ain't gon' be the one gets burned."

"NO MORE MOVEMENTS, STEVEN," Elaina says. She's your fiancée now, and the two of you are sharing late afternoon drinks, the place all to yourselves while the bartenders prep and the band sets up its merch booth. You've earned the opportunity to be here and to just sit and work on your laptop whenever you want, and that feels almost like a fulfillment of the dream of your blog, but Elaina's saying, "Baby, from now on, you need to get *paid* for your work. You deserve it, and I'm not letting anyone take advantage of you anymore."

"Take advantage?" you ask. "This is my *passion*. I'm having *fun* with it, like you said. I mean, we're *here* right now, right?"

Here is The Social, a long-standing music venue on Orange Ave, the planned #7 spot on your *Orlandofesto*, and you are the only two people at the bar because The Social does not open for several hours. You've become semi-important to this place, having taken up a graphic design gig for them several months ago; you are the first to see their monthly performance calendar, which you type into your calendar template, and which you decorate with photos of the bands; you design the glossy tabletop tents that feature the upcoming headliners, too, and carefully place them onto every table, and at fifteen-inch intervals along the bartop. You swing by on Wednesday afternoons to meet with management, and afterward they pull you Dogfish Head drafts and let you work on your laptop at the bar. Sometimes, too, in the curious sober lighting of 4 PM, you see someone with a guitar, someone sound-checking, and you think: I am an essential part of the machinery that makes the city's music culture spin!

"All I'm saying is that you've put a lot of work into your blog," Elaina says. "Everyone wants you to write about their business, to share their event. All of it for free. I care about you. It kills me to see someone using you."

You see it differently. The blog is no longer in trouble. The Other City Beautiful is going strong, every post short, bullet-pointed, numbered, filled with high-quality photographs or low-quality animated gifs. After your conversation with Anderson, you knew you had to give up the serious, immersive posts and just go with what the people wanted. You not only made 7-Eleven #9 on your Top Fifty list, you wrote the whole post from the perspective of the Slurpee Machine, and damn did it feel good, the goofiness. The following week you wrote "25 Things That Only Orlandoans Think," and "5 Orlando Intersections That'll Make You Want to Burn Your Beloved City to the Ground," and all quick zippy sentences, and damn was it easy, and when the immediate likes and shares came in, damn did it feel good. Fun, Anderson said. Snappy. Now you're writing weekly "what's happening in your hood?" posts breaking down events from "Date Night at Leu Gardens" to the *Orlando Weekly* "Best of Orlando" party, subscribers doubling, tripling, faithful readers looking to you for weekend plans here in *Authentic Orlando*. And the people at the places you write up—at

Stardust, at Park Ave CDs, at Pom Pom's, at The Social—they *know* you now, and they love your project, love the attention you lavish upon them.

"Not everyone can get paid for their passions," you protest, implying Elaina's furniture blog, the reputation she's built, the money she commands for sanding down a dresser. Hell, she's just returned from a furniture convention, and to see the photos on her blog, you'd think she was a guest of honor or something.

By now, of course, it's late 2008, and you have proposed to Elaina, and cute smiles and giggles have given way to sacrifices and negotiations and deep discussions about the future. But still, you're both happy in the way that anxious young people are happy: you're over-confident and you're making tons of mistakes, sure, but you're *happy*, and committed to your life together. More important, you know she has your best interests at heart, that she has all along.

And yet.

There are things Elaina does not understand about you, things you cannot tell her, reasons why—despite the stupid happiness pulsing through you both—you want to fight her on this.

"This is the next spot on your big list, huh?" Elaina asks, looking around.

"I can't believe you've never been here."

"I'm not from here," she says. "I was never—how do you say—in the *scene*? Do I sound lame saying that?"

You laugh, place your hand over her knee. Her jeans are ripped and torn in about a hundred places, frayed and shredded so much your hand is touching more skin than denim. You're not sure if these are beat-up work pants, the kind in which she paints and varnishes and cracks apart broken drawers, or if these pants are trendy and expensive. It's all the same to you. "You can get away with it," you say.

"Gee, thanks."

"I've probably invited you to fifty different shows here."

"Oh, the *shows*," she says. "With Eli and Tyler and"—she shudders—"Goat."

"Goat is artistic. You'd like him if you gave him a chance."

"He's not artistic. Does he even know how to draw?"

"He worked on the zine with me, back in high school."

"He's a complainer. This movie sucks, that album blows. That's not the same thing as being artistic."

"He's been my friend since we were thirteen."

"Every time I see 'Goat'"—she makes air quotes, a tic that's lately begun to irritate you—"he's shirtless. Damn close to pantless, too."

"*One time.* One time he answered the door in boxers!"

"I saw *testicle*, Steven."

"He's a good friend. First friend I made in Orlando."

"Would he loan you money if you needed it?" Elaina asks.

"He doesn't have money."

"Would he help you move?"

"He doesn't have a truck."

"Would you want him to sit next to my parents at our wedding?"

Shit. How is it that she seems to always claim the most reasonable ground in any argument? How do you always get stuck arguing for some patch of indefensible soil? You stare straight ahead, pretend to search the draft taps for something new. "Your point has been made."

Elaina nods, satisfied. Always the victor. "Well, it must have taken a lot of restraint to hold out on writing about this place for so long. Your beloved *scene.*"

"A list of the most authentic places in any city should be varied," you say. "Food, shopping, recreation—"

"Antique shops."

"Sure. Antique shops. But the most important is music. Because what, really, is any city without its music? The bands who've made it big, the singers, the rappers—I mean, think of all the raps song stamped with Eastside or Westside or ATL—but also the bars and dives and backyard shacks where they performed."

And you're off on another rant, asking her, What's New Orleans without The Civic Theater and the Blue Nile and The Howlin' Wolf, the sounds of the horns always floating above the graveyards? What's Gainesville without its swamp-punk, its Less Than Jake, its Fest, its post-rock? What is *Orlando* without the music that bursts from *its* open doorways downtown and along Mills, or that is contained deep within soundproof theme park chambers for paying customers, music held there as tight as oxygen in a spaceship, the endless "It's a Small World" chant, the pianists at the top-tier I-Drive hotels, the big band at Disney's Grand Floridian forever roaring like the twenties? The music of Orlando. (You're vaguely aware that this whole monologue is the first draft of your eventual blog post. She's aware, too. That's why she doesn't tell you to shut up.)

The Social should, of course, take #1 in your Top 50, but that'd be too obviously personal. Still, is there anywhere that means more to you? Elaina would never suspect it. Elaina has never met Punk Rock Steven, who was himself a first draft of the current you.

Back in high school, fueled by father-loathing and by your hatred for the dozens of cities and towns you'd been dumped into and ripped from and dumped into, you were punk rock. *Punk* fucking *rock*. Elaina knows you love "shows," but your actual musical past is far too vulgar for her tastes. Hell, when you finally settled in Orlando, you started a zine called *24 Pages Up Your Ass*, a nod to the band 88 Fingers Louie, whose *88 Fingers Up Your Ass* defined your senior year. Your friend Goat wrote CD reviews and drew stick-figure comics in which asshole football players found themselves trampled beneath the pass-rush of hard-core pits. You and Goat and Eli and a cadre of other angry, semi-reject high schoolers traveled the I-4 Corridor every Thursday to see shows at the St. Petersburg State Theatre and Jannus Landing, and sometimes got lucky when one of your favorite bands chose Orlando over Tampa. You saw Millencolin at The Beacham, Unwritten Law at Firestone, No Fraud at the Edge, and you swirled in mosh pits with shirtless skinheads and mohawked dropouts and granite-chested bruisers who worked highway construction by day and pounded suburban kids like you at night. One of your shoulders still hasn't recovered from the hits. Once, you got so drunk at a Goldfinger show that you didn't even feel someone elbow your face, didn't feel your head slam against the floor, but Goat was there (inexplicably wearing those fake glasses with nose and mustache attached) to lift you back up, and the two of you summoned the rest of your Orlando crew and you singled out the motherfucker who'd blindsided you and together descended on him and battered him into something unrecognizable.

Elaina doesn't know that this is the genesis of so much of what you do and who you are, that this is why you hated (*still* hate) late-90s radio rock, Creed and Smash Mouth and the Goo Goo Dolls, why you moshed through the late '90s oblivious to Orlando's own contribution to pop music, the rise of the Backstreet Boys and 'NSYNC and 98 Degrees. It was only after the success of MTV's boy band reality show, *Making the Band*, that you began to notice that the world assumed *your city* was the epicenter of bubblegum pop. Other cities found their names chanted in gangsta rap songs, but Orlando was represented by a fucking *boy band called O-Town?* And what made it worse, you discovered, was that none of the boys were *from* Orlando. They came from elsewhere, but were assembled here, labeled "O-Town" because the city itself had the persona the producers were looking for, the persona of a middle school girl's pink poster-covered bedroom. "Can you believe this shit?" you asked Eli and Goat. "Can you believe what they're doing with our city? Can you?" Totally, they said. Totally fucked up, dude. Eli and Goat had lived here their whole lives, both of them in the same Conway neighborhood through the 1980s, roads widening around them, new malls and shopping centers and subdivisions sprouting on land that had been citrus fields until the Great Freeze of '89 finally wiped everything out. They had lifelong ties to the place, but *you* had settled here in high school, saw what the rest of the country had to offer and thus had more passion for the city than either of them could've expected. O-Town: five dudes in stupid clothes, harmonizing and making the city look like an old TGIF sitcom come to life, like there was some whole boy-band *scene* here?

After the world survived Y2K and you started college, you moved from zine writing to CD reviews for the *Orlando Music Guide*, then to concert previews for *Orlando Weekly*, then your own blog, but nobody in the fraternity house knew about this. Marc, Anderson, Jimmy, Edwin. (And it's not like

Eli and Goat had followed you down the college route.) You'd pledged the fraternity to try to tame yourself, to practice normal male interaction, to prepare for a post-college life that you imagined required strict adherence to polo shirts and khaki pants, and so you never fully revealed yourself to your housemates. At your weirdest, they knew you as the music-guy who'd slip in CDs by unknown bands, or the writer-guy to visit when they needed someone to proofread their papers, but *Punk Rock Steven* was a man kept hidden during college while you tried to reinvent yourself as someone more reasonable, a Professional Steven. But the other Steven...that was the *real you*.

And now, every fucking real estate brochure you design, every advertisement for a Lone Star grand opening, every Family Dollar "New Management" campaign, prods and goads your punk rock past... Elaina knows nothing about *Punk Rock Steven,* knows nothing about the Lagwagon show at which you tore off your shirt and twirled it over your head with a hundred others and screamed along with such passion that your voice was hoarse for a week, the ecstasy of shared anger. She doesn't know how tightly you've held onto it, these memories and these bands and these people. How does a man stay *punk fucking rock* when he's married to a woman who is not, who has never been, who couldn't even explain to him why it's so necessary that the word "fucking" should always be wedged between "punk" and "rock"?

You are not yet married, but...maybe you *are* worried about your future?

"No movements, no free work," Elaina tells you. "You have to believe you're worth it. *My* blog doesn't give everything away. It forces the reader to buy something at my Etsy shop."

"But I'm not selling anything yet. I can't make people pay for the words."

"I mean generally...all this stuff you do for free, all these favors for coffee shops and beer bars. Weren't you going to sell t-shirts? Get *something* for all the work you're doing."

"I just..." You shake your head. If she knew you were losing money by working for The Social, she'd spit out her Blue Moon. She's right, though. She's always right, and here you are again, ready to defend an indefensible position. "I want to build my audience first. I don't want to seem pushy. Like, too corporate or…"

"Everybody's gotta eat. Don't feel bad about making money."

You look at your hands, the nails you clip with obsessive regularity because a slightly-too-long nail impacts the way your fingers hit the keyboard. It's not so easy. Your blog has come a long way, you've silenced the trolls, you've built a real audience. But you can't betray the trust of your readers, many of whom would unsubscribe if they sniffed inauthenticity and product peddling. But there's Elaina, too, the only woman who's ever believed in you, the (let's be honest here) only long-term girlfriend (now fiancée!) you've ever had, and she wants what's best for you, right? Are you prepared to trust her, or is this a sign that you need to make a choice between her and the blog?

"I'm going to order my first batch of t-shirts," you say finally. "And I'm going to start printing the bumper stickers."

"Steven, I'm not forcing you to—"

"I've been talking about it for the past two years. I hear what you're saying. But the campaign needs support from local businesses, see? I'm doing all these favors, building these relationships, because I need them. You have to understand that that's what I've been doing, right?"

"And you have to understand that I'm sticking up for you," Elaina says, her hand on yours. Her fingers are scraped with fresh wounds, sawdust under her cracked nails. "You're doing this, and you're gonna kill it."

If Elaina says it, how can you doubt it?

TONIGHT IS YOUR long-awaited housewarming party, and right now, twenty minutes before it starts, you're pouring cold Pinot Grigio into your nicest wine glass (one of only three nice wine glasses you own, in fact, since you're restraining yourself from buying up the wedding registry) and watching in horror as a crack forms at the bottom of the glass and etches a jagged line soundlessly toward the rim.

"Fuck," you say, expecting the wine to leak out and spill across the hardwood, but you run your finger over the smooth glass and there is no sharpness, no moisture. Somehow, the crack exists entirely within the thin glass.

"That can't be a good sign," Marc says from the living room, pointing.

"Dear God." You shut your eyes. "Can you put a fucking *shirt* on?"

He looks down, pats his chest. "It's in the dryer."

"The doorbell's going to ring any minute. This party is"—you stop, breathe—"this party is about *looking good*, okay? Looking like, against all evidence to the contrary, we have our *shit* together. A shirt, listen to me, don't look away, a shirt *matters*, do you hear me?"

"What about a dining room table?" He snickers, heading toward the laundry room.

"Not funny," you say. "I'm trying very hard not to...not to *murder* someone."

Breathe again. Breathe.

A few months ago, back when Marc first closed on this house (before he proposed, but still: you knew), you two went furniture shopping. Together you selected the living room set, and while the couches were delivered without incident, the coffee table and dining room table arrived broken. Twice. And today, you were supposed to have received the re-re-deliveries no later than noon, but it's now motherfucking 7 PM and still *nothing*, and it takes every ounce of energy in your under-nourished, wedding-dress-ready body to stop yourself from screaming.

Tonight is the night when it all comes together: your fair-weather sorority friends, who live to be impressed, whose days and nights are spent in a greedy social buffet of events and parties and open bars and wine-tastings all painstakingly planned by someone else; your Golden Citrus co-workers, who will be scrutinizing every detail of your house and your life and judging whether it reveals a woman who can succeed and move up, or whether you'll always just be relegated to an assistant role; and women from Alumni Club, too, who've heard you talk so much about your planning prowess, but who've meanwhile patronized you at every turn, holding your business card like a gum wrapper you know they'll later toss.

You've spent the full day making sure this space is convention-center-perfect, a showcase not only of the marriage you want to convey, but also of your professional expertise. As an event planner, what's a simple house party?

The things you control look fabulous. Nothing says "class" like brie baked into that warm bread-bowl thing, side of raspberry chutney. Summer sausage. Toasted pine nut hummus. Olives of many colors. A whole paycheck spent on serving plates and spreaders and charms for the martini glasses. You restrained yourself from buying up your entire wedding registry, but you made a few strategic purchases that you couldn't do without (stainless steel skewers, anyone?). The hors d'oeuvres are just grocery store finger-food dressed up to look expensive, but no one will see receipts. They will only see how *together* you have it. They'll see it in the maintenance of the front hedges, in the straight lines of a yard just-edged, the iPod playlist that will serenade them from the docking station you set up in the living room. The position of the cheese trays on the bartop, the height of the multi-colored napkin stacks, the location of the martini bar, the flow of human traffic from one room to the next so that the party never feels crowded, the space always humming, a true feat of civil engineering. They will leave this house saying, "Damn, Shelley is good at what she does," and—better—"Damn, Shelley really does *have it all.*"

But there are the things you can't control, too: the emptiness of the house, the lack of furniture, the lack of décor. A model home looks more lived-in than this place. So you've played up the "work in progress" angle. All around the house are post-its that say "Mirror Here?" and "Wedding Photo Here?" and "Potential Wedding Gift Here!"—all of it your charming attempt to make this new house feel warmer and more fun, as if crowd-sourcing a home's decor is a time-honored party game. You've even left notepads in every corner of the house that say "Help us imagine our life! Suggestions?"

When the doorbell rings for the first time, Marc is on the phone out on the lanai (wearing a shirt now, at least), and you're still arranging hors d'oeuvres on the countertop. But you know that—no matter if it's his friends or yours at the door—this is *your* party entirely. Marc will be on his phone, and then he'll be drinking, and then he'll be on the porch smoking cigars with Edwin and

Jimmy, and then, when the party is over and you're cleaning everything, he'll be in the bedroom giving you the "let's have sex" stare without having washed so much as a fork.

Deep breath. You have it all, Shelley. All of it. You rock this shit.

Now: the door.

"Shelley!" says Andrea, and—arms wide for a hug—she struggles forward in her too-short skirt, legs only able to take the smallest of steps, and she wraps her arms around you and her skin is cold from her car's air-conditioning or from her general lack of humanity, it's not clear. "Oh, your house is beautiful!"

"Thank you," you say, because this is the response you've programmed yourself to give, even though you want to say "You've only walked in the front door." Stifle that remark. Keep the smile going. You cannot be angry before the party starts.

Andrea looks behind her to her shit-bag husband Rob, then looks back at you. "Are we the first ones here?"

"Looks that way."

"Oh!" Andrea says and forces her smile brighter. (The disappointment beams from her: to be the first ones to arrive at the party? They played this wrong.)

"Let me show you to the drinks," you say.

"Rob!" Andrea says. "Rob! Drinks, this way!"

Her husband bumbles forward, trips over the foyer rug, says "oh shit," then guffaws. Rob is just another douchebag who has it all but probably shouldn't, who (based on the Facebook photos you see) golfs so much he shouldn't be able to hold down a full-time job, drinks so much he shouldn't have such a beautiful wife, and yet—against the very laws of nature—here is this Neanderthal, and he's saying "Get my motherfucking *drank* on!" and bumping past both of you without even the most minor acknowledgment of the lady of the house.

"He's had a long week," Andrea whispers.

"I'm sure," you say, but you're thinking that he probably doesn't have the word "assistant" in his title, probably gets paid twice as much as you for doing a fraction of the work. "Well, you can follow me." You lead Andrea toward the dining room, where you've set up six bottles of wine and a full martini bar on a fold-out card table (you'd wanted to set it up on the dining room table, but that's in a delivery truck somewhere). Rob has gone the wrong way, into the kitchen, is inside the refrigerator and shoving aside orange juice cartons and milk gallons to search for beer. You hear the salad dressings knocked over, the vegetable drawer opening, before he finally says "Ah!" and you know he's found *something* that Marc left in the fridge, even though there's a full cooler of party beer on the lanai.

"Do you feel relieved?" Andrea asks.

"Relieved?" you ask.

"To be *settled*, roomie," Andrea says.

Ugh. For one soul-crushing year in college, you shared a bedroom at the sorority house with Andrea. Occasionally she still calls you "roomie," even though it was clear that another minute together would've resulted in her strangulation.

"Well, I—"

"No dining room table?" Andrea asks.

"Still waiting on delivery. But nice tablecloth, right?"

"Sure," Andrea says and then immediately switches gears: "I'll do a green apple martini."

"Um." Forever a beer tub girl. Forever a bartender. "Coming right up," you say and scoop ice from the handsome, just-purchased chrome bucket, pour the prescribed ounce-age from the mix and from the vodka bottle, watch the silver mixer bead with cold condensation, and then you shake it so hard that Andrea's forced-happy expression finally cracks and she can no longer smile because she must know that you are capable of killing her with your bare hands.

"You got a bottle opener?" Rob calls from the kitchen.

"On the cooler outside," you say. "Where the *beer* is."

"Never mind!" Rob calls, and—dear God, you hear the dreaded noise— he has the bottle against the granite countertop, is slamming the heel of his hand against the bottlecap, and it clinks off and it's on the floor and there's likely a scratch in the brand-new countertop of this brand-new house, and the quickness with which Rob reappears in the great room leads you to believe that he left the bottlecap rolling on the kitchen floor for you to slip on later.

"Give us a tour!" Andrea says. "Show us the mansion!"

"It's not a mansion," you say. "Just larger than what—"

"Oh shit, there's Marc," Rob says. "I'm going out to the porch."

"Lanai," you insist.

"But, Rob…" Andrea says. "Are we going on a tour?"

"Go on your tour." Rob waves his hand at his wife. "I'll be out here."

"Such an asshole," Andrea says under her breath as her husband disappears and you both hear the sound of male greeting ("Heeeeeey!" "This guy! This guy! Holy shit!" "Got a drink? Fuck yeah!" "Pool? We gettin' in later? Throw the girls in?"), and the sounds of male embrace, male high-fiving after each not-clever comment.

"Still want to see the house?" you ask.

Andrea's frown morphs terrifyingly back to normal. "Of course! Cheers!" Martini downed. "Or maybe we go back for a refresh?"

"Already?" you say. "Sure."

There's a part of you that fears the disaster of mixing friends and colleagues and co-workers: Andrea, your old sorority roomie, and douchebag Rob, and douchebags Jimmy and Edwin, and more of Marc's old frat-star friends, and then all of your work friends, and the Alumni Club women…a million things can go wrong with such an unstable arrangement, but isn't that what drew you to event planning to begin with? Establishing order to prevent chaos. Even when you tended bar: the prep, the contingency plans, the on-the-fly thinking, the mental and physical exhaustion and then (ultimately) the blessed end to the night, and a reset button the next day. Nothing feels quite like it. So yes, there's some fear about the night, but you're confident, too, in your ability to play hostess, to group like people together, to start conversations, to fashion efficient routes to/from the bar and the hors d'oeuvres. Anyone can make a room look nice. Anyone can pop a cork and say "drink up!" But you are more than *anyone*. So here you are throttling the martini shaker again with forearm muscles built solid from years of such activity.

"You've always made such strong drinks!" Andrea says.

"You know me. Just trying to get you drunk and take advantage of you."

"Oh! Ha ha!" Andrea's discomfort makes you happy for a few seconds.

But then, moments later, it's Jimmy and Sandra at the door, and you're making a drink for Sandra while Jimmy runs off and rummages through the fridge and emerges with a slice of cold pizza (where the *fuck* did he find that?) and a Guinness that you didn't even know Marc had. "Ha ha!" Jimmy's screaming. "Motherfucking *pizza*, ya'll!"

"He had a long week," Sandra says.

"Oh my God, so did we," Andrea says. "This week."

"He's going to have one of his nights, I can already tell," Sandra sighs, and she still hasn't even made eye contact with you. "Where's Marc?"

"Out on the porch," you say. "Why?"

"Go out to the porch, Jimmy," Sandra says. "Do us a favor. Just stay out there."

"Yes, ma'am!" Jimmy says and salutes, a black olive flying from the cold pizza as he gesticulates. And then he's out to the porch but forgets to close the door and so there will be bugs in here if you don't rush to close it, but the doorbell rings again, and so you're rushing that way and—

TWENTY YEARS IN THIS HARDWARE STORE. All your life in Eatonville. You view Orlando and Winter Park from a distance. Stay on your own roads, in your own shops, on your own porches and front yards. Out there's just a world of hurt.

You're thinking Rosewood, only three years ago.

You're thinking Ocoee, couple years before that, not ten miles from here, families run from their homes, the hundreds that escaped the flames of that single day and poured into Parramore and Eatonville like refugees from some distant battleground. A Trail of Tears, a march of men and women with soot on their clothes and in their hair, children in wheelbarrows, whatever jackets or books or blankets they could manage to save from their burning homes before being driven from that ruined place forever. You remember them washing ashore here in Eatonville, remember how long that night was when you thought them white-robed vigilantes on horseback would be following with torches, with nooses, that night when you thought this town would get it next.

They're still here, the refugees, absorbed into your town like family who come to visit but decide to stay forever. Children in your schools. Men working the land, just for different white folk who don't know they're from Ocoee, 'cause to say it aloud is to mark yourself an agitator even if you didn't rise up, even if you stayed quiet and got your house burned down anyway.

You're wont to think that central Florida—this whole linked system of towns and cities, Winter Park and Maitland and Ocoee and Orlando and Altamonte Springs and Bithlo—is the weirdest damned place in the world. Something in the water maybe. Or something in the soil itself makes men crazy. Shit, who'd know it better than you? Your family been around here for centuries. Somewhere down the bloodline, there was a runaway slave from Carolina who got taken in by the Spanish at St. Augustine, won his freedom by fighting the British in the year 1728. Moved deeper into the state, married a native woman. Your great-grandaddy took up arms with a band of Seminoles to fight the Union, stormed Aaron Jernigan's farm and freed a slave woman named *Tampa*, married her too. Granddaddy was one of the founding fathers of Eatonville. This place is *you*, and *you* this place, and this hardware store been in the family forty years, and this's all you need.

But listen, here's this thing happens to you.

One day a white man walks in, says, "How'd you like to live in a fantasy world? A city of dreams?"

You say, "Mister, that's very kind. But I do think I'm already living in one."

The man laughs, all chesty-like, says, "Ho ho! This place?"

"Ain't much," you tell him, "but I own it."

"This store is falling apart."

"Then I'll fix it. Got the tools, sir. It's a hardware store."

"You're a clever one," he says.

You keep quiet then. When white men say something like this, you know they're walking that line between conversation and violence, like they're just *looking* for a reason, like maybe they already *got* a reason but if you say just *one more clever comment* then they say *they had no choice* but to do what they done.

"Down the road," he says. "We're building a new neighborhood."

"Mister, don't know if you noticed," you say, "but I'm a black man, and this here is a black town. Everything just fine by me."

He laughs. "I'm talking about a city of *tomorrow*. Race won't matter. It's what we make it."

"This town here," you say, "we already made this."

Nothing's ever good enough for folks these days. Build an all-black town, a model community, and someone'll come along with some new idea. Someday there'll be a village of all women, maybe, or all babies, or all comic strip characters, or whatever. A city where circus workers retire. A city of psychics. Every crazy idea's on the table.

"It'll be an experimental prototype," he says, "a city of tomorrow. I want it to be a place where every type of man can live side by side. Or, at the very least, in small villages, you see? A whole international community, a row of houses for the Irish, a row of houses for the Chinese, a row of houses for Cubans. Get in early, and I can make you a rich man."

Almost two hundred years your family's been in Florida, and you feel the ground shifting, the land whispering its disapproval. You know about the coasts, men getting rich from the Boom. They can't get enough, so they steamrolling their way into the swamps now, too, and hell, right up against Callahan and Jonestown and Black Bottom, where every time your people have tried to expand their territory the tiniest bit, your houses seem to mysteriously catch fire. Then *they* come, the white builders, and as soon as the ashes are cold build more white housing. Change is in the air in this year of our Lord, 1926. Changes everywhere. But the air still reeks of the past.

You look this white man up and down. Even your dog looks skeptical.

He's carrying a binder full of properties, ready to take the savings from the first dreamy-eyed black man he comes across. You see what's happenin' here.

"A rich man, you say?"

"Yessir, this land I got here in this binder—"

"Your fantasy land."

"Yessir, you—"

"You desperate, ain't you?"

He looks shocked. "Why, nossir, I—"

"Everyone buyin' up the coasts, and you got stuck with some weird chunk of land you thought was worth somethin'. Now it ain't. Shame when fantasies fall apart, ain't it?"

AND IT'S 1999, and you join a fraternity. You hear the derisive comments in your classes during Rush Week, other guys saying "I'd never pay for friends," but this is the *reason* you join. If you pay to live with forty other guys, there's no way they can run away from Edwin the Weirdo. They are financially obligated to hang out with you. And bonus: all fraternity expenses are tacked onto your tuition and housing bill, which your father's paying, so fuck it, let him. In fact, you ask them to charge double so you can have a bedroom to yourself. He'll never find out.

Your pledge semester is hell. Everyone mocks you for being the spoiled rich kid in a fraternity house full of working-class students paying for school on their own. Kids with sputtering cars. Kids who go the whole semester without getting a haircut. During Hell Week, the Pledge Master forces you to dress like a hobo and carry a sign around campus that says "Will Perform Odd Jobs For Spare Change." You take the hits because you've always taken the hits, because despite the hazing and the insults you are a part of something, but after initiation you know something has to change. You're not paying to be a laughingstock. Your father gave you a credit card for "college expenses," and though you've been scared to test its limits you feel you no longer have a choice. You spend lavishly, selflessly, and suddenly your brothers' attitudes change: everyone loves that there's a rich kid in their midst. Want a drink? On me. Want dinner? On me. Now it's super-easy to make friends! The expenses are easy enough to hide, too. What's $25 at TGIFriday's to your father, who spends how many thousands of dollars on his weekend trips? He sees statements, a grand total by month, and pays. You're a headache he doesn't want, the dumb son. "At least Edwin's in college," you overhear him say to your Uncle Jim at a 4th of July grill-out, "not roaming the streets." The fuck does *that* mean? Like, you're a criminal in the making?

Sophomore year, you push further. A couple hundred bucks at Wal-Mart, sporting goods. You buy a weight set for the fraternity house, mention it in casual conversation with your father: "Getting bigger," you say and expect him to ask the price, but he just says, "Maybe a good thing. You're short, like your mother." You want him to ask how much you bench, but conversations with your father are, without fail, interrupted by something more pressing, and rarely last sixty seconds.

Soon you realize that the credit card is likely on autopay, that your father is so indifferent to you that he isn't even paying attention to the money you're spending, so you buy a new TV, sell the old one, pocket the cash, then again buy something bigger and cooler. Eventually you buy something called a plasma screen that costs several grand and that you pay to have mounted to your bedroom wall. No one's seen anything like it. Out at bars, where your tabs run in the hundreds, the phrase "plasma screen in my room" actually gets you laid.

You buy a cactus, get tired of it and put it out in the yard. Your pledge brother Darrell gets fired from his barback job, has no money in his bank account, so you pay him to plant it. You buy an avocado tree and pay him to plant that, too.

You work out twice daily, go to the campus pool every afternoon, delight in removing your shirt. In high school, guys and girls alike laughed. The word "birdcage" was a go-to insult. Now they can't stop looking. Each day at the pool, when you lie on your stomach to tan your back, you pull your board shorts down just a little more. You'll have a fully tanned ass by the start of summer break. How far will you get before someone complains?

No one complains.

Not about you. Not ever.

You're Edwin. With your credit card, you bring joy to the world. Your friends think you're Santa Claus, but you prefer to think of yourself as Robin Hood, doing some good at the expense of someone awful.

For the sake of your credit card, of course, you do need to keep your GPA reasonable. So, in another act of altruism, you pay your suitemate Steven to write papers for you, and you tip him for an A. 'Cause you're a good fucking guy. Your buddy Marc is the most meticulous kid you know, so you pay *him* to take notes, but rarely study them, because you find that it's easier to pay some other desperate student to take your tests. When you can't do that, you pay people to smuggle exams from classrooms and study *them*. It's a game, this whole education business, and you'd be foolish to play by the stated rules when it's so easy to establish your own.

By junior year, you run a small empire, selling notes, selling tests, selling a file cabinet of recycled essays. Shoes, shorts, pants, too: one semester, you decide you won't even do laundry, not once, you'll just buy new clothes and sell the old stuff all semester long (you ultimately pay a kid to wash your boxers and socks and workout gear because you can't keep Axe-spraying your closet into submission forever).

It's funny, all of this, and then one day it kind of isn't anymore. Because about the time you're set to graduate (five-year plan, who can blame you?), a nagging panic sets in. Have you wasted college? You remember nothing from any single class, know zero professors, took zero internships. Whatever work ethic you developed back in high school as you fought to pass your classes and eek out a higher SAT score has all but atrophied. You know less than you did five years ago. You're better-looking and you're well-loved, but you have nothing to contribute to the world, and when you're sober, this scares you. You can buy a degree, but you can't buy education.

When you're drunk or high, though, you forget about this reality, so when you're not lifting weights, you drink and get high. Oh, and you have lots of sex, too. It makes you feel good when you tell your fraternity brothers about the girls you bang, and they—4.0 GPAs, jobs lined up after graduation—look at you with seething jealousy. You're dumb, but you're fucking awesome.

By graduation, your bank account is flush, too. For the last two years, every time you've gone out to eat, you've added gift cards to your bill. All told, you've spent tens of thousands of dollars on gift cards, and this has become another business of yours: buy them on Dad's card, then sell them for ten bucks less than face value. By the time you actually graduate, you hope he knows you've scammed him, that his continued payments of your credit card have been his penance for being a dick to you.

In 2004, you graduate and beg your friend Marc to get you a job at Wachovia, where he slaved over thick applications and went through like ten interviews before he was finally hired. Marc gets you through all the bullshit, no sweat, even lets you copy his own application materials, which is a good thing because the short response section is so damned tedious you want to slam your face into your computer screen.

First day on the job, you tuck the credit card deep into your wallet. Time to renew the old work ethic. You can do this. Let's go! But early in the day, some boss who's never before visited your floor comes to your cubicle and says to you, "I saw your father speak at a conference last year. Expecting big things, young man!" All the other entry-level guys are stunned. You shrug, smile, tell him—loud enough for everyone to hear—that he won't be disappointed.

But it isn't long before you're taking three-hour lunches, extended cigarette breaks and personal phone calls, full mornings spent fucking around on the internet. In six months, your total work output is likely less than forty solid hours. Still, that's because the job is so obviously *beneath* you. You are destined for something greater than this. Big things, he said. You are *better* than this. Sitting around all day, this is for other people, the ones who didn't create their own business in college (in fact, you sold the test archiving business to a Sigma Chi for ten grand, an amount the kid will easily earn back in a year or two). You should be making deals, doing important stuff, not…not *this*. Maybe your education is spotty, but you know how to make money. That's what matters.

One night at Wall Street, you talk to a kid who lives in a downtown condo, a kid who's flipping houses. "This is the life, bro," the kid says. "Buy, wait, sell. It's all just numbers on a computer screen, you know? Like getting a high score in a video game. Only reason more people aren't rich is 'cause they're too scared to play."

Maybe in Atlanta you'd be too scared to enter the fray. But this is Orlando. You know this town. This is what you've been waiting for. So you make the official ask: Dad, can I have money?

"What do you know about real estate investment?" he asks.

"I've got a Business degree," you say. "I'm going to a conference next weekend on house-flipping. I'm ready. I have a spreadsheet of properties I could've bought already, made over a mil on resale, if only I'd had some capital to get started."

"Spreadsheet?" he asks, and can you detect *surprise* in his voice? From his perspective, it must be tempting to believe that his idiot son could be on the verge of great things. Making it in the world. So your father transfers money to your account, and after the conference you buy your first property, straight cash, flip it, then buy another, wait, sell it, and in this way your father's investment becomes three houses in as many months.

The kid at Wall Street was right. If you're smart, and you sell to someone else who's just getting in, you're making tens of thousands for doing *nothing*, really. Maybe, if you're ambitious, you can make a couple nice remodels to appeal to a potential homeowner and not just the speculators. Hell, you don't even need to invest in useful shit, just something that impresses upon first sight, like upgraded kitchen cabinets and fixtures. A $20,000 investment will increase asking price by 40K. Shit's too easy.

You impress yourself with how quickly you learn the neighborhoods of Metro Orlando, how many contacts you gather, how many builders trust you and are willing to let you in on the ground floor. Years and years of buying drinks and dinners, just to piss off your father, and now all these kids are out in real-world jobs and they know you and fucking love you. It's just as you thought: a difficult childhood in Atlanta prepared you for what is, by comparison, an easy city.

Of course, all through college, you paid others to draft your essays, to scribble notes in class, and now the worst part of your job is in the details: loan paperwork, spreadsheets to track target purchase prices, target sale prices. You want to spend more time lunching, golfing, back-slapping and connecting, less time with the busywork. So you tell Marc that you owe him for scoring you the job back at Wachovia, and tell him you're already making a shit-ton of money on your own but together you could fucking rule the galaxy, and just like that you pry him away from the bank. Now you've got a partner to handle the bullshit, to keep careful inventory of the hundreds of pieces of staging furniture that you mix and match and move across a dozen properties, to monitor credit card payments for lord knows how many vendors (the big-box stores where you buy the furniture and appliances with 0% interest, yes, but also fence companies, AC companies, painters, electricians, landscapers). Dude lives in these sorts of details.

So now it's you and Marc, and you're moving a property every two weeks, seems like. Calling the boys at Movers Plus to haul staging furniture from Winter Springs to the Osceola Loop, and they know you by name and know that a phone call means you sold a property, and they congratulate you as soon as they answer, and you take them out after the furniture's been staged in the next property and you buy them drinks late into the night, and so what if you're blowing through an inadvisable amount of cash? You're *generous*, remember? You are loved.

To treat yourself, you buy a condo at the Waverly downtown, overlooking Lake Eola. You don't care that you spent way too much on it. Location, location, location. Who wants to live out in the suburbs in those plywood houses you're turning over quick as hotel rooms? You put down payments on condos in five other soon-to-be-built high-rises because downtown is the *future*, and if you don't get in *now*, you might never get another chance.

You've still got your father's credit card, too, and there are days when you force yourself to use it just to see if you can. Lunch at Dubsdread. Dinner at Kres. Tips so big you almost want to stick around to watch the waitress gasp.

You drink a lot of vodka. Snort a lot of coke. Fuck a lot of women, and make a lot of dudes jealous. Everyone loves you, but does everyone *love* you? Does anyone respect you? Without the…?

Shut up! Don't kill the *vibe*, yo.

This is awesome. You are awesome. Top down. Hair blown back. Yes. *Yes!*

And then the houses stop selling.

Down every street, lines of "For Sale" signs swinging in the wind. On every news station, blood-red arrows pointing down, analysts trying to "make sense of what we're seeing." You had such a good thing going; it's these amateurs coming in, flooding the market!

"Gonna be fine," you say to Marc.

"We should slow down, right?" he says.

"This is America!" you say and wipe the hair from your eyes. "We'll be fine. No, we'll be *exceptional*. You trusted me this far, bro."

Your father calls, and you tell him the same. You're good. *Goooooood.*

He says, "I see you made some charges on that credit card, the one I gave you for college."

Charges? You wipe your forehead again. Wipe your nose. You bought gas a few weeks ago, mistakenly using that old card because you spilled mojito on yourself and your other was stuck inside the wallet. Tiny charge. Maybe thirty bucks? You want to tell your father that you have your own money, you don't need his.

"You're not in college anymore," he says. "You're a big boy."

"I'm sorry," you say, and though you don't intend it this way, it sounds like an apology not just for the gas, but for a lifetime of having disappointed him.

"I'm canceling the card," he says, and while he doesn't tell you whether he's gone back through old statements to examine the full measure of your spending, you know he has. How much, you wonder? What was the grand total?

That's when it hits you. Is he pinching pennies? The self-made man who, in the last decade, seemed to finally surrender his thriftiness and accept the worry-free life of true wealth?

"You're on your own, Edwin."

STEPS OF CITY HALL, night quiet but the smell of *riot* thick in the air, and standing before you like an audience at an amphitheater are twelve of the most important black men you could think to summon. There's Father Pinder front and center, Orlando's own civil rights superhero, the *Street Priest*, and he's silent and too-calm, barely looking up to acknowledge you while a handful of his fellow pastors and ministers—men whose names you don't know—cluster around him like he's their damn general. They sway and crackle with an energy that could shatter your building's first-floor windows. To the left of the churchmen is Coach Williams of Jones High School, along with a cadre of assistants and other coaches—baseball, wrestling—who, even now in the middle of the night, wear tight shirts and look ready for physical combat. Your wimpy Yankee assistant Greg is at your side, clipboard pressed to his chest; you're Superman, but faced with this collection of muscle and prominence, you worry if Greg's geeky presence has made 'em think you're Clark Kent.

"Pillars of the Black Community!" you say, arms spread wide like a Greek orator in some classical painting, voice no different than if you were speaking to the Kiwanis Club (equality, see?). "All right now, we ain't got much time, so let's get to it, shall we? Ain't no part of me believes you want to see this city fall, am I right?"

In response, you expect the sort of impassioned "No, sir!" that you screamed through your helmet's face mask during your own football practices so long ago, but what you get is something more tepid, wet grunts, the pastors shifting their weight impatiently, the wrestling coach crossing his arms and exhaling for far too long. Ain't these men athletes?

"Hey now!" you say. "I invited you here, steps of City Hall—"

"We down here on the sidewalk," the wrestling coach says. "You standing all the way up there, looking down on us."

"You didn't even invite us into your office," Coach Williams adds.

"Well," you say, "I was running low on scotch, what can I say? We'll find another time, once this is all done. I'll get you all up, bring out some extra rocks glasses—" You're looking at Father Pinder as you say this, and they all know it: if anyone's getting an invite, it's just this one man, the one who appears on TV and has the sort of relationship with Chief Johnstone that you still ain't been able to develop.

"What is this about, *Langford?*" one of the other pastors asks. You don't know him, and yet the familiarity with which he says "Langford" is upsetting.

"Hell, gentlemen," you snort, "this is about saving the city from—" and you catch yourself before you assign blame, seeing as to how there are twelve black men before you and only white-bread Greg at your side. "This is about saving the city. This is about the riots. Gentlemen, tonight we can be heroes!"

"The riots?" Father Pinder says, finally looking up. "*What?*"

"The gathering storm! The hell that them boys is gonna unleash on our City Beautiful!" And you're stabbing your finger in the direction of...of...of *over there*, that side of town, *their* side of town!

Two coaches are looking at each other, mouthing "what the hell?"

"You don't know about the riots?" you ask, and there's an adolescent crack in your voice. "You *have* to know about the riots! All the blacks—" and you stop yourself again.

"*All* of us?" Wrestling Coach asks.

"There are riots going on right now?" Coach Williams asks. "I'm lost."

"They're gathering," you say. "They got pipes. Bricks. Bombs."

"Bombs," one of the pastors says. "Bombs, you say."

"They're going door to door. They're conscripting—why are you *laughing*? The whole city's gon' be on fire! Chicago! Detroit! It's—it's—it's not *funny*, damn it!"

"Riots," Father Pinder says and shakes his head, and again he's staring into the sidewalk like it's of greater interest than the man above him trying to warn of the coming doom. If only he knew what you buried beneath these sidewalks he strolls so often, Perfect Father Pinder, man of the people, beloved mentor to the kids, social justice warrior.

"Is this some crazy old lady calling ya'll's office again?" Wrestling Coach asks.

Now you're stabbing your right pointer finger into your left palm, like this shit couldn't be more clear: "We have reliable info—" But again, you stop. You pulled police from Parramore, from Washington Shores, from everywhere west of Division. Your staff. Your aides. All of you been relying on the telephone, not one of you's seen a thing.

"Riots," Coach Williams says. "Aw hell, he's probably talking about Greg."

"*Me?*" Greg shrieks and nearly drops his clipboard.

"Not you, cupcake," Wrestling Coach says. "Greg Washington. Thinks he's a tough guy. Played linebacker three years at Jones. I bet he—"

Coach Williams meets his gaze, shakes his head, and they share a laugh. "Yeah. I hear you. Come on, ya'll," he says.

"Don't go!" you scream. "Don't you leave! We got a city to save!"

"We're gonna go talk to Greg," Coach Williams says, "set that boy straight."

"He's got a lot going on in his life," Wrestling Coach says. "Lost his momma. Been talking a lot of shit lately, but ain't nothing we can't handle. But do me a favor, Mr. Mayor?"

You stop. Was that respect in the man's voice? Do they now understand who you are, what you represent, that you are the man charged with transforming Orlando? Do they get it now? "Yes?"

"You ever see reason to cross Division, don't come our way wearing that fuckin' cowboy hat."

Father Pinder snorts, collects himself.

"Wait," you say, and here atop the steps you hold out your hands as if to grab them, keep them beneath you on that sidewalk. "So that's it?"

"We got this," Father Pinder says. "You go upstairs, finish that Scotch."

"Riots," Wrestling Coach says, all the men laughing as they walk away.

Now it's just you and the cowboy hat and the baseball bat and Greg, standing here on Orange Avenue, empty this late at night, and far in the distance the sound of a hammer pounding wood or metal. Ten minutes ago, you'd have thought this was the sound of imminent destruction, weapons being gathered or constructed, but now? Could be a man fixing his house, or a skeleton crew building a roller coaster at Disney. Who knows?

"We did it," Greg says. "We stopped the riots. I can't believe it!"

"What's this 'we' stuff?" you say. You cross your arms over your chest, adjust your cowboy hat. "Got-damn, Greg, ain't you see what happened here? It was *me*. Superman saved the whole dadgum city."

"EVERYTHING THAT MATTERS for the future of Orlando is happening *right here*," you say to the crowd at Bar-BQ-Bar, the #6 spot on your Top 50. This place, you've decided, is on the front lines of the war between two competing visions for the city's identity. "Orange Avenue, at any given moment, is a snapshot of the city's future," you say, "of what the city thinks of itself, of what the city *wants* to think of itself."

You're on the floor-level stage, standing before the window that looks out on Orange Avenue, and the indie congregation of Bar-BQ-Bar is nodding. Goat, with his tattered "We Can't Help It If We're From Florida" tank top. Eli, smelling of garlic because he mostly just eats canned soup with garlic swirled in. Tonight's band (the OBT All-Stars) behind you on stage, smashing the cymbals every time you say something awesome. Dozens of others on barstools and in booths *hear-hear*-ing and *amen*-ing as you stand on stage, microphone in hand, rallying them to your cause. See, you are giving voice to everything this contingent has ever believed about downtown Orlando.

The "war" is on display every night on Orange Avenue. On one side of the road is the block party of Wall Street, its turnstile always spinning with homogeneity, a group of bars that may as well be corporate chains…and then, here on the other side of Orange, is Bar-BQ-Bar, the centerpiece of a row of venues—I-Bar, the Social, Backbooth around the corner—that feel like Wall Street's evil twin, that feel like the very embodiment of your blog and mission. It's like a frat row for all the kids who'd never join fraternities (you, the obvious exception, but don't think about it too hard). It's Mr. T t-shirts and fixies and English majors and kids in bands and kids who carry Noam Chomsky books around in public, or who drop out one semester short of graduation because, like, they no longer buy into the corporate behemoth of the State University System. It's kids who smell like soggy couches and who complain for hours on end about George W. Bush and how he turned the country into a surveillance state or a theocracy or a theocratic surveillance state.

"There are two possible futures for this city," you say to the packed room.

"Two futures!" the lead singer of the OBT All-Stars repeats, hype-man-style.

"One of them is a unique, united, diverse Orlando, a place where the jukeboxes are full of local music, where the dumpsters are painted in murals and there are craft beer bars and vegan bakeries and indie coffee shops lining Mills and Ivanhoe and leading into a rich and varied downtown music scene!" You are pointing in every direction, toward Mills, toward Ivanhoe, and the band's lead singer is so caught up shouting "Hell yeah!" that he forgets to repeat any of the words that you've said. "Bar-BQ-Bar!" you scream. "The Social! Backbooth! All those bars where you don't need to style your hair and wear an Armani Exchange t-shirt that costs as much as your electric bill!"

"Fuckin' A!" someone shouts from the back of the room.

"Preach it, Steven!" Eli shouts.

And holy hell, how long it took to memorize this. You typed it out, deleted pages, added paragraphs. Tortured yourself night after night to get your inflection just right. If Elaina wasn't so consumed with designing a playroom for a rich housewife in Winter Park, she might have even noticed your absence.

To truly see and feel Orlando, you tell the crowd, one must walk the downtown strip and watch the two clusters of young people, the two *futures*, one on either side of Orange Avenue. But to truly know *you* (and this part you do not say aloud), one must watch *you* move back and forth, to your fraternity brothers at Wall Street, to your indie friends at Bar-BQ-Bar, watch you down PBRs on one side of the road, and watch you buy Mich Ultras with Anderson and Jimmy from a beer tub girl on the other side, witness the eternal struggle within you. A life as a freelance graphic designer, decent income but agonized soul because oh, do you despise the people you work for. But then there's *this* life as a blogger and cultural revolutionary, zero income until that inventory of t-shirts starts selling, a fiancée growing ever more impatient because her own artistic endeavors have exploded in popularity, and she's going places, and holy shit it's January already, you're getting married in four months, and this whole time you've just been spinning your wheels, half-assing two different lives, two different sides of the road.

So here you are making your move, trying to monetize your blog, to sell the products that will get the movement rolling, to sign the sponsors who will compose the Coalition of the Weird, your grand vision for an indie chamber of commerce, to leave behind the corporate contracts and the khakis and finally—*finally*—launch the career you want.

"Keep Austin Weird!" you exclaim to your crowd here at Bar-BQ-Bar, pointing to a bumper sticker on the wall that you tap each time you come in. "That's what we're doing here. That's our model. You've heard this story before, right? No?"

And you seize the opportunity, tell your audience the story of Austin in the 1990s, a city besieged by corporate chains and big-box stores. *Austin, Texas!* The home of South by Southwest, the city that probably came up with the word "indie." So there was this local business owner, and he came up with this idea, this slogan that embodied everything they stood to lose: "Keep Austin Weird." It started as a bumper sticker, a way to support a handful of local businesses. But there was an undercurrent of rebellion in the city, the college kids, the music scene, and soon enough the bumper stickers were everywhere, and then they were t-shirts, a physical protest but also a state of mind. *You will not take what we love*! they said. Keep Austin Weird, and soon enough it it had entered the national consciousness as the very identity of the city.

"We *need* something like that," you say, and you jab your finger in the direction of Wall Street. "We need to fight for our identity, fight for local businesses, or sooner or later we're *all* going to get swallowed! We'll be the artificial city, just like those fuckers across the street, and there'll be no hope for us, for the little guys who give the city its flavor."

"Yasssssss!" Goat shouts. "Dude, you're making my nipples hard!"

"This is *our* city," you say. "We could *lose* it. We need to embrace our weird side, fight back against the conformity. We need to…*Make* Orlando Weird.'"

"Make Orlando Weird," the lead singer voices into his microphone, then holds it out to the crowd.

"Make Orlando Weird," they repeat.

"Make Orlando Weird," you say again. "Take over the city."

You've been thinking this catchphrase for years, but this is the first time you've uttered it aloud to your indie friends. But tonight they've gathered. They're listening. The centerpiece for your campaign, your coalition of small businesses, your mission to save the city. The centerpiece for your online store, your vintage t-shirts, your income stream, and now it's been spoken, and the reaction will tell you whether to proceed.

"Perfect!" someone yells. "Motherfucking *perfect!*"

"WHOOOOO!"

"Fuck the man! Fuck those assholes!"

And you're crackling with so much energy you can barely speak, the words all threatening to flood out at once: "I've got bumper stickers up here," you manage. "A buck each, and it supports the start of the movement. Online, I've got t-shirts. Soon, it's my hope that you'll be able to find them at our whole linked web of local businesses."

The lead singer steps next to you; he's wearing a "Conway: Great Freeze of '89" t-shirt, a cartoon image of a frozen orange dead-center. He points to the drummer, who's wearing a t-shirt that says "FTU: The Fightin' Citronauts, 1968." The other guitarist wears a shirt that says "Sapphire Supper Club."

"Steven Hart," the singer says, "he's the man. Blog address is on the flier, y'all. Let's make sure this blows up and we take the city *back*, know what I'm saying?"

And it's like a record release party, the official start to the Make Orlando Weird campaign, everything you've worked for, the flood of joy evident with your every breath, and you can't stop smiling as you preach to your friends through the band's final set. Who could ask for a better night for Steven Hart, the Chosen One, the savior of the city's culture?

"So, are you guys gonna buy a t-shirt?" you ask your friends at their table. "Help support the start of the movement?"

"Um," Goat says.

Silence.

"I don't have much cash right now," Eli says.

"You just got another tattoo," you point out.

"That's why," Eli says.

"Can't we, like, get rich people on board? Have them do all this?" Goat asks.

And you get it now. You're preaching to the choir…a positive step taken tonight, no doubt, but for you to achieve your dream, you need to work harder to get the businesses to buy in, just as you told Elaina. Your impoverished indie friends won't do much for you. Even the managers at Bar-BQ-Bar: they love the affection showered upon them in your blog, but they've taken a "wait and see" approach with regard to your pitch. They're not yet buying ads on your blog, or paying dues to become charter members of the Coalition of the Weird. You need someone on the other side of Orange Ave, someone who doesn't paint murals on the sides of dumpsters, someone who doesn't shop at thrift stores, someone who doesn't smell perpetually of weed and Cap'n Crunch. Someone with a business that isn't celebrated because it's "quirky" and "such a neat addition to this area." You need someone who's part of that *other* Orlando, who's part of the buying and selling and brokering and sociopathic development, someone with money, but who can be *flipped*.

YOU'RE TOO FRAZZLED TO WORRY about how frazzled you look when you open the door and greet Amanda Linda from Alumni Club, standing there with her assembly-line husband (goatee, golf shirt).

"Very nice house, Shelley." Amanda Linda points to the porch and sends her husband that way. To his credit, he obeys, doesn't take a detour into the kitchen, even closes the sliding glass door behind him. Within seconds, the whole group of men outside will be talking college football, or LeBron James, or Tiger Woods, or whateverthefuck allows individual men to become a herd without effort, and there will soon be a table full of empty beer bottles, and even the strangers will feel as if they've made new best friends. The ease of male friendship makes you unhappy. The women inside are not strangers; they are your *friends*, and you don't even like them.

Amanda Linda is beside you with her own not-happy half-smile, like she wants to tell you the straight scoop that she wouldn't dare reveal to anyone else (maybe that's the secret: never commit to a full smile, never wear yourself out). "A darling neighborhood," she says.

"Thank you. We were lucky. One of the best lots in this subdivision, too."

"How do you like the gate?" Amanda Linda asks.

"It's nice. I've never lived behind a gate before."

"It's a pain." She rolls her eyes as if you got the answer to the question wrong. "We've only lived in gated communities the last ten years, and honestly, I would *love* to move out."

"Oh."

"The traffic. It takes so long some days when you have to wait behind…" And she stops, motions her hand at your house, the party that's starting to build. "Well, when there are parties and the dopey security guard has to pull out his clipboard and verify names on a guest list. Halloween is the worst. The. Worst."

"I see. Did you have to wait long tonight?"

"No, no," Amanda Linda says, in a voice that really means *yes, yes.* "Do you like your pool?"

"We haven't used it yet."

Amanda Linda sips her pinot grigio. "And you probably won't, truthfully. Pools are a money pit. The cost of the filter running. The cleaning company. And when something breaks? And listen, something is *always* broken. The things we burden ourselves with, am I right?"

"Rich people problems," you say.

Amanda Linda's drink is frozen at her lips. She's not the type, you realize, to allow someone *else* to poke fun at her lifestyle.

This is the thing you've learned from growing up lower-middle-class, working as a hostess and waitress and babysitter through high school, working as a full-time nanny your freshman year, a waitress your sophomore year, a bartender the years after…there is a large subset of the population that takes its accomplishments deathly serious, as if joking about the ease of their moneyed lives is a judgment against their having all that they have, a judgment against their work ethic or their worthiness to have such money. And who knows?

Maybe it is. Maybe you do harbor some bitterness toward women (and men) whose paths seem easier than your own.

"Are you the joking type?" Amanda Linda asks.

You force a laugh. "I enjoy…humor?"

"I remember when I made jokes all the time. When everything in the world seemed funny." She holds her wine glass in a way that seems menacing, the pinot unnaturally still no matter how she moves or gestures, and with deepening horror you realize she has somehow wound up with the cracked glass.

"Well, it's not that *everything* is funny—"

"I look back at the *young* me, and I think: you could've accomplished so much more, if only you'd taken the world seriously. I thought I was too *good* for the world. I didn't respect the women who'd worked for years to achieve what they had."

"I *do* take the world—"

"So young, and such a wonderful house," Amanda Linda says. "The first of many parties here, I predict." And she raises her wine glass in a mock toast to you, and finally—now that a smile has returned to her face—the liquid in the glass seems to come unfrozen, rolling from side to side again around the crack buried deep in the glass, though maybe she hasn't noticed?

Then it's the doorbell again. "Oh. If you'll give me a mo—"

"I know, dear. Your party. I'll go outside to introduce myself to your husband."

You pause mid-step. "Some of the guys out there are…" You're picturing Amanda Linda in conversation with Jimmy. "They're kind of…"

"It's nothing new to me, sweetie. I was young once. I remember thinking that I'd invented bad behavior, and then again that I'd invented maturity."

And then it's Tonya at the door in a skirt shorter than Andrea's (where the fuck did they think they were coming? what kind of party did they think this was going to be?), and soon thereafter, there's Steven and Elaina at the door, and before you can show them to the bar Tara and Jennifer arrive together, sans boyfriends, and Laurie from work, and Michelle and Mike, and Cassandra and Cindy from Alumni Club arrive together, and it seemed only the span of minutes but the house is now buzzing with these friends and colleagues and miscellaneous acquaintances and *still the dining room table hasn't arrived*. With every ringing of the doorbell you picture this grimy furniture deliveryman there with a carbon copy form for you to sign and a truck bigger than a basketball court, ready to lecture you about how there are too many cars on the street and he can't pull close enough, and the more you imagine and re-imagine this conversation in your head, the more you want to punch one of these freshly painted walls. What would happen if you were planning an awards ceremony and the plaques were delivered mid-ceremony? All of it would—all of it *does*—reflect on you.

"Sconces," someone's saying from afar and laughing, and is the laughter at your expense?

"Valances!"

"Plantation shutters."

"Bamboo."

"Yes! Bamboo!"

"Cork."

"Do it yourself."

"Brazilian."

"No. Always hire an electrician."

You see Todd from work holding one of the "Help us imagine our lives" notepads, pointing to what he's written, saying, "The house *needs* this, okay? It cannot be allowed to stand without it! I'm adamant. *Adamant!*"

"Oh my God, your bathroom!" Laurie says, spilling riesling on the floor, and when did she wander off to your bathroom? All corners: the party has spread to all corners of the house, and there is no controlling it. The more you spin around to follow the activity and all the new arrivals who have seeped into every square inch of your home, the more quickly time passes. Outside, Amanda Linda has her hand on Jimmy's shoulder, and Jimmy is pantomiming a—what the *fuck*?

"Your tub is fantastic," Michelle tells you.

"Jacuzzi tub?" Mike asks. "Perfect for some bow-chicka-wow-wow."

"Mike!" Michelle says.

"Haven't even turned the faucet yet," you say.

Marc's inside now, sliding door wide open, and is something splashing in the pool? You can't see from this angle. You want things to slow down. You need them to slow down. Somehow everything has slipped out of your control, and every time someone stops you, tells you to make them a drink, you feel further disconnected from the agenda you'd set for the night.

"Shelley! Shelley!" Marc is screaming. "You heat up the mozzarella sticks?"

"No, I was—"

"Heat 'em up, heat 'em up!"

"There are baking pans in the styrofoam cooler over there," you say. "Five of them. Stacked. I was just about to start the first one."

"But I want them *now*, is the thing."

"You can do it, you know?" you say. "Or do you not know how to work the oven?"

"Oooooooohhhhh!" says Edwin, who appears behind him.

"She told you, Marc. She *told* you!" Jimmy says, appearing behind Edwin.

"Liquid diet tonight!" Marc says. "No food for anyone!"

"Or you can enjoy the twenty other things spread out around the room," you say, and Edwin says "Oooooooohhhhh!" again, and you know that—at the very least—you've won this round, even if you might have (maybe, just a little) given the impression of relationship conflict.

And then—oh shit.

Somehow, inexplicably, Amanda Linda is talking to Andrea. Andrea, the stupidest fucking girl here. And Amanda Linda, whose validation is so tremendously tough to earn. So far, she approves of the house, despite any snark to indicate the contrary, and she was able to converse with your fiancé and his friends without incident, so that's positive, right? But...

"Andrea! Amanda Linda!" you say, rushing toward the two of them, hoping you're not too late to prevent disaster.

"I just don't see why people have children, you know?" Andrea is saying to Amanda Linda, who's nodding as one would when listening to a toddler. "I mean, babies are just gross, am I right? The diapers?"

As you weave through every party-goer in your great room, you hear the stream of stupid comments continue—"I'd have to hire a babysitter, like, every night, 'cause I'd need to get away from that little vomit-bag"—and it feels like a flashback to your sophomore year of college. You were 19, had vowed to never nanny or babysit again, were going out to the bars and clubs four nights a week, drinking till blackout so often that there are stretches of weeks months semesters that feel foggier in your mind than memories from elementary school. You, and Andrea, and every girl you hung out with at school, you were all so certain that this was life, that *growing up* was just, like, so fucking stupid. Why would anyone have children? Who wants to spend their whole life sitting at fucking soccer practice, and driving minivans? But you grew up.

"Andrea! Andrea!" you say, out of breath. You place your hands on each of their shoulders. "I see you've met Amanda Linda, from Alumni Club. Amanda Linda, Andrea is my old roommate."

"Your friend," Amanda Linda says, "was just educating me on why the human race should cease propagation."

"Um," you say. "You don't have to listen to—"

"Oh no," Amanda Linda says. "I'm very interested to hear what she has to say." You hold your breath.

"Kids are *creepy!*" Andrea is saying. "I was in line at Publix the other day, and there was this kid in the cart in front of me, and he was just staring at me. Like, full-on horror movie stare. Like, deep into my soul or something."

"Mmm. What do you think he saw?" Amanda Linda asks, cracked wine glass at her lips.

Your eyes are closed. This girl is your *friend?*

"I have two children, myself," Amanda Linda says, savoring the reveal, "though I've never quite considered your…interesting perspective."

"Oh my God," Andrea says, and you think maybe she realizes how idiotic she sounds, how immature, that maybe she's rewinding the tape and taking a second look at the full transcript of stupidity, thinking of recanting. But then she says: "I totally didn't even think of this. Are you, like, Shelley's mom?"

Oh dear God. Amanda Linda is, what, *fifteen years* older than you?

"Excuse me?" Amanda Linda asks. The vicious smile has disappeared. A comment this dumb…this is a true shock.

But Andrea's attention has already shifted, and she's staring into her drink. "I want to drink vodka with, like, gold flakes in it. Wouldn't that be fucking *awesome*?"

Sometime recently, you realized you were walking a tightrope between two very different worlds: the world of *real women*, the ones who work hard both in their careers and relationships and try to maintain reasonable perspectives, and who try to make positive contributions to the world, and whose words you genuinely want to hear (some of whom *have it all*, others who do not); and then, conversely, the world of straight-up *stupid bitches*. Not *can't tie my own shoes* stupid, nothing that offensive…just, *I'd rather not think* stupid. *I'm loud and having a good time and boys love me so everything's just fine* stupid (*stupidity* often graphed parallel to *hotness*, the two traits rising together in tandem). Stupid bitches, you realized, had been in your life for a long time. In college, you sought them out, reveled in their company, became them; they were your roommates, your classmates, your sorority sisters; they were your co-workers at the Wall Street beer tubs; but then one day, a tectonic shift occurred within you, and it was as if you suddenly heard what they were saying, understood that they would never change, but you knew you had to.

"If I had a baby," Andrea is saying, "I'd take it to the fire department and just leave it."

Holy sweet hell.

You interrupt, hoping there's a shred of reputation you can salvage: "Ladies! You've noticed the notepads, right? We're trying to get opinions… what should we do with the place?"

"Yes, it's all very bare, isn't it?" Amanda Linda says, motioning to the walls.

"Blank canvas! Waiting for the right brush strokes! We want to make good long-term choices."

"The ceiling is so high," Andrea says. "Could you, like, make it lower?"

"I don't…" you start.

"High ceilings are a good thing, dear." Amanda Linda pats Andrea's shoulder.

"So who changes your light bulbs, then?" Andrea asks.

Amanda Linda coughs, nearly chokes.

"Andrea," you say. "We get a ladder."

"Ahhhh," Andrea says and taps her forehead. "Smart thinking. So you'll probably, like, never move again, huh? Big house in Orlando. Pool. Hubby."

"The real estate industry reports that we move every six years," Amanda Linda says. "No matter how happy we are when we move in, we find reasons."

"Whoa, ha ha," Andrea says, and her words and her laugh sound like vodka and unpredictability. "You can be a real Debbie Downer!" Andrea takes a sip and, with ice in her mouth, says, "I just don't know why anyone would want to live outside of Florida."

"You're familiar with the concept of a round world, correct?" Amanda Linda asks. "With the fact that there are several large continents? That our own, North America, is a gigantic piece of land with unimaginably diverse geographies and ecosystems and peoples spread from one ocean to another? That there are cities speckled throughout, glowing with opportunities you simply cannot understand until you've visited?"

"Sure," Andrea says. "Miami's an upgrade, for sure."

You are very nearly breaking your wine glass by its stem, sending new cracks up into the bowl. You are smarter than Andrea. You work harder. And yet she moves through life like a bubble carried by the breeze and still has more than you do.

"I don't understand how people can drink red wine," Andrea says now. "A warm drink? It's like drinking blood."

Make it stop.

"I…" Amanda Linda is saying. "Where to start with you?"

"I want a boat," Andrea says. "A really big boat. I mean, that's how you know you've made it, right?"

"Young lady," Amanda Linda says.

"Or, like, *Tiffany's* luggage. Am I right?" Andrea says.

"I want to retire by, like, age 35 or something," Andrea says.

"If something was built before, like, 1980, it should just be torn down, you know?" Andrea says. "That should be a *law*."

"Amanda Linda," Andrea says. "Why two names? Was that hard to memorize as a kid?"

Amanda Linda's hand is on your shoulder. "This has been enlightening, but if I don't leave the vicinity, I feel I'll be lost within the black hole forever."

You nod, but you wonder if she has only left you to be sucked into the vortex, or if she thinks you are *part* of the vortex.

"Andrea," you say.

"Obama," Andrea is saying. "*Obama.*"

"I've..." You point to the other end of the room. "I've got..." And then, blessedly, you spot your way out: you see Elaina, wandering into the hallway with a notepad in her hand.

"Shelley, we've got a problem," Elaina says. Since she arrived, she's been madly scribbling into the "Help us imagine our life!" notepads, writing full essays on each page about what sort of bookshelf should go where, what sort of lamp, what sort of light fixture. Some pages contain diagrams, instructions on how to re-appropriate old dresser drawers as nightstands. Elaina: the smartest and most talented young woman you know, someone who seems like she has it all...and yet also seems curiously *happy* in a way that you are not. "Did you see this?" Elaina holds up a notepad. "Someone's been writing nasty notes. But in really elegant handwriting?"

Ugh. Edwin. He's like a male version of Andrea, but for all his idiocy and vulgarity, writes with almost aristocratic handsomeness.

"I put a lot of effort into my comments," Elaina says. "And now someone is drawing penises all over them?"

This is the last fucking thing you need tonight. Imagine if this had occurred at the Orlando Regional Health awards banquet, some douchebag drawing cocks on every program...you're losing control of your house, losing control right in front of your co-workers, in front of the alumni women...

"I'll find him," you say. "I will save the notepads."

AND THEN, FINALLY, it's Friday night, and you're walking through the tailgates in the fields outside of Orlando Speed World in Bithlo, a thousand charcoal grills cooking ten thousand hot dogs and Italian sausages and Bubba burgers. The air's thick with cigarette smoke, coarse with redneck laughter, footballs flying like arrows in the sky above. It's the end of May, the end of your first week closing loans on your own, and you're ready for some damn school bus races. You're ready for the Crash-o-Rama, for crunching metal and flying shrapnel, for tens of thousands of pounds of wreckage set on fire to the soundtrack of (one can hope) AC/DC or Guns 'N' Roses.

"Bithlo?" Marc asked when you first told him about it. "You want to go to *Bithlo?*"

"Hell yeah," you said. "School bus races. This thing's famous."

You'd read about it in an old issue of *Car and Driver* magazine years ago, couldn't believe your luck when you saw it was still happening, and that Bithlo was so close. Life in Metro Orlando was bizarre and unpredictable. That a potential Redneck Paradise could be so close to the international resort and theme park destinations…

"I have to go to this thing?" Marc asked.

"No Magic game tonight."

"It's been a bad week." He closed his eyes and rubbed the tired folds of his forehead. The vividness of the purple flesh under his eye had peaked at the start of the week and was now yellowing. His cracked lips had almost healed, and his limp had started to fade. Other good news: as of this morning, he was under contract to sell his Lake Nona property, which would see a minor flood of income back into his account. Didn't seem like such a bad week to you, though apparently Marc had also been moments from accepting an offer on a property he called the "oil stain house" (you've mowed so many damn lawns and cleared so many wasp nests, you're not sure which house this is), before negotiations ultimately fell through; Marc seems to think this was his last shot to sell the "oil stain house" before crippling price reductions. "Fine," he said. "School bus races. I just…I would prefer to not get punched in the face again."

You took this as an encouraging sign: that he was speaking again, making jokes about the fight. Maybe he was starting to become *himself* again.

"Hey, me neither. There will be no punched faces," you said.

"The people there. They don't like people like me."

"People like you?"

"People who wear polo shirts. Who comb their hair."

"Get off it. I know where you come from. You *are* people like them."

"Not anymore."

"I'll let *you* borrow a shirt this time," you said. "I'll remind you how the other half lives."

For weeks you've been learning your brother's trade, seeing the world as he sees it, but tonight, *you're* in charge. Marc is here with *you*.

Orlando, you've discovered, is a city of stark contrasts. Down south are the Disney Worlds and the Universal Studios and the Holy Land Experiences and the convention centers and spinning spotlights of I-Drive, but—after a month of traveling with Marc for these loan-closings—you've now seen the Black side of town, the Hispanic side, the College side, the Suburban White Side, the Gay side, the Hipster side, the Douchebag side, and the wealthy side, each an overlapping sphere. You knew there had to be a Redneck side, and now, hallelujah, you've found it. Hell, Bithlo feels like a redneck *theme park*, all exhaust and gravel and cut-off jean shorts and Gators hats with hooks through the bills; it's Confederate flag blankets spread out on the ground picnic-style, and "Ducks Unlimited" bumper stickers, and Budweiser products *only*; it's men who still wear leather Joe Camel jackets purchased two decades ago with stacks of Camel Cash, and packs of dudes who look like Larry the Cable Guy, and it's Kenny Chesney and Brad Paisley, and you know a *woman* is controlling someone's truck stereo when you walk past a tailgate party and Carrie Underwood is belting out "Before He Cheats" and the guys are all kind of staring at the ground. You imagine this place as a beacon summoning the 'necks throughout Metro Orlando to come and breathe in the toxically awesome fumes.

Past the tailgates and into the stadium, you lead your brother along the chainlink fence separating spectators from the track, and the central field where tire marks have been burned into the weary grass in a hundred different directions. At the far end of the track, someone is revving his engine, and then someone else, and someone else, so many men pushing gas pedals you're sure they can hear the noise all the way out at Disney. These sounds, your father might say, are the sounds of life itself, of progress, these guttural explosions that remind us what we are capable of producing with our brains and our two calloused hands, but still...it's a little weird that they're booming from school buses.

You've never been here before but you lead your brother up the bleachers with redneck confidence. According to the *Sentinel*, the stands seat 6,000, which you imagine must be roughly the size of Bithlo, but add the folks outside at the tailgates and 6,000's a lowball estimate. Sad thing is, you've been here four weeks and already you know "Bifflo" is a local punchline. Depending on who you ask, it's the *armpit* of Orlando, or the *asshole*, or the *taint*. If Marc hadn't already branded Apopka as Meth-lando, perhaps Bifflo would be Meth-lo. It is what happens when you sweep all the automotive garbage and waste, the torn tires and used-up engines, the broken glass and burned frames, into a place where everyone can carve out huge fucking yards on which to store all their vehicular projects. Even as you were driving here, Marc tried to convince you to turn around. "Your truck'll get broken into," he said. "They don't even have, like, clean water out there." A wasteland, mocked and spit-upon, where the suburban grocery stores and meticulous side-of-the-road landscaping disappear in favor of Family Dollars and junkyards sunk beneath slash pines, but...this place...everyone's got grease under their fingernails here. Nobody cares if your t-shirt could double as a shop rag. Cheap beer, All-American Beer, not the craft shit Marc keeps in his fridge. Cheetos and Oreos and Big Gulps and "FUCK YOU" to anyone who wants to tell you about the dangers of high-fructose corn syrup. This place is everything that—in Marc's clean antiseptic vision of life—you've been missing.

You spy two empty seats in the packed stands and head that way.

"Starting to feel better, Marc?"

"Feel better?"

"The head. The concussion."

"I'm fine," he says.

"You sleep so much. You've been so quiet."

"I'm thinking. A lot."

"About what?"

He shrugs.

In the center of the track, one man stands atop a school bus and howls like a werewolf, rips the metal tab off a Busch Light with his teeth, spits it onto the ground. The crowd erupts. Something's about to happen, and you know it's going to make up for all the paperwork bullshit of these past few weeks.

"Whenever you want to talk," you say.

"I'm fine."

"I mean, you still haven't told me what happened with Shelley. Clearly that's a big deal. Are you—"

"I'm fine."

"And that oil stain house. If there's anything you want me to do for you?"

Marc doesn't answer.

From the speakers comes Ratt's "Round and Round," and then the school buses follow in a parade around the track, each painted in a different deranged way: it's a scene from Mad Max except more colorful, a replica of the Scooby Doo Mystery Machine circling a General Lee school bus, both of them trailed by drivers who didn't try quite so hard, just spraypainted slogans onto the crackling yellow paint: "Hot For Teacher" and "School's Out For Summer!" and "Death to Honor Students."

Marc spends the night squirming in his seat, never smiling when the school buses rev their engines, never cheering the crunching collisions. Exhaust. Bud Lite. Popcorn and peanut shells and no apologies. You want this to never end.

"See this one?" the guy beside you says.

"The bus with the Christmas lights?" you ask.

"Yep," he says. "That's my neighbor."

Marc is looking at you like he's disappointed, like how-dare-you-talk-to-the-locals?, *they might rub off on you*. But these are your people. Unlike Marc, you don't want to *conquer* this city, you only want to find your place in it.

"You come to a lot of these?" you ask the guy beside you.

"Wouldn't miss 'em."

To your right, Marc is holding his head in his hands.

"Ya'll got NASCAR nearby, too," you say. "You like this better or worse?"

"Daytona's fun. Make a weekend of it. But it's so commercial now. This here, this is what happens when average folks cut loose."

Within moments, the school bus races have ended, and the track fills with an absolutely random assortment of vehicles grumbling over the tire tracks left behind by the buses. One man kisses the hood of his T-bird, and another tosses a bucket of mud over the top of his souped-up camper in some sort of pre-race ritual.

"You live out this way?" you ask him.

"Christmas. Yourself?"

Christmas? Another town you've never heard of.

"Up near, uh…" You stop, think of all the neighborhood and town names to which you've been introduced these past few weeks. "North of Orlando. Near…is it Lake Mary? Maitland?"

"Shit, son," he says. "Long drive all the way out here. You slummin' it tonight?"

You try to laugh, try to show that this is your natural habitat, that perhaps you come from some small corner of Maitland where events such as this are common. "Livin' with my brother. Just moved here from Georgia."

"Barnes," the man says and you introduce yourself.

Barnes extends his hand to Marc, too, who regards it curiously. "I'm not feeling well," he says. "The hot dogs. I need to go to the bathroom."

"Whoo." Barnes retracts his hand. "Sorry, my man."

Marc stands and brushes himself off, then retreats stiffly to whatever outdoor facility he'll be forced to use. You aren't sure if he's actually sick, or if maybe he's just looking for any reason to escape.

"So what do you do?" you ask him. "What kinda work is out this way?"

"I'm a contractor," Barnes says.

"What kind of contracting?"

"Anything. Paint houses. Do crown molding. Lay tile. Someone needs a job done, I'll find a way to do it."

"That's your life? Your job?"

Your first week in town, you spent the entirety of your days doing yardwork and fix-ups at Marc's properties. Hauled the lawn mower around town, pushed it through tall weedy grass that always seemed to end abruptly at a next-door yard well-clipped. Marc kept telling you that he felt bad, that he'd teach you how to close loans so you wouldn't need to spend your days sweating out your water-weight, but you loved it. You brought along your screwdriver, tightened what you could. Corrected the tipped-over solar lights on the sidewalks. "I can fix that fence," you told him about the Eagle's Nest property. It just needed a power wash, a re-stain, one day's work, but Marc's told you that the schedule's too packed for more repairs.

"Got four guys working with me," Barnes says. "Between us, got the whole range of services covered. Lot of work needs to be done, but the economy's shit, you know. So not a lot of people willing to spend, that's the real problem. They put things off, and problems get worse—"

"That's what I been saying," you say. "My brother is, like, a house-flipper. Or was. Now he's stuck with the properties. I been fixing 'em up wherever I can. We close loans, too, and *everywhere*, it's just like...people bought these houses but don't know what to do with 'em."

"Sad state of affairs."

"I worked in an auto shop," you say. "People come in with 20-year-old cars don't need as much work as the living room of one of these houses."

"People don't take care of cars, neither."

"Some people do." You point to the demolition derby. "And if they don't, at least they know how to get rid of 'em in style."

"Shame we can't have the same for houses." He laughs.

"Shame," you agree. "So. You only work out on this side of town?"

"I go wherever," he says. "Advertise with Service Magic, and in the Clipper

Magazine. I get phone calls from all over. I'll drive to St. Augustine if the job is substantial. Service Magic charges you for every tip they give, so sometimes I'll do jobs that're break-even."

"Charges you for every tip?"

"Like, someone searches for 'tree-trimming,' and these web services give a list of companies who'll call them back and give a quote. We gotta call back quick, too, or else the next company'll call, and whether we do the job or not, we get charged for the tip."

"Damn." You think about the money made off each batch of documents that your brother drops off to FedEx, the signing, the dating, the emptiness of the task. "The people that do the hardest work get screwed the most."

"Ain't all bad."

"Sounds better than what I'm doing," you say. "Fucking paperwork for my brother."

Barnes nods like he's been there, done that, got no love for paperwork.

Moments later, when Marc returns with a beer, he looks frustrated. "Wouldn't take cash at the bar," he says. "Had to go to this shitty little ATM—"

"I could've warned you about that," Barnes says.

"Thought you were sick," you say. "Thought you were going to the bathroom."

"Hmm?" Marc says. "Right. Yeah. I'm still…not with it. Not myself."

"No beer for me?" you ask.

"I…" Marc starts. "I forgot. I wasn't thinking."

"I'm getting up in a minute," Barnes says. "I'll take care of you."

"Perfect," you say, and Marc looks down into his beer as if he's spotted a fly. Disgusted, like this was an inevitability, bound to happen at an event like this.

It's a sad moment for you. You know there's a world where the two of you match up like an eclipse, where you work on engines together, go boating and fishing, but this world, the one where he moved to Orlando long ago, and you just now joined him, this isn't it. That other world—where brothers are brothers—that world has been dead a long time, and only now as the mess of cars and trucks collide in the dead mud-grass in the center of the Orlando Speed World track do you admit it: he is your brother in name only.

AND NOW YOU'RE TRAVELING down I-75 from Georgia to Orlando for your annual Disney World trip, up since 4 AM and the kids haven't slept. Kyle spent the first hour of the trip drawing a picture of Donald Duck, precise to the thickness of line from the Disney book you bought him for Christmas, and he's been clutching it in his hands all morning and telling the family over and over how he'll find the *real* Donald at the park and he'll show him the picture and he'll give it to him as a gift.

"That's very generous," you say.

"Where does Donald live?" Kyle asks.

"I'm sure he has a house."

"At Disney World?"

"I, uh…" It is impossible to answer a child's question to his satisfaction, as every response seems only to lead to a maze of deeper questions from which there is no return, until suddenly you're talking about the Cuban Missile Crisis or the advent of the printing press. "Most likely his house is at Disney World, yes," you say and take a deep breath and wait and—blessedly—that seems to have staunched the flow.

Your husband is at the wheel and so you zone out. When you regain focus, you're on I-4, only a few miles from the exit for Buena Vista Drive, which will lead you directly down the throat of Disney World. Thomas doesn't say anything; you've been trying to convince yourself that he's happy, that he wants to be here with his family, but his expression for the entire drive: a brick wall. Sips of coffee from his thermos, only occasional comments about "concentrating on the road." Marc even asked whether Dad was mad at everyone, and his response was unclear.

"Are you sure you want to give away your drawing, honey?" you ask Kyle.

In the backseat, Kyle is searching through the Disney book, has his fingers stopped at one page with a full-color illustration of skeletons dancing. It's a Grateful Dead-style cartoon, and—while there are many Disney movies you've never seen—you have no clue where these skeletons ever appeared. *Fantasia?* The universe of Disney characters is so vast, it isn't all just Mickey and Goofy and *Cinderella*; the Disney vaults are more frighteningly deep than that final image from *Raiders of the Lost Ark*, rows upon rows upon rows of forgotten or hidden materials, awkward animated characters, failed experiments, racist stereotypes hidden away like they never existed. Kyle has tried to draw these skeletons dozens of times, but it's the one character he can't quite master… strange, since he's usually so good at fitting pieces together, understanding the logic of the body, how fingers bend and arms connect to torsos, how Mickey's ears rise from his head, how a nose casts shadow on the face. Perhaps because the skeletons are stripped of muscle and tendon, there is no logic: how can a skeleton dance? Wouldn't it simply collapse? It is a machine half-built, doomed to failure.

"There *is* no Donald Duck," Marc says.

"Shut up, Marc!" Kyle says.

"Both of you," you say from the front seat. "Let's not be mean to one another. We talked about this."

"I'm not being mean," Marc says. "I'm being honest. There is no Donald Duck. He's just a man in a costume."

"That's not true," Kyle says.

"Both of you," you say again. "This is a family vacation. Let's cut this out."

"There are gators in the water at Disney, too," Marc says.

"Noooo," Kyle says.

"I read in the newspaper. Gators in the lake, and if you get too close they'll *snatch* you."

"That's a horrible thing to say." You close your eyes, squeeze the bridge of your nose. A headache feels imminent. "That family…they lost their child. We didn't show you that article so you could tease your brother, Marc. We showed it to you so you'd be careful."

"There *are* gators?" Kyle asks, and his eyes are large and fearful. Crap.

They argue, Kyle and Marc, and never about anything worthwhile. Usually a movie, which to watch: *Back to the Future* or *Indiana Jones* or *What About Bob?* Occasionally the naiveté of their comments is heartwarming in its innocence, but too often you worry about whether it will continue and continue, the two of them shouting even when Thomas comes home from work grumbling about "never a moment's peace." Years ago, he lost the ability to fall asleep, just a fraction of the overall toll taken by the death of both his parents in a three-year window. (God, the cost of those funerals, and even though he's one of five children the burden somehow fell upon him alone. And the money he loaned to Uncle Mike, who repaid him by falling into a series of idiotic schemes that sent him tumbling across the country, Mississippi to Texas to Colorado to Utah to New Mexico, before he disappeared completely.) Since then, it's as if Thomas has steeled himself against further trauma by purging himself of all feeling. He only engages those moments in life that can be easily solved through step-by-step instructions, and petty arguments between children do not fall into this category. Thus, it seems as if he'd rather have the *idea* of Family than actually immerse himself in the messy day-to-day tragicomedy that truly *is* family…You watch him driving, squinting at the road, and you need these boys to remind him how delightful family can be—

"He started it," Kyle says.

Something is thrown and hits the back window.

"I don't care who started it," you say.

"But it was *him*."

Thomas sighs through his nose, and you almost expect to see Disney-cartoon steam shooting from the nostrils. "We gonna *enjoy* ourselves today, boys?" he asks.

The kids nod, but this question is heavy with meaning.

Because here's the other thing: the annual Disney World trip has become almost an obligation, and you know you can't afford it. Not now. The first time you were here, it *was* the happiest place on Earth. The Epcot golf ball, the manicured gardens, the parades, the castle, and—your favorite—the world of Tomorrowland. The Carousel of Progress, where you watched a family evolve from ice boxes and outhouses to 3-D televisions, always together despite the new technologies; it was your own life on display in that presentation, your own parents, your own childhood home in rural Tennessee. Marc and Kyle had been so filled with wonder that anyone could live without electricity, it was the first time they'd truly understood history.

But the problem with Disney World was the return home, the difficulty in accepting that *that world* was not the *real world*. That the rest of the world—gas stations and restaurants and customer-service desks—could never live up to the standards that Disney set. The rest of the world was a disappointment, roads not as beautiful, grass not as green, families not as happy. And then there was the further complication of the next year's trip to Disney, the sequel, an expectation that it would be *better*, that Disney would one-up itself, but nothing was ever as good as the first time. Rides not as exciting. Weather more horridly hot. The feeling of wonder sinking beneath a feeling of entitlement.

"We're gonna enjoy ourselves, Thomas," you say. "We're gonna *conquer* the park today, aren't we, boys?"

Again, the sheepish nods that hide the energy surging through them both.

Thomas parks the car, and you herd the children from the parking lot—Goofy lot? Pluto lot? oh God, you've already forgotten—to the tram, which spirits you into MGM Studios, the newest of the Disney parks. There's a *Honey! I Shrunk the Kids* play area, and a *Star Wars* ride, and it's a full day of Toon Town, of Muppets, of the Great Movie Ride and Sigourney Weaver and an alien popping out and an old animatronic 1930s gangster saying, "You dirty rat! You killed my brother!" over and over throughout the day.

Thomas pushes lunchtime past noon, pushes it back, tells the kids to drink out of the water fountains. "We're having too much fun," he says, "can't stop now," but there's an emptiness in his voice. "Back to Star Tours," he says without feeling. Maybe he's trying to get his money's worth by ensuring that every ride is ridden, every sight seen, not a single penny of the ticket price wasted. The same approach he takes with the weekly groceries. Not a sip of milk left to expire.

"We have to *eat*," you tell him eventually. "It's 2:30, Thomas. The kids are exhausted. Dehydrated." The kids are sitting on a bench in the shade, leaning on each other. Earlier, this was the best day of their lives, high-fiving with Chewbacca; now they look like they could throw up, a day of sugar and pixie dust but no sandwich or glass of milk, not even a potato chip or a dill pickle slice. You feel your headache worsening, and you've been eating Tic Tacs to stave it off.

"We *have* to eat?" he asks.

"Yes. Slow down. If we get in that line, we're going to wait another 45 minutes before we can get food."

"We *have* to eat," he says, "and we *had* to come to Disney?"

"It's *lunch*. Don't tell me you've never heard of it."

"We can have an early dinner instead," he says. "Go on this ride, and maybe one more, and then we do an early dinner. Makes sense, right?"

You hold your head. "Oh," you say. "Oh, that's what this is."

The kids briefly look up from their spot on the bench. Exhausted, but they can always sense an argument.

"What?" Thomas asks. "*What's* what this is?"

"You want to skip lunch so you only have to buy one meal today for your family."

"That's not it," he says. "It's just…the way the day worked out."

"Combine dinner and lunch," you say. "One less receipt."

"No."

"Yes."

"Honey, this place is…" He shakes his head. "This place will bleed you dry if you're not careful. I'm just being careful."

The money, the money. The things the children will never know. The funerals, yes, and the money given over to Mike. But the house repairs, too, after the fire, the tens of thousands of dollars Thomas borrowed from John-John as you were all living in that rental house and Thomas was rebuilding the walls of the burned shell all on his own…And your operation, the growth removed from your midsection. Benign but terrifying, an ordeal that lasted far too long and that seemed to produce a new four-figure bill every other week. You understand your husband's trepidation, but you also wonder what solution he might propose: never leave the house, never spend a dime?

"I know you're being careful," you say. "But food is part of the deal. You're not going to skip lunch to save a buck."

"That wasn't my plan," he says.

"Sure it was." You whisper: "You're *not* doing this, do you hear me? You're not doing this to the kids. This is their vacation. They get this *once a year.* That's it."

He throws up his hands. He's hungry, too, you can tell, but he'd starve himself to stick to whatever budget he's created for this vacation.

Ultimately, you win the battle: you find an air-conditioned sandwich place in the park, and the kids devour the first few bites but look exhausted again by the time you stand from the table. They were dehydrated, and now they're stuffed, their bodies on shutdown in order to digest the bowling ball of food that just suddenly splashed into their stomachs. They need a siesta, but there are no siestas at Disney World, not when Thomas insists that you move quickly to the next ride, the next line, get your money's worth. For the rest of the day, the excitement is gone, the enthusiasm depleted. You see momentary flashes of the children enjoying themselves, a chant of "Star Tours! Star Tours! Star Tours!" But your husband doesn't speak to you, and you're fearful of the long drive home.

This is how Thomas operates: he refuses to let you see the budget, refuses to hear your input into the family finances. He'll hold a grudge for a week when you go clothes shopping with the boys, oblivious to the tattered shoes you wear, or the number of 50-cent pot pie dinners you have each week. He doesn't lament that there's no juice in the fridge, only cheap jugs of multi-colored sugar-water engineered to taste like some vaguely imagined fruit. But still he holds against you any negative impact you make on his planned budget.

He even suggested that you not go to Orlando this year, so deep was the hole you all found yourselves in, but the Disney trip, you told him, *is our chance to get out.* Once a year. Enjoy a different life. A day in the parks. Then a day at Kennedy Space Center, or the beaches, or down to the Everglades, or Hilton Head or Myrtle Beach or Stone Mountain or Charleston. A real place. Whatever. *Wherever.* Two days. A chance to reward ourselves once a year and live life like it's worth living, not like we're just crossing days off the calendar until we die. But Thomas sees a video rental and a frozen pizza as a more sensible way to spend a weekend. Fifteen bucks, and everyone's just as entertained!

"You deserve the world," you say to Marc at dinnertime. It's dark now. You've left the parks, driven over to a "sensible" buffet on I-Drive, where Thomas counts the number of plates he plows through and brags that he "got the price of dinner down to 60 cents a plate!" (he'll keep bragging about this for weeks), and scolds the children if they forsake the carving station and head to the soft-serve ice cream too early. "You deserve the world," you tell Marc. "You deserve all of this."

"Okay, Mom."

You'd never contradict your husband, would never tell your children that he's wrong about the way he structures his life, how much he works, but *this* you will tell your children: there should be room in the world for fun and recklessness, and you shouldn't feel bad about it.

"Your father is going to grumble the whole ride home," you say. He's back up at the carving station; maybe he's gotten the price down to 50 cents a plate. "Don't listen to him. He's just in a bad mood."

You imagine the comments about savings accounts, about bills, and excess, and how he might try to say, "You guys don't want to come back to Disney next year, do you? You remember how *hot* it was?" and drop subtle comments for weeks about the long lines, the stupid tourists who ruin the experience, trying all the while to make the kids hate what they actually love. You imagine the kids feeling awful for wanting what everyone else has, a day at a theme park.

"You deserve the world, Marc," you say. "You deserve to get out. These days…" You stop yourself, because you're afraid you'll cry. "You should remember these family vacations. You should cherish them. All the time you spend with family. This is what it's all about."

"Okay, Mom," he says again.

He's too young to really understand this, of course, but you say it because it needs to be said.

And it's a good thing, too. You don't know it yet, but this is the last time you'll make the trip as a full family. Next year, Thomas will refuse to go, claiming to be "backed up" at the shop, and so it'll just be you and your two children. The next year, your family reunion in Knoxville will prevent it. The next, and Marc will start high school and have so many JV practices you'll barely be able to schedule *any*thing. And the next: well, you'll be dead by that point (forgive the callousness with which you are now learning this fact), a car wreck that will forever divide the lives of your husband and your sons into two distinct eras: When You Were Alive, and After You Were Gone. When There Was a Family, and When Family Ceased to Exist. Some tragedies bring people together. Others shatter lives, turn children into different people entirely. And although this moment—buffet, post-MGM Studios—is far from perfect, you hope Marc will remember it that way. Maybe it's a fantasy, here in the heart of the heart of the country's most fantastic mirage, a family sitting together at a table and slopping mashed potatoes and fried chicken and dinner rolls onto their plates, everyone so tired they're nearly face-planting into their self-serve sundaes. Or maybe this isn't a mirage. Maybe it doesn't need to be commercial-perfect for it to truly be perfect. Maybe perfection is in the sweat and the exhaustion, the sunburns and the arguments, all the stuff that would never make it into a commercial, anything so long as you're all together.

AND THEN IT'S ANOTHER damn Monday, and the thought of driving around closing loans for eight damn hours fills you with such dread that you tell Marc you can't work today, that you've got some things of your own that need taking care of: setting up a new checking account, meeting with an old friend who moved to Central Florida…but it's all a lie. You're meeting with Barnes, installing cabinets at a home in East Orlando. "You don't need to pay me, even," you told him over the phone on Sunday. "I just need to work. Real work. It feels like my hands are dying."

"I can pay you," he said. "I'm no cheapskate."

"I can't take your money. Let's think of it as a try-out. You try me out, I try you out, see if we get along. And I'll figure out how to tell my brother that his job, his life, ain't for me."

Destroying the old kitchen is the most fun you've had in a long time, swinging a sledgehammer to outdated cabinets that look plucked from an '80s family sitcom, the doors breaking apart and misting the air with pulp-dust and splinters. By the time you set about collecting the chunks and tossing them into the industrial garbage cans, it looks like someone dumped a wagonload of sawdust onto the floor, and you have to wear a mask so you don't breathe in the '80s.

"This is the life," you say, though your words are muffled by the mask. Your muscles feel great today, but you know they'll soon be sore on account of all that sedentary living the last couple weeks.

"Layin' tile ain't so fun," Barnes says. "Layin' down floorboards, neither, not when there's stairs. But when you get paid to destroy shit, can't beat it."

You hold up a cabinet door that's still mostly intact, but that's also a piece of shit, warped from humidity because the occupants probably left windows open during summer. Or maybe it was just the cheapest possible cabinet installed when the house went up, and now the new owners finally want to see this place realize its potential. Either way, it does feel good to sledgehammer something gross and to know you'll soon be making improvements in someone's life.

"I have some jobs coming up," Barnes says. "One of my guys is moving to Dallas with his family. Gettin' the hell out of Orlando, though I don't know that there's some place in America these days where the economy's golden. But that's not my call, is it? Anyway. His spot's yours if you want it."

You pull the mask down your face and let it cover your neck. You came all the way to Orlando to hook back up with your brother, to repair the only bit of family you thought might be salvageable. Marc made a place for you, trained you, did everything he could on his own end. And now look at what you're doing.

You kick a cabinet door and your boot goes through the wood; you have to shake your foot to get the door to drop, and you're so forceful when you slam your boot against the floor that the remains barely resemble a door at all.

There's no repairing a relationship that you purposely shatter, is there? Once that wood's snapped into pieces, there's no putting it back together. There's only you, standing in the dust and splinters, looking into the other room at the brand-new cabinets that—five minutes ago—you were so damn eager to install.

But you can't take it anymore: his moping, his zombie-face, his attempts to make *you* into *him*. You're in a new city. You've got to do this, make your own path. You've got to leave him behind.

You shake hands with Barnes.

"Next week," Barnes says. "I'll give you a call. There's a bathroom renovation, takes about three weeks. You game?"

"I am." And you are.

AND NOW YOU'RE SITTING across the table from Marc Turner at Mills/ 50 Coffee, ready to finally pitch to him your big idea, "Make Orlando Weird," the campaign to unite local businesses and save the *whole fucking city*. It's the end of May 2009, the final days of the NBA Eastern Conference playoffs, a time when the words "Orlando Magic" are on the lips of every sports commentator who matters, and you know that you need to take advantage of your city's moment in the national spotlight, but things are not looking good. Contrary to the "start-of-something" elation you felt at Bar-BQ-Bar five months ago, this meeting today feels like "last chance" desperation. Every other business has "respectfully declined" to join your coalition, from the surf/skate shops to the taco palaces to the tea shops to the beer bars, and there are no other friendly managers you can ask. You've even given free "Diamond Member" sponsorship rights to The Social, Mills/50 Coffee, the Audabon Park Garden District, Bar-BQ-Bar, and half a dozen other venues you love and want involved, but this—giving away your product—is the surest way to draw Elaina's ire. You thought it would be easy, that everyone would rally around you. But if not Marc, and if not now, your blog will never be monetized, will never grow into what you need it to be.

So here goes. But Marc is pointing at the screen of your laptop, lips curled like he knows what you're going to say and doesn't want to hear it. "What's The Other City Beautiful?" he asks, voice as dry as cracked firewood.

"Oh, my blog. Forgot I left that tab open." You try at nonchalance, as if this wasn't your plan along, as if you didn't lure him to this coffee shop under the pretense of redesigning his closing company's digital platform but with the true intention of revealing your blog and your Coalition of the Weird and foisting upon him a completely unrelated business venture. No, no! You wouldn't do that! (You did. You are doing it. You suck.)

"You have a blog?" Marc asks.

"Has over 20,000 followers."

"Hmm."

"It's me and Elaina, going to local restaurants and bars. Taking pictures. Talking with the owners about their vision. I spotlight local businesses, local artists. How did you *not* know about my blog? I share the shit out of it on Facebook."

"I deleted my account." His face is still puffy and red from the beating at Wall Street, the skin under his eye still purple and frightening. You feel bad that you didn't ask "how are you?" or "how's your face?" when he first arrived, instead pretending you didn't notice.

"I'm trying to create the most comprehensive look at Orlando culture on the web," you say. "That's my mission. And I want *you* and *your business* to be linked to that effort. You care about your city, right?"

Marc points to his black eye. "I don't think it cares much for me, to be honest." His voice sounds damaged, deeper and incapable of changing pitch or tone, more robotic voicemail message than human.

"Ha ha!" you say, joylessly. "Not true. Listen, you need your city to be prosperous if you wanna survive, right? Like, if everyone stopped buying houses, what would *you* do? No more loans to close. This is about *all of us*. Together."

"I came here for a meeting about my digital presence," Marc says, his bruise seemingly darker now. "That's what you told me we'd talk about."

He's right to be skeptical. Marc has been blowing off your phone calls for so damn long, and the only way you could finally sit face to face with him was to conjure an afternoon "digital strategy session." You told him that you knew it was tough out there in the housing market, that you could help him stand out, that you'd transform his Kwik Closings business into a slick and credible brand.

You sip your coffee, tap a few keys on your laptop. During these coffee shop meetings, you try to create the impression that you've been here all day, just sitting and working and refilling your bottomless cup, that you're a workaholic whose efforts are all funneled into this one specific client, this one specific project. This is your home field, Mills/50 Coffee, and not uncoincidentally, it's also the #5 spot on the "Fifty Places in Orlando That Define the *Real Orlando*" series, a place beloved by creatives from all walks of life. Like all your favorite spots, it's indie, low-budget, looks as if the chairs have all come from a closed-down Wendy's, the tables from an old Cracker Barrel, and the wall kitsch from an old lady's yard sale.

You take another sip of coffee, then turn your laptop to show Marc the web shell you constructed for Kwik Closings, the font you picked, the stock photos you selected to give the online space warmth and humanity. "The first order of business is to create a branding infrastructure," you tell him. It's strange to you that Marc has such an extensive business that's seemingly held together by bubblegum and shoestring and sheer willpower, like he thought he'd get rich without careful thought to his brand and his online presence.

Marc is staring in that soulless, possessed way again, like he's looking into the screen and seeing something beyond what you've produced. But it's just the front page, your mockup of Marc's first logo. It isn't world-changing, but it's something to put on letterhead, on invoices, on business cards, something that shows the world that Kwik Closings (despite that stupid motherfucking misspelling) is legitimate. (A company without a logo? Baffling.) At the bottom of the page is a photo of a woman in a headset, and a caption that reads "Our staff is standing by, ready to take your calls."

"I don't have a staff," Marc says.

"Use your imagination," you say. "The image doesn't say that *this girl* is on your staff. Maybe you actually work out of your house, but the image creates the *impression* that your business has an office, and phones, and a receptionist."

"But I don't *have* a staff."

"I have a license to a stock-photo site," you say, and how much of your days are spent in such repositories, sifting through the millions of gleaming generic photographs, searching out the perfect blandest photos for your clients' web products? "I've got others. A guy with a clipboard. A row of people sitting behind computers. But this girl, she's—nobody will say this out loud, but if you're trying to target some d-bag banker, the sex appeal seals the deal."

"But she's not my employee."

"Obviously. No girl *this hot* works the phones!"

"But if this is a stock photo, couldn't she be on *every* small-business site?"

"That's not…" you start. "No. No." The meeting is getting away from you. You wipe your forehead. Though you love this coffee shop, it gets hot. An Orlando structure built in the early years of air conditioning, when nobody really knew how to build a place that'd keep cool. "You *do* have a staff," you say, patting your chest. "A whole web team."

Marc doesn't respond, just continues regarding the site like it's a document he doesn't want to sign. He is not his typical self today. Definitely not himself. "What's this 'links' page?" He points to the screen like an old man just introduced to computers.

"Well," you say and take a deep breath. You click the link and bring up the page; the first few links are resources for banking customers, but the next few are for Bar-BQ-Bar, for Mills/50 Coffee, for The Social. "You want to give the impression that you're larger than you are, more connected, right?" you ask. "So we're linking you with other Orlando businesses. And you own property, right? So we can even create *another* site for your property company, and they'll both be unique sites, but part of the same community. Linked together. Again, creating the perception that each business is bigger than it is. It's a coalition, a grassroots Chamber of Commerce for small businesses."

"All right," Marc says, but he's looking at the "links" page even more skeptically. "But your blog is linked there. And there's, like, a whole paragraph about the blog."

"Haha. Yes! All part of the plan." No turning back now. "So this is the idea, right? The city is, like, *drowning* in artificiality, you know?" You talk about Red Lobster and Olive Garden, about *Tupperware*, about a plasticized city. You talk about the threat of the exurbs, about Avalon Park and the Disney-founded town of Celebration, whole regions where everything is pre-approved for the best chance at franchising. You hear yourself saying the same things, making the same pitch, and you're tired of failing but accustomed to it.

"That's not the business I'm in," Marc says. "I'm doing everything I can just to stay afloat. I don't need some cultural cause, too."

"We can change the city, is what I'm saying," you say, "you and me."

"This isn't about *me*, seems like," Marc says.

"The website! I bought the domain name! It's yours, Marc!"

"I think I have to go," Marc says.

"Look," you say and slam your hands on the table. "I need your help, all right? Is it too much to ask a friend for help? Can I *count* on you as my friend?"

Marc is holding up his hands, looking at you sideways.

You dial it back: "We go back, don't we?"

"Sure." Marc still looks ready to stand, but he hasn't, not yet.

"What I'm saying is, we used to talk, all the time, about what we were going to do with our lives."

"Sure."

You want this moment to be impactful, want him to feel something, but if you were to create a list of your current friends, where would he fall? In a week and a half, understand, you are marrying Elaina. And Marc *would have* been one of your groomsmen had this wedding occurred last year or the year before, but after Marc's engagement broke off he stopped returning your phone calls, stopped going out. Worked through weekends. Vanished from social media. A shell of a man with (as far as you can tell) no real life anymore.

Back when Marc was still engaged to Shelley, you and Elaina would call the two of them, and you'd all head to "Cocktails & Cosmos" at the Orlando Science Center, or maybe the Florida Music Festival downtown, or the German American Society Oktoberfest. You'd take trips to Cocoa Beach, to Clearwater. You traveled together to Memphis, and to Seattle for that Bucs-Seahawks game, even though—with your coach-father and your family history—you detest the sport of football. Still: Seattle! Savannah! Double dates every other weekend. You were a unit. Hell, Shelley loved Elaina so much that you were almost worried she might propose before you could get a shot! But then there was Labor Day of '08, the great break-up, Shelley stuffing her boxes in Elaina's car and leaving Marc's house, and there was you and Elaina going out to dinner alone, no longer a thought to even call Marc anymore.

"We're brothers, right?" you ask.

Marc blinks a few times, perhaps struggling to make sense of what he's hearing. Are you begging? Are you trying to move him back from potential client to occasional friend to best friend, all in one desperate swoop? "Fraternity brothers, yes," he says, and this is the most deflating response possible. Your relationship is an organizational happenstance.

You reach for your coffee, nearly knock it over. Your hand is shaking. Did you overestimate where your friends fall in your life? A couple weeks ago, you gave Goat a box of bumper stickers to pass out, entrusted him with a stack of t-shirts he seemed eager to sell, and now…you haven't seen Goat since. Voicemails, but no return calls. Knocks on his door, and no one's ever home. But it goes beyond Goat. Online, you tweet about an historic building under threat of demolition, and you'll get a hundred *favorites*, or you'll post a Throwback Thursday update about Terror on Church Street and get five hundred *likes*, but when it comes to something as simple as going to an Orlando Predators game ("Free tickets, Anderson. Wanna go?"), or to Wekiva Springs ("Anyone want to do a day at the park? I'll make sandwiches!"), it's crickets. Of course you've got your fiancée, but she's often out of town collecting old furniture for refurb projects, was out of town all of Memorial Day weekend for that job interview, too. She's got her own projects, and you can't burden her with lifting up yours. You need your friends—your real flesh and blood friends—to buy into your idea, to support it in a way that goes beyond just saying "I support it."

God, when did you become so fucking isolated?

And now Marc is saying that he needs to go. "I have narrow windows in which to eat," he's saying.

"I'll buy lunch," you say. "This shop has an amazing gluten-free turkey melt. It'll brighten your day, my friend, make you forget about…um…" (You almost say "your face," but you stop yourself.)

"I'm not allergic to gluten."

You want to tell him that gluten is, like, bad for digestion, but you can't really explain how or why, your knowledge of this issue having come mostly from photo slideshows linked from some Orlando food blog.

"Well. The vegan brownies—"

"I'm not vegan, either."

Now you want to advocate for veganism, too, explain how meat addiction is actually killing our environment and contributing to climate change, and why we should all do a "Meatless Monday" just to make a small impact and—

"I've got work to do," Marc says.

"Please," you say.

He sighs. "Does this place have salads?"

"Yes! There's a tremendous goat cheese and beet salad that—"

"That's fine."

In the back of your mind, you're aware that friendships cannot survive hard business propositions, that this could be it for you and Marc, that Marc could forever think of you through the lens of this moment. You're also aware that there are very real things that—with the two of you alone together, friend to friend—you *should* talk to Marc about instead. Marc is a man in a giant home, now empty, a man devastated by the housing market, a man who was just beaten so badly that he was rushed to the hospital. A man who (and oh, this is the big one, isn't it, the one you've been avoiding?) doesn't know that his ex-fiancée—after breaking up with him last Labor Day—needed help packing and moving out, and so she called Elaina, who called you (and by proxy, Anderson, the guy with the truck who is always enlisted to help everyone haul their shit). "I can't do that," you told your own fiancée, "Marc will hate me." "They're broken up," she said. "The way I see it, he'll probably be happy you helped her move out." There were space-saver bags, tons of clothes vacuum-sealed inside giant plastic blocks that wound up being heavier than boxes of books, and as you loaded the truck until it was overflowing with crap, Elaina suggested that maybe Shelley could take that third bedroom up in Anderson's condo, and Anderson's face lit up because *yesssssss!*, extra rent!, and that was how you came to live with Shelley for four months, all the way through the holidays until she could move in with a friend at the start of the new year. As far as you know, this was all kept secret from Marc. In the back of your mind, you know that these things need to be discussed, that maybe…maybe it wasn't Marc who wouldn't return phone calls, maybe it wasn't Marc who faded to "occasional friend," maybe it was instead you and Anderson who *avoided* him. For months. *We're brothers*, you said to him. Right. So many things you could talk with him about, and yet— here at the coffee shop—you know you will keep the conversation centered upon your flailing cultural campaign.

"So you made bumper stickers," Marc says once you've settled back at the table, two heaping salads between you. "That's what this is about?"

"The point is a *movement*," you say. "There are pockets of this city, people and businesses who *do* have an identity, who *are* doing cool things. We can be the ones behind the movement."

"Pockets of people," he says.

"Artists. Musicians. I want to create a dialogue that celebrates the *true* culture of our city, that makes people proud of what we are, and saves us from the developers."

"Saves us? Development is progress."

"Yes, but with a *cost*."

"So you want people to care about, what? The old Colonial Plaza? The round building downtown? Some abandoned stretch of land in Parramore? I heard you started some Facebook group to, like, save an intersection."

"Yes! See, that's what—"

"Wasn't there something on that land before those businesses at that intersection?"

You stop. Shake your head. "Well. Maybe. But you're missing the point."

"No. I get it. You want a hipster movement that keeps the city exactly as it is, forever." He has the most perfect bite poised on his fork: chicken, avocado, beet, goat cheese, arugula. How is it possible to gather them all together, in such equal proportions? How can you win an argument with a man whose salad bites are flawless?

"It's not *hipsters*—"

"Sorry. You want to celebrate *cultural authenticity*."

"Yes! Preserve what's real."

"Who decides what's real and what isn't?"

You stop again, shake your head again. Your own arugula looks wilted, soggy in the balsamic vinaigrette. "This is a movement," you say again.

"A movement effected by a 'links' page on my loan closing website?"

"I mean, that's one piece of it."

"Many have tried to conquer this city," Marc says. "Many have failed."

"Wha—what are you—"

"You convinced me that I needed a better web presence," Marc says, his voice deep and rumbling, suddenly strange and otherworldly. "You're my friend, so I listened. But I don't go to I-Bar. I don't vote in the *Orlando Weekly* polls. I don't go to 'shows' and stay out till 3 AM on work nights. I don't even like bumper stickers."

"It's not just *bumper* stickers!" you say and throw your hands up. "It's a statement. If we don't assert our identity, we're going to fucking *lose*—" You're shaking. Shaking. "I'll tell it to you as straight as I can. I need sponsors. I need local businesses who want to take a stand and say, 'Let's do this. Let's be what we can be.' Have you read—"

"Sponsorship?" Marc shakes his head, dabs his lips with a napkin. He's nearly finished with his salad, and yet yours remains mostly untouched, unattractive, acid reflux on a plate. "The thing is, Austin *is* weird," he says. "You get that, right? We're Orlando. You can't make us into what you want us to be. Culture is—" and his voice is rumbling again, and he's looking deep into your eyes and soul—"culture is a living, organic entity. *Your* words, correct? It's not ever going to change because of a 'links' page, or a bumper sticker, or a blog, or a handful of misfit businesses."

You hold out your hand, as if to keep your friend from leaving, but Marc is checking his cell phone, standing up.

"I've gotta get to Casselberry for my appointment."

"Make Orlando Weird," you say, and is your voice cracking? You pull out a bumper sticker that you'd saved for this moment, and it trembles in your grip as you reach forward to hand it to him. "Just, like, remember it. I mean. Marc, this could be the campaign that puts *me* on the map in this town, too, buddy. This is a big deal. Help a brother out?"

The sticker is in your hand, but Marc is at the door, and then the door is closing behind him.

THE DECADES REWIND. From 2009 to 1999 to 1989, and soon you are sweeping through the '60s, the Roaring Twenties, Orlando at the turn of the century. Now the 1890s, the 1870s, to the days before there ever was a city, a town, an idea of Florida as anything but angry wilderness. Aaaand…ah yes, here you are. September 1835.

Your name is Orlando Reeves, and someday a city will be named for *you*, schoolchildren for centuries forced to remember key details about your life and your contribution to the region.

But that is many years away. Right now, you are a soldier in the bitter Seminole War. There is no city yet, only a fort called Gatlin. (Even the homesteader Aaron Jernigan, who will give the area the name "Jernigan" for about a decade, is still years away from settling here.) You've trudged through the thickness of the state's interior, picking off sniper Seminoles hiding in the tall oaks, your aim so true, your vision so clear, that your men believe you almost magical. You are *Orlando Reeves*, the man who shimmers through the forest like a spirit and with just five bullets kills ten Indians, the man who hides in the brown waters of this swamp or that, breathing through hollow bamboo, waiting in ambush through the day, rising once darkness comes and the Seminoles sit safely around their fire, and you rise from the water and the mud, rise so slowly and quietly that the extinguishing of the fire—of all light—is noticed only seconds before your sword burns into one man's heart, then another's, and another's. *Orlando Reeves*: you are an action hero before the words "action hero" mean anything. Boston can have its Paul Revere, but *you* are Central Florida's legend, a man who—with his last bullet, and his camp about to be overrun—fires a shot into the air to warn his fellow soldiers of the encroaching danger, a man who draws his sword and makes his final stand to give his brothers time to escape, a man finally felled by the Seminoles but whose sacrifice is never forgotten. Later, your men bury your body on the banks of Lake Eola, where it will forever guard the land. For years they call this place "Orlando's Grave," as if you still hover over the land and the water.

You are Orlando Reeves. Orlando. Reeves.

But the thing is, that story is kind of bullshit. And the lights of the Dead Zone have no time for bullshit.

There was never any soldier named Orlando Reeves, never any battles on the banks of Lake Eola, or at Fort Gatlin, or in the eventual town of Jernigan. The Seminole War touched a great number of swamps, forests, and towns in Central Florida, even reaching as far as the someday-site of Walt Disney World, but not *Orlando*. And not Lake Eola. That story was conjured from thin air, a fantasy.

You are Orlando Reeves, and here in the Dead Zone, you're grasping at your own dissipating narrative. It's tough to hear, but it's the truth: you do not exist. Despite the town founders, who needed a history worth telling, a history exciting enough to lure the world into the city's embrace, and despite schoolteachers struggling to make the city's history engaging for their students, and despite (oh, this is heartbreaking!) the junior high class who erected the monument to your memory in Lake Eola Park in the 1930s...*you do not exist*. No military records. Only whispers and folklore, tall tales and urban legends.

Orlando's Grave, the people of this town were told, and there was even evidence that the name "Orlando" had been long ago carved into a tree on the banks of Lake Eola. That much is true, but you are no less an invention. The man who carved the city's namesake was not an action hero named Orlando Reeves, but Orlando Rees of South Carolina, owner of a sugar mill thirty miles away.

No battles, no soldier. The city is named after a tourist.

Orlando Rees, a slave-owning sugar peddler from far away. Not a glamorous history, but better to *actually exist* than to be completely fabricated, right?

But what sort of life did you have, Orlando Rees? Is there anything that the city can celebrate, that residents can hold up and say, "Yes! We are proud our city is named after *you!*" Is there anything that anyone should remember about you, other than your name?

You ran a sugar mill, and you liked to carve your name into trees. That's something? You were made of flesh and blood, too. And listen, maybe that's enough. After all, Lake Eola was named after a beautiful and beloved woman from the city's early history, but no one remembers a damn thing about her, either. Grand scheme, what's the difference between the two of you?

But look ahead 170 years, and the history buffs are disputing your very existence. There was never a man named Orlando anywhere at all in this region, they say. No soldier. No slave owner. Just a word scratched into a tree, a city named after 19th-century graffiti, and a century and a half of writers scrambling for theories to give meaning to this act.

Here's the hard truth, Orlando Ree(ve)s. You don't belong here among the lights. You are a fleeting dream, a figment of the imaginations of the dead men buried deep in this muck.

DRIVING THE OVERBUILT STRETCH of 17-92 that pushes past Winter Park and north into Maitland, the natural world fades into power lines and parking lots and gravel and stoplights and construction cones even where there's no construction. But it's within this urban grit that one finds the Enzian Theater, #3 on your list of "Top Fifty Places in Orlando That Define the *Real* Orlando," and perhaps the only true indie cinema left in the Metro Orlando region, a green garden in that gray stretch, a lime-colored Key West structure beneath oak branches grown long as city blocks, a building nestled so deep beneath all those centuries-old trees it seems to pre-date them.

The Enzian is included on your list because it's an historical marker in your life: it was the site of the first double date between you, Elaina, Marc and Shelley. Sometime in 2007, as you recall. It was on one of Shelley's lists, her "Weird Florida" list or her "Orlando Bucket List," or whatever. Together, the four of you sat at a table and ate hummus and drank wine and watched *Sideways*. It's a night you still remember, even as your memories of a hundred other date nights have faded: the moment when Marc tried to cut his cannoli in half, and his fork slipped and sent the cannoli rocketing off the table; or the moment in the film when Paul Giamatti flees the house of the married woman, and her naked husband chases after him and his penis flops onto the car window, Elaina laughing so hard she nearly choked on the maraschino cherry from her whatever-tini.

Oh, for fuck's sake! Why talk about this place and these people?

Because the blog, the dream…it's *never going to happen*.

It's over. Everything. Make Orlando Weird. You as culture warrior. Everything is—

Wait, wait. Hold up. Step back from the ledge, Steven.

Go outside. Take a walk. You've been on your computer all day long, the curtains in your bedroom closed tight, nighttime-dark as you slump in your chair all through an afternoon that outside is probably bright and cheerful but how would you ever know it? It's wearing on you, trying to finish all of these blog posts, trying to imagine and describe all the places that mean so much to you. So get off the computer, get out of the darkness.

Scenic Langford Park is a good destination! And hey, perfect as a #2 spot for your list! Not obvious, like downtown's Lake Eola Park (which *every other listicle* would mention). Langford's a hidden gem, a park deep within the Colonialtown neighborhood, bordered by no major thoroughfares and highlighted on no travel guides. Langford Park, named after…some guy? You should probably brush up on your city history, but…well, what's it matter now?

Langford Park. Number two spot.

So…how to describe the park in your blog post? Well, the houses nearby are mostly historic Florida bungalows, and then there's Reeves Terrace beyond the park's grass fields, a one-story housing project hidden in Florida shade and looking a bit like a camping retreat. The park itself: Florida boardwalks over Florida creeks and Florida swamps, heavy humid Florida air settling over the Florida grass and Florida oaks, creepy Florida cypress trees rising from the stagnant Florida water. The Florida Florida is Florida, also, with Florida Florida Florida Florida, Floridaing but yet Florida Florida Florida. Florida! Florida! Florida!

Little else to say about Langford Park. As far as parks go, it's just kind of there.

But you would love to walk it again, to stand beside a creek and just listen. To sit on a bench on a March morning, laptop open, smell of wet pavement in the air, smell of newly laid mulch. This was where you wanted to live, an old bungalow in Colonialtown within walking distance of this park, hammock in your backyard, Adirondack chairs on the sloping front lawn, big trees, because there's no joy quite like oak shade on a hot Florida day. But now you're phoning-in these final blog posts in your Top 50 and the words are…just text. Florida your easy adjective to fill the space. What is Florida sunshine? What is Florida dirt, Florida water, Florida heat?

It's memories. It's a place where you *used* to live, that's what.

Elaina has accepted a job in North Carolina. You're both leaving. And your blog, it's

THE CITY'S MOVED ON without your leadership. Ain't that always the way? Through the '80s, through the '90s, into the new century. There were hurricanes, but never any riots. The world takes to water quite often, but the city never took to fire; and the garbage—as far as you've seen—never poured out of the gutters. It's always stayed buried.

You're sitting at Lakeside Wine Bar and staring across at the bandshell, where earlier there was a middle-school choral performance going on. Kids from all over Orlando singing in unison, the sort of shit that'd make a perfect Visit Orlando commercial. But it's 2009 and ain't nobody care what Carl T. Langford thinks, some codger who ran the city back before Universal Studios and Sea World and the Orlando Magic. Back when downtown didn't have a skyline, and UCF was just a tiny college with two buildings and a whole lotta sandspurs, not the second-largest university in the country. Back when I-4 was a modern marvel, a boon, not a parking lot, a daily-cursed deathtrap. You ran this city in the 1970s, but in the end, does anyone care about what happened in that decade? Does anyone want to understand the men that made it all what it is today?

When you look around the city, you see their names. The Walt Disney Amphitheatre at Lake Eola, as if he ever done anything in the city itself. Hell, he was dead before Disney World even opened! You see road names like Bumby and Summerlin and Curry Ford and occasionally you'll regale someone with the inside story of how a road was named, who Joseph Bumby was, or Jacob Summerlin (King of the Crackers!, Homestead Hero!), how the Curry family created their road as a ford over the Econ River, or even—for the youngsters—why that big club downtown used to be called Zuma Beach even though there are no beaches in Orlando. "It was the *Beach*am Theatre originally," you say, "second theater built in the city, first to show 'talkies.' Built on the site of the city's first jail!" Of course, your anecdote is useless now: most kids don't even know what Zuma Beach is anymore, and as soon as you'd rehearsed that anecdote, the club changed owners. Tabu, it's called now. Justin Timberlake's an owner, someone said. Tabu this week. Next week, who knows? Maybe someone else will take over, re-name it Beacham Theatre, and then you can tell the story behind the structure again.

Names. You know the stories behind them all. The city of Orlando itself named after that old warrior-hero Orlando Reeves. Lake Eola, Lake Underhill, Lake Ivanhoe. Names. The history of the city singing to you from a thousand stages. Orange Blossom Trail. College Park. Boone High School. The Green Way. Parramore. The Rosalind Club. You know every story.

The point is, the reason you been thinkin' so much on this, is you look around and see these other names, marks left on the city, but who ever sees *your* name? Mayor Bob Carr, the man who beat you in your first election, then dropped dead in office (thus paving the way for a new election and—*boom!*— your victory), has a performing arts center named for him. And that astronaut, the hometown boy John Young? Was admonished by NASA for taking a sandwich into space, but the city damn-near gave him everything they got. And Dr. Phillips? (Not a real doctor, by the way. Just a millionaire who had enough money to convince the world he was a doctor.) All these guys, with their auditoriums and high schools and expressways named after them. But Carl T.? All throughout your time in office, you thought you were a legend in the making. Orlando going from *backwater* to *metropolis* on your watch, people giving you credit, calling you Supermayor, but all along you must have known that the city had a life of its own. That the university might have opened its doors in '68, gone from tiny FTU to massive UCF on your watch, but the foundation was set in '63, before you were in office. Disney, too: Walt made his decision in 1963, but *you* were the one invited to the grand opening like you'd earned it. And I-4? The highway that truly built the city? The Orlando stretch completed in '62. You didn't build it. You only reaped the benefits of being a "highway city." Orlando had already willed itself into existence, education and tourism and transportation aligning perfectly without you, and you sat on the saddle and yelled giddy-up and took credit. You put it all down in your memoir and published that shit before you even left office! It's 2009, and how arrogant that seems now. Great men don't write history, they make it.

Langford.

They named a park after you, your daughter's always quick to remind you. And that sounds nice, only the park is built on your Got-damn secret trash heap! Thank Hizzoner the Mayor for all them hills, kids!

So here you are at Lakeside Wine Bar, sneaking peeks at the TV inside to catch the score of the Magic game, surrounded by 20-year-olds with fake titties. You can feel how these kids are looking at you: some weird old man in a cowboy hat? They still let Florida Crackers come downtown? Didn't we sweep the city clean of *their type*, dump them all out in Chuluota and Bithlo? Ain't we cosmopolitan now? Two tables down, there's a quiet couple, a blonde girl who looks so expressionless she's gotta be on drugs, and a guy who's looking out at the pedicabs like he'd rather be on a bicycle than where he's at.

"Daddy," your daughter says.

"Yeah," you say.

"What do you think of the wine?"

"Ahh," you say and turn away from the sad couple. "You know me." Your daughter's been trying for the past two years to get you on the Wine Bandwagon now that "wine bars" seem to be the new thing, she and her husband out every weekend and bragging to the world about the tastes they've encountered.

"I know," she says. "You'd rather have a scotch."

"Whatever makes you happy, baby," you tell her. "I promised you I'd come."

Her husband is here, too, on his phone. These kids and their phones.

"We should've come down here earlier," she says. "Taken a swan boat on the lake."

"Ain't my thing," you say. "Can you picture me in one of them?"

The wine tastes sharp but lacks the hard bite of scotch, that ancient feeling of the oak and the earth, of history, the sense that you're drinking as God intended.

"Lake Eola wasn't always so pretty," you say.

"Oh, Daddy, you're not gonna start talking about the *garbage* again, are you?"

"Do I talk about it that much?"

"Only when we're trying to have a nice time."

"Sorry."

"The garbage story, or the riot story."

"I tell both of 'em that much, huh?"

"But the riots never happened, so that story is sort of disappointing."

"Yeah, I guess."

"But I like the story about the Disney riots," she says.

"I don't remember that one. Disney riots?"

"You only told it once. The strike during the Disney World construction? The rally at the Citrus Bowl?"

"I must have...forgotten." Things are fading these days, your memories like ghosts, as intangible as Old Orlando. You will not survive, and they will not survive you. The city's young. For most of these kids, the way it is now is the way it's always been. But you remember a different Orlando. You remember Ronnie's, the country cookin', the pies under the glass. You remember Lake Eola before the swan boat rides and high-rise condos and concession stands.

"Daddy?" your daughter asks.

"Yeah?"

"You were saying something about the lake?"

"Nothing important," you say. "Better turn around, sweetie. They're showing Magic highlights."

The image is there in your mind, one memory that hasn't yet left you. You were a child, a boy of maybe ten or eleven, in the very center of Lake Eola, your arms spread out, and you weren't riding no damn paddleboat. You were standing on a sandbar in the center of the lake, your feet just below the surface. The lake was brown and filled with wild critters, hadn't yet been drained to improve the color, hadn't yet been filled with swans. In the spring, before the summer rains hit, the water levels would recede, and sometimes you'd see sandbars in the middle of the lake. Once, you swam to the center. You timed it just right, before the water levels dropped enough to actually show the sand over the lake's surface. You swam out and stood on the sandbar and the lake was at your ankles and if anyone was watching from shore, it would've looked like you were walking on water. Even now, after all these years, there's been no other moment when you felt so truly alive, so powerful; you felt like the city was yours. It was palpable, the energy, and though for years you wanted to recapture it, even in business, even as mayor, you never could. That was it: that day, walking on Lake Eola. Nobody will ever do that again.

AND THE "GREAT HURRICANE OF 1926" is what the papers are calling it. *Hurricane.* Who in God's name would think such a storm possible, and that it could devastate so far inland! This is why you chose *Central* Florida, after all, wilderness you could tame, nature you could improve upon, but still the land and the sea attack your dream.

For months you'd been sleeping on your land, on cleared foundations where you set your tent and your lamp to make a temporary home. But when news of the storm came, you took refuge in the biggest damn hotel you could find, the gorgeous Seminole Hotel in Winter Park, with a hundred other guests, women shrieking each time the chandeliers shook. One man kept trying to play it cool, told everyone to calm down. "Ha ha!" he said. "Haven't you ever seen a Florida thunderstorm?" He kept going outside to smoke cigarettes under the awning, as if enjoying the spectacle of the palm trees bent sideways with fronds toe-touching the ground. "Ha ha!" he said late in the night and went outside to smoke another cigarette, and then you heard a loud smack, and the rain was horizontal and it was darker than midnight had ever been for you, and no one could see him anymore. His wife asked the other men to go out and search for him, but there were flashes of lightning, black shapes whizzing past like witches on broomsticks. Interior of the hotel lit only by candles and fireplace. The night had grown dangerous in a real way, the sound of wood cracking and metal shifting. Immersed in the storm, in its colors and violent sounds, in its unendingness, in its waters rising just past the entryway (from *whence* came this inky water, which soaked even the carpet beneath the second and third-floor windows?), it was as unreal as if you'd been transported to another world entirely.

"For God's sake!" the woman wailed. "He's out there! Someone help him!"

So you looked to the biggest man in the room, a Cuban named Vincent who you were certain was muscle for some gangster running Bolita operations from Tampa to Orlando. You motioned for him to help, that simple cock of the head that said "we're men, we gotta do something." Before this moment, Vincent hadn't moved for anybody, but suddenly he was with you. You were all in this together.

When you opened the lobby door it damn-near screamed off into the wind, and you with it. Rain pelting without pause, like your skin was being sanded off. And then through squinted eyes you saw him, the man who'd been carried off. The man with no fear. Thirty yards away in the darkness and rain, crumpled against a tree. He looked discarded, no different than the branches and leaves and palm fronds that covered him. When you finally made your way to him, you and Vincent had to drag him sled-style back to the lobby. He was unconscious, his jacket ripped and face smeared with mud; likely he'd been hit by a flying tree branch, though it might also have been a lamppost or a street sign or an umbrella, who knew? He was alive, but this man would never again laugh at a hurricane.

All night it raged, and continued to rage until sunup, and even then you couldn't leave the hotel grounds, couldn't drive your car through these continuing winds. So you waited it out another day, until the world went ghostly calm and—perhaps like the battlefields of Europe after the armistice—the quiet of death settled in. And it was only then that you could brave the flooded roads and return to your development, your investment, to see if it had survived.

It hadn't.

All is deathly hot and humid and you are clearing bricks and broken concrete from the once-epic entryway into your massive Central Florida community. Your equipment is mostly crushed by felled pines, your supplies buried beneath the muck of advancing lake. The few houses that had been finished are now scattered toothpicks floating in a lake three times the size it's supposed to be, the landscape reimagined just as you'd finished fashioning it to meet your vision.

"Have you ever seen anything like this?" you ask Davis, the only man to report to work this morning.

"It's worse elsewhere," Davis says. "The other men, some of 'em had family down Okeechobee." Down there, he tells you, the flooding is more severe, dikes in the Everglades ruptured, floods over fifty square miles of agricultural land, death toll in the thousands. "They say they stackin' bodies, burnin' 'em. Ain't enough caskets. Ain't enough time."

"My God," you say.

Hurricane. Florida Apocalypse. What sort of evil is this? You'd admired the land's fierceness, but only because you thought *you* were ferocious enough to handle it. It seems as if there's something, some invisible force, that doesn't want you here, that doesn't want *anyone* here. You know that now. The land will not be conquered. You aren't a church-going man, but this is enough to make you believe that He does issue warnings, that He does exact his wrath. This is a warning from God, is it not?

You hold up the gigantic letter "S," once a gleaming part of the golden-lettered gate but now scratched and bent in several directions, and you think of the future you'd imagined for yourself down here in the City of Dreams. You think of the money you could have made, and how it's all gone now, every penny to your name, letters from your wife unanswered for too long. Her last letter said someone had taken the hotel, she couldn't stop them, and where was she supposed to go? Then: not another word. Where *did* she go? Where *is* she? Was she on her way here?

Here in Florida, you've been swallowed by a state—you will soon learn—whose land boom has been proclaimed "dead" by the New York papers. There's no way you can rebuild, no way you can count on Northern buyers, no way to recoup the costs of all that equipment bobbing and sinking in the lake. It is 1926, and for you, it is the end of the world.

Your dreams are over. Your visions of a fantasyland are over. Hell, your time as a businessman—here, anywhere—is over. Elsewhere, the tycoons are probably putting bullets in their brains, everything lost. The Binder Boys are moving on. But you can't leave. Hell, maybe you *wanted* this; maybe it was always your intention to escape the old life, to be unburdened entirely.

So you know what you'll do: you'll live here in the wilderness. You'll follow the river the storm has altered to snake into your centerpiece lake (Lake Opportunity, you'd named it, but someone else will come along and name it something new), and somewhere, you'll clear just enough brush for a domicile made of oak. That sounds pleasant, doesn't it? You'll fish the river. You'll make a fire pit, and every night you'll eat what you catch. Maybe you'll grow hardened enough to wrestle a gator, cook the tail. You'll let your hair grow long, till no one recognizes you as the man you once were. You will become Florida, as cracker as they come.

You remember your first thoughts about the state, the region: staring inland from Daytona, thinking how it was beautiful but dangerous, how it was a frontier that could swallow a man whole, an observation that will soon turn prophecy. There is no *conquering* this state, no re-making it in your own image; there is only fighting against it, fighting the wind, fighting the soil, fighting the rain until the land swallows you whole.

You collect what you can, lay your hand on Davis' shoulder and say, "How long does a man last, living off the land?"

Davis shakes his head. "Out there, a man lasts only if he gives up being a man."

"Yeah," you say. "Sounds right." And then you walk the perimeter of the lake until the river appears. Four dead deer are piled like driftwood on its bank. You look back once more before following the river and, into the brush, you disappear

WILD BERRY, THE NEIGHBORHOOD IS CALLED, and you drive in during the night with your U-Haul, park beside a van that some stranger's left in your driveway. Another day, maybe you'd care. Not today. This is the third house you've visited today, one final cross-town mission before you leave this city. You unlock the door, flip on the lights, and as the living room comes to life in the radiance of the ceiling fan and accent lights, you are reminded what a beauty this house is, how stunning the staging photos you took. Mirror on the wall (Pottery Barn, voluptuous curves like scooped gelato), accent artwork from Anthropologie, framed print of a white tiger dashing through water (scored at some damned gala's silent auction), espresso-brown coffee table, couches the color of blue steel. Silver lamps on glass end tables. Furniture you've used to stage a dozen flips, but in this room, amid the white plantation shutters and upgraded ceiling fans, it's a fucking knockout.

"How much you put into this place, Edwin?" Wes asks. He's a kid from the fraternity house, and you're paying him twenty dollars an hour to help you today. That and the cost of your U-Haul, and you'll be out a couple hundred. But when you sell off all this furniture? Small price to pay.

"Twenty grand in renovations and remodels," you say. "Some landscaping. Some minor repairs. But it's the appliances and the countertops that move units. The wow factor. This house should've sold itself."

"But no one's buying?"

You shrug, feign nonchalance. "Shame I can't pop out the shutters."

"I can try?"

"They're custom. Worthless outside these window frames."

"So, uh, what goes?"

"All of it." You sweep your hand across the room. "Focus on the fridge, the stove, big-ticket items first. Same as the last two houses. After that, we take every damn thing we can fit in the U-Haul. If we had a ladder, I'd take the ceiling fans, too."

"Bedrooms?"

"Full master set. Crappy mattress, sandpaper sheets, but I can find some joker who's doing flips, sell it to him for his own staging. People trust me."

"This neighborhood's nice. You really don't think this'll sell?"

"I don't give a fuck anymore," you say. "Not paying another dime to the banks. I want money, cash money they can't take. The bankers, the Wall Street ass-hats, they were playing a game and didn't let anyone else know the real rules. Bunch of cheats." You're thinking of posters and baseball cards, handshakes and fine print, the illusion of fair transactions.

It's dark in Wild Berry as you and Wes cram the furniture into the U-Haul. Tomorrow you'll drive it to your father's warehouse outside Atlanta, and you'll place Craigslist ads to earn back whatever you can. As a goodwill gesture, maybe you'll pay your father 20%. Well. *If* he notices you're using the warehouse. Also, if he cares, asks for a cut. See, you can still be generous, even when you're down and out!

"Found a ladder in the master closet!" Wes yells from the other end of the house.

"Well, shit," you say, vaguely remembering the day that you hung the palm tree painting in the bedroom, and vaguely remembering the ladder—unseen since that day, one of several you own. "We can get these fans, after all. And those decorative vases high in the alcove." The ladder itself is another fifty bucks. "Things are looking up!" you say.

YOU'RE OFF, SCREECHING DOWN THE HALL and out into the great room as if lit like a bottlerocket. You grab the notepads from this floor, that one, this table, that one, never stopping. Moving through the foyer, through the kitchen, peeking into the office, into the guest bedrooms and hallway, rushing out onto the porch, until finally you find Edwin in the laundry room with a notepad in hand. Caught in the act.

"Have you been writing these notes, Edwin?" you ask. You hope it comes across as playful rather than scornful. But you know that you've failed, that your eyes communicate a DEF CON-1 rage.

"Who, meeeee?" he says, jiggling his vodka tonic so the ice cubes clink the glass.

Suddenly you hate vodka tonics. Suddenly you hate vodka, too, and anyone who'd drink it, anyone who'd say *Who, meeeee?* "These are your suggestions for our house?" you ask, and read: "'Breast implants for Shelley, and penile implants for Marc. Right now you're both average, but imagine the awesomeness of a well-endowed life.'"

"Don't think I wrote that one," Edwin says, "but that's some funny shit."

"That was from the bedroom notepad. Almost every notepad has similar comments, in exactly the same handwriting."

"Well, I don't like writing by hand. So, you know, couldn't be me."

"Your handwriting is meticulous, Edwin."

"Aw, thanks!"

"Here's the notepad for the kitchen. 'Start with a walk-in wine and cheese cooler. Then a walk-in humidor. Then a walk-in coffee bean pantry and grindery. Then, hire a full-time smoothie technician to live and sleep in the fruit closet (which you'll need to build, also) and boom: smoothies whenever you want them. Also, slave labor is acceptable.'"

"Again," Edwin says, "didn't write it, but it's hi-*lar*-ious."

"While I do appreciate your unique sense of humor, Edwin, you *do* realize that there are people here outside of, um…outside of your own social circle? That there should be a certain degree of maturity…an acknowledgment that this party *means* something to some of us?"

Edwin is a grade-A *douchebag*, a word that you've come to love for the genuine offense that douchebags take when called "douchebag," a word that functions as a sort of companion to "white trash" except higher on the wealth scale. If your youth on the Gulf Coast was populated by white trash, then your twenties have been overtaken by douchebags, hundreds of them, *thousands*, in college and at bars and in the workplace. In fact, you've frequently wondered if Orlando is a "Douchebag" and "Stupid Bitch" nexus, if they're all pulled here like insects to a bug zapper…These are *not* the most talented young people of the Southeast, but the place—the high percentage of *new* houses and *new* restaurants and *new* stores and *new* buildings, the year-round warmth, the everywhere amusements and attractions and never a dull moment…it makes them all feel as if they're somehow responsible for this fantasy world around them, as if the sunshine was their own creation.

"Come on, Shelley. Take it easy."

"Don't, Edwin."

"I was just joking. Live a little. Smile."

This is the Douchebag Way. Everything's funny. Everything's a joke. And if you get offended, it's your own fault, indicative of your larger problem: that you have no sense of humor, that you're a stereotypical not-funny girl.

"Did you tell me to—" Pause. Don't play into his trap. "Some of this stuff is not appropriate, okay? The comment about the dead hookers under the floorboards?"

"It's *funny*!"

"Just because you're laughing at your own joke doesn't mean it's funny."

"Laughing. That's the *definition* of funny. Try it sometime."

"No. Humor is about the right joke for the right occasion."

"I'm laughing," he says. "Right here, right now." Points to his mouth. "Ha. Ha. Ha."

"Don't be a dick."

"What, are you afraid I'm going to embarrass you in front of your old-lady friends?"

"Edwin."

He leans close, and—though he's shorter than Marc—he's still several inches taller than you. And he whispers in Bud-heavy breath: "Fuck the old ladies." Leans closer. "They're just old sorority bitches. Nothing special about them, and I'm not changing for 'em. You shouldn't either."

"This isn't about changing. This is…"

"I know you, Shelley. I know who you are. Don't let them change you."

"I…" You stop. "Are you *lecturing* me?"

"Naw, dude, I—"

"Stop saying 'dude.' You sound like a fucking idiot."

"A fucking idiot who made your boyfriend—'scuse me, fi-an-*cée*!—the money to buy this giant house. Show a little respect."

"I don't owe you anything. He doesn't owe you anything."

Edwin rubs his nose, pinches his nostrils, backs away. "Enjoy it while you can, Shelley. This shit can end quick. And then, think about where Marc would be if I up and left."

You search his eyes, but they're as blank and soulless and douchey as usual. You wonder if Edwin is trying to tell you something, if this is his first-ever serious moment. "Are you going somewhere?"

"We all want to get away, you know. Start over. You're not the only one."

"I don't want to get away. I'm just getting *started* here. This is step one."

"Just think, before you talk shit. Just think, what would life be like without Edwin? You think Marc could handle this on his own?" He spreads his arms and grins, and then he's backing up, out of the hallway, absorbed back into the thick of the party, right beside Marc, and you hear his voice over the crowd noise, Edwin saying, "Shelley fucking *loves* my suggestions, bro. You should read them. You'll laugh your ass off."

And then it's the doorbell, and your hands are shaking you're so fucking furious, and when you open the door to find that it's the furniture deliveryman with his grimy-greasy hands and his clipboard and his stupid blue-collar beard, you're actually delighted. As soon as he starts speaking—"Got a table here for, uh"—you don't let him complete the sentence before you're unleashing your own atomic hydrogen nuclear bomb onto this fucking clown, telling him that he's a worthless piece of shit, that he *does* know that a day is twenty-four hours long, right?, that there's an AM and a PM?, and that a delivery that's twelve hours late is about as unacceptable as performing CPR on a man who's already been embalmed, right?

Right?

Look at me.

And you do know what will happen if there is any damage—*any* damage—to my table this time around? Any damage to my floors, as you bring that table into my house? Any damage to my doorframe? You do realize that my rage won't come in the form of a dissatisfied post-delivery survey, that I will *literally fucking kill you*. I'm half your size, motherfucker, but I'm a wolverine. I will tear into your fucking neck. I will feed on your soul. Give me my dining room table, and then get the *fuck* out of my house and get back to your *shit* home, and your *shit* wife, and your *shit* life that you don't even deserve because you don't know how to fucking tell time, you elementary school son of a bitch.

Silence, then applause from the den of douchebags, affirmation from Edwin and from Jimmy and from Andrea and from Laurie and from Marc, but—though your anger-bomb has dropped, and you couldn't have stopped it even if you had control over gravity itself—you can only close your eyes and say "Excuse me" and rush to your bedroom with your phone in your hand pretending like someone's calling you urgently. You shut the door so no one can see what happens next. Your work friends. The women from Alumni Club. Your fiancé.

Beneath the noise of a hundred other conversations resuming throughout the house, beneath the noise of the iPod docking station speakers, beneath the noise of a beer bottle crashing on the pool deck, beneath the noise of the humiliated delivery team assembling a dining room table half a house away, you unleash a megaton scream into your pillow. The world around you does not hear it, but there are stars in your vision. And when you catch your breath you hold the pillow to your face and scream again.

How did this happen?

How did this happen?

How did this happen that you hate everyone around you?

This is not who you are, you are not yourself.

Or are you?

Is this exactly what you've become?

Are you the problem, the thing that you hate the most?

When you emerge from the bedroom eventually, you pour another drink and you're congratulated by co-workers and stupid bitches alike. Amanda Linda slides next to you and says, "Quite the dismantling of that poor furniture man," and when you look up and into her eyes to see whether she intends this as an insult or a compliment, she flinches and and says, "Honest. I rather enjoyed it. You're not one to cross, dear."

And it's another hour of this, Jimmy calling you "Killer" and then holding up his hands in mock surrender and saying, "Don't hit me! Don't hit me!", your co-worker Greg saying, "Looks like she's ready for the big accounts, eh?" Elaina sort of slinking away when you approach as if fearful of what you might do next.

Another hour, but then the party passes into memory, the house empties. Well, the *people* vacate, but they leave behind a trash heap of upper-middle-class waste. Empty Three Olives bottles. Tipped-over two-liters. Cheese gone hard, brie gone cold like a pool of melted candle wax. Summer sausage slices sitting in grease trails. Party plates discarded in every room, plastic cups on floors, in bathroom sinks.

"Is the house officially warmed?" Marc asks. Suddenly he's behind you, wraps his arms around your waist.

"It's been warmed," you say. "I don't think I want to have another party for a while."

"Why not? That went great."

"I berated the deliveryman."

"You were awesome."

You close your eyes. A year ago, you were doing couples nights at the Enzian. You were doing late-night picnics in Oviedo, searching for those famous Oviedo Lights. You were rolling down Spook Hill. You were doing midnight Swamp Ape hunts. You were Weird Florida. That was you. You were once a beertub girl, sure, but maybe Edwin was right: you weren't trying to force yourself to be anything else. This, the future you're barreling toward, the men, the women you've surrounded yourself with…this *you* that you're becoming…

"Marc," you say, "promise me that when we have children, you'll never refer to Edwin as Uncle Edwin."

His chin is resting on your shoulder, and he kisses your neck. "Where'd that come from?"

"He's just not good, Marc. He's ruinous."

Marc slips his arms from around your waist. "What's this 'when we have kids' stuff?" he asks. "Can you imagine *me-eeee* as a father? God, I wouldn't wish that on my worst enemy."

And in this moment, his vocal inflection matches Edwin's so perfectly that you half-expect him to call you "dude." You understand now, don't you, that for all his good qualities, his ambitions, his passion, the things that so attracted you while you felt like a tiny, disrespected college kid, Marc has by now been on Edwin's douchebag diet so long that his body mass is probably more douchebag than man, and are you prepared to be with that for the rest of your life? You don't expect a *perfect man*, but until now, you'd never have considered calling your fiancé a douchebag. And if you do allow yourself to call him that, there's no turning back. He will be irredeemable, and this house will be irredeemable, this life you've built—no matter how many other girls look at you and commend you for having it all—will be irredeemable. The longer you stay, the angrier and more awful you will become, and it will go on and on.

"I'm going to clean up," you say.

"Awesome. I'll be waiting…" he says, "in the bedroom."

Here you are, Shelley, holding a roll of paper towels and a trash bag and surveying the wreckage left behind by people you never want to see again. You are yourself, Shelley, this is you, but you don't want to be this person anymore, and while you do not yet act on it, it is now that the decision to leave this house and leave your job and leave the city and make a life and a family elsewhere first enters your mind, because there is something toxic here, in this house, in this land, something that has worked its way into you, but you will not let it win, you will not let it consume you, you will not let it win, you will not

IN LESS THAN TWENTY-FOUR HOURS, you'll be married, but right now, right this very second, you are slogging your way through your *bachelor party* (you sigh just thinking these words). Against your own wishes, your extended family—all of them staying on or near Disney property, living it up with 5-day Park Hopper passes—has not simply decreed that you have this ceremonial all-male gathering, but also that you have it *at the parks*. And so you now find yourself deep within the international absurdity of Epcot's World Showcase, "drinking around the world," as the corny tourists say.

"Steven, you cannot have your bachelor party at motherfucking Disney World!" Jimmy argued a few weeks ago. "Please tell me you're joking."

"I didn't even want a bachelor party," you told him. "I went to see a show with some old friends in Gainesville last weekend. Got a hotel. Drank a lot. I told Elaina that was enough. But now I'm stuck entertaining relatives at Disney."

"The relatives are invited to your *bachelor party*?"

"It was *their idea*!"

"You're getting married downtown," Jimmy said. "Why did they get hotels all the way out there?"

"Elaina's family lives in *Texas*," you told him. "I doubt they even want to come to the city proper for the ceremony. We had to charter a bus to drive them from their hotels."

"This is very off-brand for you," Jimmy said.

Understatement of the year. You are Steven Hart, Mr. *Other* City Beautiful, blogging your way through Authentic Orlando one indie sandwich shop at a time, and you *never* go to Disney World, to the Magic Kingdom, to Epcot or Blizzard Beach or Hollywood Studios or Animal Kingdom, never to Disney's Boardwalk, nor Downtown Disney, never to SeaWorld or Universal Studios (special points for not having gone to Halloween Horror Nights in a decade!) or Universal CityWalk, never Pointe Orlando, nor any of the other tourist-sector theme parks and theme-park-malls that make Orlando *Orlando* for the rest of the world, their interior walkways flooded with families rushing to get photos with people in animal suits, or bumping into one another while rushing to hour-long waits at tourist-trap restaurants owned by celebrities and flashing with "gotta have a t-shirt" appeal. These places are hell on Earth.

But here you are: a Friday night bachelor party at Epcot Center. Just three of your own friends (Jimmy, Anderson, Marc) and a Where's Waldo spread of relatives who inspire various degrees of aggravation (your brother Todd, an engineer at Lockheed; Elaina's two brothers, Brandon and Pete, both of whom wear baseball caps low on their brows and constantly push their sleeves up to reveal their biceps and (best of all!) dismissively refer to you as "my sister's hipster boyfriend," a source of endless amusement for them; and finally, your Christian warrior cousins, of whom there are enough to field a football team, offense and defense, and all of whom—predictably— applauded the idea of a family-friendly bachelor party). This entourage is scattered around the grand Mayan pyramid that Disney constructed to represent "Mexico," everyone drinking too-sour margaritas from a quick- service kiosk (the Christian cousins opted for the non-alcoholic slushie, a stomachache in a souvenir cup). Twenty feet away, Jimmy is modeling a gift- shop sombrero and saying "El correcto politico, muchachos!" while Anderson and Marc shake maracas painted with the likeness of Donald Duck. This can only end badly.

You and your brother stand on the edge of the Mexican pavilion, leaning against the railings overlooking Epcot's centerpiece lake. "So when were you gonna tell me you're moving?" Todd asks. This is the first the two of you have spoken in months, mostly because you're not sure *how* to have a conversation with him. Your relationship with your brother is all surface, decades of three- minute conversations that include the words "fine" and "okay," and rarely move beyond thoughts on the weather.

"I didn't know I had to clear everything with my older brother," you say.

"You don't have to clear anything with me. But it'd be nice if you told me."

"Okay," you say. "I'm moving."

"Out of Orlando? You love this city, man. What are you gonna do?"

You shake your head and look out toward the water, whitecaps from all the energy and noise in this place. Somewhere behind you, a mariachi band has drifted out from the pyramid and is playing in the streets. The sky is darkening and twisting to twilight purples. Todd is not being mean-spirited, you know that. He's not capable of it. Still, you hate him for bringing this up, this thing you don't want to think about.

"When are you moving?" he asks.

"Soon. Weeks."

"I can help you pack. Just let me know."

"Fine."

"A big deal, moving out of Orlando. You put all that time into the blog."

Your teeth are clenched. You tell yourself to breathe.

"Did you ever finish that top fifty series?"

"Just do me a favor, Todd. Just…just shut up, okay?"

"What the hell, bro?" he says, face in genuine shock.

You grip the railing tighter, close your eyes. Elaina has accepted a design job in North Carolina with an "artisan furniture start-up" financed by a consortium of celebrities and athletes who want to eventually grow the brand and (in ten years) become a big box to compete with IKEA. As a freelance graphic designer with a side-project blog that will never generate meaningful revenue, how could *you* tell her no?

Oh, Steven. For so long in love with Orlando, with your passion-project blog and your "Make Orlando Weird" campaign. In love with the city, and in love with Elaina. And if the two should be in conflict, who should win?

Not even a discussion. And that's what makes this excruciating. You *want* Elaina to succeed. You want to give her everything you have, and if that means moving to Charlotte and giving up your city, then that's what will happen. This is her shot, *her* dream.

Oh, you. Either the most supportive fiancé (husband, tomorrow) the world has ever seen, or the biggest pussy in the world, having offered no fight, having just said "whatever makes you happy," and then cried on the inside.

Shit. Enough of that.

You'd do anything for her.

It's just…it had to be *this*, didn't it?

"I'm sorry," you say. "There's a lot on my mind."

"I get it. The wedding," he says. "Lot of stress." He slaps your back and steps away, sucking his margarita through the straw, a rubber-band man who snaps back to a good mood like *that*. Moments later, true to form, Todd's chatting up one of the church cousins, your remark forgotten. He stands there with Dull Darrell, one hand in pocket, nodding and smiling, involved in a conversation that—from here—seems so utterly bland that its transcription might bring you to tears. Life is just fine for him, isn't it? Life is just fine for *all* of them.

You try to remember what it was like to be close to them, to feel like family, but you can't. After the wedding, it'll be another few years before you see the cousins again. Are you the only one to whom this feels like a charade? Or are you over-thinking *everything*, by this point?

You're alone at the railing, replaying your brother's comment over and over in your head: "What are you gonna do?" *What* are you gonna do? What are you gonna *do*? In twenty-four hours you and Elaina will be married at the Orange County Regional History Center (which could've been a *great* #1 location for your Top Fifty, now that you think about it), your ceremony in the preserved courtroom on the third floor, the most authentically Orlando wedding anyone could draw up. And yet here you are at Epcot, fake Orlando, fake Mexico. What little time you have left in the only place you've ever called home, and you're *here*.

"Hey Steven, we gotta talk," Jimmy says, materializing beside you. "These guys seriously don't drink?" He points to the blonde-haired, milk-skinned Midwesterners standing beside the coffee and pastry vendor.

"That's what *non-drinker* means," you say.

"They realize they aren't driving? That a couple *margz* won't kill them?"

"I think so."

"Maybe I should, like, slip 'em something."

"Not a good idea, Jimmy. And it worries me that you thought of that."

"Well, shit. How we gonna drink around the world if we're not all drinking?"

"I think we'll survive."

Jimmy takes one last gulp, shakes the ice at the bottom of his cup. "All right, then. One nation at a time, right? Onward!"

Despite never being an option for your Best Man, Jimmy is indeed the de facto leader for the night, summoning all disparate elements of your party. From Mexico, you all press forward into "The Grandeur of Kazakhstan," a camp of flimsy tents and food kiosks likely erected to take advantage of some post-*Borat* interest in a country that otherwise never would've managed to squeak into Epcot's World Showcase. Hell, Russia's not even here. Three of the Earth's continents, in fact, have no representation in the international village. But Kazakhstan is clearly not destined for permanence; once the sales of the "Kazak Bomb" drinks and the beef jerky and the souvenir horse whips slow, this bewildering pop-up encampment will likely be reimagined as an Australian outback or a Pacific island paradise or a African future-market, depending upon what movie is breaking box office records at the moment. Only at Disney could the nations of the world be monetized and hierarchized in such a way.

"Kazak Bombs!" Jimmy yells, trying on his Borat accent. "Verrry nice!"

Anderson and Marc trade movie quotes, and then Elaina's brothers join in with *Anchorman* quotes for some reason, and then you hear some *Wedding Crashers* too, and it's maybe the most depressing thing you've ever witnessed, all the different voices and pantomimes and butchered quotes and guffaws. "Dear God," you whisper to yourself. "Please, are you listening? Please." Briefly, you make eye contact with the girl working the Horse Whip kiosk, and there's an endless sadness in her eyes, too, the agony of smiling through ten thousand unfunny Borat impressions, and you see that sadness and that agony reflecting back and forth like mirrors all the way down into her soul.

You want time to speed up so the night can end.

And suddenly Anderson shoves a Kazak Bomb in your hand and he's dragging you into a shoulder-to-shoulder circle with Marc and Jimmy and Todd and Pete and Brandon, and Jimmy's screaming something about your last night on Earth, *last night on Earth!*, so let's drink like there's no tomorrow, and then the bomb is down your throat and it tastes like sugar and grass and icicles and bonfire smoke and how the fuck is it that you want another?

Disney.

"Onward, my Viking comrades, to motherfucking Norwaaay!" Jimmy bellows.

"Viking *comrades?*" the girl at the kiosk says and shakes her head. She's close to cracking, you can tell.

"Don't judge me," you tell her. "Please don't judge me."

The bachelor party crew is moving. From Kazakhstan to Norway, then to China, where Anderson models the straw hat of the Chinese rice farmer and bounces on his heels like a character out of Mortal Kombat. "I will finish you!" he screams at Marc.

At some point there's a Tsingtao in your hand, and you manage only a single sip before Jimmy yells into a bullhorn (where the fuck did he get that?)—"Germany, mein brothers! The fatherland!"—and you're suddenly walking again, all of you, to the land of lederhosen. For the drinker's Epcot, Germany—giant pretzels and tall beers in the biergarten—is a sort of capital. No other nation's pavilion seems to suggest the notion of "drinking around the world" quite like Germany, but to get there, you must pound through the sea of sweaty tourists, their just-purchased merchandise gleaming everywhere like the floating remains on the ocean surface after a cruise ship catastrophe. Tea pots. Kimonos. Soccer jerseys. Samurai swords.

"It's so damn corny," you say to Anderson as you walk.

"I don't know why you hate Disney. This is a blast."

"*This*? Are you kidding me?"

Anderson ruffles your hair. "At least we didn't make you take pictures with the princesses."

Soon enough, your bachelor party crew makes it through the crowds and into Germany, and once again, Jimmy's ordering drinks for everyone, and once again, he mistakenly orders beers for the cousins, thrusts cups into their hands and says "sorry, sorry" like he forgot they don't drink alcohol but hey, whatareyougonnado?, and they're left trying to return the beers to the St. Pauli girl at the kiosk.

You're allowing yourself one more drink. But because you drove—*drove*, to your own bachelor party!—this has gotta be the last one, which means that, after the next twenty ounces, you'll endure the remainder of the hell that Disney pours upon you without the blessed aid of any intoxicants.

As you settle against a dark wooden post and swirl your Hefeweizen, wanting only to enjoy a moment to yourself after an evening of asses-to-elbows crowds, you see your worst nightmare approaching: Elaina's brother Brandon.

Though they also live within a half-hour of the parks, you barely know either brother. Still, you've felt pressured to maintain a squeaky-clean image around them, as they've entrusted you with their precious sister.

"I like your friend Jimmy," Brandon says and wraps his arm around your shoulders. It's a power move; he's a former collegiate baseball player, and he likes you to have a close look at his massive forearms. "Thought this night was gonna be lame, but that cat knows how to party."

Brandon's arm-hair tickles your nose, but if you try to fight him off, you'll only embarrass yourself. "Good thing my friends are cooler than me," you say.

"No argument here," Brandon says, finally letting you free. You've spilled only a negligible amount of beer, so you count yourself lucky. "So tell me, brother-in-law. Where you gonna work in North Carolina?"

"I'm freelance. Have to find local clients, but I can still do long-distance with a lot of my current base."

"Sounds precarious."

"Good word, Brandon."

"You talking shit? Growing a backbone, hipster?"

"No," you say, but you were answering the first question, not the second, and this is why her brothers think you're a jellyfish.

"The blog, then: is it done-zo?"

"Done-zo?"

"I've read that shit. 'Make Orlando Weird.' All the crap about authenticity, local-grown culture. How's that gonna fly if the author's living in Charlotte?"

"I'd rather not talk about it right now, man."

"Did you finish the list?" he asks.

The list. Years of your life spent before the keyboard, hunched over, positioning photos and inserting hyperlinks and responding to comments. More hours invested in that damn list than in any other relationship you've had in your life, your forthcoming marriage included. You can't tell if Brandon's joking, if he's trying to get under your skin, but you answer honestly. "No. I've got one more posting."

"Holy shit, *one* more? Number one spot? Some timing!"

You nod. Yes, years leading to this, the moment when you were supposed to publish the final blog post in the series, the #1 spot. Anticipation heavy among lovers of all things Authentic Orlando. But that #1 spot? Does it matter now?

"Kinda sucks, huh," Brandon says. "Leaving just as it's done."

There's a "FUCK YOU" that wants to come out, but you swallow it.

"Well, for what it's worth," Brandon says, "I tried out some of the places on your list. Beefy King. The coffee place. I go there every day now."

"Huh," you say.

"Some bullshit prices, so I steal Splenda packets and toilet paper rolls just to get my money's worth."

"Of course you do."

"Looking forward to that #1 spot, little buddy." He punches your arm. It hurts like hell, a knuckle to flesh collision that tremors all the way into your belly and up to your brain, but there's something encouraging about it, too, and about the conversation, like maybe he's warming to the idea of you as a brother. Of course, upon further consideration, there's also something unsettling about the revelation that Elaina's a-hole brothers now frequent *your* favorite places, that they might be the reason why you can no longer find a barstool at Fifty Brews, or a table at Pom Pom's during lunch.

You think you've managed through the obligatory brother-in-law conversation and now you're free to enjoy your beer, but Elaina's other brother Pete emerges next, and so Brandon stays put, and they surround you. "Sup, hipster," Pete says, and moves to fake-punch your gut.

You flinch, then say, "Good morning." (You feel obligated to give snarky responses, to never allow yourself to be serious around them, but it's wearying.)

Pete has typically been more aggressive than Brandon, despite being about six inches shorter and less athletic. It's as if the same asshole ingredients were packed into a smaller space, their taste more pungent as a result. "You should write *this* place up on the blog," Pete says. "Drinking around the world."

"That's what *I'm* talking about," Brandon says.

"Yeah, that's not exactly what I do—"

"Too good for Disney?" Pete asks.

"No, I just—"

"Everything's gotta be fucking *indie* with you."

"Not *everything* is—"

"This right here," and Pete holds up his beer, "Bud *Heavy*. Hiked all the way over to *America* to get it. Love this shit. Red label. Patriotic. But you hate it, don't you? It offends your hipster sensibilities. Gotta drink shit that was brewed in some hemp farmer's garage."

"Drink whatever you—"

"Hey, so anyway, the reason I'm over here," Pete says. "Uncle Jesse texted. They're at the tequila bar in Downtown Disney."

"I don't know Uncle Jesse," you say.

"*Our* Uncle Jesse," Pete says. "He's the man."

"Epcot's closing soon, right?" Brandon asks. "Downtown Disney's open late. Feels like a natural progression to me."

"I don't want to—"

"Uncle Jesse's buying shots," Pete says.

"Verrry nice," Brandon says, and the Borat impressions are back, dear God. "How do we get there? Trams?"

"Hipster hasn't been drinking much," Pete says and backhands your chest. "He drove."

"Oh," you say, like the blood has all drained from your body. "Oh no." Nothing sounds less appealing than this, extending your night, further torture on Disney property, further encounters with Wisconsinites who smell of thickly applied sunscreen, further fights for a place in line at a restaurant that smells like ribs or fried shrimp or hamburgers, but somehow not genuine, like they're just pumping an artificial smell to make everyone *think* they're eating ribs on Beale Street, or coconut shrimp in Key West. No, please no. "I said I don't want—"

"Your last chore," Pete tells you, "in the service of your new family. After this, we will gladly accept you, and all your quirky eccentricities, as our brother."

"If we remember tomorrow," Brandon adds.

"Drive us to Downtown Disney," Pete says, "and *boom:* you are family."

"Wait," you say. "You just want me to drop you off? Not drink?"

"You wanna catch an early bedtime, brother, that's your choice," Pete says.

"Well, then." You look around and can't find a single member of the entourage except Todd. This is your *one chance* to bail. For the last hour, Jimmy's been urging you to come downtown afterward and get wasted, and you've smiled and declined, but that motherfucker is so persistent. So you grab Todd, who you'd earlier picked up from his resort, and you're off, pushing out of the World Showcase, past Epcot's iconic golfball, to the trams, the parking lot, with these three men who are all kind of your brothers, but kind of not.

"Why the hurry?" Todd asks.

"I've still got a lot to do before tomorrow," you say.

"You probably should've just planned your wedding down here. It would've been so much easier."

"But that's—" You stop yourself. What's the point?

Minutes later, you're pulling into the neighborhood-sized parking lot for Downtown Disney, a walled pseudo-city of Disney-approved money-sucks. Celebrity restaurants, Lego stores, candy cauldrons. You picture yourself on the "streets" of Downtown Disney, everywhere you move the crowds congealing around you, *American Idol* rejects wearing headset microphones and belting out pop hits from makeshift stages. No thank you.

"Goodbye," you tell your brothers-in-law. "Good luck in there!"

Brandon's leaning over your window. "No shots? You're sure?"

"Positive."

"Number one spot, I'm telling you," Brandon says. "Get some Disney on that blog, and that shit'll take off."

"This is everything my blog is *not*. The money these people are spending on this bullshit…if we took those dollars to places in the city that really deserve it…"

"The fuck's it matter?" Pete asks from farther away, his voice diminishing as he walks. "Shit's over. You're off to North Carolina."

"Burn," Brandon says, and steps back from the car.

"I—" you say, but they're gone. It's just you and Todd in the car, and he's scrolling through his phone, oblivious to the whole exchange. "Damn it," you say instead. "Damn it!" and slam your hands on the wheel.

"It's all right," Todd says from the passenger seat, looking over now. "They're messing with you, but Pete and Brandon, they're your brothers now."

"Yeah," you say. "Cool."

But it's sinking in now, isn't it?

You probably knew it from the moment you agreed to move, but still you've spent the last week or two asking whether the blog still has a chance at life, whether you might be able to change the city from afar, after you move to North Carolina, or is there a chance that *Elaina* can work remotely, that you can *stay* here? Or, maybe, is there a shot that you can return here in two years, three, that you can return to your blog, that you will be celebrated, not forgotten…is there a chance that you mattered, that you could *still* matter?

But really, you know it's over, the dream of The Other City Beautiful. You put the car back into drive, ready to drop off your brother at Coronado Springs, thankful the bachelor party is over, and that—in fifteen minutes, when you exit the Disney property—you will no longer feel like a sell-out.

As you leave the Downtown Disney parking lot, you watch a couple twenty-somethings in Tennessee Volunteers t-shirts hijack a "SLOW – PEDESTRIANS" sign from the crosswalk. It's a portable sign, but heavy, weighed down by the sort of shit used for roadwork signs in construction zones. In other words, it's not meant to be lifted by human hands, and it takes both of these ass pirates to lift it six inches off the ground. And they're trying to run with it, even make you slam on the brakes as they trudge past with their stolen sign. A couple hundred feet away is an old security guard on his walkie talkie, witnessing the theft but unable to do more than raise his hand impotently and say, "Hey there. Hey there. You're not supposed to take that!"

You let your foot off the brake pedal, still watching them grunt and tug and take tiny lumbering steps through the parking lot, still transfixed by the idiocy of the vandalism, and when you turn your head back to the road there's someone in the crosswalk and you slam on your brakes. "What the frick, man?" you hear the guy say, and he spreads his arms wide. You wave, mouth "sorry," but then you notice the t-shirt he's wearing: "Keep Disney Weird!" With Mickey and Goofy beneath the letters, the ghosts and ghouls of the Haunted Mansion spilling around them, Donald running away in terror.

"No," you say. "God no."

This place. A hell that keeps on punishing.

Deep breath. Foot off the brakes, and then you're driving your brother back to his room.

"Sleep well," Todd says before he heads inside. "Biggest day of your life tomorrow."

"Is it?" you ask.

"That's what they say."

"Who's 'they,' Todd?"

Your brother squints in confusion, like he's trying to read a blurry computer screen. "I don't understand. What are you so upset about?"

"Who says I'm upset?"

"All night, you've been acting like an asshole. We got together to celebrate *you*."

You shake your head. "It's this place." You don't say "Isn't it obvious? Doesn't this place get to you, too?" but you hope your voice conveys it.

"I just don't understand the anger," Todd says. "This was a fun night."

"What anger are you—" you start, but then take a deep breath and change course. "Good night, Todd. I don't want to have this discussion. I just want to get a good night's sleep."

"Is this because the parents are here?"

"What? No."

"Is this about Dad? About moving so much? You're an adult now, man. You can't keep complaining about that your whole life. Be happy."

"You really don't know me at all, do you? This has nothing to do with that." You're putting all of your energy into a stranglehold on the steering wheel. "Please. I would like to go now. I will see you tomorrow, okay?"

"All right," Todd says, and you breathe easier when your brother is out of the car; you loosen your grip on the wheel and the blood returns to your fingers. Perspiration has broken out across your forehead, so you turn the AC to max, then cruise back down the two-lane road from your brother's resort to Buena Vista, which will lead you to I-4 and back to your condo downtown. Back to the real Orlando, to a place where you are human again.

The resorts are on the left side of the road, thick trees on the right, a sort of natural-world buffer between the resort communities and the highways. It should be an uneventful drive out of this place, but something's wrong. Up ahead, shapes move among the trees at road's edge. Deer? Does Disney allow deer to roam the property? Certainly they can control such a thing, right? Animatronic deer? You let the car coast to 35, just in case. The last thing you want is to slay Bambi and ruin some kid's magical vacation.

But when you round the bend, you see that it's a cluster of boys—high-school-age, eight of them, maybe—standing together on the curb and laughing and pointing at your car, and why the hell are they so close to the road, *in the road* like it's no different than the super-safe car-free walkways of Downtown Disney? Then one of the boys shoves another into the road, *directly* into your lane, and you shriek and jerk the steering wheel left to avoid the kid, and now you're suddenly in the opposite lane and then pounding over the curb and scratching against a speed limit sign, your side-mirror snapped off, and you're swerving back into the road—headlights coming at you, a bus—and you're swerving, fish-tailing, before you stop the car in your own northbound lane again, and breathe, breathe…

In your rearview mirror you see the kids, see them still in the road high-fiving. They're all wearing matching t-shirts. Maybe this is a band trip, or Key Club, or soccer, high school jerk-offs from Atlanta or Jacksonville or Alabama, a heap of them brought to Orlando without parental supervision. When you open the car door and run at them screaming, they scatter and you have no chance of catching them. "Fuck you!" you scream at the vanishing shapes. "Fuck you, you little fucking pussies! Go home! Go back wherever you came from!"

Downtown Disney. The parks, the resorts. Forty-two thousand acres of safety. Oh, just do whatever you want because this is *Theme Park City* where all is safe and no punishment will be visited upon you and everyone is a customer and everyone is entitled and everyone is the worst possible human they can be. Go ahead, play chicken with the passing cars!

There is no changing this, not ever. The city's visitors will always be this way, and they will keep coming, keep coming, keep coming.

And now the stoplight a block away has turned green, and there are buses and SUVs headed your way, other vacationers shuttling from dinner and drinks and Cirque du Soleil shows to their hotels, and it's *you* they see, still standing in the road like a maniac. So you collect your broken-off side mirror and run back to your car, the headlights growing larger before you. As you pull away, you see dark shapes in the trees, gathering again to try another round of chicken with one of the approaching vehicles.

What was the point of an Orlando manifesto anyway? you finally allow yourself to think. Do you want *more* of these people coming to Orlando? Do you want them streaming into *downtown*, into the *real* city, taking over your coffee shop, taking over your Beefy King? Won't building the city's image just bring developers to Mills/50 to tear down city blocks for new mixed-use developments, new high-rise condos overtaking artists' warehouses? All that you love? Won't your online opus destroy what's authentic and true? The thought is terrible, but it will not go away.

It stays with you as you careen down I-4, past the damned mouse-ear electrical towers (at which so many visitors squeal with delight, like it's the city's Gateway Arch or Statue of Liberty) and Central Casting and the I-Drive t-shirt shops; and just as you approach the "Orlando" sign at Millenia, it finally hits you, and a feeling of manic joy washes over you. You've decided on your #1 spot in the "Fifty Places in Orlando That Define the *Real* Orlando."

Drum roll, please!

Downtown Disney.

Yes! The corporate monster, the antithesis of all that your blog stands for.

Because it isn't just the visitors, either, is it? In Central Florida, there are hordes of Disney fanatics roaming about, hordes of mini-vans stamped with Annual Passholder bumper stickers, hordes of fierce advocates for Gay Days or the Epcot Food and Wine Festival, hordes of homeowners whose living rooms overflow with Disney DVDs and Disney stuffed characters and Disney paintings and whose lawns, come Christmastime, are crowded with inflatable Santa Mickeys, hordes of retirees who still work Main Street USA retail 20 hours a week just to be a part of it all, hordes, hordes, hordes who make this region into the Mickey Mouse Town that civic leaders desperately want to convince the world it's not. It's a lie to say that any "Other Orlando" is the "*Real* Orlando," isn't it?

Yes. For years you've taken readers to places best defined as indie, alternative, off-the-beaten-path, hidden, local, homegrown. A constant argument for culture and blah blah blah. But the place that best defines Orlando? Maybe it *is* Disney. A place that—as the #1 spot on your *Orlandofesto*—will sap you of street cred and undermine all the work you've done.

Its inclusion will bring about the end. End of the manifesto. End of the blog. Yes, you are going to kill your blog. Kill it fucking *dead*!

You don't matter. You are not the Chosen One. You could write a million more blog posts, and what will it all be worth? A trillion more comments on message boards. A waste, all of it. You don't matter, except to the woman who believes in you, who fights for you no matter your project. The woman, more importantly, that *you* believe in.

And so, on the morning of your wedding, you'll click "delete" on the draft you've been working on for years, all your ideas and anecdotes for the perfect #1 spot, and type some bullshit about the gloriousness of the parks, and by the time you return home from your honeymoon, you'll click "delete" on the whole damn site, zap it into the place where old web pages go to die, the internet dead zone, and it'll be glorious.

And that's why, when you arrive at the History Center for the ceremony, you are glowing, *glowing*, lit from within by the freedom to end your misguided conquest of the city, to love a person and not a concept.

And then

You are Gatorland.

Xanadu.

Walt Disney.

Justin Timberlake.

You are Wesley Snipes.

You are John Young. John Hitt. John Morgan, for the people.

Mike Bianchi.

You are Dog-lando, and Cake-lando, and Car-lando, and Porn-lando, and a thousand other landos...

You are Shaq, mumbling his way through the nineties.

You are Aaron Jernigan, and you are a murderer, and no one knows that, do they? The original homesteader, the man who settled the land, who made it all possible, and you...

Oh ho ho! Gather 'round, children, and hear Jernigan's awful tale!

YOU…

You…

You…

You are awakened by your cell phone at 4:56 AM, and though you try to ignore it, the caller is insistent. The phone rings again and again and again, and so finally you succumb. You grab the phone, answer it, and it's Jimmy: "Hey bro," he says. He sounds drunk, and not just had-some-drinks drunk; no, his level of intoxication is definitely appropriate for the hour at which he's dialing.

"I'm sleeping, Jimmy," you say. "What do you want?"

"I'm, uh," he starts, and you can picture his eyes wandering, his mind falling into dark pits before somehow clawing back out and regaining direction. "I'm outside your house."

"You're what?"

"In my car. I'm parked at your curb."

You can feel the last wisps of a good night's sleep falling away, sand grains through your fingers. It feels as if you've been sleeping for days, weeks even, as if this body has been on autopilot while your mind has been elsewhere. There are memories returning, but they are as elusive as old dreams in the light of morning, and you're unsure which are real, which are yours, which belong to others. Memories. You and Steven at the coffee shop. You and Kyle at a school bus race. And were you at Disney last night?

"Jimmy," you say.

"Dude," he says.

"Maybe I shouldn't even bother asking," you say and look at your clock again, "but what the hell are you doing outside my house?" Nothing makes sense right now, but it seems like *forever* since anything's made sense.

"I need, um," he says. "I need a place to, like, crash for a while."

You toss the sheets from your body and stagger across the length of your house to the front door, your wood floors cold under the air conditioning. But now you remember this, at least: last night, your friends left Disney to go drinking downtown, but *you* drove home early, called it a night and fell asleep watching *Entourage* reruns. You were not yourself last night, but you are now, and the tiles of the foyer beneath your feet feel right. This is your world, Marc Turner, your life, and you are in control of your body once again.

When you open the door, Jimmy's car is indeed parked on the street, headlights off, dark shape in the driver's seat. You walk to the curb, hold your arms out and say, "What's the deal? It's 5 AM." You're spotlighted by the streetlamp, as if this is your dramatic monologue about to begin.

The driver-side door pops open. A little at first, and then it falls shut, as if Jimmy lost his grip. Then it opens again and Jimmy emerges from the car in one fluid motion like smoke from a bottle, and he's all smiles. "Hey buddy," he says, pushing himself against his side mirror in a way that makes you think the door will shut and his hands will be caught and there will be blood. But he's drunk Jimmy, and nothing bad ever happens to drunk Jimmy.

"Did you *drive* here?" you ask.

"Huh?"

"Did you drive all the way from downtown?"

"I drive better when I'm drunk," he says, and makes a dismissive motion with his hand.

"Nobody drives better when they're drunk. You could've killed someone."

"Could've, but *didn't*. That's life. Game of inches and all that. So listen, bro," Jimmy says. "I need, like, a huge favor."

"You need a couch to crash on?" You don't understand why he drove all the way here, past his house in College Park, but it's tough to unravel the logic of a drunk man.

"No," he says. "Well, yes. But more than that."

"Do tell."

"Come here," he says and come-hithers with his finger.

"Out into the street?"

"Come here," he says again and winks, sloshing back and forth against that side mirror; you expect to see alcohol literally spilling from his ears like his head's a too-full glass.

"What's in there?" You step from your driveway to the street, and shuffle around the front of his car, joining him as he leans against the mirror and points at his driver-side window; your gaze follows the direction of his outstretched finger until you're staring inside the car, staring at a woman passed out in the passenger seat, slumped down so far that the seatbelt acts as a noose around her neck.

"Um," you say.

"I, like, have a problem," he says.

She's dead, you know it, and Jimmy is going to ask if you have a chainsaw... tonight, you will be forced to chop her apart, stuff her into trash bags, carry her to some alligator farm on the outskirts of Orlando. "Is she dead?" you ask him, choking on your words.

"What?" he asks, sliding away from the door, away from you, looking suddenly sober and reasonable. "Dead? What? No. Come on, man, get your head out of the gutter."

"I just..."

"Naw, bro, I need somewhere to take her."

You shake your head. "You could, um, take her *home*?"

"Are you blind? She's fucking passed out. I couldn't even wake her to ask where she lives."

"What were you doing with her in your car to begin with?"

"Questions, questions," he says and slaps your shoulder. "Listen, I can't take her to my place, obviously. Sandra would freak. And I can't, like, push her out of my car and just leave her someplace. That would be messed up, I think. So help me out. Let's get her inside till she wakes up."

You know that your friend is a scumbag, that—if there were some way to chart douchebaggery, to plot it on a spectrum like political ideology—he would certainly be at one far end of the spectrum, the douchiest of the douche-canoes. And you know that he was cheating on his wife tonight, again, that this pile of glitter and lipstick and hair and heels collapsed in the passenger seat like dirty laundry was not an innocent and friendly encounter, two people shooting the shit and then one of them offering the other a ride. She was not even another human being to Jimmy, but instead a warm body he hoped to ride hard. And while there are elements of this scenario that even now—in this moment—play out as fantasy in your mind (what if this girl wakes up, and she's beautiful, and she looks at you like you've saved her, and then she wants to have sex as gratitude?), there is more *good* than *bad* in you. You have to believe this about yourself. You have to believe that there is good in you, that the proper choices can earn redemption against the debt of all your mistakes, that it's never too late.

And so this is the one thing you know right now: you should not be so quick to accommodate your friend. You should not enable him. Marc, seriously. You should be on the phone with his wife, telling her the truth for her own well-being as a woman; you should not be worming into the deplorable position of accomplice. If you do, you are terrible, flat-out *terrible*, because—after all this—you fucking *know better*. You know who you are, have seen from a thousand angles the sad shape of your character, and you understand how to stop the corrosion. This is real life. You are yourself again. Will you do what's right?

Yes. You picture yourself sending Jimmy away, standing triumphant and noble in your driveway as he swerves back down the—

Shit. What about the other drivers on the road? And what about the girl?

Shit shit shit.

God, why can't anything be fucking *simple*?

You don't know if it's right or wrong, your best judgment or your worst, but you tell Jimmy "*okay*, come on inside."

And because Jimmy is so drunk that he's falling on his ass every few steps, it is *you* who must unbuckle his plaything's seatbelt, who must gingerly unwrap her from the car's embrace, slide her from the seat—her skirt catching on the door and you see her full ass exposed and there's a part of you that wants it to be sexy, flesh blue-lit by moonlight, but another part of you is ashamed that you looked. You lift her out, carry her, fingers on the skin of her smooth legs, the fabric of her skirt brushing against you. In a sexual fantasy, her arms would be wrapped around your neck. In a sexual fantasy, she would be curled up cute, eyes open and staring at you, so thankful, so ready to repay the favor you've done her. But here in your arms her mouth is open so wide that you hope she doesn't swallow a bug.

"Get the door," you tell Jimmy, and he does. You lay the girl across the couch, put her into a comfortable sleeping position, stretch the bottom of her skirt so she's not exposed.

"I'm gonna go to sleep," he says, lumbering down the hall toward your guest room.

"You can't go in there," you say. "Kyle's in there, sleeping."

"Who?"

"*Kyle.* My brother."

"You have a brother?"

"For the love of…Jimmy, you met him the other night."

"Where am I supposed to sleep?"

You hold up your hands. There's no furniture in the other bedrooms, and you won't let him sleep out here with this girl. You're not going to wake up Kyle, though chances are that this early-morning racket has roused him already. "Go to my bedroom," you say.

"Your bedroom? I'm not gay, homeboy."

"Neither am I. But I'm awake," you say. "In it for the long haul, unfortunately. I'm gonna make some coffee and get caught up on—I don't know, something. Just…go get some sleep so you don't look like a complete asshole when you go home to your wife. When this—" you point to the girl— "when *she* wakes up, I'll drive her home."

"Thanks, buddy."

"I'm doing this for her, not for you." You think you sound authoritative as you make this statement, that this excuses your sexual fantasies and your enabling of your idiot friend. You think that you are a moral and ethical man. A Man. You think your father would be proud. For a few seconds, you allow yourself this reassuring thought, but then you squash it because it too is another fantasy, isn't it?

"You got extra pillows?" Jimmy asks.

After a terse stare-down in which you offer no answer, Jimmy forgets what he asked and stumbles to your bedroom. Blessed with silence and this hard-earned reprieve from your friend, you make coffee, then take a seat on the sofa chair and read emails on your laptop. Then you read some online sports news. Then you come to the end of the internet, and decide that you want the day to start for this girl, too, so you can drive her home and be rid of her; so you unload the dishwasher, each plate clanking hard against the last, silverware a metal cacophony. But still the girl doesn't wake, only shifts on the couch, one arm drifting from stomach to cushion to floor.

And then the second coffee pot is at the end of its brew cycle, steam and that gurgling noise like it's dying, whole house smelling of Starbucks Breakfast Blend, and still she's unconscious, and it's now 6:45 AM on a Saturday and you wonder if she's one of those college-aged never-worked-a-day-in-my-life types who can sleep till noon, no sweat.

You stir the creamer and Splenda into your fifth or sixth cup of coffee, and you take another scalding sip. How much of your day will this consume?

If last night was the bachelor party at Disney, that means tonight is Steven's wedding. Shelley will be there…You remember that you wanted to be well-rested. You wanted to do the chicken dance, the electric slide. You know that Shelley is planning to move to San Diego. You know that this is the last time you might ever see her. You want to tell her that you're not sunk, you're a fighter. You want her to see the fight in your eyes, the future. Maybe a moment will present itself for you to make some climactic declaration to her about who you will be. You picture your entire life going differently if you are just able to spend a night with Shelley, if you are able to speak to her and maybe convince her to sit at your table, and maybe…can you imagine that far ahead without getting light-headed? You feel more like yourself than ever, alive with anticipation, with a chance to change everything.

Except.

Except right now, you're sitting in your sofa chair five feet from a passed-out 21-year-old, sipping coffee from a Wachovia mug and flipping through an old issue of *GQ*. It's the Fall Fashion issue, and everything is scarves and jackets and flannel and your air-conditioning kicks on every ten minutes and you wonder why you subscribe to these New York publications even though you live in a year-round sauna that will never be New York, a place where Fall Fashion is really the same as Summer Fashion and Spring Fashion.

You sip your coffee again, and when you look past the pages of an interview with James Franco, you see that your houseguest's eyes have opened.

"Oh," you say and you toss the magazine onto the table.

Her eyes are wide open, but she hasn't moved.

"Hello," you say. "Um. I'm…"

Her eyes dart from side to side, and she notices her body sprawled along the couch, the blanket you've given her somehow kicked to her feet, her legs bare and her skirt hiked up, her shirt bunched up, belly-button and stomach visible for all the world to see, the tanned flesh color of her stomach fading at waistline to never-seen-the-sun white.

"Who *are* you?" she asks, and her legs are regaining life, kicking so that she can back up against the couch's armrest, blanket hitting the floor. Her arms cover her chest, like someone has yanked off her clothing.

"I'm, uh…" you start, and this isn't a good start.

"Where the fuck *am* I?" she asks, eyes searching all around, and what is this place telling her? What is her frame of reference? This is bad. This is going to be very bad. "Who the fuck *are* you?" she asks, leg whipping around and knocking over your lamp.

"Listen, I'm Jimmy's friend," you say, and you half-rise from your chair but she scoots back even more terrified so you stop there, don't stand entirely. Jimmy's friend? Is that how you want to be identified? "I'm Marc. This is my house," you try.

The room is dark now, the lamp on the floor, its power cord ripped from the socket.

"Jimmy," she says and her eyes burn with distrust. "I don't know any Jimmy," and she's slithering off the couch, tumbling to the floor and the fullness of her ass is now on display as her skirt rips, and you hold out your hand in the best *be calm* gesture you can manage, but she's crawling on the rug now, crawling away from you and making a horrible scared-mumble noise—"ah, ah, ah, ah!"—that doesn't yet qualify as a scream, and she's crawling, and looks like one of those clumsy female victims in a horror movie that get axed super-quick because they don't ever think to stand up and dart away, only stumble and crawl on the ground.

"It's okay," you say and now you stand, too. "You got here with Jimmy, and—"

But now she's standing also, all the way over in your kitchen, and she's gone from Victim to Heroine, grabbing your butcher's knife from the block. "Stay away!" she screams. "You stay the *fuck* away from me, do you *hear me*?" And she swings the butcher's knife even though she's twenty feet away.

"Please, please," you say, arms in front of you like a hostage negotiator. "Please just listen."

"Stay the fuck away from me!" she screams and she sprints to your porch door, fiddling with the lock and panting and looking back over at you like you're going to get her so she's got to be quick and smart, but you're not even moving, and then the door opens unexpectedly and she collapses out to the porch, and through the vertical blinds you can't see her fall, but you hear an "oof" and clanging metal and a sound like raw beef slapped against the countertop, and then an "Ahh! Ahh! Ahh!" and footsteps and the screen door opening and then slamming shut.

You're still standing, still have the coffee mug in your hand, but you haven't taken a single step. Did all of this just happen? You look around. Your bedroom door is closed; your guest bedroom door is closed; Jimmy and Kyle still seem to be asleep, despite the noise. You wake up, finally feeling like yourself again, and this is what you're given?

"For fuck's sake," you say, and you wipe your forehead, then walk to the porch door. You step slowly, half-expecting her to lunge at you from around the corner with the butcher's knife, but when you peer outside, she's gone. The knife sits on the floor of your patio, its blade darkened by a strip of blood and a large chunk of purple fabric from her skirt. Along the floor, leading to the screen door and the backyard: a trail of blood droplets. It's nothing gratuitous, not like a scene from *Dawn of the Dead*, but God, this really happened. Some blood on the backyard stone steps, too, and another piece of fabric—more skirt?—hanging from your vinyl fence. Her shoes are probably still in your living room, along with her purse, but she's now running through the backyards of Stoney Creek wearing only a tight club shirt and half a skirt, and she's bloody like she escaped a serial killer, and the sun is still barely pinking the horizon.

You hear rustling from behind you, and again your first thought is that there's an attacker somewhere, so convincing was her terror. Did she know something about your house that *you* don't?

"What was all that?" It's just Kyle, still in his boxers, shuffling through the living room. "Why the hell are you up so early?"

"I don't know," you say.

"Whose purse is that?"

"I don't know."

He's at your side, staring at the porch with you. "Is that blood? Holy shit, Marc, what happened out here?"

"Just leave it," you say. "We're going to let Jimmy clean this up."

"What the hell *happened*?"

"It's okay," you say. "I feel like I've been away, but I'm here now. I'm ready… I'm…Everything is going to be okay. You can trust me, Kyle."

You want to feel these words, want them to animate you, want the world to quiet and watch as you take the stage and act out the role for which you've prepared and practiced. You want this to be a moment, you and your brother, the Earth growing brighter at the horizon as the sun rises and you stand beside him and radiate with goodness. But as you take in one long breath and think of grandiose comments to make, there is a crashing noise against your roof, and then a golf ball skittering from shingles to the porch screen over your pool, and it rolls softly to a rest on the flat middle over the pool's deep end.

"The fuck?" Kyle says, looking around, searching beyond your backyard for the source of the golf ball. Yours is not a golf course home. The ball came from so far away that you can't even imagine its origin. "Ain't that some luck? It's not gonna move, is it?" Kyle asks, now pointing to the screen. "Stuck there. Just stuck there."

"No," you say. "I see it. I see the ball moving." It *has* to.

"Want me to spray it off with the hose?"

There. There! It's rolling. No. "I see the ball moving," you say, and how you want to believe it. You'd wait here forever, if only it would

L ate Saturday morning.

It's just hours after a young woman woke shrieking on your couch, and now you're in suit and tie, dizzy and foggy and still re-acclimating to your birth-born body, driving I-4 toward downtown on your way to Steven's wedding where your friends—all of them, Steven and Anderson and Jimmy and Sandra and Edwin and Shelley—will be gathered in one place. The whole damn cast, but it's Shelley and Edwin that matter most. The two of them. Before the night is over, you've got to find them. This could be your last chance to confront either of them, to make the world right.

As you drive, you get a phone call from your realtor, Samantha.

"The Wild Berry offer fell through," she tells you.

That was your lifeline, the cash to get you through a couple more months.

"I figured," you say.

"We'll have to lower the asking price if we don't get another offer soon. That'll put us into short-sale territory. You'll have to bring money to the table, if you really want to get rid of it."

"I know." You're at a red light now. You close your eyes, try to remember what it was like to be someone else. "It's all over, isn't it?"

"Don't get discouraged," she says. "We got that offer on Lake Nona, too, asking price. So things aren't as bleak as they could be."

"I can't keep doing this," you say. "I need to..."

"Other news," she says. "There's interest in your Stoney Creek property."

"My home?" She called it a "property," as if it's a thing to be bought and sold. This is the place you eat and sleep, this is your present and your future, this is the last shred of Shelley that hasn't been torn from you. "My house isn't on the market."

"The area is hot, I told you. After our last conversation, I sent around some feelers, got some comps. Your house has amazing square footage, solid amenities, an enviable neighborhood. Turnkey ready. The market for homes in that income bracket still has a heartbeat."

"So I'm supposed to sell the one thing I have that matters," you say, "just because it's the one thing that'll sell?"

You know it's over between you and Shelley, and she'd never move back into that tomb of yours, but you can't shake the feeling that…maybe there's a shot…This house…everything you built…maybe you *can* rise again, if only you have her by your side.

"You'd be selling for profit, Marc."

"My house is not for sale," you tell her. "My house is my house."

•

Saturday afternoon in downtown Orlando.

Both the wedding and the reception are taking place here in the History Center, a structure built in the late 1920s as the Orange County Courthouse and which tries hard to convey the power of justice: stone façade, high arched windows, thick columns, and broad ledges from which you imagine gangster-movie criminals crawling to escape their "guilty" verdict. Back then, it was probably the biggest building in town. Now it's lost in the shadows of the metal and glass skyscrapers around it. The new courthouse is a half-mile away on Orange Avenue, 23 stories tall, a high-rise free of early-century ornamentation, instead designed as if it desperately wants to leave the twentieth century behind, bright blue glass windows rising from the ground like reflective landing strips to a new Orlando that the old courthouse couldn't even imagine.

On the History Center's third floor is a large chamber, once a functioning courtroom, now preserved as life-sized diorama, and it is here where you currently find yourself sitting in anticipation of Steven's wedding ceremony. A hundred and fifty people fill the wooden gallery seats, but for all you care, it's just Shelley and Edwin. You alternate looks between Shelley on the bride's side, Edwin on the groom's.

The gallery seats are varnished wood, creaky and uncomfortable as church pews, some etched with the initials of teenagers, others bejeweled with petrified gum, decades of high school field trip vandalism. Before history becomes valuable, it must first be forsaken, a scene that's played out in Orlando again and again, what little history the city has torn down and then (years later) its loss lamented. A few years back, there was an uproar over the San Juan Hotel near Wall Street, a tall brick building like something out of a Dick Tracy comic strip, outdoor fire escapes and all that, remarkably unprofitable for its owners and in dire need of renovation and repair, and so demolished. And lately, there's the "Save the Round Building" campaign that Steven never shuts up about. But this place has prevailed somehow, against all odds. Steven and Elaina will be exchanging vows in front of the judge's bench, and (as the wedding program informs you) they will be "standing in the exact spot as Ted Bundy when he was set to receive his second death sentence for the murder of Kimberly Leach, and asked witness Carole Ann Boone to marry him. If you look closely, you can see Bundy's name carved into the defendants' table." They're a bizarre couple, Elaina and Steven. They share an irreverence that breaks every rule you'd once devised for how your life should proceed.

Your own wedding with Shelley was supposed to have been held a few miles north of here, outdoors beneath the twisting oaks of Loch Haven Park on the shores of Lake Formosa, your vows exchanged as the sun set just west of the skyline and the orange light melted into the angled Spanish-tiled rooftops on the lake's far shore. Across the street from that park is the Orlando Science Center, and you'd booked its rooftop terrace for the reception. That—your unique wedding venue—was actually what gave Steven and Elaina the idea to seek out this courtroom. "Engaging with the city!" Steven had screamed when you told him, clapping. "Screw the corporate hotel banquets! Perfect!"

And so you are here rather than some I-Drive hotel or Disney resort. Steven: a man in love with the city and eager to share its history and intertwine it with his own, even if it means printing serial killer factoids in the wedding program. Sitting in the courtroom, you find that you feel for Steven in a way you never had before. That thing he wanted to do, that ridiculous "Make

Orlando Weird" campaign, is…noble. It *mattered* to him, even if to no one else. It's like wearing an awful "World's Best Dad" hat, goofy and lame, but also authentic and passionate. You admire that. You want that.

You feel, in fact, like there are two reflections of yourself in the room: in one mirror is Edwin the Douchebag, a man without a care for anyone but himself, a man who'd bulldoze this very venue, would pave the swamps of the Dead Zone, steal money straight from the wallets of his friends, anything to get what he felt he was due…and in the other mirror is Steven, the man who respects the place and the people, even if ultimately it doesn't respect him back. You don't know which reflection is *you*, and whether you can choose, or whether it's too late.

You direct your gaze to Edwin. Seated amid a crowd of men in jackets, men you don't know, Edwin looking far too polished for a man who ran away from two million dollars' worth of properties—charcoal suit, red tie and matching pocket square, banker's hair combed perfectly and shiny as onyx. Does he have a job now? Is his father still financing his life, despite the failed investments he dumped onto you?

And then there's Shelley, who sits across the room with camera in hand, occasionally smiling when something new happens (flower girl toddling in, too-young ring-bearer needing to be led down the aisle by his father, then the exchanging of rings in a room so crypt-silent the wood-creaking is all you hear), Shelley in a long row of sorority girls young and old. Shelley, who is not a reflection of you, but a doorway into a room where you could be a different, better man.

You never used to care about weddings, not as anything more than open bars. Jimmy was the first of your friends to marry, and his wedding set the tone for your entire crew because his wedding *was* little more than an open bar. In fact, you only began caring about the meaningful stuff—the ceremonies and the vows and the visiting family—when it became clear that your own engagement was over. You tried to hold onto it all, the reservations, the florist, the caterer; even after you canceled everything, you bought up your gift registry and stocked your house full of lonely pots and pans and blenders and hand-mixers and fondue sets, objects as stand-ins for the life you'd never have. Now you see scenes like this—the rows of siblings and cousins in the pews, the friends from Dallas and Nebraska and New York puddled together here in the warmth of Orlando history, the embraces, the cheek-kisses, the aunts pinching nephews, the grandmas embracing daughters and granddaughters together, the mom with the screaming baby who leaves during the ceremony to change a diaper and who will inevitably dance with both husband and child together during the reception—the things that are wedding clichés and yet *must occur* at every wedding because they are glowing with real love, the sort of clichés that everyone with a soul cherishes.

When the ceremony ends, you huddle in the hallway outside the courtroom with Jimmy and Sandra and Anderson, listening to them mull possibilities for hors d'oeuvres and entrées, scrutinize the bridesmaids, and weigh odds on whether a particular aunt will get drunk and break a hip on the dance floor, or whether the father of the bride will become a slobbery wreck whose sob-slurred words no one can decipher? So many possibilities for this evening.

"So where's the reception?" Sandra asks.

"'Florida Land Boom of the 1920s,'" Jimmy says.

"1920s?" Anderson asks. "Sounds boring."

"Didn't even know people lived here in the '20s," Jimmy says.

"Didn't you read the program? This building was built in the '20s," you say. You also have a flickering memory of the Hurricane of 1926, of wind-whipped palms and darkness at the Seminole Hotel, of a nameless monster lake opening its mouth and swallowing your land…You shake your head and will it away, this memory of another man's demise.

You're looking over Jimmy's head and into the massive congregation that's bottlenecked at the courtroom exit, trying to spot Shelley or Edwin, but you can't see either of them, not individually, because (a) they're both short, always lost in crowds, and (b) it's all retina-stinging fluorescent overhead lights, and clusters of women in spring-colored dresses, radioactive yellows and limes and tangerines, the sort of colors that astronaut wives wear in every Space Race movie ever made. Huddled at the doorway are

Steven's *other* Nebraskan cousins, a troupe of pint-sized twenty-something girls with hair as gold as corn who—in contrast to Steven's puritanical male cousins—all seem to think Orlando is Las Vegas or something, a place to shed their inhibitions and go wild, and they've been giggling and generally looking devious all afternoon. Every damn one of them looks like Shelley. Is *that* her? You stare hard, squint, try to connect heads with bodies, and maybe *that one* is the slim body of your old fiancée…

But before you can be sure, Jimmy's grabbing your arm and saying, "Time to head downstairs, homeboy." He's pointing to a man in a tuxedo shirt and bowtie who's pushing a cart of alcohol into the service elevator. "Open bar. No time to waste."

"I was going to wait for Shel—"

"Now," he repeats and tugs.

•

The History Center's top floor—the fourth—is mostly dedicated to early Florida history. Murals of the Timucuans battling dinosaur-sized alligators, twelve men spearing a creature that looks capable of consuming them all. Drift down to the third floor and you're in the thick of the nineteenth century, the birth of the citrus industry, the history of the "Florida Cracker," the transition from Spanish colony to English to Spanish to English and the weird journey to a uniquely Florida culture. The Seminole Wars. Camps and tribes and towns full of guerrilla Seminoles and runaway slaves building families. Civil War. A brief stint as part of the Confederacy, forever imbedding in the public mind the idea of Florida as a "Southern state." It is, and it isn't, and the conversation on the subject is old, ongoing. Hell, maybe someday there'll be wedding receptions in the "Is Florida Southern?" wing.

One more floor and you're at the Florida Land Boom of the 1920s, an exhibit ambitious in design, rows of maze-like black partitions displaying thousands of photos, aerial black-and-white shots of the glut of new homes constructed in the '20s, one partition showcasing a "Wall of Gates" that tells the story of neighborhood entrances: College Park, Orwin Manor, Colonialtown, all the downtown bungalow communities. Another partition examines the influence of Spanish architecture in Tampa, Mediterranean architecture in Miami and Palm Beach, and the ill-fated efforts of one developer to create a single neighborhood whose subdivisions each reflected a different European influence. There are scale models of golf courses, and one partition profiles the oft-forgotten construction workers, the men who toiled in the heat to create this new Florida: close-up photos of weather-cracked faces, lips swollen and bloody, skin tattooed with mud and dust in open wounds. Ultimately the exhibit circles the room until the end of the land boom is mere feet from the beginning. Within spitting distance of one another, there are large-scale newspaper reproductions whose headlines announce the crash, and large-scale brochure reproductions advising the hopeful to "take advantage now *while there's still land available!*"

You've been to the History Center a half-dozen times, but never sober. You've come only to the "culture and cocktails" events, when the exhibit spaces fill with twenty-somethings who want to drink wine and martinis and dance beside taxidermied alligators. You remember, on one such evening, staring in a drunken daze at a scale model of downtown Orlando, with its plastic buildings and street signs and cars, and marveling at how easy it was to reduce the real world to something so tiny. How big you seemed as you hovered over it all. But that was a long time ago.

"This is depressing," Jimmy says, leading the way inside the Land Boom room.

"You sure we should be down here?" you ask. "Everyone else is still upstairs."

"Pssh," Jimmy says, then opens his arms wide as he approaches the bar: "Donny, buddy, working this *yourself?*"

"Jimmy!" says a man at the bar with a ponytail.

"Donny!"

"Jimmy!"

"Donny runs the catering company," Jimmy tells you. "But sometimes he likes to slum it with the working folk, serve drinks or slice meat at the carving station."

Donny holds up his palms. "Keeping it humble." He runs a washrag along the makeshift bartop, arranges a cup of plastic swords just-so, then motions to the liquor bottles at his disposal. "So what can I get you gentlemen?"

"Two Jack and Cokes," Jimmy says.

You hadn't planned on starting the night with hard liquor. There are important things to be accomplished tonight with Shelley and Edwin, and it's been a recurring theme in your life that giving alcohol the control yields poor results. You know this. And yet.

"And you?" Donny asks you.

"Me?" you say. "I guess I'll do two, also. Avoid standing in line."

"Quite the set-up, eh?" Donny says after he pushes the plastic cups your way. He holds his hand out to indicate the entirety of the room, the blue and silver balloons tied to the museum's partitions, balloons tied to the replica of an old subdivision called "Fantasyland," balloons tied to the six-foot-tall reproduction of the newspaper headline "FLORIDA BOOM IS OVER!" Blue and silver glitter on the floor. Blue and silver glass balls in hurricane vases situated in the centers of thirty tables draped in black tablecloth. The dance floor is in the center of it all, the DJ booth set up inside a replica of a 1920s front porch.

"Only one bar?" Jimmy asks. "Come on!"

"It's the History Center," Donny says apologetically. "Apparently there was a wedding last year where some drunk groomsmen messed up the Florida Cracker exhibit. Stole the straw hat off the mannequin, tossed around the citrus crates, took pictures riding the fake cows." Donny shakes his head. "Anyway, just one bar tonight. Try not to let history repeat itself."

"Ha ha!" Jimmy says and they high-five.

Jimmy finishes one Jack and Coke, places it onto the bar. Donny refills.

"Should we…" you say and point up at the ceiling. "Your wife?"

"Oh yeah," Jimmy says. "I'll text her."

You aren't *worried* about Sandra, necessarily, but instead about time spent removed from the larger congregation (and within that larger congregation, Shelley and Edwin). Every second you're down here is a second wasted.

You finish your first drink. Donny refills you, too.

What next? What's your next move? Go upstairs, find Shelley?

But Jimmy doesn't give you a chance to make your own decisions. He texts his wife, and seconds later Anderson and Sandra are walking downstairs, followed closely by the full crowd from the ceremony. Within moments, the Land Boom room is packed, couples taking pictures beneath large-scale photos of distraught businessmen examining the empty fields they thought would be million-dollar housing developments. A few remain in the hallway, though, huddling around the tall windows and hoping to capitalize on the sunset, so it's out there that you wander, thinking you might casually bump into your ex-fiancée. The sun sits just above the horizon, the sky washed pink and lavender, whites twisting throughout like cigar smoke from the angels, a perfect sunset for wedding photos, but a beauty you're too anxious to appreciate, your focus so consumed on scanning the crowds for—

Suddenly there's a hard elbow to your chest, and you nearly spill your drink. "Shit, sorry," you say to the dark-suited body you bumped, "I wasn't…" But you trail on the final syllable when you notice who it is. "Edwin."

"Marc," he says flatly. "How, uh…how are you?"

You cross your arms over your chest. How to answer such a question?

Edwin stuffs his hands in his pockets, lifts his head to look up at you. He's short, yes, but built like a beer keg, and when he looks up he makes sure to flex his traps so his shirt collar stretches to the ripping point.

Time seems to stand still, both of you awaiting one another's next move.

You thought you wouldn't be in this position again, where the choices appear before you and wait for you to select and proceed.

Well, here we are again.

But this time, no page-turning. No second chances. Just one selection. Consider it a final exam, to see if this book has taught you a damned thing. Are you a good man, Marc? Are you ready to rise again as something more than a heartless heedless conqueror?

Question #1: Edwin is here before you. At long last. What do you do?

A) Punch Edwin in the face. Send this motherfucker into the Dead Zone.

B) Tell him, "Fine," the world's most generic response. Let him decide if he's going to pursue an altercation.

C) Get sarcastic. Say "No, how are you, good sir?" Smile goofily.

D) Walk away without starting a fight. Maybe say, "I need a moment," as the red of anger rises to your ears.

Note: teacher's guide included behind the red tab.

Note: make sure to circle the response as completely as possible. An unclosed circle could be labeled "pregnant," with your intention considered noncommittal.

Note: while this particular question does not have a time limit, you don't want to spend too much time thinking on it…this is an easy one…seriously, just answer it and move on.

D. You choose **D.** You say "I need a moment" and walk away and collect your breath, try to allow the intensity of your heartbeat to subside. You walk away, back toward the bar, Edwin still standing back there and perhaps thinking you've gone insane, but whatever.

Breathe.

The time will come to confront Edwin, to say to him what needs to be said, to reacquire some of what he stole from you, but not yet. Patience. Remember, there can be no conversation with Shelley if you're thrown out of here before the cocktail hour is even over.

By the time you return to the bar for a refresher, the line has become Disney-long, all aunts and uncles, Nebraskans and Texans and occasional Floridians. Up at the bar, ordering a Pabst, is Steven's high school friend Goat, wearing a jacket over a torn Sex Pistols t-shirt.

"Been waiting for this," an old man behind you says. You look around to see who he's with, but it seems he's talking to you.

"The wedding?" you ask.

"The open bar," he says. "Four days at Disney with the family…didn't think I'd get out alive. You know there no alcohol at the Magic Kingdom?"

You laugh, the image of the tourist-thick walkways at Epcot still fresh in your mind. "I feel the same way. First time in Orlando?"

"Naw," he says. He's wearing the type of decades-old brown suit you see only in fading family photos in dark hallways of houses where the owner has long since forgotten the photos are even up, but he's got an I-don't-care expression that suggests maybe he owns nicer clothes but wanted to make a point about how a man should dress on vacation. "Came down here, me and the wife, for our honeymoon. Way back in the '70s."

"Back when this place was still a courthouse?"

"This place was a courthouse?"

"The ceremony was in an old courtroom. Didn't *anyone* read the program?"

"Hmmm," he says, and smooths the long gray hair from one side of his scalp to the other to re-create the comb-over that continuously unravels under the gust of air conditioning. "Epcot was still an idea. That was when they were still touting it as the experimental prototype community of tomorrow, like people were gonna live there or something. Still remember that damn acronym."

"Wait. So you went to the Magic Kingdom for your honeymoon?"

"Stayed in a little off-site hotel that probably doesn't exist no more. Grimy place, smaller than the master bedroom of my house. Honeymoons were different back then. Florida was more exotic."

The line is moving closer to Donny the bartender, who's shaking a martini for another old man in a vacation suit. You've always been fascinated by random wedding conversations; under what other circumstances might you pair off with this old man for ten minutes and listen to his life? Who will be next? At one wedding, you spoke for an hour with a man who tinkered with mosquito repellent recipes for a living.

"We had to fly into Tampa, actually." He licks his fingers and tries to fix his comb-over again, but once the humidity takes hold it's like trying to manage a melting ice cream cone in summertime. "All orange groves, as I remember.

Land along the interstate looked as empty as any of the highways out in west Texas: that's where we're from."

"You're part of Elaina's family?"

"Smartest thing that girl's mother did," he says, "was to move out here."

"Elaina was born in Florida?"

"Virginia. That family, they're always moving. That kid," the man says, pointing to Steven, "he better be prepared for life as a gypsy or something. Those girls do *not* like staying in one place. But hey, that's Orlando, right? From what I hear, this is the most transitory city in the country. This and Vegas."

"Some people stay."

The line is closer now, and you weigh whether to argue: everyone seems to think that the city is brand-new, but in your bones, you know the truth of the land.

"Listen," he says. "We stayed at the Got-damned Grand Floridian the last few nights. Supposed to be historic Florida and all that. Looks like one of the ritzy hotels in these Land Boom photos. Palm Beach or Miami Beach."

"Or the Seminole Hotel in Winter Park," you say.

"Sure." He motions for you to approach the bartender. "You're up, son."

You turn, and in your face is a new question. Right there. Text hanging in front of you.

Oh, haha, you thought the exam was over? No, sir! There are nearly *40 questions*, my friend, that will collectively *decide your value as a human being*. Yes. That is what's at stake tonight. Onward!

Question #2: Second drink. What to order?

A) **Wine**

B) **Water**

C) **Beer**

D) **More Liquor**

Note: teacher's guide included in the appendix.

You choose **C) Beer.** Switch to beer. The safest choice.

"Yuengling," you tell Donny.

"You got it, chief," the bartender says, though he doesn't recognize you as Jimmy's accomplice from earlier.

A second later the Yuengling is in your hands. You feel like this is a responsible choice, since you're already three-deep with Jack and Cokes. And with beer in hand, you feel much better prepared to re-engage with the world.

"Impossible not to like the Grand Floridian, of course," the old man is saying. "Except the price." He tells the bartender whiskey and water. "Hell, better make it two."

"Going heavy," you say.

"Gonna drink the price of that Disney resort."

"That bad, huh?"

"Historic Florida didn't look like that," he says. "Historic Florida didn't have air conditioning, or sparkling pools, or monorails. Even that lake on the Boardwalk? The color ain't right. Florida lakes should be *brown*. Everything here is artificial, even the history."

"Hmm," you say. "I gotta—"

"I know. You gotta run. See you back in line in fifteen minutes." He nudges you in the ribs. "Name's Jesse. Uncle Jesse, everyone calls me. We'll do shots later."

"Oh, no. I—"

"Ain't no saying no. You're one of the boys."

And the cocktail hour is a mass of bodies, of bowties and black jackets, spring dresses and too-loud music from the just-warming-up DJ, and things are spinning as you step around and try to find breathing room.

Soon enough, you've finished your Yuengling (your fourth drink (at least you're keeping tabs!)), and the bride and groom are still elsewhere, taking pictures, and you're trying to spot Shelley while also trying to avoid Edwin, who (you notice) is now chatting with Anderson by the "Wall of Gates," both of them pointing to one of the mangled post-1926 hurricane gates and laughing as if disaster could never befall them. The bridal party is likely with Steven and Elaina, too. And the parents. All of them posing in one spot, smiling smiling smiling while fifteen different cameras snap pictures, then all of them shuffling to a new spot where the process is repeated, facial muscles straining.

You wander the Land Boom room looking for Shelley, step into the Hurricane House, which rocks to simulate the crashing of storms, thus making it nearly impossible to read the text inside about the thousands killed in 1926, the billions of dollars lost, the pre-Depression death of Florida. Once inside the Hurricane House, the building shakes, and fake lightning cracks, and a park ranger voice intones that "The Hurricane of 1926 came out of nowhere, but its damage was deep and lasting." You step out quickly (someone should have cordoned this exhibit off; your drunk friends will make short work of it), and there is Jimmy, waiting for you.

"Shots!" he says.

"I don't want to get too sloppy," you say.

"You're not even *sloppy* yet. Why worry about getting *too* sloppy?"

Damn it.

Oh no, here it comes—

Question #3: Taking this one little shot will destroy your entire evening.
(Circle the correct response.)

A) True

B) False

Note: teacher's guide included in the appendix.

You choose **False**. How can you not, with the question worded that way? *Destroy* your *entire* evening?

"Circle the correct response," the exam says. For fuck's sake. What does "correct" even mean? This isn't a math exam; this isn't algorithm. This isn't history, with its indisputable dates and names. This is—and shit, what if you turn down the shots, and Shelley avoids you all night *anyway*?

Wait.

Did it say "teacher's guide" up there in the fine print? Is that…is that a joke?

Read again: "Note: teacher's guide included in the appendix."

What if it's real? What if you *could* cheat and peek ahead to see where the night goes?

Hell. If life is playing tricks on you, why not take the shot with Jimmy and flip the pages? That's how you'd treat a test back in college, always jumping ahead to the part that said "assignment instructions" and then deciding how much work was necessary.

"Fuck it," you say to Jimmy and down the Jack Daniels and then the world goes black. You're floating in the darkness now, floating toward glowing white pages, an open book. The teacher's guide, it's calling to you, and here in the darkness, you're taking control.

You are driving. It's the morning after the wedding and you're driving a horror-movie stretch of the Turnpike, fog drifting between pine trees and consuming the road ahead, anti-abortion billboards rising through the gray at mile-marker intervals, the faces of babies ("I love you, Mommy. Why do you want to kill me?") and shattered women ("You can still be saved") blurring, disappearing from mile to mile. The fog seems always to retreat in anticipation of your car, but all the world is milky and thick and wet, only pinpricks of southbound headlights struggling through the gloom. You're still half-drunk, but it's early morning and you cannot wait, not after Kyle's note, his voicemails. Many hundreds of thousands of pine trees later and you will be in Georgia.

It's a long drive back home. Which CD would you most like to listen to?

A) Gym Class Heroes. It reminds you of two years ago, when life was good and your relationships were healthy and happy.

B) Sublime. It reminds you of high school's end, the soaring optimism you felt as you left backwoods Georgia for UCF.

C) Rod Stewart. Yes, you own a Rod CD. No smart-ass comments, please. It was your mother's. Somehow it wound up in your CD case, and on depressing days "Rhythm of My Heart" makes you feel upbeat. And fuck anyone who doesn't enjoy "Downtown Train."

D) CCR. One of your father's favorites. It is for him that you are returning, after all, and nothing captures the spirit of your father quite like Fogerty's pained wail on "Have You Ever Seen the Rain?"

FLLLIIIIPPP

Question #37: Final Chance with Shelley.

Here you are at the end of the night, once again standing in Heritage Square, that city block that sweeps outward from the front doors of the History Center, that plaza of pavement and brick and custom-cut rubber mulch fit between the rolling sidewalks. Scattered about are bronze gators and other photo opportunities for daytime families and nighttime drunks. It's the History Center's friendly outdoor reconstruction of Old Florida, but there's no dirt, no mud, not even *real* mulch that could be kicked about, no chance of being swallowed whole.

Two hundred feet to your right is the outdoor block party at Wall Street, howling-mad on a Saturday night, thousands of drunk twenty-somethings doing the things that drunk twenty-somethings do. To your left, a quarter-mile away, is Lake Eola and Lakeside Wine Bar and all the high-rise condos of upscale Central Boulevard. In this way, if no other, you are mere feet from where you were when this adventure began, back when you were sitting with Sandra and measuring the distance you'd fallen.

Your suit jacket is folded over one arm and you're stumbling forward, leading with your head as if it is a separate entity pulling your body along. This is how toddlers look when they first learn to walk, every step a near-disaster. Upstairs, where everyone was drunk, you didn't feel this close to debacle. But now in the fresh air and empty space of Heritage Square, you can't shake the last few hours of Jack and Cokes, Yuenglings, shots. "Shelley," you say, but it's a moan lost in the bass from Wall Street.

She's forty or fifty feet ahead of you, a shadow walking the darkness beneath the cypress trees.

It's just the two of you walking down Central. Everyone else from the reception is either still at the History Center, or already walking through the parking garage. Viewed without context (for instance: in a teacher's guide, by a cheater who's skipped forty questions), this might seem like a good sign: that it's just the two of you, here at the end of the night. Isn't this what you wanted? But Shelley isn't stumbling. She's dead-sober, moves forward with the authority and grace of an event planner who watches the world drink but denies herself a glass.

"I was *nervous*," you say.

She doesn't respond. She's farther away.

"I was nervous to talk to you."

Even drunk, you know that things shouted across courtyards and streets and parks—desperate man to fleeing woman, late-night—inevitably sound not just cheesy but downright *stupid*. They're never as memorable as in romantic comedies, they're never backgrounded by killer pop soundtracks. You don't want to sound cheesy, but your mouth is betraying your brain: "I still love you, Shelley!" you sort-of shout and she stops but doesn't turn, just holds her clutch tighter against her hip, then keeps moving.

You pick up speed.

You're almost running now, and when Shelley stops to open the door to the parking garage's stairwell, she hears your approach. She turns and sees your lurching frame, and if this was indeed a romantic comedy the camera would zoom out so that the audience could see the both of you backgrounded by the parking garage and its spectacular floral mural, and you'd run to one another and embrace...but here, now, her face crumbles in disappointment. There is nowhere she'd like to be less than face to face with her drunk ex. My God, how did you come to this?

Essay Prompt: Given the above scenario, write what you will do and say next. Keep in mind that your response must be written in a way that reflects your aforementioned level of intoxication. Consider drafting the response with your non-dominant hand in order to ensure that the handwriting is sufficiently impacted.

Perhaps use the following question as a means of generating your response: If you were face to face with the ex-fiancé that you desperately wanted to win back, the woman you now realize you'd treated poorly, and you had just this one chance to say something to her before she left town for good...what would you say?

Note For Teachers: Essay responses are subjective. Score the essay based on the following rubric.

5 – Essay demonstrates critical thinking skills, is complete, and demonstrates attention to detail at sentence level.

3 – Essay demonstrates some insight, but is incomplete, or is flawed at either local or global level.

1 – Essay does not demonstrate critical thinking, and/or is incomplete, and/or is highly flawed at local or global levels.

FLLLIIIIPPP

Question #38: Getting Home.

After your final encounter with Shelley in the stairwell, you drive out of the downtown parking garage and camp at a Denny's on Colonial for a couple hours, drinking water after water, maybe a coffee or two, and—what is that?—a plate of hash browns, and, like, chicken-fried steak and white gravy? Scrambled eggs in there, too? Oh dear God.

Your fork slips.

You see two of everything, sometimes four, and you nearly pass out in the gristle. Cheap diner breakfast after late-night drinking: this was a thing back in college, but this is the first time you've done it in years. How you manage to eat so much without throwing up is concrete evidence of the existence of miracles.

The drive back to your place is a little easier than the drive from downtown to Denny's, a little more coherent after the sober-up period and the greasy food. At your first major intersection, you pass a company of lit-up police cars that seem to have pulled over a drunk driver, former passengers now sitting on the sidewalk with heads resting in their hands. A mile later, a speed demon Mustang passes you and shoots through a yellow light, but you come to a slow and sensible stop and wait for the red rather than following like a maniac.

As always, you're reminded of the woman you lost to a car accident, and you know you should be ashamed at what you're currently doing but you kind of don't care right now because it almost doesn't matter if you live or die. What value are you to the world? From the moment you watched the girl run scared from your living room, butcher knife in hand, you knew it: you are an awful person. No final exam can change that. The world is better without you.

By the time you wake up in the morning, though, you can barely remember the drive.

When you rise from bed and wander the house, you discover that Kyle isn't home.

Eventually you find a note from your brother magnet-clipped to the fridge, and you've got two choices here:

(A) Read it now.

B) **Collapse on the couch** and watch *Entourage* on HBO On Demand and just worry about that shit later.

Question #19: Spotting Shelley for the First Time.

Here you are, drink in hand but loitering at the bar nonetheless, waiting for the moment when Shelley finishes filling her plate at the buffet so you can make contact.

You know exactly what you'll say, but you just hope you can manage the words in the correct order, without sounding rehearsed. You have doubts about your ability to manage anything right now, though you're proud that you've mapped the geography of the room and have tracked the moving pieces with enough skill to put yourself in position to intercept her—

—but now Jimmy is here, right behind you, hands on your shoulders as he shouts something to Donny the bartender, the two of them laughing and you can't move because Jimmy is holding you in place and shaking your shoulders every couple seconds and he says "Yahtzee!" and both he and Donny laugh and

Jimmy slaps your back and says "Shots, buddy! Donny made us some Kazak-bombs!"

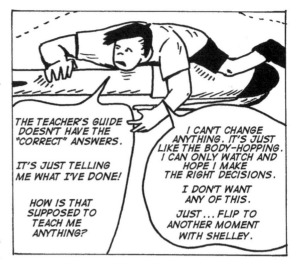

"Okay," you say, "okay," because you need to fill the time until Shelley is finished at the dinner station, and you need to not look like you're stalking her.

But just as you down the shot, Shelley walks past and sees. She rolls her eyes and says, "Pace yourself, guys. The night just started."

Fuck.

Still, we must choose how to proceed from here. This moment, after all, is pivotal to your ability to win her back, to your entire future as a man who matters and does the right things. What do you do next?

A) Shout, "Hell yeah! Just gettin' started!" and hope she turns and laughs. You're the life of the party, and what woman doesn't want to be with the life of the party?

B) Follow her back to her table. She doesn't seem interested in further conversation with you, but maybe if…if you don't let her get away?

C) Take the next shot that Jimmy is now handing you, and…and *hope* you'll run into Shelley again later.

D) Tell Jimmy, "I should probably call it quits. I need to talk to Shelley eventually." In so doing, you will face scorn. Be called a pussy, etc. And at this point, you will be no more sober for having declined, so why fucking bother?

FLLLIIIIPPP

Question #31: Your Second Shelley Encounter.

The Electric Slide is over, but before anyone can settle back into their seats, the DJ transitions to Frank Sinatra and calls all couples to the dance floor. "You know what time it is," he says. "We're going to celebrate everlasting love, folks. Everyone who's in a relationship: on the dance floor!" After a few moments of swaying, he asks the unmarried couples to leave the dance floor ("Good luck to you all, and hopefully you can stick around on the dance floor longer at the next wedding!"); a few beats later, and it's everyone married for less than a year who's leaving, and then everyone married less than five years, and the newlyweds and the second marriages and the young parents are all throwing up their hands and laughing in faux exasperation, but politely stepping away and leaving the floor to the marriages with more rings on their trunks.

Obviously, as a partner-less bachelor, you were never allowed out there to begin with, but with so much shuffling on and off the dance floor, you make your way to Shelley's table for the first time. As a single woman, she isn't out on the floor, either. Maybe she was even tasked by a married friend to watch the purses. The curse of being single.

You're worried that your breath is pungent from the garlic mashed potatoes, so you swish the Jack and Coke around your mouth and hope this makes some difference. Twice as you walk, you nearly trip on the floor—not on an extension cord, or a purse left in your way, or a warped floorboard, no, you're stumbling through thin air.

Once across the room, you plop into an empty chair beside Shelley. Her table's covered in empty plates and party favor chocolate bars upon which each guest's name has been candy-embossed. Shelley won't meet your eyes, just shakes her head and stares at her purse. The Frank Sinatra song is ending, the eighty-year-old couple on the dance floor holding hands and shakily returning to their seats to boisterous applause, their annual moment of marriage glory now over.

Sinatra out. Craig David's "Key to My Heart" in.

"It's a slow dance," you say to Shelley. "We're allowed back on the dance floor."

"Marc, you smell like *girl*."

You swirl another sip of Jack. Not garlic, not Jack Daniels…but *girl*?

"It's Sandra, probably," you say.

"Sandra?"

"We were at the same table. She tends to be…overpowering."

Shelley looks past you, across the room. "Jimmy's passed out right now."

You look over and confirm. "That's a first."

"There's lip gloss on your neck."

"Lip gloss?" You touch your neck, and it does indeed feel sticky. "It's a good *song*," you say to change the subject. "Slow dance! Please?"

"Maybe later."

"Promise?"

"You're wasted, Marc. I need you to go away." Shelley's entrenched in her seat, has her elbows on the table and a water glass in hand; she's not rising, not leaving this spot to go anywhere with you. It is a nightmarish moment, the worst-case scenario made real before you. She is the reason for the evening, and yet you face flat-out rejection. How does a "good man" recover from this, make a night meaningful after being told to go away?

A) Let your anger speak for you, and put her in her place. Tell her "Fuck you! I needed this, do you hear me? Tonight could've been spectacular, but you're ruining it." Women. Women! Let it out. Even if it's not what you actually believe. Sometimes it feels good to let the anger take control. Tell her, "My life has been *shit* for the last six months. I had to make a list of things to be *happy* about, and still I wanted to kill myself." Tell her, "This is all *your* fault. The drinking. The black eye. The ribs. The chipped tooth. Every foreclosure. Everything I did was for *you*." Tell her, "You want to blame everything in *your* life on me, don't you? How *your* life was going? How you didn't like your friends? How you felt trapped, depressed, demeaned at work? You want to blame *me*? That's convenient, Shelley. You don't get to fucking *do* that. It doesn't happen like that, okay? I fucking love you, and I made every…I did everything…*you* don't tell *me*…Do you *hear* me?" Let it out Let it out.

B) Or, if it's anger you want to unleash, maybe go find Edwin. Flick a bottlecap in his face. That worked well on at least one other recent occasion, right? Maybe your anger is *his* fault instead, and you can use the above speech to get worked up before shoving him into the coffee carafes. Oh, the anger. The anger. It is a living creature, feeding on itself once again, growing.

C) **Remove yourself from this situation.** Realize that you're not thinking straight. Say "I've gotta talk to Anderson," and walk away. Hell, you got a promise for a slow dance, right? "Maybe later," she said. Whoop whoop!

Question #12: Your Best Friend, Jimmy Bastion.

"The girl in the red, the girl in the red," Jimmy's saying, and you're both in line at the bar once again. You've spent more time here than at your table, and you feel yourself dissolving into fuzzy-headed uselessness, your ability to achieve anything this evening slipping, slipping...

"Calm down, Jimmy. Your wife is, like, fifteen feet away."

"Whatever. Who goes to a wedding to stare at *his wife?*" There are spit particles flying, tangible objects the size of raisins, and you watch as one of them crashes and settles in the curly hair of the woman in front of you, where it jiggles every time she moves. A few older folks from a nearby table are watching, and they back away to avoid becoming the next victims.

"I don't know, Jimmy," you say. "Not me, clearly."

"You're so lucky you're not married." He turns to the man behind him, the kind of buttoned-up humorless type who could easily be the father of one of the Christian cousins, and says, "This guy knows what I'm talking about, right?"

The man says, "Uhhhh."

"Ignore him," you say.

"Let's go find her, the girl in red." And Jimmy humps the air spastically, his shirt untucking as he thrusts. On the final thrust, he comes dangerously close to hitting the woman upon whom he already spit, but you pat his shoulder in a "that's enough" signal that you're surprised he obeys.

"I told you, Jimmy. You *don't* want to find her. You don't understand who she—"

"Oh, I want to find her. I want to *find* her." He pauses. "When I say 'I want to find her,' I actually mean that I want to have sex with her. Get it?"

"Holy shit, man. I—"

"But not until I smoke a cig."

"We just smoked fifteen minutes ago."

The couple in front of you turns around, freshly poured drinks in hands, mild grimaces on their faces as if they've heard your conversation and couldn't be more disappointed. But Jimmy doesn't care, just says "We're up. Time for some shots of Jack, Donny! Nah, lemme at that bottle!" Whereupon he reaches across the bar and knocks the tip cup into the ice bin below, and there are limes on the floor and olives rolling madly toward—

Okay. You get the idea. Here's the question: What is it about all of the above that you find most unfortunate?

A) **Your proximity** to a man who, fifteen feet from his wife, would pantomime the fucking of another woman (and with such intensity!).

B) **The terrible waste** of limes and olives and maraschino cherries.

C) Cigarette?

D) **That you can't just laugh** and roll with it. Dude, stop thinking so much.

FLLLIIIIPPP

Question #6: Cigarette Break.

You're outside the doors of the History Center, under the dusk sky in Heritage Square. A block away at Wall Street, a beer tub girl holds a lighter to each in a row of unlit tiki torches, and as she moves on, each new fire whooshes upward and bends in a different way. All of this is in anticipation of the glorious chaos that will commence upon sunset, and you watch with Jimmy and Uncle Jesse, the old guy from the bar line. You've all three stepped out of the reception for "fresh air," but you check your hand and there's a lit cigarette trailing a thin gray plume. Right. Fresh air. You're *smoking*, something you only do when unreasonably drunk, something that reflexively makes you think of your father and his disgusting cough and his stubborn declaration that this was what a man *did* to calm down, and to hell with consequences, something's gonna kill us one day anyway, right?

"Wanna go out to the bars after the reception?" Jimmy asks the old guy, pointing to the beertub girl across the street.

"Vegas has lots of good bars and hot girls, too," Uncle Jesse says and a ball of smoke emerges from his mouth. "I remain unconvinced that this city is anything more than an airport."

"We should take him to Wall Street, right?" Jimmy says and nudges you.

"That would certainly be an experience," you say.

"I still don't understand why this city exists," he says. "Why would anyone *live* here, except to take advantage of tourists?"

Jimmy shrugs. "It's a city. There are bars. There are girls. Why ask why?"

"We visited Disneyland in Anaheim, too. And the problem *there* is the surrounding area. When Disney built the park, the riff-raff swooped in, encircled it. The shitty souvenir stores, the crummy hotels. No matter what the parks do to update themselves, there are these sedimentary layers encircling them."

"Sure," Jimmy says.

"Here in Orlando, though, Disney built the parks. Made himself a whole city down there. Hell, Disney World is a fucking *county*, right? I read that somewhere."

"Reedy Creek Improvement District," Jimmy says, and where did this knowledge come from? Jimmy never knows anything of value. "We distribute to Disney, too," he says, feeling your stare. "They're our biggest customer. Anyway, it's common knowledge. Disney World has its own, like, government. Because Epcot was originally supposed to be a real city. Then they decided to make it a theme park, not a city, but they still have their own government."

"Jimmy, you surprise me."

"Fuck you," he says. "I'm motherfucking smart."

"The point is," the old man's saying, "Walt Disney wanted a carnival, but didn't want anyone to see the carnies. Their apartments, their cars. So where'd the garbage wind up? Orlando. The city is all the runoff and sprawl that services the theme parks, four decades' worth of crap. The low-income housing, the roach motels, the crumbling gift shops."

You shake your head. "Don't say any of that to Steven."

"See, I know what a real city should look like," the old man says. "I been all over. Dallas? Nashville? New Orleans? Orlando ain't got what those cities got. The history? Local flavor? This place, it's like a port city on a cruise."

"Preach," Jimmy says.

"No," you say. "What are you even—" Deep within you there is mud, there are cypress knees, there are Mangrove Men and dead golf courses and celery farmers and hurricanes. They are still with you, could overtake you at any moment, do not speak ill of the muck—

But Uncle Jesse is already blowing out smoke, has his arm wrapped around Jimmy, and is whispering conspiratorially in his ear. "That girl in the red dress, I think she likes you."

"Yeah?"

"Nice ass. I mean *niiiice*. Like, flexes every step she takes, flexes so hard that red dress is gonna rip. Mmmmm."

"The things I would do, my man. Tenderize that meat."

"She likes you. I saw her staring at you."

"The girl in the red does *not* like him," you say, maybe too loud. The ancients have receded, like a vomit burp after a sip of water.

"Don't be a hater," Jimmy says.

You, of course, know who she is, and you know the complicated history that all three of you share. Jimmy doesn't remember.

"She keeps looking at him," the old guy says. "Lust, pure and simple."

"The girl in the red does *not* like him," you repeat. "If she was 'staring hard,' it was not a good thing."

"Jealous," Jimmy says. "She wants my D. But whatever. I'm, like, married." He holds up his ring finger, and you're impressed that he hasn't pocketed the ring at the first possibility of play. The old man is sliding two new cigarettes from the pack.

"I'm not jealous," you say. "You don't understand who she is, Jimmy."

Should you tell Jimmy what you know? It would greatly benefit him. Or maybe it wouldn't. Maybe it would only ruin his night. What would a good person do?

A) **Don't tell him.** He's not even going to listen.

B) **Tell him.** Wipe that smirk off his face.

C) **No.** Don't tell him. It's not about whether or not he'll listen. It's about revenge. He's a douchebag, and this whole situation could blow up in his face. Let it. He deserves it.

D) **Yes.** Tell him. Regardless of *his* value as a human, this choice is about *you*. It's not your place to judge someone else, to determine their punishment for past sins. You should tell him because a decent person would warn his friend about something like this.

Question #4: A Status Report on Edwin and Shelley, and a Girl in Red.

Cocktail hour swirls around you madly, the room a Tilt-A-Whirl from both the mad rush of reception-goers thirsty for open bar and from your own pleasant four-drink lift (*Four?* Yes. That sounds right.), and your head's on a swivel trying to keep track of the people who matter most.

Status report on Edwin: he has now wandered to parts unknown. You'll bump into him again soon enough, and you worry about what will happen then. Will you throw a punch? Will the crowd form a circle and let you go at it? Or will it be broken up immediately, men in tuxedos bear-hugging you away from one another? And who will be on your side? Will Anderson support *you*, or *Edwin?* Edwin never wronged Anderson, never wronged Steven or Jimmy or anyone else but *you*, and Edwin—for all his faults—never carries himself so gloomily as you do. Everywhere you go, you bring the dark storm clouds. Who wants to side with that?

Status report on Shelley: just moments ago, you asked Anderson if he'd seen her, and he told you she was with the bridesmaids and other sorority friends at a "Sisterhood Ceremony." Unfortunately, you know what this is. They pass a candle, sing a song, wish the bride good health, good fortune, a strong marriage for many years…you don't know the exact words, but at a friend's wedding a year ago, you took a wrong turn and wound up in the middle of one of these sisterhood ceremonies and it felt like you'd interrupted a coven of witches raising the dead, women in dresses with solemn faces, heads rising in unison to look at the intruder as you backed out the door.

And so it's you and Jimmy and Sandra, in the Land Boom room surrounded by cousins and work friends and old sorority sisters and former roommates and high school classmates, everyone not important enough to be in the wedding party, Jimmy going on and on about how the Magic, despite having lost the first game of the NBA Finals, are *still* the team to beat ("Can you imagine if they win Game Two in LA tomorrow? Pandemonium in Orlando."), and Sandra's looking acerbic as usual, her face sinking into scowl as she watches a mob of girls take their place in line at the bar—girls in their early 20s, the still-in-college sorority friends of the bride, just moments ago released from that sisterhood ceremony, girls who clump together as if the outside world (the families and marriages and children and real jobs) is a thing to be feared and avoided, like it will infect them.

Shelley isn't with them, but in the midst of these sorority girls, in a lipstick-red dress so bright that the world around might as well be black and white, is a familiar face. You've seen her before. She looks like someone you know intimately, someone you maybe hooked up with once, but she's too young to have been some drunken one-nighter from your college days. You know her from a different world, one where she wasn't made up to be this gorgeous, one where she wasn't dazzling the world in a red dress, one where…Wait. There's a bandage on her arm, a scab on her knee, as if she fell on a sidewalk, or—

She looks in your direction, and years of casual checking-out have trained you to anticipate this and look away so she doesn't notice you.

When you look back, she looks quickly away like *you've* caught *her* checking you out.

But who is she?

In the space below, write out your best guess.

Have we given you enough clues? If you're a man who truly sees women as something more than objects for fucking (or fantasy-fucking), this should not be tough. Are you better than your friend Jimmy? Write out your guess.

Question #5: The Mystery Solved, the Danger Revealed.

You should remember the face. You stared at it, after all, when she was passed out on your couch this very morning, a tangle of dress and hair and intoxication. Makeup smeared. Hair a crunchy tangle, body exposed and contorted in ways she'd never intended a man to see. This—the girl in red—is who Jimmy deposited on your couch, the girl who awoke and screamed and grabbed a knife and accidentally *cut herself* as she ran to the backyard and climbed the fence and disappeared. She's alive. She's *here*, dressed up and cleaned up and hiding the bandage on the underside of her forearm.

"Um, Jimmy," you say.

"—the fucking three-point shot," Jimmy is saying to you or to Sandra, or to himself maybe. "Can't defend it. *Can't* defend it."

"We've got to *go*, Jimmy."

"What crawled up your ass?" he asks. "Chill, brother."

You lean close, whisper. "The girl, Jimmy. The one you brought to my house. She's here."

Sandra has learned to not pay attention to you, just stares at the dance floor oblivious.

"What girl?" Jimmy asks. "What are you talking about?"

"The girl," you whisper, but you know it already…He was blackout-drunk last night. The second he hit your mattress and passed out, the night became an Etch A Sketch shaken from his memory: the drive to your place, the girl, all of it dust dropped to the bottom of his mind.

Some moments, some emergencies, are of your own creation. There is no one else to blame when, for instance, your actions resulted in violent retribution for the Cavaliers fans at Wall Street. But this one, when someone else t-boned you?

Which statement best represents how you view the current situation?

A) **You didn't do anything wrong!** Hell, you were trying to be a "good guy." You gave her a blanket. You shouldn't feel bad. If she comes over here, just be calm, be honest, and narrate the morning as you remember it.

B) **You're being punished, cosmically.** Why, oh why, do bad things keep happening to you? Did you let food spoil in the fridge again? Did you run a red light? Why you? Why *yoouuuuuu?* Etc.

C) **This is the consequence** of making poor choices in your selection of friends, and shouldn't be surprising. Because your father is a big fan of Dr. Phil expressions, you should be familiar with this one: "sleep with dogs, and you'll wake up with fleas." Are you just now starting to see what Shelley realized at your housewarming party? Can you ultimately blame your d-bag friends when you wind up looking like a date-rapist by association? Still, in this situation, here's the only thing you can do. Grab Jimmy, and get the hell out of there.

D) **Why bother** with a fourth choice? You're just not getting it.

527

"Pace yourself," Shelley said as she passed by with her plate of carefully selected low-carb fare, broccolini, kale salad, walnuts, salmon, Shelley in her yellow dress bright as headlights off a hazard sign. How quickly she brushed you aside while you stood at the bar with Jimmy, made you feel like a disgrace with just two words. Nearly forty minutes have now passed, but you thought about that comment all through dinner, every bite of your mashed potatoes. You're thinking about it *now* as you stand in line at the bar for another drink, how embarrassing to be reprimanded by the woman who once wanted to call you husband. You're thinking, I understand *her*, so why doesn't she just take a moment to understand *me*?

And, the shame sinking heavy into your soul, *that's* when your eyes drift to a clump of thick-haired bros with American flag and Florida Gator lapel pins, good-looking goons with the sort of natural-born handsomeness that's likely earned them years of handouts and good fortune: first jobs, second chances, promotions, rounds of golf with important people. And indeed, among them is Edwin, who's had no trouble re-assimilating post-failure, who still looks like his life is a golf course. Edwin.

"Vodka cranberry," you tell Donny.

Edwin is everything wrong with America, the meltdown entirely. Edwin is the reason for everything that's gone wrong in your life.

You take the drink and you walk, working your way through the crowd with your vodka cranberry, lowering your shoulders, turning sideways, like you're at a packed concert trying to squeeze your way to the stage. Closer, and you see he's in full storyteller mode (his face alight, his arms wide like he's describing a fish he caught), and with the vodka cranberry held weakly in your grip, you allow an old woman's elbow to knock into the drink, sending cranberry juice downward across Edwin's chest in sharp wet slashes like he's been mauled by a grizzly.

"The fuck?" he yells. Even his face is wet.

"Oh my!" the old woman says. "I'm so—"

"This motherfucker," Edwin says. Cranberry juice dripping from his eyebrows.

"—did not even see—" the old woman is saying.

"This motherfucker," Edwin is saying.

"Now, fellas," a grandfather is saying. The old woman is apologizing, touching arms, damn-near crying but no one's listening to her. It is you and it is Edwin and you are both standing face to face with clenched fists and the sort of hate in your hearts that's been brewing just long enough to explode and shatter the world around you, and then Edwin is barreling forward through the bodies and cocking his arm to take a swing but Anderson is there somehow, Anderson holding Edwin's massive bicep and one of the middle-aged golfers saying, "Whoa, son, it was an accident," and he has his arms out and Anderson's managed Edwin into a headlock but it will not hold and he's saying, "Marc, walk away. *Walk away*, Marc," and that's what you do: hold up your hands and say, "Just an accident," and then it's back to the bar for something that's not a vodka cranberry and Donny's saying "What happened over there?" And maybe it's best he didn't see: you don't want to get cut off.

"Nada," you say. "Jack and Coke please."

Certainly a good man—the most moral and virtuous among us—is entitled to some sort of retribution when wronged, correct? Personal justice? With that thought in mind, then, circle the response that is most appropriate:

This is the coolest thing you've done in a long time.

Ⓐ True

B) False

Question #20: The Buffet Line.

FLLLIIIIPPP

Five seconds ago, back in the bathroom, you felt fine. You were going to approach Shelley for the first time. Things were looking good. Then Jimmy fed you another shot (two, actually) and Shelley walked by and said "Pace yourself" and everything inside you tumbled like a felled Jenga tower. Beside you, Anderson downs the rest of his water bottle, says "It might be smart to hydrate, my friend. We're drinking a lot on empty stomachs."

"Fuck that!" Jimmy says and slaps your back. "Let's go straight to the buffet line!"

"I don't think our table's been called," you say, maybe coherently. Even drunk, you know the rules of wedding dinners.

"Who gives a fuck? You think they'll notice?"

Anderson shrugs, like he's powerless to resist the pull of Jimmy's gravity.

So you follow them both to the buffet line, where you all squeeze behind some grandmas, then fill your plates with more food than you should reasonably be able to eat, gigantic scoops of garlic mashed potatoes, stacks of carved roast beast, a sloppy heap of bread-crumb-topped mac and cheese. You're so drunk you've lost all sense of proportion...you want to eat the *entire fucking buffet*! You even snatch the last bacon-wrapped scallop before some great-aunt can get it. She shakes her head, mutters something mean, but you just shrug and follow your friends as they shuffle back toward your table, laughing and bragging about bucking the system, and you're all three walking across the dance floor just as the father of the bride is beginning his speech: "Thank you all so much for—"

And you're walking directly in front of him—HAW! HAW HAW!—louder with your drunk guffaw than he is with his speech, and he has to stop speaking and wait for you to pass. Everyone in the room watching the three of you stumbling oblivious to your table, dripping au jus along the dance floor as you go.

"Okay," the father says and sighs. "Now that I have the floor."

And everyone applauds him and Jimmy is so oblivious that he yells "Whooop! Speech!" When you sit, struggling to stifle your laughter, you look across the room and Shelley is shaking her head.

With the above scene having played out, what would be the most fortuitous course of action for a man who wants to win back the affections of his ex-fiancée, to become that shining beacon of "decent person" that he should be capable of becoming?

A) Go over to her table. Turn on the charm, man! How can she resist?

B) Sit and scarf some free *foooooood*, mothafucka!

C) Jump out of your seat and yell, "I want to make a toast!" Be the center of attention. She'll love that! Everybody loves Party Guy!

D) Tell Shelley to calm. the fuck. down. Weddings, bee-otch!

MY GOD, HOW DRUNK AM I? HOW ABOUT (E) GO BACK TO THE START OF THE NIGHT AND DECLINE EVERY DAMNED DRINK?

EVERY ONE OF THESE CHOICES... THIS IS NOT...

FLIP BACK. PLEASE.

Question #18: Bathroom.

You're peeing into the urinal and having trouble standing and you're holding your hand out to the tiled wall to steady yourself and you're pissing on the floor and it's a wonder you haven't hit your shoes. So, like, for this question, fill in the blanks with the correct word to form the year's top hits most likely to be played at this wedding.

I'm _____.

I Gotta_____.

Tik_____.

Paper_____.

Good Girls Go_____.

_____'N Cold.

_____Your Life.

_____Boy.

Bad_____.

I HAVEN'T LEARNED A DAMN THING, HAVE I? LIKE I'M WATCHING AN OLD VERSION OF MYSELF RUIN MY CURRENT LIFE.

HOW BAD DOES THIS NIGHT GET FOR ME? SKIP AHEAD AGAIN.

Question #27: Sandra.

Sandra is pressed against you, rubbing herself against your erection.

She's putting her soft hand onto your pants and saying, "My thoughts exactly," and now her hand is undoing your belt and you're laughing because this is really happening, and how is it possible that she's able to so easily—with a single hand—unclasp your belt and slip it from the loops and slide her hand into your suit pants?, and her hands are cold when her fingers wrap around you but it's the best kind of cold—

This is:

A) **Going very well.**

B) **Extremely confusing to you.**

C) **A situation you'd like to escape.**

D) **Such a bizarre moment** that you can't actually enjoy what is happening, so consumed are you by the questions of how you got here, how this even came to fruition, and her hand is grabbing your cock and even as you consider the correct reaction you're aware that she's jerking you off—and why aren't you the kind of guy who can instinctively act in all the right ways, like slap her hand away and say, "You're married!" or—God, she's still going—oh God…so…so why not let her?

Question #23: Orlando.

Are you tired of this gimmick? Weary?

Think of how we feel. All of us, our lives one big gimmick.

Think of what it must feel like to drive down I-4 with 3D billboards exploding toward you, Aerosmith's Rock 'n' Roller Coaster shooting from the sign, Spider-Man swinging out, the slides of waterparks curling around like giant balloon animals, all of it just twenty feet from your car. Think of what it feels like to live in a place where the winter months are endless streams of salty muddy cars stamped with Ontario and New York and Wisconsin license plates and the drivers behind the wheels don't give a holy fuck that you're a real town with real residents and real lives. Think of what it feels like to pass electrical towers shaped like mouse ears on your way to visit a friend at the hospital, to—even as you contemplate where your next month's mortgage payment will come from—see a thousand SUVs with those Annual Passholder bumper stickers with the mouse ears in the center, to mistakenly get off on an exit backed up for miles with Disney cruise buses whose back windows are overlaid with the silhouettes of Goofy and Minnie and Donald waving out at you; would that make you feel *happier* in a traffic jam? To be human, to have real problems and real struggles, maybe not always of consequence to the greater world, but *your* struggles and *yours* entirely. Think of how it feels to have them dismissed by outsiders because, *tee hee*, you live in the happiest place on Earth! As if it makes debt feel any happier when you're staring at a replica of the Roman Coliseum, or fighting for a parking space with a man dressed as a court jester and wearing a nametag that identifies him as "Sir Craig." Oooh, or when a man still dressed as Jesus snags the last pump at the gas station, and you've got to wait behind him as he takes his time, his whole damn ensemble an insult that won't quit.

To live in Orlando.

To live in Orlando.

Think of what it must feel like to live in a place where the spotlights are always swirling, the fireworks always blasting, the fanny packs and the bad sunburns and the Brazilian hordes, and the resort hotels where there are giraffes—like, *real fucking giraffes*—walking the fields outside your window, and the hotels where there are full waterparks and pirate ships out back, and no matter how expensive the restaurant there's always a family in swimsuits and sandals leaving wet footprints on the floors. Think not just of the bustling theme parks but consider also the ruins, stretches of city as theme park junkyard, Xanadu and Skull Kingdom, an abandoned stretch of scale-model Great Wall of China. Think of what it must feel like to live in a place where everyone's always pointing with two fingers and forcing smiles that hurt their faces, everything and everyone held to the Disney Standard, the performance unending.

This gimmick is making *you* weary?

Please.

We're sooooo sorry for you.

Perhaps we were just preoccupied with watching the rise of this new monstrous Ferris wheel on International Drive, this high-rise mall/ hotel mash-up that'll bring ten billion more cars to the two-lane roads that we (sadly) must drive.

Feel free to use the space below to rewrite the novel in a more straightforward style that still somehow evokes the personality of the region, and what it truly feels like to live here. Really. Take a moment. Write it down. Photograph it with your stupid fucking smartphone. Send it to brightlights@gmail.com. You want to judge *us*? You do it better, you magnanimous fuck.

We're sorry.

We didn't mean that.

Really, we didn't.

Please come back to Orlando. Call us whatever you'd like. Complain about the heat and the humidity, and say things like "God, who would ever want to live here?" as loud as you can while walking through areas crowded with Orlando residents. When you're at Universal Studios or SeaWorld or Disney World, say things like "It must fucking *suck* to work at a place like this," within earshot of someone sweating his ass off in a Tigger costume. Make fun of Central Florida for the weirdos you see in our Wal-Marts, our 7-Elevens, no matter how closely our weirdos resemble the weirdos in a rural Missouri Wal-Mart, or a Staten Island Wal-Mart, or a Fresno Wal-Mart. Make fun of us for the national news stories of bizarre violence and incompetent court proceedings, no matter your own region's history of violence and incompetence, as if somehow we are *more* deranged, or *less* educated, or *more* racist, or *less* empathetic, or just *subhuman* in general. Say whatever you like. Really.

Just, like, don't take your conference to Las Vegas instead.

Don't vacation to California.

Look at these resorts we've got. *Look* at them. Please don't go.

Don't leave a poor review on Yelp, TripAdvisor, Expedia, Urbanspoon, or any other websites or social media outlets now or in the future.

Gosh, we'll even give you the space below to write something worse, provided you don't share it on the internet. Will that make it better? Also, here's a park-hopper pass for this weekend, along with some Disney dining credits. We can probably throw in some limited-edition *Bright Lights, Medium-Sized City* mouse ears as well. (You'll just need to attend a brief, no-hassle presentation for our new time-share development at Little Lake Grand. Ten minutes of your time, tops. Maybe thirty or forty.)

Question #25: Dinner.

You're bulldozing a forkful of garlic mashed potatoes into a green bean, ramming beef into potatoes now red with blood. To be carnivorous is to be *alive.* You bite down, fumble for your red wine. Yes, that's right, you've covered all the bases tonight: beer, hard liquor, wine…this is a *rock star* night, and you're back on top, baby!

"With the camera?" Jimmy's saying.

"Supposed to *wait* to drink the champagne," Sandra says. She somehow ended up seated between you and Jimmy.

Here at your table in the farthest corner of the room, this wedding reception feels like a fraternity formal, one of those old college events for which you pre-gamed in someone's room at the house, rounds and rounds of shots with a scattering of girls in dresses and boys in tuxedos, and then everyone piling aboard a charter bus with flasks tucked in suit jackets and bellowing drinking songs ("There are no SAEs on the bus! They're all down below, givin' head to ATO, there are no SAEs on the bus!") and everyone sloshed, black-out drunk by the time dinner rolls were dumped on tables. In college you all were frat stars, and now it's impossible to change the behavior so deeply embedded.

"Alcohol in the mashed potatoes!" Jimmy says. "Ha ha!"

"You're embarrassing, Jimmy." Sandra's pushing away from him, toward you.

"How much have we had?" you ask. You want to take stock, a self-inventory…Dizzy, though… the words take effort.

"Come on," Jimmy says.

"Why am I drinking *red wine*?" you ask. "When did I…?"

"You said you wanted to slow down," Sandra says.

You mumble something: "Whereddidthisbruisecomefrom?"

In Anderson's place at the table, there's only an empty plate stained with carving board blood. You vaguely recall hearing him say that he was going back for another cut of prime rib, and you vaguely recall him saying that he was only going to eat meat tonight, just mothereffin' protein, that the potatoes would kill his carb intake for the week. He's been here all night, but now it's just you and Jimmy and Sandra and two of Elaina's high school friends who long ago made it clear they were uncomfortable at this table and are now openly discussing where else they might sit.

"Need another *drank*," Jimmy says. "Donny! Donny!" But the room is loud, the DJ playing Flo Rida and the sorority girls grinding against one another on the dance floor and shouting along. Far away, as if viewed through the wrong end of a telescope, Steven's old high school friend Goat is trying to creep on a sorority girl in a peach dress, but you watch as Anderson plucks him off, lifts him from the floor, and deposits him at the black partition detailing the coastal destruction wrought by the 1926 hurricane. Meanwhile, Donny the bartender is pouring shots for a group of drunk uncles, a reassuring development, as your table no longer appears to be the drunkest here in the History Center. Jimmy tries to stand but collapses in his chair. "Sandra," he says, "get me another *drank*. Get me…" His words are becoming intangible, formless as melted butter, and that *never* happens; Jimmy's blood is more alcohol than blood.

"Get your own Goddamned drink," Sandra tells him.

"Sandra!" he says. Then more gibberish.

"Stop it," she says. "God, you can be so fucking embarrassing."

He slaps the table, nearly toppling her cosmo. "Did you…are you even *listening* to me?"

Your smile is getting harder to hold.

You've forgotten what you were smiling about.

Weren't you supposed to *do* something tonight? Here we are at Question #25, more than halfway through the exam, and it appears you've consumed so much alcohol that you've forgotten how this Final Exam began, the mission you were on, the point of the test.

Sandra throws her hands up in surrender. "Fine, if it'll get you to shut up, I'll get you a drink." And she turns to you and says something she's never said before: "Marc, will you come with me?"

"Will I…" For as long as you can remember, you've always just *wound up* with Sandra while Jimmy wanders off. At a table outside Lakeside Wine Bar, for instance, or on barstools at Buffalo Wild Wings, or at your seats at Magic games while Jimmy spends a half-hour at the bar. Two castaways, Sandra exuding disdain for this sourest of circumstances. Very rarely has she asked you a question without sighing, without closing her eyes and brushing the hair from her forehead so you can see the fullness of contempt in her face.

"Please," she says and opens her eyes wide, that icicle-sharp blonde hair falling across her face in a way that somehow makes her seem not just tired but…vulnerable? She nods in Jimmy's direction like maybe she wants you to *save* her from this abomination she's been cursed with. "Come with me, Marc."

"Sure," you say and wobble-stand.

Does she realize how drunk *you* are, too? How fitting it would be to disappoint her even in this moment, when all she needs is someone *not Jimmy*.

After a moment, though, you shake it off and move cleanly, your drunkenness noticeable perhaps only to yourself, and you follow Sandra toward the bar line while Jimmy leans back in his chair and nearly falls over backward. He's still talking about the NBA Finals, saying something about Kobe Bryant, but no one's around to listen. His eyes are closed and he's talking, his lips not parting wide enough to enunciate. Only caveman sounds. This, you imagine, is Jimmy in fifteen years, this moment, this image, a man who will more and more frequently find himself alone at the party, eyes vacant, blabbering incoherently, a ten-foot radius around him as if he's radioactive… this is Future Jimmy, and you know that Sandra's time enduring it is almost over, that soon enough the marriage will be finished…this is Future Jimmy, and it is toxic and irredeemable, and why has it taken you until now to realize that—whatever past you share with him—*you* do not need to be committed to this man either?

Just like Steven, you've been too quick to bestow upon someone the title of "friend," to give away your loyalty without any return commitment. Too many of these people are only reciting emptily the lines of friendship, and you understand now that you've shaped your life around another rule—your father's?, your mother's?—that needs to be reconsidered: "A friendship is permanent. When someone is a *friend*, they just…are. Forever." Even as others have jettisoned *you* for their own benefit—Shelley, Edwin—you couldn't do the same to them.

Sandra holds out her hand. You grip her fingertips, and she leads you across the room and to the bar, but—just as you take a spot in line—she tugs and leads you out into the hallway, then finally lets go of your hand and puts her palms on her thighs and bends forward. "I just had to get out of there," she says, staring into the floor as if winded.

"He's in rare form tonight," you say.

"I can't take it. I can't take it anymore." Her breaths, they are almost sobs.

"Weddings."

"Not the wedding. *Him*. My fucking husband."

"Oh." This is the comment you knew was coming, but still you're unsure of what to say.

She stands up straight, then turns toward the stairwell. "I need a break. Will you walk with me?"

You don't know where this is leading. Until a minute ago, you thought Sandra was repulsed by you in the same way some people are repulsed by the smell of fish or the texture of oysters or the word "moist." And yet somehow you've become one another's only hopes this evening.

Consider the above scene and context, and—after calculating the number of poor encounters and decisions you've already had tonight—circle the response that most correctly describes how you should now behave.

A) Don't walk with her. Maybe say "Aw shucks, I should probably go back in with Jimmy." (Hmmm, that won't work, will it? He's maniacally drunk, unstable.) Or maybe say "A walk? Um. My leg hurts." (But again, if you park yourself in one spot, you could run into the girl in the red dress, who you've skillfully avoided thus far but who will now likely remember your face. Or you could bump into *Edwin* again, who's almost certainly ready to fight you.)

B) Follow her. Just say "Sure." Sandra is a friend, after all. It's not like you're going to have sex in the middle of the History Center. It's. A. Walk.

Question #26: Following Sandra.

Up the stairs to the third floor, then the fourth, and you're following Sandra into the Famous Florida Disasters exhibit, the entrance of which has been cordoned off with a red velvet rope and a "Please Do Not Enter" sign.

"Let's go in *here!*" Sandra says, voice lifted by the thrill of adventure and danger, and hearing her speak like this rouses in you a reckless exhilaration so deliciously different from your everyday melancholy—and haven't you been trying to get back to the way things were just a year ago, two years ago, when you could quiet the voices inside your head?

She gifts you an unfakeable smile, the opposite of the mechanical mouth reconfiguration she usually forces when speaking to you, the one seemingly created by the pulling of heavy levers. This smile, right here and now, it is genuine: it lights up her face, makes you feel exactly what Jimmy must have felt when he fell in love with her. It's heartbreaking to think that she has such joy inside her but that it's been so deeply buried. When did this happen? How long after she married? Is this the same thing that happened to Shelley, a growing bitterness overtaking a joyful soul? Is there a woman like Shelley hidden inside Sandra?

You follow, and the the two of you stumble into the darkness of Famous Florida Disasters. As your eyes adjust, she leads you toward the 1981 Winter Park Sinkhole exhibit. It's a story most Central Floridians know: a natural disaster only possible in a state so otherworldly, so fantasy-novel, a state where dinosaurs still crawl and slither through backyards and swamps, and where the ground groans open at random and just *inhales* the world above. *Sinkholes.* The geologic explanation is that there are dried-up lakes and rivers beneath the shallow Florida topsoil, pits that—given the right rainfall, the right erosion, the right shifting of weight—are just waiting to reveal themselves, and at some unknowable moment the sinkhole opens its mouth and the dirt falls like sand down the chute of an hourglass, everything built upon the land crumbling and falling with it. Twenty feet deep, thirty feet, forty, fifty, something within reach one moment and then seventy feet below you the next. Sinkholes. An earth-*suck* rather than an earth*quake*, striking highways, schools, neighborhoods, or—in the case of this exhibit—one gigantic block of Winter Park, sycamore trees and houses sucked underground, streets, stop signs, a row of Porsches from a car dealership, the Winter Park municipal pool, all gone *like that*, a sinkhole ninety feet deep opening *like that*, all of the act-of-God devastation re-created here as diorama and as photos on walls, a TV monitor looping news footage from the aftermath.

Still holding hands, you and Sandra enter a tube-like chamber, encircled by the sloping dirt walls of the simulated sinkhole. "Do you ever feel like your life is just this series of stupid mistakes?" she asks. All around you, descending a mock ninety feet, are glued-in dollhouse pieces, streetlights and mailboxes and wooden boards and corrugated metal that one is supposed to imagine as having broken free from some now-destroyed building.

"I don't know," you lie. "Sometimes, I guess."

"And, like, everything could've been different," she says, "if you'd made one different decision? Completely different future, I mean, traced back to one decision."

You're silent. You're waiting for the sinkhole re-creation to start sinking again, the sand in the walls to move, the floor to disappear. Here inside the tube, it is disconcerting to realize that this hole has no bottom, that even though there is a floor, the dirt just abruptly cuts off at the carpet, like the sinkhole goes on without end.

"One choice," she says. "Different life."

"I think you're describing the plot of *Mr. Destiny*," you say.

"Haha," she says, the first real laugh you've ever earned from her, and it moves you in a way you couldn't have expected. "I remember that movie. You're funny, Marc."

"I am?"

"What I'm saying is," she says and with her fingertips gently turns your face to stare into the model. "Those lives were changed in a single moment. But it wasn't something they could control."

You nod. You wonder if she's seen this exhibit before, if these thoughts are recited or if—you at her side—she's coming to an honest understanding of what's happened in her life.

At the bottom of the sinkhole, very near the floor and half-buried in the dirt, is a tan late-'70s camper twice the size of a Matchbox car. And is there a tiny hand reaching out of the dirt wall, too? Are you imagining that, is the darkness playing tricks on you? You try to look closer, but you'd have to move away from Sandra to do so, and there's a heat between you that you don't want to give up.

"Like, how different would things be if you *did* marry Shelley," Sandra says. "Do you ever think about that?"

"Not really."

"Liar." She smiles again in that way that can't be faked. God, that smile is enough to get you breathing heavy, to make you want to hold her, press your lips to hers and just devour her. When you saw your ex-fiancée earlier, she didn't give you a look this warm. Hell, she wanted nothing to do with you. Maybe you've been pursuing the wrong things. Maybe there *is* a woman at this ceremony—here, right in front of you—who needs you, who's *asking* you to save her, a woman to whom you can *prove* that you're a good man.

"Okay. Sometimes I think about it."

"Or how different would things be if I'd never married Jimmy," she says.

You swallow. "Well. I never got married. And, like, you probably don't want to think that way. It's not, um, healthy for your marriage."

"I can't help it," Sandra says. "Nights like tonight, it's all I can think about."

"He's drunk. But he'll sober up."

"He'll still be an asshole."

"Right. But, I mean…"

"Don't tell me you disagree."

"He has some redeeming qualities."

"I live with him. No, he doesn't. I was just…with him, so long. It was like we were *supposed* to get married."

"He means well, I'm sure."

"No. He's worse than you can imagine. The things I've seen in his email."

You reflexively raise your hand to take a drink but your drink is…shit, did you even bring a drink up here?

"It isn't easy being *me*, you know," she says.

"I know it. I never said it was."

"But that's what you think, that I'm just some spoiled bitch." She's closer now, her hip against yours, fingers intertwined with yours. If she moves her hand an inch it'll touch your erection through your pants, and *then* what? "You look at me like you hate me. Why do you hate me?"

And then she's turning toward you and you're turning toward her and you're saying "I don't hate you," but it's more like you're breathing it because her face is now just inches from yours.

"I get so nervous around you," she says. "I've just imagined this so many times."

"Imagined?" Breathe. "This?"

Her fingers are at your waistline and she's asking, "Do you ever think about what it would be like if the two of *us* were together?"

And now, of course, we've arrived at a crisis moment, after which nothing will be the same. What should you do?

A) Break away. Get *out* of here. Now! You know that this is the wrong thing to do. No matter how attractive this situation seems, this is your friend's *wife*.

B) But she said it herself. He's unredeemable. And you've already said that you don't need to commit yourself to friendship with Jimmy, that he's a fucking villain. Why protect the friendship?

C) Motherfucking *commit* to the moment. This could be the one productive thing you've done in months! Enjoy Sandra, with her soft hands and short black dress, moving into you. You're right up against her, after all, and she pulls you forward and backs her ass onto a metal railing and she whispers, "Let's fuck in the sinkhole," and you say "Holy shit."

Question #27: Sandra.

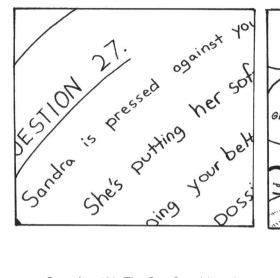

Question #28: The Sex Considered.

You can't help yourself: you run your hands down her hips, her thighs, and you're overtaken by this heat between you, this incredible heat that's been so absent from your life for so long that you almost cry even as her face is on your face, and you're both tearing into each other like children into just-sliced birthday cake, your tie on the floor, suit jacket splashed over the railing, her hand on your dick and yours up the back of her dress and grabbing her ass lifting her onto the railing inside the chamber. You're not sure how you're gonna do this, but you'd better do it right. One gets so few opportunities to fuck over a sinkhole.

And it feels good to be here, to be pressed against her like this, to be submerged together beneath the collapsed topsoil of the Winter Park Sinkhole, the empty underground lakes and rivers that have emptied and drained and left the Earth's surface unsupported.

If this was a romantic comedy, someone would walk in and stop it. Or witness it, at least, and then report back to Shelley, and that'd be the final complication before both parties ultimately made up and got together. But you're not likeable enough to be the star of a romantic comedy. You're just a garden variety taint pirate. And this isn't a misunderstanding: this is the clearest image *ever* that a relationship is truly over, both of you naked and Sandra unwrapping a condom (wait, she carries a *condom* with her to weddings?), your back pushed into the glued-in Matchbox cars of the sinkhole wall as she breathes anticipation, world smelling like hairspray and perfume and body heat and latex.

Even tonight, on a night when you had such a singular focus—*talk to Shelley, win her back*—*this* is where you wind up? With your friend's wife, in the sinkhole exhibit at another friend's wedding, Sandra settling onto you while Jimmy passes out or pukes downstairs? Sandra saying "Fuck, yes!" and grabbing your ass and pushing you deep within her while somewhere beneath you Shelley does the chicken-dance with the bridal party, the cousins, Steven and Elaina? Why does this happen? And when it does, why can't you be like Jimmy and just do whatever you want and not give a fuck? Why can't you *stop* with this awful inhibitive empathy, *stop caring* so you can *rise back to the top* like all the other heartless douchebags out there?

You don't want to be here anymore.

You don't want to feel the thrust, the spread of ecstasy from your outermost extremities into the deepest pit of yourself, the odd mix of pleasure and sadness, like masturbation back in high school, jerking off in the bathroom real quick while your father or mother or brother wandered outside in the hallway, the release as you finish, the look of joy on Sandra's face as she claims some revenge on her husband…You don't want any of that.

Because that's what this is, right? *Revenge.* It's her face. You're not *saving* her. She's biting her lip and moving faster up and down. It's *angry joy*. She doesn't love you, want you, need you. You are a prop to her. You don't want that, and you are no longer willing to make anyone else a prop in *your* life, either.

So this is your one "Get Out of Jail Free" card, Marc. You've witnessed one possible future. This is your only chance to turn back time. Is this the life you want?

A) Yes

B) No

Question #29: Rewind.

So now you know how it *would* play out. Maybe, over the sinkhole, you'd both experience an implosion/ explosion of ecstasy, the sort that would destroy city blocks, the sort that would leave craters in its wake…But the thing is, you know that the sex—its aftermath—*would* be paired with abject misery.

So here at the sinkhole exhibit, you slide your hands out from under her dress, take her wrists and move her hands away from your waist.

"I can't do this," you say.

It feels like a cop-out, like you're less of a man for not following through.

And the response from Sandra is just as poisonous as you might imagine. There's a part of you that wants to fuck her just to take the murder out of her eyes, like if you can give her the revenge-fuck she wants and make her happy then maybe you'll have actually done something good, but no: you cannot have sex another man's wife over a sinkhole and ever again in your life think yourself a good man. If you did, there'd be no need to even finish the exam.

You leave Sandra in the Famous Florida Disasters room and stagger to the bathrooms to rearrange your clothes, straighten your tie, wash your face.

Tonight was supposed to be a final chance at glorious redemption, but do you deserve redemption? Do truly good men screw up as much as you do? Or do they all—like your father—live by codes, die by codes, easily answering A-B-C-D questions and scoring 100%? Tonight was supposed to be about Shelley, and the faucet is still on, and you're saying into the mirror, "Swallow me whole, swallow me whole," and the sinkhole is out there but the sinkhole is you.

Short Response.

Now is a good time to ask: what *is* a good man? Is it better/ more noble to be a good man because you've seen the error of your ways and *changed*? Or is it better to never have experienced or enacted badness, to never have crawled out of anything? Can you be a good man if you've never been tempted to be otherwise?

Question #30: Back in the World.

Still in the men's room, you sit on the toilet, your head in your hands, crying the sort of tears you cried after your mother's accident. Tears not associated with any singular thought, any singular sadness, they just come and they overwhelm you. Fifteen minutes. More. When you stand up from the toilet, the world is spinning more than before, and so you sit back down. It's past 9 PM, maybe almost 10 by now, precious few ticks left on the clock before reception's end.

You drink from the faucet. Splash water on your face.

You decide that this state—the lack of balance, the weird feeling of zooming in/out, camera going in circles—is not going away, and you'll just have to deal with it. You need to see Shelley, after all. This is all for her, the decision you made, the *you* that you want to be.

You leave the bathroom, lurch back down to the third floor, nearly tumble down the stairs. You wobble through the hallways and by the time you make it back to the reception, the world spinning a little less but still off-axis, you spot Shelley and you approach her and summon your focus. The Electric Slide is in full swing.

Pause here, and put down your pencil.

Short response.

Stand up.

Do the electric slide.

We will watch.

Each misstep will result in the deduction of a single point.

Now. Do it.

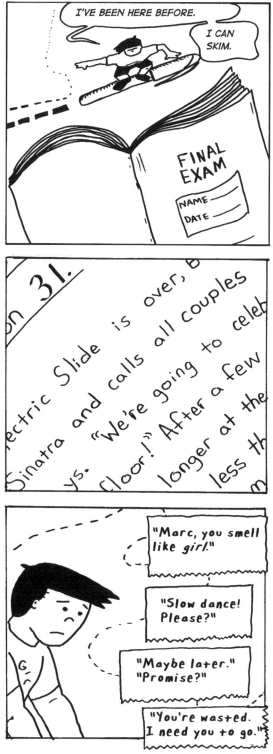

When you return to your table, you find that it's empty. Just Anderson's suit jacket. Perhaps he's also shed his dress shirt, is now shirtless on the dance floor, just bowtie over bulging bare pecs, a bridesmaid unapologetically rubbing his smooth muscles. But when you search the dance floor, you can't find him. Where is he? And *Jimmy*, for that matter?

On the far side of the Land Boom room, Sandra has now fixed her attention upon Edwin, the only man in the room more putrid than Jimmy, and she's running her finger down his cranberry-stained tie and not really caring whether anyone sees her aggressive flirting. Revenge was only tabled for a mere fifteen minutes; the motion will still be carried, seconded.

You look right, left, twirl around like a character in a horror movie who's just realized he's entered a room full of the undead…but there's no sign of them, not anywhere. Something's happened.

You rush to the back stairwell, away from the crowds. When you reach the History Center's first-floor lobby, you see through the glass of the long front window the dark shapes of your three friends. Anderson is carrying Jimmy as best he can, Jimmy's left arm slung around Anderson's neck. Steven is backing away, as if he's helped them get this far but can't go another step. You see Anderson saying "thank you" before dragging Jimmy's drunk corpse away, and Steven turns and comes back inside, straightening his bowtie, adjusting his sleeves.

That's when he sees you. "Holy shit, where *were* you?"

"Sorry, I…I was in the bathroom. I had a moment."

"We just had to haul Jimmy out of here. Anderson's driving him home." Steven puts his hands in his hair. "I thought Sandra would take care of it, but she just kept saying 'Fuck him,' so I don't know what's going on there. I don't want their drama tonight." He wipes the sweat from his forehead. "Fuck. Humid Florida nights. Once you start sweating, you can't stop."

"God bless our state," you say.

"Land of dreams. Paradise found."

"The City Beautiful." You chuckle. "Not to be confused with The Other City Beautiful."

Steven takes a deep breath. "Yeah. Well. We're leaving, Marc." Another deep breath, and he shakes his head. "Moving to North Carolina, buddy. I'm sorry I didn't tell you at the bachelor party, but I'm still…processing it."

"You're getting out of Orlando. I'm glad for you."

"The truth, Marc, is that I don't know if I can move. This place. I've been here since…"

"Listen, Steven—" you start, but how to tell him that you know more about his life than he does, that you understand more completely than he ever will how much he *needs* this move? That he and his city are growing apart, and you can't force a soured relationship back into sweetness? How to tell him that it's okay?

"And I know you're going to make fun of me for the bumper stickers. I know," Steven is saying. "But that's not it, okay? It's about more than that. I mean, I *am* Orlando. Like, to the bone. And Elaina just…she doesn't *care*, you know? It's just, like, *land* to her."

You take a deep breath, adjust your tie. How to tell him…what to tell him…? But something strange is happening deep within you, the rumble and the light of centuries coursing like swamp-mud through your veins. You feel words emerging from your lips that you—just a month ago—would not have said. "Will anyone know that you're gone?"

He turns to you, lips parted but unsure how to respond. "Don't be a dick, Marc."

"What happens when your coffee shop gets demolished," you say, "and some New York developer builds a high-rise condo and shopping center at that intersection? What then?"

"Your voice, Marc."

"What *then*?" you say, the words deep and earthy.

"That won't happen. We band together. We fight the encroachment together. This city and its independent businesses, its artists…we have an *identity*."

"So what happens when you arrive at Mills and Virginia and find a Fresh Market there?" you ask. "An upscale chain restaurant, a Cheesecake Factory, say? What then? Will you still love the city when your quirky neighborhoods are big-boxified and condo-ized? Commodified? When some out-of-town investor reads the name 'Mills/50' or 'Milk District' in a listicle in *USA Today* and thinks: those spots are hip! I'm gonna tear down those old buildings and make something *bigger*!"

"Marc, you're…freaking me out, man."

"What happens when Bar-BQ-Bar is gone?"

"That place is an institution! It's never—"

"The round building will be demolished, and though there will be a fight to save the elaborate concrete work you all celebrate as Orlando's architectural treasure, no one will know what to do with it, and it'll be lost forever."

"That—no!"

"The Merita Bread Factory will close. No one driving I-4 will ever again smell fresh-baked bread on their commutes."

"Stop it."

"Ivanhoe will become a cluster of high-rises. 4Rivers will become a chain. This moment in time. The city you love—"

"How do you—"

"It will be an entirely different creature in five years. The city will no longer wear Magic blue. Everyone will wear purple, and no one will remember 'Make Orlando Weird' because there will be a thousand new slogans battling it out in bloody hashtag wars. In seven years, the city's identity will change so entirely that it'll seem this decade never happened."

Mouth agape, but he's silent. He wants to know what you've become.

"Steven, this place doesn't need you. You are of no consequence. We are all destined to be mud and muck together. Get out now."

"It does," Steven says, "it *does* need me," but his bowtie is crooked and his body looks deflated beneath his rumpled tuxedo. And he backs away from you.

You feel the centuries recede and your voice becomes your own again, and you say: "I thought about something tonight," and Steven stops his retreat. "You're fiercely loyal, Steven. To the city you call home, to the people you call friends. You care about us, but we're not good people. Jimmy. Edwin. Me. You'll move, and Anderson will get a new roommate and nothing will change in his life. Jimmy will ruin another wedding next year. That Goat guy…he'll be borrowing money from someone else next year, and he'll be glad you've moved so you won't ever collect what's owed. These people you call friends…we're *rotten*."

"Don't say that. You guys are my *brothers*! All my life, I was—"

"Steven, I get it," you say. "You went so long without friends that you think this"—and you motion at yourself, and at the now-long-gone spectacle that was Jimmy, and at Goat upstairs in his Sex Pistols t-shirt, probably stuffing beer bottles down his pants to take home—"is what it's supposed to be. It's *not*. You're the best of us, and this is the best thing that could happen to you, escaping the tyranny of shitty friends."

"Stop it."

"Steven, trust me: your life is going to be so much better." You put your arm around Steven's shoulders. On the other side of the History Center's front windows, there's a twenty-something drunkard who's wandered over from Wall Street, his dick in one hand and his other arm out so he can lean against the glass as he pees. He either can't see inside or hasn't bothered to look. He's wobbling, a jet of urine spraying across the glass, and he's rolling his hips as if attempting to piss-spell his name. "Wooo," he says and his eyes are half-closed. "Wooo."

With this image in mind, you say:

A) **"Do you understand,** Steven? Do you get it now?"

B) **Nothing.** There is nothing left to say.

And, arm around Steven's shoulder as if you're counseling a man at his wife's funeral, you lead him back to the reception. Perhaps you've crushed him. Perhaps it was unnecessary. Perhaps he will hate you forever. Or perhaps you've finally done something selfless, something positive for another human being. Perhaps there is hope for you after all?

And here in the hallway outside the Land Boom room, the bass from the dance floor seeping out and traveling up the walls and through the carpet and tickling your toes, that's when you see her and she sees you, and there is sudden and terrifying recognition in her eyes.

The girl in red.

The girl—the one you saved from Jimmy last night—has spotted you finally, and she knows who you are.

Your arm falls from Steven's shoulder as you watch her whisper the words "Oh. My. God," and reflexively touch the bandage on her arm. She grabs her blonde friend beside her. Dear God, what must she be thinking right now? In her mind, she escaped a slaughterhouse.

And you can't look away; she's staring at you with that hypnotizing scream-queen mix of victim/ heroine, her mouth a perfect "o," her eyes conveying horrors unimaginable. Terror, but…no, not terror entirely…she looks *strong*. Remember, she is the type to grab a butcher knife, and swing it. Oh, and that's far worse for you, isn't it?

The girl in red is now slapping her blonde friend's shoulder, saying her friend's name, repeating it louder, louder to get her attention. And now both girls are looking over at you, the blonde's face white with shock as she distinctly mouths the word "*Him?*"

And before you can grab Steven and make a run for it, she's there before you, this girl in the red dress, atomic hate in her eyes. "You're a fucking *psycho!*" she's saying, stabbing her finger at you. Her blonde sidekick stands beside her, nodding with increasing boldness.

You did nothing wrong last night, but how to convey that fact?

"Listen. I didn't do *anything*," you try, but she's advancing, forcing you back into a corner. She is powered by bloodlust. She will slit your throat, slice off your balls, and stand over the corpse with one bloody fist held high. You are doomed.

"What's going on?" Steven asks, his expression alternating between amusement and shock. *Is this*, he must be wondering, *some flirty inside joke between Marc and the girl?*

"I'm calling the police," she says, and the sidekick nods vigorously.

"What's, um…" Steven's saying. "The *police*? Sarah, is this a joke?"

Sarah is her name, then, the girl in the red dress, and she ignores Steven and says, "I'll let you tell *them*. Tell the police you didn't kidnap me, you fucking *psycho*."

Her friend's nodding, aflame with you-go-girl. *Kick ass!* her face says. *Kick ass!*

"Kidnap?" Steven says. "What the fuck's *happening*? Jenna…someone talk to me?"

But Jenna, the blonde sidekick, just shakes her head and says, "Steven, you need to pipe down. This is way more important than your wedding."

Oh, this could get very bad.

"Come on, everyone," Steven says. "Do we have to do this here?"

"*Do we—*" Jenna starts. "Don't silence us. Don't be a fucking *accomplice*."

"Marc, tell her who you are," Steven says. "Tell her! She's got you confused!"

"She knows who I am," you say. "Sort of."

"I will fucking end you," Sarah says, and you believe it. You didn't feel any strength in the dead weight you carried to your couch last night, but you see and feel it now: her muscles taut, her arms lean and fierce, body rippling like she pushes herself through spin class five days a week, muscle toning classes on the weekend, maybe yoga, maybe Zumba, maybe rock climbing, everything the gym has to offer.

"Stop, please," you say, and you finally muster a defense. "Listen, you woke up on my couch in your clothes, not naked or tied to a post in my basement or something. It was my *couch*. I was drinking coffee in my living room and you were under a blanket. That's all. You know it. There's nothing—"

"You *kidnapped* me," Sarah says. "I was probably drugged. And I'm *bloodied* now." She flips her arm around and points at the bandage. "I could've gone to the Special Victims Unit. I could've called my uncle. He's a *Marine*."

"Holy *shit!*" Steven says, hands in his hair, looking around to see if any of his family is nearby. That comment about the tyranny of shitty friends is likely resonating now. "Can we just keep our voices down? Please? That's…that's my wife's *father* over there!"

"This is crazy," you tell Sarah, the girl in red. "I'm not what you think I am."

"*You're* crazy," Sarah says.

"You don't know the half of it."

"Guys like *you* need to get what's coming to them." And she's pointing to you and Steven.

"Whoa. What did *I* do?" Steven asks. "How am I…involved with this? I need to get back to my…to the—"

"You're going nowhere, accomplice," Jenna says.

The entire room is cast in red at this moment, the long hallway and its semi-gloss walls, the crown molding, the industrial carpeting. All of it—the doorway into the Land Boom room, the bathroom and water fountain, all filtered red through an angry kaleidoscope. There's so much anger in this hallway now, anger at the way things are and the way they're supposed to be, and for once in your life you can see it physically manifest, but it isn't just yours anymore.

You close your eyes and shake your head and still you feel the weight of the two girls, the weight of Steven's horrified stare, the weight of what you did with Sandra upstairs, the weight of a life poorly lived for half a decade.

The specifics of what did or did not happen last night are unimportant in establishing this central fact: it is not enough to concede that you have awful friends. You must accept your own vileness, too.

"Maybe," you say softly. "Maybe I deserved to get punched in the face, maybe I deserve it again and again. But I never touched you, except to carry you from the car."

"Don't listen to him," Jenna says.

"You woke up on my couch," you say. Hands out again, like you're begging for your life. "You didn't know where you were. You got spooked and grabbed a butcher's knife and ran away. You *know* that's all that happened."

"*Fuck* you," Jenna says. "He's distorting reality, Sarah."

"Hold on. Who are you again?" you ask.

"Please," Steven is pleading, making prayer hands. "*Please*, the *voices*."

"I'm someone who actually cares—"

"You weren't at my house this morning," you say. "So you didn't see what happened, did you? You have no clue."

"I have *every* clue," Jenna says. Her phone is in her hand, but she hasn't typed any numbers, hasn't hit "call" yet. Jenna is all fire and rage, no different than you, maybe, always craving something to fuel her anger, a particularly dangerous quality when you are on the receiving end of the fury.

"Wait, this happened *last night?*" Steven asks. "After the bachelor party? Marc was with *me* last night. He was at *Disney!*"

You meet Jenna's gaze. She doesn't know what to do anymore. She's looking for the right answer and A seems just as good as B seems just as good as C or D. And she knows the gravity of words like "rape" and "police," words not easily discarded once invoked. "Wait," she says. "Wait wait."

Silence as Jenna attempts to make sense of the moment.

Then she says, "Your bachelor party was at *Disney?*" And her face is intense, but suddenly it cracks, and she's laughing, and then—what the hell?—Sarah beside her is laughing, too.

"Well, I'm glad this is all amusing to—" Steven starts.

"Disney!" Jenna's saying through the guffaws, and she's holding up a finger to give her a minute. "The big bad frat boys, bachelor party at Disney!"

"Come on," Steven says. "Okay. Okay, everyone's having a laugh."

"Were you trying on Goofy ears, Steven?" Jenna says. "Photos with Ariel? Did you post them on your blog?"

You exhale slowly, adrenaline receding. How this potentially catastrophic moment turned into a moment of levity, you're not sure, but you run your hands down your wrinkled dress shirt, down your soaked-with-Yuengling tie. Your hands are shaking now, and your forehead is cold…it's what happens after the fight-or-flight moment has passed, the body trying to use up that adrenaline somehow.

"So how did I get to your house, then?" Sarah asks, wiping at the corner of her eye, the laughter now past.

She's willing to listen. That was the tough part.

You try to control yourself, to speak clearly, though you know you're slurring again. You tell her about Jimmy, about how and when the two of them arrived. She's lucky to be alive, drunk as he was. Hell, you're lucky he didn't plow his car through the front door. You tell her that you carried her inside, sequestered Jimmy to the bedroom. You tell her that you've turned your head too many times when horrible evil things were happening, and maybe it took you too long to finally intervene, but you're not going to watch someone get taken advantage of again. That's your pledge, not just to her but to the world. Maybe it's grandiose, but you believe it now. You believe it about yourself. As weird as this whole episode has been, you know that you made one strong, good decision on your own (you can see it now, you can see it), and you know that you now have (at the very least) the foundation of a code by which you can live. Not anyone else's. Yours.

"I appreciate what you did," she says. "But don't you get it?"

"Get what?" you ask.

"You think this is all about you."

"Well." You look to Steven. You look to Jenna. "I mean. Isn't it?" After all, these are your actions they are discussing. Had Jenna placed a phone call to the police, it would be you who'd have to defend your life and reputation against the merest hint that you'd—

"How can this be all about you," Sarah asks, "when I'm the one who woke up where I did? When I was so fucking terrified that I ran from your house screaming? How can that be about *you*?"

"It's just…I'm being blamed."

"I don't know what happened to me last night," she says. "Do you understand that feeling? I don't know if I was drugged. Fine, I woke up on a suburban couch, and maybe nothing happened, and I'm at a wedding and able to have fun tonight with my friends. But maybe…" And she shakes her head, stares out the window and into the night, tears at her eyes even as the dance floor explodes in merriment, a doorway away. "I walked, half-naked, to a gas station three miles from your house to make a phone call. I had to beg to borrow someone's cell phone. And you're worried about getting blamed."

"It's…I mean, it's a legitimate worry in this, um, political climate."

"Legitimate worry?"

"Legitimate worry."

"Wanna trade lives? Trade worries?"

No thank you, you want to say, but still you want to ask her, "Do you know what *I've* been through?" What, because you're a straight white male, you can't go through some shit, too? You want to tell her that of course your reputation matters. You want to tell her…You want…but it's all so damn exhausting, and maybe it's exhausting because you've been forcing yourself away from just saying the right thing, the only thing.

"I'm sorry," you say. "I feel terrible about everything. You're right. I wouldn't want that. I'm sorry."

Sarah exhales. "Not so bad, was it?"

Jenna pats your shoulder. "That's a nice step, asshole. You're learning."

"I'm one of the good guys?" you say.

"I wouldn't go that far," Sarah says.

"Well. I'm not Jimmy, at least."

"But he's your best friend. So."

And as the women walk back toward the reception with Steven, you nod to yourself. "I'm not so bad. Yeah. I'm not so bad, really."

Hey there! This moment feels good, doesn't it? With these realizations having occurred, it almost doesn't seem necessary to even have an exam anymore, right?

So here are your options:

A) Close the book. Just end on a high note. Drop the mic and walk away! Hell, you can place a bookmark here—right here—and put the book onto your shelf, somewhere between that *Moby Dick* you'll never read, and maybe your college anthropology textbook that they wanted to give you $1.50 for on buyback, and that was just insulting so you kept it for years and there it sits. Anyway, the point is that this moment can last forever, if you just stop now.

B) Turn the page if you think "not quite." There's more to figure out, and more choices to make.

Question #34: Apologies, Forgiveness, Grudges, Revenge.

What, in the end, have you learned about forgiveness? Is it a thing that you want lavished upon *you* when you reconsider your own regrettable actions, but a thing (conversely) you withhold from others? You wanted Sarah's forgiveness, right? There is something productive about apologizing, making yourself vulnerable and accountable, asking for forgiveness, but it's self-serving. It nourishes your guilty soul. What of forgiving others? Should a strong man *never forget*? It has become the motto of a nation attacked, after all, to never forget, but a good businessman—the paragon of capitalism!—is one who can move on from poor deals, insulting offers; what is negotiation if not a series of slights, a series of forgivenesses? Under what conditions, then, do you forgive freely, and under what conditions are you allowed to maintain a grudge? Read the following narrative, which begins just as you leave Sarah behind and re-enter the Land Boom room in search of Shelley. Then, follow the prompt at the end.

Narrative:

It's after 10 PM and you are racing across the room with the singular mission of apologizing to your ex-fiancée for years of awfulness, the exact words forming in your head like a speech to be recited, and then Edwin—the man who started you on your downward spiral—is right there, right in front of you, a barrel of muscle and cranberry stains and bad vibes.

Edwin's just as drunk as you, a dystopian wasteland of a man, those strands of usually-combed-back hair now falling down his forehead sloppy as untied shoelaces. He slouches when drunk, you've learned, and smiles and says "yeahman" (all one word) constantly, his need to please and have a good time intensified by his blood alcohol level.

"So here we are," you say to him.

"Haha, yeahman." He stuffs his hands in his pockets. He's bouncing up and down on his heels, face sweaty. "Guess we didn't talk earlier."

Out on the dance floor it's Kanye West's "Amazing," the anthem for this season's NBA playoffs, and the twenty-something male contingent is excitedly hopping around the makeshift parquet floor and using their beer bottles and cocktail cups as microphone props, but everyone over thirty has vacated the dance floor and is now hovering around the espresso bar.

"Sorry about the drink," you say, an easy apology.

He raises his arms, nods. This is as close to forgiveness as you'll get for such a mean-spirited, stupid act.

There's a long silence between the two of you, during which he could offer apologies of his own. But he doesn't. He just takes his shirt cuff to his forehead and wipes the sweat away. But, like a windshield in early-morning humidity, his forehead immediately glazes over again.

The more you think about your apology, the more you question whether it *was* an "easy" one. How much money does Edwin owe you, how much did he steal, and yet you were restrained enough to only *spill a drink* on him?

"I guess you're lucky I didn't punch you in the face instead," you say.

"I hear you've got some experience with that."

You touch your eye, where the bruise has all but faded. "I got assaulted, two on one."

"You don't have to convince me. Honestly, I don't care."

"Of course you don't. You don't care about anything."

Edwin scratches his nose, wipes his brow again. There are three long hairs that remain sweat-glued to the tan expanse of his forehead even as—with a toss of his head—he tries to bounce the others away. They remain there, unmoved, once-liquid and now frozen with product, stiff strands that will only come loose if scraped off.

"Thank you," he says. "You've just spared me, like, months of counseling."

"Wait. Why are *you* being an asshole to *me*? What right do you have?"

Edwin leans close, pats your shoulder with his sweatiest hand. "I hear the shit you talk about me. Don't think I don't hear it."

"It's not 'shit-talking' when it's true. You damn near ruined my life, you know that?"

"Oh, did I? So *I* asked Shelley to break up with you?" He jerks his head again and his main body of hair bounces as one, those three problematic strands still stuck to his skin. "I made you take out the mortgage on your golf course house?"

Forgiveness. How do you forgive a man like this? It seems that, at the very least, you should issue forgiveness only to those wrong-doers who express awareness of what they did wrong. That seems a reasonable criterion, doesn't it?

"Listen to me, Edwin: my house wouldn't be a problem if I still had a functioning business. That's on *you*."

"You do have a functioning business," he says, "you just don't know it."

"I know that you fucked me over."

And if he'd just acknowledge this…then perhaps you'd be able to forgive him. Damn him for making this tough.

"Way I see it," he says, "I gifted you with a business. If the business isn't going well, turn it around. Don't whine about the gift."

"You didn't *gift me* with anything. You left when things got tough. Left me with all the work, and yet I still don't own anything outright." You stop, considering something you hadn't even vocalized until now. "Your name is on all the mortgage documents, right along with mine. I have to work my ass off to sell these properties, and then if I'm successful, I've *still* gotta hunt you down for signatures and pay you back your share. That's not a gift."

Edwin shifts on his feet impatiently, pushes up his sleeves. "Blame your problems on me," he says and the hair is in his eyes but there's anger beneath those black icicles.

"You drained the bank account when you left!" you say. "You sold the staging furniture. Who else would I blame for that?"

"Do you know where I'm living?"

"Your parents' place. Living well, I imagine."

He rolls his eyes. "God, you're clueless. Do you know how much my parents lost, how much they still stand to lose?"

The DJ is playing something indistinct now. It's all bass pops, air horn noises, the moaning noises of a woman presumably mid-coitus. The dancing seems uncertain, Goat in his t-shirt cackling and mocking the very concept of dancing, gesticulating wildly, the girl Jenna eying him like he just farted, and maybe he did. God, how you'd love to see the two of them dance together.

"I'm sure they're fine," you say finally. The losses of the wealthy are of no concern to you. You are now a firm believer in "trickle-down empathy," the desire to feel and understand only those whose income is equal to or less than your own. Millionaires? Fuck them. Fuck them up their wealthy asses. They deserve all that's coming to them.

"Everything," Edwin says. "They lost everything. They were building this condo complex…" One arm is stretched out in mid-gesture, shirt all bunched up at the elbow and wet from sweat and red with cranberry, but he puts his hand back in his pocket. He stops, shakes his head. "Why bother? The explanation is the same for everyone, isn't it? My father sold off his investments, everything he had. Cashed in his retirement when he couldn't get the credit he needed for the first phase of construction. And in the end, it's a shell, this development, and still they're going to lose it."

To have one's entire life reduced to unusable, unfinished real estate: is that enough to elicit feeling? To know that someone has worked a lifetime, but must now start over with nothing at age 60? Does this sad scenario erase their years of financial excess? "At least you're getting to crash at their mansion for free rent, right?"

He meets your eyes, won't look away, doesn't even appear to be blinking. "I'm sleeping on the couch at my sister's place, smart guy. Much to the chagrin of her boyfriend, who's convincing her on a daily basis how much of a parasite I am."

"Free rent is free rent," you say.

"Only for another month. I'm working. Saving for first and last month's rent."

"You could've taken one of the rental properties. Made it your home."

"Yeahman, sure," he says, and he's trying to look tough but the sweat is pooled at his eyebrows. How does a man get so damned sweaty in a place so heavily air-conditioned? "I'm sorry. I could've stayed in Orlando. I just…I needed to get out. I needed a fresh start." He wipes at his nose again, wipes his hand through his hair. "I needed to get clean."

And there it was.

Edwin apologized to you. Did you hear it?

After so long, after you'd nearly given up on life because of what he did to you, he's standing before you in a stained dress shirt, sweaty helmet of hair deflated over his face, and he's telling you that he made a mistake, he knows it. Acknowledgment. Is this enough for you to forgive him?

"Get clean?" you ask, something else suddenly clicking.

He sniffs. "Yeahman."

But this is too much. Certainly there's a point where it just becomes *too much*: too much whining, too many excuses, too many bad decisions and willful errors for a grown-ass man to make, too much too much too much, and you're thinking—here in this moment, that so much of your daily anger focuses on things that don't matter (sports, traffic, grocery cart wheels that don't spin properly) because the few things that you *should* be legitimately angry about (*this* motherfucker, for instance) have been inaccessible. Forgiveness? If ever there was a reason to deny forgiveness, it is *here*, *now*. Right? Right?

Forgiveness is such an easy concept, isn't it? So. Given the above narrative, create a flow chart that will show what Edwin must do to gain forgiveness. Space is provided below.

Note For Teachers: Essay responses are subjective. Score the essay on a 1-5 scale, while immediately disregarding any/ all artwork that is superior in quality to the work found in this book. We don't like to be shown up.

But Edwin is still talking, going deeper into his drug story, saying "can't believe you never knew," and "don't judge me" and "you really should've stopped me" and it's that last comment that jerks you back to reality.

"Wait. So this is my fault?"

"I mean, not entirely," he says. "You were my *best friend*. You should've noticed. You should've *done* something. I was, like, relying on *you* to make the right decisions."

You shake your head, picture yourself grabbing Edwin by his stupid bangs and yanking his stupid skull down into your upward-thrusting knee. As the image plays in your mind, you savor the crack, the droplets of sweat that'll shake outward from impact. But you don't want to give in that easily.

"I guess I could move into the Lake Nona house and—"

"I'm lost here," you say. "Didn't you say *two seconds ago* that you needed to *move away* to get clean? Now you're talking about *coming back* from Atlanta?"

He wipes his nose. "You got me thinking," he says. "We own those houses. Why would I bother *renting?*"

"We own them because I've been busting my ass to make ends meet and keep them. If it was up to you, they'd all…" You shake your head. "And anyway, Orlando enables your addictions, apparently, which until now I didn't know were addictions."

"I mean, I'm fine now. I've learned how to handle myself," he says. "I'll just move into that house, get myself clean again, and we can get back to work. Together. Like, we make a couple sales and we're right back on top, you know?"

Hand on your forehead. Eyes shut. There was indeed a time when this act would've sold you, Cool Guy Edwin buddy-buddying back up, the party life a panacea for your bad moods. "That house is off limits. That's the best property we've got. That house is going to *sell*."

"Not if I don't sign the paperwork. Come on, Marky Marc. Old times, my man."

You need your hands to do something. You run your fingers over your shirt buttons, smooth the shirt at your belt line. "I've told you a thousand times. 'Marky Marc' doesn't work. You can't just pretend there's a *k* in my name. Anyway, I thought you said you had a job."

"I do. It's just…it sucks." He's looking at the wall now, and you're not sure what he's picturing, what he even does with his days. "Back when things were working for us, like *really* working, that's the life I want. I want to get back to *that*. Come on, bro."

Hands smoothing your shirt again. "If I were anyone else," you say, "I would've knocked you out a long time ago. You defy the traditional definition of douchebag. Edwin, you are in a class all your own."

"Thanks," he says. Sniffs. "Dude, just siphon the *bad* investments into your loan-closing business, then let *that* go bankrupt so it doesn't affect our personal credit. Easy-peasy." The loan-closing business. Your only steady income, your honest business you've worked so damn hard to build, your reputation. "Then we keep and sell the *good houses*, use *that* cash to buy some cheap foreclosures, rock-bottom prices…I mean, it's can't-lose."

"Are you kidding me?"

"Bro," he says, winks. "Bro-ooooo."

"Here's my counterplan," you say.

"Yeah?" Sniffs.

Yeah. Here we are. The end of your encounter with Edwin. And it is time to choose, once and for all, how to proceed through this relationship that— like a bad property in your portfolio—cannot be easily dumped. You should now have your flow chart for forgiveness, and a "code" by which to operate. What would a good man do in this situation, a *good man* who's cognizant of his prior awfulness, who is serious about making amends to the community around him? Let's apply your code to this real-world situation. In the space below, explain how you could forgive a man you once deemed unforgivable. Feel free to do so in comic form, since of course we have seen your cartoon persona lurking in the margins:

YEAHMAN.

Sniff

THERE ARE A LOT OF CHOICES I HAVE RIGHT NOW, AND THIS ONE I'M CERTAIN ABOUT: I HAVE TO FORGIVE YOU. WHATEVER YOUR REASONS, AND WHATEVER BULLSHIT YOU GOT INTO, THIS CAN'T GO ON ANY LONGER.

I WAS ABLE TO TAKE YOU OFF THE BANK ACCOUNT SO YOU COULDN'T STEAL EVERY PENNY I DEPOSIT, BUT I CAN'T TAKE YOU OFF THE MORT-GAGE DOCUMENTS.

24 HOUR BANKING

WELCOME

SO SURE, I DO NEED YOU. BUT I DON'T TRUST YOU. SO YOU'RE GOING TO LIVE THERE, AND PAY RENT--

AND WORK AS A NOTARY, AND CLOSE EVERY DAMN LOAN I SEND YOUR WAY-

AND LIVE A BORING LIFE IN A SUBURB OF '80S-CONSTRUCTION STARTER HOMES UNTIL THAT HOUSE SELLS...

YEAHMAN?

YOU'RE GOING TO DO THAT, BECAUSE THE
ALTERNATIVE IS THAT WE BOTH WALK AWAY
FROM OUR FINANCIAL OBLIGATIONS, AND
THEN WE BOTH SPEND TEN MISERABLE
YEARS TRYING TO RECOVER.

AND LISTEN TO ME:
THE SECOND YOU MISS
AN APPOINTMENT...

OR SHOW UP HUNG-OVER,
OR WHAT-THE-FUCK-EVER,
WE'RE DONE.

FORGIVENESS IS
EASY, BUT TRUST HAS
A STEEP PRICE.

I DON'T KNOW IF ANY OF THIS
GETS ME CREDIT.

I DON'T KNOW IF YOU'VE GOT A
FINAL EXAM YOU'RE TAKING, TOO.

HELL, I DON'T KNOW WHAT THE
FUCK A PASSING SCORE
EVEN GETS ME, ANYWAY.

BUT THIS IS THE BEST I'VE GOT.

OKAY.

OKAY, MAN.

THEN WE'RE DONE FOR TONIGHT, EDWIN.

Question #36: A Dance with Shelley.

There's one thing left to do tonight. One person left to speak with.

Far away, beyond the clutter of a reception that has built to a dozen different climaxes, Steven and Elaina are clinking champagne glasses with her parents. From here, it all looks hazy, soft focus, but Elaina appears to be all smiles, while Steven's joy looks tentative, a smile that he can only force so wide before it crumbles back on itself. He'll be fine. You know it. If Shelley asked you to move to San Diego with her, after all, you'd make it happen. You'd work as a janitor in California. You'd do anything. She is the answer to any question that you could possibly ask.

From afar, you watch Shelley engaged in hearty conversation with one of Steven's cousins, an attractive Nebraskan who's benefited from country life in all the right ways. This is not a man who spends his days driving from house to office to house, then forcing himself to the gym lest his muscles quit him. This is a man who builds, who operates real-man machinery, who produces, and who in turn the lord has blessed with a torso that'd burst your clothes apart Incredible Hulk-style. Probably he operates by a code similar to your father's and never needs to settle internal conflicts over rightness and wrongness, never needs to interrogate his life's decisions or struggle toward goodness. He simply *is*. There's strength in that kind of self-assurance, there's power. There's a lot to like about it, a life made easier by the avoidance of nuance and choice. But it's also…it's *country*, is what it is, not city, not even medium-sized city, a life without complexity.

You cross the dance floor, your feet carrying you ever closer to her table. The thing to remember, despite the clear prose of this final exam, is that you're still sloppy drunk. The end of the reception is near, and the alcohol has come to collect.

Still, Shelley earlier agreed to one dance, or maybe she kinda sorta acquiesced just so you'd leave her alone? Either way, you're going to make it happen. And—in a night filled with sinkholes and mystery women and drunk uncles—it's comforting to know that the song crackling to life as you approach her table is something as calming and earnest as Garth Brooks' "The Dance." You don't listen to country music anymore, not since your freshman year of college when you took white-out to the sketchpad that was your personality, trying desperately to conceal any trace of backwoods Georgia—but when you hear Elaina shout "Oh *yes*! Garth!" you think, Well, cool, dancing to "The Dance." Simple enough. Nothing to unpack here. One thing in the narrative of your life that can be literal, easy.

"Will you dance with me?" you try to say, but everyone at Shelley's table— from the Nebraskan cousin to the waifish heartland blonde who looks like she spends too many hours each day at church activities—looks horrified by the degree to which enunciation eludes you.

"…the dance we shared," Garth is singing, "neath the stars a-bove." (And oh God, Garth is so down-home, so regular, so trustworthy. Garth is good people, and the contrast between his voice and yours is almost enough to make you cry.)

The Nebraskan is confident, looks like he's about to ask Shelley "is this guy bothering you?" A tough-guy cliché waiting to happen.

But Shelley takes a deep breath and says, "I suppose?" Not exactly a rousing endorsement, and her nod is heavy with let's-get-this-over-with, but once you're on the dance floor you fit together still, your body and Shelley's.

Your hand at her waist, hers between your shoulder and neck. It's so natural that it might never have ended between you.

"Holding you," Garth is singing, "I held everything…"

"So here we are," she says. Beneath the thickness of your suit jacket, you feel her fingers resting upon you, and you want them to press tighter.

"This is…" (and you want to say "the only thing I really wanted tonight," but it's too bold, too much, even now your mind cycles through choices, weighs pros/cons) "…nice."

"Have a good time tonight?" she asks.

"Funny to think that we gave them the idea for their wedding reception," you say. "We should've been credited in the program."

"That's not how it happened."

"Yeah. After we told them about our plans to book the Science Center, they booked the History Center."

"Nope," Shelley says. "Elaina's good friends with one of the women on the board here. She, like, completely redesigned this lady's living room. They got an amazing deal, paid almost nothing."

"Oh. I guess I, uh, remember differently."

You kick into her foot as you shuffle and she says "Ow! I'm wearing heels, be careful." You mumble apologies, but step on her toe again moments later. The more you try to force yourself to move with her naturally, the more your body betrays you.

"I hear you met Sarah," she says.

Oh dear God. "You talked to her? Tonight?"

"She asked how we ever got together. I told her I was a different person a few years back. Wilder."

"We all were."

"She asked why we broke up, too."

You wipe your forehead. You know the answer to this question, know it with such deepness of understanding that to hear euphemism vocalized would break your heart far more than the truth. "What did you tell her?"

"Our lives," Garth is singing, "are bet-ter left to chance…"

"I told her the truth," Shelley says, her hand curling away from its spot on your back, returning to her side as if holstered. "Our futures weren't compatible. We were going in two different directions. Not the most interesting break-up story, is it?"

"But what if…" Song ending, Garth singing that he could've missed the pain, but then he'd have had to miss…the…dance. You forgot that this song is actually a downer. It's one of those songs that sounds upbeat but then gets uncomfortable when—after you've finished dancing or singing along—you replay the lyrics in your head. Elaina and Steven are a few yards away on the dance floor, her head on his shoulder, his eyes glassy. This is the last you'll see of either of them for a long time, probably. And Shelley…

"What if I was a different me?" you ask. "What if my future has changed? What would it take to be compatible?"

Garth fading out, Outkast fading in, DJ telling the room that this is our last chance to get rowdy on the dance floor, and Shelley drifts away like a moon set free of orbit to join a sparkling new galaxy, drifting to the system of sorority girl friends who are together shaking it like a Polaroid picture, but before Shelley disappears into them entirely she says, in lieu of goodbye, "We'll never know, will we?"

And now you're alone at one far edge of the dance floor, a world abandoned, trying to conjure something to say but there's nothing, no way to prove to her that you've changed, because *have you*? She wants a real marriage; she wants a man who will make responsible decisions, and she doesn't want to sink into deeper and darker anger with him; she wants children, and she wants to be good to them. She wants joy in her life, wants to rediscover what that means on her own. These things seem so simple when you think about it, and yet you've confused them into such a long fucking test.

"Ladies and gentlemen," the DJ is saying, "the bride and groom would like to thank you for standing by them, for being their pillars, their community, their family…Let's wish them off as they take their leave, and journey across the European continent for their honeymoon!" The room shakes with applause, and then—as the hollering fades—you see that the bride and groom are gone too, Land Boom exhibit becoming just another empty trashed room in your life's floor plan. And so now it's time to wonder what this night has meant. This is not how it is supposed to end. Just one quiet dance? You pay close attention to endings in movies, and they don't end like this. "This can't be it," you say. "That can't have been it."

There's a full Jack and Coke on your dinner table still, left presumably by Jimmy, and it's in your hand and down your throat and in your belly to power you through, because you must have another moment, *must*, cannot give up so easily. If you can just talk to her one more time… If you can just…

And as Shelley walks off the dance floor, you're there to intercept her, asking if she'll join you at the espresso bar, "I need a cappuccino, maybe two? I need caffeine and hydration."

"How responsible of you," she says.

"Believe it! I left a full Yuengling on the table." (You didn't. You chugged that, too.)

"A full beer untouched? Very proud of you."

At the espresso bar, you down a water and stuff another into your jacket for the road. "Who drove you here?" Shelley asks.

"Myself."

"*You* drove?"

"I wasn't planning on drinking so much."

"Your plans changed, obviously. Are you calling a cab?"

"Have to get my car out of the parking garage tonight, or it gets towed."

"A DUI is more expensive, you know."

"I *have* to drive," you say. "What else am I supposed to do?"

She throws up her hands and suddenly the frustration—the look you recognize from your brief time together at the house, the housewarming party, the moment she confronted Edwin over those notepads—is back. She'd been stifling it, had maybe *quit it* for months, but it's back fully. "That's how it goes with you, isn't it? Always some excuse for doing the wrong thing. You love convincing yourself that there's *no other choice*."

"That's not true. I'm always—"

"Always what?"

"Always thinking about different choices. Different outcomes."

"Right," she says.

"You don't know what it's like inside my head. It's…It's maddening."

"You think it isn't like that for *everyone*? God, Marc," she says. "I'm going back to the table." A few steps into her retreat, she stops and turns back to you, and she's stunning in her fury and in her heels, looks taller than she ever has, calves tensed like she's doing lifts, her body in that yellow dress like a piece of unbreakable hard candy. "I was anxious about tonight. You need to know that. I was anxious about seeing you again, almost couldn't come. Because I figured the night could've gone one of two ways: either you'd be super-nice and we'd stay friends after I move, or you'd be a drunk asshole. A few minutes ago, I thought: well, he proved me wrong…he was actually nice. But now this is my final impression of you, the image I'll always remember when I think about you."

"But I had some good moments, too. You can't ignore that."

"They're crowded out by the asshole moments."

"Come on."

"You smell like *another girl*," and she shakes her head in a way that gives you pause, like maybe there *was* a chance for the two of you tonight and you ruined it, "you had a dozen drinks at least, and you're about to *drive drunk*, and you're going to argue that you had *good* moments? I saw them carrying Jimmy out of here. When will you guys fucking *grow up*?"

"I've tried so hard, though," you say. "Give me another chance. Let me show you that I've changed. Let me…"

"This isn't about trying hard. It's about you making bad choices, and more bad choices, and more. If you're doing shitty things, who cares if you *want* to be good? I don't want to keep doing this, Marc. I've *decided*."

"But that's what all this has led to, don't you see?"

"Oh my," she says. "You've played out this whole fucking story in your mind, haven't you? Your life as some epic hero's journey, and tonight you were going to, what, sweep me off my feet and we'd have some happily ever after?"

"That's…it sounds dumb when you say it like that."

"You made me into the answer, but the question has nothing to do with me. Shit, when was the last time you even saw me?"

"I don't know."

"Let's refresh our memories. The day I moved out of that house of yours?"

You remember how angry she was that day. *Why can't she smile?* You remember thinking that. This gigantic house, this pool, *why can't she just fucking smile?* And that night, after she'd left you for good, you punched a wall that you'd later need to call a handyman to patch. You were angry that she was angry, angry that she'd left, angry that you were alone on Labor Day and how could you enjoy your holiday now? Shit, you couldn't go drink with your friends, not that night, not the next night, not till the hurt and humiliation passed. Angry at her, angry at the world for not being everything to which you felt entitled.

"I've got two weeks left in town," she says. "There's no magic that can keep me here."

"But maybe…" you try, even though you know it's beyond futile. "I mean, maybe…"

"Whatever the hell is going on in your head: *leave me out of it.*" She's walking back to her table. She's grabbing her purse, kissing Nebraska on the cheek, telling the others she'll see them at the after-party, and then she's heading for the stairwells and you are following her. Slowly, subtly, so Nebraska doesn't decide you're a threat.

"I can be a good father," you say too loudly across the first-floor lobby, so close you can feel her disgust radiating like body heat. "If that's what you were worried about? I took stupid chances, I know. I was too self-centered. I get reckless, I get angry…I get…I get these days where everything just infuriates me, and it's stupid, it kills me. But I know that I just need to open up. Live for someone else. I can be a good father, Shelley."

She turns around and comes close, and there's a feeling of finality to the way she takes your hands and looks you in the eyes and nods. "I know. Maybe it took all of this for you to get there, Marc, to realize it. I'm sure there's a good man in you. I don't hate you. I know that you can be a good father, too, a good husband." She lets go of your hands. "But I also know that it won't be with me."

And then she's gone, one final time, out the door and into the night.

What next?

Where do you go now?

A) You know the answer to that one, don't you? You've already skipped ahead to Question #37. Hell, that was the first thing you read.

B) So go ahead. Push open the door.

C) And slowly, sloppily, stumble-chase her through Heritage Park, a drunken pursuit that ends outside the parking garage with the giant Florida landscape mural.

D) And there you are, face to face. Maybe it's time to write that essay, the prompt you saw when you first flipped to Question #37, then dismissed? Yeah. Let's give that a try. Now that you're sober, reading this final exam, what would you say to this woman who's meant so much to you?

Yesss

into this room ... finally

...

Okay.

Maybe I should start with this.

I, um. I saw you a couple weeks ago, Shelley.

I was at a gas station.

You were across the street.

Well, I think you were. It was your car, anyway.

So the odds were good that, despite the randomness of our lives, we had come together...

That meant something, right?

So...I guess I was angry that day, too.

And those few seconds when I thought I might see you, and reconnect... it was the first time I'd felt happiness in so long.

And I thought, maybe I could make things up to you. And if I did that, maybe you could make me a good person again.

And I know that isn't fair. I understand now that you were angry when you were with me, that you didn't like the person you'd become.

I don't like the person I've become, either.

It kills me now to watch it, divorced of myself, this man in my skin acting outside of my mind.

The more I think about our time together, the more certain I am...

My mistake wasn't just the house, or the business, or even the anger I invited into our lives...

My mistake, the big one, was in how I saw you at the gas station...

And how I saw you here, at the wedding...

My mistake has nothing to do with why you left me.

My mistake is why I wanted you back.

I wanted you to be my redemption.

That's what men like me always want from women, isn't it?

I'm glad you're leaving. You deserve better than me.

You're important because you're important.

EX

I hope that San Diego is everything you need it to be.

I hope you find a job where you're respected. I hope your wine glasses are not cracked, that your house is not empty and your furniture is not broken.

I hope that, if you want a family, you find someone who'll help you to build it, and everything about the experience brings out the best in you.

And years from now, you have memories of having lived in this place, with this man, but the memories aren't clouded by anger or resentment.

That's it.
That's all.

These are the things I wish I could say in person, outside the parking garage, but I don't know what's real or not anymore, what's the page and what's the margin, what's the answer and what's the trick.

I just know that this is me.
This is who I am now.

Question #38:
Getting Home.

Question #39: Your Brother's Note.

"Marc, tried calling. Left a voicemail, but I know you're at that wedding. Leaving for Georgia. Call me when you wake up and I'll give you an update."

Kyle is indeed gone. His truck, his duffel bag. The house is again your tomb.

You check your messages. Sometime in the night, Kyle did call, but the wedding was chaotic, the music too loud, and at some point your battery died.

Kyle's voicemail tells you this: your father has had another heart attack.

Hold on. You must've heard wrong.

Listen again.

Your father has had another heart attack.

With such a message hanging in the stagnant emptiness of your house, there are two choices:

(A) **Rush to your father.** Go home to Georgia. Settle the grudges. Family.

B) **Fuck family.** Isn't that the decision you made a decade ago? Stay here. Stay in Florida, and stretch out in the life you've built on your own. Call Jimmy or Anderson and do Sunday brunch at, like, Dexter's or something. Take a nap. Consider potential travel plans once you consult your week's schedule.

You are driving. It's the morning after the wedding and you're driving a horror-movie stretch of the Turnpike, fog drifting between pine trees and consuming the road ahead, anti-abortion billboards rising through the gray at mile-marker intervals, the faces of babies ("I love you, Mommy. Why do you want to kill me?") and shattered women ("You can still be saved") blurring, disappearing from mile to mile. The fog seems always to retreat in anticipation of your car, but all the world is milky and thick and wet, only pinpricks of southbound headlights struggling through the gloom. You're still half-drunk, but it's early morning and you cannot wait, not after Kyle's note, his voicemails. Many hundreds of thousands of pine trees later and you will be in Georgia.

It's a long drive back home. Which CD would you most like to listen to?

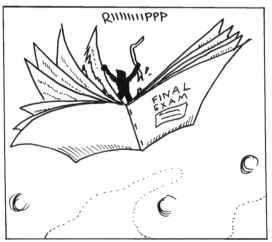

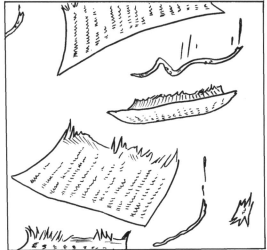

We understand that you're upset, Marc. You should be. But we also know that you'll make the right choice. This was a 40-question exam, after all, and the final question has already been written. You've *seen* the answer. If we didn't think you'd be changed by all of this, what was the point?

All right, then.

And so, Sunday morning, sky outside the color of your hangover, all the world looking sick and drained, you assume your place in your car and you turn the key and you drive and you don't look back. There are still choices in your life—what CD to pop in, for instance—but it's clear that an exam is no longer necessary.

Arrival in Georgia

Mid-afternoon, you exit the interstate and twist through back roads, through back roads behind back roads, past power lines and fields and buildings that once were gas stations but now are weeds and crackled concrete. The closer you get to your father's house, the more these anonymous objects and landscapes begin to feel like landmarks, mailboxes and ponds that you once memorized as you go-karted far from home. Closer, then closer still, until you are in the vague geography you've always called "the neighborhood" even though it's definitely not a neighborhood in the suburban sense; out here, the houses have been built at infrequent intervals amid the sprawling forest, some well-kept, others shrouded beneath low oak branches and draping nets of Spanish moss. There is no aesthetic consistency to the designs, no demographic or socioeconomic consistency to the occupants: some houses are points of pride, castles for retirees escaping city life, while others are 70-year-old relics inhabited by old-timers who still watch TVs that can only be fixed with a caveman bang. This is the world outside the domain of any HOA, settlements in the wilderness.

When you arrive at your father's house, Kyle answers the door wearing an old work uniform from the auto shop, cap turned backward. "Wondered when you'd wash up," he says.

Even now, with your father in the hospital, the lawn is meticulously maintained, azaleas clipped in a perfect line, grass edged along the long wooden posts your father has laid on either side of the gravel driveway like poor man's curbs.

"I'm sorry it took so long."

"You're here," he says. "That's what's important."

You crunch forward and step into the house, past the hand-carved sign that says "Welcome to the Turner's" (you never had the heart to tell your father that the apostrophe was a mistake), and wrap your arms around Kyle, hug him the way you should have when he showed up in your driveway *a month ago.* "I'm sorry," you tell him again. "Kyle, I'm sorry."

You're so fragile it almost feels like your bones will break if you hug too hard, but you do it anyway.

"It's all right, brother. Let me breathe, huh?"

"Sorry," you say, backing away from him.

You've been sitting in your car for the past four and a half hours, and still you crumble to your knees in your father's doorway, as if there's no strength left in your legs. You raise your hand to your eyes and you try to say more but you can only manage a pained wet croak. You didn't want to wind up back here, not ever, not for any reason. You were better than this place, you thought, better than where you came from. But now that you're here, you understand that you should've come a long time ago.

"Come on," Kyle says and lifts you by your shirt. "Inside, buddy. Work to do."

•

Inside the house are stacks and stacks of boxes, some flat, others fully assembled and bearing the logos of familiar alcohol brands—Smirnoff, Bacardi, Tanqueray—boxes taken from liquor store dumpsters, no doubt. The floor looks like the sorting room at a Goodwill, shit of questionable worth and salvageability gathered in piles, stacked canned goods, stacked records, three VCRs one on top of the next, extension cords leading everywhere.

"What's going on here?" you ask.

"I'm packing," Kyle says.

"Packing what?"

"The whole house."

"Did I miss something?"

"Dad's not staying here anymore," Kyle says. "He's alone. Friends gone, family gone, job gone. This is his second heart attack. Do you know the only reason he's still alive?"

You bend at the knees and lift an old plastic ice cream bucket now filled with screws and pegs and allen wrenches. Either your father collected spare hardware, or Kyle collected it from all over, from wall corners, beneath cushions, under couches. "The hospital?" you ask. "The doctors? Medicaid?"

"Don't be a smart-ass," Kyle says.

You hold out your arms in surrender. "I'm not trying to start a fight, Kyle."

"He was outside watering the flowers." Kyle leans over to grab a stack of old newspapers, lifts them and tosses them into a white trashbag with RECYCLE drawn in Sharpie across the plastic. "Doris—from down the street?—was walking her dog."

"Doris," you repeat. You have no idea who that is.

"Older woman? Husband died of throat cancer when we were in middle school?"

You shake your head. This place. How fully you've purged it all from your hard drive.

"Dad fell over, sprayed her with the hose."

"He had the heart attack *outside*?"

"Since the shop closed, it's been yardwork 24/7. You should see the size of his garden out back. It's like he thought he'd never afford another grocery run. Rows of corn, green beans, peppers, preparing for a damn zombie apocalypse. I think he was buying gold, too, but I'm not sure."

"Gold," you say. Likely a fear-based investment, but still, that's progress, right? Your father investing? "A shame he didn't maintain the inside the way he maintained the outside."

"You know Dad. A walking contradiction."

He pulls the strings on the recycle bag and lugs it past you to the garage, opens the door and tosses it into the darkness. "Threw out his cigarettes," Kyle says. "Rounded up the liquor. It's his diet, more than anything: red meat every meal. Full sticks of butter in his baked potato. That Turner family metabolism. Burns through it like it's nothing, and he thinks it's a sign of good health."

"So where will he go?" you ask, and when Kyle walks past you to grab another trash bag without answering, it hits you: Kyle isn't talking about your father moving *somewhere*, in the abstract. He isn't talking about Dad in an old folks' home; Dad's too young for that, and he'd never agree to such a thing.

He's talking about Dad moving in with *him*, with *Kyle*, and by extension, since Kyle lives in the guest bedroom of your house, with *you*. Kyle's packing up your father's stuff to bring to *Orlando*. The Old Man coming down to the Big City? It's a scenario out of a bad sitcom.

You can see it now: your father sitting in the living room late on Saturday night, watching *Cops* as you bring a girl home, grumbling to you that *nothin' good ever happens after midnight, son*; your friends over for a Magic game and your father wobbling out from his bedroom to tell you all to *keep it down* and *watch your language*; your friends over for a barbecue and your father questioning how quickly you turn the steaks on the grill; your father drinking his chocolate milk from your pub glasses, OJ from your rocks glasses, sneaking cigarettes into the bathroom during his "morning constitution" and yellowing the walls; your father taking note of every artifact that Kyle saw on his house tour, the empty photo frames, the glass coffee table, the makeup dotted on electrical outlets, then making the cutting observations that Kyle was too polite to say ("Why the hell you listing *things to be happy about* on a damned dry erase board? You depressed? Grow up."); your father asking how much money you're spending to live alone, saying you could buy a tractor for all the money you're paying for lawn service, and *close the refrigerator* for God's sake, Marc, you're racking up one hell of a power bill, aint'cha?

Your father in your life. The rulebook in the flesh.

These are the things you want to say to Kyle, give voice to the anxiety suddenly gripping you, and in your former life you'd actually be stuck lingering between choices and unsure of which to pick.

"We're bringing him back with us," he says.

You look around the room, at the old *National Geographic*s, at the old Polaroid camera atop the old Monopoly box atop a dozen cans of baked beans atop some sort of black crate that probably used to hold shop rags or boxes of wiper blades.

Kyle knows what you're thinking.

"I've ordered one of those pod things," he says. "It's getting here tomorrow morning. We pack it, and they ship it down to you, park it right in your driveway."

"In my driveway? My HOA," you say. "I don't know if…"

"Marc, this is *happening*," he says. "Sometimes you get choices, other times you just get life, and you deal with it."

Where the fuck is the happy-go-lucky youth group smile? How is it that the kid who couldn't even think to buy new t-shirts is making the mature decisions here?

You look around again: empty mason jars, dozens of pooper scoopers/ chocolate milk cups, old two-liter bottles now filled with seeds.

"We're not taking all of this, if that's what's on your mind," he says. "Dad doesn't need the *Atlanta Journal-Constitution* from 1981. A lot of this, we dump."

"Will he even come?" you ask.

That's the question, isn't it? Convenient for you to bring up, because it puts the burden of the decision back on your father.

"No," Kyle says.

"So why bother with any of—"

"Unless *you* ask him," Kyle says. He tosses you a Wheaties box, circa '97, Jordan pictured mid-jump shot. You remember saving this for some reason… part of your anti-Shaq tirade? You fling the box into a stack of recyclables.

"You want *me* to ask him?"

"We're going to the hospital," Kyle says, "and there's two things that can happen. Either you keep up the petty bullshit, or you put an end to it and do what's right."

"It's not petty," you say.

"What's right is right."

"I fucking *hate* that expression. What does it even mean?"

"It means you've gotta stop the damned excuses. You're a grown-ass man. You know this will save his life, and ain't nothing more right—more clear— than that. Tomorrow we pack. Then we head back to Orlando, Dad in my passenger seat."

You sigh as violently as you can manage. So often when you've thought of your father, there was an anger that rose with the memory of his voice, and you know now that you came to *love* that anger. It was yours, an affirmation of your *rightness*, your blamelessness in all things: no matter what bullshit you encountered, you were *superior*.

"This isn't about trying to find the thing that makes *you* happiest, like you're the only one in the world who fucking matters," Kyle says. "Sometimes if you really care, there's only ever one option."

•

On the 15-inch TV bolted into the corner of the hospital's fluorescent-lit waiting room, the local news replays footage from the horrendous Magic loss in Game One of the NBA Finals. Every Magic player looks smaller on the game's biggest stage. Kobe Bryant and Pau Gasol and Derek Fisher and the Lakers all look quicker, stronger, smarter, a varsity team playing the JV squad. "The Magic have their second shot at LA tonight at the Staples Center," the local sports guy says. This guy's been around forever, looks like he's wearing the same baggy dress shirt and frumpy blazer as when you were in high school. "Dwight Howard and company looking for a chance at redemption!" he says.

You wonder if that's possible for Dwight and the Magic, if they do have a shot at winning the championship, or if the dream is over, if it died in that Game One loss. A magical run to the NBA Finals, a bright shining moment for the city of Orlando conquering Boston's Celtics and smashing LeBron's Cavaliers: is it over now? Should everyone just move on?

You want to stop thinking that sports—that the Magic—are some metaphor for everything happening to you, but you're in a motherfucking hospital. Everything becomes a sign when bad news is so close, death so palpable. A fly on the overhead lights. A broken faucet in the bathroom. A nurse banging on the soda machine, saying "Will one thing please work today?"

"Let's go," Kyle says. "We've only got a few minutes left."

And he leads you into your father's room, where there is a man who looks like your father except two decades older. His face is bloodless, waxen.

Eyes drained of fight. His stubble, once so uniform, is now sporadic, so that there are whiskers on his chin but a smooth spot on one cheek. Is this all because of the heart attack, or have you missed the slow graying of his hair, the deepening of his crow's feet? Two minutes ago you were thinking time moved slower in small towns, but now it feels like maybe—while you were livin' it up in Central Florida—time started to sprint, and you missed it.

"Dad," you say. He turns his head to look at you. Forehead lines more severe, seemingly permanent, as if they don't go away even under times of zero stress. "This isn't a bad time, is it?"

He closes his eyes tight, like he just heard the stupidest comment ever spoken. "What's a *good* time?"

Kyle moves past you to take his place beside your father. He shuffles a few different items on the windowsill, cards and flowers delivered by neighbors or old shop-friends. One of the cards actually says "Happy Birthday," but it's crossed out and there's a long handwritten note on the inside.

"Are you going to watch the Magic game tonight?" you ask him.

"The TV stations. They come in funny here."

"Can't be any worse than the house," Kyle says. He leans back against the windowsill.

"I'll be out tomorrow morning," your father says. "I'll watch the third game wherever I want."

Wherever, he says. The freedom of such a word. The freedom he doesn't yet know you are seeking to steal.

Kyle looks at you, motions for you to speak. "I'm going to grab a Coke." He pushes away from the windowsill and pats your father's sheet-covered knee, then—like a parent leaving two warring siblings to make up—disappears from the room and it's you and the old man.

"Glad you could come," he says. "Glad you could clear your busy schedule."

"Glad you're glad," you say.

Your father clears his throat and shifts his jaw; it's this weird tic he has, like he's chewing on something but really he's not. He smoked, but he also chewed tobacco at the shop; maybe this habit dates back to then, or maybe it goes back further. "You don't have to pretend to be nice to me just 'cause I'm in the hospital," he says. "Go on. I know it makes you happy to see me where I am."

"That's a kind characterization," you say. "Why would this *ever* make me happy?"

He clears his throat again, backs up in his bed. "Follow all the rules, and look where it gets me. You go off, you do what you like, and you come back here—Mr. Big Shot, cheating the system, playing by his own rules—and you see Dad on his deathbed. You got everything you wanted, while I got *this*?"

You hold your fingers to the bridge of your nose, squeeze as if seized by migraine. "There's so much wrong with what you just said."

"That right?" he says.

"Followed every rule," you say. "Like, you quit smoking?"

He chews the inside of his cheek.

"Didn't think so. Cut down on the red meat? Stopped cooking pork chops in butter?"

He shifts his jaw again but narrows his eyes. Back in high school when you had a mini-obsession with calories, you would carefully slice the strip of fat off your steak; you'd sacrifice just a hint of beef in order to be rid of that quivering chunk of fat, and then your father would swoop in with his fork and say, "What the hell's wrong with you? That's the best part," and eat the fat straight-up. The superhuman metabolism of your father and Kyle somehow skipped you.

"There's no cosmic judge weighing your adherence to your code," you say. "You smoke, and bad shit happens to your body. You eat like Fred Flintstone, and you get the life expectancy of a caveman. Not tough to figure out."

"So you're the big-time scientist now, too?"

"Holy shit, Dad. Arguing with me won't make you right."

"Ain't nothing'll make me right, will it?"

"You know, the one reason I was able to go off to college and leave you alone with Kyle after Mom died," you say, "the one reason I never felt guilty? It's because I *know* you don't indulge in self-pity. You've always been stronger than that. *I'm* the one, don't you understand? I'm the one who's a self-pity black hole.

I'm the one too weak for this family, the one who needed to leave and become a different person. Not you, though. Self-pity doesn't run in your blood."

"Just speaking the truth, is all."

"When someone says, 'speaking the truth,' it's usually an excuse to say something negative. I've spent the last six months being negative enough for both of us. I'm done with it. So seriously: you, too: get over it."

And you do see the strength in his eyes as you lecture him, the grit, a man who'd work for thirty years in one auto shop, who'd work eighteen hours a day if he could, gas pedal to the floor, but who never really understood the expression "work smarter, not harder." You see the muscle, the toil, the sweat, the concentration creases in his brow etched from accumulated years spent wrench-turning. You see—despite the defensiveness—how happy it makes him to hear he's "too strong" for any of that, and that—if he were out of the hospital—he'd pick up a hammer or a drill or a hammer-drill and get to work on something. "Stronger than that," you said, and you see how easy it'd be to sabotage Kyle's plan, support your father's insistence upon staying alone in Georgia. *You can do it, Dad! And don't let anyone tell you otherwise!* God, you'd be the good son again. Can you imagine that? The best of both worlds: you get to keep your house father-free, while also making up with the man. Everybody wins.

Except Kyle, of course.

And really, your father, who'd be utterly alone, working himself to death.

Oh, for fuck's sake. Here you are considering choices again, when you know there isn't one, not if you're determined to be a better man.

"You're strong, but you're not strong *enough*, Dad," you say.

He rolls his eyes. "Shit," he says disdainfully.

"You need help."

"Who the hell are *you* to—"

"You can't take care of that house alone. That yard. Not like you used to."

"I was watering *plants*. I'm not 80. I don't need some nurse changing my bedpan." The blood is returning to his face. When he stops speaking, he starts chewing again. "Men my age should just be reaching the top. Coaching football teams. Running for president. Not—"

"I'm not saying 'nursing home.' Two heart attacks, though? You're not a kid anymore."

"This is *nothing*."

"What is it you love to say? No Turner man has lived past 65? I see why. We sabotage our bodies to fulfill the prophecy."

"I want you to go." He points at the door.

"I'm leaving here on Tuesday," you say. "And you're coming with me."

"The hell I am."

"You're going to live in Orlando with me and Kyle. I don't expect you'll like it, not at first, but I don't care."

"You're kidnapping me?"

"You're a grown man. You can fight us if you want, but you know you won't win. Not now, not anymore."

"Bullshit."

"Kyle's packing your house. By the time you're out of here, the house'll be empty."

"He's just cleaning up for me."

"A ruse. He's clever."

"So I move in with you? That's your plan? And what happens when you lose *your* house? When we're all living on the street? Mr. Big Shot. Don't think I don't know what kind of trouble you're in, you and everyone else like you."

"I thought I was the successful one, the rule-breaker who got rewarded."

"You'll get yours."

"I'm selling my house," you say.

This is the other realization you've come to, and it's so obvious that (once again) you can't believe it was ever a choice.

"The McMansion?"

"People love that expression," you say. "It's not a mansion, especially compared to the other houses in the neighborhood. But I can't afford it, and it's one of the few properties I own that'll sell easy. I can use the money from that house to short-sell another. Then keep renting the ones that'll rent. Baby steps."

"So where are we supposed to live, then?"

"I've been going about this all wrong, see," you say. "Living in a tomb, while the real houses go to shit. I don't belong there. I need to be somewhere that *needs* me."

"You're not making sense."

"I've got the perfect house for us, one that's empty and just waiting for the right family," you say. You're thinking of the oil stains in the driveway, the work that house needs outside and in. You're thinking that the city is a mess because of people like you, that neighborhoods and subdivisions and condo developments died because of the people who bought but never lived in their houses. "It's three times the size of what you got here, and it needs serious attention," you say. "When you're well, you can help, but I'll make sure you're not over-exerting yourself."

"I got work to do *here*," he says, and he jabs his finger into his palm. "Why would I wanna help you with something *you* couldn't take care of?"

"All of us," you say, "are going to meet with a real estate agent on Monday. And when your house is cleared out, you're going to sell, and you're going to take what you can get. Cash-money in your pocket, replenish that bank account of yours, and you'll have zero expenses moving forward."

"That's my *life* in there," he says. "The money I spent. Thirty years of it. The money I put into the yard, the structure. I *built* that. My back still aches from the work."

"It'll pay off when we put it on the market, then," you say. "You need to start looking at it as property, not a life."

"Same difference."

"Absolutely not," you say. You know better than to give some physical space power over you—another new rule by which you will now live your life. So many rules to abandon, but *this one* you like. "If I have to hit you over the head with a shovel, I'm prying you away from that place. You're coming to Orlando, and we're—*listen* to me—it's been a long time coming, and every one of us has made our mistakes, and none of us has healed since Mom died— but you're *coming* to Orlando and—*listen*—we're going to get right again."

•

From the hospital you drive back to your father's house, where you clear space from the living room couch to sit. Visiting hours have ended, and you can't tell if things are looking up or down, if life is getting better or worse, but it's reassuring that maybe there's an equal chance of things going right or wrong. "Let's get out of this mess," Kyle tells you.

Minutes later he's driving the both of you to 8-Ball for the Magic game, your first 8-Ball experience in years. You are mentally preparing yourself for the cigarette smoke, for your jeans to be unwearable forever more, for the hard looks from men with NASCAR driver facial hair. Who knows what you will step in, what you will sit in? Who knows whether you will be pegged "city boy," whether you will be punched in the face again? But fuck it. Beer. Wings. Basketball. And your brother. Right?

You drive to the bar in silence, the weight of June pressing down on you. Elsewhere in the country, summertime is cause for optimism, things blossoming and growing, yards vibrant, fathers throwing baseballs to their sons. A world alive! In Florida and southern Georgia, it is like passing the first mile marker as you run a marathon. The months of May and June—the first hot breath of nighttime humidity—are Nature's warning to get prepared. Soon it's gonna get hotter, the humidity smothering, the sunshine stealing more and more time from the cool night, the AC kicking nonstop, sunglasses glazing with condensation, yards growing up and out, world covered in green. There's a part of you that longs for seasons, for Nature's refresh button that allows other regions to start over every new calendar year, but another part of you thinks Florida's lack of seasons might be more honest to the way the world works: you never truly get to start over.

"Is he convinced?" Kyle asks.

"No," you say.

"So what do we do?"

"Drag him to Florida, like you said. He'd never come willingly, you know that."

"Shit, Marc. I was *counting* on you to change his mind." He says it like you'd expect a little brother to say this, and it helps to hear that—despite everything—Kyle has *some* faith in you.

"He knows it's happening. He doesn't like it, but it's happening."

"So tomorrow we pack?"

"Tomorrow we pack."

But that's a long way away.

Right now he's 25 and you're 29 and you're two twenty-something dudes headed to 8-Ball and the Magic are playing in Game Two of the NBA Finals, and it's Bud Lite on draft and you're back in a place you've always been ashamed to call home, but it's a place that just *is*, and that's fine.

The bartender has long wrinkle-ridges down his cheeks, and a way of breathing that rustles both his mustache and the wisps of thinning rust-colored hair drifting across his scalp. He doesn't know you, but he knows Kyle, and soon you're splitting a pitcher of Bud Lite with a bag of ice dropped into it. At one far end of the bar, an old guy demands the TV be turned to CSI reruns, but Kyle says "Shut your face, Franklin, we're watching the Magic," and the bartender laughs through his nose and the guy shuts up and goes back to staring into his beer and mumbling and otherwise fulfilling the role of Stereotypical Drunk Guy at End of Bar that nearly every establishment seems to have.

The game starts. Dwight with the ball. Hedo with the ball. Kobe the Black Mamba slithering through the Magic defense, pulling back, striking. It's tough to watch on the bar's old TV, tough to make out one player from the next, and it's tough to think of anything but your father, his house, your house, oil stains.

At some point you snap back to cognizance and the first quarter is over.

"We're making the same mistakes we made last game!" Coach Stan is screaming on the "wired-up" feed that the network loves to air during time-outs. "When's it gonna change?" His voice is scratchy, tinged with the familiar Van Gundy panic, but you can't argue with Stan, can you? The announcers agree: this was a shitty first quarter for the Magic. They are not themselves. They need to wake up.

You tell yourself this game doesn't mean anything. Keep silent, refrain from throwing your glass across the bar. A good man is allowed to care about sports, but there must be a limit to how deep his passions run, how he acts as a result of things over which he has no control.

On the television is a commercial for some explosive and effects-heavy new summer film. You remember it from a few weeks ago, back in the house of the frat stars. There's a green monster, and someone in a superhero cape flying around a fireball spit from the monster's mouth. There's a sexy woman, standing sexily and looking so fierce you might be forgiven for thinking she actually has a role in the film aside from standing sexily and looking fierce, and there's the movie-announcer voice saying "This summer…" but he sounds disinterested, and the action in the trailer just sort of stops, the woman exhaling and letting her shoulders slump, her once-blowing hair falling around her shoulders motionless; the flying superhero lands on the ground, runs his hands through his hair. The soundtrack stops. Even the monster groans, as if he's tired of being in the same fucking movie every summer.

You shake your head, rub your eyes. "Do you even like me, Kyle?" you ask before you can stop yourself.

A new pitcher has just arrived. Kyle's stuck here with you, no choice but to answer.

"Um," he says. "You're my *brother*."

"That's not what I asked."

"Well, I don't know how to answer."

"You don't have to tie yourself to me, or to Dad, just 'cause we've got the same last name."

"I know that."

"I know you know. What I'm saying is, I'm giving you permission to leave me. Us."

"*Permission?*"

"Freedom from guilt, I mean. No regret over having broken some family rule. I take responsibility for being an asshole brother, for being someone who's generally unlikeable. Who doesn't deserve your loyalty. I'm telling you that you can leave."

"What does that even mean, unlikeable?"

You're thinking of Shelley, how she untethered herself from you, from her friends and her job and from the city, sparing herself a hideous future. How good you would've felt if you had have sensed her misery and offered her that option first. You can't bear the thought of embittering another joyful person.

"Life is short," you say. "You should be with people whose company you enjoy."

Kyle pours himself a beer from a new pitcher, foam rising over the top and down the sides of the glass. He doesn't care, just lifts the cup—coaster still stuck to the bottom—and drinks. "Seems to me that the person who'd call someone else *unlikeable* is part of the problem," he says. "It's easy to not like someone. I know some people, they spend their whole lives not liking people, not liking things in their lives. You remember my friend Andy?"

"Sure."

"He was dating this girl. When we were both at community college. Beautiful girl named Vanessa. Could sing, came from a nice family, loved him even though he was mostly a terrible dude to her."

"Okay."

"Out of the blue he breaks up with her. Tells me he woke up and had this image in his head of, like, how she laughed. Couldn't get it out of his head. Said she looked like a raccoon."

A typical Kyle anecdote. You laugh. "Did she?"

"She looked like a *girl laughing*. I don't know. But he said, once he pictured it, that was the end. She became ugly to him. Like that."

You pour your own beer and raise your eyebrows, waiting for the point.

"He's a fucking idiot is the point. Looking for *reasons* to dislike everyone and everything. If that's your mindset, you're never *really* going to like anyone."

"That wasn't what I was saying, Kyle."

"You asked whether I like you? We have good times, bad times. If I saw the world like Andy, I could find reasons to always dislike you."

"This feels like a cop-out answer."

"I don't want to be the person your question's trying to make me. I'm not so damn naive to say, 'ignore the raccoon laugh.' I'm just saying that, when you love another person, shit's deeper than 'like' or 'dislike.'"

You stare into your beer. You imagined he'd say the word "love," but you thought it would sound generic; you thought you'd be able to make a joke about it and show how superficial was his concept of love.

In the second quarter, the Magic are a different team, Rashard Lewis tearing off 18 points to keep the offense clicking, the score close. But still they're playing the battle-tested Lakers, from the bright lights and the big city of Los Angeles, and it's the Kobe show. Kobe under the Hollywood spotlights, driving the basket. Kobe spitting the ball to Derek Fisher on the perimeter for three-pointers, the ball traveling to the hoop as smooth as if it'd been rolled down a bowling lane, Jack Nicholson howling in support courtside, any pregame high-fives and *how-ya-doin's* with Dwight Howard now forgotten, the Lakers leading by five points when halftime begins.

You take a deep breath. There's something else to address, too, something you wish you could put off, but it's there in the bubbles of your Bud Lite. A proposal you have to make. "We're moving," you tell your brother finally.

"Right."

"No, really," you say. "Out of Stoney Creek. Across Orlando." He needs to know what you've been planning, so you tell him about the other house, the one from which Edwin stole the ceiling fans. "It needs work, this house. A lot of my houses need work. You're right about that."

"So you need help, then, fixing 'em up?"

"A lot of houses in *Orlando* need work."

"That's what I've been saying."

"Kyle, I want to help you start a contracting business," you say. "You don't want to be a loan-closer, I know that. I won't force you. I can see what I was doing, and I'm sorry. But that house I'm selling? And Dad's house? I don't want to just get stuck in the same rut. When we sell, we'll have enough money for you to get started."

"My own business?"

"It'll be all of ours, I guess," you say. "Dad wants to, he can help. It's hard work, Kyle. I've seen some of these guys. Contractors. End of the day, sweating buckets, covered in paint, hands calloused. Hell if I'd do that shit."

"Hard work's nothing to be afraid of."

"Of course not, but we've got to build *smart*," you say. "Don't try to be the muscle every time. Find high school kids, college kids looking for weekend work, summer work. We'll be *running* a business. By the time you're 40, you should only be lifting a hammer or a screwdriver if you want to. By the time you're 50, you shouldn't be having your first heart attack. This is a cycle we have to break."

You've made your pitch. Whether Kyle accepts is up to him.

By the start of the third quarter, Kyle's taken over your role as over-passionate fan and is throwing peanut shells at the TV. It's okay, though. His passion never becomes angry like yours. You're the one who's got to keep it in check. Every dribble, every bounce, every shot, remind yourself: *My father is in the hospital, and he's okay, and my team is in the Finals, and, win or lose, everything's okay because this is so much better than planning a funeral.* Your life is not a tragedy. You are going to see the world as Kyle does.

Dwight Howard slam-dunks the basketball and the announcer says "That's Dwight Howard's first dunk of the series!" and you're tempted to say, "It's a sign! This move is going to go so easy, so easy!" but you breathe slowly and stifle that comment, because you know the inevitable blocked shot on the next possession will only lead you back to those darker rooms.

You play darts during the third quarter. You and Kyle lose to some rattailed joker and his friend in a "Fuck Your Feelings" t-shirt, so you owe them a pitcher, and even *that* doesn't bother you. It doesn't mean anything, that errant dart in the wall you'd intended for the bull's-eye. It doesn't mean you and your brother are destined to fail. The darts are darts.

Now it's the fourth quarter and the score is going back and forth, Kobe putting the Lakers up by three, then JJ Redick nailing an outside shot to tie it up. The cameras make the rounds from JJ to Kobe to Dwight to Stan (who's sweating and tugging on his turtleneck) to Rashard to Derek Fisher to Pau to Jack Nicholson to Shia LeBouf to Rafer Alston to Leonardo DiCaprio to Carrot Top. Then it's Kobe snaking through the entire Magic roster to deliver a dagger, Hedo racing up-court on the next possession to sink a jumper. Forty-seven seconds of game-time remaining, and the Magic are up 88-86, so close to victory! But then it's Derek Fisher on the other end passing the ball to— *wait*, the ball is tipped by outstretched Magic arms, the ball nearly falls into the waiting hands of Rashard Lewis, who only needs to hold the ball to secure the victory—but *no*, the ball is poked away and falls into Pau Gasol's palms, and then Pau rises and rolls the ball into the basket to tie the game at 88-88.

You remind yourself not to rise from your seat, not to swear, that the only thing that matters for your future is the way *you* act, how *you* will continue to view the world, not how Rafer Alston reacts on the court, not whether Dwight gets a technical foul for mouthing off to the ref. You are the metaphor for yourself. Do not find excuses to be angry.

Nine seconds left and the Lakers have the ball. You've seen this before, of course. How many times has your team lost in the final seconds?

Kobe squares up to take the final shot and you expect that this will be the end, that Kobe will produce one of his patented heart-breaking buzzer-beaters to win the game, and you inhale and watch as one long pale arm reaches over Kobe's head and with stiffened fingertips knocks the ball away.

Hedo! Hedo Fucking Türkoğlu blocked Kobe's shot, saved the day!

For once, there's optimism. Game One was a disaster. No other way to describe it. But here we are in Game Two and the Magic have fought back and there's now six-tenths of a second left, possession arrow pointing to Orlando. If they inbound and score in six-tenths of a second, they'll win the game and tie the series at 1-1, before Game Three shifts to Orlando, where the Magic will suddenly have *home-court advantage* for the series. The hard work! The effort! Is this a sign that *your* hard work will pay off? That your gamble— selling your house, moving to Wild Berry—will work?

No, no. Stop that. Breathe.

It's just the end of a game (biggest game in Magic *history*, though!), and just a single shot opportunity (but a big shot!).

Breathe. Don't make this more than it is.

Sign or no sign, it has all come down to this moment for the Orlando Magic, 88-88 with 0.6 left on the clock. Hedo inbounds the ball from just beyond the Lakers logo near Staples Center's half-court and it sails high… not intended for Rashard Lewis on the perimeter or even Dwight Howard standing outside the paint and too far from the basket to make a play, no, the ball slices the air above the heads of *every* player as they look up and watch it go past, a rocket of orange that is all at once strong *and* delicate. You see Courtney Lee materialize from nowhere—the Orlando Magic's Courtney Lee with his plastic face mask, Courtney Lee the rookie from Western Kentucky who no one would suspect as the Magic's go-to assassin for the final shot of the biggest game in franchise history—Courtney Lee spins away from his defender and sprints to the basket, and he is super-quick but the moment is also slow-motion, so that all of the arena sees it happen, microsecond by microsecond, all of Los Angeles knows, all of Orlando knows, Courtney Lee breaking free and running to the hoop and the inbounded ball traveling through the blackness and the brightness overhead and floating his way and Courtney Lee is jumping, jumping—an inbound alley-oop to Courtney Lee! This is gonna happen! Orlando will win, if he can just tip the ball into the hoop! As the microseconds tick down, it's tempting to allow yourself the fantasy that you are watching the rest of your life, watching the culmination of four decades of Orlando history that will determine the next four. It's tempting to say that this is *everything*, this alley-oop, this opportunity. Courtney Lee is rising and the ball is almost at his fingertips and it is a split second but in this single fraction of a single frame of the motion picture of your life, you see all the possibilities, all the different ways it could end. The ball is in the air, and Courtney Lee could tap it in and *Game Over*, Magic win! The ball is in the air, and Kyle could be your partner and run a prosperous business, the real brother you never should've forsaken for phonies like Edwin, and you can fix those houses, make those sales, build your business back up! The ball is in the air, and here you are at your father's house and you can *make things right*, bring him to Orlando, take care of him, rebuild the family. Maybe this will be the greatest moment *ever* for the Magic—here in the Finals, on the verge of a winning basket—and it is *so* tempting, *so* seductive to consider what this means, that you could become champions! What a metaphor *that* could be for your future, for Orlando's future! The ball is in the air, but (oh God) maybe the Magic will squander the opportunity and lose the game in overtime and lose the Finals and the years will collapse upon one another and you'll relive the humiliation of fourteen years ago (fourteen years ago, this very day!) when Nick Anderson missed four straight free throws to lose the Magic their first NBA Finals game ever, that day and this one as mirror images of futility. Maybe it will be even worse, the ball glancing off Courtney Lee's fingertips as he smashes his face into the backboard, or Dwight falls down on the court and dies of a heart attack inexplicably because he's a monster too gigantic to be human. Or maybe next year they'll trade Courtney Lee away, and then all the local favorites, or maybe they'll just regress and *lose* to the mighty Celtics in the Eastern Conference Finals next time around, and maybe LeBron James will leave Cleveland for a sexier market and the spurned Ohioans will light his jersey on fire and this whole era of the NBA—the 2000s, the LeBron Cavs and the Dwight Magic and the Kobe Lakers—will officially end, and Dwight will leave Orlando for the bright lights and big city of LA or New York or, fuck it, Houston, and maybe all the small and medium-sized markets are doomed, Orlando doomed, you, doomed, your father stubborn till the end and refusing to leave Georgia, Kyle hating you in that particularly intense way that little brothers can hate their older siblings, and Shelley moving away and never talking to you again… the ball is in the air, and Courtney Lee is jumping, and you could rise out of your seat and scream every profanity and shake your fist and let your anger feed on itself and grow and grow, but you could also remind yourself that maybe the outcome doesn't matter, not really, that the ball is just a ball and the game is just a game and neither signifies anything more.

The ball is floating.

Courtney Lee is rising to meet it.

The ball is floating in the air, and you watch with Kyle, holding your breath as the ball floats and spins forever and never falls. Eventually, you slip a couple twenties under the empty pitcher, the ice bag in the center now only a melted reminder of the cooler, better times, and you push away the basket of gnawed chicken bones. The ball is floating, and you look to Kyle and he looks back, and for the first time you see traces of what will become permanent worry lines in Kyle's forehead, a vision of the future for that perfect babyface complexion, and you know they've been there this whole time but that you've just chosen to not see them, to not see him. The ball is floating. The ball is floating, and you leave it there on the bad television in the dark humid interior of a smoky Georgia bar called 8-Ball, and you both go back to your father's place because that's where the real work begins.

Nathan Holic is the author of the novels *The Things I Don't See* and *American Fraternity Man*. He is the editor of Burrow Press' "15 Views" series, and Graphic Narrative editor for *The Florida Review*.

ACKNOWLEDGEMENTS

I began writing Bright Lights, Medium—Sized City shortly after purchasing my first house in May 2008. I remember watching too many Orlando Magic games in that living room, excited that I could shout as loud as I wanted, and—through the miracle of home ownership—feeling more a part of the city than ever.

But that excitement faded when my neighbor—hood wilted into a foreclosure zone, and the price of my home dropped by nearly a hundred thousand dollars.

And I was just a humble "Visiting Instructor" at the University of Central Florida at this time, not the superwealthy, world famous writer I am today! (jk, obvi)

I felt stupid...my first real investment as an adult, and this is what I was left with?

Soon thereafter, even Magic games grew painful, with Dwight Howard beginning the slow tortured process of whining himself out of Orlando. The Dwightmare.

Meanwhile, Orlando was being derided on a national scale. As TD Allman wrote in an extended essay at National Geographic, our city was merely a "brand name," a "characterless connorbation of congested freeways and parking lots."

For years we had been growing, our region teeming with anticipation, but after the housing bubble burst, we were just a sprawling suburb whose national identity was theme parks, foreclosure, traffic jams, and chain restaurants.

It was out of this time period that
Bright Lights, Medium—Sized City
was born.

Or, rather, the idea of a city novel—a book
that treated the city and its inhabitants
as characters worth exploring, their human
struggles worthy of our empathy—came at
me, sucked me in. So nobody on a national
scale was taking us seriously? Well, shit. I
would try to do that for Orlando.

With this mission in mind, I began
consuming the rich and fascinating
history of Central Floridar. While
this book cannot hope to capture it all,
I do want to mention some of the works
that were helpful as I underwent my
initiation as a True Orlandoan.

For a sense of the city's complicated
relationship with Disney, I found Carl
Hiassen's Team Rodent: How Disney
Devoured the World, Richard Foglesong's
Married to the Mouse, and Chad Denver
Emerson's Project Future,
to be particularly illuminating.

And for a sense of how the city
existed before Disney, I am indebted to
James Clark's Orlando: A Brief History,
and Joy Wallace Dickinson's Orlando: City
of Dreams and Remembering Orlando: Tales
From Elvis to Disney. Lost Orlando, from
Stephanie Gaub Antequino and Tana Mosier
Porter, is also a fantastic visualization
of a version of the city that will never be
seen again.

I'm also indebted to Paradise For Sale, Nick Wynne and Richard
Moorhead's look at Florida's 1920s land boom and inevitable bust.
I was also helped in understanding the machinations and scope of
the 2000s housing crisis by Edmund Andrews' Busted: Life Inside
the Great Mortgage Meltdown and Alyssa Katz's Our Lot. And
although I was sadly unable to force this material into my own
novel, Celebration USA: Living in Disney's Brave New Town, by
Douglas Franz and Catherine Collins, offers a great look at how
the housing boom came to Central Florida.

And while there are countless other short histories, I must also mention Joe A. Akerman Jr. and J. Mark Akerman's Jacob Summerlin: King of the Crackers, Carl Langford's bizarre memoir Hizzoner the Mayor, and Crossing Division Street by Benjamin Brotemarkle.

I took a lot of liberties in this book, as I'm sure I will be reminded by experts in banking, real estate, Florida history, and Orlando Magic basketball. But if you're inspired by this novel to learn more about our weird past, I hope that the above will prove a fascinating starting point.

To that end, I need to thank Brandon Lee and Alex Scharf, who helped me understand the strange world of notary work and loan closing, and who set me up to interview a notary who turned out to also be running an illegal sex dungeon. So. Thanks?

And thank you to Richard Varner, my friend and realtor, who probably didn't realize my casual questions about his job were often motivated by troublesome book details I was attempting to work through. And thank you to Tonio Bianca, also, for sharing his expertise in house flipping.

Which leads me to my next dilemma. How to say thank you to everyone who helped shape this book into reality? Let me give it a try.

Thank you to Jamie Poissant, and Lindsay Hunter, and James Clark. Generous with their time, generous with their encouraging words. And double thanks to Terry Godbey, for her careful read.

I'm thankful to Jennifer Flynn and Meghann Stubel Batchelor, who both offered some extremely useful feedback on some trickier moments in the book. I'm thankful also to Mark Pursell and Sarah Prevatt Harris for their long—ago feedback on early chapters, as well.

I'm thankful, of course, to the Orlando Magic, who gave us a great season in 2009 and then closed up shop thereafter.

Wait, is the team still around?

And especially to Ryan Rivas, editor and publisher and friend, who has asked since 2011 how the project was going, whose genuine interest and enthusiasm kept me reassured for years and years. Ryan has been the literary champion and advocate that this city and state always needed. We all (writers, artists, readers) owe him so much, myself most of all.

And I'm thankful to Jared Silvia, John King, Hunter Choate, Susan Lilley, Susan Fallows, Matt Peters, Vanessa Blakeslee, J. Bradley, and everyone else I conscripted into "15 Views of Orlando," thankful to Lisa Roney and everyone at The Florida Review past and present, thankful to Blake Scott and Vanessa Calkins and Matt Bryan and Stephanie Vie and everyone at UCF who has helped to make it a great place to teach writing, thankful to everyone at the Orange County Libraries who has invited me to give a talk, and (of course) Drunken Monkey and Vespr Coffee for the seats, and the fuel.

I am thankful for a rich and supportive community that has encouraged this project through nearly a decade of authorial agony, thankful and lucky for every damn one of you, but thankful and lucky most of all for Heather, the woman who's never let me give up or doubt myself, and who loves me no matter what sort of bullshit I write.

(I write a lot of bullshit.)

It's done, the book?

Everyone should have a Heather, but this one is mine, and I'm not letting go.

SUBSCRIBE

We thrive on the direct support of enthusiastic readers like you. Your generous support has helped Burrow, since our founding in 2010, provide over 1,200 opportunities for writers to publish and share their work.

Burrow publishes four, carefully selected books each year, offered in an annual subscription package for a mere $60 (which is like $5/month, $0.20/day, or 1 night at the bar). Subscribers are recognized by name in the back of our books, and are inducted into our not-so-secret society: the illiterati.

Glance to your right to view our 2019 line-up. Since you've already (presumably) read *this* book, enter code **BRIGHT25** at checkout to knock 25% off this year's subscriber rate:

BURROWPRESS.COM/SUBSCRIBE

VENUS IN RETROGRADE
poetry by Susan Lilley

$20 | Hardcover | 136 pages

In a voice both lyrical and conversational, Lilley interprets various stages of womanhood while parsing the beauty and decay of her beloved homestate of Florida.

RADIO DARK
a novel by Shane Hinton

$16 | Paperback | 140 pages

Somewhere in Florida, where the sprawling suburbs meet a dying citrus grove, a janitor at a small community radio station, an FCC field agent, and a DJ attempt to restore humanity to a fallen world.

BRIGHT LIGHTS, MEDIUM-SIZED CITY
a novel by Nathan Holic

$25 | Hardcover | 620 pages
+ comic panels & watercolor illustrations

In the spirit of city novels like Tom Wolfe's *The Bonfire of the Vanities*, this sprawling period piece follows a hopeless house-flipper caught amid the 2009 housing bubble in Orlando, FL.

BONUS BOOK ARTIFACT
in collaboration with Obra/Artifact

For subscribers only. A limited edition book-as-object created in partnership with Stetson University's MFA-run literary journal, Orba/Artifact.

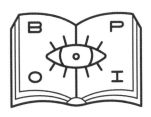

the illiterati

Florida isn't known as a bastion of literature. Being one of the few literary publishers in the state, we embrace this misperception with good humor. That's why we refer to our subscribers as "the illiterati," and recognize them each year in our print books and online.

To follow a specific publishing house, just as you might follow a record label, requires a certain level of trust. Trust that you're going to like what we publish, even if our tastes are eclectic and unpredictable. Which they are. And even if our tastes challenge your own. Which they might.

Subscribers support our dual mission of publishing a lasting body of literature and fostering literary community in Florida. If you're an adventurous reader, consider joining our cult—er, cause, and becoming one of us...

One of us! One of us! One of us!

2019 illiterati

Park Ave CDs
Secret Society Goods
Emily Dziuban
Linda Buckmaster
Robert Veith
Pam Escarcega
Randi Brooks
Lauren Salzman
Drew Hoffmann
Michael Wheaton
Kristen Arnett
Cindy & Frank Murray
Naomi Butterfield

Ted Greenberg
Gene Albamonte
Vicki Entreken
Cooper Levey-Baker
Whatever Tees
Nayma Russi
Lauren Mitchell
Roberta Alfonso
Terry Godbey
Bob Morris
Mary T. Duerksen
Debbie Goetz
Mary Reed

Grover Austin

Paula Bowers

Jean Dowdy

Stephen Cagnina

Yana Keyzerman

Amy Suzanne Parker

Jonathan Fink

Brian Turner

Joe McGee and Jess Rinker

Kim Britt

Martha Brenckle

John Henry Fleming

Thomas M. Bunting Projects

Rebecca Evanhoe

Adam C. Margio

Joshua Moye

Kelly Schumer

Jason Holic

Hunter Choate

Erica McCay

Shelby Nathanson

J. Thomas Wright

John & Pam Holic

Aaron & Patti Holic

Susan Scrupski

Catherine Carson

Mary Ann de Stefano

Michelle Riddle

Michael Gualandri

Richard Varner

Victoria Webster-Perez

Peter M. Gordon

Bonnie Frenkel

Jean West

NM Greenberg

Jason Katz

J.C. Carnahan

Pamela Melear

Patty Daoust

Marc Vaughan

Lisa Hinton

Chuck Dinkins

Tania Parada

Dystacorp Light Industries

Emily Webber

Abigail and Henry Craig

Jeanan Davis

Matthew Lang

Courtney Clute

Michael Cuglietta

Anna

Virginia Beeson

Mistie Watkins

Jane Trimble and Robert Ambes

The Taitts

Paul L. Bancel

Martha Sarasua

Jeff Ferree

Barbara Van Horn

Benjamin Noel

Pat Rushin

Sara Isaac

Nancy Pate
Amy Letter
Rita Ciresi
Dirt Dog Dustin
Alissa Barber Torres and
Anthony Torres
Heather Owens
Alicia Marini
Peter Bacopoulos
Lora Waring
Giti Khalsa
Chris Wiewiora
Travis Kiger
pete !
Alexandra Mariano
Erich Schwarz
Alison Townsend
Kim Rose
Neil and Sarah Asma
Valerie and Ross Blakeslee
A John Gosslee
Martin Fulmer
Dainon Moody
J. Stroup
Robert Lipscomb
Irene L. Pynn
Libby Ludwig
Kimberly Lojewski
Amy Copeland
Rebecca Renner
Chrissy Kolaya

Alison Jennings
Elena Postal
Anonymous
Suzannah Gilman
Blaine Strickland
Danielle Kessinger
Melanie
Margaret Nolan
Erin Hartigan
Stuart Buchanan
RC Wahl
Georgia Parker
Jackie Pappas
David James Poissant
Stacey Matrazzo
Nikki Fragala Barnes
Stacy Barton
Cindy Simmons
Sarah Hicks
Chelsea Torregrosa and
Matthew H. Bowlin
David Lilley
Spencer Orenstein
Ciarra Johnson
Cristina Wright
Lucianna Chixaro Ramos
Elena Shapiro-Albert
Sue Ann
Melissa K.
Teresa Carmody
V Loomie